OUTCAST

George Webber has written a successful novel about his family and hometown. When he returns to that town, he is shaken by the force of outrage and hatred that greets him. Family and life-long friends feel naked and exposed by the truths they have seen in his book, and their fury drives him from his home.

Outcast, Webber begins a search for his own identity. It takes him to New York and a hectic social whirl; to Paris with an uninhibited group of expatriots; to Berlin, lying cold and sinister under Hitler's shadow. The journey comes full circle when Webber returns to America and rediscovers it with love, sorrow, and hope.

Seldom has a writer caught the essence of a nation and a time as Thomas Wolfe did when he completed this novel in 1938, shortly before he died. It stands as one of the greatest books ever written by an American.

"If there still lingers any doubt as to Wolfe's right to a place among the immortals of American letters, this work should dispel it."   —CLEVELAND NEWS

"Wolfe wrote as one inspired. No one in his generation had his command of language, his passion, his energy."
          —THE NEW YORKER

There came to him an image of man's whole life upon the earth. It seemed to him that all man's life was like a tiny spurt of flame that blazed out briefly in an illimitable and terrifying darkness, and that all man's grandeur, tragic dignity, his heroic glory, came from the brevity and smallness of this flame. He knew his life was little and would be extinguished, and that only darkness was immense and everlasting. And he knew that he would die with defiance on his lips, and that the shout of his denial would ring with the last pulsing of his heart into the maw of all-engulfing night.

Thomas Wolfe

YOU CAN'T GO HOME AGAIN

PERENNIAL LIBRARY
Harper & Row, Publishers
New York • Hagerstown
San Francisco • London

Contents

BOOK I

The Native's Return

Chapter One

The Drunken Beggar on Horseback

It was the hour of twilight on a soft spring day toward the end of April in the year of Our Lord 1929, and George Webber leaned his elbows on the sill of his back window and looked out at what he could see of New York. His eye took in the towering mass of the new hospital at the end of the block, its upper floors set back in terraces, the soaring walls salmon colored in the evening light. This side of the hospital, and directly opposite, was the lower structure of the annex, where the nurses and the waitresses lived. In the rest of the block half a dozen old brick houses, squeezed together in a solid row, leaned wearily against each other and showed their backsides to him.

The air was strangely quiet. All the noises of the city were muted here into a distant hum, so unceasing that it seemed to belong to silence. Suddenly, through the open windows at the front of the house came the raucous splutter of a truck starting up at the loading platform of the warehouse across the street. The heavy motor warmed up with a full-throated roar, then there was a grinding clash of gears, and George felt the old house tremble under him as the truck swung out into the street and thundered off. The noise receded, grew fainter, then faded into the general hum, and all was quiet as before.

As George leaned looking out of his back window a nameless happiness welled within him and he shouted over to the waitresses in the hospital annex, who were ironing out as usual their two pairs of drawers and their flimsy little dresses. He heard, as from a great distance, the faint shouts of children playing in the streets, and, near at hand, the low voices of the people in the houses. He watched the cool, steep shadows, and saw how the evening light was moving in the little squares of yards, each of which had in it something intimate, familiar, and revealing —a patch of earth in which a pretty woman had been setting out flowers, working earnestly for hours and wearing a big straw hat and canvas gloves; a little plot of new-sown grass, solemnly watered every evening by a man with a square red face and a bald head; a little shed or playhouse or workshop for some

9

business man's spare-time hobby; or a gay-painted table, some easy lounging chairs, and a huge bright-striped garden parasol to cover it, and a good-looking girl who had been sitting there all afternoon reading, with a coat thrown over her shoulders and a tall drink at her side.

Through some enchantment of the quiet and the westering light and the smell of April in the air, it seemed to George that he knew these people all around him. He loved this old house on Twelfth Street, its red brick walls, its rooms of noble height and spaciousness, its old dark woods and floors that creaked; and in the magic of the moment it seemed to be enriched and given a profound and lonely dignity by all the human beings it had sheltered in its ninety years. The house became like a living presence. Every object seemed to have an animate vitality of its own—walls, rooms, chairs, tables, even a half-wet bath towel hanging from the shower ring above the tub, a coat thrown down upon a chair, and his papers, manuscripts, and books scattered about the room in wild confusion.

The simple joy he felt at being once more a part of such familiar things also contained an element of strangeness and unreality. With a sharp stab of wonder he reminded himself, as he had done a hundred times in the last few weeks, that he had really come home again—home to America, home to Manhattan's swarming rock, and home again to love; and his happiness was faintly edged with guilt when he remembered that less than a year before he had gone abroad in anger and despair, seeking to escape what now he had returned to.

In his bitter resolution of that spring a year ago, he had wanted most of all to get away from the woman he loved. Esther Jack was much older than he, married and living with her husband and grown daughter. But she had given George her love, and given it so deeply, so exclusively, that he had come to feel himself caught as in a trap. It was from that that he had wanted to escape—that and the shameful memory of their savage quarrels, and a growing madness in himself which had increased in violence as she had tried to hold him. So he had finally left her and fled to Europe. He had gone away to forget her, only to find that he could not; he had done nothing but think of her all the time. The memory of her rosy, jolly face, her essential goodness, her sure and certain talent, and all the hours that they had spent together returned to torture him with new desire and longing for her.

Thus, fleeing from a love that still pursued him, he had

10

become a wanderer in strange countries. He had traveled through England, France, and Germany, had seen countless new sights and people, and—cursing, whoring, drinking, brawling his way across the continent—had had his head bashed in, some teeth knocked out, and his nose broken in a beer-hall fight. And then, in the solitude of convalescence in a Munich hospital, lying in bed upon his back with his ruined face turned upward toward the ceiling, he had had nothing else to do but think. There, at last, he had learned a little sense. There his madness had gone out of him, and for the first time in many years he had felt at peace within himself.

For he had learned some of the things that every man must find out for himself, and he had found out about them as one has to find out—through error and through trial, through fantasy and illusion, through falsehood and his own damn foolishness, through being mistaken and wrong and an idiot and egotistical and aspiring and hopeful and believing and confused. As he lay there in the hospital he had gone back over his life, and, bit by bit, had extracted from it some of the hard lessons of experience. Each thing he learned was so simple and obvious, once he grasped it, that he wondered why he had not always known it. All together, they wove into a kind of leading thread, trailing backward through his past, and out into the future. And he thought that now, perhaps, he could begin to shape his life to mastery, for he felt a sense of new direction deep within him, but whither it would take him he could not say.

And what had he learned? A philosopher would not think it much, perhaps, yet in a simple human way it was a good deal. Just by living, by making the thousand little daily choices that his whole complex of heredity, environment, conscious thought, and deep emotion had driven him to make, and by taking the consequences, he had learned that he could not eat his cake and have it, too. He had learned that in spite of his strange body, so much off scale that it had often made him think himself a creature set apart, he was still the son and brother of all men living. He had learned that he could not devour the earth, that he must know and accept his limitations. He realized that much of his torment of the years past had been self-inflicted, and an inevitable part of growing up. And, most important of all for one who had taken so long to grow up, he thought he had learned not to be the slave of his emotions.

Most of the trouble he had brought upon himself, he saw, had come from leaping down the throat of things. Very well, he would look before he leaped hereafter. The trick was to get his reason and his emotions pulling together in double harness, instead of letting them fly off in opposite directions, tearing him

11

apart between them. He would try to give his head command and see what happened: then if head said, "Leap!"—he'd leap with all his heart.

And that was where Esther came in, for he had really not meant to come back to her. His head had told him it was better to let their affair end as it had ended. But no sooner had he arrived in New York than his heart told him to call her up—and he had done it. Then they had met again, and after that things followed their own course.

So here he was, back with Esther—the one thing he had once been sure would never happen. Yes, and very happy to be back. That was the queerest part of it. It seemed, perversely, that he ought to be unhappy to be doing what his reason had told him not to do. But he was not. And that was why, as he leaned there musing on his window sill while the last light faded and the April night came on, a subtle worm was gnawing at his conscience and he wondered darkly at how great a lag there was between his thinking and his actions.

He was twenty-eight years old now, and wise enough to know that there are sometimes reasons of which the reason knows nothing, and that the emotional pattern of one's life, formed and set by years of living, is not to be discarded quite as easily as one may throw away a battered hat or worn-out shoe. Well, he was not the first man to be caught on the horns of this dilemma. Had not even the philosophers themselves been similarly caught? Yes—and then written sage words about it:

"A foolish consistency," Emerson had said, "is the hobgoblin of little minds."

And great Goethe, accepting the inevitable truth that human growth does not proceed in a straight line to its goal, had compared the development and progress of mankind to the reelings of a drunken beggar on horseback.

What was important, perhaps, was not that the beggar was drunk and reeling, but that he was mounted on his horse, and, however unsteadily, was *going somewhere.*

This thought was comforting to George, and he pondered it for some time, yet it did not altogether remove the edge of guilt that faintly tinged his contentment. There was still a possible flaw in the argument:

His inconsistency in coming back to Esther—was it wise or foolish? . . . Must the beggar on horseback forever reel?

Esther awoke as quick and sudden as a bird. She lay upon her back and stared up at the ceiling straight and wide. This was her body and her flesh, she was alive and ready in a moment.

12

She thought at once of George. Their reunion had been a joyous rediscovery of love, and all things were made new again. They had taken up the broken fragments of their life and joined them together with all the intensity and beauty that they had known in the best days before he went away. The madness that had nearly wrecked them both had now gone out of him entirely. He was still full of his unpredictable moods and fancies, but she had not seen a trace of the old black fury that used to make him lash about and beat his knuckles bloody against the wall. Since he returned he had seemed quieter, surer, in better control of himself, and in everything he did he acted as if he wanted to show her that he loved her. She had never known such perfect happiness. Life was good.

Outside, on Park Avenue, the people had begun to move along the sidewalks once more, the streets of the city began to fill and thicken. Upon the table by her bed the little clock ticked eagerly its pulse of time as if it hurried forward forever like a child toward some imagined joy, and a clock struck slowly in the house with a measured, solemn chime. The morning sun steeped each object in her room with casual light, and in her heart she said, "It is now."

Nora brought coffee and hot rolls, and Esther read the paper. She read the gossip of the theatre, and she read the names of the cast that had been engaged for the new German play that the Community Guild was going to do in the fall, and she read that, "Miss Esther Jack has been engaged to design the show." She laughed because they called her "Miss," and because she could see the horrified look on *his* face when he read it, and because she remembered his expression when the little tailor thought she was his wife, and because it gave her so much pleasure to see her name in the paper—"Miss Esther Jack, whose work has won her recognition as one of the foremost modern designers."

She was feeling gay and happy and pleased with herself, so she put the paper in her bag, together with some other clippings she had saved, and took them with her when she went downtown to Twelfth Street for her daily visit to George. She handed them to him, and sat opposite to watch his face as he read them. She remembered all the things they had written about her work:

". . . subtle, searching, and hushed, with a wry and rueful humor of its own. . . ."

". . . made these old eyes shine by its deft, sure touch of whimsey as nothing else in this prodigal season of dramatic husks has done. . . ."

". . . the gay insouciance of her unmannered settings, touched with those qualities which we have come to expect in

13

all her ardent services to that sometimes too ungrateful jade, the drama. . . ."

". . . the excellent fooling that is implicit in these droll sets, elvishly sly, mocking, and, need we add or make apology for adding, expert? . . ."

She could hardly keep from laughing at the scornful twist of his mouth and the mocking tone of his comment as he bit off the phrases.

"'Elvishly sly!' Now isn't that too God-damned delightful!" he said with mincing precision. "'Made these old eyes shine!' Why, the quaint little bastard! . . . 'That sometimes too ungrateful jade!' Oh, deary me, now! . . . 'And need we add—!' I am swooning, sweetheart: pass the garlic!"

He threw the papers on the floor with an air of disgust and turned to her with a look of mock sternness that crinkled the corners of his eyes.

"Well," he said, "do I get fed, or must I starve here while you wallow in this bilge?"

She could control herself no longer and shrieked with glee. "I didn't do it!" she gasped. "I didn't write it! I can't help it if they write like that! Isn't it awful?"

"Yes, and you hate it, don't you?" he said. "You lap it up! You are sitting there licking your lips over it now, gloating on it, and on my hunger! Don't you know, woman, that I haven't had a bite to eat all day? Do I get fed, or not? Will you put your deft whimsey in a steak?"

"Yes," she said. "Would you like a steak?"

"Will you make these old eyes shine with a chop and a delicate dressing of young onions?"

"Yes," she said. "Yes."

He came over and put his arms about her, his eyes searching hers in a look of love and hunger. "Will you make me one of your sauces that is subtle, searching, and hushed?"

"Yes," she said. "Whatever you like I will make it for you."

"Why will you make it for me?" he asked.

It was like a ritual that both of them knew, and they fastened upon each word and answer because they were so eager to hear it from each other.

"Because I love you. Because I want to feed you and to love you."

"Will it be good?" he said.

"It will be so good that there will be no words to tell its goodness," she said. "It will be good because I am so good and beautiful, and because I can do everything better than any other woman you will ever know, and because I love you with all my heart and soul, and want to be a part of you."

"Will this great love get into the food you cook for me?"

"It will be in every morsel that you eat. It will feed your

14

hunger as you've never been fed before. It will be like a living miracle, and will make you better and richer as long as you live. You will never forget it. It will be a glory and a triumph."

"Then this will be such food as no one ever ate before," he said.

"Yes," she said. "It will be."

And it was so. There was never anything like it in the world before April had come back again.

So now they were together. But things were not quite the same between them as they had once been. Even on the surface they were different. No longer now for them was there a single tenement and dwelling place. From the first day of his return he had flatly refused to go back to the house on Waverly Place which the two of them had previously shared for work and love and living. Instead, he had taken these two large rooms on Twelfth Street, which occupied the whole second floor of the house and could be made into one enormous room by opening the sliding doors between them. There was also a tiny kitchen, just big enough to turn around in. The whole arrangement suited George perfectly because it gave him both space and privacy. Here Esther could come and go as she liked; here they could be alone together whenever they wished; here they could feed at the heart of love.

The most important thing about it, however, was that this was *his* place, not *theirs*, and that fact reestablished their relations on a different level. Henceforth he was determined not to let his life and love be one. She had her world of the theatre and of her rich friends which he did not want to belong to, and he had his world of writing which he would have to manage alone. He would keep love a thing apart, and safeguard to himself the mastery of his life, his separate soul, his own integrity.

Would she accept this compromise? Would she take his love, but leave him free to live his life and do his work? That was the way he told her it must be, and she said yes, she understood. But could she do it? Was it in a woman's nature to be content with all that a man could give her, and not forever want what was not his to give? Already there were little portents that made him begin to doubt it.

One morning when she came to see him and was telling him with spirit and great good humor about a little comedy she had witnessed in the street, suddenly she stopped short in the middle of it, a cloud passed over her face, her eyes became troubled, and she turned to him and said:

"You do love me, don't you, George?"

"Yes," he said. "Of course. You know I do."

"Will you never leave me again?" she asked, a little breathless. "Will you go on loving me forever?"

Her abrupt change of mood and her easy assumption that he or any human being could honestly pledge himself to anyone or anything forever struck him as ludicrous, and he laughed.

She made an impatient gesture with her hand. "Don't laugh, George," she said. "I need to know. Tell me. Will you go on loving me forever?"

Her seriousness, and the impossibility of giving her an answer annoyed him now, and he rose from his chair, stared down blankly at her for a moment, and then began pacing back and forth across the room. He paused once or twice and turned to her as if to speak, but, finding it hard to say what he wanted to say, he resumed his nervous pacing.

Esther followed him with her eyes; their expression betraying her mixed feelings, in which amusement and exasperation were giving way to alarm.

"What have I done now?" she thought. "God, was there ever anybody like him! You never can tell what he'll do! All I did was ask him a simple question and he acts like this! Still, it's better than the way he used to act. He used to blow up and call me vile names. Now he just stews in his own juice and I can't tell what he's thinking. Look at him—pacing like a wild animal in a cage, like a temperamental and introspective monkey!"

As a matter of fact, in moments of excitement George did look rather like a monkey. Barrel-chested, with broad, heavy shoulders, he walked with a slight stoop, letting his arms swing loosely, and they were so long that they dangled almost to the knees, the big hands and spatulate fingers curving deeply in like paws. His head, set down solidly upon a short neck, was carried somewhat forward with a thrusting movement, so that his whole figure had a prowling and half-crouching posture. He looked even shorter than he was, for, although he was an inch or two above the middle height, around five feet nine or ten, his legs were not quite proportionate to the upper part of his body. Moreover, his features were small—somewhat pug-nosed, the eyes set very deep in beneath heavy brows, the forehead rather low, the hair beginning not far above the brows. And when he was agitated or interested in something, he had the trick of peering upward with a kind of packed attentiveness, and this, together with his general posture, the head thrust forward, the body prowling downward, gave him a distinctly simian appearance. It was easy to see why some of his friends called him Monk.

Esther watched him a minute or two, feeling disappointed

16

and hurt that he had not answered her. He stopped by the front window and stood looking out, and she went over and quietly put her arm through his. She saw the vein swell in his temple, and knew there was no use in speaking.

Outside, the little Jewish tailors were coming from the office of their union next door and were standing in the street. They were pale, dirty, and greasy, and very much alive. They shouted and gesticulated at one another, they stroked each other gently on the cheek in mounting fury, saying tenderly in a throttled voice: "Nah! Nah! Nah!" Then, still smiling in their rage, they began to slap each other gently in the face with itching finger tips. At length they screamed and dealt each other stinging slaps. Others cursed and shouted, some laughed, and a few said nothing, but stood darkly, somberly apart, feeding upon their entrails.

Then the young Irish cops charged in among them. There was something bought and corrupt about their look. They had brutal and brainless faces, full of pride. Their jaws were loose and coarse, they chewed gum constantly as they shoved and thrust their way along, and they kept saying:

"Break it up, now! Break it up! All right! Keep movin'!"

The motors roared by like projectiles, and people were passing along the pavement. There were the faces George and Esther had never seen before, and there were the faces they had always seen, everywhere: always different, they never changed; they welled up from the sourceless springs of life with unending fecundity, with limitless variety, with incessant movement, and with the monotony of everlasting repetition. There were the three girl-friends who pass along the streets of life forever. One had a cruel and sensual face, she wore glasses, and her mouth was hard and vulgar. Another had the great nose and the little bony features of a rat. The face of the third was full and loose, jeering with fat rouged lips and oily volutes of the nostrils. And when they laughed, there was no warmth or joy in the sound: high, shrill, ugly, and hysterical, their laughter only asked the earth to notice them.

In the street the children played. They were dark and strong and violent, aping talk and toughness from their elders. They leaped on one another and hurled the weakest to the pavement. The policemen herded the noisy little tailors along before them, and they went away. The sky was blue and young and vital, there were no clouds in it; the trees were budding into leaf; the sunlight fell into the street, upon all the people there, with an innocent and fearless life.

Esther glanced at George and saw his face grow twisted as he looked. He wanted to say to her that we are all savage, foolish, violent, and mistaken; that, full of our fear and confusion, we

17

walk in ignorance upon the living and beautiful earth, breathing young, vital air and bathing in the light of morning, seeing it not because of the murder in our hearts.

But he did not say these things. Wearily he turned away from the window.

"There's forever," he said. "There's your forever."

Chapter Two

Fame's First Wooing

In spite of the colorings of guilt that often tinged his brighter moods, George was happier than he had ever been. There can be no doubt about that. He exulted in the fact. The old madness had gone out of him, and for long stretches at a time he was now buoyed up by the glorious belief—not by any means a new one with him, though it was much stronger now than it had ever been before—that he was at last in triumphant control of his destiny. From his early childhood, when he was living like an orphan with his Joyner relatives back in Libya Hill, he had dreamed that one day he would go to New York and there find love and fame and fortune. For several years New York had been the place that he called home, and love was his already; and now he felt, with the assurance of deep conviction, that the time for fame and fortune was at hand.

Anyone is happy who confidently awaits the fulfillment of his highest dreams, and in that way George was happy. And, like most of us when things are going well, he took the credit wholly to himself. It was not chance or luck or any blind confluence of events that had produced the change in his spirits: his contentment and sense of mastery were the reward of his own singular and peculiar merit, and no more than his just due. Nevertheless, fortune had played a central part in his transformation. A most incredible thing had happened.

He had been back in New York only a few days when Lulu Scudder, the literary agent, telephoned him in great excitement. The publishing house of James Rodney & Co. was interested in his manuscript, and Foxhall Edwards, the distinguished editor of this great house, wanted to talk to him about it. Of course, you couldn't tell about these things, but it was always a good idea to strike while the iron was hot. Could he go right away to see Edwards?

As he made his way uptown George told himself that it was silly to be excited, that probably nothing would come of it. Hadn't one publisher already turned the book down, saying that it was no novel? That publisher had even written—and the words of his rejection had seared themselves in George's brain— "The novel form is not adapted to such talents as you have." And it was still the same manuscript. Not a line of it had been changed, not a word cut, in spite of hints from Esther and Miss Scudder that it was too long for any publisher to handle. He had stubbornly refused to alter it, insisting that it would have to be printed as it was or not at all. And he had left the manuscript with Miss Scudder and gone away to Europe, convinced that her efforts to find a publisher would prove futile.

All the time he was abroad it had nauseated him to think of his manuscript, of the years of work and sleepless nights he had put into it, and of the high hopes that had sustained him through it; and he had tried not to think of it, convinced now that it was no good, that he himself was no good, and that all his hot ambitions and his dreams of fame were the vaporings of a shoddy aesthete without talent. In this, he told himself, he was just like most of the other piddling instructors at the School for Utility Cultures, from which he had fled, and to which he would return to resume his classes in English composition when his leave of absence expired. They talked forever about the great books they were writing, or were going to write, because, like him, they needed so desperately to find some avenue of escape from the dreary round of teaching, reading themes, grading papers, and trying to strike a spark in minds that had no flint in them. He had stayed in Europe almost nine months, and no word had come from Miss Scudder, so he had felt confirmed in all his darkest forebodings.

But now she said the Rodney people were interested. Well, they had taken their time about it. And what did "interested" mean? Very likely they would tell him they had detected in the book some slight traces of a talent which, with careful nursing, could be schooled to produce, in time, a publishable book. He had heard that publishers sometimes had a weather eye for this sort of thing and that they would often string an aspiring author along for years, giving him just the necessary degree of encouragement to keep him from abandoning hope altogether and to make him think that they had faith in his great future if only he would go on writing book after rejected book until he "found himself." Well, he'd show them that he was not their fool! Not by so much as a flicker of an eyelash would he betray his disappointment, and he would commit himself to nothing!

If the traffic policeman on the corner noticed a strange young man in front of the office of James Rodney & Co. that morning, he would never have guessed at the core of firm resolution with which this young man had tried to steel himself for the interview that lay before him. If the policeman saw him at all, he probably observed him with misgiving, wondering whether he ought not to intervene to prevent the commission of a felony, or at any rate whether he ought not to speak to the young man and hold him in conversation until the ambulance could arrive and take him to Bellevue for observation.

For, as the young man approached the building at a rapid, loping stride, a stern scowl upon his face and his lips set in a grim line, he had hardly crossed the street and set his foot upon the curb before the publisher's building when his step faltered, he stopped and looked about him as if not knowing what to do, and then, in evident confusion, forced himself to go on. But now his movements were uncertain, as if his legs obeyed his will with great reluctance. He lunged ahead, then stopped, then lunged again and made for the door, only to halt again in a paroxysm of indecision as he came up to it. He stood there facing the door for a moment, clenching and unclenching his hands, then looked about him quickly, suspiciously, as though he expected to find somebody watching him. At last, with a slight shudder of resolution, he thrust his hands deep into his pockets, turned deliberately, and walked on past the door.

And now he moved slowly, the line of his mouth set grimmer than before, and his head was carried stiffly forward from the shoulders as if he were trying to hold himself to the course he had decided upon by focusing on some distant object straight before him. But all the while, as he went along before the entrance and the show windows filled with books which flanked it on both sides, he peered sharply out of the corner of his eye like a spy who had to find out what was going on inside the building without letting the passers-by observe his interest. He walked to the end of the block and turned about and then came back, and again as he passed in front of the publishing house he kept his face fixed straight ahead and looked stealthily out of the corner of his eye. For fifteen or twenty minutes he repeated this strange maneuver, and each time as he approached the door he would hesitate and half turn as if about to enter, and then abruptly go on as before.

Finally, as he came abreast of the entrance for perhaps the fiftieth time, he quickened his stride and seized the door knob—but at once, as though it had given him an electric shock, he snatched his hand away and backed off, and stood on the curb looking up at the house of James Rodney & Co. For several minutes more he stood there, shifting uneasily on his feet and watching all the upper windows as for a sign. Then, suddenly, his jaw muscles tightened, he stuck out his under lip in desperate resolve, and he bolted across the sidewalk, hurled himself against the door, and disappeared inside.

An hour later, if the policeman was still on duty at the corner, he was no doubt puzzled and mystified as before by the young man's behavior as he emerged from the building. He came out slowly, walking mechanically, a dazed look on his face, and in one of his hands, which dangled loosely at his sides, he held a crumpled slip of yellow paper. He emerged from the office of James Rodney & Co. like a man walking in a trance. With the slow and thoughtless movements of an automaton, he turned his steps uptown, and, still with the rapt and dazed look upon his face, he headed north and disappeared into the crowd.

It was late afternoon and the shadows were slanting swiftly eastward when George Webber came to his senses somewhere in the wilds of the upper Bronx. How he got there he never knew. All he could remember was that suddenly he felt hungry and stopped and looked about him and realized where he was. His dazed look gave way to one of amazement and incredulity, and his mouth began to stretch in a broad grin. In his hand he still held the rectangular slip of crisp yellow paper, and slowly he smoothed out the wrinkles and examined it carefully.

It was a check for five hundred dollars. His book had been accepted, and this was an advance against his royalties.

So he was happier than he had ever been in all his life. Fame, at last, was knocking at his door and wooing him with her sweet blandishments, and he lived in a kind of glorious delirium. The next weeks and months were filled with the excitement of the impending event. The book would not be published till the fall, but meanwhile there was much work to do. Foxhall Edwards had made some suggestions for cutting and revising the manuscript, and, although George at first objected, he surprised himself in the end by agreeing with Edwards, and he undertook to do what Edwards wanted.

George had called his novel, *Home to Our Mountains*, and in it he had packed everything he knew about his home town in Old Catawba and the people there. He had distilled every line of it out of his own experience of life. And, now that the issue was decided, he sometimes trembled when he thought that it would be only a matter of months before the whole world knew what he had written. He loathed the thought of giving pain to anyone,

21

and that he might do so had never occurred to him till now. But now it was out of his hands, and he began to feel uneasy. Of course it was fiction, but it was made as all honest fiction must be, from the stuff of human life. Some people might recognize themselves and be offended, and then what would he do? Would he have to go around in smoked glasses and false whiskers? He comforted himself with the hope that his characterizations were not so true as, in another mood, he liked to think they were, and he thought that perhaps no one would notice anything.

Rodney's Magazine, too, had become interested in the young author and was going to publish a story, a chapter from the book, in their next number. This news added immensely to his excitement. He was eager to see his name in print, and in the happy interval of expectancy he felt like a kind of universal Don Juan, for he literally loved everybody—his fellow instructors at the school, his drab students, the little shopkeepers in all the stores, even the nameless hordes that thronged the streets. Rodney's, of course, was the greatest and the finest publishing house in all the world, and Foxhall Edwards was the greatest editor and the finest man that ever was. George had liked him instinctively from the first, and now, like an old and intimate friend, he was calling him Fox. George knew that Fox believed in him, and the editor's faith and confidence, coming as it had come, at a time when George had given up all hope, restored his self-respect and charged him with energy for new work.

Already his next novel was begun and was beginning to take shape within him. He would soon have to get it out of him. He dreaded the prospect of buckling down in earnest to write it, for he knew the agony of it. It was like demoniacal possession, driving him with an alien force much greater than his own. While the fury of creation was upon him, it meant sixty cigarettes a day, twenty cups of coffee, meals snatched anyhow and anywhere and at whatever time of day or night he happened to remember he was hungry. It meant sleeplessness, and miles of walking to bring on the physical fatigue without which he could not sleep, then nightmares, nerves, and exhaustion in the morning. As he said to Fox:

"There are better ways to write a book, but this, God help me, is mine, and you'll have to learn to put up with it."

When *Rodney's Magazine* came out with the story, George fully expected convulsions of the earth, falling meteors, suspension of traffic in the streets, and a general strike. But nothing happened. A few of his friends mentioned it, but that was all. For several days he felt let down, but then his common sense reassured him that people couldn't really tell much about a new author from a short piece in a magazine. The book would show them who he was and what he could do. It would be different then. He could afford to wait a little longer for the fame which he was certain would soon be his.

It was not until later, after the first excitement had worn off and George had become accustomed to the novelty of being an author whose book was actually going to be published, that he began to learn a little about the unknown world of publishing and the people who inhabit it—and not till then did he begin to understand and appreciate the real quality of Fox Edwards. And it was through Otto Hauser—so much like Fox in his essential integrity, so sharply contrasted to him in other respects—that George got his first real insight into the character of his editor.

Hauser was a reader at Rodney's, and probably the best publisher's reader in America. He might have been a publisher's editor—a rare and good one—had he been driven forward by ambition, enthusiasm, daring, tenacious resolution, and that eagerness to seek and find the best which a great editor must have. But Hauser was content to spend his days reading ridiculous manuscripts written by ridiculous people on all sorts of ridiculous subjects—"The Breast Stroke," "Rock Gardens for Everybody," "The Life and Times of Lydia Pinkham," "The New Age of Plenty"—and once in a while something that had the fire of passion, the spark of genius, the glow of truth.

Otto Hauser lived in a tiny apartment near First Avenue, and he invited George to drop in one evening. George went, and they spent the evening talking. After that he returned again and again because he liked Otto, and also because he was puzzled by the contradictions of his qualities, especially by something aloof, impersonal, and withdrawing in his nature which seemed so out of place beside the clear and positive elements in his character.

Otto did all the housekeeping himself. He had tried having cleaning women in from time to time, but eventually he had dispensed entirely with their services. They were not clean and tidy enough to suit him, and their casual and haphazard disarrangements of objects that had been placed exactly where he wanted them annoyed his order-loving soul. He hated clutter. He had only a few books—a shelf or two—most of them the latest publications of the house of Rodney, and a few volumes sent him by other publishers. Usually he gave his books away as soon as he finished reading them because he hated clutter, and books made clutter. Sometimes he wondered if he didn't hate books, too. Certainly he didn't like to have many of them around: the sight of them irritated him.

23

George found him a curious enigma. Otto Hauser was possessed of remarkable gifts, yet he was almost wholly lacking in those qualities which cause a man to "get on" in the world. In fact, he didn't want to "get on." He had a horror of "getting on," of going any further than he had already gone. He wanted to be a publisher's reader, and nothing more. At James Rodney & Co. he did the work they put into his hands. He did punctiliously what he was required to do. He gave his word, when he was asked to give it, with the complete integrity of his quiet soul, the unerring rightness of his judgment, the utter finality of his Germanic spirit. But beyond that he would not go.

When one of the editors at Rodney's, of whom there were several besides Foxhall Edwards, asked Hauser for his opinion, the ensuing conversation would go something like this:

"You have read the manuscript?"

"Yes," said Hauser, "I have read it."

"What did you think of it?"

"I thought it was without merit."

"Then you do not recommend its publication?"

"No, I do not think it is worth publishing."

Or:

"Did you read that manuscript?"

"Yes," Hauser would say. "I read it."

"Well, what did you think of it? (Confound it, can't the fellow say what he thinks without having to be asked all the time!)"

"I think it is a work of genius."

Incredulously: "You *do*!"

"I do, yes. To my mind there is no question about it."

"But look here, Hauser—" excitedly—"if what you say is true, this boy—the fellow who wrote it—why, he's just a kid—no one ever heard of him before—comes from somewhere out West—Nebraska, Iowa, one of those places—never been anywhere, apparently—if what you say is true, we've made a discovery!"

"I suppose you have. Yes. The book is a work of genius."

"But— (Damn it all, what's wrong with the man anyway? Here he makes a discovery like this—an astounding statement of this sort—and shows no more enthusiasm than if he were discussing a cabbage head!)—but, see here, then! You—you mean there's something wrong with it?"

"No, I don't think there's anything wrong with it. I think it is a magnificent piece of writing."

"But—(Good Lord, the fellow *is* a queer fish!)—but you mean to say that—that perhaps it's not suitable for publication in its present form?"

"No. I think it's eminently publishable."

"But it's overwritten, isn't it?"

24

"It *is* overwritten. Yes."

"I thought so, too," said the editor shrewdly. "Of course, the fellow shows he knows very little about writing. He doesn't know how he does it, he repeats himself continually, he is childish and exuberant and extravagant, and he does ten times too much of everything. We have a hundred other writers who know more about writing than he does."

"I suppose we have, yes," Hauser agreed. "Nevertheless, he is a man of genius, and they are not. His book is a work of genius, and theirs are not."

"Then you think we ought to publish him?"

"I think so, yes."

"But—(Ah, here's the catch, maybe—the thing he's holding back on!)—but you think this is all he has to say?—that he's written himself out in this one book?—that he'll never be able to write another?"

"No. I think nothing of the sort. I can't say, of course. They may kill him, as they often do——"

"(God, what a gloomy Gus the fellow is!)"

"—but on the basis of this book, I should say there's no danger of his running dry. He should have fifty books in him."

"But—(Good Lord! What *is* the catch?)—but then you mean you don't think it's time for such a book as this in America yet?"

"No, I don't mean that. I think it *is* time."

"Why?"

"Because it has happened. It is always time when it happens."

"But some of our best critics say it's not time."

"I know they do. However, they are wrong. It is simply not their time, that's all."

"How do you mean?"

"I mean, their time is critic's time. The book is creator's time. The two times are not the same."

"You think, then, that the critics are behind the time?"

"They are behind creator's time, yes."

"Then they may not see this book as the work of genius which you say it is. Do you think they will?"

"I can't say. Perhaps not. However, it doesn't matter."

"Doesn't *matter*! Why, what do you mean?"

"I mean that the thing is good, and cannot be destroyed. Therefore it doesn't matter what anyone says."

"Then—Good Lord, Hauser!—if what you say is true, we've made a great discovery!"

"I think you have. Yes."

"But—but—is that *all* you have to say?"

"I think so, yes. What else *is* there to say?"

Baffled: "Nothing—only, I should think *you* would be excited about it!" Then, completely defeated and resigned: "Oh, *all* right! *All* right, Hauser! Thanks very much!"

The people at Rodney's couldn't understand it. They didn't know what to make of it. Finally, they had given up trying, all except Fox Edwards—and Fox would never give up trying to understand anything. Fox still came by Hauser's office—his little cell—and looked in on him. Fox's old grey hat would be pushed back on his head, for he never took it off when he worked, and there would be a look of troubled wonder in his sea-pale eyes as he bent over and stooped and craned and stared at Hauser, as if he were regarding for the first time some fantastic monster from the marine jungles of the ocean. Then he would turn and walk away, hands hanging to his coat lapels, and in his eyes there would be a look of utter astonishment.

Fox couldn't understand it yet. As for Hauser himself, he had no answers, nothing to tell them.

It was not until George Webber had become well acquainted with both men that he began to penetrate the mystery. Foxhall Edwards and Otto Hauser—to know them both, to see them working in the same office, each in his own way, was to understand them both as perhaps neither could have been understood completely by himself. Each man, by being what he was, revealed to George the secret springs of character which had made the two of them so much alike—and so utterly different.

There may have been a time when an intense and steady flame had been alive in the quiet depths of Otto Hauser's spirit. But that was before he knew what it was like to be a great editor. Now he had seen it for himself, and he wanted none of it. For ten years he had watched Fox Edwards, and he well knew what was needed: the pure flame living in the midst of darkness; the constant, quiet, and relentless effort of the will to accomplish what the pure flame burned for, what the spirit knew; the unspoken agony of that constant effort as it fought to win through to its clear purpose and somehow to subdue the world's blind and brutal force of ignorance, hostility, prejudice, and intolerance which were opposed to it—the fools of age, the fools of prudery, the fools of genteelness, fogyism, and nice-Nellyism, the fools of bigotry, Philistinism, jealousy, and envy, and, worst of all, the simple, utter, sheer damn fools of nature!

Oh, to burn so, so to be consumed, exhausted, spent by the passion of this constant flame! And for what? For *what*? And *why*? Because some obscure kid from Tennessee, some tenant farmer's son from Georgia, or some country doctor's boy in

North Dakota—untitled, unpedigreed, unhallowed by fools' standards—had been touched with genius, and so had striven to give a tongue to the high passion of his loneliness, to wrest from his locked spirit his soul's language and a portion of the tongue of his unuttered brothers, to find a channel in the blind immensity of this harsh land for the pent tides of his creation, and to make, perhaps, in this howling wilderness of life some carving and some dwelling of his own—all this before the world's fool-bigotry, fool-ignorance, fool-cowardice, fool-faddism, fool-mockery, fool-stylism, and fool-hatred for anyone who was not corrupted, beaten, and a fool had either quenched the hot, burning passion with ridicule, contempt, denial, and oblivion, or else corrupted the strong will with the pollutions of fool-success. It was for this that such as Fox must burn and suffer—to keep that flame of agony alive in the spirit of some inspired and stricken boy until the world of fools had taken it into their custody, and betrayed it!

Otto Hauser had seen it all.

And in the end what was the reward for such a one as Fox? To achieve the lonely and unhoped-for victories one by one, and to see the very fools who had denied them acclaim them as their own. To lapse again to search, to silence, and to waiting while fools greedily pocketed as their own the coin of one man's spirit, proudly hailed as *their* discovery the treasure of another's exploration, loudly celebrated their own vision as they took unto themselves the fulfillment of another's prophecy. Ah, the heart must break at last—the heart of Fox, as well as the heart of genius, the lost boy; the frail, small heart of man must falter, stop at last from beating; but the heart of folly would beat on forever.

So Otto Hauser would have none of it. He would grow hot over nothing. He would try to see the truth for himself, and let it go at that.

This was Otto Hauser as George came to know him. In the confidence of friendship Otto held up a mirror to his own soul, affording a clear, unposed reflection of his quiet, unassuming, and baffling integrity; but in the same mirror he also revealed, without quite being aware of it, the stronger and more shining image of Fox Edwards.

George knew how fortunate he was to have as his editor a man like Fox. And as time went on, and his respect and admiration for the older man warmed to deep affection, he realized that Fox had become for him much more than editor

27

and friend. Little by little it seemed to George that he had found in Fox the father he had lost and had long been looking for. And so it was that Fox became a second father to him—the father of his spirit.

Chapter Three

The Microscopic Gentleman from Japan

In the old house where George lived that year Mr. Katamoto occupied the ground floor just below him, and in a little while they got to know each other very well. It might be said that their friendship began in mystification and went on to a state of security and staunch understanding.

Not that Mr. Katamoto ever forgave George when he erred. He was always instantly ready to inform him that he had taken a false step again (the word is used advisedly), but he was so infinitely patient, so unflaggingly hopeful of George's improvement, so unfailingly good-natured and courteous, that no one could possibly have been angry or failed to try to mend his ways. What saved the situation was Katamoto's gleeful, childlike sense of humor. He was one of those microscopic gentlemen from Japan, scarcely five feet tall, thin and very wiry in his build, and George's barrel chest, broad shoulders, long, dangling arms, and large feet seemed to inspire his comic risibilities from the beginning. The first time they met, as they were just passing each other in the hall, Katamoto began to giggle when he saw George coming; and as they came abreast, the little man flashed a great expanse of gleaming teeth, wagged a finger roguishly, and said:

"Tramp-ling! Tramp-ling!"

For several days, whenever they passed each other in the hall, this same performance was repeated. George thought the words were very mysterious, and at first could not fathom their recondite meaning or understand why the sound of them was enough to set Katamoto off in a paroxysm of mirth. And yet when he would utter them and George would look at him in a surprised, inquiring kind of way, Katamoto would bend double with convulsive laughter and would stamp at the floor like a child with a tiny foot, shrieking hysterically: "Yis—yis—yis!

You are tramp-ling!"—after which he would flee away.

George inferred that these mysterious references to "trampling" which always set Katamoto off in such a fit of laughter had something to do with the bigness of his feet, for Katamoto would look at them quickly and slyly as he passed, and then giggle. However, a fuller explanation was soon provided. Katamoto came upstairs one afternoon and knocked at George's door. When it was opened, he giggled and flashed his teeth and looked somewhat embarrassed. After a moment, with evident hesitancy, he grinned painfully and said:

"If you ple-e-eze, sir! Will you—have some tea—with me—yis?"

He spoke the words very slowly, with deliberate formality, after which he flashed a quick, eager, and ingratiating smile.

George told him he would be glad to, and got his coat and started downstairs with him. Katamoto padded swiftly on ahead, his little feet shod in felt slippers that made no sound. Halfway down the stairs, as if the noise of George's heavy tread had touched his funnybone again, Katamoto stopped quickly, turned and pointed at George's feet, and giggled coyly: "Trampling! You are tramp-ling!" Then he turned and fairly fled away down the stairs and down the hall, shrieking like a gleeful child. He waited at the door to usher his guest in, introduced him to the slender, agile little Japanese girl who seemed to stay there all the time, and finally brought George back into his studio and served him tea.

It was an amazing place. Katamoto had redecorated the fine old rooms and fitted them up according to the whims of his curious taste. The big back room was very crowded, intricate, and partitioned off into several small compartments with beautiful Japanese screens. He had also constructed a flight of stairs and a balcony that extended around three sides of the room, and on this balcony George could see a couch. The room was crowded with tiny chairs and tables, and there was an opulent-looking sofa and cushions. There were a great many small carved objects and bric-a-brac, and a strong smell of incense.

The center of the room, however, had been left entirely bare save for a big strip of spattered canvas and an enormous plaster figure. George gathered that he did a thriving business turning out sculptures for expensive speakeasies, or immense fifteen-foot statues of native politicians which were to decorate public squares in little towns, or in the state capitals of Arkansas, Nebraska, Iowa, and Wyoming. Where and how he had learned this curious profession George never found out, but he had mastered it with true Japanese fidelity, and so well that his products were apparently in greater demand than those of American sculptors. In spite of his small size and fragile build, the man was a dynamo of energy and could perform the labors of a Titan. God knows how he did it—where he found the strength.

George asked a question about the big plaster cast in the center of the room, and Katamoto took him over and showed it to him, remarking as he pointed to the creature's huge feet:

"He is—like you! . . . He is tramp-ling! . . . Yis! . . . He is tramp-ling!"

Then he took George up the stairs onto the balcony, which George dutifully admired.

"Yis!— You like it?" He smiled at George eagerly, a little doubtfully, then pointed at his couch and said: "I sleep here!" Then he pointed to the ceiling, which was so low that George had to stoop. "You sleep there?" said Katamoto eagerly.

George nodded.

Katamoto went on again with a quick smile, but with embarrassed hesitancy and a painful difficulty in his tone that had not been there before:

"I here," he said pointing, "you there—yis?"

He looked at George almost pleadingly, a little desperately —and suddenly George began to catch on.

"Oh! You mean I am right above you—" Katamoto nodded with instant relief—"and sometimes when I stay up late you hear me?"

"Yis! Yis!" He kept nodding his head vigorously. "Sometimes—" he smiled a little painfully—"sometimes—you will be tramp-ling!" He shook his finger at George with coy reproof and giggled.

"I'm awfully sorry," George said. "Of course, I didn't know you slept so near—so near the ceiling. When I work late I pace the floor. It's a bad habit. I'll do what I can to stop it."

"Oh, no-o!" he cried, genuinely distressed. "I not want—how you say it?—change your life! . . . If you ple-e-ese, sir! Just little thing—not wear shoes at night!" He pointed at his own small felt-shod feet and smiled up at George hopefully. "You like slippers—yis?" And he smiled persuasively again.

After that, of course, George wore slippers. But sometimes he would forget, and the next morning Katamoto would be rapping at his door again. He was never angry, he was always patient and good-humored, he was always beautifully courteous—but he would always call George to account. "You were tramp-ling!" he would cry. "Last night—again—trampling!" And George would tell him he was sorry and would try not to do it again, and Katamoto would go away giggling, pausing to turn and wag his finger roguishly and call out once more, "Tramp-ling!"—after which he would flee downstairs, shrieking with laughter.

They were good friends.

In the months that followed, again and again George would come in the house to find the hall below full of sweating, panting movers, over whom Katamoto, covered from head to foot with clots and lumps of plaster, would hover prayerfully and with a fearful, pleading grin lest they mar his work, twisting his small hands together convulsively, aiding the work along by slight shudders, quick darts of breathless terror, writhing and shrinking movements of the body, and saying all the while with an elaborate, strained, and beseeching courtesy:

"Now, if—*you*—gentleman—a little! . . . *You* . . . yis—yis—yis-s!" with a convulsive grin. "*Oh-h-h!* Yis—yis-s! If you *ple-e-ese*, sir! . . . If you would down—a little—yis-s!—yis-s!—yis-s!" he hissed softly with that prayerful and pleading grin.

And the movers would carry out of the house and stow into their van the enormous piecemeal fragments of some North Dakota Pericles, whose size was so great that one wondered how this dapper, fragile little man could possibly have fashioned such a leviathan.

Then the movers would depart, and for a space Mr. Katamoto would loaf and invite his soul. He would come out in the backyard with his girl, the slender, agile little Japanese —who looked as if she had some Italian blood in her as well —and for hours at a time they would play at handball. Mr. Katamoto would knock the ball up against the projecting brick wall of the house next door, and every time he scored a point he would scream with laughter, clapping his small hands together, bending over weakly and pressing his hand against his stomach, and staggering about with delight and merriment. Choking with laughter, he would cry out in a high, delirious voice as rapidly as he could:

"Yis, yis, yis! Yis, yis, yis! Yis, yis, yis!"

Then he would catch sight of George looking at him from the window, and this would set him off again, for he would wag his finger and fairly scream:

"You were tramp-ling! . . . Yis, yis, yis! . . . Last night—again tramp-ling!"

This would reduce him to such a paroxysm of mirth that he would stagger across the court and lean against the wall, all caved in, holding his narrow stomach and shrieking faintly.

It was now the full height of steaming summer, and one day early in August George came home to find the movers in the house again. This time it was obvious that a work of more than usual magnitude was in transit. Mr. Katamoto, spattered with plaster, was of course hovering about in the hall, grinning nervously and fluttering prayerfully around the husky truckmen. As George came in, two of the men were backing slowly down the hall, carrying between them an immense head, monstrously jowled and set in an expression of far-seeing statesmanship. A moment later three more men backed out of the studio, panting and cursing as they grunted painfully around the flowing fragment of a long frock coat and the vested splendor of a bulging belly. The first pair had now gone back in the studio, and when they came out again they were staggering beneath the trousered shank of a mighty leg and a booted Atlantean hoof, and as they passed, one of the other men, now returning for more of the statesman's parts, pressed himself against the wall to let them by and said:

"Jesus! If the son-of-a-bitch stepped on you with that foot, he wouldn't leave a grease spot, would he, Joe?"

The last piece of all was an immense fragment of the Solon's arm and fist, with one huge forefinger pointed upward in an attitude of solemn objurgation and avowal.

That figure was Katamoto's masterpiece; and George felt as he saw it pass that the enormous upraised finger was the summit of his art and the consummation of his life. Certainly it was the apple of his eye. George had never seen him before in such a state of extreme agitation. He fairly prayed above the sweating men. It was obvious that the coarse indelicacy of their touch made him shudder. The grin was frozen on his face in an expression of congealed terror. He writhed, he wriggled, he wrung his little hands, he crooned to them. And if anything had happened to that fat, pointed finger, George felt sure that he would have dropped dead on the spot.

At length, however, they got everything stowed away in their big van without mishap and drove off with their Ozymandias, leaving Mr. Katamoto, frail, haggard, and utterly exhausted, looking at the curb. He came back into the house and saw George standing there and smiled wanly at him.

"Tramp-ling," he said feebly, and shook his finger, and for the first time there was no mirth or energy in him.

George had never seen him tired before. It had never occurred to him that he could get tired. The little man had always been so full of inexhaustible life. And now, somehow, George felt an unaccountable sadness to see him so weary and so strangely grey. Katamoto was silent for a moment, and then he lifted his face and said, almost tonelessly, yet with a shade of wistful eagerness:

"You see statue—yis?"

"Yes, Kato, I saw it."

"And you like?"

"Yes, very much."

"And—" he giggled a little and made a shaking movement with his hands—"you see foot?"

"Yes."

"I sink," he said, "he will be tramp-ling—yis?"—and he made a laughing sound.

"He ought to," George said, "with a hoof like that. It's almost as big as mine," he added, as an afterthought.

Katamoto seemed delighted with this observation, for he laughed shrilly and said: "Yis! Yis!"—nodding his head emphatically. He was silent for another moment, then hesitantly, but with an eagerness that he could not conceal, he said:

"And you see finger?"

"Yes, Kato."

"And you like?"—quickly, earnestly.

"Very much."

"Big finger—yis?"—with a note of rising triumph in his voice.

"Very big, Kato."

"And *pointing*—yis?" he said ecstatically, grinning from ear to ear and pointing his own small finger heavenward.

"Yes, pointing."

He sighed contentedly. "Well, zen," he said, with the appeased air of a child, "I'm glad you like."

For a week or so after that George did not see Katamoto again or even think of him. This was the vacation period at the School for Utility Cultures, and George was devoting every minute of his time, day and night, to a fury of new writing. Then one afternoon, a long passage completed and the almost illegible pages of his swift scrawl tossed in a careless heap upon the floor, he sat relaxed, looking out of his back window, and suddenly he thought of Katamoto again. He remembered that he had not seen him recently, and it seemed strange that he had not even heard the familiar thud of the little ball against the wall outside or the sound of his high, shrill laughter. This realization, with its sense of loss, so troubled him that he went downstairs immediately and pressed Katamoto's bell.

There was no answer. All was silent. He waited, and no one came. Then he went down to the basement and found the janitor and spoke to him. He said that Mr. Katamoto had been ill. No, it was not serious, he thought, but the doctor had advised a rest, a brief period of relaxation from his exhausting labors, and had sent him for care and observation to the near-by hospital.

George meant to go to see him, but he was busy with his writing and kept putting it off. Then one morning, some ten days later, coming back home after breakfast in a restaurant, he found a moving van backed up before the house. Katamoto's door was open, and when he looked inside the moving people had already stripped the apartment almost bare. In the center of the once fantastic room, now empty, where Katamoto had performed his prodigies of work, stood a young Japanese, an acquaintance of the sculptor, whom George had seen there several times before. He was supervising the removal of the last furnishings.

The young Japanese looked up quickly, politely, with a toothy grin of frozen courtesy as George came in. He did not speak until George asked him how Mr. Katamoto was. And then, with the same toothy, frozen grin upon his face, the same impenetrable courtesy, he said that Mr. Katamoto was dead.

George was shocked, and stood there for a moment, knowing there was nothing more to say, and yet feeling somehow, as people always feel on these occasions, that there was something he *ought* to say. He looked at the young Japanese and started to speak, and found himself looking into the inscrutable, polite, untelling eyes of Asia.

So he said nothing more. He just thanked the young man and went out.

Chapter Four

Some Things Will Never Change

Out of his front windows George could see nothing except the somber bulk of the warehouse across the street. It was an old building, with a bleak and ugly front of rusty, indurated brown and a harsh webbing of fire escapes, and across the whole width of the façade stretched a battered wooden sign on which, in faded letters, one could make out the name—"The Security Distributing Corp." George did not know what a distributing corporation was, but every day since he had come into this street to live, enormous motor vans had driven up before this dingy building and had backed snugly against the worn plankings of the loading platform, which ended with a sharp, sheared emptiness four feet above the sidewalk. The drivers and their helpers would leap from their seats, and instantly the quiet depths of the old building would burst into a furious energy of work, and the air would be filled with harsh cries:

"Back it up, deh! Back it up! Cuh-*mahn*! Cuh-*mahn*! Givvus a hand, youse guys! Hey-y! *You!*"

They looked at one another with hard faces smiling derision, quietly saying "Jesus!" out of the corners of their mouths. Surly, they stood upon their rights, defending truculently the narrow frontier of their duty:

"Wadda *I* care where it goes! Dat's *yoeh* lookout! Wat t'hell's it got to do wit *me*?"

They worked with speed and power and splendid aptness, furiously, unamiably, with high, exacerbated voices, spurred and goaded by their harsh unrest.

The city was their stony-hearted mother, and from her breast they had drawn a bitter nurture. Born to brick and asphalt, to crowded tenements and swarming streets, stunned into sleep as children beneath the sudden slamming racket of the elevated trains, taught to fight, to menace, and to struggle in a world of savage violence and incessant din, they had had the city's qualities stamped into their flesh and movements, distilled through all their tissues, etched with the city's acid into their tongue and brain and vision. Their faces were tough and seamed, the skin thick, dry, without a hue of freshness or of color. Their pulse beat with the furious rhythm of the city's stroke: ready in an instant with a curse, metallic clangors sounded from their twisted lips, and their hearts were filled with a dark, immense, and secret pride.

Their souls were like the asphalt visages of city streets. Each day the violent colors of a thousand new sensations swept across them, and each day all sound and sight and fury were erased from their unyielding surfaces. Ten thousand furious days had passed about them, and they had no memory. They lived like creatures born full-grown into present time, shedding the whole accumulation of the past with every breath, and all their lives were written in the passing of each actual moment.

And they were sure and certain, forever wrong, but always confident. They had no hesitation, they confessed no ignorance or error, and they knew no doubts. They began each morning with a gibe, a shout, an oath of hard impatience, eager for the tumult of the day. At noon they sat strongly in their seats and, through fumes of oil and hot machinery, addressed their curses to the public at the tricks and strategies of cunning rivals, the tyranny of the police, the stupidity of pedestrians, and the errors of less skillful men than they. Each day they faced the perils of the streets with hearts as calm as if they were alone upon a country road. Each day, with minds untroubled, they embarked upon adventures from which the bravest men bred in the wilderness would have recoiled in terror and desolation.

In the raw days of early spring they had worn shirts of thick black wool and leather jackets, but now, in summer, their arms were naked, tattooed, brown, and lean with the play of whipcord muscles. The power and precision with which they worked stirred in George a deep emotion of respect, and also touched him with humility. For whenever he saw it, his own life, with its conflicting desires, its uncertain projects and designs, its labors begun in hope and so often ended in incompletion, by comparison with the lives of these men who had learned to use their strength and talents perfectly, seemed faltering, blind, and baffled.

At night, too, five times a week, the mighty vans would line up at the curb in an immense and waiting caravan. They were covered now with great tarpaulins, small green lamps were burning on each side, and the drivers, their faces faintly lit with the glowing points of cigarettes, would be talking quietly in the shadows of the huge machines. Once George had asked one of the drivers the destination of these nightly journeys, and the man had told him that they went to Philadelphia, and would return again by morning.

The sight of these great vans at night, somber, silent, yet alive with powerful expectancy as their drivers waited for the word to start, gave George a sense of mystery and joy. These men were part of that great company who love the night, and he felt a bond of union with them. For he had always loved the night more dearly than the day, and the energies of his life had risen to their greatest strength in the secret and exultant heart of darkness.

He knew the joys and labors of such men as these. He could see the shadowy procession of their vans lumbering through the sleeping towns, and feel the darkness, the cool fragrance of the country, on his face. He could see the drivers hunched behind the wheels, their senses all alert in the lilac dark, their eyes fixed hard upon the road to curtain off the loneliness of the land at night. And he knew the places where they stopped to eat, the little all-night lunchrooms warm with greasy light, now empty save for the dozing authority of the aproned Greek behind the

36

counter, and now filled with the heavy shuffle of the drivers'
feet, the hard and casual intrusions of their voices.

They came in, flung themselves upon the row of stools, and
gave their orders. And as they waited, their hunger drawn into
sharp focus by the male smells of boiling coffee, frying eggs and
onions, and sizzling hamburgers, they took the pungent,
priceless, and uncostly solace of a cigarette, lit between cupped
hand and strong-seamed mouth, drawn deep and then exhaled
in slow fumes from the nostrils. They poured great gobs and
gluts of thick tomato ketchup on their hamburgers, tore with
blackened fingers at the slabs of fragrant bread, and ate with
jungle lust, thrusting at plate and cup with quick and savage
gulpings.

Oh, he was with them, of them, for them, blood brother of
their joy and hunger to the last hard swallow, the last deep ease
of sated bellies, the last slow coil of blue expiring from their
grateful lungs. Their lives seemed glorious to him in the magic
dark of summer. They swept cleanly through the night into the
first light and bird song of the morning, into the morning of new
joy upon the earth; and as he thought of this it seemed to him
that the secret, wild, and lonely heart of man was young and
living in the darkness, and could never die.

Before him, all that summer of 1929, in the broad window of
the warehouse, a man sat at a desk and looked out into the
street, in a posture that never changed. George saw him there
whenever he glanced across, yet he never saw him do anything
but look out of the window with a fixed, abstracted stare. At
first the man had been such an unobtrusive part of his surroundings that he had seemed to fade into them, and had gone
almost unnoticed. Then Esther, having observed him there,
pointed to him one day and said merrily:

"There's our friend in the Distributing Corp again! What do
you suppose he distributes? I've never seen him do anything!
Have you noticed him—hah?" she cried eagerly. "God! It's the
strangest thing I ever saw!" She laughed richly, made a shrug of
bewildered protest, and, after a moment, said with serious
wonder: "Isn't it queer? What do you suppose a man like that
can do? What do you suppose he's thinking of?"

"Oh, I don't know," George said indifferently. "Of nothing, I
suppose."

Then they forgot the man and turned to talk of other things,
yet from that moment the man's singular presence was pricked
out in George's mind and he began to watch him with hypnotic

37

fascination, puzzled by the mystery of his immobility and his stare.

And after that, as soon as Esther came in every day, she would glance across the street and cry out in a jolly voice which had in it the note of affectionate satisfaction and assurance that people have when they see some familiar and expected object:

"Well, I see our old friend, The Distributing Corp, is still looking out of his window! I wonder what he's thinking of today."

She would turn away, laughing. Then, for a moment, with her childlike fascination for words and rhythms, she gravely meditated their strange beat, silently framing and pronouncing with her lips a series of meaningless sounds—"Corp-Borp-Forp-Dorp-Torp"—and at length singing out in a gleeful chant, and with an air of triumphant discovery:

"The Distributing Corp, the Distributing Corp,
He sits all day and he does no Worp!"

George protested that her rhyme made no sense, but she threw back her encrimsoned face and screamed with laughter.

But after a while they stopped laughing about the man. For, obscure as his employment seemed, incredible and comical as his indolence had been when they first noticed it, there came to be something impressive, immense, and formidable in the quality of that fixed stare. Day by day, a thronging traffic of life and business passed before him in the street; day by day, the great vans came, the drivers, handlers, and packers swarmed before his eyes, filling the air with their oaths and cries, irritably intent upon their labor; but the man in the window never looked at them, never gave any sign that he heard them, never seemed to be aware of their existence—he just sat there and looked out, his eyes fixed in an abstracted stare.

In the course of George Webber's life, many things of no great importance in themselves had become deeply embedded in his memory, stuck there like burs in a scottie's tail; and always they were little things which, in an instant of clear perception, had riven his heart with some poignant flash of meaning. Thus he remembered, and would remember forever, the sight of Esther's radiant, earnest face when, unexpectedly one night, he caught sight of it as it flamed and vanished in a crowd of grey, faceless faces in Times Square. So, too, he remembered two deaf mutes he had seen talking on their fingers in a subway train; and a ringing peal of children's laughter in a desolate street at sunset; and the waitresses in their dingy little rooms across the backyard, washing, ironing, and rewashing day after day the few adornments of their shabby finery, in endless preparations for a visitor who never came.

And now, to his store of treasured trivia was added the memory of this man's face—thick, white, expressionless, set in its stolid and sorrowful stare. Immutable, calm, impassive, it became for him the symbol of a kind of permanence in the rush and sweep of chaos in the city, where all things come and go and pass and are so soon forgotten. For, day after day, as he watched the man and tried to penetrate his mystery, at last it seemed to him that he had found the answer.

And after that, in later years, whenever he remembered the man's face, the time was fixed at the end of a day in late summer. Without violence or heat, the last rays of the sun fell on the warm brick of the building and painted it with a sad, unearthly light. In the window the man sat, always looking out. He never wavered in his gaze, his eyes were calm and sorrowful, and on his face was legible the exile of an imprisoned spirit.

That man's face became for him the face of Darkness and of Time. It never spoke, and yet it had a voice—a voice that seemed to have the whole earth in it. It was the voice of evening and of night, and in it were the blended tongues of all those men who have passed through the heat and fury of the day, and who now lean quietly upon the sills of evening. In it was the whole vast hush and weariness that comes upon the city at the hour of dusk, when the chaos of another day is ended, and when everything—streets, buildings, and eight million people—breathe slowly, with a tired and sorrowful joy. And in that single tongueless voice was the knowledge of all their tongues.

"Child, child," it said, "have patience and belief, for life is many days, and each present hour will pass away. Son, son, you have been mad and drunken, furious and wild, filled with hatred and despair, and all the dark confusions of the soul—but so have we. You found the earth too great for your one life, you found your brain and sinew smaller than the hunger and desire that fed on them—but it has been this way with all men. You have stumbled on in darkness, you have been pulled in opposite directions, you have faltered, you have missed the way—but, child, this is the chronicle of the earth. And now, because you have known madness and despair, and because you will grow desperate again before you come to evening, we who have stormed the ramparts of the furious earth and been hurled back, we who have been maddened by the unknowable and bitter mystery of love, we who have hungered after fame and savored all of life, the tumult, pain, and frenzy, and now sit quietly by our windows watching all that henceforth never more shall touch us—we call upon you to take heart, for we can swear to you that these things pass.

"We have outlived the shift and glitter of so many fashions, we have seen so many things that come and go, so many words forgotten, so many fames that flared and were destroyed; yet we know now we are strangers whose footfalls have not left a print upon the endless streets of life. We shall not go into the dark again, nor suffer madness, nor admit despair: we have built a wall about us now. We shall not hear the clocks of time strike out on foreign air, nor wake at morning in some alien land to think of home: our wandering is over, and our hunger fed. O brother, son, and comrade, because we have lived so long and seen so much, we are content to make our own a few things now, letting millions pass.

"Some things will never change. Some things will always be the same. Lean down your ear upon the earth, and listen.

"The voice of forest water in the night, a woman's laughter in the dark, the clean, hard rattle of raked gravel, the cricketing stitch of midday in hot meadows, the delicate web of children's voices in bright air—these things will never change.

"The glitter of sunlight on roughened water, the glory of the stars, the innocence of morning, the smell of the sea in harbors, the feathery blur and smoky buddings of young boughs, and something there that comes and goes and never can be captured, the thorn of spring, the sharp and tongueless cry—these things will always be the same.

"All things belonging to the earth will never change—the leaf, the blade, the flower, the wind that cries and sleeps and wakes again, the trees whose stiff arms clash and tremble in the dark, and the dust of lovers long since buried in the earth—all things proceeding from the earth to seasons, all things that lapse and change and come again upon the earth—these things will always be the same, for they come up from the earth that never changes, they go back into the earth that lasts forever. Only the earth endures, but it endures forever.

"The tarantula, the adder, and the asp will also never change. Pain and death will always be the same. But under the pavements trembling like a pulse, under the buildings trembling like a cry, under the waste of time, under the hoof of the beast above the broken bones of cities, there will be something growing like a flower, something bursting from the earth again, forever deathless, faithful, coming into life again like April."

Chapter Five

The Hidden Terror

He looked at the yellow envelope curiously and turned it over and over in his hand. It gave him a feeling of uneasiness and suppressed excitement to see his name through the transparent front. He was not used to receiving telegrams. Instinctively he delayed opening it because he dreaded what it might contain. Some forgotten incident in his childhood made him associate telegrams with bad news. Who could have sent it? And what could it be about? Well, open it, you fool, and find out!

He ripped off the flap and took out the message. He read it quickly, first glancing at the signature. It was from his Uncle Mark Joyner:

"YOUR AUNT MAW DIED LAST NIGHT STOP FUNERAL THURSDAY IN LIBYA HILL STOP COME HOME IF YOU CAN."

That was all. No explanation of what she had died of. Old age, most likely. Nothing else could have killed her. She hadn't been sick or they would have let him know before this.

The news shook him profoundly. But it was not grief he felt so much as a deep sense of loss, almost impersonal in its quality—a sense of loss and unbelief such as one might feel to discover suddenly that some great force in nature had ceased to operate. He couldn't take it in. Ever since his mother had died when he was only eight years old, Aunt Maw had been the most solid and permanent fixture in his boy's universe. She was a spinster, the older sister of his mother and of his Uncle Mark, and she had taken charge of him and brought him up with all the inflexible zeal of her puritanical nature. She had done her best to make a Joyner of him and a credit to the narrow, provincial, mountain clan to which she belonged. In this she had failed, and his defection from the ways of Joyner righteousness had caused her deep pain. He had known this for a long time; but now he realized, too, more clearly than he had ever done before, that she had never faltered in her duty to him as she saw it. As he thought about her life he felt an

41

inexpressible pity for her, and a surge of tenderness and affection almost choked him.

As far back as he could remember, Aunt Maw had seemed to him an ageless crone, as old as God. He could still hear her voice—that croaking monotone which had gone on and on in endless stories of her past, peopling his childhood world with the whole host of Joyners dead and buried in the hills of Zebulon in ancient days before the Civil War. And almost every tale she had told him was a chronicle of sickness, death, and sorrow. She had known about all the Joyners for the last hundred years, and whether they had died of consumption, typhoid fever, pneumonia, meningitis, or pellagra, and she had relived each incident in their lives with an air of croaking relish. From her he had gotten a picture of his mountain kinsmen that was constantly dark with the terrors of misery and sudden death, a picture made ghostly at frequent intervals by supernatural revelations. The Joyners, so she thought, had been endowed with occult powers by the Almighty, and were forever popping up on country roads and speaking to people as they passed, only to have it turn out later that they had been fifty miles away at the time. They were forever hearing voices and receiving premonitions. If a neighbor died suddenly, the Joyners would flock from miles around to sit up with the corpse, and in the flickering light of pine logs on the hearth they would talk unceasingly through the night, their droning voices punctuated by the crumbling of the ash as they told how they had received intimations of the impending death a week before it happened.

This was the image of the Joyner world which Aunt Maw's tireless memories had built up in the mind and spirit of the boy. And he had felt somehow that although other men would live their day and die, the Joyners were a race apart, not subject to this law. They fed on death and were triumphant over it, and the Joyners would go on forever. But now Aunt Maw, the oldest and most death-triumphant Joyner of them all, was dead. . . .

The funeral was to be on Thursday. This was Tuesday. If he took the train today, he would arrive tomorrow. He knew that all the Joyners from the hills of Zebulon County in Old Catawba would be gathering even now to hold their tribal rites of death and sorrow, and if he got there so soon he would not be able to escape the horror of their brooding talk. It would be better to wait a day and turn up just before the funeral.

It was now early September. The new term at the School for Utility Cultures would not begin until after the middle of the month. George had not been back to Libya Hill in several years, and he thought he might remain a week or so to see the town again. But he dreaded the prospect of staying with his Joyner relatives, especially at a time like this. Then he remembered Randy Shepperton, who lived next door. Mr. and Mrs.

Shepperton were both dead now, and the older girl had married and moved away. Randy had a good job in the town and lived on in the family place with his sister Margaret, who kept house for him. Perhaps they could put him up. They would understand his feelings. So he sent a telegram to Randy, asking for his hospitality, and telling what train he would arrive on.

By the next afternoon, when George went to Pennsylvania Station to catch his train, he had recovered from the first shock of Aunt Maw's death. The human mind is a fearful instrument of adaptation, and in nothing is this more clearly shown than in its mysterious powers of resilience, self-protection, and self-healing. Unless an event completely shatters the order of one's life, the mind, if it has youth and health and time enough, accepts the inevitable and gets itself ready for the next happening like a grimly dutiful American tourist who, on arriving at a new town, looks around him, takes his bearings, and says, "Well, where do I go from here?" So it was with George. The prospect of the funeral filled him with dread, but that was still a day off; meanwhile he had a long train ride ahead of him, and he pushed his somber feelings into the background and allowed himself to savor freely the eager excitement which any journey by train always gave him.

The station, as he entered it, was murmurous with the immense and distant sound of time. Great, slant beams of moted light fell ponderously athwart the station's floor, and the calm voice of time hovered along the walls and ceiling of that mighty room, distilled out of the voices and movements of the people who swarmed beneath. It had the murmur of a distant sea, the languorous lapse and flow of waters on a beach. It was elemental, detached, indifferent to the lives of men. They contributed to it as drops of rain contribute to a river that draws its flood and movement majestically from great depths, out of purple hills at evening.

Few buildings are vast enough to hold the sound of time, and now it seemed to George that there was a superb fitness in the fact that the one which held it better than all others should be a railroad station. For here, as nowhere else on earth, men were brought together for a moment at the beginning or end of their innumerable journeys, here one saw their greetings and farewells, here, in a single instant, one got the entire picture of the human destiny. Men came and went, they passed and vanished, and all were moving through the moments of their lives to death, all made small tickings in the sound of time—but the voice of time remained aloof and unperturbed, a drowsy and

43

eternal murmur below the immense and distant roof.

Each man and woman was full of his own journey. He had one way to go, one end to reach, through all the shifting complexities of the crowd. For each it was *his* journey, and he cared nothing about the journeys of the others. Here, as George waited, was a traveler who was afraid that he would miss his train. He was excited, his movements were feverish and abrupt, he shouted to his porter, he went to the window to buy his ticket, he had to wait in line, he fairly pranced with nervousness and kept looking at the clock. Then his wife came quickly toward him over the polished floor. When she was still some distance off, she shouted:

"Have you got the tickets? We haven't much time! We'll miss the train!"

"Don't I know it?" he shouted back in an annoyed tone. "I'm doing the best I can!" Then he added bitterly and loudly: "We *may* make it if this man in front of me ever gets done buying his ticket!"

The man in front turned on him menacingly. "Now wait a minute, *wait* a minute!" he said. "You're not the only one who has to make a train, you know! I was here before you were! You'll have to wait your turn like everybody else!"

A quarrel now developed between them. The other travelers who were waiting for their tickets grew angry and began to mutter. The ticket agent drummed impatiently on his window and peered out at them with a sour visage. Finally some young tough down the line called out in tones of whining irritation:

"Aw, take it outside, f' Chris' sake! Give the rest of us a chance! You guys are holdin' up the line!"

At last the man got his tickets and rushed toward his porter, hot and excited. The Negro waited suave and smiling, full of easy reassurance:

"You folks don't need to hurry now. You got lotsa time to make that train. It ain't goin' away without you."

Who were these travelers for whom time lay coiled in delicate twists of blue steel wire in each man's pocket? Here were a few of them: a homesick nigger going back to Georgia; a rich young man from an estate on the Hudson who was going to visit his mother in Washington; a district superintendent, and three of his agents, of a farm machinery company, who had been attending a convention of district leaders in the city; the president of a bank in an Old Catawba town which was tottering on the edge of ruin, who had come desperately, accompanied by two local politicians, to petition New York bankers for a loan; a Greek with tan shoes, a cardboard valise, a swarthy face, and eyes glittering with mistrust, who had peered in through the ticket seller's window, saying: "How mucha you want to go to Pittsburgh, eh?"; an effeminate young man from one of the city

44

universities who was going to make his weekly lecture on the arts of the theatre to a club of ladies in Trenton, New Jersey; a lady poetess from a town in Indiana who had been to New York for her yearly spree of "bohemianism"; a prize fighter and his manager on their way to a fight in St. Louis; some Princeton boys just back from a summer in Europe, on their way home for a short visit before returning to college; a private soldier in the United States army, with the cheap, tough, and slovenly appearance of a private soldier in the United States army; the president of a state university in the Middle West who had just made an eloquent appeal for funds to the New York alumni; a young married couple from Mississippi, with everything new— new clothes, new baggage—and a shy, hostile, and bewildered look; two little Filipinos, brown as berries and with the delicate bones of birds, dressed with the foppish perfection of manikins; women from the suburban towns of New Jersey who had come to the city to shop; women and girls from small towns in the South and West, who had come for holidays, sprees, or visits; the managers and agents of clothing stores in little towns all over the country who had come to the city to buy new styles and fashions; New Yorkers of a certain class, flashily dressed, sensual, and with a high, hard finish, knowing and assured, on their way to vacations in Atlantic City; jaded, faded, bedraggled women, scolding and jerking viciously at the puny arms of dirty children; swarthy, scowling, and dominant-looking Italian men with their dark, greasy, and flabby-looking women, sullen but submissive both to lust and beatings; and smartly-dressed American women, obedient to neither bed nor whip, who had assertive, harsh voices, bold glances, and the good figures but not the living curves, either of body or of spirit, of love, lust, tenderness, or any female fullness of the earth whatever.

There were all sorts and conditions of men and travelers: poor people with the hard, sterile faces of all New Jerseys of the flesh and spirit; shabby and beaten-looking devils with cheap suitcases containing a tie, a collar, and a shirt, who had a look of having dropped forever off of passing trains into the dirty cinders of new towns and the hope of some new fortune; the shabby floaters and drifters of the nation; suave, wealthy, and experienced people who had been too far, too often, on too many costly trains and ships, and who never looked out of windows any more; old men and women from the country on first visits to their children in the city, who looked about them constantly and suspiciously with the quick eyes of birds and animals, alert, mistrustful, and afraid. There were people who saw everything, and people who saw nothing; people who were weary, sullen, sour, and people who laughed, shouted, and were exultant with the thrill of the voyage; people who thrust and jostled, and people who stood quietly and watched and waited;

45

people with amused, superior looks, and people who glared and bristled pugnaciously. Young, old, rich, poor, Jews, Gentiles, Negroes, Italians, Greeks, Americans—they were all there in the station, their infinitely varied destinies suddenly harmonized and given a moment of intense and somber meaning as they were gathered into the murmurous, all-taking unity of time.

George had a berth in car K 19. It was not really different in any respect from any other Pullman car, yet for George it had a very special quality and meaning. For every day K 19 bound together two points upon the continent—the great city and the small town of Libya Hill where he had been born, eight hundred miles away. It left New York at one thirty-five each afternoon, and it arrived in Libya Hill at eleven twenty the next morning.

The moment he entered the Pullman he was transported instantly from the vast allness of general humanity in the station into the familiar geography of his home town. One might have been away for years and never have seen an old familiar face; one might have wandered to the far ends of the earth; one might have got with child a mandrake root, or heard mermaids singing, or known the words and music of what songs the Sirens sang; one might have lived and worked alone for ages in the canyons of Manhattan until the very memory of home was lost and far as in a dream; yet the moment that he entered K 19 it all came back again, his feet touched earth, and he was home.

It was uncanny. And what was most wonderful and mysterious about it was that one could come here to this appointed meeting each day at thirty-five minutes after one o'clock, one could come here through the humming traffic of the city to the gigantic portals of the mighty station, one could walk through the concourse forever swarming with its bustle of arrival and departure, one could traverse the great expanses of the station, peopled with Everybody and haunted by the voice of time—and then, down those steep stairs, there in the tunnel's depth, underneath this hivelike universe of life, waiting in its proper place, no whit different outwardly from all its other grimy brethren, was K19.

The beaming porter took his bag with a cheerful greeting:

"Yes, suh, Mistah Webbah! Glad to see you, suh! Comin' down to see de folks?"

And as they made their way down the green aisle to his seat, George told him that he was going home to his aunt's funeral. Instantly the Negro's smile was blotted out, and his face took on an expression of deep solemnity and respect.

"I'se sorry to hear dat, Mistah Webbah," he said, shaking his head. "Yes, suh, I'se pow'ful sorry to hear you say dat."

Even before these words were out of mind, another voice from the seat behind was raised in greeting, and George did not have to turn to know who it was. It was Sol Isaacs, of The Toggery, and George knew that he had been up to the city on a buying trip, a pilgrimage that he made four times a year. Somehow the knowledge of this commercial punctuality warmed the young man's heart, as did the friendly beak-nosed face, the gaudy shirt, the bright necktie, and the dapper smartness of the light grey suit—for Sol was what is known as "a snappy dresser."

George looked around him now to see if there were any others that he knew. Yes, there was the tall, spare, brittle, sandy-complexioned figure of the banker, Jarvis Riggs, and on the seat opposite, engaged in conversation with him, were two other local dignitaries. He recognized the round-featured, weak amiability of the Mayor, Baxter Kennedy; and, sprawled beside him, his long, heavy shanks thrust out into the aisle, the bald crown of his head with its tonsured fringe of black hair thrown back against the top of the seat, his loose-jowled face hanging heavy as he talked, was the large, well-oiled beefiness of Parson Flack, who manipulated the politics of Libya Hill and was called "Parson" because he never missed a prayer meeting at the Campbellite Church. They were talking earnestly and loudly, and George could overhear fragments of their conversation:

"Market Street—oh, give me Market Street any day!"

"Gay Rudd is asking two thousand a front foot for his. He'll get it, too. I wouldn't take a cent less than twenty-five, and I'm not selling anyway."

"You mark my word, she'll go to three before another year is out! And that's not all! That's only the beginning!"

Could this be Libya Hill that they were talking about? It didn't sound at all like the sleepy little mountain town he had known all his life. He rose from his seat and went over to the group.

"Why, hello, Webber! Hello, son!" Parson Flack screwed up his face into something that was meant for an ingratiating smile and showed his big yellow teeth. "Glad to see you. How are you, son?"

George shook hands all around and stood beside them a moment.

"We heard you speaking to the porter when you came in," said the Mayor, with a look of solemn commiseration on his weak face. "Sorry, son. We didn't know about it. We've been away a week. Happen suddenly? . . . Yes, yes, of course. Well, your aunt was pretty old. Got to expect that sort of thing at her time of life. She was a good woman, a *good* woman. Sorry, son,

47

that such a sad occasion brings you home."

There was a short silence after this, as if the others wished it understood that the Mayor had voiced their sentiments, too. Then, this mark of respect to the dead being accomplished, Jarvis Riggs spoke up heartily:

"You ought to stay around a while, Webber. You wouldn't know the town. Things are booming down our way. Why, only the other day Mack Judson paid three hundred thousand for the Draper Block. The building is a dump, of course—what he paid for was the land. That's five thousand a foot. Pretty good for Libya Hill, eh? The Reeves estate has bought up all the land on Parker Street below Parker Hill. They're going to build the whole thing up with business property. That's the way it is all over town. Within a few years Libya Hill is going to be the largest and most beautiful city in the state. You mark my words."

"Yes," agreed Parson Flack, nodding his head ponderously, knowingly, "and I hear they've been trying to buy your uncle's property on South Main Street, there at the corner of the Square. A syndicate wants to tear down the hardware store and put up a big hotel. Your uncle wouldn't sell. He's smart."

George returned to his seat feeling confused and bewildered. He was going back home for the first time in several years, and he wanted to see the town as he remembered it. Evidently he would find it considerably changed. But what was this that was happening to it? He couldn't make it out. It disturbed him vaguely, as one is always disturbed and shaken by the sudden realization of Time's changes in something that one has known all one's life.

The train had hurtled like a projectile through its tube beneath the Hudson River to emerge in the dazzling sunlight of a September afternoon, and now it was racing across the flat desolation of the Jersey meadows. George sat by the window and saw the smoldering dumps, the bogs, the blackened factories slide past, and felt that one of the most wonderful things in the world is the experience of being on a train. It is so different from watching a train go by. To anyone outside, a speeding train is a thunderbolt of driving rods, a hot hiss of steam, a blurred flash of coaches, a wall of movement and of noise, a shriek, a wail, and then just emptiness and absence, with a feeling of "There goes everybody!" without knowing who anybody is. And all of a sudden the watcher feels the vastness and loneliness of America, and the nothingness of all those little lives hurled past upon the immensity of the continent. But if

48

one is *inside* the train, everything is different. The train itself is a miracle of man's handiwork, and everything about it is eloquent of human purpose and direction. One feels the brakes go on when the train is coming to a river, and one knows that the old gloved hand of cunning is at the throttle. One's own sense of manhood and of mastery is heightened by being on a train. And all the other people, how real they are! One sees the fat black porter with his ivory teeth and the great swollen gland on the back of his neck, and one warms with friendship with him. One looks at all the pretty girls with a sharpened eye and an awakened pulse. One observes all the other passengers with lively interest, and feels that he has known them forever. In the morning most of them will be gone out of his life; some will drop out silently at night through the dark, drugged snoring of the sleepers; but now all are caught upon the wing and held for a moment in the peculiar intimacy of this Pullman car which has become their common home for a night.

Two traveling salesmen have struck up a chance acquaintance in the smoking room, entering immediately the vast confraternity of their trade, and in a moment they are laying out the continent as familiarly as if it were their own backyard. They tell about running into So-and-So in St. Paul last July, and——

"Who do you suppose I met coming out of Brown's Hotel in Denver just a week ago?"

"You don't mean it! I haven't seen old Joe in years!"

"And Jim Withers—they've transferred him to the Atlanta office!"

"Going to New Orleans?"

"No, I'll not make it this trip. I was there in May."

With such talk as this one grows instantly familiar. One enters naturally into the lives of all these people, caught here for just a night and hurtled down together across the continent at sixty miles an hour, and one becomes a member of the whole huge family of the earth.

Perhaps this is our strange and haunting paradox here in America—that we are fixed and certain only when we are in movement. At any rate, that is how it seemed to young George Webber, who was never so assured of his purpose as when he was going somewhere on a train. And he never had the sense of home so much as when he felt that he was going there. It was only when he got there that his homelessness began.

At the far end of the car a man stood up and started back down the aisle toward the washroom. He walked with a slight limp and leaned upon a cane, and with his free hand he held onto the backs of the seats to brace himself against the lurching of the train. As he came abreast of George, who sat there gazing out the window, the man stopped abruptly. A strong, good-natured voice, warm, easy, bantering, unafraid, unchanged —exactly as it was when it was fourteen years of age— broke like a flood of living light upon his consciousness:

"Well I'll be dogged! Hi, there, Monkus! Where you goin'?"

At the sound of the old jesting nickname George looked up quickly. It was Nebraska Crane. The square, freckled, sunburned visage had the same humorous friendliness it had always had, and the tar-black Cherokee eyes looked out with the same straight, deadly fearlessness. The big brown paw came out and they clasped each other firmly. And, instantly, it was like coming home to a strong and friendly place. In another moment they were seated together, talking with the familiarity of people whom no gulf of years and distance could alter or separate.

George had seen Nebraska Crane only once in all the years since he himself had first left Libya Hill and gone away to college. But he had not lost sight of him. Nobody had lost sight of Nebraska Crane. That wiry, fearless little figure of the Cherokee boy who used to come down the hill on Locust Street with the bat slung over his shoulder and the well-oiled fielder's mitt protruding from his hip pocket had been prophetic of a greater destiny, for Nebraska had become a professional baseball player, he had crashed into the big leagues, and his name had been emblazoned in the papers every day.

The newspapers had had a lot to do with his seeing Nebraska that other time. It was in August 1925, just after George had returned to New York from his first trip abroad. That very night, in fact, a little before midnight, as he was seated in a Child's Restaurant with smoking wheatcakes, coffee, and an ink-fresh copy of next morning's *Herald-Tribune* before him, the headline jumped out at him: "Crane Slams Another Homer." He read the account of the game eagerly, and felt a strong desire to see Nebraska again and to get back in his blood once more the honest tang of America. Acting on a sudden impulse, he decided to call him up. Sure enough, his name was in the book, with an address way up in the Bronx. He gave the number and waited. A man's voice answered the phone, but at first he didn't recognize it.

"Hello! . . . Hello! . . . Is Mr. Crane there? . . . Is that you, Bras?"

"Hello." Nebraska's voice was hesitant, slow, a little hostile, touched with the caution and suspicion of mountain people when speaking to a stranger. "Who is that? . . . Who? . . . Is that *you*, Monk?"—suddenly and quickly, as he recognized who it

50

was. "Well I'll be dogged!" he cried. His tone was delighted, astounded, warm with friendly greeting now, and had the somewhat high and faintly howling quality that mountain people's voices often have when they are talking to someone over the telephone: the tone was full, sonorous, countrified, and a little puzzled, as if he were yelling to someone on an adjoining mountain peak on a gusty day in autumn when the wind was thrashing through the trees. "Where'd you come from? How the hell are you, boy?" he yelled before George could answer. "Where you been all this time, anyway?"

"I've been in Europe. I just got back this morning."

"Well I'll be dogged!"—still astounded, delighted, full of howling friendliness. "When am I gonna see you? How about comin' to the game tomorrow? I'll fix you up. And say," he went on rapidly, "if you can stick aroun' after the game, I'll take you home to meet the wife and kid. How about it?"

So it was agreed. George went to the game and saw Nebraska knock another home run, but he remembered best what happened afterwards. When the player had had his shower and had dressed, the two friends left the ball park, and as they went out a crowd of young boys who had been waiting at the gate rushed upon them. They were those dark-faced, dark-eyed, dark-haired little urchins who spring up like dragon seed from the grim pavements of New York, but in whose tough little faces and raucous voices there still remains, curiously, the innocence and faith of children everywhere.

"It's Bras!" the children cried. "Hi, Bras! Hey, Bras!" In a moment they were pressing round him in a swarming horde, deafening the ears with their shrill cries, begging, shouting, tugging at his sleeves, doing everything they could to attract his attention, holding dirty little scraps of paper toward him, stubs of pencils, battered little notebooks, asking him to sign his autograph.

He behaved with the spontaneous warmth and kindliness of his character. He scrawled his name out rapidly on a dozen grimy bits of paper, skillfully working his way along through the yelling, pushing, jumping group, and all the time keeping up a rapid fire of banter, badinage, and good-natured reproof:

"All right—give it here, then! . . . Why don't you fellahs pick on somebody else once in a while? . . . Say, boy!" he said suddenly, turning to look down at one unfortunate child, and pointing an accusing finger at him—"What you doin' aroun' here again today? I signed my name fer you at least a dozen times!"

"No sir, Misteh Crane!" the urchin earnestly replied. "Honest—not me!"

"Ain't that right?" Nebraska said, appealing to the other children. "Don't this boy keep comin' back here every day?"

51

They grinned, delighted at the chagrin of their fellow petitioner, "Dat's right, Misteh Crane! Dat guy's got a whole book wit' nuttin' but yoeh name in it!"

"Ah-h!" the victim cried, and turned upon his betrayers bitterly. "What youse guys tryin' to do—get wise or somep'n? Honest, Misteh Crane!"—he looked up earnestly again at Nebraska—"Don't believe 'em! I jest want yoeh ottygraph! Please, Misteh Crane, it'll only take a minute!"

For a moment more Nebraska stood looking down at the child with an expression of mock sternness; at last he took the outstretched notebook, rapidly scratched his name across a page, and handed it back. And as he did so, he put his big paw on the urchin's head and gave it a clumsy pat; then, gently and playfully, he shoved it from him, and walked off down the street.

The apartment where Nebraska lived was like a hundred thousand others in the Bronx. The ugly yellow brick building had a false front, with meaningless little turrets at the corners of the roof, and a general air of spurious luxury about it. The rooms were rather small and cramped, and were made even more so by the heavy, overstuffed Grand Rapids furniture. The walls of the living room, painted a mottled, rusty cream, were bare except for a couple of sentimental colored prints, while the place of honor over the mantel was reserved for an enlarged and garishly tinted photograph of Nebraska's little son at the age of two, looking straight and solemnly out at all comers from a gilded oval frame.

Myrtle, Nebraska's wife, was small and plump, and pretty in a doll-like way. Her corn-silk hair was frizzled in a halo about her face, and her chubby features were heavily accented by rouge and lipstick. But she was simple and natural in her talk and bearing, and George liked her at once. She welcomed him with a warm and friendly smile and said she had heard a lot about him.

They all sat down. The child, who was three or four years old by this time, and who had been shy, holding onto his mother's dress and peeping out from behind her, now ran across the room to his father and began climbing all over him. Nebraska and Myrtle asked George a lot of questions about himself, what he had been doing, where he had been, and especially what countries he had visited in Europe. They seemed to think of Europe as a place so far away that anyone who had actually been there was touched with an unbelievable aura of strangeness and romance.

"Whereall did you go over there, anyway?" asked Nebraska.

"Oh, everywhere, Bras," George said—"France, England, Holland, Germany, Denmark, Sweden, Italy—all over the place."

52

"Well I'll be dogged!"—in frank astonishment. "You sure do git aroun', don't you?"

"Not the way *you* do, Bras. You're traveling most of the time."

"Who—*me?* Oh, hell, I don't git anywhere—just the same ole places. Chicago, St. Looie, Philly—I seen 'em all so often I could find my way blindfolded!" He waved them aside with a gesture of his hand. Then, suddenly, he looked at George as though he were just seeing him for the first time, and he reached over and slapped him on the knee and exclaimed: "Well I'll be dogged! How you doin', anyway, Monkus?"

"Oh, can't complain. How about you? But I don't need to ask that. I've been reading all about you in the papers."

"Yes, Monkus," he said. "I been havin' a good year. But, boy!"—he shook his head suddenly and grinned—"Do the ole dogs feel it!"

He was silent a moment, then he went on quietly:

"I been up here since 1919—that's seven years, and it's a long time in this game. Not many of 'em stay much longer. When you been shaggin' flies as long as that you may lose count, but you don't need to count—your legs'll tell you."

"But, good Lord, Bras, *you're* all right! Why, the way you got around out there today you looked like a colt!"

"Yeah," Nebraska said, "maybe I *looked* like a colt, but I felt like a plough horse." He fell silent again, then he tapped his friend gently on the knee with his brown hand and said abruptly: "No, Monkus. When you been in this business as long as I have, you know it."

"Oh, come on, Bras, quit your kidding!" said George, remembering that the player was only two years older than himself. "You're still a young man. Why, you're only twenty-seven!"

"Sure, sure," Nebraska answered quietly. "But it's like I say. You cain't stay in this business much longer than I have. Of course, Cobb an' Speaker an' a few like that—they was up here a long time. But eight years is about the average, an' I been here seven already. So if I can hang on a few years more, I won't have no kick to make. . . . Hell!" he said in a moment, with the old hearty ring in his voice, "I ain't got no kick to make, no-way. If I got my release tomorrow, I'd still feel I done all right. . . . Ain't that so, Buzz?" he cried genially to the child, who had settled down on his knee, at the same time seizing the boy and cradling him comfortably in his strong arm. "Ole Bras has done all right, ain't he?"

"That's the way me an' Bras feel about it," remarked Myrtle, who during this conversation had been rocking back and forth, placidly ruminating on a wad of gum. "Along there last year it looked once or twice as if Bras might git traded. He said to me

53

one day before the game, 'Well, ole lady, if I don't git some hits today somethin' tells me you an' me is goin' to take a trip.' So I says, 'Trip where?' An' he says, 'I don't know, but they're goin' to sell me down the river if I don't git goin', an' somethin' tells me it's now or never!' So I just looks at him," continued Myrtle placidly, "an' I says, 'Well, what do you want me to do? Do you want me to come today or not?' You know, gener'ly, Bras won't let me come when he ain't hittin'—he says it's bad luck. But he just looks at me a minute, an' I can see him sort of studyin' it over, an' all of a sudden he makes up his mind an' says, 'Yes, come on if you want to; I couldn't have no more bad luck than I been havin', no-way, an' maybe it's come time fer things to change, so you come on.' Well, I went—an' I don't know whether I brought him luck or not, but somethin' did," said Myrtle, rocking in her chair complacently.

"Dogged if she didn't!" Nebraska chuckled. "I got three hits out of four times up that day, an' two of 'em was home runs!"

"Yeah," Myrtle agreed, "an' that Philadelphia fast-ball thrower was throwin' 'em, too."

"He sure was!" said Nebraska.

"I know," went on Myrtle, chewing placidly, "because I heard some of the boys say later that it was like he was throwin' 'em up there from out of the bleachers, with all them men in shirt-sleeves right behind him, an' the boys said half the time they couldn't even see the ball. But Bras must of saw it—or been lucky—because he hit two home runs off of him, an' that pitcher didn't like it, either. The second one Bras got, he went stompin' an' tearin' around out there like a wild bull. He sure did look mad," said Myrtle in her customary placid tone.

"Maddest man I ever seen!" Nebraska cried delightedly. "I thought he was goin' to dig a hole plumb through to China. . . . But that's the way it was. She's right about it. That was the day I got goin'. I know one of the boys said to me later, 'Bras,' he says, 'we all thought you was goin' to take a ride, but you sure dug in, didn't you?' That's the way it is in this game. I seen Babe Ruth go fer weeks when he couldn't hit a balloon, an' all of a sudden he lams into it. Seems like he just cain't miss from then on."

All this had happened four years ago. Now the two friends had met again, and were seated side by side in the speeding train, talking and catching up on one another. When George explained the reason for his going home, Nebraska turned to him with open-mouthed astonishment, genuine concern written in the frown upon his brown and homely face.

54

"Well, what d'you know about that!" he said. "I sure am sorry, Monk." He was silent while he thought about it, and embarrassed, not knowing what to say. Then, after a moment: "Gee!"—he shook his head—"your aunt was one swell cook! I never will fergit it! Remember how she used to feed us kids—every danged one of us in the whole neighborhood?" He paused, then grinned up shyly at his friend: "I sure wish I had a fistful of them good ole cookies of hers right this minute!"

Nebraska's right ankle was taped and bandaged; a heavy cane rested between his knees. George asked him what had happened.

"I pulled a tendon," Nebraska said, "an' got laid off. So I thought I might as well run down an' see the folks. Myrtle, she couldn't come—the kid's got to git ready fer school."

"How are they?" George asked.

"Oh, fine, fine. All wool an' a yard wide, both of 'em!" He was silent for a moment, then he looked at his friend with a tolerant Cherokee grin and said: "But I'm crackin' up, Monkus. Guess I cain't stan' the gaff much more."

Nebraska was only thirty-one now, and George was incredulous. Nebraska smiled good-naturedly again:

"That's an ole man in baseball, Monk. I went up when I was twenty-one. I been aroun' a long time."

The quiet resignation of the player touched his friend with sadness. It was hard and painful for him to face the fact that this strong and fearless creature, who had stood in his life always for courage and for victory, should now be speaking with such ready acceptance of defeat.

"But, Bras," he protested, "you've been hitting just as well this season as you ever did! I've read about you in the papers, and the reporters have all said the same thing."

"Oh, I can still hit 'em," Nebraska quietly agreed. "It ain't the hittin' that bothers me. That's the last thing you lose, anyway. Leastways, it's goin' to be that way with me, an' I talked to other fellahs who said it was that way with them." After a pause he went on in a low tone: "If this ole leg heals up in time, I'll go on back an' git in the game again an' finish out the season. An' if I'm lucky, maybe they'll keep me on a couple more years, because they know I can still hit. But, hell," he added quietly, "they know I'm through. They already got me all tied up with string."

As Nebraska talked, George saw that the Cherokee in him was the same now as it had been when he was a boy. His cheerful fatalism had always been the source of his great strength and courage. That was why he had never been afraid of anything, not even death. But, seeing the look of regret on George's face, Nebraska smiled again and went on lightly:

"That's the way it is, Monk. You're good up there as long as

55

you're good. After that they sell you down the river. Hell, I ain't kickin'. I been lucky. I had ten years of it already, an' that's more than most. An' I been in three World's Serious. If I can hold on fer another year or two—if they don't let me go or trade me—I think maybe we'll be in again. Me an' Myrtle has figgered it all out. I had to help her people some, an' I bought a farm fer Mama an' the Ole Man—that's where they always wanted to be. An' I got three hundred acres of my own in Zebulon—all paid fer, too!—an' if I git a good price this year fer my tobacco, I stan' to clear two thousand dollars. So if I can git two years more in the League an' one more good World's Serious, why—" he turned his square face toward his friend and grinned his brown and freckled grin, just as he used to as a boy—"we'll be all set."

"And—you mean you'll be satisfied?"

"Huh? Satisfied?" Nebraska turned to him with a puzzled look. "How do you mean?"

"I mean after all you've seen and done, Bras—the big cities and the crowds, and all the people shouting—and the newspapers, and the headlines, and the World's Series—and—and—the first of March, and St. Petersburg, and meeting all the fellows again, and spring training——"

Nebraska groaned.

"Why, what's the matter?"

"Spring trainin'."

"You mean you don't like it?"

"Like it! Them first three weeks is just plain hell. It ain't bad when you're a kid. You don't put on much weight durin' the winter, an' when you come down in the spring it only takes a few days to loosen up an' git the kinks out. In two weeks' time you're loose as ashes. But wait till you been aroun' as long as I have!" He laughed loudly and shook his head. "Boy! The first time you go after a grounder you can hear your joints creak. After a while you begin to limber up—you work into it an' git the soreness out of your muscles. By the time the season starts, along in April, you feel pretty good. By May you're goin' like a house a-fire, an' you tell yourself you're good as you ever was. You're still goin' strong along in June. An' then you hit July, an' you git them double-headers in St. Looie! Boy, oh boy!" Again he shook his head and laughed, baring big square teeth. "Monkus," he said quietly, turning to his companion, and now his face was serious and he had his black Indian look—"you ever been in St. Looie in July?"

"No."

"All right, then," he said softly and scornfully. "An' you ain't played *ball* there in July. You come up to bat with sweat bustin' from your ears. You step up an' look out there to where the pitcher ought to be, an' you see four of him. The crowd in the

56

bleachers is out there roastin' in their shirt-sleeves, an' when the pitcher throws the ball it just comes from nowheres—it comes right out of all them shirt-sleeves in the bleachers. It's on top of you before you know it. Well, anyway, you dig in an' git a toe-hold, take your cut, an' maybe you connect. You straighten out a fast one. It's good fer two bases if you hustle. In the old days you could've made it standin' up. But now—boy!" He shook his head slowly. "You cain't tell me nothin' about that ball park in St. Looie in July! They got it all growed out in grass in April, but after July first—" he gave a short laugh—"hell!—it's paved with concrete! An' when you git to first, them dogs is sayin', 'Boy, let's stay here!' But you gotta keep on goin'—you know the manager is watching you—you're gonna ketch hell if you don't take that extra base, it may mean the game. An' the boys up in the press box, they got their eyes glued on you, too—they've begun to say old Crane is playin' on a dime—an' you're thinkin' about next year an' maybe gittin' in another Serious—an' you hope to God you don't git traded to St. Looie. So you take it on the lam, you slide into second like the Twentieth Century comin' into the Chicago yards—an' when you git up an' feel yourself all over to see if any of your parts is missin', you gotta listen to one of that second baseman's wisecracks: 'What's the hurry, Bras? Afraid you'll be late fer the Veterans' Reunion?' "

"I begin to see what you mean, all right," said George.

"See what I mean? Why, say! One day this season I ast one of the boys what month it was, an' when he told me it was just the middle of July, I says to him: 'July, hell! If it ain't September I'll eat your hat!' 'Go ahead, then,' he says, 'an' eat it, because it ain't September, Bras—it's July.' 'Well,' I says, 'they must be havin' sixty days a month this year—it's the longest damn July *I* ever felt!' An' lemme tell you, I didn't miss it fer, either—I'll be dogged if I did! When you git old in this business, it may be only July, but you think it's September." He was silent for a moment. "But they'll keep you in there, gener'ly, as long as you can hit. If you can smack that ole apple, they'll send you out there if they've got to use glue to keep you from fallin' apart. So maybe I'll git in another year or two if I'm lucky. So long's I can hit 'em, maybe they'll keep sendin' me out there till all the other players has to grunt every time ole Bras goes after a ground ball!" He laughed. "I ain't that bad yet, but soon's I am, I'm through."

"You won't mind it, then, when you have to quit?"

He didn't answer at once. He sat there looking out the window at the factory-blighted landscape of New Jersey. Then he laughed a little wearily:

"Boy, this may be a ride on the train to you, but to *me*—say!—I covered this stretch so often that I can tell you

57

what telephone post we're passin' without even lookin' out the window. Why, hell yes!"—he laughed loudly now, in the old infectious way—"I used to have 'em numbered—now I got 'em *named*!"

"And you think you can get used to spending all your time out on the farm in Zebulon?"

"Git used to it?" In Nebraska's voice there was now the same note of scornful protest that it had when he was a boy, and for a moment he turned and looked at his friend with an expression of astonished disgust. "Why, what are you talkin' about? That's the greatest life in the world!"

"And your father? How is he, Bras?"

The player grinned and shook his head: "Oh, the Ole Man's happy as a possum. He's doin' what he wanted to do all his life."

"And is he well?"

"If he felt any better he'd have to go to bed. Strong as a bull," said Nebraska proudly. "He could wrastle a bear right now an' bite his nose off! Why, hell yes!" the player went on with an air of conviction—"he could take any two men I know today an' throw 'em over his shoulder!"

"Bras, do you remember when you and I were kids and your father was on the police force, how he used to wrestle all those professionals that came to town? There were some good ones, too!"

"You're damn right there was!" said the player, nodding his head. "Tom Anderson, who used to be South Atlantic champion, an' that fellah Petersen—do you remember him?"

"Sure. They called him the Bone-Crushing Swede—he used to come there all the time."

"Yeah, that's him. He used to wrastle all over the country—he was way up there, one of the best in the business. The Ole Man wrastled him three times, an' throwed him once, too!"

"And that big fellow they called the Strangler Turk——"

"Yeah, an' he was good, too! Only he wasn't no Turk—he only called hisself one. The Ole Man told me he was some kind of Polack or Bohunk from the steel mills out in Pennsylvania, an that's how he got so strong."

"And the Jersey Giant——"

"Yeah——"

"And Cyclone Finnegan——"

"Yeah——"

"And Bull Dakota—and Texas Jim Ryan—and the Masked Marvel? Do you remember the Masked Marvel?"

"Yeah—only there was a whole lot of them—guys cruisin' all over the country callin' theirselves the Masked Marvel. The Ole Man wrastled two of 'em. Only the real Masked Marvel never came to town. The Ole Man told me there *was* a real Masked

Marvel, but he was too damn good, I guess, to come to Libya Hill."

"Do you remember the night, Bras, up at the old City Auditorium, when your father was wrestling one of these Masked Marvels, and we were there in the front row rooting for him, and he got a strangle hold on this fellow with the mask, and the mask came off—and the fellow wasn't the Masked Marvel at all, but only that Greek who used to work all night at the Bijou Café for Ladies and Gents down by the depot?"

"Yeah—haw-haw!" Nebraska threw back his head and laughed loudly. "I'd clean fergot that damn Greek, but that's who it was! The whole crowd hollered frame-up an' tried to git their money back.—I'll swear Monk! I'm glad to see you!" He put his big brown hand on his companion's knee. "It don't seem no time, does it? It all comes back!"

"Yes, Bras—" for a moment George looked out at the flashing landscape with a feeling of sadness and wonder in his heart—"it all comes back."

George sat by the window and watched the stifled land stroke past him. It was unseasonably hot for September, there had been no rain for weeks, and all afternoon the contours of the eastern seaboard faded away into the weary hazes of the heat. The soil was parched and dusty, and under a glazed and burning sky coarse yellow grasses and the withered stalks of weeds simmered and flashed beside the tracks. The whole continent seemed to be gasping for its breath. In the hot green depths of the train a powder of fine cinders beat in through the meshes of the screens, and during the pauses at stations the little fans at both ends of the car hummed monotonously, with a sound that seemed to be the voice of the heat itself. During these intervals when the train stood still, enormous engines steamed slowly by on adjacent tracks, or stood panting, passive as great cats, and their engineers wiped wads of blackened waste across their grimy faces, while the passengers fanned feebly with sheaves of languid paper or sat in soaked and sweltering dejection.

For a long time George sat alone beside his window. His eyes took in every detail of the changing scene, but his thoughts were turned inward, absorbed in recollections which his meeting with Nebraska Crane had brought alive again. The great train pounded down across New Jersey, across Pennsylvania, across the tip of Delaware, and into Maryland. The unfolding panorama of the land was itself like a sequence on the scroll of time. George felt lost and a little sick. His talk with his boyhood friend had driven him back across the years. The changes in

Nebraska and his quiet acceptance of defeat had added an undertone of sadness to the vague, uneasy sense of foreboding which he had gotten from his conversation with the banker, the politician, and the Mayor.

At Baltimore, when the train slowed to a stop in the gloom beneath the station, he caught a momentary glimpse of a face on the platform as it slid past his window. All that he could see was a blur of thin, white features and a sunken mouth, but at the corners of the mouth he thought he also caught the shadow of a smile—faint, evil, ghostly—and at sight of it a sudden and unreasoning terror seized him. Could that be Judge Rumford Bland?

As the train started up again and passed through the tunnel on the other side of the city, a blind man appeared at the rear of the car. The other people were talking, reading, or dozing, and the blind man came in so quietly that none of them noticed him enter. He took the first seat at the end and sat down. When the train emerged into the waning sunlight of this September day, George looked around and saw him sitting there. He just sat quietly, gripping a heavy walnut walking stick with a frail hand, the sightless eyes fixed in vacancy, the thin and sunken face listening with that terrible intent stillness that only the blind know, and around the mouth hovered that faint suggestion of a smile, which, hardly perceptible though it was, had in it a kind of terrible vitality and the mercurial attractiveness of a ruined angel. It *was* Judge Rumford Bland!

George had not seen him in fifteen years. At that time he was not blind, but already his eyes were beginning to fail. George remembered him as he was then, and remembered, too, how the sight of the man, frequently to be seen prowling the empty streets of the night when all other life was sleeping and the town was dead, had struck a nameless terror into his boy's heart. Even then, before blindness had come upon him, some nocturnal urge had made him seek deserted pavements beneath the blank and sterile corner lights, past windows that were always dark, past doors that were forever locked.

He came from an old and distinguished family, and, like all his male ancestors for one hundred years or more, he had been trained in the profession of the law. For a single term he had been a police court magistrate, and from then on was known as "Judge" Bland. But he had fallen grievously from the high estate his family held. During the period of George Webber's boyhood he still professed to be a lawyer. He had a shabby office in a disreputable old building which he owned, and his name was on the door as an attorney, but his living was earned by other and more devious means. Indeed, his legal skill and knowledge had been used more for the purpose of circumventing the law and defeating justice than in maintaining them.

60

Practically all his "business" was derived from the Negro population of the town, and of this business the principal item was usury.

On the Square, in his ramshackle two-story building of rusty brick, was "the store." It was a second-hand furniture store, and it occupied the ground floor and basement of the building. It was, of course, nothing but a blind for his illegal transactions with the Negroes. A hasty and appalled inspection of the mountainous heap of ill-smelling junk which it contained would have been enough to convince one that if the owner had to depend on the sale of his stock he would have to close his doors within a month. It was incredible. In the dirty window was a pool table, taken as brutal tribute from some Negro billiard parlor. But what a pool table! Surely it had not a fellow in all the relics in the land. Its surface was full of lumps and dents and ridges. Not a pocket remained without a hole in the bottom big enough to drop a baseball through. The green cloth covering had worn through or become unfixed in a dozen places. The edges of the table and the cloth itself were seared and burnt with the marks of innumerable cigarettes. Yet this dilapidated object was by all odds the most grandiose adornment of the whole store.

As one peered back into the gloom of the interior he became aware of the most fantastic collection of nigger junk that was ever brought together in one place. On the street floor as well as in the basement it was piled up to the ceiling, and all jumbled together as if some gigantic steam-shovel had opened its jaws and dumped everything just as it was. There were broken-down rocking chairs, bureaus with cracked mirrors and no bottoms in the drawers, tables with one, two, or three of their legs missing, rusty old kitchen stoves with burnt-out grates and elbows of sooty pipe, blackened frying pans encased in the grease of years, flat irons, chipped plates and bowls and pitchers, washtubs, chamber pots, and a thousand other objects, all worn out, cracked, and broken.

What, then, was the purpose of this store, since it was filled with objects of so little value that even the poorest Negroes could get slight use from them? The purpose, and the way Judge Rumford Bland used it, was quite simple:

A Negro in trouble, in immediate need of money to pay a police court fine, a doctor's bill, or some urgent debt, would come to see Judge Bland. Sometimes he needed as little as five or ten dollars, occasionally as much as fifty dollars, but usually it was less than that. Judge Bland would then demand to know what security he had. The Negro, of course, had none, save perhaps a few personal possessions and some wretched little furniture—a bed, a chair, a table, a kitchen stove. Judge Bland would send his collector, bulldog, and chief lieutenant—a ferret-faced man named Clyde Beals—to inspect these miserable possessions, and if he thought the junk important enough to its owner to justify the loan, he would advance the money, extracting from it, however, the first installment of his interest.

From this point on, the game was plainly and flagrantly usurious. The interest was payable weekly, every Saturday night. On a ten dollar loan Judge Bland extracted interest of fifty cents a week; on a twenty-dollar loan, interest of a dollar a week; and so on. That is why the amount of the loans was rarely as much as fifty dollars. Not only were the contents of most Negro shacks worth less than that, but to pay two dollars and a half in weekly interest was beyond the capacity of most Negroes, whose wage, if they were men, might not be more than five or six dollars a week, and if they were women—cooks or house-servants in the town—might be only three or four dollars. Enough had to be left them for a bare existence or it was no game. The purpose and skill of the game came in lending the Negro a sum of money somewhat greater than his weekly wage and his consequent ability to pay back, but also a sum whose weekly interest was within the range of his small income.

Judge Bland had on his books the names of Negroes who had paid him fifty cents or a dollar a week over a period of years, on an original loan of ten or twenty dollars. Many of these poor and ignorant people were unable to comprehend what had happened to them. They could only feel mournfully, dumbly, with the slavelike submissiveness of their whole training and conditioning, that at some time in the distant past they had got their money, spent it, and had their fling, and that now they must pay perpetual tribute for that privilege. Such men and women as these would come to that dim-lit place of filth and misery on Saturday night, and there the Judge himself, black-frocked, white-shirted, beneath one dingy, fly-specked bulb, would hold his private court:

"What's wrong, Carrie? You're two weeks behind in your payments. Is fifty cents all you got this week?"

"It doan seem lak it was three weeks. Musta slipped up somewheres in my countin'."

"You didn't slip up. It's three weeks. You owe a dollar fifty. Is this all you got?"

With sullen apology: "Yassuh."

"When will you have the rest of it?"

"Dey's a fellah who say he gonna give me——"

"Never mind about that. Are you going to keep up your payments after this or not?"

"Dat's whut Ah wuz sayin'. Jus' as soon as Monday come, an' dat fellah——"

Harshly: "Who you working for now?"

"Doctah Hollandah——"

62

"You cooking for him?"

Sullenly, with unfathomable Negro mournfulness: "Yassuh."

"How much is he paying you?"

"Three dollahs."

"And you mean you can't keep up? You can't pay fifty cents a week?"

Still sullen, dark, and mournful, as doubtful and confused as jungle depths of Africa: "Doan know. . . . Seem lak a long time since Ah started payin' up——"

Harshly, cold as poison, quick as a striking snake: "You've never started paying up. You've paid nothing. You're only paying interest, and behind in that."

And still doubtfully, in black confusion, fumbling and fingering and bringing forth at last a wad of greasy little receipts from the battered purse: "Doan know, seem lak Ah got enough of dese to've paid dat ten dollahs up long ago. How much longer does Ah have to keep on payin'?"

"Till you've got ten dollars. . . . All right, Carrie: here's your receipt. You bring that extra dollar in next week."

Others, a little more intelligent than Carrie, would comprehend more clearly what had happened to them, but would continue to pay because they were unable to get together at one time enough money to release them from their bondage. A few would have energy and power enough to save their pennies until at last they were able to buy back their freedom. Still others, after paying week by week and month by month, would just give up in despair and would pay no more. Then, of course, Clyde Beals was on them like a vulture. He nagged, he wheedled, and he threatened; and if, finally he saw that he could get no more money from them, he took their household furniture. Hence the chaotic pile of malodorous junk which filled the shop.

Why, it may be asked, in a practice that was so flagrantly, nakedly, and unashamedly usurious as this, did Judge Rumford Bland not come into collision with the law? Did the police not know from what sources, and in what ways, his income was derived?

They knew perfectly. The very store in which this miserable business was carried on was within twenty yards of the City Hall, and within fifty feet of the side entrance to the town calaboose, up whose stone steps many of these same Negroes had time and again been hauled and mauled and hurled into a cell. The practice, criminal though it was, was a common one, winked at by the local authorities, and but one of many similar practices by which unscrupulous white men all over the South feathered their own nests at the expense of an oppressed and ignorant people. The fact that such usury was practiced chiefly against "a bunch of niggers" to a large degree condoned and

63

pardoned it in the eyes of the law.

Moreover, Judge Rumford Bland knew that the people with whom he dealt would not inform on him. He knew that the Negro stood in awe of the complex mystery of the law, of which he understood little or nothing, or in terror of its brutal force. The law for him was largely a matter of the police, and the police was a white man in a uniform, who had the power and authority to arrest him, to beat him with his fist or with a club, to shoot him with a gun, and to lock him up in a small, dark cell. It was not likely, therefore, that any Negro would take his troubles to the police. He was not aware that he had any rights as a citizen, and that Judge Rumford Bland had violated those rights; or, if he was aware of rights, however vaguely, he was not likely to ask for their protection by a group of men at whose hands he had known only assault, arrest, and imprisonment.

Above the shambles of the nigger junk, upon the second floor, were Judge Bland's offices. A wooden stairway, worn by the tread of clay-booted time, and a hand rail, loose as an old tooth, smooth, besweated by the touch of many a black palm, led up to a dark hallway. Here, in Stygian gloom, one heard the punctual monotone of a single and regularly repeated small drop of water dripping somewhere in the rear, and caught the overpowering smell of the tin urinal. Opening off of this hallway was the glazed glass of the office door, which bore the legend in black paint, partly flaked off:

RUMFORD BLAND

ATTORNEY AT LAW

Within, the front room was furnished with such lumber as lawyers use. The floor was bare, there were two roll-top desks, black with age, two bookcases with glass doors, filled with battered volumes of old pigskin brown, a spittoon, brass-bodied and capacious, swimming with tobacco juice, a couple of ancient swivel chairs, and a few other nondescript straight-backed chairs for visitors to sit and creak in. On the walls were several faded diplomas—Pine Rock College, Bachelor of Arts; The University of Old Catawba, Doctor of Laws; and a certificate of The Old Catawba Bar Association. Behind was another room with nothing in it but some more bookcases full of heavy tomes in musty calf bindings, a few chairs, and against the wall a plush sofa—the room, it was whispered, "where Bland took his women." Out front, in the windows that looked on the Square, their glass unwashed and specked with the ghosts of flies that died when Gettysburg was young, were two old, frayed, mottled-yellow window shades, themselves as old as Garfield, and still faintly marked with the distinguished names of "Kennedy and Bland." The Kennedy of that old law firm had been the father of Baxter Kennedy, the Mayor, and his partner, old General Bland, had been Rumford's father. Both had been dead for years, but no one had bothered to change the lettering.

Such were the premises of Judge Rumford Bland as George Webber remembered them. Judge Rumford Bland—"bondsman," "furniture dealer," usurious lender to the blacks. Judge Rumford Bland—son of a brigadier of infantry, C.S.A., member of the bar, wearer of immaculate white and broadcloth black.

What had happened to this man that had so corrupted and perverted his life from its true and honorable direction? No one knew. There was no question that he possessed remarkable gifts. In his boyhood George had heard the more reputable attorneys of the town admit that few of them would have been Judge Bland's match in skill and ability had he chosen to use his talents in an honest way.

But he was stained with evil. There was something genuinely old and corrupt at the sources of his life and spirit. It had got into his blood, his bone, his flesh. It was palpable in the touch of his thin, frail hand when he greeted you, it was present in the deadly weariness of his tone of voice, in the dead-white texture of his emaciated face, in his lank and lusterless auburn hair, and, most of all, in his sunken mouth, around which there hovered constantly the ghost of a smile. It could only be called the ghost of a smile, and yet, really, it was no smile at all. It was, if anything, only a shadow at the corners of the mouth. When one looked closely, it was gone. But one knew that it was always there—lewd, evil, mocking, horribly corrupt, and suggesting a limitless vitality akin to the humor of death, which welled up from some secret spring in his dark soul.

In his early manhood Judge Bland had married a beautiful but dissolute woman, whom he shortly divorced. The utter cynicism that marked his attitude toward women was perhaps partly traceable to this source. Ever since his divorce he had lived alone with his mother, a stately, white-haired lady to whom he rendered at all times a faithful, solicitous, exquisitely kind and gentle duty. Some people suspected that this filial devotion was tinged with irony and contemptuous resignation, but certainly the old lady herself had no cause to think so. She occupied a pleasant old house, surrounded with every comfort, and if she ever guessed by what dark means her luxuries had been assured, she never spoke of it to her son. As for women generally, Judge Bland divided them brutally into two groups—the mothers and the prostitutes—and, aside from the single exception in his own home, his sole interest was in the second division.

He had begun to go blind several years before George left
65

Libya Hill, and the thin, white face, with its shadowy smile, had been given a sinister enhancement by the dark spectacles which he then wore. He was under treatment at the Johns Hopkins Hospital in Baltimore, and made trips there at intervals of six weeks, but his vision was growing steadily worse, and the doctors had already told him that his condition was practically hopeless. The malady that was destroying his sight had been brought on by a loathesome disease which he thought had been checked long since, and which he frankly admitted had been engendered in his eyes.

In spite of all these sinister and revolting facts of character, of spirit, and of person, Judge Bland, astonishing as it may seem, had always been an enormously attractive figure. Everyone who met him knew at once that the man was bad. No, "bad" is not the word for it. Everyone knew that he was evil—genuinely, unfathomably evil—and evil of this sort has a grandeur about it not unlike the grandeur of supreme goodness. And indeed, there was goodness in him that had never altogether died. In his single term upon the bench as a police court magistrate, it was universally agreed that Judge Bland had been fair and wise in his disposal of swift justice. Whatever it was that had made this fact possible—and no one pretended to understand it—the aura of it still clung to him. And it was for just this reason that people who met him were instantly, even if they fought against it, captivated, drawn close to him, somehow made to like him. At the very moment that they met him, and felt the force of death and evil working in him, they also felt— oh, call it the phantom, the radiance, the lost soul, of an enormous virtue. And with the recognition of that quality came the sudden stab of overwhelming regret, the feeling of "What a loss! What a shame!" And yet no one could say why.

As the early dusk of approaching autumn settled swiftly down, the train sped southward toward Virginia. George sat by the window watching the dark shapes of trees flash by, and thought back over all that he had ever known about Judge Rumford Bland. The loathing and terror and mysterious attraction which the man had always had for him were now so great that he felt he could not sit alone there any longer. Midway in the car the other people from Libya Hill had gathered together in a noisy huddle. Jarvis Riggs, Mayor Kennedy, and Sol Isaacs were sitting down or sprawling on the arms of the seats, and Parson Flack was standing in the aisle, leaning over earnestly as he talked, with arms outstretched on the backs of the two seats that enclosed the group. In the center of this huddle, the focus of all their attention, was Nebraska Crane. They had caught him as he went by, and now they had him cornered.

George rose and went over to join them, and as he did so he glanced again in the direction of Judge Bland. He was dressed with old-fashioned fastidiousness, just as he had always dressed, in loose-fitting garments of plain and heavy black, a starched white shirt, a low collar and a black string necktie, and a wide-brimmed Panama hat which he had not removed. Beneath the brim of the hat his once auburn hair was now a dead and lifeless white. This and the sightless eyes were the only changes in him. Otherwise he looked just as he had looked fifteen years ago. He had not stirred since he came in. He sat upright, leaning a little forward on his cane, his blindly staring eyes fixed before him, his white and sunken face held in an attitude of intense, listening stillness.

As George joined the group in the middle of the car, they were excitedly discussing property values—all of them, that is, except Nebraska Crane. Parson Flack would bend over earnestly, showing his big teeth in a smile and tell about some recent deal, and what a certain piece of land had sold for —"Right out there on Charles Street, not far from where you used to live, Bras!" To each of these new marvels the player's response was the same:

"Well I'll be dogged!" he said, astounded. "What d'you know about that!"

The banker now leaned forward and tapped Nebraska confidentially on the knee. He talked to him persuasively, in friendly wise, urging him to invest his savings in the real estate speculations of the town. He brought up all his heaviest artillery of logic and mathematics, drawing forth his pencil and notebook to figure out just how much a given sum of money could be increased if it was shrewdly invested now in this or that piece of property, and then sold when the time was right.

"You can't go wrong!" said Jarvis Riggs, a little feverishly. "The town is bound to grow. Why, Libya Hill is only at the beginning of its development. You bring your money back home, my boy, and let it go to work for you! You'll see!"

This went on for some time. But in the face of all their urgings Nebraska remained his characteristic self. He was respectful and good-natured, but a little dubious, and fundamentally stubborn.

"I already got me a farm out in Zebulon," he said, and, grinning—"It's paid fer, too! When I git through playin' baseball, I'm comin' back an' settle down out there an' farm it. It's three hundred acres of the purtiest bottom land you ever seen. That's all I want. I couldn't use no more."

As Nebraska talked to them in his simple, homely way, he

spoke as a man of the earth for whom the future opened up serenely, an independent, stubborn man who knew what he wanted, a man who was firmly rooted, established, secure against calamity and want. He was completely detached from the fever of the times—from the fever of the boom-mad town as well as from the larger fever of the nation. The others talked incessantly about land, but George saw that Nebraska Crane was the only one who still conceived of the land as a place on which to live, and of living on the land as a way of life.

At last Nebraska detached himself from the group and said he was going back to take a smoke. George started to follow him. As he passed down the aisle behind his friend and came abreast of the last seat, suddenly a quiet, toneless voice said:

"Good evening, Webber."

He stopped and spun around. The blind man was seated there before him. He had almost forgotten about him. The blind man had not moved as he spoke. He was still leaning a little forward on his cane, his thin, white face held straight before him as if he were still listening for something. George felt now, as he had always felt, the strange fascination in that evil shadow of a smile that hovered about the corners of the blind man's mouth. He paused, then said:

"Judge Bland."

"Sit down, son." And like a child under the spell of the Pied Piper, he sat down. "Let the dead bury the dead. Come sit among the blind."

The words were uttered tonelessly, yet their cruel and lifeless contempt penetrated nakedly throughout the car. The other men stopped talking and turned as if they had received an electric shock. George did not know what to say; in the embarrassment of the moment he blurted out:

"I—I—there are a lot of people on the train from home. I —I've been talking to them—Mayor Kennedy, and——"

The blind man, never moving, in his terrible toneless voice that carried to all ears, broke in:

"Yes, I know. As eminent a set of sons-of-bitches as were ever gathered together in the narrow confines of a single Pullman car."

The whole car listened in an appalled silence. The group in the middle looked at one another with fear in their eyes, and in a moment they began talking feverishly again.

"I hear you were in France again last year," the voice now said. "And did you find the French whores any different from the home-grown variety?"

The naked words, with their toneless evil, pierced through the car like a flash of sheer terror. All conversation stopped. Everyone was stunned, frozen into immobility.

"You'll find there's not much difference," Judge Bland

68

observed calmly and in the same tone. "Syphilis makes the whole world kin. And if you want to lose your eyesight, you can do it in this great democracy as well as anywhere on earth."

The whole car was as quiet as death. In another moment the stunned faces turned toward one another, and the men began to talk in furtive whispers.

Through all of this the expression on that white and sunken face had never altered, and the shadow of that ghostly smile still lingered around the mouth. But now, low and casually, he said to the young man:

"How are you, son? I'm glad to see you." And in that simple phrase, spoken by the blind man, there was the suggestion of a devilish humor, although his expression did not change a bit.

"You—you've been in Baltimore, Judge Bland?"

"Yes, I still come up to Hopkins now and then. It does no good, of course. You see, son," the tone was low and friendly now, "I've gone completely blind since I last saw you."

"I didn't know. But you don't mean that you——"

"Oh, utterly! Utterly!" replied Judge Bland, and all at once he threw his sightless face up and laughed with sardonic glee, displaying blackened rims of teeth, as if the joke was too good to be kept. "My dear boy, I assure you that I am utterly blind. I can no longer distinguish one of our most prominent local bastards two feet off.—*Now Jarvis!*" he suddenly cried out in a chiding voice in the direction of the unfortunate Riggs, who had loudly resumed his discussion of property values—"you *know* that's not true! Why, man, I can tell by the look in your eyes that you're lying!" And again he lifted his face and was shaken by devilish, quiet laughter. "Excuse the interruption, son," he went on. "I believe the subject of our discourse was bastardy. Why, can you believe it?—" he leaned forward again, his long fingers playing gently on the polished ridges of his stick— "where bastardy is concerned, I find I can no longer trust my eyes at all. I rely exclusively on the sense of smell. And—" for the first time his face was sunken deliberately in weariness and disgust—"it is enough. A sense of smell is all you need." Abruptly changing now, he said: "How are the folks?"

"Why—Aunt Maw's dead. I—I'm going home to the funeral."

"Dead, is she?"

That was all he said. None of the usual civilities, no expression of polite regret, just that and nothing more. Then, after a moment:

"So you're going down to bury her." It was a statement, and he said it reflectively, as though meditating upon it; then— "And do you think you can go home again?"

George was a little startled and puzzled: "Why—I don't understand. How do you mean Judge Bland?"

There was another flare of that secret, evil laughter. "I mean, do you think you can really go *home* again?" Then, sharp, cold, peremptory—"Now answer me! Do you think you can?"

"Why—why yes! Why—" the young man was desperate, almost frightened now, and, earnestly, beseechingly, he said— "why look here, Judge Bland—I haven't done anything— honestly I haven't!"

Again the low, demonic laughter: "You're *sure*?"

Frantic now with the old terror which the man had always inspired in him as a boy: "Why—why of course I'm sure! Look here, Judge Bland—in the name of God, what have I done?" He thought desperately of a dozen wild, fantastic things, feeling a sickening and overwhelming consciousness of guilt, without knowing why. He thought: "Has he heard about my book? Does he know I wrote about the town? Is that what he means?"

The blind man cackled thinly to himself, enjoying with evil tenderness his little cat's play with the young man: "The guilty fleeth where no man pursueth. Is that it, son?"

Frankly distracted: "Why—why—I'm not guilty!" Angrily: "Why damn it, I'm not guilty of anything!" Passionately, excitedly: "I can hold up my head with any man! I can look the whole damn world in the eye! I make no apologies to——"

He stopped short, seeing the evil ghost-shadow of a smile at the corners of the blind man's mouth. "That disease!" he thought—"the thing that ruined his eyes—maybe—maybe— why, yes—the man is crazy!" Then he spoke, slowly, simply:

"Judge Bland." He rose from the seat. "Good-bye, Judge Bland."

The smile still played about the blind man's mouth, but he answered with a new note of kindness in his voice:

"Good-bye, son." There was a barely perceptible pause. "But don't forget I tried to warn you."

George walked quickly away with thudding heart and trembling limbs. What *had* Judge Bland meant when he asked, "Do you think you can go home again?" And what had been the meaning of that evil, silent, mocking laughter? What had he heard? What did he know? And these others—did they know, too?

He sooned learned that his fear and panic in the blind man's presence were shared by all the people in the car. Even the passengers who had never seen Judge Bland before had heard his naked, brutal words, and they were now horrified by the sight of him. As for the rest, the men from Libya Hill, this feeling was greatly enhanced, sharpened by all that they knew of him. He had pursued his life among them with insolent shamelessness. Though he still masked in all the outward aspects of respectability, he was in total disrepute, and yet he met the opinion of the town with such cold and poisonous contempt that everyone held him in a kind of terrified respect. As for Parson Flack, Jarvis Riggs, and Mayor Kennedy, they were afraid of him because his blind eyes saw straight through them. His sudden appearance in the car, where none had expected to meet him, had aroused in all of them a sense of stark, underlying terror.

As George went into the washroom suddenly, he came upon the Mayor cleaning his false teeth in the basin. The man's plump face, which George had always known in the guise of cheerful, hearty amiability, was all caved in. Hearing a sound behind him, the Mayor turned upon the newcomer. For a moment there was nothing but nameless fright in his weak brown eyes. He mumbled frantically, incoherently, holding his false teeth in his trembling fingers. Like a man who did not know what he was doing, he brandished them in a grotesque yet terrible gesture indicative of—God knows what!—but despair and terror were both in it. Then he put the teeth into his mouth again, smiled feebly, and muttered apologetically, with some counterfeit of his usual geniality:

"Ho, ho!—well, son! You caught me that time, all right! A man can't talk without his teeth!"

The same thing was now apparent everywhere. George saw it in the look of an eye, the movement of a hand, the give-away expression of a face in repose. The merchant, Sol Isaacs, took him aside and whispered:

"Have you heard what they're saying about the bank?" He looked around quickly and checked himself, as if afraid of the furtive sound of his own voice. "Oh, everything's O.K.! Sure it is! They just went a little too fast there for a while! Things are rather quiet right now—but they'll pick up!"

Among all of them there was the same kind of talk that George had heard before. "It's worth all of that," they told each other eagerly. "It'll bring twice as much in a year's time." They caught him by the lapel in the most friendly and hearty fashion and said he ought to settle down in Libya Hill and stay for good—"Greatest place on earth, you know!" They made their usual assured pronouncements upon finance, banking, market trends, and property values. But George sensed now that down below all this was just utter, naked, frantic terror—the terror of men who know that they are ruined and are afraid to admit it, even to themselves.

71

It was after midnight, and the great train was rushing south across Virginia in the moonlight. The people in the little towns lay in their beds and heard the mournful whistle, then the sudden roar as the train went through, and they turned over restlessly and dreamed of fair and distant cities.

In K 19 most of the passengers had retired to their berths. Nebraska Crane had turned in early, but George was still up, and so, too, were the banker, the Mayor, and the political boss. Crass, world-weary, unimaginative fellows that they were, they were nevertheless too excited by something of the small boy in them that had never died to go to bed at their usual hour aboard a train, and were now drawn together for companionship in the smoke-fogged washroom. Behind the green curtains the complex of male voices rose and fell in talk as they told their endless washroom stories. Quietly, furtively, with sly delight, they began to recall unsavory anecdotes remembered from the open and shameless life of Judge Rumford Bland, and at the end of each recital there would be a choking burst of strong laughter.

When the laughter and the slapping of thighs subsided, Parson Flack leaned forward again, eager to tell another. In a voice that was subdued, confidential, almost conspiratorial, he began:

"And do you remember the time that he——"

Swiftly the curtain was drawn aside, all heads jerked up, and Judge Bland entered.

"Now, Parson——" said he in a chiding voice—"remember what?"

Before the blind, cold stare of that emaciated face the seated men were silent. Something stronger than fear was in their eyes.

"Remember *what*?" he said again, a trifle harshly. He stood before them erect and fragile, both hands balanced on the head of the cane which he held anchored to the floor in front of him. He turned to Jarvis Riggs: "Remember when you established what you boasted was 'the fastest-growing bank in all the state'—and weren't too particular what it grew on?" He turned back to Parson Flack: "Remember when one of 'the boys,' as you like to call them—you always look out for 'the boys,' don't you, Parson?—remember when one of 'the boys' borrowed money from 'the fastest-growing bank' to buy two hundred acres on that hill across the river?"—he turned to the Mayor —"and sold the land to the town for a new cemetery? . . . Though why," he turned his face to Parson Flack again, "the dead should have to go so far to bury their dead I do not know!"

72

He paused impressively, like a country lawyer getting ready to launch his peroration to a jury.

"Remember *what*?"—the voice rose suddenly, high and sharp. "Do I remember, Parson, how you've run the town through all these years? Do I remember what a good thing you've made of politics? You've never aspired to public office, have you, Parson? Oh, no—you're much too modest. But you know how to pick the public-spirited citizens who do aspire, and whose great hearts pant with eagerness to serve their fellow men! Ah, yes. It's a very nice little private business, isn't it, Parson? And all 'the boys' are stockholders and get their cut of the profits—is that the way of it, Parson? . . . Remember *what*?" he cried again. "Do I remember now the broken fragments of a town that waits and fears and schemes to put off the day of its impending ruin? Why, Parson, yes—I can remember all these things. And yet I had no part in them, for, after all, I am a humble man. Oh—" with a deprecating nod —"a little nigger squeezing here and there, a little income out of Niggertown, a few illegal lendings, a comfortable practice in small usury—yet my wants were few, my tastes were very simple. I was always satisfied with, say, a modest five per cent a week. So I am not in the big money, Parson. I remember many things, but I see now I have spent my substance, wasted all my talents in riotous living—while pious Puritans have virtuously betrayed their town and given their whole-souled services to the ruin of their fellow men."

Again there was an ominous pause, and when he went on his voice was low, almost casual in its toneless irony:

"I am afraid I have been at best a giddy fellow, Parson, and that my old age will be spent in memories of trivial things—of various merry widows who came to town, of poker chips, race horses, cards, and rattling dice, of bourbon, Scotch, and rye—all the forms of hellishness that saintly fellows, Parson, who go to prayer meeting every week, know nothing of. So I suppose I'll warm my old age with the memories of my own sinfulness—and be buried at last, like all good men and true, among more public benefactors in the town's expensive graveyard on the hill. . . . But I also remember other things, Parson. So can you. And maybe in my humble sphere I, too, have served a purpose—of being the wild oat of more worthy citizens."

They sat in utter silence, their frightened, guilty eyes all riveted upon his face, and each man felt as if those cold, unseeing eyes had looked straight through him. For a moment more Judge Bland just stood there, and, slowly, without a change of muscle in the blankness of his face, the ghostly smile began to hover like a shadow at the corners of his sunken mouth.

"Good evening, gentlemen," he said. He turned, and with his walking stick he caught and held the curtain to one side. "I'll be seeing you."

All through the night George lay in his dark berth and watched the old earth of Virginia as it stroked past him in the dream-haunted silence of the moon. Field and hill and gulch and stream and wood again, the everlasting earth, the huge illimitable earth of America, kept stroking past him in the steep silence of the moon.

All through the ghostly stillness of the land, the train made on forever its tremendous noise, fused of a thousand sounds, and they called back to him forgotten memories: old songs, old faces, old memories, and all strange, wordless, and unspoken things men know and live and feel, and never find a language for—the legend of dark time, the sad brevity of their days, the unknowable but haunting miracle of life itself. He heard again, as he had heard throughout his childhood, the pounding wheel, the tolling bell, the whistle-wail, and he remembered how these sounds, coming to him from the river's edge in the little town of his boyhood, had always evoked for him their tongueless prophecy of wild and secret joy, their glorious promises of new lands, morning, and a shining city. But now the lonely cry of the great train was speaking to him with an equal strangeness of return. For he was going home again.

The undertone of terror with which he had gone to bed, the sadness of the foreshadowed changes in the town, the somber prospect of the funeral tomorrow, all combined to make him dread his home-coming, which so many times in the years since he had been away he had looked forward to some day with hope and exultation. It was all so different from what he thought it would be. He was still only an obscure instructor at one of the universities in the city, his book was not yet published, he was not by any standard which his native town could know—"successful," "a success." And as he thought of it, he realized that, almost more than anything, he feared the sharp, appraising eye, the wordly judgments, of that little town.

He thought of all his years away from home, the years of wandering in many lands and cities. He remembered how many times he had thought of home with such an intensity of passion that he could close his eyes and see the scheme of every street, and every house upon each street, and the faces of the people, as well as recall the countless things that they had said and the densely-woven fabric of all their histories. Tomorrow he would see it all again, and he almost wished he had not come. It would

74

have been easy to plead the excuse of work and other duty. And it was silly, anyhow, to feel as he did about the place.

But why had he always felt so strongly the magnetic pull of home, why had he thought so much about it and remembered it with such blazing accuracy, if it did not matter, and if this little town, and the immortal hills around it, was not the only home he had on earth? He did not know. All that he knew was that the years flow by like water, and that one day men come home again.

The train rushed onward through the moonlit land.

Chapter Six

The Home-coming

When he looked from the windows of the train next morning the hills were there. They towered immense and magical into the blue weather, and suddenly the coolness was there, the winy sparkle of the air, and the shining brightness. Above him loomed huge shapes, the dense massed green of the wilderness, the cloven cuts and gulches of the mountain passes, the dizzy steepness, with the sudden drops below. He could see the little huts stuck to the edge of bank and hollow, toy-small, far below him in the gorges. The everlasting stillness of the earth now met the intimate, toiling slowness of the train as it climbed up round the sinuous curves, and he had an instant sense of something refound that he had always known—something far, near, strange, and so familiar—and it seemed to him that he had never left the hills, and all that had passed in the years between was like a dream.

At last the train came sweeping down the long sloping bend into the station. But even before it had come to a full halt George had been watching out of the windows and had seen Randy Shepperton and his sister Margaret waiting for him on the platform. Randy, tall and athletic looking, was teetering restlessly from one foot to another as his glance went back and forth along the windows of the train in search of him. Margaret's strong, big-boned figure was planted solidly, her hands clasped loosely across her waist, and her eyes were darting from car to car with swift intensity. And as George swung down from the steps of the Pullman and, valise in hand, strode toward the platform across the rock ballast of the roadbed and the gleaming rails, he knew instantly, with that intuitive feeling of strangeness and recognition, just what they would say to him at the moment of their meeting.

Now they had seen him. He saw Margaret speak excitedly to her brother and motion toward his approaching figure. And now Randy was coming on the run, his broad hand extended in a gesture of welcome, his rich tenor shouting greetings as he came:

"How are you, boy?" he shouted. "Put it there!" he cried heartily as he came up, and vigorously wrung him by the hand. "Glad to see you, Monk!"

Still shouting greetings, he reached over and attempted to take the valise. The inevitable argument, vehement, good-natured, and protesting, began immediately, and in another moment Randy was in triumphant possession and the two were walking together toward the platform, Randy saying scornfully all the time in answer to the other's protests:

"Oh, for God's sake, forget about it! I'll let you do as much for me when I come up to the Big Town to visit you! . . . Here's Margaret!" he said as they reached the platform. "I know she'll be glad to see you!"

She was waiting for him with a broad smile on her homely face. They had grown up together as next-door neighbors, and were almost like brother and sister. As a matter of fact, when George had been ten and Margaret twelve, they had had one of those idyllic romances of childhood in which each pledged eternal devotion to the other and took it for granted that they would marry when they grew up. But the years had changed all that. He had gone away, and she had taken charge of Randy when her parents died; she now kept house for him, and had never married. As he saw her standing there with the warm smile on her face, and with something vaguely spinsterish in her look in spite of her large, full-breasted figure and her general air of hearty good nature, he felt a sudden stirring of pity and old affection for her.

"Hello, Margaret!" he said, somewhat thickly and excitedly. "How are you, Margaret?"

They shook hands, and he planted a clumsy kiss on her face. Then, blushing with pleasure, she stepped back a pace and regarded him with the half bantering expression she had used so often as a child.

"Well, well, well!" she said. "You haven't changed much, George! A little stouter, maybe, but I reckon I'd have known you!"

They spoke now quietly about Aunt Maw and about the funeral, saying the strained and awkward things that people always say when they talk of death. Then, this duty done, there was a little pause before they resumed their natural selves once more.

The two men looked at each other and grinned. When they had been boys together Randy had seemed to George more like Mercutio than anybody he had ever known. He had had a small, lean head, well shaped, set closely with blond hair; he had been quick as a flash, light, wiry, active, with a wonderful natural grace in everything he did; his mind and spirit had been clear, exuberant, incisive, tempered like a fine Toledo blade. In college, too, he had been the same: he had not only done well in his classes, but had distinguished himself as a swimmer and as quarterback on the football team.

But now something caught in George's throat as he looked at him and saw what time had done. Randy's lean, thin face was deeply furrowed, and the years had left a grey deposit at his temples. His hair was thinning back on both sides of the forehead, and there were little webbings of fine wrinkles at the corners of the eyes. It saddened George and somehow made him feel a bit ashamed to see how old and worn he looked. But the thing he noticed most was the expression in Randy's eyes. Where they had once been clear and had looked out on the world with a sharp and level gaze, they were now troubled, and haunted by some deep preoccupation which he could not quite shake off even in the manifest joy he felt at seeing his old friend again.

While they stood there, Jarvis Riggs, Parson Flack, and the Mayor came slowly down the platform talking earnestly to one of the leading real estate operators of the town, who had come down to meet them. Randy saw them and, still grinning, he winked at George and prodded him in the ribs.

"Oh, you'll get it now!" he cried in his old extravagant way. "At all hours, from daybreak to three o'clock in the morning—no holds barred! They'll be waiting for you when you get there!" he chortled.

"Who?" said George.

"Haw-w!" Randy laughed. "Why, I'll bet they're all lined up there on the front porch right now, in a reception committee to greet you and to cut your throat, every damned mountain grill of a real estate man in town! Old Horse-face Barnes, Skin-'em-alive Mack Judson, Skunk-eye Tim Wagner, The Demon Promoter, and Old Squeeze-your-heart's-blood Simms, The Widder and Orphan Man from Arkansas—they're all there!" he said gloatingly. "She told them you're a prospect, and they're waiting for you! It's your turn now!" he yelled. "She told them that you're on the way, and they're drawing lots right now to see which one gets your shirt and which one takes the pants and B.V.D.'s! Haw-w!"—and he poked his friend in the ribs again.

77

"They'll get nothing out of me," George said, laughing, "for I haven't got it to begin with."

"That doesn't matter!" Randy yelled. "If you've got an extra collar button, they'll take that as the first installment, and then—haw-w!—they'll collect your cuff links, socks, and your suspenders in easy payments as the years roll on!"

He stood there laughing at the astounded look on his friend's face. Then, seeing his sister's reproving eye, he suddenly prodded her in the ribs, at which she shrieked in a vexed manner and slapped at his hand.

"I'll vow, Randy!" she cried fretfully. "What on earth's the matter with you? Why, you act like a regular idiot! I'll vow you do!"

"Haw-w!" he yelled again. Then, more soberly, but still grinning: "I guess we'll have to sleep you out over the garage, Monk, old boy. Dave Merrit's in town, and he's got the spare room." There was a slight note of deference in his voice as he mentioned Merrit's name, but he went on lightly: "Or if you like—haw-w!—there's a nice room at Mrs. Charles Montgomery Hopper's, and she'd be glad to have you!"

George looked rather uncomfortable at the mention of Mrs. Charles Montgomery Hopper. She was a worthy lady and he remembered her well, but he didn't want to stay at her boarding house. Margaret saw his expression and laughed:

"Ho, ho, ho, ho, ho! You see what you're in for, don't you? The prodigal comes home and we give him his choice of Mrs. Hopper or the garage! Now is that life or not?"

"I don't mind a bit," protested George. "I think the garage is swell. And besides—" they all grinned at each other again with the affection of people who know each other so well that they are long past knowledge—"if I get to helling around at night, I won't feel that I'm disturbing you when I come in. . . . But who is Mr. Merrit, anyway?"

"Why," Randy answered, and now he had an air of measuring his words with thoughtful deliberation, "he—he's the Company's man—my boss, you know. He travels around to all the branches to check up and see that everything's O.K. He's a fine fellow. You'll like him," said Randy seriously. "We've told him all about you and he wants to meet you."

"And we knew you wouldn't mind," Margaret said. "You know, it's business, he's with the Company, and of course it's good policy to be as nice to him as we can." But then, because such designing was really alien to her hospitable and whole-hearted spirit, she added: "Mr. Merrit is all right. I like him. We're glad to have him, anyway."

"Dave's a fine fellow," Randy repeated. "And I know he wants to see you. . . . Well," he said, and the preoccupied look was in his eyes again, "if we're all ready, let's get going. I'm due back at the office now. Merrit's there, of course. Suppose I run you out to the house and drop you, then I'll see you later."

This was agreed upon. Randy grinned once more—a little nervously, George thought—and picked up the valise and started rapidly across the station platform toward his car, which was parked at the curb.

At the funeral that afternoon the little frame house which old Lafayette Joyner—Aunt Maw's father, and George Webber's grandfather—had built with his own hands years ago looked just as it had always looked when George had lived there as a boy. Nothing about it had been changed. Yet it seemed smaller, meaner, more shabby than he remembered it. It was set some distance back from the street, between the Shepperton house on one side and the big brick house in which his Uncle Mark Joyner lived on the other. The street was lined with cars, many of them old and decrepit and covered with the red clay of the hills. In the yard in front of the house many men stood solemnly knotted in little groups, talking quietly, their bare heads and stiff Sunday clothes of austere black giving them an air of self-conscious shyness and restraint.

Inside, the little rooms were jammed with people, and the hush of death was on the gathering, broken now and then by muffled coughs and by stifled sobs and sniffles. Many of them were Joyners, who for three days had been coming in from the hills—old men and women with the marks of toil and pain upon their faces, cousins, in-laws, distant relatives of Aunt Maw. George had never seen some of them before, but they all bore the seal of the Joyner clan upon them, the look of haunting sorrow and something about the thin line of the lips that proclaimed their grim triumph in the presence of death.

In the tiny room, where on wintry nights Aunt Maw had always sat by the light of a kerosene lamp before a flickering fire, telling the boy her endless stories of death and sorrow, she now lay in her black coffin, the top and front of which were open to display as much of her as possible to the general view. And instantly, as George entered, he knew that one of her main obsessions in life had been victorious over death. A spinster and a virgin all her years, she had always had a horrible fear that, somehow, some day, some man would see her body. As she grew older her thoughts had been more and more preoccupied with death, and with her morbid shame lest someone see her in the state of nature after she was dead. For this reason she had a horror of undertakers, and had made her brother, Mark, and his wife, Mag, solemnly promise that no man would see her

79

unclothed corpse, that her laying out would be done by women, and, above all else, that she was not to be embalmed. By now she had been dead three days—three days of long hot sun and sultriness—and it seemed to George a grim but fitting ending that the last memory he would have of that little house, which in his childhood had been so filled with the stench of death-in-life, should now be the stench of death itself.

Mark Joyner shook hands cordially with his nephew and said he was glad he had been able to come down. His manner was simple, dignified, and reserved, eloquently expressive of quiet grief, for he had always been genuinely fond of his older sister. But Mag, his wife, who for fifty years had carried on a nagging, internecine warfare with Aunt Maw, had appointed herself chief mourner and was obviously enjoying the role. During the interminable service, when the Baptist minister in his twanging, nasal voice recited his long eulogy and went back over the events of Aunt Maw's life, Mag would break forth now and then in fits of loud weeping and would ostentatiously throw back her heavy black veil and swab vigorously with her handkerchief at her red and swollen eyes.

The minister, with the unconscious callousness of self-righteousness, rehearsed again the story of the family scandal. He told how George Webber's father had abandoned his wife, Amelia Joyner, to live in open shame with another woman, and how Amelia had shortly afterwards "died of a broken heart." He told how "Brother Mark Joyner and his God-fearing wife, Sister Maggie Joyner," had been filled with righteous wrath and had gone to court and wrested the motherless boy from the sinful keeping of his father; and how "this good woman who now lies dead before us" had taken charge of her sister's son and brought him up in a Christian home. And he said he was glad to see that the young man who had been the recipient of this dutiful charity had come home again to pay his last debt of gratitude at the bier of the one to whom he owed so much.

Throughout all this Mag continued to choke and sputter with histrionic sorrow, and George sat there biting his lips, his eyes fixed on the floor, perspiration streaming from him, his jaws clenched hard, his face purple .with shame and anger and nausea.

The afternoon wore on, and at last the service was over. People began to issue from the house, and the procession formed for the long, slow ride to the cemetery. With immense relief George escaped from the immediate family group and went over to Margaret Shepperton, and the two of them took possession of one of the limousines that had been hired for the occasion.

Just as the car was about to drive off and take its place in the line, a woman opened the door and got in with them. She was Mrs. Delia Flood, an old friend of Aunt Maw's. George had known her all his life.

"Why, hello there, young man," she said to George as she climbed in and sat down beside him. "This would've been a proud day for your Aunt Maw if she could've known you'd come all the way back home to be here at her funeral. She thought the world of you, boy." She nodded absent-mindedly to Margaret. "I saw you had an empty place here, so I said, 'It's a pity to let it go to waste. Hop right in,' I said. 'Don't stand on ceremony. It might as well be you,' I said, 'as the next fellow.'"

Mrs. Delia Flood was a childless widow well past middle age, short, sturdy, and physically stolid, with jet black hair and small, piercing brown eyes, and a tongue that was never still. She would fasten upon anyone she could catch and corner, and would talk on and on in a steady monotone that had neither beginning nor end. She was a woman of property, and her favorite topic of conversation was real estate. In fact, long before the present era of speculation and skyrocketing prices, she had had a mania for buying and selling land, and was a shrewd judge of values. With some sixth sense she had always known what direction the development of the growing town was likely to take, and when things happened as she predicted, it was usually found that she had bought up choice sites which she was able to sell for much more than she had paid for them. She lived simply and frugally, but she was generally believed to be well off.

For a little while Mrs. Flood sat in contemplative silence. But as the procession moved off and slowly made its way through the streets of the town, she began to glance sharply out of the windows on both sides, and before long, without any preliminary, she launched forth in a commentary on the history of every piece of property they passed. It was constant, panoramic, and exhaustive. She talked incessantly, gesturing briefly and casually with her hand, only pausing from time to time to nod deliberately to herself in a movement of strong affirmation.

"You see, don't you?" she said, nodding to herself with conviction, tranquilly indifferent whether they listened or not so long as the puppets of an audience were before her. "You see what they're goin' to do here, don't you? Why, Fred Barnes, Roy Simms, and Mack Judson—all that crowd—why, yes— here!—say!—" she cried, frowning meditatively—"wasn't I reading it? Didn't it all come out in the paper—why, here, you know, a week or two ago—how they proposed to tear down that whole block of buildings there and were goin' to put up the finest garage in this part of the country? Oh, it will take up the whole block, you know, with a fine eight-story building over it, and storage space upstairs for more cars, and doctors' offices—why, yes!—they're even thinkin' of puttin' in a roof garden and a big restaurant on top. The whole thing will cost 'em over half a million dollars before they're done with it—oh, paid two thousand dollars a foot for every inch of it!" she cried. "But pshaw! Why, those are Main Street prices—you can get business property up in the center of town for *that*! I could've told 'em—but hm!—" with a scornful little tremor of the head—"they didn't want it anywhere but here—no, sir! They'll be lucky if they get out with their skins!"

George and Margaret offered no comment, but Mrs. Flood appeared not to notice, and as the procession crossed the bridge and turned into Preston Avenue she went on:

"See that house and lot over there! I paid twenty-five thousand for it two years ago, and now it's worth fifty thousand if it's worth a penny. Yes, and I'll get it, too. But pshaw! See here!"—she shook her head emphatically. "They couldn't pull a trick like that on *me*! I saw what he was up to! Yes! Didn't Mack Judson come to me? Didn't he try to trade with me? Oh, here along, you know, the first part of last April," she said impatiently, with a dismissing gesture of her hand, as if all this must be perfectly clear to everyone. "All that crowd that's in with him—they were behind him—I could see it plain as day. Says: 'I'll tell you what I'll do. We know you're a good trader, we respect your judgment, and we want you in,' he says, 'and just to have you with us, why, I'll trade you three fine lots I own up there on Pinecrest Road in Ridgewood for that house and lot of yours on Preston Avenue.' Says: 'You won't have to put up a cent. Just to get you in with us I'll make you an even swap!' 'Well,' I said, 'that's mighty fine of you, Mack, and I appreciate the compliment. If you want that house and lot on Preston Avenue,' I said, 'why, I reckon I can let you have it. You know my price,' I said. 'It's fifty thousand. What are those lots in Ridgewood worth?'—came right out and asked him, you know. 'Why,' he says, 'it's hard to say. I don't know just exactly what they *are* worth,' he says. 'The property up there is goin' up all the time.' I looked him straight in the eye and said to him: 'Well, Mack, *I* know what those lots are worth, and they're not worth what you paid for 'em. The town's movin' the other way. So if you want my house and lot,' I said, 'just bring me the cash and you can have it. But I won't swap with you.' That's exactly what I told him, and of course that was the end of it. He's never mentioned it again. Oh, yes, I saw what he was up to, all right."

Nearing the cemetery, the line of cars passed a place where an unpaved clay road went upward among fields toward some lonely pines. The dirt road, at the point where it joined the main highway, was flanked by two portaled shapes of hewn granite blocks set there like markers of a splendid city yet unbuilt which would rise grandly from the hills that swept back into the green wilderness from the river. But now this ornate entrance and a large billboard planted in the field were the only evidences of what was yet to be. Mrs. Flood saw the sign.

"Haw? What's that?" she cried out in a sharply startled tone. "What does it say there?"

They all craned their necks to see it as they passed, and George read aloud the legend of the sign:

RIVERCREST

DEDICATED TO ALL THE PEOPLE

OF THIS SECTION AND TO THE GLORY

OF THE GREATER CITY THEY WILL BUILD

Mrs. Flood took in the words with obvious satisfaction. "Ah-hah!" she said, nodding her head slowly, with deliberate agreement. "That's just exactly it!"

Margaret nudged George and whispered in his ear:

"Dedicated!" she muttered scornfully—then, with mincing refinement: "Now ain't that nice? Dedicated to cutting your throat and bleeding you white of every nickel that you've got!"

They were now entering the cemetery, and the procession wound slowly in along a circling road and at length came to a halt near the rounded crest of the hill below the Joyner burial plot. At one corner of the plot a tall locust tree was growing, and beneath its shade all the Joyners had been buried. There was the family monument—a square, massive chunk of grey, metallic granite, brilliantly burnished, with "JOYNER" in raised letters upon its shining surface. On the ends were inscriptions for old Lafayette and his wife with their names and dates; and, grouped about them, in parallel rows set on the gentle slope, were the graves of Lafayette's children. All these had smaller individual monuments, and on each of these, below the name and dates of birth and death, was some little elegiac poem carved in a flowing script.

At one side of the burial plot the new-dug grave gaped darkly in the raw earth, and beside it was a mound of loose yellow clay. Ranged above it on the hill were several rows of folding chairs. Toward these the people, who were now getting out of the cars, began to move.

Mark and Mag and various other Joyners took the front rows, and George and Margaret, with Mrs. Flood still close beside them, found chairs at the back. Other people—friends, distant relatives, and mere acquaintances—stood in groups behind.

The lot looked out across a mile or two of deep, dense green, the wooded slopes and hollows that receded toward the winding river, and straight across beyond the river was the central business part of town. The spires and buildings, the old ones as well as some splendid new ones—hotels, office buildings, garages, churches, and the scaffolding and concrete of new construction which exploded from the familiar design with glittering violence—were plainly visible. It was a fine view.

While the people took their places and waited for the pallbearers to perform their last slow and heavy service up the final ascent of the hill, Mrs. Flood sat with her hands folded in her lap and gazed out over the town. Then she began shaking her head thoughtfully, her lips pursed in deprecation and regret, and in a low voice, as if she were talking to herself, she said:

"Hm! Hm! Hm! Too bad, too bad, too bad!"

"What's that, Mrs. Flood?" Margaret leaned over and whispered. "What's too bad?"

"Why, that they should ever have chosen such a place as this for the cemetery," she said regretfully. She had lowered her voice to a stage whisper, and those around her could hear everything she said. "Why, as I told Frank Candler just the other day, they've gone and deliberately given away the two best building sites in town to the niggers and the dead people! That's just exactly what they've done! I've always said as much—that the two finest building sites in town for natural beauty are Niggertown and Highview Cemetery. I could've told 'em that long years ago—they should've known it themselves if any of 'em could have seen an inch beyond his nose—that some day the town would grow up and this would be valuable property! Why, why on earth! When they were lookin' for a cemetery site—why on earth didn't they think of findin' one up there on Buxton Hill, say, where you get a beautiful view, and where land is not so valuable? But this!" she whispered loudly. "This, by rights, is *building* property! People could have fine homes here! And as for the niggers, I've always said that they'd have been better off if they'd been put down there on those old flats in the depot section. Now it's too late, of course—nothin' can be done—but it was certainly a serious mistake!" she whispered, and shook her head. "I've always known it!"

"Well, I guess you're right," Margaret whispered in reply. "I never thought of it before, but I guess you're right." And she nudged George with her elbow.

The pallbearers had set the coffin in its place, and the minister now began to read the brief and movingly solemn commitment service. Slowly the coffin was lowered in its grave. And as the black lid disappeared from sight George felt such a stab of

84

wordless pain and grief as he had never known. But he knew even as he felt it that it wasn't sorrow for Aunt Maw. It was an aching pity for himself and for all men living, and in it was the knowledge of the briefness of man's days, and the smallness of his life, and the certain dark that comes too swiftly and that has no end. And he felt, too, more personally, now with Aunt Maw gone and no one left in all his family who was close to him, that one whole cycle of time had closed for him. He thought of the future opening blankly up before him, and for a moment he had an acute sense of terror and despair like that of a lost child, for he felt now that the last tie that had bound him to his native earth was severed, and he saw himself as a creature homeless, uprooted, and alone, with no door to enter, no place to call his own, in all the vast desolation of the planet.

The people had now begun to move away and to walk back slowly toward their cars. The Joyners, however, kept their seats until the last spadeful of earth was heaped and patted into place. Then they arose, their duty done. Some of them just stood there now, talking quietly in their drawling voices, while others sauntered among the tombstones, bending over to read the inscriptions and straightening up to recall and tell each other some forgotten incident in the life of some forgotten Joyner. At last they, too, began to drift away.

George did not want to go back with them and be forced to hear the shreds of Aunt Maw's life torn apart and pieced together again, so he linked his arm through Margaret's and led her over the brow of the hill to the other side. For a little while they stood in the slanting light, silent, their faces to the west, and watched the great ball of the sun sink down behind the rim of distant mountains. And the majestic beauty of the spectacle, together with the woman's quiet presence there beside him, brought calm and peace to the young man's troubled spirit.

When they came back, the cemetery appreared to be deserted. But as they approached the Joyner plot they saw that Mrs. Delia Flood was still waiting for them. They had forgotten her, and realized now that she could not go without them, for there was only one car on the graveled roadway below and the hired chauffeur was slumped behind his wheel, asleep. In the fast-failing light Mrs. Flood was wandering among the graves, stopping now and then to stoop and peer closely at an inscription on a stone. Then she would stand there meditatively and look out across the town, where the first lights were already beginning to wink on. She turned to them casually when they came up, as though she had taken no notice of their absence, and spoke to them in her curious fragmentary way, plucking the words right out of the middle of her thoughts.

"Why, to think," she said reflectively, "that he would go and move her! To think that any man could be so hard-hearted! Oh!" she shuddered with a brief convulsive pucker of revulsion. "It makes my blood run cold to think of it—and everybody told him so!—they told him so at the time—to think he would have no more mercy in him than to go and move her from the place where she lay buried!"

"Who was that, Mrs. Flood?" George said absently. "Move who?"

"Why, Amelia, of course—your *mother*, child!" she said impatiently, and gestured briefly toward the weather-rusted stone.

He bent forward and read the familiar inscription:

Amelia Webber, née Joyner

and below her dates the carved verse:

> Still is the voice we knew so well,
> Vanished the face we love,
> Flown her spirit pure to dwell
> With angels up above.
> Ours is the sorrow, ours the pain,
> And ours the joy alone
> To clasp her in our arms again
> In Heaven, by God's throne.

"That's the thing that started all this movin'!" Mrs. Flood was saying. "Nobody'd ever have thought of comin' here if it hadn't been for Amelia! And here," she cried fretfully, "the woman had been dead and in her grave more than a year when she gets this notion in his head he's got to move her—and you couldn't reason with him! Why, your uncle, Mark Joyner—that's who it was! You couldn't argue with him!" she cried with vehement surprise. "Why, yes, of course! It was back there at the time they were havin' all that trouble with your father, child. He'd left Amelia and gone to live with that other woman—but I *will* say this for him!" and she nodded her head with determination. "When Amelia died, John Webber did the decent thing and buried her himself—claimed her as his wife and buried her! He'd bought a plot in the old cemetery, and that's where he put her. But then, more than a year afterwards—*you* know, child—when Mark Joyner had that trouble with your father about who was to bring you up—yes, and took it to the courts and won!—why, that's when it was that Mark took it in his head to move Amelia. Said he wouldn't let a sister of his lie in Web-

86

ber earth! He already had this plot, of course, way over here on this hill where nobody'd ever thought of goin'. It was just a little private buryin' ground, then—a few families used it, that was all."

She paused and looked out thoughtfully over the town, then after a moment she went on:

"Your Aunt Maw, she tried to talk to Mark about it, but it was like talkin' to a stone wall. She told me all about it at the time. But no, sir!" she shook her head with a movement of strong decision. "He'd made up his mind and he wouldn't budge from it an inch! 'But see here, Mark,' she said. 'The thing's not right! Amelia ought to stay where she's buried!' She didn't like the looks of it, you know. 'Even the dead have got their rights,' she said. 'Where the tree falls, there let it lie!'—that's what she told him. But no! He wouldn't listen—you couldn't talk to him. He says, 'I'll move her if it's the last thing I ever live to do! I'll move her if I have to dig her up myself and carry the coffin on my back all the way to the top of that hill across the river! That's where she's goin',' he says, 'and you needn't argue any more!' Well, your Aunt Maw saw then that he had his mind made up and that it wouldn't do any good to talk to him about it. But ho! an awful mistake! an *awful* mistake!" she muttered, shaking her head slowly. "All that movin' and expense for nothin'! If he felt that way, he should've brought her over here in the first place, when she died! But I guess it was the lawsuit and all the bad blood it stirred up that made him feel that way," she now said tranquilly. "And that's the reason all these other people are buried here—" she made a sweeping gesture with her arm—"that's what started it, all right! Why, of course! When the old cemetery got filled up and they had to look around for a new site—why, one of those fellows in Parson Flack's gang at City Hall, he remembered the rumpus about Amelia and thought of all these empty acres way out here beside the old buryin' ground. He found he could buy 'em cheap, and that's what he did. That's exactly how it was," she said. "But I've always regretted it. I was against it from the start."

She fell silent again, and stood looking with solemn-eyed memory at the weather-rusted stone.

"Well, as I say, then," she went on calmly, "when your Aunt Maw saw he had his mind made up and that there was no use to try to change him—well, she went out to the old cemetery the day they moved her, and she asked me to go with her, you know. Oh, it was one of those raw, windy days you get in March! The very kind of day Amelia died on. And old Mrs. Wrenn and Amy Williamson—they had both been good friends of Amelia's—of course they went along, too. And, of course, when we got there, they were curious—they wanted to have a look, you know," she said calmly, mentioning this grisly desire

87

with no surprise whatever. "And they tried to get me to look at it, too. Your Aunt Maw got so sick that Mark had to take her home in the carriage, but I stood my ground. 'No,' I said, 'you go on and satisfy your curiosity if that's what you want to do, but I won't look at it!' I said, 'I'd rather remember her the way she was.' Well, sir, they went ahead and did it then. They got old Prove—you know, he was that old nigger man that worked for Mark—they got him to open up the coffin, and I turned my back and walked away a little piece until they got through lookin'," she said tranquilly. "And pretty soon I heard 'em comin'. Well, I turned around and looked at 'em, and let me tell you somethin'," she said gravely, "their faces were a study! Oh, they turned pale and they trembled! 'Well, are you satisfied?' I said. 'Did you find what you were lookin' for?' 'Oh-h!' says old Mrs. Wrenn, pale as a ghost, shakin' and wringin' her hands, you know. 'Oh, Delia!' she says, 'it was awful! I'm sorry that I looked!' she says. 'Ah-ha!' I said. 'What did I tell you? You see, don't you?' And she says, 'Oh-h, it was all gone!—all gone!—all rotted away to nothin' so you couldn't recognize her! The face was all gone until you could see the teeth! And the nails had all grown out long! But Delia!' she says, 'the hair!—the hair! Oh, I tell you what,' she says, 'the hair was beautiful! It had grown out until it covered everything—the finest head of hair I ever saw on anyone! But the rest of it—oh, I'm sorry that I looked!' she says. 'Well, I thought so! I thought so!' I said. 'I knew you'd be sorry, so I wouldn't look!' . . . But that's the way it was, all right," she concluded with the quiet satisfaction of omniscience.

Through this recital George and Margaret had stood transfixed, a look of horror on their faces, but Mrs. Flood did not notice them. She stood now looking down at Amelia's tombstone, her lips puckered thoughtfully, and after a little while she said:

"I don't know *when* I've thought of Amelia and John Webber—both of 'em dead and in their graves through all these years. She lies here, and he's all alone in his own lot over there on the other side of town, and that old trouble that they had seems very far away. You know," she said, looking up and speaking with a tone of deep conviction, "I believe that they have joined each other and are reconciled and happy. I believe I'll meet them some day in a Higher Sphere, along with all my other friends—all happy, and all leading a new life."

She was silent for a moment, and then, with a movement of strong decision, she turned away and looked out toward the town, where the lights were now burning hard and bright and steady in the dusk.

"Come now!" she cried briskly and cheerfully. "It's time we were goin' home! It's gettin' dark!"

The three of them walked in silence down the slope toward

the waiting car. As they came up to it and were about to get in, Mrs. Flood stopped and laid her hand on George's shoulder in a warm and easy gesture.

"Young man," she said, "I've been a long time livin' on this earth, and as the fellow says, the world do move! You've got your life ahead of you, and lots to learn and many things to do—but let me tell you somethin', boy!" and all at once she looked at him in a straight and deadly fashion. "Go out and see the world and get your fill of wanderin'," she cried, "and then come back and tell me if you've found a better place than home! I've seen great changes in my time, and I'll see more before I die. There are great things yet in store for us—great progress, great inventions—it will all come true. Perhaps I'll not live to see it, but *you* will! We've got a fine town here, and fine people to make it go—and we're not done yet. I've seen it all grow up out of a country village—and some day we will have a great city here."

She waited an instant as if she expected him to answer and corroborate her judgment, and when he merely nodded to show that he had heard her, she took it for agreement and went on:

"Your Aunt Maw always hoped that you'd come home again. And you *will*!" she said. "There's no better or more beautiful place on earth than in these mountains—and some day you'll come home again to stay."

Chapter Seven

Boom Town

During the week that followed Aunt Maw's funeral George renewed his acquaintance with his home town, and it was a disconcerting experience. The sleepy little mountain village in which he had grown up—for it had been hardly more than that then—was now changed almost beyond recognition. The very streets that he had known so well, and had remembered through the years in their familiar aspect of early-afternoon emptiness and drowsy lethargy, were now foaming with life, crowded with expensive traffic, filled with new faces he had never seen before.

Occasionally he saw somebody that he knew, and in the strangeness of it all they seemed to him like lights shining in the darkness of a lonely coast.

But what he noticed chiefly—and once he observed it he began watching for it, and it was always there—was the look on the people's faces. It puzzled him, and frightened him, and when he tried to find a word to describe it, the only thing he could think of was—madness. The nervous, excited glitter in the eyes seemed to belong to nothing else but madness. The faces of natives and strangers alike appeared to be animated by some secret and unholy glee. And their bodies, as they darted, dodged, and thrust their way along, seemed to have a kind of leaping energy as if some powerful drug was driving them on. They gave him the impression of an entire population that was drunk—drunk with an intoxication which never made them weary, dead, or sodden, and which never wore off, but which incited them constantly to new efforts of leaping and thrusting exuberance.

The people he had known all his life cried out to him along the streets, seizing his hand and shaking it, and saying: "Hi, there, boy! Glad to see you home again! Going to be with us for a while now? Good! I'll be seeing you! I've got to go now—got to meet a fellow down the street to sign some papers! Glad to see you, boy!" Then, having uttered this tempestuous greeting without a pause and without the loss of a stride, pulling and dragging him along with them as they wrung his hand, they vanished.

On all sides he heard talk, talk, talk—terrific and incessant. And the tumult of voices was united in variations of a single chorus—speculation and real estate. People were gathered in earnestly chattering groups before the drug stores, before the post office, before the Court House and the City Hall. They hurried along the pavements talking together with passionate absorption, bestowing half-abstracted nods of greeting from time to time on passing acquaintances.

The real estate men were everywhere. Their motors and busses roared through the streets of the town and out into the country, carrying crowds of prospective clients. One could see them on the porches of houses unfolding blueprints and prospectuses as they shouted enticements and promises of sudden wealth into the ears of deaf old women. Everyone was fair game for them—the lame, the halt, and the blind, Civil War veterans or their decrepit pensioned widows, as well as high school boys and girls, Negro truck drivers, soda jerkers, elevator boys, and bootblacks.

Everyone bought real estate; and everyone was "a real estate man" either in name or practice. The barbers, the lawyers, the grocers, the butchers, the builders, the clothiers—all were

90

engaged now in this single interest and obsession. And there seemed to be only one rule, universal and infallible—to buy, always to buy, to pay whatever price was asked, and to sell again within two days at any price one chose to fix. It was fantastic. Along all the streets in town the ownership of the land was constantly changing; and when the supply of streets was exhausted, new streets were feverishly created in the surrounding wilderness; and even before these streets were paved or a house had been built upon them, the land was being sold, and then resold, by the acre, by the lot, by the foot, for hundreds of thousands of dollars.

A spirit of drunken waste and wild destructiveness was everywhere apparent. The fairest places in the town were being mutilated at untold cost. In the center of town there had been a beautiful green hill, opulent with rich lawns and lordly trees, with beds of flowers and banks of honeysuckle, and on top of it there had been an immense, rambling, old wooden hotel. From its windows one could look out upon the vast panorama of mountain ranges in the smoky distance.

George could remember its wide porches and comfortable rockers, its innumerable eaves and gables, its labyrinth of wings and corridors, its great parlors and their thick red carpets, and the lobby with its old red leather chairs, hollowed and shaped by the backs of men, and its smell of tobacco and its iced tinkle of tall drinks. It had a splendid dining room filled with laughter and quiet voices, where expert Negroes in white jackets bent and scraped and chuckled over the jokes of the rich men from the North as with prayerful grace they served them delicious foods out of old silver dishes. George could remember, too, the smiles and the tender beauty of the rich men's wives and daughters. As a boy he had been touched with the unutterable mystery of all these things, for these wealthy travelers had come great distances and had somehow brought with them an evocation of the whole golden and unvisited world, with its fabulous cities and its promise of glory, fame, and love.

It had been one of the pleasantest places in the town, but now it was gone. An army of men and shovels had advanced upon this beautiful green hill and had leveled it down to an ugly flat of clay, and had paved it with a desolate horror of white concrete, and had built stores and garages and office buildings and parking spaces—all raw and new—and were now putting up a new hotel beneath the very spot where the old one had stood. It was to be a structure of sixteen stories, of steel and concrete and pressed brick. It was being stamped out of the same mold, as if by some gigantic biscuit-cutter of hotels, that had produced a thousand others like it all over the country. And, to give a sumptuous—if spurious—distinction to its patterned uniformity, it was to be called The Libya-Ritz.

One day George ran into Sam Pennock, a boyhood friend and a classmate at Pine Rock College. Sam came down the busy street swiftly at his anxious, lunging stride, and immediately, without a word of greeting, he broke hoarsely into the abrupt and fragmentary manner of speaking that had always been characteristic of him, but that now seemed more feverish than ever:

"When did you get here? . . . How long are you going to stay? . . . What do you think of the way things look here?" Then, without waiting for an answer, he demanded with brusque, challenging, and almost impatient scornfulness: "Well, what do you intend to do—be a two-thousand-dollar-a-year school teacher all your life?"

The contemptuous tone, with its implication of superiority—an implication he had noticed before in the attitude of these people, big with their inflated sense of wealth and achievement—stung George to retort sharply:

"There are worse things than teaching school! Being a paper millionaire is one of them! As for the two thousand a year, you really get it, Sam! It's not real estate money, it's money you can spend. You can buy a ham sandwich with it."

Sam laughed. "You're right!" he said. "I don't blame you. It's the truth!" He began to shake his head slowly. "Lord, Lord!" he said. "They've all gone clean out of their heads here. . . . Never saw anything like it in my life. . . . Why, they're all crazy as a loon!" he exclaimed. "You can't talk to them. . . . You can't reason with them. . . . They won't listen to you . . . . They're getting prices for property here that you couldn't get in New York."

"Are they *getting* it?"

"Well," he said, with a falsetto laugh, "they get the first five hundred dollars. . . . You pay the next five hundred thousand on time."

"How much time?"

"God!" he said. "I don't know. . . . All you want, I reckon. . . . Forever! . . . It doesn't matter. . . . You sell it next day for a million."

"On time?"

"That's it!" he cried, laughing. "You make half a million just like that."

"On time?"

"You've got it!" said Sam. "On time. . . . God! Crazy, crazy, crazy," he kept laughing and shaking his head. "That's the way they make it."

"Are you making it, too?"

At once his manner became feverishly earnest: "Why, it's the damnedest thing you ever heard of!" he said. "I'm raking it in hand over fist! . . . Made three hundred thousand dollars in the last two months. . . . Why, it's the truth! . . . Made a trade yesterday and turned around and sold the lot again not two hours later. . . . Fifty thousand dollars just like that!" he snapped his fingers. "Does your uncle want to sell that house on Locust Street where your Aunt Maw lived? . . . Have you talked to him about it? . . . Would he consider an offer?"

"I suppose so, if he gets enough."

"How much does he want?" he demanded impatiently. "Would he take a hundred thousand?"

"Could you get it for him?"

"I could get it within twenty-four hours," he said. "I know a man who'd snap it up in five minutes. . . . I tell you what I'll do, Monk, if you persuade him to sell—I'll split the commission with you. . . . I'll give you five thousand dollars."

"All right, Sam, it's a go. Could you let me have fifty cents on account?"

"Do you think he'll sell?" he asked eagerly.

"Really, I don't know, but I doubt it. That place was my grandfather's. It's been in the family a long time. I imagine he'll want to keep it."

"Keep it! What's the sense in keeping it? . . . Now's the time when things are at the peak. He'll never get a better offer!"

"I know, but he's expecting to strike oil out in the backyard any time now," said George with a laugh.

At this moment there was a disturbance among the tides of traffic in the street. A magnificent car detached itself from the stream of humbler vehicles and moved in swiftly to the curb, where it came to a smooth stop—a glitter of nickel, glass, and burnished steel. From it a gaudily attired creature stepped down to the pavement with an air of princely indolence, tucked a light Malacca cane carelessly under its right armpit, and slowly and fastidiously withdrew from its nicotined fingers a pair of lemon-colored gloves, at the same time saying to the liveried chauffeur:

"You may go, James. Call for me again in hal-luf an houah!"

The creature's face was thin and sunken. Its complexion was a deathly sallow—all except the nose, which was bulbous and glowed a brilliant red, showing an intricate network of enlarged purple veins. Its toothless jaws were equipped with such an enormous set of glittering false teeth that the lips could not cover them, and they grinned at the world with the prognathous bleakness of a skeleton. The whole figure, although heavy and shambling, had the tottering appearance which suggested a stupendous debauchery. It moved forward with its false, bleak grin, leaning heavily upon the stick, and suddenly George recognized that native ruin which had been known to him since childhood as Tim Wagner.

J. Timothy Wagner—the "J" was a recent and completely arbitrary addition of his own, appropriated, no doubt, to fit his ideas of personal grandeur, and to match the eminent position in the town's affairs to which he had belatedly risen—was the black sheep of one of the old, established families in the community. At the time George Webber was a boy, Tim Wagner had been for so long the product of complete disillusion that there was no longer any vestige of respect attached to him.

He had been preëminently the town sot. His title to this office was unquestioned. In this capacity he was even held in a kind of affection. His exploits were notorious, the subjects of a hundred stories. One night, for example, the loafers in McCormack's pharmacy had seen Tim swallow something and then shudder convulsively. This process was repeated several times, until the curiosity of the loafers was aroused. They began to observe him furtively but closely, and in a few minutes Tim thrust out his hand slyly, fumbled around in the gold fish bowl, and withdrew his hand with a wriggling little shape between his fingers. Then the quick swallow and the convulsive shudder were repeated.

He had inherited two fortunes before his twenty-fifth year and had run through them both. Hilarious stories were told of Tim's celebrated pleasure tour upon the inheritance of the second fortune. He had chartered a private car, stocked it plentifully with liquor, and selected as his traveling companions the most notorious sots, vagabonds, and tramps the community could furnish. The debauch had lasted eight months. This party of itinerant bacchuses had made a tour of the entire country. They had exploded their empty flasks against the ramparts of the Rocky Mountains, tossed their empty kegs into San Francisco Bay, strewn the plains with their beer bottles. At last the party had achieved a condition of exhausted satiety in the nation's capital, where Tim, with what was left of his inheritance, had engaged an entire floor at one of the leading hotels. Then, one by one, the exhausted wanderers had drifted back to town, bringing tales of bacchanalian orgies that had not been equaled since the days of the Roman emperors, and leaving Tim finally in solitary possession of the wreckage of empty suites.

From that time on he had slipped rapidly into a state of perpetual sottishness. Even then, however, he had retained the traces of an attractive and engaging personality. Everyone had had a tolerant and unspoken affection for him. Save for the

94

harm he did himself, Tim was an inoffensive and good-natured creature.

His figure on the streets of the town at night had been a familiar one. From sunset on, he might be found almost anywhere. It was easy to tell what progressive state of intoxication he had reached simply by observing his method of locomotion. No one ever saw him stagger. He did not weave drunkenly along the pavement. Rather, when he approached the saturation point, he walked very straight, very rapidly, but with funny little short steps. As he walked he kept his face partly lowered, glancing quickly and comically from side to side, with little possumlike looks. If he approached complete paralysis, he just stood quietly and leaned against something—a lamp post or a doorway or the side of a building or the front of the drug store. Here he would remain for hours in a state of solemn immobility, broken only by an occasional belch. His face, already grown thin and flabby-jowled, with its flaming beacon of a nose, would at these times be composed in an expression of drunken gravity, and his whole condition would be characterized by a remarkable alertness, perceptiveness, and control. He rarely degenerated into complete collapse. Almost always he could respond instantly and briskly to a word of greeting.

Even the police had had a benevolent regard for him, and they had exercised a friendly guardianship over him. Through long experience and observation, every policeman on the force was thoroughly acquainted with Tim's symptoms. They could tell at a glance just what degree of intoxication he had reached, and if they thought he had crossed the final border line and that his collapse in doorway or gutter was imminent, they would take charge of him, speaking to him kindly, but with a stern warning:

"Tim, if you're on the streets again tonight, we're going to lock you up. Now you go on home and go to bed."

To this Tim would nod briskly, with instant and amiable agreement: "Yes, sir, yes, sir. Just what I was going to do, Captain Crane, when you spoke to me. Going home right this minute. Yes, sir."

With these words he would start off briskly across the street, his legs making their little fast, short steps and his eyes darting comically from side to side, until he had vanished around the corner. Within ten or fifteen minutes, however, he might be seen again, easing his way along cautiously in the dark shadow of a building, creeping up to the corner, and peeking around with a sly look on his face to see if any of the watchdogs of the law were in sight.

As time went on and his life lapsed more and more into total vagabondage, one of his wealthy aunts, in the hope that some employment might partially retrieve him, had given him the use of a vacant lot behind some buildings in the business section of the town, a short half block from Main Street. The automobile had now come in sufficient numbers to make parking laws important, and Tim was allowed by his aunt to use this lot as parking space for cars and to keep the money thus obtained. In this employment he succeeded far better than anyone expected. He had little to do except stay on the premises, and this was not difficult for him so long as he was plentifully supplied with corn whiskey.

During this period of his life some canvassers at a local election had looked for Tim to enroll him in the interest of their candidate, but they had been unable to find out where he lived. He had not lived, of course, with any member of his family for years, and investigation failed to disclose that he had a room anywhere. The question then began to go around: "Where does Tim Wagner live? Where does he sleep?" No one could find out. And Tim's own answers, when pressed for information, were slyly evasive.

One day, however, the answer came to light. The automobile had come, and come so thoroughly that people were even getting buried by motor car. The day of the horse-drawn hearse had passed forever. Accordingly, one of the local undertaking firms had told Tim he could have their old horse-drawn hearse if he would only take it off their premises. Tim had accepted the macabre gift and had parked the hearse in his lot. One day when Tim was absent the canvassers came back again, still persistent in their efforts to learn his address so they could enroll him. They noticed the old hearse, and, seeing that its raven curtains were so closely drawn that the interior was hidden from view, they decided to investigate. Cautiously they opened the doors of the hearse. A cot was inside. There was even a chair. It was completely furnished as a small but adequate bedroom.

So at last his secret had been found out. Henceforth all the town knew where he lived.

That was Tim Wagner as George had known him fifteen years ago. Since then he had been so constantly steeped in alcohol that his progressive disintegration had been marked, and he had lately adopted the fantastic trappings of a clown of royalty. Everyone knew all about him, and yet—the fact was incredible!—Tim Wagner had now become the supreme embodiment of the town's extravagant folly. For, as gamblers will stake a fortune on some moment's whimsey of belief, thrusting their money into a stranger's hand and bidding him to play with it because the color of his hair is lucky, or as race track men will rub the hump upon a cripple's back to bring them luck, so the people of the town now listened prayerfully to every word Tim Wagner uttered. They sought his opinion in all their speculations, and acted instantly on his suggestions. He had become—in what way and for what reason no one knew—the high priest and prophet of this insanity of waste.

They knew that he was diseased and broken, that his wits were always addled now with alcohol, but they used him as men once used divining rods. They deferred to him as Russian peasants once deferred to the village idiot. They now believed with an absolute and unquestioning faith that some power of intuition in him made all his judgments infallible.

It was this creature who had just alighted at the curb a little beyond George Webber and Sam Pennock, full of drunken majesty and bleary-eyed foppishness. Sam turned to him with a movement of feverish eagerness, saying to George abruptly:

"Wait a minute! I've got to speak to Tim Wagner about something! Wait till I come back!"

George watched the scene with amazement. Tim Wagner, still drawing the gloves off of his fingers with an expression of bored casualness, walked slowly over toward the entrance of McCormack's drug store—no longer were his steps short and quick, for he leaned heavily on his cane—while Sam, in an attitude of obsequious entreaty, kept at his elbow, bending his tall form toward him and hoarsely pouring out a torrent of questions:

". . . Property in West Libya. . . . Seventy-five thousand dollars. . . . Option expires tomorrow at noon. . . . Joe Ingram has the piece above mine. . . . Won't sell. . . . Holding for hundred fifty. . . . Mine's the best location. . . . But Fred Bynum says too far from main road. . . . What do you think, Tim? . . . Is it worth it?"

During the course of this torrential appeal Tim Wagner did not even turn to look at his petitioner. He gave no evidence whatever that he heard what Sam was saying. Instead, he stopped, thrust his gloves into his pocket, cast his eyes around slyly in a series of quick glances, and suddenly began to root into himself violently with a clutching hand. Then he straightened up like a man just coming out of a trance, and seemed to become aware for the first time that Sam was waiting.

"What's that? What did you say, Sam?" he said rapidly. "How much did they offer you for it? Don't sell, don't sell!" he said suddenly and with great emphasis. "Now's the time to buy, not to sell. The trend is upward. Buy! Buy! Don't take it. Don't sell. That's my advice!"

"I'm not selling, Tim," Sam cried excitedly. "I'm thinking of buying."

"Oh—yes, yes, yes!" Tim muttered rapidly. "I see, I see." He turned now for the first time and fixed his eyes upon his questioner. "Where did you say it was?" he demanded sharply. "Deepwood? Good! Good! Can't go wrong! Buy! Buy!"

He started to walk away into the drug store, and the lounging idlers moved aside deferentially to let him pass. Sam rushed after him frantically and caught him by the arm, shouting:

"No, no, Tim! It's not Deepwood! It's the other way.... I've been telling you.... It's West Libya!"

"What's that?" Tim cried sharply. "West Libya? Why didn't you say so? That's different. Buy! Buy! Can't go wrong! Whole town's moving in that direction. Values double out there in six months. How much do they want?"

"Seventy-five thousand," Sam panted. "Option expires tomorrow.... Five years to pay it up."

"Buy! Buy!" Tim barked, and walked off into the drug store.

Sam strode back toward George, his eyes blazing with excitement.

"Did you hear him? Did you hear what he said?" he demanded hoarsely. "You heard him, didn't you? . . . Best damned judge of real estate that ever lived. . . . Never known to make a mistake! . . . 'Buy! Buy! Will double in value in six months!' . . . You were standing right here—" he said hoarsely and accusingly, glaring at George—"you heard what he said, didn't you?"

"Yes, I heard him."

Sam glanced wildly about him, passed his hand nervously through his hair several times, and then said, sighing heavily and shaking his head in wonder:

"Seventy-five thousand dollars' profit in one deal! . . . Never heard anything like it in my life! . . . Lord, Lord!" he cried. "What are we coming to?"

Somehow the news had gotten around that George had written a book and that it would soon be published. The editor of the local paper heard of it and sent a reporter to interview him, and printed a story about it.

"So you've written a book?" said the reporter. "What kind of a book is it? What's it about?"

"Why—I—I hardly know how to tell you," George stammered. "It—it's a novel——"

"A Southern novel? Anything to do with this part of the country?"

"Well—yes—that is—it's about the South, all right—about an Old Catawba family—but——"

98

LOCAL BOY WRITES ROMANCE OF THE OLD SOUTH

George Webber, son of the late John Webber and nephew of Mark Joyner, local hardware merchant, has written a novel with a Libya Hill background which the New York house of James Rodney & Co. will publish this fall.

When interviewed last night, the young author stated that his book was a romance of the Old South, centering about the history of a distinguished antebellum family of this region. The people of Libya Hill and environs will await the publication of the book with special interest, not only because many of them will remember the author, who was born and brought up here, but also because that stirring period of Old Catawba's past has never before been accorded its rightful place of honor in the annals of Southern literature.

"We understand you have traveled a great deal since you left home. Been to Europe several times?"

"Yes, I have."

"In your opinion, how does this section of the country compare with other places you have seen?"

"Why—why—er—why *good*! . . . I mean, *fine!* That is——"

LOCAL PARADISE COMPARES FAVORABLY

In answer to the reporter's question as to how this part of the country compared to other places he had seen, the former Libya man declared:

"There is no place I have ever visited—and my travels have taken me to England, Germany, Scotland, Ireland, Wales, Norway, Denmark, Sweden, to say nothing of the south of France, the Italian Riviera, and the Swiss Alps—which can compare in beauty with the setting of my native town.

"We have here," he said enthusiastically, "a veritable Paradise of Nature. Air, climate, scenery, water, natural beauty, all conspire to make this section the most ideal place in the whole world to live."

"Did you ever think of coming back here to live?"

"Well—yes—I *have* thought of it—but—you see——"

WILL SETTLE AND BUILD HERE

When questioned as to his future plans, the author said: "For years, my dearest hope and chief ambition has been that one day I should be able to come back here to live. One who has ever known the magic of these hills cannot forget them. I hope, therefore, that the time is not far distant when I may return for good.

"Here, I feel, as nowhere else," the author continued wistfully, "that I will be able to find the inspiration that I must have to do my work. Scenically, climatically, geographically, and in every other way, the logical spot for a modern renaissance is right here among these hills. There is no reason why, in ten years' time, this community should not be a great artistic colony, drawing to it the great artists, the music and the beauty lovers, of the whole world, as Salzburg does now. The Rhododendron Festival is already a step in the right direction.

"It shall be a part of my purpose from now on," the earnest young author added "to do everything in my power to further this great cause, and to urge all my writing and artistic friends to settle here—to make Libya Hill the place it ought to be—The Athens of America."

"Do you intend to write another book?"
"Yes—that is—I hope so. In fact——"
"Would you care to say anything about it?"
"Well—I don't know—it's pretty hard to say——"
"Come on, son, don't be bashful. We're all your home folks here. . . . Now, take Longfellow. *There* was a great writer! You know what a young fellow with your ability ought to do? He ought to come back here and do for this section what Longfellow did for New England. . . ."

PLANS NATIVE SAGA

When pressed for details about the literary work he hopes to do hereafter the author became quite explicit:
"I want to return here," he said, "and commemorate the life, history, and development of Western Catawba in a series of poetic legends comparable to those with which the poet Longfellow commemorated the life of the Acadians and the folklore of the New England countryside. What I have in mind is a trilogy that will begin with the early settlement of the region by the first pioneers, among them my own forebears, and will trace the steady progress of Libya Hill from its founding and the coming of the railroad right down to its present international prominence and the proud place it occupies today as 'The Gem City of the Hills.'"

George writhed and swore when he read the article. There
100

was hardly an accurate statement in it. He felt angry and sheepish and guilty all at the same time.

He sat down and wrote a scathing letter to the paper, but when he had finished he tore it up. After all, what good would it do? The reporter had spun his story out of nothing more substantial than his victim's friendly tones and gestures, a few words and phrases which he had blurted out in his confusion, and, above all, his reticence to talk about his work; yet the fellow had obviously been so steeped in the booster spirit that he had been able to concoct this elaborate fantasy—probably without quite knowing that it was a fantasy.

Then, too, he reflected, people would take an emphatic denial of the statements that had been attributed to him as evidence that he was a sorehead, full of conceit about his book. You couldn't undo the effect of a thing like this with a simple negative. If he gave the lie to all that gush, everybody would say he was attacking the town and turning against those who had nurtured him. Better let bad enough alone.

So he did nothing about it. And after that, strangely enough, it seemed to George that the attitude of people changed toward him. Not that they had been unfriendly before. It was only that he now felt they approved of him. This in itself gave him a quiet sense of accomplishment, as if the stamp of business confirmation had been put upon him.

Like all Americans, George had been amorous of material success, so it made him happy now to know that the people of his home town believed he had got it, or at any rate was at last on the highroad to it. One thing about the whole affair was most fortunate. The publisher who had accepted his book had an old and much respected name; people knew the name, and would meet him on the street and wring his hand and say:

"So your book is going to be published by James Rodney & Co.?"

That simple question, asked with advance knowledge of the fact, had a wonderful sound. It had a ring, not only of congratulation that his book was being published, but also of implication that the distinguished house of Rodney had been fortunate to secure it. That was the way it sounded, and it was probably also the way it was meant. He had the feeling, therefore, that in the eyes of his own people he had "arrived." He was no longer a queer young fellow who had consumed his substance in the deluded hope that he was—oh, loaded word! —"a writer." He *was* a writer. He was not only a writer, but a writer who was about to be published, and by the ancient and honorable James Rodney & Co.

There is something good in the way people welcome success, or anything—no matter what—that is stamped with the markings of success. It is not an ugly thing, really. People love

101

success because to most of them it means happiness, and, whatever form it takes, it is the image of what they, in their hearts, would like to be. This is more true in America than anywhere else. People put this label on the image of their heart's desire because they have never had an image of another kind of happiness. So, essentially, this love of success is not a bad thing, but a good thing. It calls forth a general and noble response, even though the response may also be mixed with self-interest. People are happy for *your* happiness because they want so much to be happy themselves. Therefore it's a good thing. The idea behind it is good, anyhow. The only trouble with it is that the direction is misplaced.

That was the way it seemed to George. He had gone through a long and severe period of probation, and now he was approved. It made him very happy. There is nothing in the world that will take the chip off of one's shoulder like a feeling of success. The chip was off now, and George didn't want to fight anybody. For the first time he felt that it was good to be home again.

Not that he did not have his apprehensions. He knew what he had written about the people and the life of his home town. He knew, too, that he had written about them with a nakedness and directness which, up to that time, had been rare in American fiction. He wondered how they would take it. Even when people congratulated him about the book he could not altogether escape a feeling of uneasiness, for he was afraid of what they would say and think after the book came out and they had read it.

These apprehensions took violent possession of him one night in a most vivid and horrible dream. He thought he was running and stumbling over the blasted heath of some foreign land, fleeing in terror from he knew not what. All that he knew was that he was filled with a nameless shame. It was wordless, and as shapeless as a smothering fog, yet his whole mind and soul shrank back in an agony of revulsion and self-contempt. So overwhelming was his sense of loathing and guilt that he coveted the place of murderers on whom the world had visited the fierceness of its wrath. He envied the whole list of those criminals who had reaped the sentence of mankind's dishonor—the thief, the liar, the trickster, the outlaw, and the traitor—men whose names were anathema and were spoken with a curse, but which *were* spoken; for *he* had committed a crime for which there was no name, *he* was putrescent with a taint for which there was neither comprehension nor cure, *he* was rotten with a vileness of corruption that placed him equally beyond salvation or vengeance, remote alike from pity, love, and hatred, and unworthy of a curse. Thus he fled across the immeasurable and barren heath beneath a burning sky, an exile

102

in the center of a planetary vacancy which, like his own shameful self, had no place either among things living or among things dead, and in which there was neither vengeance of lightning nor mercy of burial; for in all that limitless horizon there was no shade or shelter, no curve or bend, no hill or tree or hollow: there was only one vast, naked eye—searing and inscrutable—from which there was no escape, and which bathed his defenseless soul in its fathomless depths of shame.

And then, with bright and sharp intensity, the dream changed, and suddenly he found himself among the scenes and faces he had known long ago. He was a traveler who had returned after many years of wandering to the place he had known in his childhood. The sense of his dreadful but nameless corruption still hung ominously above him as he entered the streets of the town again, and he knew that he had returned to the springs of innocence and health from whence he came, and by which he would be saved.

But as he came into the town he became aware that the knowledge of his guilt was everywhere about him. He saw the men and women he had known in childhood, the boys with whom he had gone to school, the girls he had taken to dances. They were engaged in all their varied activities of life and business, and they showed their friendship toward one another, but when he approached and offered his hand in greeting they looked at him with blank stares, and in their gaze there was no love, hatred, pity, loathing, or any feeling whatsoever. Their faces, which had been full of friendliness and affection when they spoke to one another, went dead; they gave no sign of recognition or of greeting; they answered him briefly in toneless voices, giving him what information he asked, and repulsed every effort he made toward a resumption of old friendship with the annihilation of silence and that blank and level stare. They did not laugh or mock or nudge or whisper when he passed; they only waited and were still, as if they wanted but one thing—that he should depart out of their sight.

He walked on through the old familiar streets, past houses and places that lived again for him as if he had never left them, and by people who grew still and waited until he had gone, and the knowledge of wordless guilt was rooted in his soul. He knew that he was obliterated from their lives more completely than if he had died, and he felt that he was now lost to all men.

Presently he had left the town, and was again upon the blasted heath, and he was fleeing across it beneath the pitiless sky where flamed the naked eye that pierced him with its unutterable weight of shame.

Chapter Eight

The Company

George considered himself lucky to have the little room over the Shepperton garage. He was also glad that his visit had overlapped that of Mr. David Merrit, and that Mr. Merrit had been allowed to enjoy undisturbed the greater comfort of the Shepperton guest room, for Mr. Merrit had filled him with a pleasant glow at their first meeting. He was a ruddy, plump, well-kept man of forty-five or so, always ready with a joke and immensely agreeable, with pockets bulging with savory cigars which he handed out to people on the slightest provocation. Randy had spoken of him as "the Company's man," and, although George did not know what the duties of a "Company's man" were, Mr. Merrit made them seem very pleasant.

George knew, of course, that Mr. Merrit was Randy's boss, and he learned that Mr. Merrit was in the habit of coming to town every two or three months. He would arrive like a benevolent, pink-cheeked Santa Claus, making his jolly little jokes, passing out his fat cigars, putting his arm around people's shoulders, and, in general, making everyone feel good. As he said himself:

"I've got to turn up now and then just to see that the boys are behaving themselves, and not taking in any wooden nickels."

Here he winked at George in such a comical way that all of them had to grin. Then he gave George a big cigar.

His functions seemed to be ambassadorial. He was always taking Randy and the salesmen of the Company out to lunch or dinner, and, save for brief visits to the office, he seemed to spend most of his time inaugurating an era of good feeling and high living. He would go around town and meet everybody, slapping people on the back and calling them by their first names, and for a week after he had left the business men of Libya Hill would still be smoking his cigars. When he came to town he always stayed "out at the house," and one knew that Margaret would prepare her best meals for him, and that there would be some good drinks. Mr. Merrit supplied the drinks himself, for he always brought along a plentiful store of expensive beverages.

George could see at their first meeting that he was the kind of man who exudes an aura of good fellowship, and that was why it was so pleasant to have Mr. Merrit staying in the house.

Mr. Merrit was not only a nice fellow. He was also "with the Company," and George soon realized that "the Company" was a vital and mysterious force in all their lives. Randy had gone with it as soon as he left college. He had been sent to the main office, up North somewhere, and had been put through a course of training. Then he had come back South and had worked his way up from salesman to district agent—an important member of the sales organization.

"The Company," "district agent," "the sales organization" —mysterious titles all of them, but most comforting. During the week George was in Libya Hill with Randy and Margaret, Mr. Merrit was usually on hand at meal times, and at night he would sit out on the front porch with them and carry on in his jolly way, joking and laughing and giving them all a good time. Sometimes he would talk shop with Randy, telling stories about the Company and about his own experiences in the organization, and before long George began to pick up a pretty good idea of what it was all about.

The Federal Weight, Scales, and Computing Company was a far-flung empire which had a superficial aspect of great complexity, but in its essence it was really beautifully simple. Its heart and soul—indeed, its very life—was its sales organization.

The entire country was divided into districts, and over each district an agent was appointed. This agent, in turn, employed salesmen to cover the various portions of his district. Each district also had an "office man" to attend to any business that might come up while the agent and his salesmen were away, and a "repair man" whose duty it was to overhaul damaged or broken-down machines. Together, these comprised the agency, and the country was so divided that there was, on the average, an agency for every unit of half a million people in the total population. Thus there were two hundred and sixty or seventy agencies through the nation, and the agents with their salesmen made up a working force of from twelve to fifteen hundred men.

The higher purposes of this industrial empire, which the employees almost never referred to by name, as who should speak of the deity with coarse directness, but always with a just perceptible lowering and huskiness of the voice as "the Company"—these higher purposes were also beautifully simple. They were summed up in the famous utterance of the Great Man himself, Mr. Paul S. Appleton, III, who invariably repeated it every year as a peroration to his hour-long address before the assembled members of the sales organization at their national convention. Standing before them at the close of each year's session, he would sweep his arm in a gesture of magnificent command toward an enormous map of the United States of America that covered the whole wall behind him, and say:

"There's your market! Go out and sell them!"

What could be simpler and more beautiful than this? What could more eloquently indicate that mighty sweep of the imagination which has been celebrated in the annals of modern business under the name of "vision"? The words had the spacious scope and austere directness that have characterized the utterances of great leaders in every epoch of man's history. It is Napoleon speaking to his troops in Egypt: "Soldiers, from the summit of yonder pyramids, forty centuries look down upon you." It is Captain Perry: "We have met the enemy, and they are ours." It is Dewey at Manila Bay: "You may fire when ready, Gridley." It is Grant before Spottsylvania Court House: "I propose to fight it out on this line, if it takes all summer."

So when Mr. Paul S. Appleton, III, waved his arm at the wall and said: "There's your market! Go out and sell them!"—the assembled captains, lieutenants, and privates in the ranks of his sales organization knew that there were still giants in the earth, and that the age of romance was not dead.

True, there had once been a time when the aspirations of the Company had been more limited. That was when the founder of the institution, the grandfather of Mr. Paul S. Appleton, III, had expressed his modest hopes by saying: "I should like to see one of my machines in every store, shop, or business that needs one, and that can afford to pay for one." But the self-denying restrictions implicit in the founder's statement had long since become so out of date as to seem utterly mid-Victorian. Mr. David Merrit admitted it himself. Much as he hated to speak ill of any man, and especially the founder of the Company, he had to confess that by the standards of 1929 the old gentleman had lacked vision.

"That's old stuff now," said Mr. Merrit, shaking his head and winking at George, as though to take the curse off of his treason to the founder by making a joke of it. "We've gone way beyond that!" he exclaimed with pardonable pride. "Why, if we waited nowadays to sell a machine to someone who *needs* one, we'd get nowhere." He was nodding now at Randy, and speaking with the seriousness of deep conviction. "We don't wait until he *needs* one. If he says he's getting along all right without one, we make him buy one anyhow. We make him *see* the need, don't we, Randy? In other words, we *create* the need."

This, as Mr. Merrit went on to explain, was what is known in more technical phrase as "creative salesmanship" or "creating the market." And this poetic conception was the inspired work of one man—none other than the present head of the Company, Mr. Paul S. Appleton, III, himself. The idea had come to him in a single blinding flash, born full-blown like Pallas Athene from the head of Zeus, and Mr. Merrit still remembered the momentous occasion as vividly as if it had been only yesterday. It was at one of the meetings of the assembled parliaments of the Company that Mr. Appleton, soaring in an impassioned flight of oratory, became so intoxicated with the grandeur of his own vision that he stopped abruptly in the middle of a sentence and stood there as one entranced, gazing out dreamily into the unknown vistas of magic Canaan; and when he at last went on again, it was in a voice surcharged with quivering emotion:

"My friends," he said, "the possibilities of the market, now that we see how to create it, are practically unlimited!" Here he was silent for a moment, and Mr. Merrit said that the Great Man actually paled and seemed to stagger as he tried to speak, and that his voice faltered and sank to an almost inaudible whisper, as if he himself could hardly comprehend the magnitude of his own conception. "My friends—" he muttered thickly, and was seen to clutch the rostrum for support—"my friends—seen properly—" he whispered, and moistened his dry lips—"seen properly—the market we shall create being what it is—" his voice grew stronger, and the clarion words now rang forth—"there is no reason why one of our machines should not be in the possession of every man, woman, and child in the United States!" Then came the grand, familiar gesture to the map: "There's your market, boys! Go out and sell them!"

Henceforth this vision became the stone on which Mr. Paul S. Appleton, III, erected the magnificent edifice of the true church and living faith which was called "the Company." And in the service of this vision Mr. Appleton built up an organization which worked with the beautiful precision of a locomotive piston. Over the salesman was the agent, and over the agent was the district supervisor, and over the district supervisor was the district manager, and over the district manager was the general manager, and over the general manager was—if not God himself, then the next thing to it, for the agents and salesmen referred to him in tones of proper reverence as "P. S. A."

Mr. Appleton also invented a special Company Heaven known as the Hundred Club. Its membership was headed by P. S. A., and all the ranks of the sales organization were eligible, down to the humblest salesman. The Hundred Club was a social order, but it was also a good deal more than that. Each agent and salesman had a "quota"—that is to say, a certain amount of business which was assigned to him as the normal average of his district and capacity. A man's quota differed from another's according to the size of his territory, its wealth, and his own experience and ability. One man's quota would be sixty, another's eighty, another's ninety or one hundred, and if he was a district agent, his quota would be higher than that of a mere salesman. Each man, however, no matter how small or how large his quota might be, was eligible for membership in the Hundred Club, the only restriction being that he must average one hundred per cent of his quota. If he averaged more—if he got, say, one hundred and twenty per cent of his quota—there were appropriate honors and rewards, not only social but financial as well. One could be either high up or low down in the Hundred Club, for it had almost as many degrees of merit as the Masonic order.

The unit of the quota system was "the point," and a point was forty dollars' worth of business. So if a salesman had a quota of eighty, this meant that he had to sell the products of the Federal Weight, Scales, and Computing Company to the amount of at least $3200 every month, or almost $40,000 a year. The rewards were high. A salesman's commission was from fifteen to twenty per cent of his sales; an agent's, from twenty to twenty-five per cent. Beyond this there were bonuses to be earned by achieving or surpassing his quota. Thus it was possible for an ordinary salesman in an average district to earn from $6000 to $8000 a year, while an agent could earn from $12,000 to $15,000, and even more if his district was an exceptionally good one.

So much for the rewards of Mr. Appleton's Heaven. But what would Heaven be if there were no Hell? So Mr. Appleton was forced by the logic of the situation to invent a Hell, too. Once a man's quota was fixed at any given point, the Company never reduced it. Moreover, if a salesman's quota was eighty points and he achieved it during the year, he must be prepared at the beginning of the new year to find that his quota had been increased to ninety points. One had to go onward and upward constantly, and the race was to the swift.

While it was quite true that membership in the Hundred Club was not compulsory, it was also true that Mr. Paul S. Appleton, III, was a theologian who, like Calvin, knew how to combine free will and predestination. If one did *not* belong to the Hundred Club, the time was not far distant when one would not belong to Mr. Appleton. Not to belong to it was, for agent or salesman, the equivalent of living on the other side of the railroad tracks. If one failed of admission to the Company Heaven, or if one dropped out, his fellows would begin to ask guardedly: "Where's Joe Klutz these days?" The answers would be vague, and in the course of time Joe Klutz would be spoken of no more. He would fade into oblivion. He was "no longer with the Company."

Mr. Paul S. Appleton, III, never had but the one revelation—the one which Mr. Merrit so movingly described —but that was enough, and he never let its glories and allurements grow dim. Four times a year, at the beginning of each quarter, he would call his general manager before him and say: "What's the matter, Elmer? You're not getting the business! The market is *there*! You know what you can do about it—or else . . . !" Thereupon the general manager would summon the district managers one by one and repeat to them the words and manner of P. S. A., and the district managers would reenact the scene before each of the district supervisors, who would duplicate it to the agents, who would pass it on to the salesmen, who, since they had no one below them, would "get out and hustle—or else!" This was called "keeping up the morale of the organization."

As Mr. David Merrit sat on the front porch and told of his many experiences with the Company, his words conveyed to George Webber a great deal more than he actually said. For his talk went on and on in its vein of mellow reminiscence, and Mr. Merrit made his little jokes and puffed contentedly at one of his own good cigars, and everything he said carried an overtone of "What a fine and wonderful thing it is to be connected with the Company!"

He told, for example, about the splendid occasion every year when all the members of the Hundred Club were brought together for what was known as "The Week of Play." This was a magnificent annual outing conducted "at the Company's expense." The meeting place might be in Philadelphia or Washington, or in the tropic opulence of Los Angeles or Miami, or it might be on board a chartered ship—one of the small but luxurious twenty-thousand-tonners that ply the transatlantic routes—bound to Bermuda or Havana. Wherever it was, the Hundred Club was given a free sweep. If the journey was by sea, the ship was theirs—for a week. All the liquor in the world was theirs, if they could drink it—and Bermuda's coral isles, or the unlicensed privilege of gay Havana. For that one week everything on earth that money could buy was at the command of the members of the Hundred Club, everything was done on the grand scale, and the Company—the immortal, paternal, and great-hearted Company—"paid for everything."

But as Mr. Merrit painted his glowing picture of the fun they had on these occasions, George Webber saw quite another image. It was an image of twelve or fifteen hundred men—for on these pilgrimages, by general consent, women (or, at any rate, wives) were debarred—twelve or fifteen hundred men,

109

Americans, most of them in their middle years, exhausted, overwrought, their nerves frayed down and stretched to the breaking point, met from all quarters of the continent "at the Company's expense" for one brief, wild, gaudy week of riot. And George thought grimly what this tragic spectacle of business men at play meant in terms of the entire scheme of things and the plan of life that had produced it. He began to understand, too, the changes which time had brought about in Randy.

The last day of his week in Libya Hill, George had gone to the station to buy his return ticket and he stopped in at Randy's office a little before one o'clock to go home to lunch with him. The outer salesroom, with its shining stock of scales and computing machines imposingly arrayed on walnut pedestals, was deserted, so he sat down to wait. On one wall hung a gigantic colored poster. "August Was the Best Month in Federal History," it read. "*Make September a Better One!* The Market's There, Mr. Agent. The Rest Is Up to You!"

Behind the salesroom was a little partitioned space which served Randy as an office. As George waited, gradually he became aware of mysterious sounds emanating from beyond the partition. First there was the rustle of heavy paper, as if the pages of a ledger were being turned, and occasionally there would be a quick murmur of hushed voices, confidential, ominous, interspersed with grunts and half-suppressed exclamations. Then all at once there were two loud bangs, as of a large ledger being slammed shut and thrown upon a desk or table, and after a moment's silence the voices rose louder, distinct, plainly audible. Instantly he recognized Randy's voice—low, grave, hesitant, and deeply troubled. The other voice he had never heard before.

But as he listened to that voice he began to tremble and grow white about the lips. For its very tone was a foul insult to human life, an ugly sneer whipped across the face of decent humanity, and as he realized that that voice, these words, were being used against his friend, he had a sudden blind feeling of murder in his heart. And what was so perplexing and so troubling was that this devil's voice had in it as well a curiously familiar note, as of someone he had known.

Then it came to him in a flash—it was Merrit speaking! The owner of that voice, incredible as it seemed, was none other than that plump, well-kept, jolly-looking man who had always been so full of hearty cheerfulness and good spirits every time he had seen him.

Now, behind that little partition of glazed glass and varnished wood, this man's voice had suddenly become fiendish. It was inconceivable, and as George listened he grew sick, as one does in some awful nightmare when he visions someone he knows doing some perverse and abominable act. But what was most dreadful of all was Randy's voice, humble, low, submissive, modestly entreating. Merrit's voice would cut across the air like a gob of rasping phlegm, and then Randy's voice—gentle, hesitant, deeply troubled—would come in from time to time in answer.

"Well, what's the matter? Don't you want the job?"

"Why—why, yes, you know I do, Dave—haw-w—" and Randy's voice lifted a little in a troubled and protesting laugh.

"What's the matter that you're not getting the business?"

"Why—haw-w!—" again the little laugh, embarrassed and troubled—"I *thought* I was——"

"Well, you're not!" that rasping voice cut in like a knife. "This district ought to deliver thirty per cent more business than you're getting from it, and the Company is going to have it, too—or else! You deliver or you go right out on your can! See? The Company doesn't give a damn about you! It's after the business! You've been around a long time, but you don't mean a damn bit more to the Company than anybody else! And you know what's happened to a lot of other guys who got to feeling they were too big for their job—don't you?"

"Why—why, yes, Dave—but—haw-w!" the little laugh again—"but—honestly, I never thought——"

"We don't give a damn what you never thought!" the brutal voice ripped in. "I've given you fair warning now! You get the business or out you go!"

The glazed glass door burst open violently and Merrit came striding out of the little partitioned office. When he saw George, he looked startled. Then he was instantly transformed. His plump and ruddy face became wreathed in smiles, and he cried out in a hearty tone:

"Well, well, well! Look who's here! If it's not the old boy himself!"

Randy had followed him out, and Merrit now turned and winked humorously at him, in the manner of a man who is carrying on a little bantering byplay:

"Randy," he said, "I believe George gets better looking from day to day. Has he broken any hearts yet?"

Randy tried to smile, grey-faced and haggardly.

"I bet you're burning them up in the Big Town," said Merrit, turning back to George. "And, say, I read that piece in the paper about your book. Great Stuff, son! We're all proud of you!"

He gave George a hearty slap on the back and turned away

with an air of jaunty readiness, picked up his hat, and said cheerfully:

"Well, what d'ya say, folks? What about one of Margaret's famous meals, out at the old homestead? Well, you can't hurt my feelings. I'm ready if you are. Let's go!"

And, smiling, ruddy, plump, cheerful, a perverted picture of amiable good will to all the world, he sauntered through the door. For a moment the two old friends just stood there looking at each other, white and haggard, with a bewildered expression in their eyes. In Randy's eyes there was also a look of shame. With that instinct for loyalty which was one of the roots of his soul, he said:

"Dave's a good fellow. . . . You—you see, he's got to do these things. . . . He—he's with the Company."

George didn't say anything. For as Randy spoke, and George remembered all that Merrit had told him about the Company, a terrific picture flashed through his mind. It was a picture he had seen in a gallery somewhere, portraying a long line of men stretching from the Great Pyramid to the very portals of great Pharoah's house, and great Pharoah stood with a thonged whip in his hand and applied it unmercifully to the bare back and shoulders of the man in front of him, who was great Pharoah's chief overseer, and in the hand of the overseer was a whip of many tails which he unstintedly applied to the quivering back of the wretch before him, who was the chief overseer's chief lieutenant, and in the lieutenant's hand a whip of rawhide which he laid vigorously on the quailing body of his head sergeant, and in the sergeant's hand a wicked flail with which he belabored a whole company of groaning corporals, and in the hands of every corporal a knotted lash with which to whack a whole regiment of slaves, who pulled and hauled and bore burdens and toiled and sweated and built the towering structure of the pyramid.

So George didn't say anything. He couldn't. He had just found out something about life that he had not known before.

Chapter Nine

The City of Lost Men

Late that afternoon George asked Margaret to go with him to the cemetery, so she borrowed Randy's car and drove him out. On the way they stopped at a florist's and bought some chrysanthemums, which George placed on Aunt Maw's grave. There had been a heavy rain during the week and the new-made mound had sunk an inch or two, leaving a jagged crack around its edges.

As he laid the flowers on the damp, raw earth, suddenly it struck him as strange that he should be doing it. He was not a sentimental person, and for a moment it puzzled him that he should be making this gesture. He hadn't planned to do it. He had simply seen the florist's window as they drove along and, without thinking, had stopped and got the flowers, and now there they were.

Then he realized why he had done it—and why he had wanted to come back to the cemetery at all. This visit to Libya Hill, which he had dreamed about so many times as his homecoming, and which had not turned out in any way as he had thought it would be, was really his leave-taking, his farewell. The last tie that had bound him to his native earth was severed, and he was going out from here to make a life for himself as each man must—alone.

And now, once again, the dusk was falling in this place, and in the valley below the lights were beginning to come on in the town. With Margaret at his side, he stood there and looked down upon it, and she seemed to understand his feelings, for she was quiet and said nothing. Then, in a low voice, George began to speak to her. He needed to tell someone all that he had thought and felt during his week at home. Randy was not available, and Margaret was the only one left to whom he could talk. She listened without interruption as he spoke about his book and his hopes for it, telling her as well as he could what kind of book it was, and how much he feared that the town would not like it. She pressed his arm reassuringly, and the gesture was more eloquent than any words could be.

113

He did not say anything about Randy and Merrit. There was no need to alarm her unduly, no sense in robbing her of that security which is so fundamental to a woman's peace and happiness. Sufficient unto the day . . .

But he spoke at length about the town itself, telling her all that he had seen of its speculative madness, and how it had impressed him. What did the future hold for that place and its people? They were always talking of the better life that lay ahead of them and of the greater city they would build, but to George it seemed that in all such talk there was evidence of a strange and savage hunger that drove them on, and that there was a desperate quality in it, as though what they really hungered for was ruin and death. It seemed to him that they *were* ruined, and that even when they laughed and shouted and smote each other on the back, the knowledge of their ruin was in them.

They had squandered fabulous sums in meaningless streets and bridges. They had torn down ancient buildings and erected new ones large enough to take care of a city of half a million people. They had leveled hills and bored through mountains, making magnificent tunnels paved with double roadways and glittering with shining tiles—tunnels which leaped out on the other side into Arcadian wilderness. They had flung away the earnings of a lifetime, and mortgaged those of a generation to come. They had ruined their city, and in doing so had ruined themselves, their children, and their children's children.

Already the town had passed from their possession. They no longer owned it. It was mortgaged under a debt of fifty million dollars, owned by bonding companies in the North. The very streets they walked on had been sold beneath their feet. They signed their names to papers calling for the payment of fabulous sums, and resold their land the next day to other madmen who signed away their lives with the same careless magnificence. On paper, their profits were enormous, but their "boom" was already over and they would not see it. They were staggering beneath obligations to pay which none of them could meet—and still they bought.

And when they had exhausted all the possibilities of ruin and extravagance that the town could offer, they had rushed out into the wilderness, into the lyrical immensities of wild earth where there was land enough for all men living, and they had staked off little plots and wedges in the hills as one might try to stake a picket fence out in the middle of the ocean. They had given fancy names to all these foolish enterprises—"Wild Boulders" —"Shady Acres"—"Eagle's Crest." They had set prices on these sites of forest, field, and tangled undergrowth that might have bought a mountain, and made charts and drawings showing populous communities of shops, houses, streets, roads,

114

and clubs in regions where there was no road, no street, no house, and which could not be reached in any way save by a band of resolute pioneers armed with axes. These places were to be transformed into idyllic colonies for artists and writers and critics; and there were colonies as well for preachers, doctors, actors, dancers, golf players, and retired locomotive engineers. There were colonies for everyone, and, what is more, they sold the lots—to one another!

But under all this flash and play of great endeavor, the paucity of their designs and the starved meagerness of their lives were already apparent. The better life which they talked about resolved itself into a few sterile and baffled gestures. All they really did for themselves was to build uglier and more expensive homes, and buy new cars, and join a country club. And they did all this with a frenzied haste, because—it seemed to George —they were looking for food to feed their hunger and had not found it.

As he stood upon the hill and looked out on the scene that spread below him in the gathering darkness, with its pattern of lights to mark the streets and the creeping pin-pricks of the thronging traffic, he remembered the barren nighttime streets of the town he had known so well in his boyhood. Their dreary and unpeopled desolation had burned its acid print upon his memory. Bare and deserted by ten o'clock at night, those streets had been an aching monotony, a weariness of hard lights and empty pavements, a frozen torpor broken only occasionally by the footfalls of some prowler—some desperate, famished, lonely man who hoped past hope and past belief for some haven of comfort, warmth, and love there in the wilderness, for the sudden opening of a magic door into some secret, rich, and more abundant life. There had been many such, but they had never found what they were searching for. They had been dying in the darkness—without a goal, a certain purpose, or a door.

And that, it seemed to George, was the way the thing had come. That was the way it had happened. Yes, it was there—on many a night long past and wearily accomplished, in ten thousand little towns and in ten million barren streets where all the passion, hope, and hunger of the famished men beat like a great pulse through the fields of darkness—it was there and nowhere else that all this madness had been brewed.

As he remembered the bleak, deserted streets of night which he had known here fifteen years before, he thought again of Judge Rumford Bland, whose solitary figure ranging restlessly through the sleeping town had been so familiar to him and had struck such terror in his heart. Perhaps he was the key to this whole tragedy. Perhaps Rumford Bland had sought his life in darkness not because of something evil in him—though certainly there was evil there—but because of something good that had not died. Something in the man had always fought against the dullness of provincial life, against its prejudice, its caution, its smugness, its sterility, and its lack of joy. He had looked for something better in the night, for a place of warmth and fellowship, a moment of dark mystery, the thrill of imminent and unknown adventure, the excitement of the hunt, pursuit, perhaps the capture, and then the fulfillment of desire. Was it possible that in the blind man whose whole life had become such a miracle of open shamelessness, there had once been a warmth and an energy that had sought for an enhancement of the town's cold values, and for a joy and a beauty that were not there, but that lived in himself alone? Could that be what had wrecked him? Was he one of the lost men—lost, really, only because the town itself was lost, because his gifts had been rejected, his energies unused, the shoulder of his strength finding no work to bend to—because what he had had to give of hope, intelligence, curiosity, and warmth had found no place there, and so were lost?

Yes, the same thing that explained the plight the town had come to might also explain Judge Rumford Bland. What was it he had said on the train: "Do you think you can go home again?" And: "Don't forget I tried to warn you." Was this, then, what he had meant? If so, George understood him now.

Around them in the cemetery as George thought these things and spoke of them, the air brooded with a lazy, drowsy warmth. There was the last evening cry of robins, and the thrumming bullet noises in undergrowth and leaf, and broken sounds from far away—a voice in the wind, a boy's shout, the barking of a dog, the tinkle of a cow bell. There was the fragrance of intoxicating odors—the resinous smell of pine, and the smells of grass and warm sweet clover. All this was just as it had always been. But the town of his childhood, with its quiet streets and the old houses which had been almost obscured below the leafy spread of trees, was changed past recognition, scarred now with hard patches of bright concrete and raw clumps of new construction. It looked like a battlefield, cratered and shell-torn with savage explosions of brick, cement, and harsh new stucco. And in the interspaces only the embowered remnants of the old and pleasant town remained—timid, retreating, overwhelmed —to remind one of the liquid leather shuffle in the quiet streets at noon when the men came home to lunch, and of laughter and low voices in the leafy rustle of the night. For this was lost!

An old and tragic light was shining faintly on the time-enchanted hills. George thought of Mrs. Delia Flood, and what she had said of Aunt Maw's hope that some day he'd come home again to stay. And as he stood there with Margaret quietly by his side the old and tragic light of fading day shone faintly on their faces, and all at once it seemed to him that they were fixed there like a prophecy with the hills and river all around them, and that there was something lost, intolerable, foretold and come to pass, something like old time and destiny—some magic that he could not say.

Down by the river's edge, in darkness now, he heard the bell, the whistle, and the pounding wheel of the night express coming into town, there to pause for half an hour and then resume its northward journey. It swept away from them, leaving the lonely thunder of its echoes in the hills and the flame-flare of its open firebox for a moment, and then just heavy wheels and rumbling cars as the great train pounded on the rails across the river—and, finally, nothing but the silence it had left behind. Then, farther off and almost lost in the traffic of the town, he heard again and for the last time its wailing cry, and it brought to him once more, as it had done forever in his childhood, its wild and secret exultation, its pain of going, and its triumphant promise of morning, new lands, and a shining city. And something in his heart was saying, like a demon's whisper that spoke of flight and darkness: "Soon! Soon! Soon!"

Then they got in the car and drove rapidly away from the great hill of the dead, the woman toward the certitude of lights, the people, and the town; the man toward the train, the city, and the unknown future.

BOOK II

The World that Jack Built

Back in New York the autumn term at the School for Utility Cultures had begun, and George Webber took up again the old routine of academic chores. He hated teaching worse than ever, and found that even in his classes he was thinking about his new book and looking forward eagerly to his free hours when he could work upon it. It was hardly more than just begun, but for some reason the writing was going well, and George knew from past experience that he'd better take advantage of every moment while the frenzy of creation was upon him. He felt, too, almost desperately, that he ought to get as much of the new book written as he could before the first was published. That event, at once so desired and dreaded, now loomed before him imminently. He hoped the critics would be kind, or at least would treat his novel with respect. Fox Edwards said it ought to have a good critical reception, but that you couldn't tell anything about sales: better not think too much about it.

George was seeing Esther Jack every day, just as always, but in his excitement over the approaching publication of Home to Our Mountains and his feverish absorption in the new writing he was doing, she no longer occupied the forefront of his thoughts and feelings. She was aware of this and resented it, as women always do. Perhaps that's why she invited him to the party, believing that in such a setting she would seem more desirable to him and that thus she could recapture the major share of his attention. At any rate, she did invite him. It was to be an elaborate affair. Her family and all her richest and most brilliant friends were to be there, and she begged him to come.

He refused. He told her he had his work to do. He said he had his world and she had hers, and the two could never be the same. He reminded her of their compromise. He repeated that he did not want to belong to her world, that he had seen enough of it already, and that if she insisted on trying to absorb him in her life she was going to destroy the foundation on which their whole relationship had rested since he had come back to her.

But she kept after him and brushed his arguments aside. "Sometimes you sound just like a fool, George!" she said impatiently. "Once you get an idea in your head, you cling to it in the face of reason itself. Really, you ought to go out more. You spend too much time cooped up here in your rooms," she said. "It's unhealthy! And how can you expect to be a writer if you don't take part in the life around you? I know what I'm talking about," she said, her face flushed with eager seriousness. "And, besides, what has all this nonsense about your *world and* my *world got to do with us? Words, words, words! Stop being silly, and listen to me. I don't ask much of you. Do as I say this once, just to please me."*

In the end she beat him down and he yielded. "All right," he muttered at last, defeated, without enthusiasm. "I'll go."

So September slid into October, and now the day of the great party had dawned. Later, as George looked back upon it, the date took on an ominous significance, for the brilliant party was staged exactly a week before the thunderous crash in the Stock Market which marked the end of an era.

Chapter Ten

Jack at Morn

At seven twenty-eight Mr. Frederick Jack awoke and began to come alive with all his might. He sat up and yawned strongly, stretching his arms and at the same time bending his slumber-swollen face into the plump muscle-hammock of his right shoulder, a movement coy and cuddlesome. "Eee-a-a-a-ach!" He stretched deliciously out of thick, rubbery sleep, and for a moment he sat heavily upright rubbing at his eyes with the clenched backs of his fingers. Then he flung off the covers with one determined motion and swung to the floor. His toes groped blindly in soft grey carpet stuff, smooth as felt, for his heelless slippers of red Russian leather. These found and slipped into, he padded noiselessly across the carpet to the window and stood, yawning and stretching again, as he looked out with sleepy satisfaction at a fine, crisp morning. Instantly he knew that it was October 17th, 1929, and the day of the party. Mr. Jack liked parties.

Nine floors below him the cross street lay gulched in steep morning shadow, bluish, barren, cleanly ready for the day. A truck roared past with a solid rattling heaviness. An ash can was banged on the pavement with an abrupt slamming racket. Upon the sidewalk a little figure of a man, foreshortened from above and covered by its drab cone of grey, bobbed swiftly along, turned the corner into Park Avenue, and was gone, heading southward toward work.

Below Mr. Frederick Jack the cross street was a narrow bluish lane between sheer cliffs of solid masonry, but to the west the morning sunlight, golden, young, immensely strong and delicate, cut with sculptured sharpness at the walls of towering buildings. It shone with an unearthly rose-golden glow upon the upper tiers and summits of soaring structures whose lower depths were still sunk in shadow. It rested without violence or heat upon retreating pyramids of steel and stone, fumed at their peaks with fading wisps of smoke. It was reflected with dazzling brilliance from the panes of innumerable lofty windows, and it made the wall surfaces of harsh white-yellow brick look soft and warm, the color of rose petals.

Among the man-made peaks that stood silhouetted against the sky in this early sun were great hotels and clubs and office buildings bare of life. Mr. Jack could look straight into high office suites ready for their work: the morning light shaped patterns out of pale-hued desks and swivel chairs of maple, and it burnished flimsy partition woods and thick glazed doors. The offices stood silent, empty, sterile, but they also seemed to have a kind of lonely expectation of the life that soon would well up swiftly from the streets to fill and use them. In that eerie light, with the cross street still bare of traffic and the office buildings empty, suddenly it seemed to Mr. Jack as if all life had been driven or extinguished from the city and as if those soaring obelisks were all that remained of a civilization that had been fabulous and legendary.

With a shrug of impatience he shook off the moment's aberration and peered down into the street again. It was empty as before, but already along Park Avenue the bright-hued cabs were drilling past the intersection like beetles in flight, most of them headed downtown in the direction of Grand Central Station. And everywhere, through that shining, living light, he could sense the slow-mounting roar of another furious day beginning. He stood there by his window, a man-mite poised high in the air upon a shelf of masonry, the miracle of God, a plump atom of triumphant man's flesh, founded upon a rock of luxury at the center of the earth's densest web—but it was as the Prince of Atoms that he stood there and surveyed the scene, for he had bought the privileges of space, silence, light, and steel-walled security out of chaos with the ransom of an emperor, and he exulted in the price he paid for them. This grain of living dust had seen the countless insane accidents of shape and movement that daily passed the little window of his eye, but he felt no doubt or fear. He was not appalled.

Another man, looking out upon the city in its early-morning nakedness, might have thought its forms inhuman, monstrous, and Assyrian in their insolence. But not Mr. Frederick Jack. Indeed, if all those towers had been the monuments of his own special triumph, his pride and confidence and sense of ownership could hardly have been greater than they were. "My city," he thought. "Mine." It filled his heart with certitude and joy because he had learned, like many other men, to see, to marvel, to accept, and not to ask disturbing questions. In that arrogant boast of steel and stone he saw a permanence surviving every danger, an answer, crushing and conclusive, to every doubt.

He liked what was solid, rich, and spacious, made to last. He liked the feeling of security and power that great buildings gave him. He liked especially the thick walls and floors of this apartment house. The boards neither creaked nor sagged when he walked across them; they were as solid as if they had been

122

hewn in one single block from the heart of a gigantic oak. All this, he felt, was as it should be.

He was a man who liked order in everything. The rising tide of traffic which now began to stream below him in the streets was therefore pleasing to him. Even in the thrust and jostle of the crowd his soul rejoiced, for he saw order everywhere. It was order that made the millions swarm at morning to their work in little cells, and swarm again at evening from their work to other little cells. It was an order as inevitable as the seasons, and in it Mr. Jack read the same harmony and permanence which he saw in the entire visible universe around him.

Mr. Jack turned and glanced about his room. It was a spacious chamber, twenty feet each way and twelve feet high, and in these noble proportions was written quietly a message of luxurious well-being and assurance. In the exact center of the wall that faced the door stood his bed, a chaste four-poster of the Revolutionary period, and beside it a little table holding a small clock, a few books, and a lamp. In the center of another wall was an antique chest of drawers, and tastefully arranged about the room were a gate-legged table, with a row of books and the latest magazines upon it, two fine old Windsor chairs, and a comfortable, well-padded easy chair. Several charming French prints hung on the walls. On the floor was a thick and heavy carpet of dull grey. These were all the furnishings. The total effect was one of modest and almost austere simplicity, subtly combined with a sense of spaciousness, wealth, and power.

The owner of this room read its message with pleasure, and turned once more to the open window. With fingers pressed against his swelling breast, he breathed in a deep draft of the fresh, living air of morning. It was laden with the thrilling compost of the city, a fragrance delicately blended of many things. There was, strangely, the smell of earth, moist and somehow flowerful, tinged faintly with the salt reek of tidal waters and the fresh river smell, rank and a little rotten, and spiced among these odors was the sultry aroma of strong boiling coffee. This incense-laden air carried a tonic threat of conflict and of danger, and a leaping, winelike prophecy of power, wealth, and love. Mr. Jack breathed in this vital ether slowly, with heady joy, sensing again the unknown menace and delight it always brought to him.

All at once a trembling, faint and instant, passed in the earth below him. He paused, frowning, and an old unquiet feeling to which he could not give a name stirred in his heart. He did not like things to shake and tremble. When he had first come here to live and had awaked at morning thinking he felt a slight vibration in the massive walls around him, a tremor so brief and distant that he could not be certain of it, he had asked a few questions of the doorman who stood at the Park Avenue entrance of the building. The man told him that the great apartment house had been built across two depths of railway tunnels, and that all Mr. Jack had felt was the vibration that came from the passing of a train deep in the bowels of the earth. The man assured him that it was all quite safe, that the very trembling in the walls, in fact, was just another proof of safety.

Still, Mr. Jack did not like it. The news disturbed him vaguely. He would have liked it better if the building had been anchored upon the solid rock. So now, as he felt the slight tremor in the walls once more, he paused, frowned, and waited till it stopped. Then he smiled.

"Great trains pass under me," he thought. "Morning, bright morning, and still they come—all the boys who have dreamed dreams in the little towns. They come forever to the city. Yes, even now they pass below me, wild with joy, mad with hope, drunk with their thoughts of victory. For what? For what? Glory, huge profits, and a girl! All of them come looking for the same magic wand. Power. Power. Power."

Thoroughly awake now, Mr. Jack closed the window and moved briskly across his chamber to the bathroom. He liked lavish plumbing, thick with creamy porcelain and polished silver fixtures. For a moment he stood before the deep wash basin with bared lips, looking at himself in the mirror, and regarding with considerable satisfaction the health and soundness of his strong front teeth. Then he brushed them earnestly with stiff, hard bristles and two inches of firm, thick paste, turning his head from side to side around the brush and glaring at his image in the glass until he foamed agreeably at the mouth with a lather that tasted of fresh mint. This done, he spat it out and let running water wash it down the drain, and then he rinsed his mouth and throat with gently biting antiseptic.

He liked the tidy, crowded array of lotions, creams, unguents, bottles, tubes, jars, brushes, and shaving implements that covered the shelf of thick blue glass above the basin. He lathered his face heavily with a large silver-handled shaving brush, rubbing the lather in with firm finger tips, brushing and stroking till his jaws were covered with a smooth, thick layer of warm shaving cream. Then he took the razor in his hand and opened it. He used a straight razor, and he always kept it in excellent condition. At the crucial moment, just before the first long downward stroke, he flourished slightly forward with his plump arms and shoulders, raising the glittering blade aloft in one firm hand, his legs widened stockily, crouching gently at the knees, his lathered face craned carefully to one side and upward, and his eyes rolled toward the ceiling, as if he were getting braced and ready beneath a heavy burden. Then, holding one cheek delicately between two arched fingers, he advanced deliberately upon it with the gleaming blade. He grunted gently, with satisfaction, at the termination of the stroke. The blade had mown smoothly, leaving a perfect swath of pink, clean flesh across his face from cheek to jowl. He exulted in the slight tug and rasping pull of wiry stubble against the deadly sharpness of the razor, and in the relentless sweep and triumph of the steel.

And while he shaved Mr. Jack occupied his mind with pleasant thoughts of all the good things in his life.

He thought about his clothes. Elegant in dress, always excellently correct, he wore fresh garments every day. No cotton touched him. He bought underclothes of the finest silk, and he had more than forty suits from London. Every morning he examined his wardrobe studiously, choosing with care and with a good eye for harmony the shoes, socks, shirt, and necktie he would wear, and before he selected a suit he was sometimes lost in thought for several minutes. He loved to open wide the door of his great closet and see his suits hanging there in rows in all their groomed and regimented elegance. He liked the strong, clean smell of honest cloth, and in those forty several shapes and colors he saw as many pleasing reflections and variations of his own character. They filled him, as did everything about him, with a sense of morning confidence, joy, and vigor.

For breakfast he would have orange juice, two leghorn eggs, soft boiled, two slices of crisp, thin toast, and tasty little segments of pink Praguer ham, which looked so pretty on fresh parsley sprigs. And he would have coffee, strong coffee, cup after cup of it. So fortified, he would face the world with cheerful strength, ready for whatever chance the day might bring him.

The smell of earth which he had caught in the air this morning was good, and the remembrance of it laid a soothing unction on his soul. Although city-bred, Mr. Jack was as sensitive to the charms of Mother Earth as any man alive. He liked the cultivated forms of nature—the swarded lawns of great estates, gay regiments of brilliant garden flowers, and rich masses of clumped shrubbery. All these things delighted him. The call of the simple life had grown stronger every year, and he had built a big country house in Westchester County.

He liked the more expensive forms of sport. He would frequently go out in the country to play golf, and he loved bright sunlight on the rich velvet of the greens and the new-mown smell of fairways. And afterwards, when he had stood below the bracing drive of the shower and had felt the sweat of competition wash cleanly from his well-set form, he liked to loaf upon the cool verandah of the club and talk about his score, joke and laugh, pay or collect his bets, and drink good Scotch with other men of note. And he liked to watch his country's flag flap languidly upon the tall white pole because it looked so pretty there.

Mr. Jack also liked the ruder and more natural forms of beauty. He liked to see tall grasses billowing on a hillside, and he liked old shaded roads that wound away to quietness from driven glares of speed and concrete. He was touched by the cosmic sadness of leafy orange, gold, and russet brown in mid-October, and he had seen the evening light upon the old red of a mill and felt deep stillness in his heart ("all—could anyone believe it?—within thirty miles of New York City"). On those occasions the life of the metropolis had seemed very far away. And often he had paused to pluck a flower or stand beside a brook in thought. But after sighing with regret as, among such scenes, he thought of the haste and folly of man's life, Mr. Jack always came back to the city. For life was real, and life was earnest, and Mr. Jack was a business man.

He was a business man, so of course he liked to gamble. What *is* business but a gamble? Will prices go up or down? Will Congress do this or that? Will there be war in some far corner of the earth, and a shortage of some essential raw material? What will the ladies wear next year—big hats or little ones, long dresses or short? You make your guess and back it with your money, and if you don't guess right often enough you don't remain a business man. So Mr. Jack liked to gamble, and he gambled like the business man he was. He gambled every day upon the price of stocks. And at night he often gambled at his club. It was no piker's game he played. He never turned a hair about a thousand dollars. Large sums did not appall him. He was not frightened by Amount and Number. That is why he liked great crowds. That is why the beetling cliffs of immense and cruel architectures lapped his soul in strong security. When he saw a ninety-story building he was not one to fall down groveling in the dust, and beat a maddened brain with fists, and cry out: "Woe! O woe is me!" No. Every cloud-lost spire of masonry was a talisman of power, a monument to the everlasting empire of American business. It made him feel good. For that empire was his faith, his fortune, and his life. He had a fixed place in it.

Yet his neck was not stiff, nor his eye hard. Neither was he very proud. For he had seen the men who lean upon their sills at evening, and those who swarm from rat holes in the ground, and often he had wondered what their lives were like.

Mr. Jack finished shaving and rinsed his glowing face, first with hot water, then with cold. He dried it with a fresh towel, and he rubbed it carefully with a fragrant, gently stinging lotion. This done, he stood for a moment, satisfied, regarding his image, softly caressing the velvet texture of close-shaved, ruddy cheeks with stroking finger tips. Then he turned briskly away, ready for his bath.

He liked the morning plunge in his great sunken tub, the sensual warmth of sudsy water, and the sharp, aromatic cleanness of the bath salts. He had an eye for aesthetic values, too, and he liked to loll back in the tub and watch the dance of water spangles in their magic shift and play upon the creamy ceiling. Most of all, he liked to come up pink and dripping, streaked liberally with tarry-scented soap, and then he loved the stinging drive and shock of needled spray, the sense of hardihood and bracing conflict, and he liked the glow of abundant health as he stepped forth, draining down upon a thick cork mat, and vigorously rubbed himself dry in the folds of a big, crashy bath towel.

All this he now anticipated eagerly as he let fall with a full thud the heavy silver-headed waste-pipe stopper. He turned the hot water tap on as far as it would go, and watched a moment as the tumbling water began smokily to fill the tub with its thick boiling gurgle. Then, scuffing the slippers from his feet, he rapidly stripped off his silk pajamas. He felt with pride the firm-swelling flexor muscle of his upper arm, and observed with keen satisfaction the reflection in the mirror of his plump, well-conditioned body. He was well-molded and solid-looking, with hardly a trace of unwholesome fat upon him—a little undulance, perhaps, across the kidneys, a mere suggestion of a bay about the waist, but not enough to cause concern, and far less than he had seen on many men twenty years his junior. Content, deep and glowing, filled him. He turned the water off and tested it with a finger, which he jerked back with an exclamation of hurt surprise. In his self-absorption he had forgotten the cold water, so now he turned it on and waited while it seethed with tiny milky bubbles and sent waves of trembling light across the hot blue surface of his bath. At last he tried it with a cautious toe and found it tempered to his liking. He shut the water off.

And now, stepping back a pace or two, he gripped the warm tiling of the floor with his bare toes, straightened up with military smartness, drew in a deep breath, and vigorously began his morning exercises. With stiffened legs he bent strongly toward the floor, grunting as his groping finger tips just grazed the tiling. Then he swung into punctual rhythms, counting, "One!—Two!—Three!—Four!" as his body moved. And all the time while his arms beat their regular strokes through the air, his thoughts continued to amble down the pleasant groove that his life had worn for them.

Tonight was the great party, and he liked the brilliant gayety of such gatherings. He was a wise man, too, who knew the world and the city well, and, although kind, he was not one to miss the fun of a little harmless byplay, the verbal thrust and parry of the clever ones, or the baiting of young innocents by those who were wily at the game. Something of the sort could usually be counted on when all kinds of people were brought together at these affairs. It gave a spice and zest to things. Some yokel, say, fresh from the rural districts, all hands and legs and awkwardness, hooked and wriggling on a cruel and cunning word—a woman's, preferably, because women were so swift and deft in matters of this nature. But there were men as well whose skill was great—pampered lap-dogs of rich houses, or feisty, nimble-witted little she-men whose mincing tongues were always good for one or two shrewd thrusts of poison in a hayseed's hide. There was something in the face of a fresh-baited country boy as it darkened to a slow, smoldering glow of shame, surprise, and anger and sought with clumsy and inept words to retort upon the wasp which had stung it and winged away—something so touching—that Mr. Jack, when he saw it, felt a sense of almost paternal tenderness for the hapless victim, a delightful sense of youth and innocence in himself. It was almost as if he were revisiting his own youth.

But enough was enough. Mr. Jack was neither a cruel nor an immoderate man. He liked the gay glitter of the night, the thrill and fever of high stakes, and the swift excitements of new pleasures. He liked the theatre and saw all the best plays, and the better, smarter, wittier revues—the ones with sharp, satiric lines, good dancing, and Gershwin music. He liked the shows his wife designed because she designed them, he was proud of her, and he enjoyed those evenings of ripe culture at the Guild. He also went to prize fights in his evening clothes, and once when he came home he had the red blood of a champion on the white boiled bosom of his shirt. Few men could say as much.

He liked the social swim, and the presence of the better sort of actors, artists, writers, and wealthy, cultivated Jews around his table. He had a kind heart and a loyal nature. His purse was open to a friend in need. He kept a lavish table and a royal cellar, and his family was the apple of his eye.

But he also liked the long velvet backs of lovely women, and the flash of jewelry about their necks. He liked women to be seductive, bright with gold and diamonds to set off the brilliance of their evening gowns. He liked women cut to fashion, with

128

firm breasts, long necks, slender legs, flat hips, and unsuspected depth and undulance. He liked their faces pale, their hair of bronze-gold wire, their red mouths thin, a little cruel, their eyes long, slanting, cat-grey, and lidded carefully. He liked a frosted cocktail shaker in a lady's hands, and he liked a voice hoarse-husky, city-wise, a trifle weary, ironic, faintly insolent, that said:

"Well! What happened to *you,* darling? I thought that you would never get here."

He liked all the things that men are fond of. All of them he had enjoyed himself, each in its proper time and place, and he expected everyone to act as well as he. But ripeness with Mr. Jack was everything, and he always knew the time to stop. His ancient and Hebraic spirit was tempered with a classic sense of moderation. He prized the virtue of decorum highly. He knew the value of the middle way.

He was not a man to wear his heart upon his overcoat, nor risk his life on every corner, nor throw himself away upon a word, nor spend his strength on the impulse of a moment's wild belief. This was such madness as the Gentiles knew. But, this side idolatry and madness, he would go as far for friendship's sake as any man. He would go with a friend up to the very edge of ruin and defeat, and he would even try to hold him back. But once he saw a man was mad, and not to be persuaded by calm judgment, he was done with him. He would leave him where he was, although regretfully. Are matters helped if the whole crew drowns together with a single drunken sailor? He thought not. He could put a world of sincere meaning in the three words: "What a pity!"

Yes, Mr. Frederick Jack was kind and temperate. He had found life pleasant, and had won from it the secret of wise living. And the secret of wise living was founded in a graceful compromise, a tolerant acceptance. If a man wanted to live in this world without getting his pockets picked, he had better learn how to use his eyes and ears on what was going on around him. But if he wanted to live in this world without getting hit over the head, and without all the useless pain, grief, terror, and bitterness that mortify human flesh, he had also better learn how *not* to use his eyes and ears. This may sound difficult, but it had not been so for Mr. Jack. Perhaps some great inheritance of suffering, the long, dark ordeal of his race, had left him, as a precious distillation, this gift of balanced understanding. At any rate, he had not learned it, because it could not be taught: he had been born with it.

Therefore, he was not a man to rip the sheets in darkness or beat his knuckles raw against a wall. He would not madden furiously in the envenomed passages of night, nor would he ever be carried smashed and bloody from the stews. A woman's ways

129

were no doubt hard to bear, but love's bitter mystery had broken no bones for Mr. Jack, and, so far as he was concerned, it could not murder sleep the way an injudicious wiener schnitzel could, or that young Gentile fool, drunk again, probably, ringing the telephone at one A. M. to ask to speak to Esther.

Mr. Jack's brow was darkened as he thought of it. He muttered wordlessly. If fools are fools, let them be fools where their folly will not injure or impede the slumbers of a serious man.

Yes, Men could rob, lie, murder, swindle, trick, and cheat—the whole world knew as much. And women—well, they were women, and there was no help for that. Mr. Jack had also known something of the pain and folly that twist the indignant soul of youth—it was too bad, of course, too bad. But regardless of all this, the day was day and men must work, the night was night and men must sleep, and it was, he felt, *intolerable*——

"One!"

Red of face, he bent stiffly, with a grunt, until his fingers grazed the rich cream tiling of the bathroom floor.

—*intolerable!*——

"Two!"

He straightened sharply, his hands at his sides.

—*that a man with serious work to do*——

"Three!"

His arms shot up to full stretching height above his head, and came swiftly down again until he held clenched fists against his breast.

—*should be pulled out of his bed in the middle of the night by a crazy young fool!*——

"Four!"

His closed fists shot outward in a strong driving movement, and came back to his sides again.

—*It was intolerable, and, by God, he had half a mind to tell her so!*

His exercises ended, Mr. Jack stepped carefully into the luxurious sunken tub and settled his body slowly in its crystal-blue depths. A sigh, long, lingering, full of pleasure, expired upon his lips.

Chapter Eleven

Mrs. Jack Awake

Mrs. Jack awoke at eight o'clock. She awoke like a child, completely alert and alive, instantly awake all over and with all sleep shaken clearly from her mind and senses the moment that she opened her eyes. It had been so with her all her life. For a moment she lay flat on her back and stared straight up at the ceiling.

Then with a vigorous and jubilant movement she flung the covers off of her small and opulent body, which was clothed in a long, sleeveless garment of thin yellow silk. She bent her knees briskly, drew her feet from beneath the covers, and straightened out flat again. She surveyed her small feet with a look of wonder and delight. The sight of her toes in perfect and solid alignment and of their healthy, shining nails filled her with pleasure.

With the same expression of childlike wonder and vanity she slowly lifted her left arm and began to revolve the hand deliberately before her fascinated eyes. She observed with tender concentration how the small and delicate wrist obeyed each command of her will, and she gazed raptly at the graceful, winglike movement of the hand and at the beauty and firm competence that were legible in its brown, narrow back and in the shapely fingers. Then she lifted the other arm as well, and turned both hands upon their wrists, still gazing at them with a tender concentration of delight.

"What magic!" she thought. "What magic and strength are in them! God, how beautiful they are, and what things they can do! The design for everything I undertake comes out of me in the most wonderful and exciting way. It is all distilled and brewed inside of me—and yet nobody ever asks me how it happens! First, it is all one piece—like something solid in the head," she thought comically, now wrinkling her forehead with an almost animal-like expression of bewildered difficulty. "Then it all breaks up into little particles, and somehow arranges itself, and then it starts to *move*!" she thought triumphantly. "First I can feel it coming down along my neck and shoulders, and then it is moving up across my legs and belly, then it meets and joins together like a star. Then it flows out into my arms until it

131

reaches down into my finger tips—and then the hand just does what I want it to. It makes a line, and everything I want is in that line. It puts a fold into a piece of cloth, and no one else on earth could put it in that way, or make it look the same. It gives a turn to the spoon, a prod to the fork, a dash of pepper when I cook for George," she thought, "and there's a dish the finest chef on earth could never equal—because it's got me in it, heart and soul and all my love," she thought with triumphant joy. "Yes! And everything I've ever done has been the same—always the clear design, the line of life, running like a thread of gold all through me back to the time I was a child."

Now, having surveyed her deft and beautiful hands, she began deliberately to inspect her other members. Craning her head downward, she examined the full outlines of her breasts, and the smooth contours of her stomach, thighs, and legs. She stretched forth her hands and touched them with approval. Then she put her hands down at her sides again and lay motionless, toes evenly in line, limbs straight, head front, eyes staring gravely at the ceiling—a little figure stretched out like a queen for burial, yet still warm, still palpable, immensely calm and beautiful, as she thought:

"These are my hands and these are my fingers, these are my legs and hips, these are my fine feet and my perfect toes—this is my body."

And suddenly, as if the inventory of these possessions filled her with an immense joy and satisfaction, she sat up with a shining face and placed her feet firmly on the floor. She wriggled into a pair of slippers, stood up, thrust her arms out and brought the hands down again behind her head, yawned, and then put on a yellow quilted dressing gown which had been lying across the foot of the bed.

Esther had a rosy, jolly, delicate face of noble beauty. It was small, firm, and almost heart-shaped, and in its mobile features there was a strange union of child and woman. The instant anyone met her for the first time he felt: "This woman must look exactly the way she did when she was a child. She can't have changed at all." Yet her face also bore the markings of middle age. It was when she was talking to someone and her whole countenance was lighted by a merry and eager animation that the child's face was most clearly visible.

When she was at work, her face was likely to have the serious concentration of a mature and expert craftsman engaged in an absorbing and exacting labor, and it was at such a time that she looked oldest. It was then that one noticed the somewhat fatigued and minutely wrinkled spaces around her eyes and some strands of grey that were beginning to sprinkle her dark-brown hair.

Similarly, in repose, or when she was alone, her face was

132

likely to have a somber, brooding depth. Its beauty then was profound and full of mystery. She was three parts a Jewess, and in her contemplative moods the ancient, dark, and sorrowful quality of her race seemed to take complete possession of her. She would wrinkle her brow with a look of perplexity and grief, and in the cast of her features there would be a fatal quality, as of something priceless that was lost and irrecoverable. This look, which she did not wear often, had always troubled George Webber when he saw it because it suggested some secret knowledge buried deep within the woman whom he loved and whom he believed he had come to know.

But the way she appeared most often, and the way people remembered her best, was as a glowing, jolly, indomitably active and eager little creature in whose delicate face the image of a child peered out with joyfulness and immortal confidence. Then her apple-cheeks would glow with health and freshness, and when she came into a room she filled it with her loveliness and gave to everything about her the color of morning life and innocence.

So, too, when she went out on the streets, among the thrusting throngs of desolate and sterile people, her face shone forth like a deathless flower among their dead, grey flesh and dark, dead eyes. They milled past her with their indistinguishable faces set in familiar expressions of inept hardness, betraying cunning without an end, guile without a purpose, cynical knowledge without faith or wisdom, yet even among these hordes of the unburied dead some would halt suddenly in the dreary fury of their existence and would stare at her with their harassed and driven eyes. Her whole figure with its fertile curves, opulent as the earth, belonged to an order of humanity so different from that of their own starved barrenness that they gazed after her like wretches trapped and damned in hell who, for one brief moment, had been granted a vision of living and imperishable beauty.

As Mrs. Jack stood there beside her bed, her maidservant, Nora Fogarty, knocked at the door and entered immediately, bearing a tray with a tall silver coffee pot, a small bowl of sugar, a cup, saucer, and spoon, and the morning *Times*. The maid put the tray down on a little table beside the bed, saying in a thick voice:

"Good maar-nin', Mrs. Jack."

"Oh, hello, Nora!" the woman answered, crying out in the eager and surprised tone with which she usually responded to a greeting. "How are you—hah?" she asked, as if she were really

133

greatly concerned, but immediately adding: "Isn't it going to be a nice day? Did you ever see a more beautiful morning in your life?"

"Oh, *beautiful*, Mrs. Jack!" Nora answered. "Beautiful!"

The maid's voice had a respectful and almost unctuously reverential tone of agreement as she answered, but there was in it an undernote of something sly, furtive, and sullen, and Mrs. Jack looked at her swiftly now and saw the maid's eyes, inflamed with drink and irrationally choleric, staring back at her. Their rancor, however, seemed to be directed not so much at her mistress as at the general family of the earth. Or, if Nora's eyes did swelter with a glare of spite more personal and direct, her resentment was blind and instinctive: it just smoldered in her with an ugly truculence, and she did not know the reason for it. Certainly it was not based on any feeling of class inferiority, for she was Irish, and a papist to the bone, and where social dignities were concerned she thought she knew on which side condescension lay.

She had served Mrs. Jack and her family for more than twenty years, and had grown slothful on their bounty, but in spite of a very affectionate devotion and warmth of old Irish feeling she had never doubted for a moment that they would ultimately go to hell, together with other pagans and all alien heathen tribes whatever. Just the same, she had done pretty well by herself among these prosperous infidels. She had a "cushy" job, she always fell heir to the scarcely-worn garments of Mrs. Jack and her sister Edith, and she saw to it that the policeman who came to woo her several times a week should lack for nothing in the way of food and drink to keep him contented and to forestall any desire he might have to stray off and forage in other pastures. Meanwhile, she had laid by several thousand dollars, and had kept her sisters and nieces back in County Cork faithfully furnished with a titillating chronicle (sprinkled with pious interjections of regret and deprecation and appeals to the Virgin to watch over her and guard her among such infidels) of high life in this rich New World that had such pickings in it.

No—decidedly this truculent resentment which smoldered in her eyes had nothing to do with caste. She had lived here for twenty years, enjoying the generous favor of a very good, superior sort of heathen, and growing used to almost all their sinful customs, but she had never let herself forget where the true way and the true light was, nor her hope that she would one day return into the more civilized and Christian precincts of her own kind.

Neither did the grievance in the maid's hot eyes come from a sense of poverty, the stubborn, silent anger of the poor against the rich, the feeling of injustice that decent people like herself should have to fetch and carry all their lives for idle, lazy

134

wasters. She was not feeling sorry for herself because she had to drudge with roughened fingers all day long in order that this fine lady might smile rosily and keep beautiful. Nora knew full well that there was no task in all the household range of duties, whether of serving, mending, cooking, cleaning, or repairing, which her mistress could not do far better and with more dispatch than she.

She knew, too, that every day in the great city which roared all about her own dull ears this other woman was going back and forth with the energy of a dynamo, buying, ordering, fitting, cutting, and designing—now on the scaffolds with the painters, beating them at their own business in immense, drafty, and rather dismal rooms where her designs were wrought out into substance, now sitting cross-legged among great bolts of cloth and plying a needle with a defter finger than any on the flashing hands of the pallid tailors all about her, now searching and prying indefatigably through a dozen gloomy little junk shops until she unearthed triumphantly the exact small ornament which she must have. She was always after her people, always pressing on, formidably but with good humor, keeping the affair in hand and pushing it to its conclusion in spite of the laziness, carelessness, vanity, stupidity, indifference, and faithlessness of those with whom she had to work —painters, actors, scene shifters, bankers, union bosses, electricians, tailors, costumers, producers, and directors. Upon this whole motley and, for the most part, shabbily inept crew which carried on the crazy and precarious affair known as "show business," she enforced the structure, design, and incomparably rich color of her own life. Nora knew about all this.

The maid had also seen enough of the hard world in which her mistress daily strove and conquered to convince herself that even if she had had any of the immense talent and knowledge that her mistress possessed, she did not have in all her lazy body as much energy, resolution, and power as the other woman carried in the tip of her little finger. And this awareness, so far from arousing any feeling of inferiority in her, only contributed to her self-satisfaction, making her feel that it was Mrs. Jack, not herself, who was really the working woman, and that she—enjoying the same food, the same drink, the same shelter, even the same clothing—would not swap places with her for anything on earth.

Yes, the maid knew that she was fortunate and had no cause for complaint; yet her grievance, ugly and perverse, glowered implacably in her inflamed and mutinous eyes. And she could not have found a word or reason for it. But as the two women faced each other no word was needed. The reason for it was printed in their flesh, legible in everything they did. It was not

135

against Mrs. Jack's wealth, authority, and position that the maid's rancor was directed, but against something much more personal and indefinable—against the very tone and quality of the other woman's life. For within the past year there had come over the maid a distempered sense of failure and frustration, an obscure but powerful feeling that her life had somehow gone awry and was growing into sterile and fruitless age without ever having come to any ripeness. She was baffled and tormented by a sense of having missed something splendid and magnificent in life, without knowing at all what it was. But whatever it was, her mistress seemed marvelously somehow to have found it and enjoyed it to the full, and this obvious fact, which she could plainly see but could not define, goaded her almost past endurance.

Both women were about the same age, and so nearly the same size that the maid could wear any of her mistress's garments without alteration. But if they had been creatures from separate planetary systems, if each had been formed by a completely different protoplasm, the contrast between them could not have been more extreme.

Nora was not an ill-favored woman. She had a mass of fairly abundant black hair which she brushed over to the side. Her face, had it not been for the distempered look which drink and her own baffled fury had now given it, would have been pleasant and attractive. There was warmth in it, but there was also a trace of that wild fierceness which belongs to something lawless in nature, at once coarse and delicate, murderous, tender, and savagely ebullient. She still had a trim figure, which wore neatly the well-cut skirt of rough green plaid which her mistress had given her (for, because of her long service, she was recognized as a' kind of unofficial captain to the other maids and was usually not required to wear maid's uniform). But where the figure of the mistress was small of bone and fine of line and yet at the same time lavish and seductive, the figure of the maid was, by contrast, almost thick and clumsy-looking. It was the figure of a woman no longer young, fresh, and fertile, but already heavied, thickened, dried, and hardened by the shock, the wear, the weight, and the slow accumulation of intolerable days and merciless years, which take from people everything, and from which there is no escape.

No—no escape, except for *her*, the maid was thinking bitterly, with a dull feeling of inarticulate outrage, and for *her*, for *her*, there was never anything but triumph. For *her* the years brought nothing but a constantly growing success. And why? Why?

It was here, upon this question, that her spirit halted like a wild beast baffled by a sheer and solid blank of wall. Had they not both breathed the same air, eaten the same food, been clothed by the same garments, and sheltered by the same roof? Had she not had as much—and as good—of everything as her mistress? Yes—if anything she had had the better of it, for she would *not* drive *herself* from morning to night, she thought with contemptuous bitterness, the way her mistress did.

Yet here she stood, baffled and confused, glowering sullenly into the shining face of the other woman's glorious success—and she saw it, she knew it, she felt its outrage, but she had no word to voice her sense of an intolerable wrong. All she knew was that she had been stiffened and thickened by the same years that had given the other woman added grace and suppleness, that her skin had been dried and sallowed by the same lights and weathers that had added luster to the radiant beauty of the other, and that even now her spirit was soured by her knowledge of ruin and defeat while in the other woman there coursed forever an exquisite music of power and control, of health and joy.

Yes, she saw it plainly enough. The comparison was cruelly and terribly true, past the last atom of hope and disbelief. And as she stood there before her mistress with the weary distemper in her eyes, enforcing by a stern compulsion the qualities of obedience and respect into her voice, she saw, too, that the other woman read the secret of her envy and frustration, and that she pitied her because of it. And for this Nora's soul was filled with hatred, because pity seemed to her the final and intolerable indignity.

In fact, although the kind and jolly look on Mrs. Jack's lovely face had not changed a bit since she had greeted the maid, her eye had observed instantly all the signs of the unwholesome fury that was raging in the woman, and with a strong emotion of pity, wonder, and regret she was thinking:

"She's been at it again! This is the third time in a week that she's been drinking. I wonder what it is—I wonder what it is that happens to that kind of person."

Mrs. Jack did not know clearly what she meant by "that kind of person," but she felt momentarily the detached curiosity that a powerful, rich, and decisive character may feel when he pauses for a moment from the brilliant exercise of a talent that has crowned his life with triumphant ease and success almost every step of the way, and notes suddenly, and with surprise, that most of the other people in the world are fumbling blindly and wretchedly about, eking out from day to day the flabby substance of grey lives. She realized with regret that such people are so utterly lacking in any individual distinction that each

137

seems to be a small particle of some immense and vicious life-stuff rather than a living creature who is able to feel and to inspire love, beauty, joy, passion, pain, and death. With a sense of sudden discovery the mistress was feeling this as she looked at the servant who had lived with her familiarly for almost twenty years, and now for the first time she reflected on the kind of life the other woman might have had.

"What is it?" she kept thinking. "What's gone wrong with her? She never used to be this way. It has all happened within the last year. And Nora used to be so pretty, too!" she thought, startled by the memory. "Why, when she first came to us she was really a very handsome girl. Isn't it a shame," she thought indignantly, "that she should let herself go to seed like this—a girl who's had the chances that she's had! I wonder why she never married. She used to have half a dozen of those big policemen on the string, and now there's only one who still comes faithfully. They were all mad about her, and she could have had her pick of them!"

All at once, as she was looking at the servant with kindly interest, the woman's breath, foul with a stale whiskey stench, was blown upon her, and she got suddenly a rank body smell, strong, hairy, female, and unwashed. She frowned with revulsion, and her face began to burn with a glow of shame, embarrassment, and acute distaste.

"God, but she stinks!" she thought, with a feeling of horror and disgust. "You could cut the smell around her with an axe! The nasty things!" she thought, now including all the servants in her indictment. "I'll bet they never wash—and here they are all day long with nothing to do, and they could at least keep clean! My God! You'd think these people would be so glad to be here in this lovely place with the fine life we've made for them that they would be a little proud of it and try to show that they appreciate it! But no! They're just not good enough!" she thought scornfully, and for a moment her fine mouth was disfigured at one corner by an ugly expression.

It was an expression which had in it not only contempt and scorn, but also something almost racial—a quality of arrogance that was too bold and naked, as if it were eager to assert its own superiority. This ugly look rested only for a second, and almost imperceptibly, about the edges of her mouth, and it did not sit well on her lovely face. Then it was gone. But the maid had seen it, and that swift look, with all its implications, had stung and whipped her tortured spirit to a frenzy.

"Oh, yes, me fine lady!" she was thinking. "It's too good fer the likes of us ye are, ain't it? Oh me, yes, an' we're very grand, ain't we? What wit' our fine clothes an' our evenin' gowns an' our forty pairs of hand-made shoes! Jesus, now! Ye'd think she was some kind of centipede to see the different pairs of shoes she's got! An' our silk petticoats an' step-ins that we have made in Paris, now! Yes! That makes us very fine, don't it? It's not as if we ever did a little private monkey-business on the side, like ordinary people, is it? Oh, me, no! We are gathered together wit' a friend fer a little elegant an' high-class entertainment durin' the course of the evenin'! But if it's some poor girl wit'out an extra pair of drawers to her name, it's different, now! It's: 'Oh! you nasty thing! I'm disgusted wit' you!' . . . Yes! An' there's many a fine lady livin' on Park Avenoo right now who's no better, if the truth was told! That I know! So just take care, me lady, not to give yerself too many airs!" she thought with rancorous triumph. . . .

"Ah! if I told all that I know! 'Nora,' she says, 'if anyone calls when I'm not here, I wish ye'd take the message yerself. Mr. Jack don't like to be disturbed.' . . . Jesus! From what I've seen there's none of 'em that likes to be disturbed. It's love and let love wit' 'em, no questions ast an' the devil take the hindmost, so long as ye do it in yer leisure hours. But if ye're twenty minutes late fer dinner, it's where the hell have ye been, an' what's to become of us when ye neglect yer family in this way? . . . Sure," she thought, warming with a flush of humor and a more tolerant and liberal spirit, "it's a queer world, ain't it? An' these are the queerest of the lot! Thank God I was brought up like a Christian in the Holy Church, an' still have grace enough to go to Mass when I have sinned! But then——"

As often happens with people of strong but disordered feelings, she was already sorry for her flare of ugly temper, and her affections were now running warmly in another direction:

"But then, God knows, there's not a better-hearted sort of people in the world! There's no one I'd rather work fer than Mrs. Jack. They'll give ye everything they have if they like ye. I've been here twenty years next April, an' in all that time no one has ever been turned away from the door who needed food. Sure, there's far worse that go to Mass seven days a week—yes, an' would steal the pennies off a dead man's eyes if they got the chance! It's a good home we've been given here—as I keep tellin' all the rest of 'em," she thought with virtuous content, "an' Nora Fogarty's not the one to turn an' bite the hand that's feedin' her—no matter what the rest of 'em may do!"

All this had passed in the minds and hearts of the two women with the instancy of thought. Meanwhile, the maid, having set the tray down on the little table by the bed, had gone to the windows, lowered them, raised the shades to admit more light, slightly adjusted the curtains, and was now in the bathroom drawing the water in the tub, an activity signalized at first by the rush of tumbling waters, and later by a sound more quiet and sustained as she reduced the flow and tempered the boiling fluid to a moderate heat.

While this was going on, Mrs. Jack had seated herself on the edge of her bed, crossed her legs jauntily, poured out a cup of black steaming coffee from the tall silver pot, and opened the newspaper which lay folded on the tray. And now, as she drank her coffee and stared with blank, unseeing eyes at the print before her, there was a perplexed frown on her face, and she was slipping one finger in and out of a curious and ancient ring which she wore on her right hand. It was a habit which she performed unconsciously, and it always indicated a state of impatience and nervousness, or the troubled reflection of a mind that was rapidly collecting itself for a decisive action. So, now, her first emotions of pity, curiosity, and regret having passed, the practical necessity of doing something about Nora was pressing at her.

"That's where Fritz's liquor has been going," she thought. "He's been furious about it. . . . She's got to stop it. If she keeps on at this rate, she'll be no good for anything in another month or two. . . . God! I could kill her for being such a fool!" she thought. "What gets into these people, anyway?" Her small and lovely face now red with anger, the space between her troubled eyes cleft deeply by a frown, she determined to speak plainly and sternly to the maid without any more delay.

This decision being made, she was conscious instantly of a sense of great relief and a feeling almost of happiness, for indecision was alien to the temper of her soul. The knowledge of the maid's delinquency had been nagging at her conscience for some time, and now she wondered why she had ever hesitated. Yet, when the maid came back into the room again and paused before going out, as if waiting for further orders, and looked at her with a glance that now seemed affectionate and warm, Mrs. Jack felt acute embarrassment and regret as she began to speak, and, to her surprise, she found herself beginning in a hesitant and almost apologetic tone.

"Oh, Nora!" she said somewhat excitedly, slipping the ring rapidly on and off her finger. "There's something I want to talk to you about."

"Yes, Mrs. Jack," Nora answered humbly, and waited respectfully.

"It's something Miss Edith wanted me to ask you," she went on quickly, somewhat timidly, discovering to her amazement that she was beginning her reproof quite differently from the way she had intended.

Nora waited in an attitude of studious and submissive attention.

"I wonder if you or any of the other girls remember seeing a dress Miss Edith had," she said, and went on quickly—"one of those dresses she brought back last year from Paris. It had a funny grey-green kind of color and she used to wear it in the morning when she went to business. Do you remember—hah?" she said sharply.

"Yes, ma'am," said Nora with a solemn, wondering air. "I've seen it, Mrs. Jack."

"Well, Nora, she can't find it. It's gone."

"Gone?" said Nora, staring at her with a stupid and astonished look.

But even as the servant repeated the word, a furtive smile played around her mouth, betraying her sullen humor, and a look of sly triumph came in her eyes. Mrs. Jack read the signs instantly:

"Yes! She knows where it is!" she thought. "Of course she knows! One of them has taken it! It's perfectly disgraceful, and I'm not going to stand it any longer!"—and a wave of indignation, hot and choking, boiled up in her. "Yes, gone! It's gone, I tell you!" she said angrily to the staring maid. "What's become of it? Where do you think it's gone to?" she asked bluntly.

"I don't know, Mrs. Jack," Nora answered in a slow, wondering tone. "Miss Edith must have lost it."

"Lost it! Oh, Nora, don't be stupid!" she cried furiously. "How could she lose it? She's been nowhere. She's been here all the time. And the dress was here, too, hanging in her closet, up to a week ago! How can you lose a dress?" she cried impatiently. "Is it just going to crawl off your back and walk away from you when you're not looking?" she said sarcastically. "You know she didn't lose it! Someone's taken it!"

"Yes, ma'am," Nora said with dutiful acquiescence. "That's what I think, too. Someone must have sneaked in here when all of yez was out an' taken it. Ah, I tell ye," she remarked with a regretful movement of the head, "it's got so nowadays ye never know who to trust and who not to," she observed sententiously. "A friend of mine who works fer some big people up at Rye was tellin' me just the other day about a man that came there wit' some kind of a floor-mop he had to sell—ast to try it out an' show 'em how it worked upon their floors, ye know, an' a finer, cleaner-lookin' boy, she says, ye wouldn't see again in yer whole lifetime. 'An' my God!' she says—I'm tellin' ye just the way she told it to me, Mrs. Jack—'I couldn't believe me own ears when they told me later what he'd done! If he'd been me own brother I couldn't have been more surprised!' she says.—Well, it just goes to show ye that——"

"Oh, Nora, for heaven's sake!" Mrs. Jack cried with an angry and impatient gesture. "Don't talk such rot to me! Who would

141

come in here without your knowing it? You girls are here all day long, there's only the elevator and the service entrance, and you see everyone who comes in! And besides, if anyone ever took the trouble to break in, you know he wouldn't stop with just one dress. He'd be after money or jewelry or something valuable that he could sell."

"Well, now, I tell ye," Nora said, "that man was here last week to fix the refrigerator. I says to May at the time, 'I don't like the look of him,' I says. 'There's somethin' in his face that I don't like. Keep yer eye on him,' I says, 'because ——' "

"Nora!"

At the sharp warning in her mistress's voice the maid stopped suddenly, looked quickly at her, and then was silent, with a dull flush of shame and truculence upon her face. Mrs. Jack stared back at her with a look of burning indignation, then she burst out with open, blazing anger.

"Look here!" Mrs. Jack cried furiously. "I think it's a dirty shame the way you girls are acting! We've been good to you! Nora," and now her voice grew gentler with pity, "there are no girls in this town who've been better treated than you have."

"Don't I know it, Mrs. Jack," Nora answered in a lilting and earnest tone, but her eyes were sullenly hostile and resentful. "Haven't I always said the same? Wasn't I sayin' the same thing meself to Janie just the other day? 'Sure,' I says, 'but we're the lucky ones! There's no one in the world I'd rather work fer than Mrs. Jack. Twenty years,' I says, 'I've been here, an' in all that time,' I says, 'I've never heard a cross word from her. They're the best people in the world,' I says, 'an' any girl that gets a job wit' 'em is lucky!' Sure, don't I know all of ye—" she cried richly—"Mr. Jack an' Miss Edith an' Miss Alma? Wouldn't I get down on me knees right now an' scrub me fingers to the bone if it would help ye any?"

"Who's asking you to scrub your fingers to the bone?" Mrs. Jack cried impatiently. "Lord, Nora, you girls have it pretty soft. There's mighty little scrubbing that you've had to do!" she said. "It's the rest of us who *scrub!*" she cried. "We go out of here every morning—six days in the week—and work like hell ——"

"Don't I know it, Mrs. Jack?" Nora broke in. "Wasn't I sayin' to May just the other day——"

"Oh, damn what you said to May!" For a brief moment Mrs. Jack looked at the servant with a straight, burning face. Then she spoke more quietly to her. "Nora, listen to me," she said. "We've always given you girls everything you ever asked for. You've had the best wages anyone can get for what you do. And you've lived here with us just the same as the rest of us, for you know very well that——"

"Sure," Nora interrupted in a richly sentimental tone. "It

142

hasn't been like I was *workin'* here at all! Ye couldn't have treated me any better if I'd been one of the family!"

"Oh, one of the family my eye!" Mrs. Jack said impatiently. "Don't make me laugh! There's no one in the family—unless maybe it's my daughter, Alma—who doesn't do more in a day than you girls do in a week! You've lived the life of Riley here! . . . The life of Riley!" she repeated, almost comically, and then she sat looking at the servant for a moment, a formidable little dynamo trembling with her indignation, slowly clenching and unclenching her small hands at her sides. "Good heavens, Nora!" she burst out in a furious tone. "It's not as if we ever begrudged you anything! We've never denied you anything you asked for! It's not the value of the dress! You know very well that Miss Edith would have given it to any one of you if you had gone to her and asked her for it! But—oh, it's intolerable! —intolerable!" she exclaimed suddenly in uncontrollable anger—"that you should have no more sense or decency than to do a thing like that to people who have always been your friends!"

"Sure, an' do ye think I'd be the one who'd do a thing like that?" cried Nora in a trembling voice. "Is it me ye're accusin', Mrs. Jack, when I've lived here wit' yez all this time? They could take me right hand—" in her rush of feeling she held the member up—"an' chop it from me arm before I'd take a button that belonged to one of yez. An' that's God's truth," she added solemnly. "I swear it to ye as I hope to live an' be forgiven fer me sins!" she declared more passionately as her mistress started to speak. "I never took a pin or penny that belonged to any one of yez—an' so help me God, that's true! An' yes! I'll swear it to ye by everything that's holy!" she now cried, tranced in a kind of ecstasy of sacred vows. "By the soul an' spirit of me blessed mother who is dead——"

"Ah, Nora!" Mrs. Jack said pityingly, shaking her head and turning away, and, in spite of her indignation, breaking into a short laugh at the extravagance of the servant's oaths. And she thought with a bitter, scornful humor: "God! You can't talk to her! She'll swear a thousand oaths and think that makes everything all right! Yes! and will drink Fritz's whiskey and go to Mass if she has to crawl to get there—and cross herself with holy water—and listen to the priest say words she cannot understand—and come out glorified—to act like this when she knows that one of the girls is taking things that don't belong to her! What strange and magic things these oaths and ceremonies are!" she thought. "They give a kind of life to people who have none of their own. They make a kind of truth for people who have found none for themselves. Love, beauty, everlasting truth, salvation—all that we hope and suffer for on earth is in them for these people. Everything that the rest of us have to get

143

with our blood and labor, and by the anguish of our souls, is miraculously accomplished for *them,* somehow," she thought ironically, "if they can only swear to it 'by the soul an' spirit of me blessed mother who is dead.'"

"—An' so help me God, by all the Blessed Saints, an' by the Holy Virgin, too!" she heard Nora's voice intoning; and, wearily, she turned to the maid again and spoke to her softly, with an almost pleading earnestness.

"Nora, for God's sake have a little sense," she said. "What is the use of all this swearing by the Virgin and the Saints, and getting up and going out to Mass, when all you do is come back home to swill down Mr. Jack's whiskey? Yes, and deceive the people who have been the best friends you ever had!" she cried out bitterly. Then, seeing the old mutinous look flaring again in the maid's sullen and distempered eyes, she went on almost tearfully: "Nora, try to have a little wisdom. Is this all you've been able to get from life—to come in here and act this way and blow your stinking breath on me, when all we've ever done has been to help you?" Her voice was trembling with her pity and her sense of passionate outrage, yet her anger was more than personal. She felt that the maid had betrayed something decent and inviolable in life—a faith and integrity in human feeling that should be kept and honored everywhere.

"Well, ma'am," said Nora with a toss of her black head, "as I was sayin', if it's me ye're accusin'——"

"No, Nora. Enough of that." Mrs. Jack's voice was sad, tired, dispirited, but its tone was also firm and final. She made a little dismissing gesture with her hand. "You may go now. I don't need anything more."

The maid marched to the door, her head held high, her stiff back and neck eloquently expressive of outraged innocence and suppressed fury. Then she paused, her hand upon the knob, and half turned as she delivered her parting shot.

"About Miss Edith's dress—" she said with another toss of her head—"if it's not lost, I guess it'll turn up. Maybe one of the girls borrowed it, if ye know what I mean."

With this, she closed the door behind her and was gone.

Half an hour later Mr. Frederick Jack came walking down the hall with his copy of the *Herald-Tribune* under his arm. He was feeling in very good humor. By now he had completely forgotten his momentary annoyance at the telephone call that had awakened him in the middle of the night. He rapped lightly at his wife's door and waited. There was no answer. More faintly, listening, he rapped again.

144

"Are you there?" he said.

He opened the door and entered noiselessly.

She was already deeply absorbed in the first task of her day's work. On the other side of the room, with her back to him, she was seated at a small writing desk between the windows with a little stack of bills, business letters, and personal correspondence on her left hand, and an open check book on her right. She was vigorously scrawling off a note. As he advanced toward her she put down the pen, swiftly blotted the paper, and was preparing to fold it and thrust it in an envelope when he spoke.

"Good morning," he said in the pleasant, half-ironic tone that people use when they address someone who is not aware of their presence.

She jumped and turned around quickly.

"Oh, hello, Fritz!" she cried in her jolly voice. "How are you—hah?"

He stooped in a somewhat formal fashion, planted a brief, friendly, and perfunctory kiss on her cheek, and straightened up, unconsciously shrugging his shoulders a little, and giving his sleeves and the bottom of his coat a tug to smooth out any wrinkle that might have appeared to disturb the faultless correctness of his appearance. While his wife's quick glance took in every detail of his costume for the day—his shoes, socks, trousers, coat, and tie, together with the perfection of his tailored form and the neat gardenia in his buttonhole—her face, now bent forward and held firmly in one cupped hand in an attitude of eager attentiveness, had a puzzled and good-natured look which seemed to say: "I can see that you are laughing at me about something. What have I done now?"

Mr. Jack stood before her, feet apart and arms akimbo, regarding her with an expression of mock gravity, in which, however, his good humor and elation were apparent.

"Well, what is it?" she cried excitedly.

In answer, Mr. Jack produced the newspaper which he had been holding folded back in one hand, and tapped it with his index finger, saying:

"Have you seen this?"

"No. Who is it?"

"It's Elliot in the *Herald-Tribune*. Like to hear it?"

"Yes. Read it. What does he say?"

Mr. Jack struck a pose, rattled the paper, frowned, cleared his throat in mock solemnity, and then began in a slightly ironic and affected tone, intended to conceal his own deep pleasure and satisfaction, to read the review.

" 'Mr. Shulberg has brought to this, his latest production, the full artillery of his distinguished gifts for suave direction. He has paced it brilliantly, timed it—word, scene, and gesture

145

—with some of the most subtly nuanced, deftly restrained, and quietly persuasive acting that this season has yet seen. He has a gift for silence that is eloquent—oh, devoutly eloquent!—among all the loud but for the most part meaningless vociferation of the current stage. All this your diligent observer is privileged to repeat with more than customary elation. Moreover, Mr. Shulberg has revealed to us in the person of Montgomery Mortimer the finest youthful talent that this season had discovered. Finally——' "

Mr. Jack cleared his throat solemnly—"Ahem, ahem!"—flourished his arms forward and rattled the paper expressively, and stared drolly at his wife over the top of it. Then he went on:

" 'Finally, he has given us, with the distinguished aid of Miss Esther Jack, a faultless and unobtrusive *décor* which warmed these ancient bones as they have not been warmed for many a Broadway moon. In these three acts, Miss Jack contributes three of the most effective settings she has ever done for the stage. Hers is a talent that needs make obeisance to no one. She is, in fact, in the studied opinion of this humble but diligent observer, the first designer of her time.' "

Mr. Jack paused abruptly, looked at her with playful gravity, his head cocked over the edges of the paper and said:

"Did you say something?"

"God!" she yelled, her happy face flushed with laughter and excitement. "Did you hear it? Vat is dees? Vat is dees?" she said comically, making a Jewish gesture with her hands—"an ovation?— What else does he say—hah?" she asked, bending forward eagerly.

Mr. Jack proceeded:

" 'It is therefore a pity that Miss Jack's brilliant talent should not have had better fare to feed on than was given it last evening at the Arlington. For the play itself, we must reluctantly admit, was neither——' "

"Well," said Mr. Jack, stopping abruptly and putting down the paper, "the rest of it is—*you* know—" he shrugged slightly—"sort of soso. Neither good nor bad. He sort of pans it.— But *say!*" he cried, with jocular indignation. "I like the nerve of that guy! Where does he get this Miss Esther Jack stuff? Where do *I* come in?" he said. "Don't I get any credit at all for being your husband? You know," he said, "I'd like to get in somewhere if it's only a seat in the second balcony. Of course—" and now he began to speak in the impersonal manner that people often use when they are being heavily sarcastic, addressing himself to the vacant air as if some invisible auditor were there, and as if he himself were only a detached observer—"of course, he's nothing but her husband, anyway. What is he? *Bah!*" he said scornfully and contemptuously. "Nothing but a business man who doesn't deserve to have such

146

a brilliant woman for his wife! What does *he* know about art? Can he appreciate her? Can he understand anything she does? Can he say—what is it this fellow says?" he demanded, suddenly looking at the paper with an intent stare and then reading from it again in an affected tone—" 'a faultless and unobtrusive *décor* which warmed these ancient bones as they have not been warmed for many a Broadway moon.' "

"I know," she said with pitying contempt, as if the florid words of the reviewer aroused in her no other emotion, although the pleasure which the reviewer's praise had given her was still legible in her face. "I know. Isn't it pathetic? They're all so fancy, these fellows! They make me tired!"

" 'Hers is a talent that needs make obeisance to no one,' " Mr. Jack continued. "Now that's a good one! Could her husband think of a thing like that? No!" he cried suddenly, shaking his head with a scornful laugh and waving a plump forefinger sideways before him. "Her husband is not smart enough!" he cried. "He is not good enough! He's nothing but a business man! He can't appreciate her!"—and all at once, to her amazement, she saw that his eyes were shot with tears, and that the lenses of his spectacles were being covered with a film of mist.

She stared at him wonderingly, her face bent toward him in an expression of startled and protesting concern, but at the same moment she was feeling, as she had often felt, that there was something obscure and strange in life which she had never been able to find out about or to express. For she knew that this unexpected and reasonless display of strong feeling in her husband bore no relation whatever to the review in the paper. His chagrin at having the reviewer refer to her as "Miss" was nothing more than a playful and jocular pretense. She knew that he was really bursting with elation because of her success.

With a sudden poignant and wordless pity—for whom, for what, she could not say—she had an instant picture of the great chasms downtown where he would spend his day, and where, in the furious drive and turmoil of his business, excited, prosperous-looking men would seize his arm or clap him on the back and shout:

"Say, have you seen today's *Herald-Tribune*? Did you read what it had to say about your wife? Aren't you proud of her? Congratulations!"

She could also see his ruddy face beginning to blush and burn brick-red with pleasure as he received these tributes, and as he tried to answer them with an amused and tolerant smile, and a few casual words of acknowledgment as if to say:

"Yes, I think I did see some mention of her. But of course you can hardly expect me to be excited by a thing like that. That's an old story to us now. They've said that kind of thing so often that we're used to it."

147

When he came home that night he would repeat all that had been said to him, and although he would do it with an air of faintly cynical amusement, she knew that his satisfaction would be immense and solid. She knew, too, that his pride would be enhanced by the knowledge that the wives of these rich men—handsome Jewesses most of them, as material-minded in their quest for what was fashionable in the world of art as were their husbands for what was profitable in the world of business—would also read of her success, would straightway go to witness it themselves, and then would speak of it in brilliant chambers of the night, where the glowing air would take on an added spice of something exciting and erotic from their handsome and sensual-looking faces.

All this she thought of instantly as she stared at this plump, grey-haired, and faultlessly groomed man whose eyes had suddenly, and for no reason that she knew, filled with tears, and whose mouth now had the pouting, wounded look of a hurt child. And her heart was filled with a nameless and undefinable sense of compassion as she cried warmly, in a protesting voice:

"But, Fritz! You know I never felt like that! You know I never said a thing like that to you! You know I love it when you like anything I do! I'd rather have your opinion ten times over than that of these newspaper fellows! What do they know anyway?" she muttered scornfully.

Mr. Jack, having taken off his glasses and polished them, having blown his nose vigorously and put his glasses on again, now lowered his head, braced his thumb stiffly on his temple and put four plump fingers across his eyes in a comical shielding position, saying rapidly in a muffled, apologetic voice:

"I know! I know! It's all right! I was only joking," he said with an embarrassed smile. Then he blew his nose vigorously again, his face lost its expression of wounded feeling, and he began to talk in a completely natural, matter-of-fact tone, as if nothing he had done or said had been at all unusual. "Well," he said, "how do you feel? Are you pleased with the way things went last night?"

"Oh, I suppose so," she answered dubiously, feeling all at once the vague discontent that was customary with her when her work was finished and the almost hysterical tension of the last days before a theatrical opening was at an end. Then she continued: "I think it went off pretty well, don't you? I thought my sets were sort of good—or did you think so?" she asked eagerly. "No," she went on in the disparaging tone of a child talking to itself, "I guess they were just ordinary. A long way from my best—hah?" she demanded.

"You know what I think," he said. "I've told you. There's no one who can touch you. The best thing in the show!" he said strongly. "They were by far the best thing in the show—by far!

by *far*!" Then, quietly, he added: "Well, I suppose you're glad it's over. That's the end of it for this season, isn't it?"

"Yes," she said, "except for some costumes that I promised Irene Morgenstein I'd do for one of her ballets. And I've got to meet some of the Arlington company for fittings again this morning," she concluded in a dispirited tone.

"What, again! Weren't you satisfied with the way they looked last night? What's the trouble?"

"Oh—" she said with disgust—"what do you think's the trouble, Fritz? There's only one trouble! It never changes! It's always the same! The trouble is that there are so many half-baked fools in the world who'll never do the thing you tell them to do! That's the trouble! God!" she said frankly, "I'm too good for it! I never should have given up my painting. It makes me sick sometimes!" she burst out with warm indignation. "Isn't it a shame that everything I do has to be wasted on those people?"

"What people?"

"Oh, you know," she muttered, "the kind of people that you get in the theatre. Of course there are some good ones—but God!" she exclaimed, "most of them are such trash! Did you see me in this, and did you read what they said about me in that, and wasn't I a knock-out in the other thing?" she muttered resentfully. "God, Fritz, to listen to the way they talk you'd think the only reason a play ever gets produced is to give them a chance to strut around and show themselves off upon a stage! When it ought to be the most wonderful thing in the world! Oh, the magic you can make, the things you can do with people if you want to! It's like nothing else on earth!" she cried. "Isn't it a shame no more is done with it?"

She was silent for a moment, sunk in her own thoughts, then she said wearily:

"Well, I'm glad this job's at an end. I wish there was something else I could do. If I only knew how to do something else, I'd do it. Really, I would," she said earnestly. "I'm tired of it. I'm too good for it," she said simply, and for a moment she stared moodily into space.

Then, frowing in a somber and perturbed way, she fumbled in a wooden box upon the desk, took from it a cigarette, and lighted it. She got up nervously and began to walk about the room with short steps, frowning intently while she puffed at the cigarette, and holding it in the rather clumsy but charming manner of a woman who rarely smokes.

"I wonder if I'll get any more shows to do next season," she muttered half to herself, as if scarcely aware of her husband's presence. "I wonder if there'll be anything more for me. No one has spoken to me yet," she said gloomily.

"Well, if you're so tired of it, *I* shouldn't think you'd care," he

149

said ironically, and then added: "Why worry about it till the time comes?"

With that he stooped and planted another friendly and perfunctory kiss on her cheek, gave her shoulder a gentle little pat, and turned and left the room.

Chapter Twelve

Downtown

Mr. Jack had listened to his wife's complaint with the serious attention which stories of her labors, trials, and adventures in the theatre always aroused in him. For, in addition to the immense pride which he took in his wife's talent and success, he was like most rich men of his race, and particularly those who were living every day, as he was, in the glamorous, unreal, and fantastic world of speculation, strongly attracted by the glitter of the theatre.

The progress of his career during the forty years since he first came to New York had been away from the quieter, more traditional, and, as it now seemed to him, duller forms of social and domestic life, to those forms which were more brilliant and gay, filled with the constant excitement of new pleasures and sensations, and touched with a spice of uncertainty and menace. The life of his boyhood—that of his family, who for a hundred years had carried on a private banking business in a little town—now seemed to him impossibly stodgy. Not only its domestic and social activities, which went on as steadily and predictably as a clock from year to year, marked at punctual intervals by a ritual of dutiful visits and countervisits among relatives, but its business enterprise also, with its small and cautious transactions, now seemed paltry and uninteresting.

In New York he had moved on from speed to speed and from height to height, keeping pace with all the most magnificent developments in the furious city that roared in constantly increasing crescendo about him. Now, even in the world in which he lived by day, the feverish air of which he breathed into his lungs exultantly, there was a glittering, inflamed quality that was not unlike that of the nighttime world of the theatre in which the actors lived.

At nine o'clock in the morning of every working day, Mr. Jack was hurled downtown to his office in a shining projectile of machinery, driven by a chauffeur who was a literal embodiment of New York in one of its most familiar aspects. As the driver prowled above his wheel, his dark and sallow face twisted bitterly by the sneer of his thin mouth, his dark eyes shining with an unnatural luster like those of a man who is under the stimulation of a powerful drug, he seemed to be—and was—a creature which this furious city had created for its special uses. His tallowy flesh seemed to have been compacted, like that of millions of other men who wore grey hats and had faces of the same lifeless hue, out of a common city-substance—the universal grey stuff of pavements, buildings, towers, tunnels, and bridges. In his veins there seemed to flow and throb, instead of blood, the crackling electric current by which the whole city moved. It was legible in every act and gesture the man made. As his sinister figure prowled above the wheel, his eyes darting right and left, his hands guiding the powerful machine with skill and precision, grazing, cutting, flanking, shifting, insinuating, sneaking, and shooting the great car through all but impossible channels with murderous recklessness, it was evident that the unwholesome chemistry that raced in him was consonant with the great energy that was pulsing through all the arteries of the city.

Yet, to be driven downtown by this creature in this way seemed to increase Mr. Jack's anticipation and pleasure in the day's work that lay before him. He liked to sit beside his driver and watch him. The fellow's eyes were now sly and cunning as a cat's, now hard and black as basalt. His thin face pivoted swiftly right and left, now leering with crafty triumph as he snaked his car ahead around some cursing rival, now from the twisted corner of his mouth snarling out his hate loudly at other drivers or at careless pedestrians: "Guh-wan, ya screwy bast-ed! Guh-*wan*!" He would growl more softly at the menacing figure of some hated policeman, or would speak to his master out of the corner of his bitter mouth, saying a few words of grudging praise for some policeman who had granted him privileges:

"Some of dem are all right," he would say. "*You* know!"—with a constricted accent of his high, strained voice. "Dey're not all basteds. Dis guy—" with a jerk of his head toward the policeman who had nodded and let him pass—"dis guy's all right. I know him—sure! sure!—he's a bruddeh of me sisteh-in-law!"

The unnatural and unwholesome energy of his driver evoked in his master's mind an image of the world he lived in that was theatrical and phantasmal. Instead of seeing himself as one man going to his work like countless others in the practical and homely light of day, he saw himself and his driver as two cunning and powerful men pitted triumphantly against the world; and the monstrous architecture of the city, the phantasmagoric chaos of its traffic, the web of the streets swarming with people, became for him nothing more than a tremendous backdrop for his own activities. All of this—the sense of menace, conflict, cunning, power, stealth, and victory, and, above everything else, the sense of privilege—added to Mr. Jack's pleasure, and even gave him a heady joy as he rode downtown to work.

And the feverish world of speculation in which he worked, and which had now come to have this theatrical cast and color, was everywhere sustained by this same sense of privilege. It was the privilege of men selected from the common run because of some mysterious intuition they were supposed to have—selected to live gloriously without labor or production, their profits mounting incredibly with every ticking of the clock, their wealth increased fabulously by a mere nod of the head or the lifting of a finger. This being so, it seemed to Mr. Jack, and, indeed, to many others at the time—for many who were not themselves members of this fortunate class envied those who were—it seemed, then, not only entirely reasonable but even natural that the whole structure of society from top to bottom should be honeycombed with privilege and dishonesty.

Mr. Jack knew, for example, that one of his chauffeurs swindled him constantly. He knew that every bill for gasoline, oil, tires, and overhauling was padded, that the chauffeur was in collusion with the garage owner for this purpose, and that he received a handsome percentage from him as a reward. Yet this knowledge did not disturb Mr. Jack. He actually got from it a degree of cynical amusement. Well aware of what was going on, he also knew that he could afford it, and somehow this gave him a sense of power and security. If he ever entertained any other attitude, it was to shrug his shoulders indifferently as he thought:

"Well, what of it? There's nothing to be done about it. They all do it. If it wasn't this fellow, it would be someone else."

Similarly, he knew that some of the maids in his household were not above "borrowing" things and "forgetting" to return them. He was aware that various members of the police force as well as several red-necked firemen spent most of their hours of ease in his kitchen or in the maids' sitting room. He also knew that these guardians of the public peace and safety ate royally every night of the choicest dishes of his own table, and that their wants were cared for even before his family and his guests were served, and that his best whiskey and his rarest wines were theirs for the taking.

But beyond an occasional burst of annoyance when he discovered that a case of real Irish whiskey (with rusty sea-stained markings on the bottles to prove genuineness) had

152

melted away almost overnight, a loss which roused his temper only because of the rareness of the thing lost, he said very little. When his wife spoke to him about such matters, as she occasionally did, in a tone of vague protest, saying: "Fritz, I'm sure those girls are taking things they have no right to. I think it's perfectly dreadful, don't you? What do you think we ought to do about it?"—his usual answer was to smile tolerantly, shrug, and show his palms.

It cost him a great deal of money to keep his family provided with shelter, clothing, service, food, and entertainment, but the fact that a considerable part of it was wasted or actually filched from him by his retainers caused him no distress whatever. All of this was so much of a piece with what went on every day in big business and high finance that he hardly gave it a thought. And his indifference was not the bravado of a man who felt that his world was trembling on the brink of certain ruin and who was recklessly making merry while he waited for the collapse. Quite the contrary. He gave tolerant consent to the extravagance and special privilege of those who were dependent on his bounty, not because he doubted, but because he felt secure. He was convinced that the fabric of his world was woven from threads of steel, and that the towering pyramid of speculation would not only endure, but would grow constantly greater. Therefore the defections of his servants were mere peccadillos, and didn't matter.

In all these ways Mr. Frederick Jack was not essentially different from ten thousand other men of his class and position. In that time and place he would have been peculiar if these things had *not* been true of him. For these men were all the victims of an occupational disease—a kind of mass hypnosis that denied to them the evidence of their senses. It was a monstrous and ironic fact that the very men who had created this world in which every value was false and theatrical saw themselves, not as creatures tranced by fatal illusions, but rather as the most knowing, practical, and hard-headed men alive. They did not think of themselves as gamblers, obsessed by their own fictions of speculation, but as brilliant executives of great affairs who at every moment of the day "had their fingers on the pulse of the nation." So when they looked about them and saw everywhere nothing but the myriad shapes of privilege, dishonesty, and self-interest, they were convinced that this was inevitably "the way things are."

It was generally assumed that every man had his price, just as every woman had hers. And if, in any discussion of conduct, it was suggested to one of these hard-headed, practical men that So-and-So had acted as he did for motives other than those of total self-interest and calculating desire, that he had done thus and so because he would rather endure pain himself than cause it to others whom he loved, or was loyal because of loyalty, or could not be bought or sold for no other reason than the integrity of his own character—the answer of the knowing one would be to smile politely but cynically, shrug it off, and say:

"All right. But I thought you were going to be intelligent. Let's talk of something else that we both understand."

Such men could not realize that their own vision of human nature was distorted. They prided themselves on their "hardness" and fortitude and intelligence, which had enabled them to accept so black a picture of the earth with such easy tolerance. It was not until a little later that the real substance of their "hardness" and intelligence was demonstrated to them in terms which they could grasp. When the bubble of their unreal world suddenly exploded before their eyes, many of them were so little capable of facing harsh reality and truth that they blew their brains out or threw themselves from the high windows of their offices into the streets below. And of those who faced it and saw it through, many a one who had been plump, immaculate, and assured now shrank and withered into premature and palsied senility.

All that, however, was still in the future. It was very imminent, but they did not know it, for they had trained themselves to deny the evidence of their senses. In that mid-October of 1929 nothing could exceed their satisfaction and assurance. They looked about them and, like an actor, saw with their eyes that all was false, but since they had schooled themselves to accept falseness as normal and natural, the discovery only enhanced their pleasure in life.

The choicest stories which these men told each other had to do with some facet of human chicanery, treachery, and dishonesty. They delighted to match anecdotes concerning the delightful knaveries of their chauffeurs, maids, cooks, and bootleggers, telling of the way these people cheated them as one would describe the antics of a household pet.

Such stories also had a great success at the dinner table. The ladies would listen with mirth which they made an impressive show of trying to control, and at the conclusion of the tale they would say: "I—think—that—is—simp-ly—price-less!" (uttered slowly and deliberately, as if the humor of the story was almost beyond belief), or: "Isn't it in-cred-ible!" (spoken with a faint rising scream of laughter), or: "Stop! You know he didn't!" (delivered with a ladylike shriek). They used all the fashionable and stereotyped phrases of people "responding" to an "amusing" anecdote, for their lives had become so sterile and savorless that laughter had gone out of them.

Mr. Jack had a story of his own, and he told it so well and so frequently that it went the rounds of all the best dinner tables in New York.

A few years before, when he was still living in the old brownstone house on the West Side, his wife was giving one of the open-house parties which she gave every year to the members of the "group" theatre for which she worked. At the height of the gayety, when the party was in full swing and the actors were swarming through the rooms, gorging themselves to their heart's content on the bountiful food and drink, there was suddenly a great screaming of police sirens in the neighborhood, and the sound of motors driven to their limit and approaching at top speed. The sirens turned into the street, and to the alarm of Mr. Jack and his guests, who now came crowding to the windows, a high-powered truck flanked by two motorcycle policemen pulled up before the house and stopped. Immediately, the two policemen, whom Mr. Jack instantly recognized as friends of his maids, sprang to the ground, and in a moment more, with the assistance of several of their fellows who got out of the truck, they had lifted a great barrel from the truck and were solemnly rolling it across the sidewalk and up the stone steps into the house. This barrel, it turned out, was filled with beer. The police were contributing it to the party, to which they had been invited (for when the Jacks gave a party to their friends, the maids and cooks were also allowed to give a party to the policemen and firemen in the kitchen). Mr. Jack, moved by this act of friendship and generosity on the part of the police, desired to pay them for the trouble and expense the beer had cost them, but one of the policemen said to him:

"Forget about it, boss. It's O.K. I tell you how it is," he then said, lowering his voice to a tone of quiet and confidential intimacy. "Dis stuff don't cost us nuttin', see? Nah!" he vigorously declared. "It's given to us. Sure! It's a commission dey give us," he added delicately, "for seein' dat dere stuff goes troo O.K. See?"

Mr. Jack saw, and he told the story many times. For he was really a good and generous man, and an act like this, even when it came from those who had drunk royally at his expense for years and had consumed the value of a hundred barrels of beer, warmed and delighted him.

Thus, while he could not escape sharing the theatrical and false view of life which was prevalent everywhere about him, he had, along with that, as kind and liberal a spirit as one was likely to meet in the course of a day's journey. Of this there was constant and repeated evidence. He would act instantly to help people in distress, and he did it again and again—for actors down on their luck, for elderly spinsters with schemes for the renovation of the stage that were never profitable, for friends, relatives, and superannuated domestics. In addition to this, he was a loving and indulgent father, lavishing gifts upon his only child with a prodigal hand.

And, strangely, for one who lived among all the constantly shifting visages of a feverish and unstable world, he had always held with tenacious devotion to one of the ancient traditions of his race—a belief in the sacred and inviolable stability of the family. Through this devotion, in spite of the sensational tempo of city life with its menace to every kind of security, he had managed to keep his family together. And this was really the strongest bond which now connected him with his wife. They had long since agreed to live their own individual lives, but they had joined together in a common effort to maintain the unity of their family. And they had succeeded. For this reason and on this ground Mr. Jack respected and had a real affection for his wife.

Such was the well-groomed man who was delivered to his place of business every morning by his speed-drunk and city-hardened chauffeur. And within a hundred yards of the place where he alighted from his car, ten thousand other men much like him in dress and style, in their general beliefs, and even, perhaps, in kindness, mercy, and tolerance, were also descending from their thunderbolts and were moving into another day of legend, smoke, and fury.

Having been set down at their doors, they were shot up in swift elevators to offices in the clouds. There they bought, sold, and traded in an atmosphere fraught with frantic madness. This madness was everywhere about them all day long, and they themselves were aware of it. Oh, yes, they sensed it well enough. Yet they said nothing. For it was one of the qualities of this time that men should see and feel the madness all around them and never mention it—never admit it even to themselves.

Chapter Thirteen

Service Entrance

The great apartment house in which the Jacks lived was not one of those structures which give to the Island of Manhattan its startling and fabulous quality—those cloud-soaring spires whose dizzy vertices and clifflike façades seem to belong to the sky rather than to the earth. These are the special shapes which flash in the mind of a European when he thinks about New York, and which in-bound travelers, looking from a liner's deck, see in all their appalling and inhuman loveliness sustained there lightly on the water. This building was none of these.

It was—just a building. It was not beautiful, certainly, but it was impressive because of its bulk, its squareness, its sheer mass. From the outside, it seemed to be a gigantic cube of city-weathered brick and stone, punctured evenly by its many windows. It filled an entire block, going through from one street to the next.

When one entered it, however, one saw that it had been built in the form of a hollow square about a large central court. This court was laid out in two levels. The lower and middle part was covered with loose gravel, and raised above this level was a terrace for flower beds, with a broad brick pavement flanking it on all four sides. Beyond the walk there was a span of arches which also ran the whole way around the square, giving the place something of the appearance of an enormous cloister. Leading off this cloister at regular intervals were the entrances to the apartments.

The building was so grand, so huge, so solid-seeming, that it gave the impression of having been hewn from the everlasting rock itself. Yet this was not true at all. The mighty edifice was really tubed and hollowed like a giant honeycomb. It was set on monstrous steel stilts, pillared below on vacancy, and sustained on curving arches. Its nerves, bones, and sinews went down below the level of the street to an underworld of storied basements, and below all these, far in the tortured rock, there was the tunnel's depth.

When dwellers in this imperial tenement felt a tremor at their feet, it was only then that they remembered there were trains beneath them—sleek expresses arriving and departing at all hours of the day and night. Then some of them reflected with immense satisfaction on the cleverness with which New York had reversed an order that is fixed and immutable everywhere else in America, and had made it fashionable to live, not merely "beside the tracks," but on top of them.

A little before seven o'clock that October evening, old John, who ran one of the service elevators in the building, came walking slowly along Park Avenue, ready to go on duty for his night's work. He had reached the entrance and was just turning in when he was accosted by a man of thirty or thereabouts who was obviously in a state of vinous dilapidation.

"Say, Bud——"

At the familiar words, uttered in a tone of fawning and yet rather menacing ingratiation, the face of the older man reddened with anger. He quickened his step and tried to move away, but the creature plucked at his sleeve and said in a low voice:

"I was just wonderin' if you could spare a guy a——"

"Na-h!" the old man snapped angrily. "I can't spare you anything! I'm twice your age and I always had to work for everything I got! If you was any good you'd do the same!"

"Oh yeah?" the other jeered, looking at the old man with eyes that had suddenly gone hard and ugly.

"Yeah!" old John snapped back, and then turned and passed through the great arched entrance of the building, feeling that his repartee had been a little inadequate, though it was the best he had been able to manage on the spur of the moment. He was still muttering to himself as he started along the colonnade that led to the south wing.

"What's the matter, Pop?" It was Ed, one of the day elevator men who spoke to him. "Who got your goat?"

"Ah—h," John muttered, still fuming with resentment, "it's these panhandling bums! One of 'em just stopped me outside the building and asked if I could spare a dime! A young fellow no older than you are, tryin' to panhandle from an old man like me! He ought to be ashamed of himself! I told him so, too. I said: 'If you was any good you'd work for it!'"

"Yeah?" said Ed, with mild interest.

"Yeah," said John. "They ought to keep those fellows away from here. They hang around this neighborhood like flies at a molasses barrel. They got no right to bother the kind of people we got here."

There was just a faint trace of mollification in his voice as he spoke of "the kind of people we got here." One felt that on this side reverence lay. "The kind of people we got here" were, at all odds, to be protected and preserved.

"That's the only reason they hang around this place," the old man went on. "They know they can play on the sympathy of the people in this building. Only the other night I saw one of 'em panhandle Mrs. Jack for a dollar. A big fellow, as well and strong as you are! I'd a good notion to tell her not to give him anything! If he wanted work, he could go and get him a job the same as you and me! It's got so it ain't safe for a woman in the house to take the dog around the block. Some greasy bum will be after her before she gets back. If I was the management I'd put a stop to it. A house like this can't afford it. The kind of people we got here don't have to stand for it!"

Having made these pronouncements, so full of outraged

158

propriety and his desire to protect "the kind of people we got here" from further invasions of their trusting sanctity by these cadging frauds, old John, somewhat appeased, went in at the service entrance of the south wing, and in a few minutes he was at his post in the service elevator, ready for the night's work.

John Enborg had been born in Brooklyn more than sixty years before, the son of a Norwegian seaman and an Irish serving-girl. In spite of this mixed parentage, one would have said without hesitation that he was "old stock" American—New England Yankee, most likely. Even his physical structure had taken on those national characteristics which are perhaps the result, partly of weather and geography, partly of tempo, speech, and local custom—a special pattern of the nerves and vital energies wrought out upon the whole framework of flesh and bone, so that, from whatever complex sources they are derived, they are recognized instantly and unmistakably as "American."

In all these ways old John was "American." He had the dry neck—the lean, sinewy, furrowed neck that is engraved so harshly with so much weather. He had the dry face, too, seamed and squeezed of its moisture; the dry mouth, not brutal, certainly, but a little tight and stiff and woodenly inflexible; and the slightly outcropping lower jaw, as if the jarring conflicts in the life around him had hardened the very formations of the bone into this shape of unyielding tenacity. He was not much above the average height, but his whole body had the same stringy leanness of his neck and face, and this made him seem taller. The old man's hands were large and bony, corded with heavy veins, as if he had done much work with them. Even his voice and manner of talking were distinctively "American." His speech was spare, dry, nasal, and semi-articulate. It could have passed with most people as the speech of a Vermonter, although it did not have any pronounced twang. What one noticed about it especially was its Yankee economy and tartness, which seemed to indicate a chronic state of sour temper. But he was very far from being an ill-natured old man, though at times he did appear to be. It was just his way. He had a dry humor and really loved the rough and ready exchange of banter that went on among the younger elevator men around him, but he concealed his softer side behind a mask of shortness and sarcastic denial.

This was evident now as Herbert Anderson came in. Herbert was the night operator of the passenger elevator in the south entrance. He was a chunky, good-natured fellow of twenty-four or five, with two pink, mottled, absurdly fresh spots on his plump cheeks. He had lively and good-humored eyes, and a mass of crinkly brownish hair of which one felt he was rather proud. He was John's special favorite in the whole building, although one might not have gathered this from the exchange that now took place between them.

"Well, what do you say, Pop?" cried Herbert as he entered the service elevator and poked the old man playfully in the ribs. "You haven't seen anything of two blondes yet, have you?"

The faint, dry grin about John Enborg's mouth deepened a little, almost to a stubborn line, as he swung the door to and pulled the lever.

"Ah-h," he said sourly, almost in disgust, "I don't know what you're talkin about!"

The car descended and stopped, and he pulled the door open at the basement floor.

"Sure you do!" Herbert flung back vigorously as he walked over to the line of lockers, peeled off his coat, and began to take off his collar and tie. "You know those two blondes I been tellin' you about, doncha, Pop?" By this time he was peeling the shirt off his muscular shoulders, then he supported himself with one hand against the locker while he stooped to take off his shoe.

"Ah-h," said the old man, sour as before, "you're always tellin' me about something. I don't even pay no attention to it. It goes in one ear and out the other."

"Oh yeah?" said Herbert with a rising, ironical inflection. He bent to unlace his other shoe.

"Yeah," said John drily.

From the beginning the old man's tone had been touched with this note of dry disgust, yet somehow he gave the impression that he was secretly amused by Herbert's chatter. For one thing, he made no move to depart. Instead, he had propped himself against the side of the open elevator door, and, his old arms folded loosely into the sleeves of the worn grey alpaca coat which was his "uniform," he was waiting there with the stubborn little grin around his mouth as if he was enjoying the debate and was willing to prolong it indefinitely.

"So that's the kind of guy you are?" said Herbert, stepping out of his neatly-pressed trousers and arranging them carefully on one of the hangers which he had taken from the locker. He hung the coat over the trousers and buttoned it. "Here I go and get you all fixed up and you run out on me. O.K., Pop." His voice was now shaded with resignation. "I thought you was a real guy, but if you're goin' to walk out on a party after I've gone to all the trouble, I'll have to look for somebody else."

"Oh yeah?" said old John.

"Yeah," said Herbert in the accent proper to this type of repartee. "I had you all doped out for a live number, but I see I picked a dead one."

John let this pass without comment. Herbert stood for a moment in his socks and underwear, stiffening his shoulders, twisting, stretching, bending his arms upward with tense

160

muscular effort, and ending by scratching his head.

"Where's old Organizin' Hank?" Herbert said presently. "Seen him tonight?"

"Who?" said John, looking at him with a somewhat bewildered expression.

"Henry. He wasn't at the door when I come in, and he ain't down here. He's gonna be late."

"Oh!" The word was small but it carried a heavy accent of disapproval. "Say!" The old man waved a gnarled hand stiffly in a downward gesture of dismissal. "That guy's a pain in the neck!" He spoke the words with the dry precision old men have when they try to "keep up with" a younger man by talking unaccustomed slang. "A pain in the neck!" he repeated. "No, I ain't seen him tonight."

"Oh, Hank's all right when you get to know him," said Herbert cheerfully. "You know how a guy is when he gets all burned up about somethin'—he gets too serious about it—he thinks everybody else in the world ought to be like he is. But he's O.K. He's not a bad guy when you get him talkin' about somethin' else."

"Yeah!" cried John suddenly and excitedly, not in agreement, but by way of introduction to something he had just remembered. "You know what he says to me the other day? 'I wonder what all the rich mugs in this house would do,' he says, 'if they had to get down and do a hard day's work for a livin' once in a while.' That's what he says to me! 'And these old bitches'—yeah!" cried John, nodding his head angrily—" 'these old bitches,' he says, 'that I got to help in and out of cars all night long, and can't walk up a flight of stairs by themselves —what if they had to get down on their hands and knees and scrub floors like your mother and my mother did?' That's the way he goes on all the time!" cried John indignantly —"and takin' tips from them—and then talkin' about them like he does!—Nah-h!" John muttered to himself and rapped his fingers on the wall. "I don't like that way of talkin'! If he feels that way, let him get out! I don't like that fellow."

"Oh," said Herbert easily and indifferently, "Hank's not a bad guy, Pop. He don't mean half of it. He's just a grouch."

By this time, with the speed and deftness born of long experience, he was putting on the starched shirt-front which was a part of his uniform on duty, and buttoning the studs. Stooping and squinting in the small mirror that was hung absurdly low on the wall, he said half-absently:

"So you're goin' to run out on me and the two blondes? You can't take it, hunh?"

"Ah-h," said old John with a return to his surly dryness, "you don't know what you're talkin' about. I had more girls in my day than you ever thought of."

161

"Yeah?" said Herbert.

"Yeah," said John. "I had blondes and brunettes and every other kind."

"Never had any red-heads, did you, Pop?" said Herbert, grinning.

"Yeah, I had red-heads, too," said John sourly. "More than you had, anyway."

"Just a rounder, hunh?" said Herbert. "Just an old petticoat-chaser."

"Nah-h, I ain't no rounder or no petticoat-chaser. Hm!" John grunted contemptuously. "I've been a married man for forty years. I got grown-up children older'n you are!"

"Why, you old two-timer!" Herbert exclaimed, and turned on him with mock indignation. "Braggin' to me about your blondes and red-heads, and then boastin' that you're a family man! Why, you——"

"Nah-h," said John, "I never done no such thing. I wasn't talkin' about *now*—but *then*! That's when I had 'em—forty years ago."

"Who?" said Herbert innocently. "Your wife and children?"

"Ah-h," said John disgustedly, "get along with you. You ain't goin' to get *my* goat. I've forgot more about life than you ever heard of, so don't think you're goin' to make a monkey out of me with your smart talk."

"Well, you're makin' a big mistake this time, Pop," said Herbert with an accent of regret. He had drawn on the neat grey trousers of his uniform, adjusted his broad white stock, and now, half squatting before the mirror, he was carefully adjusting the coat about his well-set shoulders. "Wait till you see 'em—these two blondes. I picked one of 'em out just for you."

"Well, you needn't pick out any for me," said John sourly. "I got no time for such foolishness."

At this point Henry, the night doorman, came hurriedly in from the stairway and began rattling the key in his locker door.

"What do you say, pal?" Herbert turned to him and cried boisterously. "I leave it to you. Here I get Pop all dated up with a couple of hot blondes and he runs out on me. Is that treatin' a guy right or not?"

Henry did not answer. His face was hard and white and narrow, his eyes had the look and color of blue agate, and he never smiled. He took off his coat and hung it in the locker.

"Where were you?" he said.

Herbert looked at him, startled.

"Where was I *when*?" he said.

"Last night."

"That was my night off," said Herbert.

"It wasn't *our* night off," said Henry. "We had a meetin'.

162

They was askin' about you." He turned and directed his cold eyes toward the old man. "And you, too," he said in a hard tone. "You didn't show up either."

Old John's face had frozen. He had shifted his position and begun to drum nervously and impatiently with his old fingers upon the side of the elevator. This quick, annoyed tapping betrayed his tension, but his eyes were flinty as he returned Henry's look, and there was no mistaking his dislike of the doorman. Theirs was, in fact, the mutual hostility that is instinctive to two opposite types of personality.

"Oh yeah?" John said in a hard voice.

Henry answered briefly: "Yeah." And then, holding his cold look leveled like a pointed pistol, he said: "You come to the union meetin's like everybody else, see? Or you'll get bounced out. You may be an old man, but that goes for you like it does for all the rest."

"Is that so?" said John sarcastically.

"Yeah, that's so." His tone was flat and final.

"Jesus!" Herbert's face was red with crestfallen embarrassment, and he stammered out an excuse. "I forgot all about it—honest I did! I was just goin'——"

"Well, you're not supposed to forget," said Henry harshly, and he looked at Herbert with an accusing eye.

"I—I'm all up on my dues," said Herbert feebly.

"That ain't the question. We ain't talkin' about dues." For the first time there was indignant passion in the hard voice as he went on earnestly: "Where the hell do you suppose we'd be if everybody ran out on us every time we hold a meetin'? What's the use of anything if we ain't goin' to stick together?"

He was silent now, looking almost sullenly at Herbert, whose red face had the hang-dog air of a guilty schoolboy. But when Henry spoke again his tone was gentler and more casual, and somehow it suggested that underneath his hard exterior he had a genuine affection for his errant comrade.

"I guess it's O.K. this time," he said quietly. "I told the guys you had a cold and I'd get you there next time."

He said nothing more, and began swiftly to take off his clothes.

Herbert looked flustered but relieved. For a moment he seemed about to speak, but changed his mind. He stooped and took a final appraising look at himself in the small mirror, and then, walking quickly toward the elevator with a return of his former buoyancy, he said:

"Well, Pop, O.K.—let's go!" He took his place in the car and went on with a simulation of regret: "Too bad you're goin' to miss out on the blondes, Pop. But maybe you'll change your mind when you get a look at 'em."

"No, I won't change my mind, either," said John with sour

implacability as he slammed the door. "About them or about you."

Herbert looked at the old man and laughed, the pink spots in his cheeks flushed with good humor, his lively eyes dancing.

"So that's the kind of guy you think I am?" he said, and gently poked the old fellow in the ribs with his closed fist. "So you don't believe me, hunh?"

"Ah-h, I wouldn't believe you on a stack of bibles," said John grouchily. He pushed the lever forward and the elevator started up. "You're a lot of talk—that's what you are. I don't listen to anything you say." He stopped the elevator and opened the heavy door.

"So that's the kind of friend you are?" said Herbert, stepping out into the corridor. Full of himself, full of delight with his own humor, he winked at two pretty, rosy-cheeked Irish maids who were waiting to go up, and, jerking his thumb toward the old man, he said: "What are you goin' to do with a guy like this, anyway? I go and get him all dated up with a blonde and he won't believe me when I tell him so. He calls me a big wind."

"Yeah, that's what he is," said the old man grimly to the smiling girls. "He's a lot of wind. He's always talkin' about his girls and I bet he never had a girl in his life. If he saw a blonde he'd run like a rabbit."

"Just a pal!" said Herbert with mock bitterness, appealing to the maids. "O.K., then, Pop. Have it your own way. But when those blondes get here, tell 'em to wait till I come back. You hear?"

"Well, you'd better not be bringin' any of 'em around here," said John. He shook his white head doggedly and his whole manner was belligerent, but it was evident that he was enjoying himself hugely. "I don't want any of 'em comin' in this building—blondes or brunettes or red-heads or any of 'em," he muttered. "If they do, you won't find 'em when you come back. I'll tell 'em to get out. I'll handle 'em for you, all right."

"*He's* a friend of mine!" said Herbert bitterly to the two girls, and jerked his thumb toward the old man again. He started to walk away.

"I don't believe you, anyhow," John called after his retreating figure. "You ain't got no blondes. You never did have. . . . You're a momma's boy!" he cried triumphantly as an afterthought, as if he had now hit upon the happiest inspiration of the evening. "That's what you are!"

Herbert paused at the door leading into the main corridor and looked back menacingly at the old man, but the look was belied by the sparkle in his eyes.

"Oh yeah?" he shouted.

He stood and glared fiercely at the old fellow for a moment, then winked at the two girls, passed through the door, and

164

pressed the button of the passenger elevator, whose operator he was to relieve for the night.

"That fellow's just a lot of talk," said John sourly as the maids stepped into the service car and he closed the door. "Always gassin' about the blondes he's goin' to bring around—but I ain't never seen none of 'em. Nah-h!" he muttered scornfully, almost to himself as the car started up. "He lives with his mother up in the Bronx, and he'd be scared stiff if a girl ever looked at him."

"Still, Herbert ought to have a girl," one of the maids said in a practical tone of voice. "Herbert's a nice boy, John."

"Oh, he's all right, I guess," the old man muttered grudgingly.

"And a nice-looking boy, too," the other maid now said.

"Oh, he'll do," said John; and then abruptly: "What are you folks doin' tonight, anyway? There's a whole lot of packages waitin' to come up."

"Mrs. Jack is having a big party," one of the girls said. "And, John, will you bring everything up as soon as you can? There may be something there that we need right away."

"Well," he said in that half-belligerent, half-unwilling tone that was an inverted attribute of his real good nature, "I'll do the best I can. Seems like all of them are givin' their big parties tonight," he grumbled. "It goes on sometimes here till two or three o'clock in the morning. You'd think all some people had to do was give parties all the time. It'd take a whole regiment of men just to carry up the packages. Yeah!" he muttered to himself. "And what d'you get? If you ever got so much as a word of thanks——"

"Oh, John," one of the girls now said reproachfully, "you know Mrs. Jack is not like that! You know yourself——"

"Oh, she's all right, I reckon," said John, unwillingly as before, yet his tone had softened imperceptibly. "If all of them was like her," he began—but then the memory of the panhandler came back to him, and he went on angrily: "She's too kind-hearted for her own good! Them panhandling bums—they swarm around her like flies every time she leaves the building. I saw one the other night get a dollar out of her before she'd gone twenty feet. She's crazy to put up with it. I'm goin' to tell her so, too, when I see her!"

The old man's face was flushed with outrage at the memory. He had opened the door on the service landing, and now, as the girls stepped out, he muttered to himself again:

"The kind of people we got here oughtn't to have to put up with it. . . . Well, then, I'll see," he said concedingly, as one of the maids unlocked the service door and went in. "I'll get the stuff up to you."

For a second or two after the inner door had closed behind the maids, the old man stood there looking at it—just a dull, blank sheet of painted metal with the apartment number on it—and his glance, had anyone seen it, would somehow have conveyed an impression of affectionate regard. Then he closed the elevator door and started down.

Henry, the doorman, was just coming up the basement stairway as the old man reached the ground floor. Uniformed, ready for his night's work, he passed the service elevator without speaking. John called to him.

"If they try to deliver any packages out front," he said, "you send 'em around here."

Henry turned and looked at the old man unsmilingly, and said curtly: "What?"

"I say," repeated John, raising his voice a trifle shrilly, for the man's habitual air of sullen harshness angered him, "if they try to make any deliveries out front, send 'em back to the service entrance."

Henry continued to look at him without speaking, and the old man added:

"The Jacks are givin' a party tonight. They asked me to get everything up in a hurry. If there are any more deliveries, send 'em back here."

"Why?" said Henry in his flat, expressionless voice, still staring at him.

The question, with its insolent suggestion of defied authority—*someone's* authority, his own, the management's, or the authority of "the kind of people we got here"—infuriated the old man. A wave of anger, hot and choking, welled up in him, and before he could control himself he rasped out:

"Because that's where they ought to come—that's why! Haven't you been workin' around places of this kind long enough to know how to do? Don't you know the kind of people we got here don't want every Tom, Dick, and Harry with a package to deliver runnin' up in the front elevator all the time, mixin' in with all the people in the house?"

"Why?" said Henry with deliberate insolence. "Why don't they?"

"Because," old John shouted, his face now crimson, "if you ain't got sense enough to know that much, you ought to quit and get a job diggin' ditches somewhere! You're bein' paid to know it! That's part of your job as doorman in a house like this! If you ain't got sense enough by now to do what you're supposed to do, you'd better quit—that's why!—and give your job to somebody who knows what it's all about!"

Henry just looked at him with eyes that were as hard and emotionless as two chunks of agate. Then:

"Listen," he said in a toneless voice. "You know what's goin' to happen to you if you don't watch out? You're gettin' old, Pop, and you'd better watch your step. You're goin' to be

166

caught in the street some day worryin' about what's goin' to happen to the people in this place if they have to ride up in the same elevator with a delivery boy. You're goin' to worry about them gettin' contaminated because they got to ride up in the same car with some guy that carries a package. And you know what's goin' to happen to you, Pop? I'll tell you what's goin' to happen. You'll be worryin' about it so much that you ain't goin' to notice where you're going. And you're goin to get hit, see?"

The voice was so unyielding in its toneless savagery that for a moment—just for a moment—the old man felt himself trembling all over. And the voice went on:

"You're goin' to get hit, Pop. And it ain't goin' to be by nothin' small or cheap. It ain't goin' to be by no Ford truck or by no taxicab. You're goin' to get hit by somethin' big and shiny that cost a lot of dough. You'll get hit by at least a Rolls Royce. And I hope it belongs to one of the people in this house. You'll die like any other worm, but I want you to push off knowin' that it was done expensive—by a big Rolls Royce—by one of the people in this house. I just want you to be happy, Pop."

Old John's face was purple. The veins in his forehead stood out like corded ropes. He tried to speak, but no words came. At length, all else having failed him, he managed to choke out the one retort which, in all its infinitely variable modulations, always served perfectly to convey his emotions.

"Oh yeah!" he snarled drily, and this time the words were loaded with implacable and unforgiving hate.

"Yeah!" said Henry tonelessly, and walked off.

Chapter Fourteen

Zero Hour

Mrs. Jack came from her room a little after eight o'clock and walked along the broad hallway that traversed her big apartment from front to rear. Her guests had been invited for half-past eight, but long experience in these matters told her that the party would not be going at full swing until after nine. As she walked along the corridor at a brisk and rapid little step she felt a tense excitement, not unpleasurable, even though it was now sharpened by the tincture of an apprehensive doubt.

Would all be ready? Had she forgotten anything? Had the girls followed her instructions? Or had they slipped up somewhere? Would something now be lacking?

A wrinkled line appeared between her eyes, and unconsciously she began to slip the old ring on and off her finger with a quick movement of her small hand. It was the gesture of an alert and highly able person who had come to have an instinctive mistrust of other people less gifted than herself. There was impatience and some scorn in it, a scorn not born of arrogance or any lack of warm humanity, but one that was inclined to say a trifle sharply: "Yes, yes, I know! I understand all that. There no need telling me that kind of thing. Let's get to the point. What can you do? What have you done? Can I depend on you to do everything that's necessary?" So, as she walked briskly down the hall, thoughts too sharp and quick for definition were darting across the surface of her mind like flicks of light upon a pool.

"I wonder if the girls remembered to do everything I told them," she was thinking. "Oh, Lord! If only Nora hasn't started drinking again!— And Janie! She's good as gold, of course, but God, she *is* a fool!— And Cookie! Well, she can cook, but after that she doesn't know April from July. And if you try to tell her anything she gets flustered and begins to gargle German at you. Then it's worse than if you'd never spoken to her at all.— As for May—well, all you can do is to hope and pray." The line between her troubled eyes deepened, and the ring slipped on and off her finger more rapidly than ever. "You'd think they'd realize how well off they are, and what a good life they lead here! You'd think they'd try to show it!" she thought indignantly. But almost instantly she was touched with a feeling of tender commiseration, and her mind veered back into its more usual channel: "Oh, well, poor things! I suppose they do the best they can. All you can do is to reconcile yourself to it—and realize that the only way you can get anything done right is to do it yourself."

By this time she had reached the entrance to the living room and was looking quickly about, assuring herself by a moment's swift inspection that everything was in its proper place. Her examination pleased her. The worried expression about her eyes began to disappear. She slipped the ring back on her hand and let it stay there, and her face began to take on the satisfied look of a child when it regards in silence some object of its love and self-creation and finds it good.

The big room was ready for the party. It was just quietly the way she always liked to have it. The room was so nobly proportioned as to be almost regal, and yet it was so subtly toned by the labor of her faultless taste that whatever forbidding coldness its essential grandeur may have had was utterly

168

subdued. To a stranger this living room would have seemed not only homelike in its comfortable simplicity, but even, on closer inspection, a trifle shabby. Almost everything in it was somewhat worn. The coverings of some of the chairs and couches had become in places threadbare. The carpet that covered the floor with its pattern of old, faded green showed long use without apology. An antique gate-legged table sagged a little under the weight of its pleasant shaded lamp and its stacks of books and magazines. Upon the mantel, a creamy slab of marble, itself a little stained and worn, was spread a green and faded strip of Chinese silk, and on top of it was a lovely little figure in green jade, its carved fingers lifted in a Chinese attitude of compassionating mercy. Over the mantel hung a portrait of herself in her young loveliness at twenty, which a painter now dead and famous had made long ago.

On three sides of the room, bookshelves extended a third of the way up the walls, and they were crowded with friendly volumes whose backs bore the markings of warm human hands. Obviously they had been read and read again. The stiff sets of tooled and costly bindings that often ornament the libraries of the rich with unread awe were lacking here. Nor was there any evidence of the greedy and revolting mania of the professional collector. If there were first editions on these utilitarian shelves, they were here because their owner had bought them when they were published, and bought them to be read.

The crackling pine logs on the great marble hearth cast their radiance warmly on the covers of these worn books, and Mrs. Jack had a sense of peace and comfort as she looked at the rich and homely compact of their colors. She saw her favorite novels and histories, plays, poems, and biographies, and the great books of decoration and design, of painting, drawing, and architecture, which she had assembled in a crowded lifetime of work, travel, and living. Indeed, all these objects, these chairs and tables, these jades and silks, all the drawings and paintings, as well as the books, had been brought together at different times and places and fused into a miracle of harmony by the instinctive touch of this woman's hand. It is no wonder, therefore, that her face softened and took on an added glow of loveliness as she looked at her fine room. The like of it, as she well knew, could nowhere else be found.

"Ah, here it is," she thought. "It is living like a part of me. And God! How beautiful it is!" she thought. "How warm—how true! It's not like a rented place—not just another room in an apartment. No—" she glanced down the spacious width of the long hall—"if it weren't for the elevator there, you'd think it was some grand old house. I don't know—but—" a little furrow, this time of reflectiveness and effort, came between her eyes as she tried to shape her meaning—"there's something sort

169

of grand—and simple—about it all."

And indeed there was. The amount of simplicity that could be purchased even in those times for a yearly rental of fifteen thousand dollars was quite considerable. As if this very thought had found an echo in her mind, she went on:

"I mean when you compare it with some of these places that you see nowadays—some of the God-awful places where all those rich people live. There's simply no comparison! I don't care how rich they are, there's—there's just something here that money cannot buy."

As her mind phrased the accusing words about "the God-awful places where all those rich people live," her nostrils twitched and her face took on an expression of sharp scorn. For Mrs. Jack had always been contemptuous of wealth. Though she was the wife of a rich man and had not known for years the economic necessity of work, yet it was one of her unshakable convictions that she and her family could not possibly be described as "rich." "Oh, not *really*," she would say. "Not the way people are who really *are*." And she would look for confirmation, not at the hundred and thirty million people there impossibly below her in the world's hard groove, but at the fabulous ten thousand who were above her on the moneyed heights, and who, by the comparison, were "really rich."

Besides, she was "a worker." She had always been "a worker." One look at the strength, the grace, the swiftness of those small, sure hands was enough to tell the story of their owner's life, which had always been a life of work. From that accomplishment stemmed deep pride and the fundamental integrity of her soul. She had needed the benefit of no man's purse, the succor of no man's shielding strength. "Is not my help within me?" Well, hers *was*. She had made her own way. She had supported herself. She had created beautiful and enduring things. She had never known the meaning of laziness. Therefore it is no wonder that she never thought of herself as being "rich." She was a worker; she had worked.

But now, satisfied with her inspection of the big room, she turned quickly to investigate other things. The living room gave on the dining room through glass doors, which were closed and curtained filmily. Mrs. Jack moved toward them and threw them open. Then she stopped short, and one hand flew to her bosom. She gasped out an involuntary little "Oh!" of wonder and delight. It was too beautiful! It was quite too beautiful! But it was just the way she expected it to look—the way it looked for all of her parties. None the less, every time she saw it, it was like a grand and new discovery.

Everything had been arranged to perfection. The great dining table glowed faultlessly, like a single sheet of walnut light. In its center, on a doily of thick lace, stood a large and handsome bowl blossoming with a fragrant harvest of cut flowers. At the four corners, in orderly array, there were big stacks of Dresden plates and gleaming rows of old and heavy English silver, knives and forks and spoons. The ancient Italian chairs had been drawn away and placed against the walls. This was to be a buffet supper. The guests could come and help themselves according to their taste, and on that noble table was everything to tempt even the most jaded palate.

Upon an enormous silver trencher at one end there was a mighty roast of beef, crisply browned all over. It had just been "begun on" at one side, for a few slices had been carved away to leave the sound, rare body of the roast open to the inspection of anyone who might be attracted by its juicy succulence. At the opposite end, upon another enormous trencher, and similarly carved, was a whole Virginia Ham, sugar-cured and baked and stuck all over with pungent cloves. In between and all around was a staggering variety of mouth-watering delicacies. There were great bowls of mixed green salads, and others of chicken salad, crab meat, and the pink, milky firmness of lobster claws, removed whole and perfect from their shells. There were platters containing golden slabs of smoked salmon, the most rare and delicate that money could buy. There were dishes piled with caviar, both black and red, and countless others loaded with *hors d'oeuvres*—with mushrooms, herring, anchovies, sardines, and small, toothsome artichokes, with pickled onions and with pickled beets, with sliced tomatoes and with deviled eggs, with walnuts, almonds, and pecans, with olives and with celery. In short, there was almost everything that anyone could desire.

It was a gargantuan banquet. It was like some great vision of a feast that has been made immortal in legendry. Few "rich" people would have dared venture on a "supper" such as this of Mrs. Jack's, and in this fear of venturing they would have been justified. Only Mrs. Jack could do a thing like this; only she could do it right. And that is why her parties were famous, and why everyone who had been invited always came. For, strange to tell, there was nowhere on that lavish board a suggestion of disorder or excess. That table was a miracle of planning and of right design. Just as no one could look at it and possibly want anything to be added, so could no one here have felt that there was a single thing too much.

And everywhere in that great dining room, with its simplicity and strength, there was evident this same faultless taste, this same style that never seemed to be contrived, that was so casual and so gracious and so right. At one side the great buffet glittered with an array of flasks, decanters, bottle, syphons, and tall glasses, thin as shells. Elsewhere, two lovely Colonial cupboards stood like Graces with their splendid wares of china and of porcelain, of cut-glass and of silver, of grand old plates and cups

171

and saucers, tureens and bowls, jars and pitchers.

After a quick, satisfied appraisal of everything, Mrs. Jack walked rapidly across the room and through the swinging door that led to the pantry and the kitchen and the servants' quarters. As she approached, she could hear the laughter and excited voices of the maids, broken by the gutturally mixed phrases of the cook. She burst upon a scene of busy order and of readiness. The big, tiled kitchen was as clean and spotless as a hospital laboratory. The great range with its marvelous hood, itself as large as those one sees in a big restaurant, looked as if it had been freshly scrubbed and oiled and polished. The vast company of copper cooking vessels—the skillets and kettles, the pots and pans of every size and shape, from those just large enough to hold an egg to those so huge it seemed that one might cook in them the rations of a regiment—had been scoured and rubbed until Mrs. Jack could see her face in them. The big table in the center of the room was white enough to have served in a surgeon's office, and the shelves, drawers, cupboards, and bins looked as if they had just been gone over with sandpaper. Above the voices of the girls brooded the curiously quiet, intent, dynamic hum of the mammoth electric refrigerator, which in its white splendor was like a jewel.

"Oh, this!" thought Mrs. Jack. "This is quite the most perfect thing of all! This is the best room in the house! I love the others—but is there anything in the world so grand and beautiful as a fine kitchen? And how Cookie keeps the place! If I could only paint it! But no—it would take a Breughel to do it! There's no one nowadays to do it justice——"

"Oh, Cookie!" Now she spoke the words aloud. "What a lovely cake!"

Cook looked up from the great layer cake on the table to which she had been adding the last prayerful tracery of frosted icing, and a faint smile illuminated the gaunt, blunt surface of her Germanic face.

"You like him, yes?" said Cook. "You think he is nice?"

"Oh, Cook!" cried Mrs. Jack in a tone of such childlike earnestness that Cook smiled this time a little more broadly than before. "It is the most *beautiful*—the most *wonderful*—!" She turned away with a comical shrug of despair as if words failed her.

Cook laughed gutturally with satisfaction, and Nora, smiling, said:

"Yes, Mrs. Jack, that it is! It's just what I was after tellin' her meself."

Mrs. Jack glanced swiftly at Nora and saw with relief that she was clean and plain and sober. Thank heaven she had pulled herself together! She hadn't taken another drink since morning—that was easy to see. Drink worked on her like poison, and you could tell the moment that she'd had a single one.

Janie and May, passing back and forth between the kitchen and the maids' sitting room in their trim, crisp uniforms and with their smiling, pink faces, were really awfully pretty. Everything had turned out perfectly, better than she could possibly have expected. Nothing had been forgotten. Everything was in readiness. It ought to be a glorious party.

At this moment the buzzer sounded sharply. Mrs. Jack looked startled and said quickly:

"The door bell rang, Janie." Then, almost to herself: "Now who do you suppose——?"

"Yes'm," said Janie, coming to the door of the maids' sitting room. "I'll go, Mrs. Jack."

"Yes, you'd better, Janie. I wonder who——" she cast a puzzled look up at the clock on the wall, and then at the little shell of platinum on her wrist. "It's only eight-fifteen! I don't think any of them would be this early. Oh!——" as illumination came—"I think, perhaps, it's Mr. Logan. If it is, Janie, show him in. I'll be right out."

"Yes, Mrs. Jack," said Janie, and departed.

And Mrs. Jack, after another quick look about the kitchen, another smile of thanks and approbation for Cookie and her arts, followed her.

It was Mr. Logan. Mrs. Jack encountered him in the entrance hall where he had just paused to set down two enormous black suitcases, each of which, from the bulging look of them, carried enough weight to strain strong muscles. Mr. Logan's own appearance confirmed this impression. He had seized the biceps of one muscular arm with the fingers of his other hand, and with a rueful look upon his face was engaged in flexing the aching member up and down. As Mrs. Jack approached he turned, a thickset, rather burly-looking young man of about thirty, with bushy eyebrows of a reddish cast, a round and heavy face smudged ruddily with the shaven grain of his beard, a low, corrugated forehead, and a bald head gleaming with perspiration, which he proceeded to mop with his handkerchief.

"Gosh!" said Mr. Piggy Logan, for by this affectionate title was he known to his more intimate acquaintance. "Gosh!"—the expletive came out again, somewhat windy with relief. At the same time he released his aching arm and offered his hostess a muscular and stubby hand, covered thickly on the back up to the very fingernails with large freckles.

"You must be simply dead!" cried Mrs. Jack. "Why didn't

173

you let me know you had so much to carry? I'd have sent a chauffeur. He could have handled everything for you."

"Oh, it's quite all right," said Piggy Logan. "I always manage everything myself. You see, I carry all of it right here—my whole equipment." He indicated the two ponderous cases. "That's it," he said, "everything I use—the whole show. So naturally," he smiled at her quickly and quite boyishly, "I don't like to take any chances. It's all I've got. If anything went wrong—well, I'd just rather do it myself and then I know where I am."

"I know," said Mrs. Jack, nodding her head with quick understanding. "You simply can't depend on others. If anything went wrong—and after all the years you must have put in making them! People who've seen it say it's simply marvelous," she went on. "Everyone is so thrilled to know you're going to be here. We've heard so much about it—really all you hear around New York these days is——"

"Now—" said Mr. Logan abruptly, in a manner that was still courteous but that indicated he was no longer paying any attention to her. He had become all business, and now he walked over to the entrance of the living room and was looking all about with thoughtful speculation. "I suppose it's going to be in here, isn't it?" he said.

"Yes—that is, if you like it here. If you prefer, we'll use another room, but this is the largest one we have."

"No, thank you," crisply, absently. "This is quite all right. This will do very nicely. . . . Hm!" meditatively, as he pressed his full lower lip between two freckled fingers. "Best place, I should think, would be over there," he indicated the opposite wall, "facing the door here, the people all around on the other three sides. . . . Hm! Yes. . . . Just about the center there, I should think, posters on the bookshelves. . . . We can clear all this stuff away, of course," he made a quick but expansive gesture with his hand which seemed to dispose of a large part of the furnishings. "Yes! That ought to do it very well! . . . Now, if you don't mind," he turned to her rather peremptorily and said, "I'll have to change to costume. If you have a room——"

"Oh, yes," she answered quickly, "here, just down the hall, the first room on the right. But won't you have a drink and something to eat before you start? You must be terribly——"

"No, thank you," said Mr. Logan crisply. "It's very nice of you," he smiled swiftly under his bushy brows, "but I never take anything before a performance. Now—" he crouched, gripped the handles of the big cases, and heaved mightily—"if you'll just—excuse me," he grunted.

"Is there anything we can do?" Mrs. Jack asked helpfully.

"No—thank you—nothing," Mr. Logan somewhat gruntingly replied, and began to stagger down the hall with his
174

tremendous freight. "I can—get along—quite nicely—thank you," he grunted as he staggered through the door of the room to which she had directed him; and then, more faintly: "Nothing—at all."

She heard the two ponderous bags hit the floor with a leaden thump, and then Mr. Logan's long, expiring "Whush!" of exhausted relief.

For a moment after the young man's lurching departure, his hostess continued to look after him with a somewhat dazed expression, touched faintly with alarm. His businesslike dispatch and the nonchalance with which he had suggested widespread alterations in her beloved room filled her with vague apprehension. But—she shook her head and reassured herself with sharp decision—it was bound to be all right. She had heard so many people speak of him: he was really all the rage this year, everyone was talking of his show, there had been writeups of him everywhere. He was the darling of all the smart society crowd—all those "rich" Long Island and Park Avenue people. Here the lady's nostrils curved again in a faint dilation of patronizing scorn; nevertheless, she could not help feeling a pleasant sense of triumph that she had landed him.

Yes, Mr. Piggy Logan *was* the rage that year. He was the creator of a puppet circus of wire dolls, and the applause with which this curious entertainment had been greeted was astonishing. Not to be able to discuss him and his little dolls intelligently was, in smart circles, akin to never having heard of Jean Cocteau or Surréalism; it was like being completely at a loss when such names as Picasso and Brancusi and Utrillo and Gertrude Stein were mentioned. Mr. Piggy Logan and his art were spoken of with the same animated reverence that the knowing used when they spoke of one of these.

And, like all of these, Mr. Piggy Logan and his art demanded their own vocabulary. To speak of them correctly one must know a language whose subtle nuances were becoming more highly specialized month by month, as each succeeding critic outdid his predecessor and delved deeper into the bewildering complexities, the infinite shadings and associations, of Mr. Piggy Logan and his circus of wire dolls.

True, at the beginning there had been those among the cognoscenti—those happy pioneers who had got in at the very start of Mr. Piggy Logan's vogue—who had characterized his performance as "frightfully amusing." But that was old stuff, and anyone who now dared to qualify Mr. Logan's art with such a paltry adjective as "amusing" was instantly dismissed as

175

a person of no cultural importance. Mr. Logan's circus had ceased to be "amusing" when one of the more sophisticated columnists of the daily press discovered that "not since the early Chaplin has the art of tragic humor through the use of pantomime reached such a faultless elevation."

After this, the procession formed on the right, and each newcomer paid his tribute with a new and more glittering coin. The articles in the daily press were followed by others in all the smarter publications, with eulogistic essays on Mr. Logan and pictures of his little dolls. Then the dramatic critics joined the chorus, and held up the offerings of the current stage to a withering fire of comparative criticism. The leading tragedians of the theatre were instructed to pay special attention to Mr. Logan's clown before they next essayed the rôle of Hamlet.

The solemn discussions broke out everywhere. Two eminent critics engaged in a verbal duel of such adeptive subtlety that in the end it was said there were not more than seven people in the civilized world who could understand the final passages at arms. The central issue of this battle was to establish whether Mr. Piggy Logan, in his development, had been influenced more by the geometric cubism of the early Picasso or by the geometric abstractions of Brancusi. Both schools of thought had their impassioned followers, but it was finally conceded that the Picassos had somewhat the better of it.

One word from Mr. Logan himself might have settled the controversy, but that word was never spoken. Indeed, he said very little about the hubbub he had caused. As more than one critic significantly pointed out, he had "the essential simplicity of the great artist—an almost childlike *naïveté* of speech and gesture that pierces straight to the heart of reality." Even his life, his previous history, resisted investigations of the biographers with the impenetrability of the same baffling simplicity. Or, as another critic clearly phrased it: "As in the life of almost all great men of art, there is little in Logan's early years to indicate his future achievement. Like almost all supremely great men, he developed slowly—and, it might almost be said, unheeded—up to the time when he burst suddenly, like a blazing light, upon the public consciousness."

However that may be, Mr. Piggy Logan's fame was certainly blazing now, and an entire literature in the higher aesthetics had been created about him and his puppets. Critical reputations had been made or ruined by them. The last criterion of fashionable knowingness that year was an expert familiarity with Mr. Logan and his dolls. If one lacked this knowledge, he was lower than the dust. If one had it, his connoisseurship in the arts was definitely established and his eligibility for any society of the higher sensibilities was instantly confirmed.

To a future world—inhabited, no doubt, by a less acute and

understanding race of men—all this may seem a trifle strange. If so, that will be because the world of the future will have forgotten what it was like to live in 1929.

In that sweet year of grace one could admit with utter nonchalance that the late John Milton bored him and was a large "stuffed shirt." "Stuffed shirts," indeed, were numerous in the findings of the critical gentry of the time. The chemises of such inflated personalities as Goethe, Ibsen, Byron, Tolstoy, Whitman, Dickens, and Balzac had been ruthlessly investigated by some of the most fearless intellects of the day and found to be largely filled with straw wadding. Almost everything and everybody was in the process of being debunked—except the debunkers and Mr. Piggy Logan and his dolls.

Life had recently become too short for many things that people had once found time for. Life was simply too short for the perusal of any book longer than two hundred pages. As for *War and Peace*—no doubt all "they" said of it was true—but as for oneself—well, one had tried, and really it was quite too—too—oh, well, life simply was too short. So life that year was far too short to be bothered by Tolstoy, Whitman, Dreiser, or Dean Swift. But life was not too short that year to be passionately concerned with Mr. Piggy Logan and his circus of wire dolls.

The highest intelligences of the time—the very subtlest of the chosen few—were bored by many things. They tilled the waste land, and erosion had grown fashionable. They were bored with love, and they were bored with hate. They were bored with men who worked, and with men who loafed. They were bored with people who created something, and with people who created nothing. They were bored with marriage, and with single blessedness. They were bored with chastity, and they were bored with adultery. They were bored with going abroad, and they were bored with staying at home. They were bored with the great poets of the world, whose great poems they had never read. They were bored with hunger in the streets, with the men who were killed, with the children who starved, and with the injustice, cruelty, and oppression all around them; and they were bored with justice, freedom, and man's right to live. They were bored with living, they were bored with dying, but—they were *not* bored that year with Mr. Piggy Logan and his circus of wire dolls.

And the Cause of all this tumult? The generating Force behind this mighty sensation in the world of art? As one of the critics so aptly said: "It is a great deal more than just a new talent that has started just another 'movement': it is rather a whole new universe of creation, a whirling planet which in its fiery revolutions may be expected to throw off its own sidereal systems." All right; *It*, then—the colossal Genius which had

177

started all this—what was It doing now?

It was now enjoying the privacy of one of the lovely rooms in Mrs. Jack's apartment, and, as if It were utterly unaware of the huge disturbance It had made in the great world, It was calmly, quietly, modestly, prosaically, and matter-of-factly occupied in peeling off Its own trousers and pulling on a pair of canvas pants.

While this momentous happening was taking place, events were moving smoothly to their consummation in other quarters of the house. The swinging door between the dining room and the kitchen domain kept slatting back and forth as the maids passed in and out to make the final preparations for the feast. Janie came through the dining room bearing a great silver tray filled with bottles, decanters, a bowl of ice, and tall, lovely glasses. As she set the tray down upon a table in the living room, the shell-thin glasses chimed together musically, and there was a pleasant jink of bottles and the cold, clean rattle of cracked ice.

Then the girl came over toward the hearth, removed the big brass screen, and knelt before the dancing flames. As she jabbed at the logs with a long brass poker and a pair of tongs there was a shower of fiery sparks, and the fire blazed and crackled with new life. For just a moment she stayed there on her knees in a gesture of sweet maiden grace. The fire cast its radiance across her glowing face, and Mrs. Jack looked at her with a softened glance, thinking how sweet and clean and pretty she was. Then the maid arose and put the screen back in its place.

Mrs. Jack, after arranging anew a vase of long-stemmed roses on a small table in the hall and glancing briefly at herself in the mirror above, turned and walked briskly and happily down the broad, deep-carpeted hallway toward her own room. Her husband was just coming from his room. He was fully dressed for the evening. She looked him over with an expert eye, and saw how well his clothes fit him and how he wore them as if they had grown on him.

His manner, in contrast to hers, was calm and sophisticated, wise and knowing. One knew just to look at him that he took excellent care of himself. Here was a man, one felt, who, if he was experienced in the pleasures of the flesh, knew how far to go, and beyond what point lay chaos, shipwreck, and the reef. His wife, taking all this in with a swift and comprehensive glance that missed nothing, despite her air of half-bewildered innocence, was amazed to see how much he knew, and a little troubled to think that he knew even more, perhaps, than she could see or fathom.

178

"Oh, hello," he said, in a tone of suave courtesy as he bent and kissed her lightly on one cheek.

For just the flick of an instant she was conscious of a feeling of distaste, but then she remembered what a perfect husband he had been, how thoughtful, how good, how devoted, and how, no matter what the unfathomed implications of his eyes might be, he had said nothing—and for all that anyone could prove, had seen nothing. "He's a sweet person," she was thinking as she responded brightly to his greeting:

"Oh, hello, darling. You're all ready, aren't you? . . . Listen—" she spoke rapidly—"will you look out for the bell and take care of anyone who comes? Mr. Logan is changing his costume in the guest room—won't you look out for him if he needs anything? And see if Edith's ready. And when the guests begin to come you can send the women to her room to take off their wraps—oh, just tell Nora—she'll attend to it! And you'll take care of the men yourself—won't you, dear? You can show them back to your room. I'll be out in a few minutes. If only everything—!" she began in a worried tone, slipping the ring quickly from her finger and slipping it back again. "I do hope everything's all right!"

"But *isn't* it?" he said blandly. "Haven't you looked?"

"Oh, everything *looks* perfect!" she cried. "It's really just too beautiful! The girls have behaved wonderfully—only—" the little furrow of nervous tension came between her eyes—"do keep an eye on them, won't you, Fritz? You know how they are if somebody's not around. Something's so likely to go wrong. So please do watch them, won't you, dear? And look out for Mr. Logan. I do hope—" she paused with a look of worried abstraction in her eyes.

"You do hope what?" he said pointedly, with just the suggestion of an ironic grin around the corners of his mouth.

"I do hope he won't—" she began in a troubled tone, then went on rapidly—"He said something about—about clearing away some of the things in the living room for his show." She looked at him rather helplessly; then, catching the irony of his faint grin, she colored quickly and laughed richly. "God! I don't know what he's going to do. He brought enough stuff with him to sink a battleship! . . . Still, I suppose it's going to be all right. Everyone's been after him, you know. Everyone's thrilled at the chance of seeing him. Oh, I'm sure it'll be all right. Don't you think so—hah?"

She looked earnestly at him with an expression of such droll, beseeching inquiry that, unmasked for a moment, he laughed abruptly as he turned away, saying:

"Oh, I suppose so, Esther. I'll look after it."

Mrs. Jack went on down the hall, pausing just perceptibly as she passed her daughter's door. She could hear the girl's voice, clear, cool, and young, humming the jaunty strains of a popular tune:

"You're the cream in my coffee—you're the salt in my stew-w ——"

A little smile of love and tenderness suffused the woman's face as she continued down the hall and entered the next door, which was her own room.

It was a very simple, lovely room, hauntingly chaste, almost needlessly austere. In the center of one wall stood her narrow little wooden bed, so small and plain and old that it seemed it might almost have served as the bed of a mediaeval nun, as perhaps it had. Beside it stood the little table with its few books, a telephone, a glass and a silver pitcher, and in a silver frame a photograph of a girl in her early twenties—Mrs. Jack's daughter, Alma.

Beside the door as one entered there was an enormous old wooden wardrobe, which she had brought from Italy. This contained all her beautiful dresses and her wonderful collection of winglike little shoes, all of them made by hand to fit her perfect little feet. On the opposite wall, facing the door, between two high windows, stood her writing desk. Between the bed and the windows there was a small drawing table. It was a single board of white, perfect wood, and on it, arranged with faultless precision, were a dozen sharpened pencils, a few feathery brushes, some crisp sheets of tracing paper on which geometric designs were legible, a pot of paste, a ruler, and a little jar of golden paint. Exactly above this table, hanging from the wall in all the clean beauty of their strength and accuracy, were a triangle and a square.

At the foot of the bed there was a chaise longue covered with a flowered pattern of old faded silk. There were a few simple drawings on the walls, and a single painting of a strange, exotic flower. It was such a flower as never was, a dream flower which Mrs. Jack had painted long ago.

Along the wall opposite the bed stood two old chests. One of them, a product of the Pennsylvania Dutch, was carved and colored in quaint and cheerful patterns, and this contained old silks and laces and the noble Indian saris which she often loved to wear. The other was an old chest of drawers, with a few silver toilet articles and a square mirror on its top.

Mrs. Jack crossed the room and stood before the mirror looking at herself. First she bent forward a little and stared at her face long and earnestly with an expression of childlike innocence. Then she began to turn about, regarding herself from first one angle, then another. She put her hand up to her temple and smoothed her brow. Obviously she found herself good, for her eyes now took on an expression of rapt complacency. There was open vanity in her look as she brooded with smoldering

180

fascination on the thick bracelet around her arm—a rich and somber chain of ancient India, studded with dull and curious gems. She lifted her chin and looked at her neck, tracing out with her finger tips the design of an old necklace which she wore. She surveyed her smooth arms, her bare back, her gleaming shoulders, and the outlines of her breasts and figure, touching, patting, and half-unconsciously arranging with practiced touches the folds of her simple, splendid gown.

She lifted her arm again and with hand extended, the other hand upon her hip, she turned about once more in her orbit of self-worship. Slowly she turned, still rapt in contemplation of her loveliness, then she gasped suddenly with surprise and fright, and uttered a little scream. Her hand flew to her throat in a gesture of alarm as she realized that she was not alone and, looking up, saw her daughter standing there.

The girl, young, slender, faultless, cold, and lovely, had entered through the bathroom that connected the two rooms, and was standing in the door, having paused there, frozen to immobility as she caught her mother in the act. The mother's face went blood-red. For a long moment the two women looked at each other, the mother utterly confused and crimson with her guilt, the daughter cold and appraising with the irony of sophisticated mirth. Then something quick and instant passed between them in their glance.

Like one who has been discovered and who knows that there is nothing more to say, the mother suddenly threw back her head and laughed, a rich, full-throated, woman's yell of free acknowledgement, unknown to the race of man.

"Well, Mother, was it good?" said the girl, now grinning faintly. She walked over and kissed her.

Again the mother was shaken with her hysteria of helpless laughter. Then both of them, freed from the necessity of argument by that all-taking moment, were calm again.

Thus was enacted the whole tremendous comedy of womankind. No words were needed. There was nothing left to say. All had been said there in that voiceless instant of complete and utter understanding, of mutual recognition and conspiracy. The whole universe of sex had been nakedly revealed for just the flick of a second in all its guile and its overwhelming humor. And the great city roared on unwittingly around that secret cell, and no man in its many millions was any the wiser about this primal force more strong than cities and as old as earth.

Chapter Fifteen

The Party at Jack's

Now the guests were beginning to arrive. The electric thring of the door bell broke sharply and persistently on accustomed quietness. People were coming in and filling the place with the ease and familiarity of old friends. In the hallway and in the rooms at the front there arose now a confused medley of many voices—the rippling laughter and quick, excited tones of the women mingled with the deeper, more vibrant sonorities of the men. It was a mixture smooth as oil, which fused and mouthed steadily. With every sharp ringing of the bell, with every opening and closing of the door, there were new voices and new laughter, a label of new greetings, new gayety, and new welcomes.

The whole place—all the rooms front to back—was now thrown open to the party. In the hall, in the bedrooms, in the great living room, and in the dining room, people were moving in and out, circulating everywhere in beautiful and spontaneous patterns. Women were coming up to Mrs. Jack and embracing her with the affectionate tenderness of old friendship. Men, drawn together in solemn discussion or in the jesting interplay of wit, were going in and out of Mr. Jack's room.

Mrs. Jack, her eyes sparkling with joy, was moving about everywhere, greeting people and stopping to talk to everyone. Her whole manner had a quality of surprised delight, as of a person who feels that wonders will never cease. Although she had invited all these people, she seemed, as she spoke to each in turn, as if she was taken aback by the happiness of an unexpected and unhoped-for encounter with an old friend whom she had not seen for a long time. Her voice, as she talked, grew a trifle higher with its excitement, even at times a little shrill, and her face glowed with pleasure. And her guests smiled at her as people smile at a happy and excited child.

Many were moving about now with glasses in their hands. Some were leaning against walls talking to each other. Distinguished-looking men were propped with their elbows on the mantel in the casual earnestness of debate. Beautiful women with satiny backs were moving through the crowd with velvet undulance. The young people were gathered together in little parties of their own, drawn to one another by the magic of their youth. Everywhere people were laughing and chattering, bending to fill glasses with frosty drinks, or moving around the loaded temptations of the dining table and the great buffet with that "choosy" look, somewhat perturbed and doubtful, which said plainly that they would like to taste it all but knew they couldn't. And the smiling maids were there to do their bidding, and to urge them to have just a little more. All in all, it was a wonderful scene of white and black and gold and power and wealth and loveliness and food and drink.

Mrs. Jack glanced happily through the crowded rooms. It was, she knew, a notable assemblage of the best, the highest, and the fairest the city had to offer. And others were arriving all the time. At this moment, in fact, Miss Lily Mandell came in, and the tall, smoldering beauty swung away along the hall to dispose of her wraps. She was followed almost at once by Mr. Lawrence Hirsch, the banker. He casually gave his coat and hat to one of the maids, and, groomed and faultless, schooled in power, he bowed greetings through the throng toward his hostess. He shook hands with her and kissed her lightly on one cheek, saying with that cool irony that was a portion of the city style:

"You haven't looked so lovely, darling, since the days when we used to dance the cancan together."

Then, polished and imperturbable, he turned away—a striking figure. His abundant hair was prematurely white, and, strangely, it gave to his clear and clean-shaven face a look of almost youthful maturity. His features, a little worn but assured, were vested in unconscious arrogance with the huge authorities of wealth. He moved, this weary, able son of man, among the crowd and took his place, assuming, without knowing he assumed, his full authorities.

Lily Mandell now returned to the big room and made her way languidly toward Mrs. Jack. This heiress of Midas wealth was tall and dark, with a shock of wild black hair. Her face, with its heavy-lidded eyes, was full of pride and sleepy eloquence. She was a stunning woman, and everything about her was a little startling. The dress she wore was a magnificent gown fashioned from a single piece of dull golden cloth, and had been so designed to display her charms that her tall, voluptuous figure seemed literally to have been poured into it. It made her a miracle of statuesque beauty, and as she swayed along with sleepy undulance, the eyes of all the men were turned upon her. She bent over the smaller figure of her hostess, kissed her, and, in a rich, yolky voice full of genuine affection, said:

"Darling, how are you?"

By now, Herbert, the elevator boy, was being kept so busy bringing up new arrivals that one group hardly had time to finish with its greetings before the door would open and a new group would come in. There was Roderick Hale, the distinguished lawyer. Then Miss Roberta Heilprinn arrived with Mr. Samuel Fetzer. These two were old friends of Mrs. Jack's "in the theatre," and her manner toward them, while not more cordial or affectionate than that toward her other guests, was a shade more direct and casual. It was as if one of those masks—not of pretending but of formal custom—which life imposes upon so many human relations had here been sloughed off. She said simply: "Oh, hello, Bertie. Hello, Sam." The shade indefinable told everything: they were "show people"—she and they had "worked together."

There were a good many show people. Two young actors from the Community Guild Theatre escorted the Misses Hattie Warren and Bessie Lane, both of them grey-haired spinsters who were directors of the theatre. And, in addition to the more gifted and distinguished people, there were a number of the lesser fry, too. There was a young girl who was understudy to a dancer at one of the repertory theatres, and another woman who was the seamstress and wardrobe mistress there, and still another who had once been Mrs. Jack's assistant in her own work. For, as success and fame had come to Mrs. Jack, she had not forgotten her old friends. Though she was now a celebrity herself, she had thus escaped the banal and stereotyped existence that so many celebrities achieve. She loved life too well to cut herself off from the common run of warm humanity. In her own youth she had known sorrow, insecurity, hardship, heartbreak, and disillusion, and she had never forgotten it. Nor had she forgotten any of the people her life had ever touched. She had a rare talent for loyal and abiding friendships, and most of the people who were here tonight, even the most famous ones, were friends whom she had known for many years, some of them since childhood.

Among the guests who now came streaming in was a mild, sad-faced woman named Margaret Ettinger. She was married to a profligate husband and had brought him with her. And he, John Ettinger, had brought along a buxom young woman who was his current mistress. This trio provided the most bizarre and unpleasantly disturbing touch to an otherwise distinguished gathering.

The guests were still arriving as fast as the elevator could bring them up. Stephen Hook came in with his sister, Mary, and greeted his hostess by holding out to her a frail, limp hand. At the same time he turned half away from her with an air of exaggerated boredom and indifference, an almost weary disdain, as he murmured:

"Oh, hello, Esther. . . . Look—" he half turned toward her again, almost as if this were an afterthought—"I brought you this." He handed her a book and turned away again. "I thought it was rather interesting," he said in a bored tone. "You might like to look at it."

What he had given her was a magnificent volume of Peter Breughel's drawings—a volume that she knew well, and the cost of which had frightened even her. She looked quickly at the flyleaf and saw that in his fine hand he had written primly: "For Esther—from Stephen Hook." And suddenly she remembered that she had mentioned to him casually, a week or two before, her interest in this book, and she understood now that this act, which in a characteristic way he was trying to conceal under a mask of labored indifference, had come swift and shining as a beam of light out of the depths of the man's fine and generous spirit. Her face burned crimson, something choked her in the throat, and her eyes grew hot with tears.

"Oh, Steve!" she gasped. "This is simply the most beautiful—the most wonderful——"

He seemed fairly to shrink away from her. His white, flabby face took on an expression of disdainful boredom that was so exaggerated it would have seemed comical if it had not been for the look of naked pleading in his hazel eyes. It was the look of a proud, noble, strangely twisted and tormented man—the look almost of a frightened child, who, even while it shrank away from the companionship and security it so desperately needed and wanted, was also pleading pitifully: "For God's sake, help me if you can! I am afraid!"

She saw that look in his eyes as he turned pompously away from her, and it went through her like a knife. In a flash of stabbing pity she felt the wonder, the strangeness, and the miracle of living.

"Oh, you poor tormented creature," she was thinking. "What is wrong with you? What are you afraid of? What's eating on you anyway? . . . What a strange man he is!" she thought more tranquilly. "And how fine and good and high!"

At this moment, as if reading her own thoughts, her daughter, Alma, came to the rescue. Cool, poised, lovely, the girl came across the room, moved up to Hook, and said casually:

"Oh, hello, Steve. Can I get you a drink?"

The question was a godsend. He was extremely fond of the girl. He liked her polished style, her elegance, her friendly yet perfectly impenetrable manner. It gave him just the foil, the kind of protection, that he so desperately needed. He answered her at once.

"What you have to say quite fascinates me," he murmured in a bored tone and moved over to the mantel, where he leaned as spectator and turned his face three-quarters away from the room, as if the sight of so many appallingly dull people was more than he could endure.

The elaborately mannered indirection of his answer was completely characteristic of Stephen Hook, and provided a key to his literary style. He was the author of a great many stories, which he sold to magazines to support himself and his mother, and also of several very fine books. The books had established his considerable and deserved reputation, but they had had almost no sale. As he himself had ironically pointed out, almost everyone, apparently, had read his books and no one had bought them. In these books, just as in his social manner, he tried to mask his shyness and timidity by an air of weary disdain and by the intricate artifice and circumlocution of an elaborately mannered style.

Mr. Jack, after staring rather helplessly at Hook, turned to his sister, a jolly-faced spinster with twinkling eyes and an infectious laugh who shared her brother's charm but lacked his tormented spirit, and whispered:

"What's wrong with Steve tonight? He looks as if he's been seeing ghosts."

"No—just another monster," Mary Hook replied, and laughed. "He had a pimple on his nose last week and he stared at it so much in the mirror that he became convinced it was a tumor. Mother was almost crazy. He locked himself in his room and refused to come out or talk to anyone for days and days. Four days ago he sent her a note leaving minute instructions for his funeral and burial—he has a horror of being cremated. Three days ago he came out in his pajamas and said good-bye to all of us. He said his life was over—all was ended. Tonight he thought better of it and decided to dress and come to your party."

Mary Hook laughed again good-naturedly and, with a humorous shrug and a shake of her head, moved away into the crowd. And Mrs. Jack, still with a rather troubled look on her face, turned to talk to old Jake Abramson, who had been holding her hand and gently stroking it during the last part of this puzzled interlude.

The mark of the fleshpots was plain upon Jake Abramson. He was old, subtle, sensual, weary, and he had the face of a vulture. Curiously enough, it was also a strangely attractive face. It had so much patience in it, and a kind of wise cynicism, and a weary humor. There was something paternal and understanding about him. He looked like an immensely old and tired ambassador of life who had lived so long, and seen so much, and been so many places, that even his evening clothes were as habitual as his breath and hung on him with a weary and accustomed grace as if he had been born in them.

He had taken off his topcoat and his silk hat and given them to the maid, and then had come wearily into the room toward Mrs. Jack. He was evidently very fond of her. While she had been talking to Mary Hook he had remained silent and had brooded above her like a benevolent vulture. He smiled beneath his great nose and kept his eyes intently on her face; then he took her small hand in his weary old clasp and began to stroke her smooth arm. It was a gesture frankly old and sensual, jaded, and yet strangely fatherly and gentle. It was the gesture of a man who had known and possessed many pretty women and who still knew how to admire and appreciate them, but whose stronger passions had now passed over into a paternal benevolence.

And in the same way he now spoke to her.

"You're looking nice!" he said. "You're looking pretty!" He kept smiling vulturesquely at her and stroking her arm. "Just like a rose she is!" the old man said, and never took his weary eyes from her face.

"Oh, Jake!" she cried excitedly and in a surprised tone, as if she had not known before that he was there. "How nice of you to come! I didn't know you were back. I thought you were still in Europe."

"I've been and went," he declared humorously.

"You're looking awfully well, Jake," she said. "The trip did you lots of good. You've lost weight. You took the cure at Carlsbad, didn't you?"

"I didn't take the cure," the old man solemnly declared, "I took the die-ett." Deliberately he mispronounced the word.

Instantly Mrs. Jack's face was suffused with crimson and her shoulders began to shake hysterically. She turned to Roberta Heilprinn, seized her helplessly by the arm, and clung to her, shrieking faintly:

"God! Did you hear him? He's been on a diet! I bet it almost killed him! The way he loves to eat!"

Miss Heilprinn chuckled fruitily and her oil-smooth features widened in such a large grin that her eyes contracted to closed slits.

"I've been die-etting ever since I went away," said Jake. "I was sick when I went away—and I came back on an English boat," the old man said with a melancholy and significant leer

187

that drew a scream of laughter from the two women.

"Oh, Jake!" cried Mrs. Jack hilariously. "How you must have suffered! I know what you used to think of English food!"

"I think the same as I always did," the old man said with resigned sadness—"only ten times more!"

She shrieked again, then gasped out, "Brussels sprouts?"

"They still got 'em," said old Jake solemnly. "They still got the same ones they had ten years ago. I saw Brussels sprouts this last trip that ought to be in the British Museum. . . . And they still got that good fish," he went on with a suggestive leer.

Roberta Heilprinn, her bland features grinning like a Buddha, gurgled: "The Dead Sea fruit?"

"No," said old Jake sadly, "not the Dead Sea fruit—that ain't dead enough. They got boiled flannel now," he said, "and that *good* sauce! . . . You remember that *good* sauce they used to make?" He leered at Mrs. Jack with an air of such insinuation that she was again set off in a fit of shuddering hysteria:

"You mean that awful . . . tasteless . . . pasty . . . *goo* . . . about the color of a dead lemon?"

"You got it," the old man nodded his wise and tired old head in weary agreement. "You got it. . . . That's it. . . . They still make it. . . . So I've been die-etting all the way back!" For the first time his tired old voice showed a trace of animation. "Carlsbad wasn't in it compared to the die-etting I had to do on the English boat!" He paused, then with a glint of cynic humor in his weary eyes, he said: "It was fit for nothing but a bunch of goys!"

This reference to unchosen tribes, with its evocation of humorous contempt, now snapped a connection between these three people, and suddenly one saw them in a new way. The old man was smiling thinly, with a cynical intelligence, and the two women were shaken utterly by a paroxysm of understanding mirth. One saw now that they really were *together*, able, ancient, immensely knowing, and outside the world, regardant, tribal, communitied in derision and contempt for the unhallowed, unsuspecting tribes of lesser men who were not party to their knowing, who were not folded to their seal. It passed—the instant showing of their ancient sign. The women just smiled now, quietly: they were citizens of the world again.

"But Jake! You poor fellow!" Mrs. Jack said sympathetically. "You must have hated it!" Then she cried suddenly and enthusiastically as she remembered: "Isn't Carlsbad just *too* beautiful? . . . Did you know that Bert and I were there one time?" As she uttered these words she slipped her hand affectionately through the arm of her friend, Roberta, then went on vigorously, with a jolly laugh and a merry face: "Didn't I ever tell you about that time, Jake? . . . Really, it was the most wonderful experience! . . . But God!" she laughed almost explosively—"Will you ever forget the first three or four days, Bert?" She appealed to her smiling friend. "Do you remember how hungry we got? How we thought we couldn't possibly hold out? Wasn't it dreadful?" she said, and then went on with a serious and rather puzzled air as she tried to explain it: "But then—I don't know—it's funny—but somehow you get used to it, don't you, Bert? The first few days are pretty awful, but after that you don't seem to mind. I guess you get too weak, or something. . . . I know Bert and I stayed in bed three weeks—and really it wasn't bad after the first few days." She laughed suddenly, richly. "We used to try to torture each other by making up enormous menus of the most delicious food we knew. We had it all planned out to go to a swell restaurant the moment our cure was over and order the biggest meal we could think of! . . . Well!" she laughed—"would you believe it?—the day the cure was finished and the doctor told us it would be all right for us to get up and eat—I know we both lay there for hours thinking of all the things we were going to have. It was simply wonderful!" she said, laughing and making a fine little movement with her finger and her thumb to indicate great delicacy, her voice squeaking like a child's and her eyes wrinkling up to dancing points. "In all your life you never heard of such delicious food as Bert and I were going to devour! We resolved to do everything in the greatest style! . . . Well, at last we got up and dressed. And God!" she cried. "We were so weak we could hardly stand up, but we wore the prettiest clothes we had, and we had chartered a Rolls Royce for the occasion and a chauffeur in livery! In all your *days*," she cried with her eyes twinkling, "you've never seen such swank! We got into the car and were driven away like a couple of queens. We told the man to drive us to the swellest, most expensive restaurant he knew. He took us to a beautiful place outside of town. It looked like a chateau!" She beamed rosily around her. "And when they saw us coming they must have thought we were royalty from the way they acted. The flunkies were lined up, bowing and scraping, for half a block. Oh, it was thrilling! Everything we'd gone through and endured in taking the cure seemed worth it. . . . Well!" she looked around her and the breath left her body audibly in a sigh of complete frustration—"would you believe it?—when we got in there and tried to eat we could hardly swallow a bite! We had looked forward to it so long—we had planned it all so carefully—and all we could eat was a soft-boiled egg—and we couldn't even finish that! It filled us up right to here—" she put a small hand level with her chin. "It was so tragic that we almost wept! . . . Isn't it a strange thing? I guess it must be that your stomach shrinks up while you're on the diet. You lie there day after day and think of the enormous meal you are going to devour just as soon as you get up—and then when

189

you try it you're not even able to finish a soft-boiled egg!"

As she finished, Mrs. Jack shrugged her shoulders and lifted her hands questioningly, with such a comical look on her face that everybody around her laughed. Even weary and jaded old Jake Abramson, who had really paid no attention to what she was saying but had just been regarding her with his fixed smile during the whole course of her animated dialogue, now smiled a little more warmly as he turned away to speak to other friends.

Miss Heilprinn and Mrs. Jack, left standing together in the center of the big room, offered an instructive comparison in the capacities of their sex. Each woman was perfectly cast in her own rôle. Each had found the perfect adaptive means by which she could utilize her full talents with the least waste and friction.

Miss Heilprinn looked the very distinguished woman that she was. Hers was the talent of the administrator, the ability to get things done, and one knew at a glance that in the rough and tumble of practical affairs this bland lady was more than a match for any man. She suggested oil—smooth oil, oil of tremendous driving power and generating force.

Along Broadway she had reigned for years as the governing brain of a celebrated art theatre, and her business acuity had wrung homage even from her enemies. It had been her function to promote, to direct, to control, and in the tenuous and uncertain speculations of the theatre to take care not to be fleeced by the wolves of Broadway. The brilliance of her success, the power of her will, and the superior quality of her metal were written plain upon her. It took no very experienced observer to see that in the unequal contest between Miss Heilprinn and the wolves of Broadway it had been the wolves who had been worsted.

In that savage and unremitting warfare, which arouses such bitter passions and undying hatreds that eyes become jaundiced and lips so twisted that they are never afterwards able to do anything but writhe like yellowed scars on haggard faces, had Miss Heilprinn's face grown hard? Had her mouth contracted to a grim line? Had her jaw outjutted like a granite crag? Were the marks of the wars visible anywhere upon her? Not at all. The more murderous the fight, the blander her face. The more treacherous the intrigues in which Broadway's life involved her, the more mellow became the fruity lilt of her good-humored chuckle. She had actually thriven on it. Indeed, as one of her colleagues said: "Roberta never seems so happy and so unconsciously herself as when she is playing about in a nest of rattlesnakes."

190

So, now, as she stood there talking to Mrs. Jack, she presented a very handsome and striking appearance. Her grey hair was combed in a pompadour, and her suave and splendid gown gave the finishing touch to her general air of imperturbable assurance. Her face was almost impossibly bland, but it was a blandness without hypocrisy. Nevertheless, one saw that her twinkling eyes, which narrowed into such jolly slits when she smiled, were sharp as flint and missed nothing.

In a curious way, Mrs. Jack was a more complex person than her smooth companion. She was essentially not less shrewd, not less accomplished, not less subtle, and not less determined to secure her own ends in this hard world, but her strategy had been different.

Most people thought her "such a romantic person." As her friends said, she was "so beautiful," she was "such a child," she was "so good." Yes, she was all these things. For she had early learned the advantages of possessing a rosy, jolly little face and a manner of slightly bewildered surprise and naïve innocence. When she smiled doubtfully yet good-naturedly at her friends, it was as if to say: "Now I know you're laughing at me, aren't you? I don't know what it is. I don't know what I've done or said now. Of course I'm not clever the way you are—all of you are so frightfully smart—but anyway I have a good time, and I like you all."

To many people that was the essential Mrs. Jack. Only a few knew that there was a great deal more to her than met the eye. The bland lady who now stood talking to her was one of these. Miss Roberta Heilprinn missed no artifice of that almost unconsciously deceptive innocence. And perhaps that is why, when Mrs. Jack finished her anecdote and looked at old Jake Abramson so comically and questioningly, Miss Heilprinn's eye twinkled a little brighter, her Buddhistic smile became a little smoother, and her yolky chuckle grew a trifle more infectious. Perhaps that is also why, with a sudden impulse of understanding and genuine affection, Miss Heilprinn bent and kissed the glowing little cheek.

And the object of this caress, although she never changed her expression of surprised and delighted innocence, knew full well all that was going on in the other woman's mind. For just a moment, almost imperceptibly, the eyes of the two women, stripped bare of all concealing artifice, met each other. And in that moment there was matter for Olympian laughter.

While Mrs. Jack welcomed her friends and beamed with happiness, one part of her mind remained aloof and preoccupied. For someone was still absent, and she kept thinking of him.

"I wonder where he is," she thought. "Why doesn't he come? I hope he hasn't been drinking." She looked quickly over the brilliant gathering with a troubled eye and thought impatiently: "If only he liked parties more! If only he enjoyed meeting people—going out in the evening! Oh, well—he's the way he is. It's no use trying to change him. I wouldn't have him any different."

And then he arrived.

"Here he is!" she thought excitedly, looking at him with instant relief. "And he's all right!"

George Webber had, in fact, taken two or three stiff drinks before he left his rooms, in preparation for the ordeal. The raw odor of cheap gin hung on his breath, his eyes were slightly bright and wild, and his manner was quick and a trifle more feverish than was his wont. Just the same he was, as Esther had phrased it to herself, "all right."

"If only people—my friends—everyone I know—didn't affect him so," she thought. "Why is it, I wonder. Last night when he telephoned me he talked so strange! Nothing he said made any sense! What could have been wrong with him? Oh, well—it doesn't matter now. He's here. I love him!"

Her face warmed and softened, her pulse beat quicker, and she went to meet him.

"Oh, hello, darling," she said fondly. "I'm so glad you're here at last. I was beginning to be afraid you were going to fail me after all."

He greeted her half fondly and half truculently, with a mixture of diffidence and pugnacity, of arrogance and humility, of pride, of hope, of love, of suspicion, of eagerness, of doubt.

He had not wanted to come to the party at all. From the moment she had first invited him he had brought forward a barrage of objections. They had argued it back and forth for days, but at last she had won and had exacted his promise. But as the time approached he felt himself hesitating again, and last night he had paced the floor for hours in an agony of self-recrimination and indecision. At last, around one o'clock, he had seized the telephone with desperate resolve and, after waking the whole household before he got her, he had told her that he was not coming. Once more he repeated all his reasons. He only half-understood them himself, but they had to do with the incompatibility of her world and his world, and his belief, which was as much a matter of instinctive feeling as of conscious thought, that he must keep his independence of the world she belonged to if he was to do his work. He grew almost desperate as he tried to explain it to her, because he couldn't seem to make her understand what he was driving at. In the end she became a little desperate, too. First she was annoyed, and told him for God's sake to stop being such a fool. Then she became hurt and angry and reminded him of his promise.

"We've been over all of this a dozen times!" she said shrilly, and there was also a tearful note in her voice. "You promised, George—you know you did! And now everything's arranged. It's too late to change it now. You can't let me down like this!"

This appeal was too much for him. He knew, of course, that the party had not been planned for him and that no arrangements would be upset if he failed to appear. No one but Esther would even be aware of his absence. But he *had* given his promise to come, however reluctantly, and he saw that the only issue he had succeeded in raising in her mind was the simple one of whether he would keep his word. So once more, and finally, he had yielded. And now he was here, full of confusion, and wishing with all his heart that he was anywhere else.

"I'm sure you're going to have a good time," Esther was saying to him eagerly. "You'll see!"—and she squeezed his hand. "There are lots of people I want you to meet. But you must be hungry. Better get yourself something to eat first. You'll find plenty of things you like. I planned them especially for you. Go in the dining room and help yourself. I'll have to stay here a little while to welcome all these people."

After she left him to greet some new arrivals, George stood there awkwardly for a moment with a scowl on his face and glanced about the room at the dazzling assemblage. In that attitude he cut a rather grotesque figure. The low brow with its frame of short black hair, the burning eyes, the small, packed features, the long arms dangling to the knees, and the curved paws gave him an appearance more simian than usual, and the image was accentuated by his not-too-well-fitting dinner jacket. People looked at him and stared, then turned away indifferently and resumed their conversations.

"So!" he thought with somewhat truculent self-consciousness—"These are her fine friends! I might have known it!" he muttered to himself, without knowing at all what it was he might have known. The poise, assurance, and sophistication of all these sleek faces made him fancy a slight where none was offered or intended. "I'll show them!" he growled absurdly beneath his breath, not having the faintest idea what he meant by that.

With this, he turned upon his heel and threaded his way through the brilliant throng toward the dining room.

"I *mean*! . . . You *know*! . . ."

At the sound of the words, eager, rapid, uttered in a rather hoarse yet strangely seductive tone of voice, Mrs. Jack smiled at the group to whom she had been talking. "There's Amy!" she said.

Then, as she turned and saw the elflike head with its unbelievable harvest of ebony curls, the snub nose and the little freckles, and the lovely face so radiant with an almost boyish quality of animation and enthusiasm, she thought:

"Isn't she beautiful! And—and—there is something so sweet, so—so good about her!"

Even as her mind framed its spontaneous tribute to the girlish apparition with the elflike head, Mrs. Jack knew that it was not true. No; Amy Carleton was many things, but no one could call her good. In fact, if she was not "a notorious woman," the reason was that she had surpassed the ultimate limits of notoriety, even for New York. Everybody knew her, and knew all about her, yet what the truth was, or what the true image of that lovely counterfeit of youth and joy, no one could say.

Chronology? Well, for birth she had had the golden spoon. She had been born to enfabled wealth. Hers had been the childhood of a dollar princess, kept, costly, cabined, pruned, confined. A daughter of "Society," her girlhood had been spent in rich schools and in travel, in Europe, Southampton, New York, and Palm Beach. By eighteen she was "out"—a famous beauty. By nineteen she was married. And by twenty she was divorced, her name tainted. It had been a sensational case which fairly reeked. Even at that time her conduct had been so scandalous that her husband had had no difficulty in winning a decree.

Since that time, seven years before, her career had defied the measurements of chronology. Although she was now only in her middle twenties, her life seemed to go back through aeons of iniquity. Thus one might remember one of the innumerable scandals that had been connected with her name, and then check oneself suddenly with a feeling of stunned disbelief. "Oh, no! It can't be! That happened only three short years ago, and since then she's—why she's—" And one would stare in stupefaction at that elflike head, that snub nose, that boyishly eager face, like one who realized that he was looking at the dread Medusa, or at some enchantress of Circean cunning whose life was older than the ages and whose heart was old as hell.

It baffled time, it turned reality to phantasmal shapes. One could behold her as she was tonight, here in New York, this freckled, laughing image of happy innocence—and before ten days had made their round one might come upon her again in the corrupt gatherings of Paris, drugged fathoms deep in opium, foul-bodied and filth-bespattered, cloying in the embraces of a gutter rat, so deeply rooted in the cesspool that it seemed she

194

must have been bred on sewage and had never known any other life.

Since her first marriage and divorce, she had been married twice again. The second marriage had lasted only twenty hours, and had been annulled. The third had ended when her husband shot himself.

And before and after that, and in between, and in and out, and during it and later on, and now and then, and here and there, and at home and abroad, and on the seven seas, and across the length and breadth of the five continents, and yesterday and tomorrow and forever—could it be said of her that she had been promiscuous? No, that could not be said of her. For she had been as free as air, and one does not qualify the general atmosphere with such a paltry adjective as "promiscuous." She had just slept with everybody—with white, black, yellow, pink, green, or purple—but she had never been promiscuous.

It was, in romantic letters, a period that celebrated the lady who was lost, the lovely creature in the green hat who was "never let off anything." Her story was a familiar one: she was the ill-starred heroine of fate, a martyr to calamitous mischance, whose ruin had been brought about through tragic circumstances which she could not control, and for which she was not responsible.

Amy Carleton had her apologists who tried to cast her in this role. The stories told about her "start upon the downward path" were numerous. One touching version dated the beginning of the end from the time when, an innocent and fun-loving girl of eighteen, she had, in a moment of daring, lighted a cigarette at a dinner party in Southampton, attended by a large number of eminent dowagers. The girl's downfall, according to this tale, had been brought about by this thoughtless and harmless little act. From that moment on—so the story went—the verdict of the dowagers was "thumbs down" on Amy. The evil tongues began to wag, scandal began to grow, her reputation was torn to shreds. Then, in desperation, the unhappy child did go astray: she took to drink, from drink to lovers, from lovers to opium, from opium to—everything.

All this, of course, was just romantic nonsense. She was the victim of a tragic doom indeed, but she herself had fashioned it. With her the fault, as with dear Brutus, lay not in her stars, but in herself. For, having been endowed with so many rare and precious things that most men lack—wealth, beauty, charm, intelligence, and vital energy—she lacked the will, the toughness, to resist. So, having almost all, but lacking this, she was the slave to her advantages. Her wealth had set a premium on every whim, and no one had ever taught her to say no.

In this she was the child of her own time. Her life expressed

195

itself in terms of speed, sensational change, and violent movement, in a feverish tempo that never drew from its own energies exhaustion or surcease, but mounted constantly to insane excess. She had been everywhere and "seen everything"—in the way one might see things from the windows of an express train traveling eighty miles an hour. And, having quickly exhausted the conventional kaleidoscope of things to be seen, she had long since turned to an investigation of things more bizarre and sinister and hidden. Here, too, her wealth and powerful connections opened doors to her which were closed to other people.

So, now, she possessed an intimate and extensive acquaintance among the most sophisticated and decadent groups in "Society," in all the great cities of the world. And her cult of the unusual had led to an exploration of the most shadowy border lines of life. She had an acquaintanceship among the underworld of New York, London, Paris, and Berlin which the police might have envied. And even with the police her wealth had secured for her dangerous privileges. In some way, known only to persons who control great power, financial or political, she had obtained a police card and was privileged to a reckless license in the operation of her low-slung racing car. Although she was near-sighted, she drove it at murderous speed through the seething highways of Manhattan, and as it flashed by she always got the courtesy of a police salute. All this in spite of the fact that she had demolished one car and killed a young man who had been driving with her, and in spite of the further fact that the police knew her as one who had been present at a drinking party at which one of the chieftains of the underworld had been slain.

It seemed, therefore, that her wealth and power and feverish energy could get her anything she wanted in any country of the world. People had once said: "What on earth is Amy going to do next?" But now they said: "What on earth is there left for her to do?" If life is to be expressed solely in terms of velocity and sensation, it seemed there was nothing left for her to do. Nothing but more speed, more change, more violence, more sensation—until the end. And the end? The end could only be destruction, and the mark of destruction was already apparent upon her. It was written in her eyes—in her tormented, splintered, and exploded vision. She had tried everything in life—except living. And she could never try that now because she had so long ago, and so irrevocably, lost the way. So there was nothing left for her to do except to die.

"If only—" people would think regretfully, as Mrs. Jack now thought as she looked at that elfin head—"oh, if only things had turned out differently for her!"—and then would seek back desperately through the labyrinthine scheme to find the clue to her disorder, saying: "Here—or here—or here—it happened here, you see!—If only——!"

If only men were so much clay, as they are blood, bone, marrow, passion, feeling! If they only were!

"I *mean*! . . . You *know*! . . ." With these words, so indicative of her undefined enthusiasm and inchoate thought, Amy jerked the cigarette away from her lips, laughed hoarsely and eagerly, and turned to her companions as if fairly burning with desire to communicate to them something that filled her with exuberant elation. "I *mean*!" she cried again—"when you compare it with the stuff they're doing nowadays!—I *mean*!—there's simply no comparison!" Laughing jubilantly, as if the thought behind these splintered phrases must be perfectly clear to everyone, she drew furiously upon her cigarette again and jerked it from her lips.

The group of young people of which Amy was the radiant center, and which included not only the young Japanese who was her current lover but also the young Jew who had been his most recent predecessor, had moved over toward the portrait of Mrs. Jack above the mantel, and were looking up at it. The portrait deserved the praise that was now being heaped upon it. It was one of the best examples of Henry Mallows' early work.

"When you look at it and *think* how long ago that was!—" cried Amy jubilantly, gesturing toward the picture with rapid thrusts of her cigarette—"and how beautiful she was *then*!—and how beautiful she is *now*!" she cried exultantly, laughed hoarsely, then cast her grey-green eyes around her in a glance of feverish exasperation—"I *mean*!—" she cried again, and drew impatiently on her cigarette—"there's *simply* no comparison!" Then, realizing that she had not said what she had wanted to say, she went on: "Oh, I *mean*!—" she said in a tone almost of desperation and tossed her cigarette angrily away into the blazing fire—"the whole thing's obvious!" she muttered, leaving everyone more bewildered than before. With a sudden and impulsive movement she turned toward Stephen Hook, who was still leaning with his elbow on one corner of the mantel, and demanded: "How long has it been, Steve? . . . I *mean*!—it's been twenty years ago, hasn't it?"

"Oh, quite all of that," Hook answered in his cold, bored voice. In his agitation and embarrassment he moved still farther away until he almost had his back turned upon the group. "It's been nearer thirty, I should think," he tossed back over his shoulder, and then with an air of casual indifference he gave the date. "I should think it was done in nineteen-one or two—wasn't it, Esther?" he said, turning to Mrs. Jack, who had now approached the group. "Around nineteen-one, wasn't it?"

"What's that?" said Mrs. Jack, and then went on immediately, "Oh, the picture! No, Steve. It was done in nineteen—" she checked herself so swiftly that it was not apparent to anyone but Hook—"in nineteen-six." She saw just the trace of a smile upon his pale, bored face and gave him a quick, warning little look, but he just murmured:

"Oh. . . . I had forgotten it was as late as that."

As a matter of fact, he knew the exact date, even to the month and day, when it had been finished. And, still musing on the vagaries of the sex, he thought: "Why will they be so stupid! She must understand that to anyone who knows the least thing about Mallows' life the date is as familiar as the fourth of July!"

"Of course." Mrs. Jack was saying rapidly, "I was just a child when it was made. I couldn't have been more than eighteen at the time—if I was that."

"Which would make you not more than forty-one now," thought Hook cynically—"if you are that! Well, my dear, you were twenty when he painted you—and you had been married for more than two years. . . . Why do they do it!" he thought impatiently, and with a feeling of sharp annoyance. He looked at her and caught a quick expression—startled, almost pleading—in her eyes. He followed her glance, and saw the awkward figure of George Webber standing ill at ease in the doorway leading from the dining room. "Ah! It's this boy!" he thought. "She's told him then that—" and, suddenly, remembering her pleading look, he was touched with pity. Aloud, however, he merely murmured indifferently:

"Oh, yes, you couldn't have been very old."

"And God!" exclaimed Mrs. Jack, "but I was beautiful!"

She spoke the words with such innocent delight that they lost any trace of objectionable vanity they might have had, and people smiled at her affectionately. Amy Carleton, with a hasty little laugh, said impulsively:

"Oh, Esther! Honestly, you're the *most* . . . ! But I *mean!*—" she cried impatiently, with a toss of her dark head, as if answering some invisible antagonist—"she *is!*"

"In all your days," said Mrs. Jack, her face suffused with laughter, "you never saw the like of me! I was just like peaches and cream. I'd have knocked your eye out!"

"But, *darling!* You do *now!*" cried Amy. "What I mean to say is—darling, you're the *most* . . . ! Isn't she, Steve?" She laughed uncertainly, turning to Hook with feverish eagerness.

And he, seeing the ruin, the loss, the desperation in her splintered eyes, was sick with horror and with pity. He looked at her disdainfully, with weary, lidded eyes, said "What?" quite

198

freezingly, and then turned away, saying with an accent of boredom: "Oh."

Beside him was the smiling face of Mrs. Jack, and, above, the portrait of the lovely girl that she had been. And the anguish and the mystery of time stabbed through him.

"My God, here she is!" he thought. "Still featured like a child, still beautiful, still loving someone—a boy!—almost as lovely now as she was then when Mallows was a boy!"

1901! Ah, Time! The figures reeled in a drunken dance and he rubbed his hand before his eyes. In 1901! How many centuries ago was that? How many lives and deaths and floods, how many million days and nights of love, of hate, of anguish and of fear, of guilt, of hope, of disillusion and defeat here in the geologic aeons of this monstrous catacomb, this riddled isle!—In 1901! Good God! It was the very Prehistoric Age of Man! Why, all *that* had happened several million years ago! Since then so much had begun and ended and been forgotten—so many untold lives of truth, of youth, of old age, so much blood and sweat and agony had gone below the bridge—why, he himself had lived through at least a hundred lives of it. Yes, he had lived and died through so many births and deaths and dark oblivions of it, had striven, fought, and hoped, and been destroyed through so many centuries of it, that even memory had failed—the sense of time had been wiped out—and all of it now seemed to have happened in a timeless dream. 1901! Looked at from here and now, it was a kind of Grand Canyon of the human nerves and bones and blood and brain and flesh and words and thought, all timeless now, all congealed, all solidified in an unchanging stratum there impossibly below, mixed into a general geologic layer with all the bonnets, bustles, and old songs, the straw hats and the derbies, the clatter of forgotten hooves, the thunder of forgotten wheels upon forgotten cobbles—all merged together now with the skeletons of lost ideas in a single stratum of the sunken world—while *she*——

—She! Why, surely she had been a part of it with him!

She had turned to speak to another group, and he could hear her saying:

"Oh yes, I knew Jack Reed. He used to come to Mabel Dodge's place. We were great friends. . . . That was when Alfred Stieglitz had started his salon——"

Ah, all these names! Had he not been with these as well? Or, was it but another shape, a seeming, in this phantasmal shadow-show of time? Had he not been beside her at the launching of the ship? Had they not been captives together among Thracian faces? Had he not lighted tapers to the tent when she had come to charm remission from the lord of Macedon?—All these were ghosts—save she! And she—devouring child of time—had of this whole huge company of ghosts alone remained immortal and herself, had shed off the chrysalis of all these her former selves as if each life that she had lived was nothing but an outworn garment, and now stood here—*here!* Good God! —upon the burnt-out candle-end of time—with her jolly face of noon, as if she had just heard of this brave new world on Saturday—and would see if *all* of it was really true tomorrow!

Mrs. Jack had turned back once more at the sound of Amy's voice and had bent forward to listen to the girl's disjointed exclamations as if, by giving more concentrated attention, she could make sense of what the girl was trying to say.

"I *mean*! . . . You *know*! . . . But Esther! Darling, you're the most . . . ! It's the most . . . ! I *mean*, when I look at both of you, I simply can't—" cried Amy with hoarse elation, her lovely face all sunning over with light—"Oh, what I *mean* to say is—" she cried, then shook her head strongly, tossed another cigarette impatiently, and cried with the expiration of a long sigh— "Gosh!"

Poor child! Poor child! Hook turned pompously away to hide the naked anguish in his eyes. So soon to grow, to go, to be consumed and die like all of us! She was, he felt, like him, too prone to live her life upon the single instant, never saving out anything as a prudent remnant for the hour of peril or the day of ruin—too prone to use it all, to give it all, burning herself out like last night's moths upon a cluster of hard light!

Poor child! Poor child! So quick and short and temporal, both you and I, thought Hook—the children of a younger kind! While these! He looked about him at the sensual volutes of strong nostrils curved with scornful mirth. These others of this ancient chemistry—unmothed, reborn, and venturesome, yet wisely mindful of the flame—these others shall endure! Ah, Time!

Poor child!

Chapter Sixteen

A Moment of Decision

George Webber had helped himself generously to the sumptuous feast so temptingly laid out in the dining room, and now, his hunger sated, he had been standing for a few minutes in the doorway surveying the brilliant scene in the great living room. He was trying to make up his mind whether to plunge boldly in and find somebody to talk to, or whether to put off the ordeal a little longer by lingering over the food. He thought with regret that there were still a few dishes that he had not even tasted. He had already eaten so much, however, that he knew he could not make a convincing show of taking more, so there seemed to be nothing for it but to screw up his courage and make the best of the situation.

He had just reached this conclusion, with a feeling of "Now you're in for it!"—when he caught a glimpse of Stephen Hook, whom he knew and liked, and with a great sense of relief he started toward him. Hook was leaning on the mantel, talking with a handsome woman. He saw George coming and extended his soft, plump hand sideways, saying casually:

"Oh. How are you? . . . Look." His tone, as always when he did something that was prompted by the generous and sensitive warmth of his spirit, was deliberately indifferent and masked with an air of heavy boredom. "Have you a telephone? I was trying to get you the other day. Can't you come and have lunch with me sometime?"

As a matter of fact, this idea had never occurred to him until that moment. Webber knew that he had thought of it in an instant reflex of sympathy to put him at his ease, to make him feel less desperately shipwrecked in these glittering, sophisticated tides, to give him something "to hold on to." Ever since he had first met Hook and had seen his desperate shyness and the naked terror in his eyes, he had understood the kind of man he was. He had never been deceived by the show of aloof weariness or the elaborately mannered speech. Beneath these disguises he had felt the integrity, the generosity, the nobility, the aspiration in the man's tortured soul. So, now, with profound gratitude, he reached out and shook his hand, feeling as he did so like a bewildered swimmer seizing on the one thing that could sustain him in these disturbing and unfathomed currents which were edged somehow with menace. He stammered out a hasty greeting, said he would be delighted to go to lunch with him sometime—any time—any time at all; and he took a place beside Hook as though he meant to stay there for the rest of the evening.

Hook talked to him a little while in his casual way and introduced the woman. George tried to engage her in conversation, but, instead of answering his remarks, she just looked at him coolly and said nothing. Embarrassed by this behavior, George looked around him as if searching for someone, and in a final effort to say something, to give some show of ease and purpose which he did not feel, he blurted out:

"Have—have you seen Esther anywhere about?"

As he said the words he knew how stiff and clumsy they

201

sounded, and how absurd, too, for Mrs. Jack, as anyone could see, was standing talking to some of her guests not ten feet away. And the woman, as if she had been waiting for just such an opening, now answered him at once. Turning to him with a bright, superior smile, she said with cool unfriendliness:

"About? Yes, I think you'll find her about—just about there," nodding in the direction of Mrs. Jack.

It was not a very witty remark. To George it seemed almost as stupid as his own words had been. He knew, too, that the unfriendliness behind it was impersonal—just the mark of fashion, a willingness to sacrifice manners to the chance of making a smart retort. Why, then, did his face now flush with anger? Why did he double up his fist and turn upon the trivial and smiling creature with such smoldering menace that it seemed he was about to commit a physical assault upon her?

In the very instant that he assumed this belligerent attitude he realized that he was acting like a baffled clodhopper, and this consciousness made him feel ten times the yokel that he looked. He tried to think of telling words with which to answer her, but his mind was paralyzed and he was conscious only of the burning sensation in his face and neck. He knew that his ill-fitting coat was sticking out around his collar, that he was cutting a sorry figure, and that the woman—"that damned bitch!" he muttered to himself—was laughing at him. So, defeated and discomfited utterly, not so much by the woman as by his own ineptitude, he turned and stalked away, hating himself, the party, and, most of all, his folly in coming.

Well, he hadn't wanted to come! That was Esther's doing! She was responsible for this! It was all her fault! Full of confusion and irrational anger at everything and everybody, he backed himself against the wall on the opposite side of the room and stood there clenching and unclenching his fists and glaring around him.

But the violence and the injustice of his feelings soon began to have a calming and sobering effect upon him. Then he saw the absurdity of the whole episode, and began to laugh and mock inwardly at himself.

"So this is why you didn't want to come!" he thought scornfully. "You were afraid some silly fool of an ill-bred woman would make an inane remark that would prick your delicate hide! God, what a fool you are! Esther was right!"

But *had* she been right, really? He had made such an issue of it with his talk about the work he had to do as a novelist, and how he had to keep clear of her world in order to do it. Was all that just a way of rationalizing his sense of social inadequacy? Had he gone to such lengths of theorizing merely to spare his tender ego the ridicule and humiliation of such a scene as he had just precipitated?

No, that was not the answer. There was more to it than that. By now he had cooled off enough to be able to look at himself objectively, and all at once he realized that he had never gotten clear in his own mind what he had meant when he had talked to Esther about her world and his world. He had used the phrases as symbols of something real, something important that he had felt instinctively but had never put into words. And that's why he hadn't been able to make her understand. Well, what was it? What had he been afraid of? It wasn't only that he didn't like big parties and knew himself to be unschooled in the social graces that such occasions demanded. That was a part of it—yes. But it was only a part—the smallest part, the petty, personal part. There was something else—something imper-sonal, something much bigger than himself, something that mattered greatly to him and that would not be denied. What was it now? Better face it and try to get it straight.

Completely cool now, and fascinated by the inner problem which the ridiculous little incident had brought into sharp focus, he began to look about him at the people in the room. He watched their faces closely and tried to penetrate behind the social masks they wore, probing, boring, searching as for some. clue that might lead him to an answer to his riddle. It was, he knew, a distinguished gathering. It included brilliant, successful men and beautiful women. They were among the best and highest that the city had to offer. But as he looked them over with an alert eye and with all his sensitivities keenly awakened by his present purpose, he saw that there were some among them who wore quite another hue.

That fellow there, for instance! With his pasty face and rolling eyes and mincing ways, and hips that wiggled suggestively as he walked—could there be any doubt at all that he was a member of nature's other sex? Webber knew that people of this fellow's type and gender were privileged personalities, the species being regarded tenderly as a cross between a lap dog and a clown. Almost every fashionable hostess considered them essential functionaries at smart gatherings like this. Why was it, George wondered. Was it something in the spirit of the times that had let the homosexual usurp the place and privilege of a hunchbacked jester of an old king's court, his deformity become a thing of open jest and ribaldry? However it had come about, the thing itself was indubitable. The mincing airs and graces of such a fellow, his antics and his gibes, and spicy sting of his feminine and envenomed wit, were the exact counterparts of the malicious quips of ancient clowns. So, now. As this simpering fellow minced along, the powdered whiteness of his parchment face held languidly to one side, the weary eyes half-closed and heavy-lidded, he would pause from time to time to wave with a maidenly gesture of his wrist at various people of his acquaintance in different parts of the big room, saying as he did so:

"Oh, hello! . . . *There* you are! . . . You *must* come over!"

The effect of all this was so irresistible that the ladies shrieked with laughter, and the gentlemen spluttered and guffawed.

And that woman over there in the corner, the one with the mannish haircut and angular lines and hard, enameled face, holding the hand of that rather pretty and embarrassed young girl—a nymphomaniac if ever he saw one.

At the sound of the splintered phrases, "I *mean*! . . . You *know*!"—Webber turned and saw the dark curls of Amy Carleton. He knew who she was, and he knew her story, but even if he had not known he thought he would have guessed a part of it by the tragic look of lost innocence in her face. But what he noticed chiefly now was the group of men who followed her about, among them the young Jew and the young Japanese—and the sight made him think of a pack of dogs trailing after a bitch in heat. It was so open, so naked, so shameless that it almost made him sick.

His eye took in John Ettinger, standing a little apart with his wife and his mistress, and he read their relationship unmistakably in their bearing toward each other.

At these repeated signs of decadence in a society which had once been the object of his envy and his highest ambition, Webber's face had begun to take on a look of scorn. Then he saw Mr. Jack moving suavely among his guests, and suddenly, with a rush of blood to his face, he thought about himself. Who was *he* to feel so superior? Did they not all know who *he* was, and why he was here?

Yes, all these people looked at one another with untelling eyes. Their speech was casual, quick, and witty. But they did not say the things they knew. And they knew everything. They had seen everything. They had accepted everything. And they received every new intelligence now with a cynical and amused look in their untelling eyes. Nothing shocked them any more. It was the way things were. It was what they had come to expect of life.

Ah, there he had it! That was part of the answer. It was not so much what they did, for in this there was no appreciable difference between themselves and him. It was their attitude of acceptance, the things they thought and felt about what they did, their complaisance about themselves and about their life, their loss of faith in anything better. He himself had not yet come to that, he did not want to come to it. This was one of the reasons, he now knew, why he did not want to be sealed to this world that Esther belonged to.

Still, there could be no question that these people were an

honored group. They had stolen no man's ox or ass. Their gifts were valuable and many, and had won for them the world's grateful applause.

Was not the great captain of finance and industry, Lawrence Hirsch, a patron of the arts as well, and a leader of advanced opinion? Yes. His views on child labor, sharecropping, the trial of Sacco and Vanzetti, and other questions that had stirred the indignation of the intellectual world were justly celebrated for their enlightenment and their liberalism. Who should cavil, then, at the fact that a banker might derive a portion of his income from the work of children in the textile factories of the South?—that another part of it might be derived from the labor of sharecroppers in the tobacco fields?—that still another might come from steel mills in the Middle West where armed thugs had been employed to shoot into the ranks of striking workers? A banker's business was to invest his money wherever he could get the best return. Business was business, and to say that a man's social views ought to come between him and his profits was caviling, indeed! As for Mr. Hirsch himself, he had his devoted champions even among the comrades of the left, who were quick to point out that theoretical criticism of this sort was childish. The sources of Mr. Hirsch's wealth and power, whatever they might be, were quite accidental and beside the point. His position as a liberal, "a friend of Russia," a leader of advanced social opinion, a searching critic, indeed, of the very capitalist class to which he belonged, was so well known as to place him in the very brain and forehead of enlightened thought.

As for these others in the illustrious company that Webber now saw on every side, not one of them had ever said, "Let them eat cake!" When the poor had starved, these had suffered. When the children toiled, these had bled. When the oppressed, the weak, the stricken and betrayed of men had been falsely accused and put to death, these tongues had been lifted in indignant protest—if only the issue had been fashionable! These had written letters to the press, carried placards upon Beacon Hill, joined parades, made contributions, lent the prestige of their names to form committees of defense.

All this was indubitably true. But as he thought about it now, Webber also felt that such as these might lift their voices and parade their placards till the crack of doom, but that in the secret and entrenched resources of their lives they had all battened on the blood of common man, and wrung their profits from the sweat of slaves, like any common overseer of money and of privilege that ever lived. The whole tissue of these princely lives, he felt, these lesbic and pederastic loves, these adulterous intrigues, sustained in mid-air now, floating on the face of night like a starred veil, had none the less been spun from man's common dust of sweated clay, unwound out of the entrails of man's agony.

Yes, that was it! That was the answer! That was the very core of it! Could he as a novelist, as an artist, belong to this high world of privilege without taking upon himself the stultifying burden of that privilege? Could he write truthfully of life as he saw it, could he say the things he must, and at the same time belong to this world of which he would have to write? Were the two things possible? Was not this world of fashion and of privilege the deadliest enemy of art and truth? Could he belong to the one without forsaking the other? Would not the very privilege that he might gain from these, the great ones of the city, come between him and the truth, shading it, tempering it, and in the end betraying it? And would he then be any different from a score of others who had let themselves be taken into camp, made captive by false visions of wealth and ease, and by the deadly hankering for respectability—that gilded counterfeit which so often passes current for the honest coin of man's respect?

That was the danger, and it was real enough. It was, he knew, no mere phantom of his distempered and suspicious mind. Had it not happened over and over again? Think of all the young writers, among them some of the best, who had won acclaim for the promise of their genius, and then had left their promise unfulfilled because they had traded their birthright for just such a mess of the world's pottage. They, too, had begun as seekers after truth, but had suffered some eclipse of vision and had ended as champions of some special and limited brand of truth. They were the ones who became the special pleaders for things as they are, and their names grew fat and sleek in the pages of the *Saturday Evening Post* and the women's magazines. Or they became escapists and sold themselves to Hollywood, and were lost and sunk without a trace. Or, somewhat differently, but following the same blind principle, they identified themselves with this or that group, clique, faction, or interest in art or politics, and led forlorn and esoteric little cults and isms. These were the innumerable small fry who became literary Communists, or single-taxers, or embattled vegetarians, or believers in salvation through nudism. Whatever they became—and there was no limit to their variety—they were like the blind men with the elephant: each one of them had accepted some part of life for the whole, some fragmentary truth or half-truth for truth itself, some little personal interest for the large and all-embracing interest of mankind. If that happened to him, how, then, could he sing America?

The problem was clearing up now. In the exhilaration of this moment of sharp vision the answers to his questions were beginning to come through. He was beginning to see what he must do. And as he saw the end of the road down which, willingly, hopefully, even joyfully, he had been traveling with Esther, he saw, too—swiftly, finally, irrevocably—that he must break with her and turn his back upon this fabulous and enchanting world of hers—or lose his soul as an artist. That is what it came down to.

But even in the very instant that he saw it, and knew that it was so, and accepted it, he was overwhelmed with such a sudden sense of loss that he all but cried out in his pain and love. Was there, then, no simple truth and certainty to be found anywhere? Must one forever be stretched out on the rack? Forever in his youth he had envisioned the starred face of the night with high exaltation and noble inspiration, longing to dream great dreams and think great thoughts in the company of the world's most honored great. And now, in this very moment of the dream come true, with the ones he had always envied from afar surrounding him here on every side—now to have the selfless grandeur turn to dust, and to see great night itself a reptile coiled and waiting at the heart of life! To find no ear or utterance anywhere for all the blazing, baffled certitudes of youth! To find man's faith betrayed and his betrayers thronged in honor, themselves the idols of his bartered faith! To find truth false and falsehood truth, good evil, evil good, and the whole web of life so changing, so mercurial!

It was all so different from the way he had once thought it would be—and suddenly, convulsively, forgetful of his surroundings, he threw out his arms in an instinctive gesture of agony and loss.

Chapter Seventeen

Mr. Hirsch Could Wait

Esther had seen George's gesture and wondered what it meant. She disengaged herself from the people to whom she had been talking and came over to him, a frown of tender solicitude on her face.

"Darling," she said eagerly, taking his hand and looking at him earnestly, "how are you getting along? Are you all right?"

In his confusion and anguish he could not answer her for a

moment, and when he did, the guilty knowledge of the decision he had just arrived at made him lash out angrily as though in self-defense.

"Who said I wasn't all right?" he demanded harshly. "Why shouldn't I be?" And, instantly, seeing her gentle face, he was filled with baffled and furious regret.

"Oh, all right, all right," she said hastily and placatingly. "I just wanted to know if—are you having a good time?" she said, with a little forced smile. "Don't you think it's a nice party—hah? You want to meet anyone? You must know some of the people here."

Before he had a chance to say anything more Lily Mandell came weaving through the crowded room to Mrs. Jack's side.

"O Esther, darling," she said in a drowsy tone, "I wonder if you've heard—" Seeing the young man, she paused. "Oh, hello. I didn't know *you* were here." There was a note of protest in her voice.

These two had met before, but only casually. They shook hands. And all at once Mrs. Jack's face was glowing with happiness. She put her own hands in a firm clasp upon those of the man and woman, and whispered:

"My two. Two of the people that I love best in the whole world. You must know and love each other as I do you."

In the grip of her deep emotion she fell silent, while the other two remained clumsily holding hands. After a moment, awkwardly, they let their hands drop to their sides and stood ill at ease, looking at each other.

Just then Mr. Lawrence Hirsch sauntered up. He was calm and assured, and did not seem to be following anyone. His hands in the trouser pockets of his evening clothes, a man fashionably at ease, urbanely social, a casual ambler from group to group in this brilliant gathering, informed, alert, suave, polished, cool, detached—he was the very model of what a great captain of finance, letters, arts, and enlightened principles should be.

"O Esther," he said, "I must tell you what we have found out about the case." The tone was matter-of-fact and undisturbed, carrying the authority of calm conviction. "Two innocent men were put to death. At last we have positive proof of it—evidence that was never allowed to come to light. It proves beyond the shadow of a doubt that Vanzetti could not have been within fifty miles of the crime."

Mr. Hirsch spoke quietly, and did not look at Miss Mandell.

"But how horrible!" cried Mrs. Jack, righteous anger blazing up in her as she turned to Mr. Hirsch. "Isn't it dreadful to know that such things can happen in a country like this! It's the most damnable thing I ever heard of!"

For the first time, now, Mr. Hirsch turned to Miss Mandell,

casually, as if he had only just become aware of her presence. "Yes, isn't it?" he said, including her with charming yet not over-zealous intimacy within the range of his quiet enthusiasm. "Don't you think——?"

Miss Mandell did not actually step on him. She just surveyed him slowly, with a smoldering look of loathing. *"What!"* she said. Then to Mrs. Jack: *"Really!* I simply can't—" She shrugged helplessly, despairingly, and moved away, a miracle of sensual undulance.

And Mr. Hirsch—he did not follow her, not even with a glance. Nor did he show by so much as the flicker of a lash that he had seen or heard or noticed anything. He went on talking in his well-modulated tones to Mrs. Jack.

In the middle of what he was saying, suddenly he noticed George Webber. "Oh, hello," he said. "How are you?" He detached one hand from his elegant pocket and for a moment bestowed it on the young man, then turned back again to Mrs. Jack, who was still burning with hot indignation over what she had heard.

"These miserable people who could be guilty of such a thing!" she exclaimed. "These despicable, horrible, rich people! It's enough to make you want a revolution!" she cried.

"Well, my dear," said Mr. Hirsch with cool irony, "you may have your wish gratified. It's not beyond the realm of possibility. And if it comes, *that* case may still return to plague them yet. The trials, of course, were perfectly outrageous, and the judge should have been instantly dismissed."

"To think that there are people living who could do a thing like that!" cried Mrs. Jack. "You know," she went on earnestly and somewhat irrelevantly, "I have always been a Socialist. I voted for Norman Thomas. You see," she spoke very simply and with honest self-respect, "I've always been a worker. All my sympathy is on their side."

Mr. Hirsch's manner had become a trifle vague, detached, as if he were no longer paying strict attention. "It is a *cause célèbre*," he said, and, seeming to like the sound of the words, he repeated them portentously: "A *cause célèbre*."

Then, distinguished, polished, and contained, with casual hands loose-pocketed beneath his tails, he sauntered on. He moved off in the general direction of Miss Mandell. And yet he did not seem to follow her.

For Mr. Lawrence Hirsch was wounded sorrowfully. But he could wait.

"Oh, *Beddoes! Beddoes!*"

At these strange words, so exultantly spoken that they rang

around the walls of the great room, people halted in the animation of their talk with one another and, somewhat startled, looked in the direction from which the sounds had proceeded.

"Oh, *Beddoes* by all means!" the voice cried even more exuberantly than before. "Hah-hah-hah! *Beddoes!*"—there was gloating in the laugh. "Everyone must, of course, they simply must!"

The speaker was Mr. Samuel Fetzer. He was not only an old friend of Mrs. Jack's, but apparently he was also a familiar of many of the people there, because when they saw who it was they smiled at one another and murmured, "Oh, it's Sam," as if that explained everything.

In the world to which he belonged Mr. Samuel Fetzer was known as "the book-lover" *par excellence*. His very appearance suggested it. One needed only to look at him to know that he was an epicure, a taster of fine letters, a collector and connoisseur of rare editions. One could see with half an eye that he was the kind of fellow you might expect to find on a rainy afternoon in a musty old bookshop, peering and poking and prowling around the stacks with a soft, cherubic glow on his ruddy features, and occasionally fingering with a loving hand some tattered old volume. He made one think somehow of a charming thatched cottage in the English countryside—of a pipe, a shaggy dog, a comfortable chair, a warm nook by the blazing fire, and an old book and a crusty bottle—a bottle of old port! In fact, the exultant way in which he now pronounced the syllables of "*Beddoes!*" suggested a bottle of old port. He fairly smacked his lips over the word, as if he had just poured himself a glass of the oldest and rarest vintage and taken his first appraising sip.

His whole appearance confirmed this impression of him. His pleasant, sensitive, glowing face, which wore a constant air of cherubic elation, and his high bald forehead were healthily browned and weathered as if he spent much time tramping in the open air. And, in contrast to the other guests, who were all in formal evening dress, he had on tan, thick-soled English walking shoes, woolen socks, grey flannel trousers, a trifle baggy but fashionably Oxonian, a tweed coat of brownish texture, a soft white shirt, and a red tie. One would have said, at sight of him, that he must have just come in from a long walk across the moors, and that now, pleasantly tired, he was looking forward with easeful contemplation to an evening spent with his dog, beside his fire, with a bottle of old port, and Beddoes. One would never have guessed the truth—that he was an eminent theatrical director whose life since childhood had been spent in the city, along Broadway and among the most highly polished groups of urban society.

He was talking now to Miss Mandell. She had wandered over to him after leaving Mrs. Jack, and had asked him the provocative question which had touched off his extraordinary demonstration of enthusiasm. Miss Mandell was herself somewhat of an adept in the arts—a delver into some of the rarer obscurities. She was forever asking people what they thought of William Beckford's *Vathek*, the plays of Cyril Tourneur, the sermons of Lancelot Andrewes, or—as now—the works of Beddoes.

What she had said, to be exact, was: "Did you ever read anything by a man named Beddoes?"

Miss Mandell had the habit of putting her questions that way, and she would even use the same form of oblique reference when she spoke of the more famous objects of her aesthetic interest. Thus she would inquire what one knew about "a man named Proust," or "a woman named Virginia Woolf." The phrase, accompanied as it always was by a dark and smoldering look, carried an air of "There's more to this than meets the eye." It made Miss Mandell appear to be a person of profound and subtle knowingness, and one whose deep and devious searchings had gone so far beyond the platitudes that might be found in the *Encyclopaedia Britannica* and other standard works that there was really no way left for her to learn anything new except, possibly, through a quiet talk with Mr. T. S. Eliot—or, since he wasn't handy, through an occasional tentative yet not very optimistic question addressed to someone of superior intelligence like oneself. And after one had answered Miss Mandell and had poured forth whatever erudition one commanded on the subject of her interest, her usual comment would be a simple and noncommittal "Um." This always produced a very telling effect. For as Miss Mandell murmured "Um" and wandered off, the victim was left flattened out, feeling that he had emptied himself dry and still had been found childishly superficial and pathetically wanting.

Not so, however, Mr. Samuel Fetzer. If Miss Mandell had hoped to work this technique on him when she wove her languorous way to his side and casually asked, "Did you ever read anything by a man named Beddoes?"—she was in for a rude surprise. She had caught a tartar—a cherubic tartar, it is true, a benevolent tartar, an exultant, exuberant, elated tartar—but a tartar nevertheless. For Mr. Fetzer had not only *read* Beddoes: he felt that he had rather *discovered* Beddoes. Beddoes was one of Mr. Fetzer's philobiblic pets. So he was not only ready for Miss Mandell: it almost seemed as if he had been waiting for her. She had hardly got the words out of her mouth before he fairly pounced upon her, and his pleasant face lit up all over with a look of cherubic glee as he cried:

"Oh, *Beddoes!*" The name rang out with such explosive

enthusiasm that Miss Mandell recoiled as if someone had thrown a lighted firecracker at her feet. *"Beddoes!"* he chortled. *"Beddoes!"*—he smacked his lips. "Hah-hah-hah! *Beddoes!"*—he cast back his head, shook it, and chuckled gloatingly. Then he told her about Beddoes' birth, about his life, about his death, about his family and his friends, about his sisters and his cousins and his aunts, about things that were well known about Beddoes, and about other things that no one in the world except Mr. Samuel Fetzer had ever known about Beddoes. "Oh, *Beddoes!"* cried Mr. Fetzer for the sixteenth time. "I love *Beddoes!* Everybody must read *Beddoes! Beddoes* is——"

"But he *was* insane, wasn't he?" The quiet, well-bred voice was that of Mr. Lawrence Hirsch, who had just wandered up casually, as if attracted by the noise of cultural enthusiasm, and without seeming to follow anyone. "I mean," he turned with an air of gracious explanation to Miss Mandell, "it's an interesting example of the schizophrenic personality, don't you think?"

She looked at him for a long moment as one might look at a large worm within the core of a chestnut that one had hoped was sound.

"Um," said Miss Mandell, and with an expression of drowsy loathing on her face she moved away.

Mr. Hirsch did not follow her. Perfectly possessed, he had already shifted his glance back to the glowing Mr. Fetzer.

"I mean," he continued, with that inflection of interested inquiry which is the mark everywhere of a cultivated intelligence, "it always seemed to me that it was a case of misplaced personality—an Elizabethan out of his time. Or do you think so?"

"Oh, absolutely!" cried Mr. Fetzer, with instant and enthusiastic confirmation. "You see, what I have always maintained——"

Mr. Hirsch appeared to be listening carefully. He really was not following anyone. He kept his eyes focused on Mr. Samuel Fetzer's face, but something in their expression indicated that his mind was elsewhere.

For Mr. Lawrence Hirsch was wounded sorrowfully. But he could wait.

So it went all evening. Mr. Hirsch moved from group to sophisticated group, bowing, smiling suavely, exchanging well-bred pleasantries with all he met. Always he was imperturbable, authoritatively assured, on his aesthetic toes. And his progress through that brilliant assemblage was marked by a phosphorescent wake composed of the small nuggets of enlightenment which he dropped casually as he passed. Here it was a little confidential gossip about Sacco and Vanzetti, there a little first-hand information from Wall Street, now a sophisticated jest or so, again an amusing anecdote about what happened only last week to the President, or a little something about Russia, with a shrewd observation on Marxian economy—and to all of this a little Beddoes had been added for good measure. It was all so perfectly informed and so alertly modern that it never for a moment slipped into cliché, but always represented the very latest mode in everything, whether art, letters, politics, or economics. It was a remarkable performance, an inspiring example of what the busy man of affairs can really accomplish if he only applies himself.

And, in addition to all this, there was Miss Mandell. He never seemed to follow her, but wherever she went he was not far behind. One always knew that he was there. All evening long, whenever he came up to any group and honored it with one of his apt observations, and then, turning casually and discovering that Miss Mandell was among the company, made as if to include her in the intimate circle of his auditors, she would just give him a smoldering look and walk away. So it was no wonder that Mr. Lawrence Hirsch was wounded sorrowfully.

Still, he did not beat his breast, or tear his hair, or cry out, "Woe is me!" He remained himself, the man of many interests, the master of immense authorities. For he could wait.

He did not take her aside and say: "Thou art fair, my love; behold, thou art fair, thou hast doves' eyes." Nor did he say: "Tell me, O thou whom my soul loveth, where thou feedest." He did not remark to her that she was beautiful as Tirzah, or comely as Jerusalem, or terrible as an army with banners. He did not ask anyone to stay him with flagons, or comfort him with apples, or confess that he was sick of love. And as for saying to her: "Thy navel is like a round goblet, which wanteth not liquor; thy belly is like a heap of wheat set about with lilies," the idea had never occurred to him.

Though he did not cry out to her in his agony, what he was thinking was: "Flaunt me with your mockery and scorn, spurn me with your foot, lash me with your tongue, trample me like a worm, spit upon me like the dust of which I am composed, revile me to your friends, make me crawl far and humbly—do anything you like, I can endure it. But, oh, for God's sake, notice me! Speak to me with just a word—if only with hate! Stay near me for just a moment, make me happy with just a touch—even if the nearness is but loathing, and the touch a blow! Treat me in any way you will! But I beg you, O beloved that thou art—" out of the corner of his eye he followed her

213

lavish undulations as she turned and walked away again—"in God's name, let me see you know that I am here!"

But he said nothing. He showed nothing of what he felt. He was sorrowfully wounded, but he could wait. And no one but Miss Mandell knew how long she intended to keep him waiting.

Chapter Eighteen

Piggy Logan's Circus

The hour had now arrived for Mr. Piggy Logan and his celebrated circus of wire dolls. Till now he had kept himself secreted in the guest room, and as he made his entrance there was a flurry of excited interest in the brilliant throng. People in the dining room crowded to the door, holding tinkling glasses or loaded plates in their hands, and even old Jake Abramson let his curiosity draw him away from the temptations of the table long enough to appear in the doorway gnawing at a chicken leg.

Mr. Piggy Logan was attired for his performance in a costume that was simple yet extraordinary. He had on a thick blue turtleneck sweater of the kind that was in favor with college heroes thirty years ago. Across the front of it—God knows why—was sewn an enormous homemade Y. He wore old white canvas trousers, tennis sneakers, and a pair of battered knee pads such as were formerly used by professional wrestlers. His head was crowned with an ancient football helmet, the straps securely fastened underneath his heavy jowls. Thus arrayed, he came forward, staggering between his two enormous valises.

The crowd made way for him and regarded him with awe. Mr. Logan grunted under his burden, which he dropped with a thump in the middle of the living room floor, and breathed an audible sigh of relief. Immediately he began pushing back the big sofa and all the chairs and tables and other furniture until the center of the room was clear. He rolled back the rug, and then started taking books from the shelves and dumping them on the floor. He looted half a dozen shelves in different parts of the room and in the vacant spaces fastened up big circus posters, yellow with age, which showed the familiar assortment of tigers, lions, elephants, clowns, and trapeze performers, and

214

bore such descriptive legends as "Barnum & Bailey—May 7th and 8th," "Ringling Brothers—July 31st."

The gathering watched him curiously as he went about this labor of methodical destruction. When he had finished he came back to his valises and began to take out their contents. There were miniature circus rings made of rounded strips of tin or copper which fitted neatly together. There were trapezes and flying swings. And there was an astonishing variety of figures made of wire to represent all the animals and performers. There were clowns and trapeze artists, acrobats and tumblers, horses and bareback lady riders. There was almost everything that one could think of to make a circus complete, and all of it was constructed of wire.

Mr. Logan was down on his kneepads extremely busy with his work, his mind as completely focused on it as though he had been alone in the room. He rigged up his trapezes and swings and took meticulous care in arranging each of the little wire figures of elephants, lions, tigers, horses, camels, and performers. He was evidently of a patient turn of mind, and it took him half an hour or more to set everything up. By the time he had finished his labors and had erected a little sign which said, "Main Entrance," all the guests, who at first had watched him curiously, had grown tired of waiting and had resumed their interrupted talking, eating, and drinking.

At length Mr. Logan was ready, and signified his willingness to begin by a gesture to his hostess. She clapped her hands as loudly as she could and asked for silence and attention.

But just then the door bell rang, and a lot of new people were ushered in by Nora. Mrs. Jack looked somewhat bewildered, for the new arrivals were utter strangers. For the most part they were young people. The young women had that unmistakable look of having gone to Miss Spence's School, and there was something about the young men which indicated that they were recently out of Yale and Harvard and Princeton, and were members of the Racquet Club, and were now connected with investment brokers in Wall Street.

With them was a large and somewhat decayed-looking lady of advanced middle age. She had evidently been a beauty in her palmy days, but now everything about her—arms, shoulders, neck, face, and throat—was blown, full, and loose, and made up a picture of corrupted elegance. It was a picture of what Amy Carleton *might* look like thirty years from now, if she were careful and survived. One felt unpleasantly that she had lived too long in Europe, probably on the Riviera, and that somewhere in the offing there was something with dark, liquid eyes, a little mustache, and pomaded hair—something quite young and private and obscene and kept.

This lady was accompanied by an elderly gentleman faultlessly attired in evening dress, as were all the others. He had a cropped mustache and artificial teeth, which were revealed whenever he paused to lick his thin lips lecherously and to stutter out, "What? . . . What?"—as he began to do almost at once. Both of these people looked exactly like characters who might have been created by Henry James if he had lived and written in a later period of decay.

The whole crowd of newcomers streamed in noisily, headed by a spruce young gentleman in white tie and tails whose name was shortly to be made known as Hen Walters. He was evidently a friend of Mr. Logan. Indeed, they all seemed to be friends of Mr. Logan. For as Mrs. Jack, looking rather overwhelmed at this invasion, advanced to greet them and was dutifully murmuring her welcome, all of them swarmed right past her, ignoring her completely, and stormed into the room shouting vociferous gayeties at Mr. Logan. Without rising from his kneepads, he grinned at them fondly and with a spacious gesture of his freckled hand beckoned them to a position along one wall. They crowded in and took the place he had indicated. This forced some of the invited guests back into the far corners, but the new arrivals seemed not to mind this at all. Indeed, they paid not the slightest attention to anybody.

Then somebody in the group saw Amy Carleton and called across to her. She came over and joined them, and seemed to know several of them. And one could see that all of them had heard of her. The débutantes were polite but crisply detached. After the formalities of greeting they drew away and eyed Amy curiously and furtively, and their looks said plainly: "So this is she!"

The young men were less reserved. They spoke to her naturally, and Hen Walters greeted her quite cordially in a voice that seemed to be burbling with suppressed fun. It was not a pleasant voice: it was too moist, and it seemed to circulate around a nodule of fat phlegm. With the gleeful elation which marked his whole manner he said loudly:

"Hello, Amy! I haven't seen you for an age. What brings *you* here?" The tone indicated, with the unconscious arrogance of his kind, that the scene and company were amusingly bizarre and beyond the pale of things accepted and confirmed, and that to find anyone he knew in such a place was altogether astounding.

The tone and its implications stung her sharply. As for herself, she had so long been the butt of vicious gossip that she could take it with good nature or complete indifference. But an

216

affront to someone she loved was more than she could endure. And she loved Mrs. Jack. So, now, her green-gold eyes flashed dangerously as she answered hotly:

"What brings *me* here—of *all* places! Well, it's a very good place to be—the best I know. . . . And I *mean!*—" she laughed hoarsely, jerked the cigarette from her mouth, and tossed her black curls with furious impatience—"I *mean!* After all, I *was* invited, you know!"

Instinctively, with a gesture of protective warmth, she had slipped her arm around Mrs. Jack, who, wearing a puzzled frown upon her face, was standing there as if still a little doubtful of what was happening.

"Esther, darling," Amy said, "this is Mr. Hen Walters—and some of his friends." For a moment she looked at the cluster of young débutantes and their escorts, and then turned away, saying to no one in particular, and with no effort to lower her voice: "God, aren't they simply dreadful! . . . I *mean!* . . . You *know!*—" she addressed herself now to the elderly man with the artificial teeth— "Charley—in the name of God, what are you trying to do? . . . You old cradle-snatcher, you! . . . I *mean!*—after all, it's not *that* bad, is it?" She surveyed the group of girls again and turned away with a brief, hoarse laugh. "All these little Junior League bitches!" she muttered. "God! . . . How do you stand it, anyway—you old bastard!" She was talking now in her natural tone of voice, good-naturedly, as though there was nothing in the least unusual in what she was saying. Then with another short laugh she added: "Why don't you come to see me any more?"

He licked his lips nervously and bared his artificial teeth before he answered:

"Wanted to see you, Amy, for ever so long. . . . What? . . . Intended to stop in. . . . Matter of fact, did stop by some time ago, but you'd just sailed. . . . What? . . . You've been away, haven't you? . . . What?"

As he spoke in his clipped staccato he kept licking his thin lips lecherously, and at the same time he scratched himself, rooting obscenely into the inner thigh of his right leg in a way that suggested he was wearing woolen underwear. In doing so he inadvertently pulled up his trouser leg and it stayed there, revealing the tops of his socks and a portion of white meat.

Meanwhile Hen Walters was smiling brightly and burbling on to Mrs. Jack:

"So nice of you to let us all come in,"—although she, poor lady, had had nothing at all to do with it. "Piggy told us it would be all right. I hope you don't mind."

"But no-o—not at all!" she protested, still with a puzzled look. "Any friends of Mr. Logan's. . . . But won't you all have a drink, or something to eat? There's loads——"

217

"Oh, *heavens,* no!" burbled Mr. Walters. "We've all been to Tony's and we simply *gorged* ourselves! If we took another mouthful, I'm absolutely positive we should explode!"

He uttered these words with such ecstatic jubilation that it seemed he might explode at any moment in a large, moist bubble.

"Well, then, if you're sure," she began.

"Oh, *absolutely!*" cried Mr. Walters rapturously. "But we're holding up the show!" he exclaimed. "And, after all, that's what we're here to see. It would simply be a tragedy to miss it. . . . O Piggy!" he shouted to his friend, who had been cheerfully grinning all the while and crawling about on his kneepads. "Do begin! Everyone's simply dying to see it! . . . I've seen it a dozen times myself," he announced gleefully to the general public, "and it becomes more fascinating every time. . . . So if you're ready, please begin!"

Mr. Logan was ready.

The new arrivals held their position along one wall, and the other people now withdrew a little, leaving them to themselves. The audience was thus divided into two distinct halves—the people of wealth and talent on one side, and those of wealth and fashion or "Society" on the other.

On a signal from Mr. Logan, Mr. Walters detached himself from his group, came over, arranged the tails of his coat, and knelt down gracefully beside his friend. Then, acting on instructions, he read aloud from a typewritten paper which Mr. Logan had handed to him. It was a whimsical document designed to put everybody in the right mood, for it stated that in order to enjoy and understand the circus one must make an effort to recover his lost youth and have the spirit of a child again. Mr. Walters read it with great gusto in a cultivated tone of voice which almost ran over with happy laughter. When he had finished, he got up and resumed his place among his friends, and Mr. Logan then began his performance.

It started, as all circuses should, with a grand procession of the performers and the animals in the menagerie. Mr. Logan accomplished this by taking each wire figure in his thick hand and walking it around the ring and then solemnly out again. Since there were a great many animals and a great many performers, this took some time, but it was greeted at its conclusion with loud applause.

Then came an exhibition of bareback riders. Mr. Logan galloped his wire horses into the ring and round and round with movements of his hand. Then he put the riders on top of the

218

wire horses, and, holding them firmly in place, he galloped these around too. Then there was an interlude of clowns, and he made the wire figures tumble about by manipulating them with his hands. After this came a procession of wire elephants. This performance gained particular applause because of the clever way in which Mr. Logan made the figures imitate the swaying, ponderous lurch of elephants—and also because people were not always sure what each act meant, and when they were able to identify something, a pleasant little laugh of recognition would sweep the crowd and they would clap their hands to show they had got it.

There were a good many acts of one kind or another, and at last the trapeze performers were brought on. It took a little while to get this act going because Mr. Logan, with his punctilious fidelity to reality, had first to string up a little net below the trapezes. And when the act did begin it was unconscionably long, chiefly because Mr. Logan was not able to make it work. He set the little wire figures to swinging and dangling from their perches. This part went all right. Then he tried to make one little figure leave its trapeze, swing through the air, and catch another figure by its downswept hands. This wouldn't work. Again and again the little wire figure soared through the air, caught at the outstretched hands of the other doll—and missed ingloriously. It became painful. People craned their necks and looked embarrassed. But Mr. Logan was not embarrassed. He giggled happily with each new failure and tried again. It went on and on. Twenty minutes must have passed while Mr. Logan repeated his attempts. But nothing happened. At length, when it became obvious that nothing was going to happen, Mr. Logan settled the whole matter himself by taking one little figure firmly between two fat fingers, conveying it to the other, and carefully hooking it onto the other's arms. Then he looked up at his audience and giggled cheerfully, to be greeted after a puzzled pause by perfunctory applause.

Mr. Logan was now ready for the grand climax, the *pièce de résistance* of the entire occasion. This was his celebrated sword-swallowing act. With one hand he picked up a small rag doll, stuffed with wadding and with crudely painted features, and with the other hand he took a long hairpin, bent it more or less straight, forced one end through the fabric of the doll's mouth, and then began patiently and methodically to work it down the rag throat. People looked on with blank faces, and then, as the meaning of Mr. Logan's operation dawned on them, they smiled at one another in a puzzled, doubting way.

It went on and on until it began to be rather horrible. Mr. Logan kept working the hairpin down with thick, probing fingers, and when some impediment of wadding got in his way he would look up and giggle foolishly. Halfway down he struck

219

an obstacle that threatened to stop him from going any farther. But he persisted—persisted horribly.

It was a curious spectacle and would have furnished interesting material for the speculations of a thoughtful historian of life and customs in this golden age. It was astounding to see so many intelligent men and women—people who had had every high and rare advantage of travel, reading, music, and aesthetic cultivation, and who were usually so impatient of the dull, the boring, and the trivial—patiently assembled here to give their respectful attention to Mr. Piggy Logan's exhibition. But even respect for the accepted mode was wearing thin. The performance had already lasted a weary time, and some of the guests were beginning to give up. In pairs and groups they would look at one another with lifted eyebrows, and quietly would filter out into the hall or in the restorative direction of the dining room.

Many, however, seemed determined to stick it out. As for the young "Society" crowd, all of them continued to look on with eager interest. Indeed, as Mr. Logan went on probing with his hairpin, one young woman with the pure, cleanly chiseled face so frequently seen in members of her class turned to the young man beside her and said:

"I think it's *frightfully* interesting—the way he does that. Don't you?"

And the young man, evidently in the approved accent, said briefly, "Eh!"—an ejaculation which might have been indicative of almost anything, but which was here obviously taken for agreement. This interchange between them had taken place, like all the conversations in the group, in a curiously muffled, clipped speech. Both the girl and the young man had barely opened their mouths—their words had come out between almost motionless lips. This seemed to be the fashionable way of talking among these people.

As Mr. Logan kept working and pressing with his hairpin, suddenly the side of the bulging doll was torn open and some of the stuffing began to ooze out. Miss Lily Mandell watched with an expression of undisguised horror and, as the doll began to lose its entrails, she pressed one hand against her stomach in a gesture of nausea, said "Ugh!"—and made a hasty exit. Others followed her. And even Mrs. Jack, who at the start of the performance had slipped on a wonderful jacket of gold thread and seated herself cross-legged on the floor like a dutiful child, squarely before the maestro and his puppets, finally got up and went out into the hall, where most of her guests were now assembled.

Almost no one was left to witness the concluding scenes of Mr. Piggy Logan's circus except the uninvited group of his own particular friends.

Out in the hall Mrs. Jack found Lily Mandell talking to George Webber. She approached them with a bright, affectionate little smile and queried hopefully:

"Are you enjoying it, Lily? And you, darling?"—turning fondly to George—"Do you like it? Are you having a good time?"

Lily answered in a tone of throaty disgust:

"When he kept on pushing that long pin into the doll and all its insides began oozing out—ugh!"—she made a nauseous face—"I simply couldn't stand it any longer! It was horrible! I had to get out! I thought I was going to puke!"

Mrs. Jack's shoulders shook, her face reddened, and she gasped in a hysterical whisper:

"I know! Wasn't it awful!"

"But what is it, anyway?" said the attorney, Roderick Hale, as he came up and joined them.

"Oh, hello, Rod!" said Mrs. Jack. "What do you make of it—hah?"

"I can't make it out," he said, with an annoyed look into the living room, where Piggy Logan was still patiently carrying on. "What is it all supposed to be, anyway? And who is this fellow?" he said in an irritated tone, as if his legal and fact-finding mind was annoyed by a phenomenon he could not fathom. "It's like some puny form of decadence," he muttered.

Just then Mr. Jack approached his wife and, lifting his shoulders in a bewildered shrug, said:

"What is it? My God, perhaps *I'm* crazy!"

Mrs. Jack and Lily Mandell bent together, shuddering helplessly as women do when they communicate whispered laughter to one another.

"Poor Fritz!" Mrs. Jack gasped faintly.

Mr. Jack cast a final bewildered look into the living room, surveyed the wreckage there, then turned away with a short laugh:

"I'm going to my room!" he said with decision. "Let me know if he leaves the furniture!"

Chapter Nineteen

Unscheduled Climax

At the conclusion of Mr. Logan's performance there was a ripple of applause in the living room, followed by the sound of voices. The fashionable young people clustered around Mr. Logan, chattering congratulations. Then, without paying attention to anybody else, and without a word to their hostess, they left.

Other people now gathered about Mrs. Jack and made their farewells. They began to leave, singly and in pairs and groups, until presently no one remained except those intimates and friends who are always the last to leave a big party—Mrs. Jack and her family, George Webber, Miss Mandell, Stephen Hook, and Amy Carleton. And, of course, Mr. Logan, who was busy amid the general wreckage he had created, putting his wire dolls back into his two enormous valises.

The atmosphere of the whole place was now curiously changed. It was an atmosphere of absence, of completion. Everybody felt a little bit as one feels in a house the day after Christmas, or an hour after a wedding, or on a great liner at one of the Channel ports when most of the passengers have disembarked and the sorrowful remnant know that the voyage is really over and that they are just marking time for a little while until their own hour comes to depart.

Mrs. Jack looked at Piggy Logan and at the chaos he had made of her fine room, and then glanced questioningly at Lily Mandell as if to say: "Can you understand all this? What has happened?" Miss Mandell and George Webber surveyed Mr. Logan with undisguised distaste. Stephen Hook remained aloof, looking bored. Mr. Jack, who had come forth from his room to bid his guests good-bye and had lingered by the elevator till the last one had gone, now peered in through the hall door at the kneeling figure in the living room, and with a comical gesture of uplifted hands said: "What is it?"—leaving everybody convulsed with laughter.

But even when Mr. Jack came into the room and stood staring down quizzically, Mr. Logan did not look up. He seemed not to have heard anything. Utterly oblivious of their

222

presence, he was happily absorbed in the methodical task of packing up the litter that surrounded him.

Meanwhile the two rosy-cheeked maids, May and Janie, were busily clearing away glasses, bottles, and bowls of ice, and Nora started putting the books back on their shelves. Mrs. Jack looked on rather helplessly, and Amy Carleton stretched herself out flat on the floor with her hands beneath her head, closed her eyes, and appeared to go to sleep. All the rest were obviously at a loss what to do, and just stood and sat around, waiting for Mr. Logan to finish and be gone.

The place had sunk back into its wonted quiet. The blended murmur of the unceasing city, which during the party had been shut out and forgotten, now penetrated the walls of the great building and closed in once more upon these lives. The noises of the street were heard again.

Outside, below them, there was the sudden roar of a fire truck, the rapid clanging of its bell. It turned the corner into Park Avenue and the powerful sound of its motors faded away like distant thunder. Mrs. Jack went to the window and looked out. Other trucks now converged upon the corner from different directions until four more had passed from sight.

"I wonder where the fire can be," she remarked with detached curiosity. Another truck roared down the side street and thundered into Park. "It must be quite a big one—six engines have driven past. It must be somewhere in this neighborhood."

Amy Carleton sat up and blinked her eyes, and for a moment all of them were absorbed in idle speculation about where the fire might be. But presently they began to look again at Mr. Logan. At long last his labors seemed to be almost over. He began to close the big valises and adjust the straps.

Just then Lily Mandell turned her head toward the hall, sniffed sharply, and suddenly said:

"Does anyone smell smoke?"

"Hah? What?" said Mrs. Jack. And then, going into the hall, she cried excitedly: "But yes! There is quite a strong smell of smoke out here! I think it would be just as well if we got out of the building until we find out what's wrong." Her face was now burning with excitement. "I suppose we'd better," she said. "Everybody come on!" Then: "O Mr. Logan!"—she raised her voice, and now for the first time he lifted his round and heavy face with an expression of inquiring innocence— "I say—I think perhaps we'd all better get out, Mr. Logan, until we find out where the fire is! Are you ready?"

"Yes, of course," said Mr. Logan cheerfully. "But fire?"—in

223

a puzzled tone. "What fire? Is there a fire?"

"I think the building is on fire," said Mr. Jack smoothly, but with an edge of heavy irony, "so perhaps we'd better all get out—that is, unless you prefer to stay."

"Oh no," said Mr. Logan brightly, getting clumsily to his feet. "I'm quite ready, thank you, except for changing my clothes——"

"I think that had better wait," said Mr. Jack.

"Oh, the girls!" cried Mrs. Jack suddenly, and, snapping the ring on and off her finger, she trotted briskly toward the dining room. "Nora—Janie—May! Girls! We're all going down-stairs—there's a fire somewhere in the building. You'll have to come with us till we find out where it is."

"Fire, Mrs. Jack?" said Nora stupidly, staring at her mistress.

Mrs. Jack saw at a glance her dull eye and her flushed face, and thought: "She's been at it again! I might have known it!" Then aloud, impatiently:

"Yes, Nora, fire. Get the girls together and tell them they'll have to come along with us. And—oh!—Cook!" she cried quickly. "Where is Cookie? Go get her, someone. Tell her she'll have to come, too!"

The news obviously upset the girls. They looked helplessly at one another and began to move aimlessly around, as if no longer certain what to do.

"Shall we take our things, Mrs. Jack?" said Nora, looking at her dully. "Will we have time to pack?"

"Of course not, Nora!" exclaimed Mrs. Jack, out of all patience. "We're not moving out! We're simply going down-stairs till we can learn where the fire is and how bad it is! . . . And Nora, please get Cook and bring her with you! You know how rattled and confused she gets!"

"Yes'm" said Nora, staring at her helplessly. "An' will that be all, mum?—I mean—" and gulped—"will we be needin' anything?"

"For heaven's sake, Nora—*no!* . . . Nothing except your coats. Tell the girls and Cook to wear their coats."

"Yes'm," said Nora dumbly, and after a moment, looking fuddled and confused, she went uncertainly through the dining room to the kitchen.

Mr. Jack, meanwhile, had gone out into the hall and was ringing the elevator bell. There, after a short interval, his family, guests, and servants joined him. Quietly he took stock of them:

Esther's face was flaming with suppressed excitement, but

her sister, Edith, who had hardly opened her mouth all evening and had been so inconspicuous that no one had noticed her, was her usual pale, calm self. Good girl, Edith! His daughter, Alma, he observed with satisfaction, was also taking this little adventure in her stride. She looked cool, beautiful, a bit bored by it all. The guests, of course, were taking it as a lark—and why not?—*they* had nothing to lose. All except that young Gentile fool—George What's-his-name. Look at him now—all screwed up and tense, pacing back and forth and darting his feverish glances in all directions. You'd think it was *his* property that was going up in smoke!

But where was that Mr. Piggy Logan? When last seen, he was disappearing into the guest room. Was the idiot changing his clothes after all?—Ah, here he comes! "At least," thought Mr. Jack humorously, "it must be he, for if it isn't who in the name of God is it?"

The figure that Mr. Logan now cut as he emerged from the guest room and started down the hall was, indeed, a most extraordinary one. All of them turned to look at him and saw that he was taking no chances of losing his little wire dolls or his street clothes in any fire. Still wearing the "costume" that he had put on for his performance, he came grunting along with a heavy suitcase in each hand, and over one shoulder he had slung his coat, vest, and trousers, his overweight tan shoes were tied together by their laces and hung suspended around his neck, where they clunked against his chest as he walked, and on his head, perched on top of the football helmet, was his neat grey hat. So accoutered, he came puffing along, dropped his bags near the elevator, then straightened up and grinned cheerfully.

Mr. Jack kept on ringing the bell persistently, and presently the voice of Herbert, the elevator boy, could be heard shouting up the shaft from a floor or two below:

"All right! All right! I'll be right up, folks, as soon as I take down this load!"

The sound of other people's voices, excited, chattering, came up the shaft to them; then the elevator door banged shut and they could hear the car going down.

There was nothing to do but wait. The smell of smoke in the hallway was getting stronger all the time, and although no one was seriously alarmed, even the phlegmatic Mr. Logan was beginning to feel the nervous tension.

Soon the elevator could be heard coming up again. It mounted steadily—and then suddenly stopped somewhere just below them. Herbert could be heard working his lever and fooling with the door. Mr. Jack rang the bell impatiently. There was no response. He hammered on the door. Then Herbert shouted up again, and he was so near that all of them could hear every word:

"Mr. Jack, will you all please use the service elevator. This one's out of order. I can't go any farther."

"Well, that's that," said Mr. Jack.

He put on his derby, and without another word started down the hall toward the service landing. In silence the others followed him.

At this moment the lights went out. The place was plunged in inky blackness. There was a brief, terrifying moment when the women caught their breaths sharply. In the darkness the smell of smoke seemed much stronger, more acrid and biting, and it was beginning to make their eyes smart. Nora moaned a little, and all the servants started to mill around like stricken cattle. But they calmed down at the comforting assurance in Mr. Jack's quiet voice speaking in the dark:

"Esther," he said calmly, "we'll have to light candles. Can you tell me where they are?"

She told him. He reached into a table drawer, pulled out a flashlight, and went through a door that led to the kitchen. Soon he reappeared with a box of tallow candles. He gave one to each person and lighted them.

They were now a somewhat ghostly company. The women lifted their candles and looked at one another with an air of bewildered surmise. The faces of the maids and Cookie, in the steady flame that each held before her face, looked dazed and frightened. Cookie wore a confused, fixed smile and muttered jargon to herself. Mrs. Jack, deeply excited, turned questioningly to George, who was at her side:

"Isn't it strange?" she whispered. "Isn't it the strangest thing? I mean—the party—all the people—and then this." And, lifting her candle higher, she looked about her at the ghostly company.

And, suddenly, George was filled with almost unbearable love and tenderness for her, because he knew that she, like himself, felt in her heart the mystery and strangeness of all life. And his emotion was all the more poignant because in the same instant, with sharp anguish, he remembered his decision, and knew that they had reached the parting of the ways.

Mr. Jack flourished his candle as a signal to the others and led the procession down the hall. Edith, Alma, Miss Mandell, Amy Carleton, and Stephen Hook followed after him. Mr. Logan, who came next, was in a quandary. He couldn't manage both his baggage and his light, so after a moment of indecision he blew out his candle, set it on the floor, seized his valises, gave a mighty heave, and, with neck held stiff to keep his hat from tumbling off of the football helmet, he staggered after the retreating figures of the women. Mrs. Jack and George came last, with the servants trailing behind.

Mrs. Jack had reached the door that opened onto the service landing when she heard a confused shuffling behind her in the line, and when she glanced back along the hallway she saw two teetering candles disappearing in the general direction of the kitchen. It was Cook and Nora.

"Oh Lord!" cried Mrs. Jack in a tone of exasperation and despair. "What on earth are they trying to do? . . . *Nora!*" she raised her voice sharply. Cook had already disappeared, but Nora heard her and turned in a bewildered way. "Nora, where *are* you going?" shouted Mrs. Jack impatiently.

"Why—why, mum—I thought I'd go back here an' get some things," said Nora in a confused and thickened voice.

"No you *won't,* either!" cried Mrs. Jack furiously, at the same time thinking bitterly: "She probably wanted to sneak back there to get another drink!" "You come right along with us!" she called sharply. "And where is Cook?" Then, seeing the two bewildered girls, May and Janie, milling around helplessly, she took them by the arm and gave them a little push toward the door. "You girls get along!" she cried. "What are you gawking at?"

George had gone back after the befuddled Nora, and, after seizing her and herding her down the hall, had dashed into the kitchen to find Cook. Mrs. Jack followed him with her candle held high in her hand, and said anxiously:

"Are you there, darling?" Then, calling out loudly: "Cook! *Cook!* Where are you?"

Suddenly Cook appeared like a spectral visitant, still clutching her candle and flitting from room to room down the narrow hall of the servants' quarters. Mrs. Jack cried out angrily:

"Oh, Cookie! What *are* you doing? You've simply got to come on now! We're waiting on you!" And she thought to herself again, as she had thought so many times before: "She's probably an old miser. I suppose she's got her wad hoarded away back there somewhere. That's why she hates to leave."

Cook had disappeared again, this time into her own room. After a brief, fuming silence Mrs. Jack turned to George. They looked at each other for a moment in that strange light and circumstance, and suddenly both laughed explosively.

"My God!" shrieked Mrs. Jack. "Isn't it the damnedest——"

At this instant Cook emerged once more and glided away down the hall. They yelled at her and dashed after her, and caught her just as she was about to lock herself into a bathroom.

"Now Cook!" cried Mrs. Jack angrily. "Come on now! You simply must!"

227

Cook goggled at her and muttered some incomprehensible jargon in an ingratiating tone.

"Do you hear, Cook?" Mrs. Jack cried furiously. "You've got to come now! You can't stay here any longer!"

"Augenblick! Augenblick!" muttered Cook cajolingly.

At last she thrust something into her bosom, and, still looking longingly behind her, allowed herself to be prodded, pushed, and propelled down the servants' hall, into the kitchen, through the door into the main hallway, and thence out to the service landing.

All the others were now gathered there, waiting while Mr. Jack tested the bell of the service elevator. His repeated efforts brought no response, so in a few moments he said coolly:

"Well, I suppose there's nothing for us to do now except to walk down."

Immediately he headed for the concrete stairs beside the elevator shaft, which led, nine flights down, to the ground floor and safety. The others followed him. Mrs. Jack and George herded the servants before them and waited for Mr. Logan to get a firm grip on his suitcases and start down, which at length he did, puffing and blowing and letting the bags bump with loud thuds on each step as he descended.

The electric lights on the service stairways were still burning dimly, but they clung to their candles with an instinctive feeling that these primitive instruments were now more to be trusted than the miracles of science. The smoke had greatly increased. In fact, the air was now so dense with floating filaments and shifting plumes that breathing was uncomfortable.

From top to bottom the service stairs provided an astounding spectacle. Doors were opening now on every floor and other tenants were coming out to swell the tide of refugees. They made an extraordinary conglomeration—a composite of classes, types, and characters that could have been found nowhere else save in a New York apartment house such as this. There were people in splendid evening dress, and beautiful women blazing with jewels and wearing costly wraps. There were others in pajamas who had evidently been awakened from sleep and had hastily put on slippers, dressing gowns, kimonos, or whatever garments they could snatch up in the excitement of the moment. There were young and old, masters and servants, a mixture of a dozen races and their excited babel of strange tongues. There were German cooks and French maids, English butlers and Irish serving girls. There were Swedes and Danes and Italians and Norwegians, with a sprinkling of White

228

Russians. There were Poles and Czechs and Austrians, Negroes and Hungarians. All of these poured out helter-skelter on the landing stages of the service stairway, chattering, gesticulating, their interests all united now in their common pursuit of safety.

As they neared the ground floor, helmeted firemen began to push their way up the stairs against the tide of downward-moving traffic. Several policemen followed them and tried to allay any feelings of alarm or panic.

"It's all right, folks! Everything's O.K.!" one big policeman shouted cheerfully as he went up past the members of the Jack party. "The fire's over now!"

These words, spoken to quiet the people and to expedite their orderly progress from the building, had an opposite effect from that which the policeman had intended. George Webber, who was bringing up the end of the procession, paused upon hearing these reassuring words, called to the others, and turned to retrace his way upstairs again. As he did so, he saw that the policeman was about to throw a fit. From the landing half a flight above, he was making agonized faces and frantic gestures at George in a silent and desperate entreaty to him not to come back any farther or to encourage the others to come back, but to leave the building as quickly as possible. The others had looked around when George had called, and had witnessed this pantomime—so now, genuinely alarmed for the first time, they turned again and fled down the stairs as fast as they could go.

George himself, seized with the same momentary panic, was hastening after them when he heard some tapping and hammering noises from the shaft of the service elevator. They seemed to come from up above somewhere. For just a moment he hesitated and listened. The tapping began, then stopped . . . began again . . . stopped again. It seemed to be a signal of some kind, but he couldn't make it out. It gave him an eerie feeling. A chill ran up his spine. He broke out in goose flesh. Stumbling blindly, he fled after the others.

As they came out into the great central courtyard of the building, their moment's terror dropped away from them as quickly as it had come upon them. They filled their lungs with the crisp, cold air, and so immediate was their sense of release and relief that each one of them felt a new surge of life and energy, a preternaturally heightened aliveness. Mr. Logan, his round face streaming with perspiration and his breath coming in loud snorts and wheezes, summoned his last remaining strength and, ignoring the tender shins of those about him, bumped and banged his burdened way through the crowd and

229

disappeared. The others of Mr. Jack's party remained together, laughing and talking and watching with alert interest everything that was going on around them.

The scene of which they were a part was an amazing one. As if it had been produced by the combining genius of a Shakespeare or a Breughel, the whole theatre of human life was in it, so real and so miraculously compressed that it had the nearness and the intensity of a vision. The great hollow square formed by the towering walls of the building was filled with people in every conceivable variety of dress and undress. And from two dozen entry ways within the arched cloisters that ran around the court on all four sides, new hordes of people were now constantly flooding out of the huge honeycomb to add their own color and movement and the babel of their own tumultuous tongues to the pageantry and the pandemonium already there. Above this scene, uplifted on the arches of the cloisters, the mighty walls soared fourteen stories to frame the starry heavens. In the wing where Mr. Jack's apartment was the lights were out and all was dark, but everywhere else those beetling sides were still blazing with their radiant squares of warmth, their many cells still burning with all the huge deposit of their just-departed life.

Except for the smoke that had been in some of the halls and stairways, there was no sign of fire. As yet, few people seemed to comprehend the significance of the event which had so unceremoniously dumped them out of their sleek nests into the open weather. For the most part they were either bewildered and confused or curious and excited. Only an occasional person here and there betrayed any undue alarm over the danger which had touched their lives and fortunes.

Such a one now appeared at a second-floor window on the side of the court directly opposite the Jack's entry. He was a man with a bald head and a pink, excited face, and it was instantly apparent that he was on the verge of emotional collapse. He threw open the window and in a tone shaken by incipient hysteria cried out loudly:

"Mary! . . . Mary!" His voice rose almost to a scream as he sought for her below.

A woman in the crowd came forward below the window, looked up, and said quietly:

"Yes, Albert."

"I can't find the key!" he cried in a trembling voice. "The door's locked! I can't get out!"

"Oh, Albert," said the woman more quietly and with evident embarrassment, "don't get so excited, dear. You're in no danger—and the key is bound to be there somewhere. I'm sure you'll find it if you look."

"But I tell you it isn't here!" he babbled. "I've looked, and it's
230

not here! I can't find it! . . . Here, you fellows!" he shouted at some firemen who were dragging a heavy hose across the graveled court. "I'm locked in! I want out of here!"

Most of the firemen paid no attention to him at all, but one of them looked up at the man, said briefly: "O.K., chief!"—and then went on about his work.

"Do you hear me?" the man screamed. "You firemen, you! I tell you . . . !"

"Dad. . . . Dad—" a young man beside the woman on the ground now spoke up quietly—"don't get so excited. You're in no danger there. All the fire is on the other side. They'll let you out in a minute when they can get to you."

Across the court, at the very entrance from which the Jacks had issued, a man in evening clothes, accompanied by his chauffeur, had been staggering in and out with great loads of ponderous ledgers. He had already accumulated quite a pile of them, which he was stacking up on the gravel and leaving under the guardianship of his butler. From the beginning this man had been so absorbed in what he was doing that he was completely unconscious of the milling throng around him. Now, as he again prepared to rush into the smoke-filled corridor with his chauffeur, he was stopped by the police.

"I'm sorry, sir," the policeman said, "but you can't go in there again. We've got orders not to let anybody in."

"But I've got to!" the man shouted. "I'm Philip J. Baer!" At the sound of this potent name, all those within hearing distance instantly recognized him as a wealthy and influential figure in the motion picture industry, and one whose accounts had recently been called into investigation by a board of governmental inquiry. "There are seventy-five millions dollars' worth of records in my apartment," he shouted, "and I've got to get them out! They've got to be saved!"

He tried to push his way in, but the policeman thrust him back.

"I'm sorry, Mr. Baer," he said obdurately, "but we have our orders. You can't come in."

The effect of this refusal was instantaneous and shocking. The one principle of Mr. Baer's life was that money is the only thing that counts because money can buy anything. That principle had been flouted. So the naked philosophy of tooth and claw, which in moments of security and comfort was veiled beneath a velvet sheath, now became ragingly insistent. A tall, dark man with a rapacious, beak-nosed face, he became now like a wild animal, a beast of prey. He went charging about among the crowds of people, offering everyone fabulous sums if they would save his cherished records. He rushed up to a group of firemen, seizing one of them by the arm and shaking him, shouting:

231

"I'm Philip J. Baer—I live in there! You've got to help me! I'll give any man here ten thousand dollars if he'll get my records out!"

The burly fireman turned his weathered face upon the rich man. "On your way, brother!" he said.

"But I tell you!" Mr. Baer shouted. "You don't know who I am! I'm——"

"I don't care who you are!" the fireman said. "On your way now! We've got work to do!"

And, roughly, he pushed the great man aside.

Most of the crowd behaved very well under the stress of these unusual circumstances. Since there was no actual fire to watch, the people shifted and moved about, taking curious side looks at one another out of the corners of their eyes. Most of them had never even seen their neighbors before, and now for the first time they had an opportunity to appraise one another. And in a little while, as the excitement and their need for communication broke through the walls of their reserve, they began to show a spirit of fellowship such as that enormous beehive of life had never seen before. People who, at other times, had never deigned so much as to nod at each other were soon laughing and talking together with the familiarity of long acquaintance.

A famous courtesan, wearing a chinchilla coat which her aged but wealthy lover had given her, now took off this magnificent garment and, walking over to an elderly woman with a delicate, patrician face, she threw the coat over this woman's thinly covered shoulders, at the same time saying in a tough but kindly voice:

"You wear this, dearie. You look cold."

And the older woman, after a startled expression had crossed her proud face, smiled graciously and thanked her tarnished sister in a sweet tone. Then the two women stood talking together like old friends.

A haughty old Bourbon of the Knickerbocker type was seen engaged in cordial conversation with a Tammany politician whose corrupt plunderings were notorious, and whose companionship, in any social sense, the Bourbon would have spurned indignantly an hour before.

Aristocrats of ancient lineage who had always held to a tradition of stiff-necked exclusiveness could be seen chatting familiarly with the plebeian parvenus of the new rich who had got their names and money, both together, only yesterday.

And so it went everywhere one looked. One saw race-proud Gentiles with rich Jews, stately ladies with musical-comedy actresses, a woman famous for her charities with a celebrated whore.

Meanwhile the crowd continued to watch curiously the labors of the firemen. Though no flames were visible, there was plenty of smoke in some of the halls and corridors, and the firemen had dragged in many lengths of great white hose which now made a network across the court in all directions. From time to time squadrons of helmeted men would dash into the smoky entries of the wing where the lights were out and would go upstairs, their progress through the upper floors made evident to the crowd below by the movement of their flashlights at the darkened windows. Others would emerge from the lower regions of basements and subterranean passages, and would confer intimately with their chiefs and leaders.

All at once somebody in the waiting throng noticed something and pointed toward it. A murmur ran through the crowd, and all eyes were turned upward searchingly to one of the top-floor apartments in the darkened wing. There, through an open window four floors directly above the Jacks' apartment, wisps of smoke could be seen curling upward.

Before very long the wisps increased to clouds, and suddenly a great billowing puff of oily black smoke burst through the open window, accompanied by a dancing shower of sparks. At this the whole crowd drew in its collective breath in a sharp intake of excitement—the strange, wild joy that people always feel when they see fire.

Rapidly the volume of smoke increased. That single room on the top floor was apparently the only one affected, but now the black and oily-looking smoke was billowing out in belching folds, and inside the room the smoke was colored luridly by the sinister and unmistakable glow of fire.

Mrs. Jack gazed upward with a rapt and fascinated expression. She turned to Hook with one hand raised and lightly clenched against her breast, and whispered slowly:

"Steve—isn't it the strangest—the most—?" She did not finish. With her eyes full of the deep sense of wonder that she was trying to convey, she just stood with her hand loosely clenched and looked at him.

He understood her perfectly—too well, indeed. His heart was sick with fear, with hunger, and with fascinated wonder. For him the whole scene was too strong, too full of terror and overwhelming beauty to be endured. He was sick with it, fainting with it. He wanted to be borne away, to be sealed hermetically somewhere, in some dead and easeful air where he would be free forevermore of this consuming fear that racked his flesh. And yet he could not tear himself away. He looked at everything with sick but fascinated eyes. He was like a man mad

233

with thirst who drinks the waters of the sea and sickens with each drop he drinks, yet cannot leave off drinking because of the wetness and the coolness to his lips. So he looked and loved it all with the desperate ardor of his fear. He saw the wonder of it, the strangeness of it, the beauty and the magic and the nearness of it. And it was so much more real than anything imagination could contrive that the effect was overpowering. The whole thing took on an aura of the incredible.

"It can't be true," he thought. "It's unbelievable. But here it is!"

And there it was. He didn't miss a thing. And yet he stood there ridiculously, a derby hat upon his head, his hands thrust into the pockets of his overcoat, the velvet collar turned up around his neck, his face, as usual, turned three-quarters away from the whole world, his heavy-lidded, wearily indifferent eyes surveying the scene with Mandarin contempt, as if to say: "Really, what is this curious assembly? Who are these extraordinary creatures that go milling about me? And why is everyone so frightfully eager, so terribly earnest about everything?"

A group of firemen thrust past him with the dripping brass-nozzled end of a great hose. It slid through the gravel like the tough-scaled hide of a giant boa constrictor, and as the firemen passed him, Hook heard their booted feet upon the stones and he saw the crude strength and the simple driving purpose in their coarse faces. And his heart shrank back within him, sick with fear, with wonder, with hunger, and with love at the unconscious power, joy, energy, and violence of life itself.

At the same moment a voice in the crowd—drunken, boisterous, and too near—cut the air about him. It jarred his ears, angered him, and made him timorously hope it would not come closer. Turning slightly toward Mrs. Jack, in answer to her whispered question, he murmured in a bored tone:

"Strange? . . . Um . . . yes. An interesting revelation of the native *moeurs*."

Amy Carleton seemed really happy. It was as if, for the first time that evening, she had found what she was looking for. Nothing in her manner or appearance had changed. The quick, impetuous speech, the broken, semi-coherent phrases, the hoarse laugh, the exuberant expletives, and the lovely, dark, crisp-curled head with its snub nose and freckled face were just the same. Still there was something different about her. It was as if all the splintered elements of her personality had now, in the strong and marvelous chemistry of the fire, been brought together into crystalline union. She was just as she had been before, except that her inner torment had somehow been let out, and wholeness let in.

Poor child! It was now instantly apparent to those who knew

her that, like so many other "lost" people, she would not have been lost at all—if only there could always be a fire. The girl could not accept getting up in the morning or going to bed at night, or doing any of the accustomed things in their accustomed order. But she could and did accept the fire. It seemed to her wonderful. She was delighted with everything that happened. She threw herself into it, not as a spectator, but as a vital and inspired participant. She seemed to know people everywhere, and could be seen moving about from group to group, her ebony head bobbing through the crowd, her voice eager, hoarse, abrupt, elated. When she returned to her own group she was full of it all.

"I *mean*! . . . You *know*!" she burst out. "These firemen here!—" she gestured hurriedly toward three or four helmeted men as they dashed into a smoke-filled entry with a tube of chemicals—"when you think of what they have to *know*!—of what they have to *do*!—I went to a big fire once!—" she shot out quickly in explanatory fashion—"a guy in the department was a friend of mine!—I *mean*—!" she laughed hoarsely, elatedly—"when you *think* of what they have to——"

At this point there was a splintering crash within. Amy laughed jubilantly and made a quick and sudden little gesture as if this answered everything.

"After *all*, I mean!" she cried.

While this was going on, a young girl in evening dress had wandered casually up to the group and, with that freedom which the fire had induced among all these people, now addressed herself in the flat, nasal, and almost toneless accents of the Middle West to Stephen Hook:

"You don't think it's very bad, do you?" she said, looking up at the smoke and flames that were now belching formidably from the top-floor window. Before anyone had a chance to answer, she went on: "I *hope* it's not bad."

Hook, who was simply terrified at her raw intrusion, had turned away from her and was looking at her sideways with eyes that were almost closed. The girl, getting no answer from him, spoke now to Mrs. Jack:

"It'll be just too bad if anything is wrong up there, won't it?"

Mrs. Jack, her face full of friendly reassurance, answered quickly in a gentle voice.

"No, dear," she said, "I don't think it's bad at all." She looked up with trouble in her eyes at the billowing mass of smoke and flame which now, to tell the truth, looked not only bad but distinctly threatening; then, lowering her perturbed gaze quickly, she said to the girl encouragingly: "I'm sure everything is going to be all right."

"Well," said the girl, "I hope you're right. . . . Because," she added, apparently as an afterthought as she turned away, "that's
235

Mama's room, and if she's up there it'll be just too bad, won't it?—I mean, if it *is* too bad."

With this astounding utterance, spoken casually in a flat voice that betrayed no emotion whatever, she moved off into the crowd.

There was dead silence for a moment. Then Mrs. Jack turned to Hook in alarm, as if she were not certain she had heard aright.

"Did you hear—?" she began in a bewildered tone.

"But there you *are!*" broke in Amy, with a short, exultant laugh. "What I *mean* is—the whole thing's *there!*"

Chapter Twenty

Out of Control

Suddenly all the lights in the building went out, plunging the court in darkness save for the fearful illumination provided by the bursts of flame from the top-floor apartment. There was a deep murmur and a restless stir in the crowd. Several young smart alecks in evening clothes took this opportunity to go about among the dark mass of people, arrogantly throwing the beams of their flashlights into the faces of those they passed.

The police now began to move upon the crowd, and, good-naturedly but firmly, with outstretched arms, started to herd everybody back, out of the court, through the arches, and across the surrounding streets. The streets were laced and crisscrossed everywhere with bewildering skeins of hose, and all normal sounds were lost in the powerful throbbing of the fire engines. Unceremoniously, like driven cattle, the residents of the great building were forced back to the opposite sidewalks, where they had to take their places among the humbler following of the general public.

Some of the ladies, finding themselves too thinly clad in the night air, sought refuge in the apartments of friends who lived in the neighborhood. Others, tired of standing around, went to hotels to wait or to spend the night. But most of the people hung on, curious and eager to see what the outcome might be. Mr. Jack took Edith, Alma, Amy, and two or three young people of Amy's acquaintance to a near-by hotel for drinks. The others stayed and looked on curiously for a while. But presently Mrs. Jack, George Webber, Miss Mandell, and Stephen Hook repaired to a drug store that was close at hand. They sat at the counter, ordered coffee and sandwiches, and engaged in eager chatter with other refugees who now filled the store.

The conversation of all these people was friendly and casual. Some were even gay. But in their talk there was also now a note note of perturbation—of something troubled, puzzled, and uncertain. Men of wealth and power had been suddenly dispossessed from their snug nests with their wives, families, and dependents, and now there was nothing they could do but wait, herded homelessly into drug stores and hotel lobbies, or huddled together in their wraps on street corners like shipwrecked voyagers, looking at one another with helpless eyes. Some of them felt, dimly, that they had been caught up by some mysterious and relentless force, and that they were being borne onward as unwitting of the power that ruled them as blind flies fastened to a revolving wheel. To others came the image of the tremendous web in which they felt they had become enmeshed—a web whose ramifications were so vast and complicated that they had not the faintest notion where it began or what its pattern was.

For in the well-ordered world in which these people lived, something had gone suddenly wrong. Things had got out of control. They were the lords and masters of the earth, vested with authority and accustomed to command, but now the control had been taken from them. So they felt strangely helpless, no longer able to command the situation, no longer able even to find out what was happening.

But, in ways remote from their blind and troubled kenning, events had been moving to their inexorable conclusion.

In one of the smoky corridors of that enormous hive, two men in boots and helmets had met in earnest communion.

"Did you find it?"

"Yes."

"Where is it?"

"It's in the basement, chief. It's not on the roof at all—a draft is taking it up a vent. But it's down there." He pointed with his thumb.

"Well, then, go get it. You know what to do."

"It looks bad, chief. It's going to be hard to get."

"What's the trouble?"

"If we flood the basement, we'll also flood two levels of railroad tracks. You know what that means."

237

For a moment their eyes held each other steadily. Then the older man jerked his head and started for the stairs.

"Come on," he said. "We're going down."

Down in the bowels of the earth there was a room where lights were burning and it was always night.

There, now, a telephone rang, and a man with a green eyeshade seated at a desk answered it.

"Hello. . . . Oh, hello, Mike."

He listened carefully for a moment, suddenly jerked forward taut with interest, and pulled the cigarette out of his mouth.

"The hell you say! . . . Where? Over track thirty-two? . . . They're going to flood it! . . . Hell!"

Deep in the honeycombs of the rock the lights burned green and red and yellow, silent in the eternal dark, lovely, poignant as remembered grief. Suddenly, all up and down the faintly gleaming rails, the green and yellow eyes winked out and flashed to warning red.

A few blocks away, just where the network of that amazing underworld of railroad yards begins its mighty flare of burnished steel, the Limited halted swiftly, but so smoothly that the passengers, already standing to debark, felt only a slight jar and were unaware that anything unusual had happened.

Ahead, however, in the cab of the electric locomotive which had pulled the great train the last miles of its span along the Hudson River, the engineer peered out and read the signs. He saw the shifting patterns of hard light against the dark, and swore:

"Now what the hell?"

And as the great train slid to a stop, the current in the third rail was shut off and the low whine that always came from the powerful motors of the locomotive was suddenly silenced. Turning now across his instruments to another man, the engineer spoke quickly:

"I wonder what the hell has happened," he said.

For a long time the Limited stood a silent and powerless thing of steel, while a short distance away the water flooded down and flowed between the tracks there like a river. And five hundred men and women who had been caught up from their lives and swiftly borne from cities, towns, and little hamlets all across the continent were imprisoned in the rock, weary, impatient,

238

frustrated—only five minutes away from the great station that was the end and goal of their combined desire. And in the station itself other hundreds waited for them—and went on waiting—restless, wondering, anxious, knowing nothing about the why of it.

Meanwhile, on the seventh landing of the service stairs in the evacuated building, firemen had been working feverishly with axes. The place was dense with smoke. The sweating men wore masks, and the only light they had was that provided by their torchlights.

They had battered open the doorway of the elevator shaft, and one of them had lowered himself down onto the roof of the imprisoned car half a floor below and was now cutting into the roof with his sharp axe.

"Have you got it, Ed?"

"Yeah—just about. . . . I'm almost through. . . . This next one does it, I think."

The axe smashed down again. There was a splintering crash. And then:

"O.K. . . . Wait a minute. . . . Hand me down that flashlight, Tom."

"See anything?"

In a moment, quietly:

"Yeah. . . . I'm going in. . . . Jim, you better come down, too. I'll need you."

There was a brief silence, then the man's quiet voice again:

"O.K. . . . I've got it. . . . Here, Jim, reach down and get underneath the arms. . . . Got it? . . . O.K. . . . Tom, you better reach down and help Jim. . . . Good."

Together they lifted it from its imprisoned trap, looked at it for a moment in the flare of their flashlights, and laid it down, not ungently, on the floor—something old and tired and dead and very pitiful.

Mrs. Jack went to the window of the drug store and peered out at the great building across the street.

"I wonder if anything's happening over there," she said to her friends with a puzzled look on her face. "Do you suppose it's over? Have they got it out?"

The dark immensity of those towering walls told nothing, but there were signs that the fire was almost out. There were fewer

239

lines of hose in the street, and one could see firemen pulling them in and putting them back in the trucks. Other firemen were coming from the building, bringing their tools and stowing them away. All the great engines were still throbbing powerfully, but the lines that had connected them with the hydrants were uncoupled, and the water they were pumping now came from somewhere else and was rushing in torrents down all the gutters. The police still held the crowd back and would not yet permit the tenants to return to their appartments.

The newspapermen, who had early arrived upon the scene, were now beginning to come into the drug store to telephone their stories to the papers. They were a motley crew, a little shabby and threadbare, with battered hats in which their press cards had been stuck, and some of them had the red noses which told of long hours spent in speakeasies.

One would have known that they were newspapermen even without their press cards. The signs were unmistakable. There was something jaded in the eye, something a little worn and tarnished about the whole man, something that got into his face, his tone, the way he walked, the way he smoked a cigarette, even into the hang of his trousers, and especially into his battered hat, which revealed instantly that these were gentlemen of the press.

It was something wearily receptive, wearily cynical, something that said wearily: "*I* know, *I* know. But what's the story? What's the racket?"

And yet it was something that one liked, too, something corrupted but still good, something that had once blazed with hope and aspiration, something that said: "Sure. I used to think I had it in me, too, and I'd have given my life to write something good. Now I'm just a whore. I'd sell my best friend out to get a story. I'd betray your trust, your faith, your friendliness, twist everything you say around until any sincerity, sense, or honesty that might be in your words was made to sound like the maunderings of a buffoon or a clown—if I thought it would make a better story. I don't give a damn for truth, for accuracy, for facts, for telling anything about you people here, your lives, your speech, the way you look, the way you really are, the special quality, tone, and weather of this moment—of this fire—except insofar as they will help to make a story. What I want to get is the special 'angle' on it. There has been grief and love and fear and ecstasy and pain and death tonight: a whole universe of living has been here enacted. But all of it doesn't matter a damn to me if I can only pick up something that will make the customers sit up tomorrow and rub their eyes—if I can tell 'em that in the excitement Miss Lena Ginster's pet boa constrictor escaped from its cage and that the police and fire departments are still looking for it while Members of Fashionable Apartment House Dwell in Terror. . . . So there I am, folks, with yellow fingers, weary eyeballs, a ginny breath, and what is left of last night's hangover, and I wish to God I could get to that telephone to send this story in, so the boss would tell me to go home, and I could step around to Eddy's place for a couple more highballs before I call it another day. But don't be too hard on me. Sure, I'd sell you out, of course. No man's name or any woman's reputation is safe with me—if I can make a story out of it—but at bottom I'm not such a bad guy. I have violated the standards of decency again and again, but in my heart I've always wanted to be decent. I don't tell the truth, but there's a kind of bitter honesty in me for all that. I'm able to look myself in the face at times, and tell the truth about myself and see just what I am. And I hate sham and hypocrisy and pretense and fraud and crookedness, and if I could only be sure that tomorrow was going to be the last day of the world—oh, Christ!—what a paper we'd get out in the morning! And, too, I have a sense of humor, I love gayety, food, drink, good talk, good companionship, the whole thrilling pageantry of life. So don't be too severe on me. I'm really not as bad as some of the things I have to do."

Such, indefinably yet plainly, were the markings of these men. It was as if the world which had so soiled them with its grimy touch had also left upon them some of its warm earthiness—the redeeming virtues of its rich experience, its wit and understanding, the homely fellowship of its pungent speech.

Two or three of them now went around among the people in the drug store and began to interview them. The questions that they asked seemed ludicrously inappropriate. They approached some of the younger and prettier girls, found out if they lived in the building, and immediately asked, with naïve eagerness, whether they were in the Social Register. Whenever any of the girls admitted that she was, the reporters would write down her name and the details of her parentage.

Meanwhile, one of the representatives of the press, a rather seedy-looking gentleman with a bulbous red nose and infrequent teeth, had called his City Desk on the telephone and, sprawled in the booth with his hat pushed back on his head and his legs sticking out through the open door, was reporting his findings. George Webber was standing with a group of people at the back of the store, near the booth. He had noticed the reporter when he first came in, and had been fascinated by something in his seedy, hard-boiled look; and now, although

241

George appeared to be listening to the casual chatter around him, he was really hanging with concentrated attention on every word the man was saying:

". . . Sure, that's what I'm tellin' yuh. Just take it down. . . . The police arrived," he went on importantly, as if fascinated by his own journalese—"the police arrived and threw a cordon round the building." There was a moment's pause, then the red-nosed man rasped out irritably: "No, no, no! Not a squadron! A cordon! . . . What's 'at? . . . *Cordon,* I say! C-o-r-d-o-n— cordon! . . . for Pete's sake!" he went on in an aggrieved tone. "How long have you been workin' on a newspaper, anyway? Didn't yuh ever hear of a cordon before? . . . Now get this. Listen—" he went on in a careful voice, glancing at some scrawled notes on a piece of paper in his hand. "Among the residents are included many Social Registerites and others prominent among the younger set. . . . What? How's that?" he said abruptly, rather puzzled. "Oh!"

He looked around quickly to see if he was being overheard, then lowered his voice and spoke again:

"Oh, sure! *Two!* . . . Nah, there was only two—that other story was all wrong. They found the old dame. . . . But that's what I'm tellin' yuh! She was all alone when the fire started—see! Her family was out, and when they got back they thought she was trapped up there. But they found her. She was down in the crowd. That old dame was one of the first ones out. . . . Yeh—only two. Both of 'em was elevator men." He lowered his voice a little more, then, looking at his notes, he read carefully: "John Enborg . . . age sixty-four . . . married . . . three children . . . lives in Jamaica, Queens. . . . You got that?" he said, then proceeded: "And Herbert Anderson . . . age twenty-five . . . unmarried . . . lives with his mother . . . 841 Southern Boulevard, the Bronx. . . . Have yuh got it? . . . Sure. Oh, sure!"

Once more he looked around, then lowered his voice before he spoke again:

"No, they couldn't get 'em out. They was both on the elevators, goin' up to get the tenants—see!—when some excited fool fumbled for the light switches and grabbed the wrong one and shut the current off on 'em. . . . Sure. That's the idea. They got caught between the floors. . . . They just got Enborg out," his voice sank lower. "They had to use axes. . . . Sure. Sure." He nodded into the mouthpiece. "That's it—smoke. Too late when they got to him. . . . No, that's all. Just those two. . . . No, they don't know about it yet. Nobody knows. The management wants to keep it quiet if they can. . . . What's that? Hey!—speak louder, can't yuh? You're mumblin' at me!"

He had shouted sharply, irritably, into the instrument, and and now listened attentively for a moment.

"Yeh, it's almost over. But it's been tough. They had trouble

242

gettin' at it. It started in the basement, then it went up a flue and out at the top. . . . Sure, I know," he nodded. "That's what made it so tough. Two levels of tracks are right below. They were afraid to flood the basement at first—afraid to risk it. They tried to get at it with chemicals, but couldn't. . . . Yeh, so they turned off the juice down there and put the water on it. They probably got trains backed up all the way to Albany by now. . . . Sure, they're pumpin' it out. It's about over, I guess, but it's been tough. . . . O.K., Mac. Want me to stick around? . . . O.K.," he said, and hung up.

Chapter Twenty-One

Love Is Not Enough

The fire was over.

Mrs. Jack and those who were with her went out on the street when they heard the first engine leaving. And there on the sidewalk were Mr. Jack, Edith, and Alma. They had met some old friends at the hotel and had left Amy and her companions with them.

Mr. Jack looked in good spirits, and his manner showed, mildly and pleasantly, that he had partaken of convivial refreshment. Over his arm he was carrying a woman's coat, which he now slipped around his wife's shoulders, saying:

"Mrs. Feldman sent you this, Esther. She said you could send it back tomorrow."

All this time she had had on nothing but her evening dress. She had remembered to tell the servants to wear their coats, but both she and Miss Mandell had forgotten theirs.

"How sweet of her!" cried Mrs. Jack, her face beginning to glow as she thought how kind everyone was in a time of stress. "Aren't people good?"

Other refugees, too, were beginning to straggle back now and were watching from the corner, where the police still made them wait. Most of the fire engines had already gone, and the rest were throbbing quietly with a suggestion of departure. One by one the great trucks thundered away. And presently the policemen got the signal to let the tenants return to their rooms.

Stephen Hook said good night and walked off, and the others

243

started across the street toward the building. From all directions people were now streaming through the arched entrances into the court, collecting maids, cooks, and chauffeurs as they came. An air of order and authority had been reestablished among them, and one could hear masters and mistresses issuing commands to their servants. The cloisterlike arcades were filled with men and women shuffling quietly into their entryways.

The spirit of the crowd was altogether different now from what it had been a few hours earlier. All these people had recaptured their customary assurance and poise. The informality and friendliness that they had shown to one another during the excitement had vanished. It was almost as if they were now a little ashamed of the emotions which had betrayed them into injudicious cordialities and unwonted neighborliness. Each little family group had withdrawn frigidly into its own separate entity and was filing back into its own snug cell.

In the Jacks' entry a smell of smoke, slightly stale and acrid, still clung to the walls, but the power had been restored and the elevator was running again. Mrs. Jack noticed with casual surprise that the doorman, Henry, took them up, and she asked if Herbert had gone home. He paused just perceptibly, and then answered in a flat tone:

"Yes, Mrs. Jack."

"You all must be simply worn out!" she said warmly, with her instant sympathy. "Hasn't it been a thrilling evening?" she went on eagerly. "In all your life did you ever know of such excitement, such confusion, as we had tonight?"

"Yes, ma'am," the man said, in a voice so curiously unyielding that she felt stopped and baffled by it, as she had many times before.

And she thought:

"What a strange man he is! And what a difference between people! Herbert is so warm, so jolly, so human. You can talk to *him*. But this one—he's so stiff and formal you can never get inside of him. And if you try to speak to him, he snubs you—puts you in your place as if he doesn't want to have anything to do with you!"

She felt wounded, rebuffed, almost angry. She was herself a friendly person, and she liked people around her to be friendly, too—even the servants. But already her mind was worrying loosely at the curious enigma of the doorman's personality:

"I wonder what's wrong with him," she thought. "He seems always so unhappy, so disgruntled, nursing some secret grievance all the time. I wonder what has done it to him. Oh, well, poor thing, I suppose the life he leads is enough to turn anyone sour—opening doors and calling cabs and helping people in and out of cars and answering questions all night long. But then, Herbert has it even worse—shut up in this stuffy elevator and riding up and down all the time where he can't see anything and where nothing ever happens—and yet he's always so sweet and so obliging about everything!"

And, giving partial utterance to her thoughts, she said:

"I suppose Herbert had a harder time of it tonight than any of you, getting all these people out."

Henry made no answer whatever. He simply seemed not to have heard her. He had stopped the elevator and opened the door at their own landing, and now said in his hard, expressionless voice:

"This is your floor, Mrs. Jack."

After they got out and the car had gone down, she was so annoyed that she turned to her family and guests with flaming cheeks, and said angrily:

"Honestly, that fellow makes me tired! He's such a grouch! And he's getting worse every day! It's got so now he won't even answer when you speak to him!"

"Well, Esther, maybe he's tired out tonight," suggested Mr. Jack pacifically. "They've all been under a pretty severe strain, you know."

"So I suppose that's *our* fault?" said Mrs. Jack ironically. And then, going into the living room and seeing again the chaos left there by Mr. Logan's performance, she had a sudden flare of her quick and jolly wit, and with a comical shrug said: "Vell, ve should have a fire sale!"—which restored her to good humor.

Everything seemed curiously unchanged—curiously, because so much had happened since their excited departure. The place smelled close and stale, and there was still a faint tang of smoke. Mrs. Jack told Nora to open the windows. Then the three maids automatically resumed their interrupted routine and quickly tidied up the room.

Mrs. Jack excused herself for a moment and went into her own room. She took off the borrowed coat and hung it in the closet, and carefully brushed and adjusted her somewhat disordered hair.

Then she went over to the window, threw up the sash as far as it would go, and filled her lungs full of the fresh, invigorating air. She found it good. The last taint of smoke was washed clean and sweet away by the cool breath of October. And in the white light of the moon the spires and ramparts of Manhattan were glittering with cold magic. Peace fell upon her spirit. Strong comfort and assurance bathed her whole being. Life was so solid and splendid, and so good.

A tremor, faint and instant, shook her feet. She paused, startled; waited, listening. . . . Was the old trouble with George there again to shake the deep perfection of her soul? He had been strangely quiet tonight. Why, he had hardly said two words all evening. What was the matter with him? . . . And what was the rumor she had heard this night? Something about stocks falling. During the height of the party she had overheard Lawrence Hirsch say something like that. She hadn't paid any attention at the time, but now it came back. "Faint tremors in the market"—that's what he had said. What was this talk of tremors?

—Ah, there it was a second time! What was it?

—Trains again!

It passed, faded, trembled delicately away into securities of eternal stone, and left behind the blue dome of night, and of October.

The smile came back into her eyes. The brief and troubled frown had lifted. Her look as she turned and started toward the living room was almost dulcet and cherubic—the look of a good child who ends the great adventure of another day.

Edith and Alma had retired immediately on coming in, and Lily Mandell, who had gone into one of the bedrooms to get her wraps, now came out wearing her splendid cape.

"Darling, it has been too marvelous," she said throatily, wearily, giving Mrs. Jack an affectionate kiss. "Fire, smoke, Piggy Logan, everything—I've simply adored it!"

Mrs. Jack shook with laughter.

"Your parties are too wonderful!" Miss Mandell concluded. "You never know what's going to happen next!"

With that she said her good-byes and left.

George was also going now, but Mrs. Jack took him by the hand and said coaxingly:

"Don't go yet. Stay a few minutes and talk to me."

Mr. Jack was obviously ready for his bed. He kissed his wife lightly on the cheek, said good night casually to George, and went to his room. Young men could come, and young men could go, but Mr. Jack was going to get his sleep.

Outside, the night was growing colder, with a suggestion of frost in the air. The mammoth city lay fathoms deep in sleep. The streets were deserted, save for an occasional taxicab that drilled past on some urgent nocturnal quest. The sidewalks were vacant and echoed hollowly to the footfalls of a solitary man who turned the corner into Park and headed briskly north toward home and bed. The lights were out in all the towering office buildings, except for a single window high up in the face of a darkened cliff which betrayed the presence of some faithful slave of business who was working through the night upon a dull report that had to be ready in the morning.

At the side entrance of the great apartment house, on the now empty cross street, one of the dark green ambulances of the police department had slid up very quietly and was waiting with a softly throbbing motor. No one was watching it.

Shortly a door which led down to a basement opened. Two policemen came out, bearing a stretcher, which had something sheeted on it that was very still. They slid this carefully away into the back of the green ambulance.

A minute later the basement door opened again and a sergeant emerged. He was followed by two more men in uniform who carried a second stretcher with a similar burden. This, too, was carefully disposed of in the same way.

The doors of the vehicle clicked shut. The driver and another man walked around and got into the front seat. And after a hushed word or two with the sergeant, they drove off quietly, turning the corner with a subdued clangor of bells.

The three remaining officers spoke together for a moment longer in lowered voices, and one of them wrote down notes in his little book. Then they said good night, saluted, and departed, each walking off in a different direction to take up again his appointed round of duty.

Meanwhile, inside the imposing front entrance, under a light within the cloistered walk, another policeman was conferring with the doorman, Henry. The doorman answered the questions of the officer in a toneless, monosyllabic, sullen voice, and the policeman wrote down the answers in another little book.

"You say the younger one was unmarried?"

"Yes."

"How old?"

"Twenty-five."

"And where did he live?"

"In the Bronx."

His tone was so low and sullen that it was hardly more than a mutter, and the policeman lifted his head from the book and rasped out harshly:

"Where?"

"The Bronx!" said Henry furiously.

The man finished writing in his book, put it away into his pocket, then in a tone of casual speculation he said:

"Well, I wouldn't want to live up there, would you? It's too damn far away."

"Nah!" snapped Henry. Then, turning impatiently away, he began: "If that's all you want——"

"That's *all*," the policeman cut in with brutal and ironic geniality. "That's all, *brother*."

And with a hard look of mirth in his cold eyes, he swung his night-stick behind him and watched the retreating figure of the doorman as it went inside and disappeared in the direction of the elevator.

Up in the Jacks' living room, George and Esther were alone together. There was now an air of finality about everything. The party was over, the fire was over, all the other guests had gone.

Esther gave a little sigh and sat down beside George. For a moment she looked around her with an expression of thoughtful appraisal. Everything was just the same as it had always been. If anyone came in here now, he would never dream that anything had happened.

"Wasn't it all strange?" she said musingly. "The party—and then the fire! . . . I mean, the *way* it happened." Her tone had grown a little vague, as if there was something she could not quite express. "I don't know, but the way we were all sitting here after Mr. Logan's performance . . . then all of a sudden the fire engines going past . . . and we didn't know . . . we thought they were going somewhere else. There was something so—sort of weird—about it." Her brow was furrowed with her difficulty as she tried to define the emotion she felt. "It sort of frightens you, doesn't it?—No, not the fire!" she spoke quickly. "That didn't amount to anything. No one got hurt. It was terribly exciting, really. . . . What I mean is—" again the vague and puzzled tone—"when you think of how . . . *big* . . . things have got . . . I mean, the way people live nowadays . . . in these big buildings . . . and how a fire can break out in the very house you live in, and you not even know about it. . . . There's something sort of *terrible* in that, isn't there? . . . And God!" she burst out with sudden eagerness. "In all your life did you ever see the like of them? I mean the kind of people who live here—the way they all looked as they poured out into the court?"

She laughed and paused, then took his hand, and with a rapt look on her face she whispered tenderly:

"But what do they matter? . . . They're all gone now. . . . The whole world's gone. . . . There's no one left but you and I. . . . Do you know," she said quietly, "that I think about you all the time? When I wake up in the morning the first thought that comes into my head is you. And from that moment on I carry you around inside me all day long—*here*." She laid her hand upon her breast, then went on in a rapt whisper: "You fill my life, my heart, my spirit, my whole being. Oh, do you think there ever was another love like ours since the world

248

began—two other people who ever loved each other as we do? If I could play, I'd make of it great music. If I could sing, I'd make of it a great song. If I could write, I'd make of it a great story. But when I try to play or write or sing, I can think of nothing else but you. . . . Did you know that I once tried to write a story?" Smiling, she inclined her rosy face toward his: "Didn't I ever tell you?"

He shook his head.

"I was sure that it would make a wonderful story," she went on eagerly. "It seemed to fill me up. I was ready to burst with it. But when I tried to write it, all that I could say was: 'Long, long into the night I lay—thinking of you.' "

She laughed suddenly, richly.

"And that's as far as I could get. But wasn't it a grand beginning for a story? And now at night when I try to go to sleep, that one line of the story that I couldn't write comes back to me and haunts me, and keeps ringing in my ears. 'Long, long into the night I lay—thinking of you.' For that's the story."

She moved closer to him, and lifted her lips to his.

"Ah, dearest, that's the story. In the whole world there's nothing more. Love is enough."

He could not answer. For as she spoke he knew that for him it was not the story. He felt desolate and tired. The memory of all their years of love, of beauty and devotion, of pain and conflict, together with all her faith and tenderness and noble loyalty—the whole universe of love which had been his, all that the tenement of flesh and one small room could hold—returned to rend him in this instant.

For he had learned tonight that love was not enough. There had to be a higher devotion than all the devotions of this fond imprisonment. There had to be a larger world than this glittering fragment of a world with all its wealth and privilege. Throughout his whole youth and early manhood, this very world of beauty, ease, and luxury, of power, glory, and security, had seemed the ultimate end of human ambition, the furthermost limit to which the aspirations of any man could reach. But tonight, in a hundred separate moments of intense reality, it had revealed to him its very core. He had seen it naked, with its guards down. He had sensed how the hollow pyramid of a false social structure had been erected and sustained upon a base of common mankind's blood and sweat and agony. So now he knew that if he was ever to succeed in writing the books he felt were in him, he must turn about and lift his face up to some nobler height.

He thought about the work he wanted to do. Somehow the

events which he had witnessed here tonight had helped to resolve much of his inner chaos and confusion. Many of the things which had been complex before were now made simple. And it all boiled down to this: honesty, sincerity, no compromise with truth—those were the essentials of any art—and a writer, no matter what else he had, was just a hack without them.

And that was where Esther and this world of hers came in. In America, of all places, there could be no honest compromise with special privilege. Privilege and truth could not lie down together. He thought of how a silver dollar, if held close enough to the eye, could blot out the sun itself. There were stronger, deeper tides and currents running in America than any which these glamorous lives tonight had ever plumbed or even dreamed of. Those were the depths that he would like to sound.

As he thought these things, a phrase that had been running through his head all evening, like an overtone to everything that he had seen and heard, now flashed once more into his consciousness:

—He who lets himself be whored by fashion will be whored by time.

Well, then—a swift thrust of love and pity pierced him as Esther finished speaking and he looked down at her enraptured, upturned face—it must be so: he to his world, she to hers.

But not tonight. He could not tell her so tonight.

Tomorrow——

Yes, tomorrow he would tell her. It would be better so. He would tell it to her straight, the way he understood it now—tell it so she could not fail to understand it, too. But tell it—get it over with—tomorrow.

And to make it easier, for her as well as for himself, there was one thing he would not tell her. It would be surer, swifter, kinder, not to tell her that he loved her still, that he would always love her, that no one else could ever take her place. Not by so much as a glance, a single word, the merest pressure of the hand, must he let her know that this was the hardest thing he would ever have to do. It would be far better if she did not know that, for if she knew, she'd never understand——

—Never understand tomorrow——

—That a tide was running in the hearts of men——

—And he must go.

They said little more that night. In a few minutes he got up, and with a sick and tired heart he went away.

BOOK III

An End and a Beginning

When a cicada comes out of the ground to enter the last stage
of its life cycle, it looks more like a fat, earth-stained grubworm
than a winged thing. Laboriously it climbs up the trunk of a
tree, pulling itself along on legs that hardly seem to belong to it,
for they move with painful awkwardness as though the creature
had not yet got the hang of how to use them. At last it stops in
its weary climb and clings to the bark by its front feet. Then,
suddenly, there is a little popping sound, and one notices that
the creature's outer garment has split down the back, as neatly
as though it had come equipped with a zipper. Slowly now the
thing inside begins to emerge, drawing itself out through the
opening until it has freed its body, head, and all its members.
Slowly, slowly, it accomplishes this amazing task, and slowly
creeps out into a patch of sun, leaving behind the brown and
lifeless husk from which it came.

The living, elemental protoplasm, translucent, pale green
now, remains motionless for a long time in the sun, but if one
has the patience to watch it further, one will see the miracle of
change and growth enacted before his very eyes. After a while
the body begins to pulse with life, it flattens out and changes
color like a chameleon, and from small sprouts on each side of
the back the wings commence to grow. Quickly, quickly now,
they lengthen out—one can see it happening!—until they
become transparent fairy wings, iridescent, shimmering in the
sun. They begin to quiver delicately, then more rapidly, and all
at once, with a metallic whirring sound, they cut the air and the
creature flashes off, a new-born thing released into a new
element.

America, in the fall of 1929, was like a cicada. It had come to
an end and a beginning. On October 24th, in New York, in a
marble-fronted building down in Wall Street, there was a sudden crash that was heard throughout the land. The dead and
outworn husk of the America that had been had cracked and
split right down the back, and the living, changing, suffering

thing within—the real America, the America that had always been, the America that was yet to be—began now slowly to emerge. It came forth into the light of day, stunned, cramped, crippled by the bonds of its imprisonment, and for a long time it remained in a state of suspended animation, full of latent vitality, waiting, waiting patiently, for the next stage of its metamorphosis.

The leaders of the nation had fixed their gaze so long upon the illusions of a false prosperity that they had forgotten what America looked like. Now they saw it—saw its newness, its raw crudeness, and its strength—and turned their shuddering eyes away. "Give us back our well-worn husk," they said, "where we were so snug and comfortable." And then they tried word-magic. "Conditions are fundamentally sound," they said—by which they meant to reassure themselves that nothing now was really changed, that things were as they always had been, and as they always would be, forever and ever, amen.

But they were wrong. They did not know that you can't go home again. America had come to the end of something, and to the beginning of something else. But no one knew what that something else would be, and out of the change and the uncertainty and the wrongness of the leaders grew fear and desperation, and before long hunger stalked the streets. Through it all there was only one certainty, though no one saw it yet. America was still America, and whatever new thing came of it would be American.

George Webber was just as confused and fearful as everybody else. If anything, he was more so, because, in addition to the general crisis, he was caught in a personal one as well. For at this very time he, too, had come to an end and a beginning. It was an end of love, though not of loving; a beginning of recognition, though not of fame. His book was published early in November, and that event, so eagerly awaited for so long, produced results quite different from any he had expected. And during this period of his life he learned a great deal that he had never known before, but it was only gradually, in the course of the years to come, that he began to realize how the changes in himself were related to the larger changes in the world around him.

Chapter Twenty-Two

A Question of Guilt

Throughout George Webber's boyhood in the little town of Libya Hill, when the great vision of the city burned forever in his brain, he had been athirst for glory and had wanted very much to be a famous man. That desire had never changed, except to become stronger as he grew older, until now he wanted it more than ever. Yet, of the world of letters in which he dreamed of cutting a great figure, he knew almost nothing. He was now about to find out a few things that were to rob his ignorance of its bliss.

His novel, *Home to Our Mountains,* was published the first week in November 1929. The date, through the kind of accidental happening which so often affects the course of human events, and which, when looked back on later, seems to have been attended by an element of fatality, coincided almost exactly with the beginning of the Great American Depression.

The collapse of the Stock Market, which had begun in late October, was in some ways like the fall of a gigantic boulder into the still waters of a lake. The suddenness of it sent waves of desperate fear moving in ever-widening circles throughout America. Millions of people in the far-off hamlets, towns, and cities did not know what to make of it. Would its effects touch them? They hoped not. And the waters of the lake closed over the fallen boulder, and for a while most Americans went about their day's work just as usual.

But the waves of fear had touched them, and life was not quite the same. Security was gone, and there was a sense of dread and ominous foreboding in the air. It was into this atmosphere of false calm and desperate anxiety that Webber's book was launched.

It is no part of the purpose of this narrative to attempt to estimate the merits or deficiencies of *Home to Our Mountains.*

It need only be said here that it was a young man's first book, and that it had a good many of the faults and virtues of the kind of thing it was. Webber had done what so many beginning writers do: he had written it out of the experience of his own life. And that got him into a lot of trouble.

He was to become convinced as he grew older that if one wants to write a book that has any interest or any value whatever, he has got to write it out of the experience of life. A writer, like everybody else, must use what he has to use. He can't use something that he hasn't got. If he tries to—and many writers have tried it—what he writes is no good. Everybody knows that.

So Webber had drawn upon the experience of his own life. He had written about his home town, about his family and the people he had known there. And he had done it in a manner of naked directness and reality that was rather rare in books. That was really what caused the trouble.

Every author's first book is important. It means the world to him. Perhaps he thinks that what he has done has never been done before. Webber thought so. And in a way he was right. He was still very much under the influence of James Joyce, and what he had written was a *Ulysses* kind of book. People at home, whose good opinion he coveted more than that of all the rest of the world combined, were bewildered and overwhelmed by it. They, of course, had not read *Ulysses*. And Webber had not read people. He thought he had, he thought he knew what they were like, but he really didn't. He hadn't learned what a difference there is between living with them and writing about them.

A man learns a great deal about life from writing and publishing a book. When Webber wrote his, he had ripped off a mask that his home town had always worn, but he had not quite understood that he was doing it. Only after it was printed and published did he fully realize the fact. All he had meant and hoped to do was to tell the truth about life as he had known it. But no sooner was the thing done—the proofs corrected, the pages printed beyond recall—then he knew that he had not told the truth. Telling the truth is a pretty hard thing. And in a young man's first attempt, with the distortions of his vanity, egotism, hot passion, and lacerated pride, it is almost impossible. *Home to Our Mountains* was marred by all these faults and imperfections. Webber knew this better than anybody else, and long before any reader had a chance to tell him so. He did not know whether he had written a great book—sometimes he thought he had, or at least that there were elements of greatness in it. He did know that it was not altogether a true book. Still, there was truth in it. And this was what people were afraid of. This was what made them mad.

As the publication day drew near, Webber felt some apprehension about the reception of his novel in Libya Hill. Ever since his trip home in September he had had a heightened sense of uneasiness and anxiety. He had seen the boom-mad town tottering on the brink of ruin. He had read in the eyes of people on the streets the fear and guilty knowledge of the calamity that impended and that they were still refusing to admit even to themselves. He knew that they were clinging desperately to the illusion of their paper riches, and that madness such as this was unprepared to face reality and truth in any degree whatever.

But even if he had been unaware of these special circumstances of the moment, he would still have had some premonitory consciousness that he was in for something. For he was a Southerner, and he knew that there was something wounded in the South. He knew that there was something twisted, dark, and full of pain which Southerners have known with all their lives—something rooted in their souls beyond all contradiction, about which no one had dared to write, of which no one had ever spoken.

Perhaps it came from their old war, and from the ruin of their great defeat and its degraded aftermath. Perhaps it came from causes yet more ancient—from the evil of man's slavery, and the hurt and shame of human conscience in its struggle with the fierce desire to own. It came, too, perhaps, from the lusts of the hot South, tormented and repressed below the harsh and outward patterns of a bigot and intolerant theology, yet prowling always, stirring stealthily, as hushed and secret as the thickets of swamp-darkness. And most of all, perhaps, it came out of the very weather of their lives, out of the forms that shaped them and the food that fed them, out of the unknown terrors of the skies above them, out of the dark, mysterious pineland all around them with its haunting sorrow.

Wherever it came from, it was there—and Webber knew it.

But it was not only in the South that America was hurt. There was another deeper, darker, and more nameless wound throughout the land. What was it? Was it in the record of corrupt officials and polluted governments, administrations twisted to the core, the huge excess of privilege and graft, protected criminals and gangster rule, the democratic forms all rotten and putrescent with disease? Was it in "puritanism"—that great, vague name: whatever it may be? Was it in the bloated surfeits of monopoly, and the crimes of wealth against the worker's life? Yes, it was in all of these, and in the daily tolling of the murdered men, the lurid renderings of promiscuous and casual slaughter everywhere throughout the land, and in the pious hypocrisy of the press with its swift-forgotten prayers for our improvement, the editorial moaning while the front page gloats.

But it is not only at these outward forms that we must look to find the evidence of a nation's hurt. We must look as well at the heart of guilt that beats in each of us, for there the cause lies. We must look, and with our own eyes see, the central core of defeat and shame and failure which we have wrought in the lives of even the least of these, our brothers. And why must we look? Because we must probe to the bottom of our collective wound. As men, as Americans, we can no longer cringe away and lie. Are we not all warmed by the same sun, frozen by the same cold, shone on by the same lights of time and terror here in America? Yes, and if we do not look and see it, we shall be all damned together.

So George Webber had written a book in which he had tried, with only partial success, to tell the truth about the little segment of life that he had seen and known. And now he was worried about what the people back in his home town would think of it. He thought a few of them would "read it." He was afraid there would be "talk." He supposed that there might even be a protest here and there, and he tried to prepare himself for it. But when it came, it went so far beyond anything he had feared might happen that it caught him wholly unawares and almost floored him. He had felt, but had not *known* before, how naked we are here in America.

It was a time when the better-known gentlemen and lady authors of the South were writing polished bits of whimsey about some dear Land of Far Cockaigne, or ironic little comedies about the gentle relics of the Old Tradition in the South, or fanciful bits about Negro mongrels along the Battery in Charleston, or, if passion was in the air, amusing and light-hearted tales about the romantic adulteries of dusky brethren and their "high-yaller gals" on a plantation somewhere. There wasn't much honesty or essential reality in these books, and the people who wrote them had not made much effort to face the facts in the life around them. One wrote about Cockaigne because it was far enough away to be safe; and if one wanted to write about adultery, or about crime and punishment of any sort, it was a good deal safer to let it happen to a group of darkies than to the kind of people one had to live with every day.

Home to Our Mountains was a novel that did not fit into any of these standardized patterns. It didn't seem to have much pattern at all. The people of Libya Hill hardly knew what to make of it at first. Then they recognized themselves in it. From that point on, they began to live it all over again. People who had never bought a book before bought this one. Libya Hill alone bought two thousand copies of it. It stunned them, it overwhelmed them, and in the end it made them fight.

For George Webber had used the scalpel in a way that that section of the country was not accustomed to. His book took the hide off of the whole community, and as a result of this it also took the hide off of George Webber.

In Libya Hill, a day or two before the publication of the book, Margaret Shepperton met Harley McNabb on the street. They exchanged greetings and stopped to talk.

"Have you seen the book?" he said.

"Yes, George sent me an advance copy," she answered, beaming at him, "and he signed it for me, too. But I haven't read it. It just came this morning. Have you seen it?"

"Yes," he said. "We have a review copy in the office."

"What do you think of it?" She looked at him with the expression of a large and earnest woman who lets herself be governed considerably by the opinion of those around her. "I mean—now you've been to college, Harley," she began jestingly, but also rather eagerly. "It may be deep stuff to me—but you ought to know—you're educated—you ought to be a judge about these things. What I mean is, do you think it's good?"

He was silent for a moment, his lean hand fingering the bowl of his blackened briar, on which he puffed thoughtfully. Then:

"Margaret," he said, "it's pretty rough. . . . Now don't get excited," he added quickly as he saw her large face contract with anxiety and concern. "No use getting excited about it—but—" he paused, puffing on his pipe, his eyes staring off into vacancy—"there—there are some pretty rough things in it. It's—it's pretty frank, Margaret."

She felt the gathering in her of sharp tensions, a white terror, personal, immediate, as she said almost hoarsely:

"About me? About *me*, Harley? Is that what you mean? Are there things in it—about *me*?" Her face was tortured now, and she felt an indescribable sense of fear and guilt.

"Not only about you," he said. "About—well, Margaret, about everybody—about a lot of people here in town. . . . You've known him all your life, haven't you? You see— well—he's put in everybody he ever knew. Some of it is going to be pretty hard to take."

For a moment, in a phrase she was fond of using, she "went all to pieces." She began to talk wildly, incoherently, her large features contorted under the strain:

257

"Well, now, I'm sure I don't know what he's got to say about me! . . . Well, now, if anyone feels *that* way—" without knowing how anyone felt. "What I mean to say is, I certainly don't feel that I've got anything to be ashamed of. . . . You know me, Harley," she went on eagerly, almost beseechingly, "I'm *known* in this town—I've got friends here—everybody knows me. . . . Well, I certainly have nothing to conceal."

"I know you haven't, Margaret," he said. "Only—well, there's going to be talk."

She felt emptied out, hollow, her knees were weak. His words had almost knocked her over. If he said it, it must be so, even though she did not yet understand what it was he had said. She only knew that she was in the book, and that Harley didn't like it; and his opinion stood for something, for a great deal, in her own eyes and in the eyes of the whole town. He represented what her mind called, somewhat vaguely, "the high-brow element." He had always been "a fine man." He stood for truth, for culture, for learning, and for high integrity. So she looked at him with her bewildered face and stricken eyes, and, just as a young soldier, with his entrails shot out in his hands, speaks to the commander of his life, saying in his deadly fear and peril: "Is it bad, General? Do you think it's bad?"—so now she said hoarsely to the editor, hanging on his words:

"Harley, do you think it's bad?"

He looked away again into blue vacancy and puffed gravely on his pipe before he answered:

"It's pretty bad, Margaret. . . . But don't worry. We'll see what happens."

Then he was gone, leaving her alone there, bleakly staring at the pavement of the small, familiar street. Unseen motes of the familiar life swept round her, the pale light of the sun fell on her, and she remained there staring with gaunt face. How much time went by she did not know, but all at once——

"O Margaret!"

At the lush voice, sugared with the honey of its owner's sweetness, she turned, blindly smiling, and stiffly blurted out a word of greeting.

"Aren't you just *so* proud of him? He always liked you better than *anybody* else! Aren't you simply thrilled to *death*?" The voice rose to a honeyed lilt, and in the pale light the face was now shaped into the doelike contours of a china doll. "I'll declayah! I'm so *thrilled*! I know you must be walkin' on ayah! Why, I just can't *wait*! I'm just *dyin'* to *read* it! I know that *you're* the proudest thing that *evah* lived!"

Margaret stammered out something through stiff, smiling lips, and then was left alone again, her big gaunt face strained into vacancy. She went about the business that had brought her to town. She went through the motions automatically. And all the while she was thinking:

"So, he's written about us! That's what it is!" Her mind rushed furiously on through a chaos of unresolved emotions. "Well, I'm sure I don't know what it's all about, but there's one thing certain—*my* conscience is clear. If anyone thinks they've got anything on *me*, they're very much mistaken. . . . Now, if he wants to criticize *me*—" in her mind the word implied a derogatory appraisal of a person's life and conduct—"why he can go right ahead. I've lived all my life in this town, and everybody knows—no matter what anybody says—that I've never done anything immoral." By this word she meant solely and simply a deviation from the standards of sexual chastity. "Now I'm sure I don't know what Harley meant by its being hard to take and people will talk, but I know *I've* got nothing to be ashamed about. . . ."

Her mind was full of frantic questions. A hundred apprehensions, fears, and terrors swept through her. But through it all there were shafts of stubborn strength and loyalty:

"Whatever it's about, I know there can't be any harm in it. We've all done things we're sorry for, but we're not bad people, any of us. No one I know is really very bad. He couldn't harm us if he wanted to. And," she added, "he wouldn't want to."

To her brother, Randy, when he came home that night, she said:

"Well, we're in for it! . . . I saw Harley McNabb on the street and he said the book is pretty bad. . . . Now, I don't know what he said about *you*—Ho! Ho! Ho!—but *my* conscience is clear!"

Randy followed her back to the kitchen and they talked about it long and earnestly while Margaret cooked supper. They were both puzzled and bewildered by what McNabb had said. Neither of them had yet read the book, so they searched their memories for all sorts of things that might be in it, but they couldn't imagine what it was.

Supper was late that night, and when Margaret brought it to the table it was burned.

Three weeks later, in New York, George sat in the back room of his dismal flat on Twelfth Street, reading his morning mail. He had always wanted letters. Now he had them. It seemed to him that all the letters he had been waiting for all his life, all the letters he had longed for, all the letters that had never come, had now descended in a flood.

He remembered all the years, all the weary and unnumbered

days and hours of waiting, after he had first left home for college. He remembered that first year away from home, his freshman year, and how it seemed to him that he was always waiting for a letter that never came. He remembered how the students gathered for their mail twice a day, at noon and then again at night when they had finished dinner. He remembered the dingy little post office on the main street of the little college town, and the swarm of students shuffling in and out—the whole street dense with them, the dingy little post office packed with them, opening their boxes, taking out their mail, milling around the delivery window.

Everyone, it seemed, got letters except himself.

Here were boys packed in the corners, leaning against the walls, propped up against trees, squatted on steps and porch rails and the verandahs of fraternity houses, walking oblivious across the village street—all immersed, all reading, all buried in their letters. Here was the boy who had only one girl and wanted no one but the girl he had, who had wormed himself away into a corner, just out of contact with that noisy and good-natured crowd, where he read slowly, carefully, word for word, the letter that she wrote him every day. Here was another lad, a sleek and handsome youth, one of the Casanovas of the campus, walking along and skimming the contents of a dozen scented epistles, shuffling through the pages and responding with a touch of complaisant satisfaction to the gibes of his fellows over his latest conquest. Here were boys reading letters from their friends, from boys in other colleges, from older brothers and from younger sisters, from fathers, mothers, and from favorite aunts and uncles. From all these people these boys received the tokens of friendship, kinship, fellowship, and love—the emotions that give a man his place, that secure him in the confident, brave knowledge of his home, that wall his soul about with comfort, and that keep him from the desolation of an utter nakedness, from the dreadful sense of his atomic nullity in the roofless openness of life.

It seemed to him that everyone had this, except himself.

And, later, he remembered his first years in the city, his years of wandering, his first years of living utterly alone. Here, too, even more than in his college days, it seemed to him that he was always waiting for a letter that never came. That was the time when he had eaten out his heart at night in the cell-like privacy of little rooms. That was the time when he had beaten his knuckles raw and bloody at the walls that hemmed him in. That was the time—and it was ten thousand times of longing, disappointment, bitter grief, and loneliness—when his unresting mind had written to himself the letters that never came. Letters from the noble, loyal, and gracious people he had never known. Letters from the heroic and great-hearted friends that he had never had. Letters from the faithful kinsmen, neighbors, schoolmates who had all forgotten him.

Well, he had them now—all of them—and he had not foreseen it.

He sat there in his room and read them, numb in the city's roar. Two shafts of light sank through the windows to the floor. Outside, the cat crept trembling at his merciless stride along the ridges of the backyard fence.

Anonymous, in pencil, on a sheet of ruled tablet paper:

"Well author old lady Flood went away to Florida yestiddy after a so called *litterary* book arrived from a so called author that she thought she knew. Oh God how can you have this crime upon your soal. I left your pore dere aunt Maggie lying on her back in bed white as a sheet where she will never rise again where you have put her with your murder pen. Your dere friend Margaret Shepperton who was always like a sister to you is ruined and disgraced for *life* you have made her out no better than a wanton woman. You have murdered and disgraced your friends never come back *here* you are the same as *dead* to all of us we never want to see your face again. I never believed in *linch* law but if I saw a mob drag that *monkyfied karkus* of yours across the Public Square I would not say a *word*. How can you sleep at night with this crime upon your soal. Destroy this *vile* and *dirty* book at once let no more copies be published the crime that you have done is worse than Cain."

On a postcard, sealed in an envelope:

"We'll kill you if you ever come back here. You know who."

From an old friend:

"My dear boy,

"What is there to say? It has come, it is here, it has happened—and now I can only say, as that good woman who brought you up and now lies dead and buried on the hill would have said: 'O God! If I had only known!' For weeks I have waited for nothing else except the moment when your book should come and I should have it in my hands. Well, it has come now. And what is there to say?

"You have crucified your family in a way that would make the agony of Christ upon the Cross seem light in the comparison. You have laid waste the lives of your kinsmen, and of dozens of your friends, and to us who loved you like our own you have driven a dagger to the heart, and twisted it, and left it fixed there where it must always stay."

From a sly and hearty fellow who thought he understood:

". . . if I had known you were going to write this kind of book, I could have told you lots of things. Why didn't you come to me? I know dirt about the people in this town you never dreamed of."

Letters like this last one hurt him worst of all. They were the ones that made him most doubt his purpose and accomplishment. What did such people think he had been trying to write—nothing but an encyclopaedia of pornography, a kind of prurient excavation of every buried skeleton in town? He saw that his book had unreefed whole shoals of unsuspected bitterness and malice in the town and set evil tongues to wagging. The people he had drawn upon to make the characters in his book writhed like hooked fish on a line, and the others licked their lips to see them squirm.

Those who were the victims of all this unleashed malice now struck back, almost to a man, at the hapless author—at him whom they considered to be the sole cause of their woe. Day after day their letters came, and with a perverse satisfaction in his own suffering, a desire to take upon himself now all the searing shame that he had so naïvely and so unwittingly brought to others, he read and reread every bitter word of every bitter letter, and his senses and his heart were numb.

They said at first that he was a monster against life, that he had fouled his own nest. Then they said he had turned against the South, his mother, and spat upon her and defiled her. Then they leveled against him the most withering charge they could think of, and said he was "not Southern." Some of them even began to say that he was "not American." This was really rather hard on him, George thought with a wry, grim humor, for if he was not American he was not anything at all.

262

And during those nightmarish first weeks following the publication of his book, only two rays of warmth and comforting assurance came to him from anyone he knew.

One was a letter from Randy Shepperton. As a boy, and later as a student at college, Randy had possessed a spirit that always burned with the quick, pure flame of a Mercutio. And now, in spite of what life had done to him—the evidence of which George had seen in his troubled eyes and deeply furrowed face—his letter showed that he was still essentially the same old Randy. What he wrote was full of understanding about the book; he saw its purpose clearly, and he gave, George thought, a shrewd appraisal of its accomplishment and its weaknesses; and he ended with a generous burst of pride and honest pleasure in the thing itself. Not a word about personalities, not a breath of all the gossip in the town, not even a hint that he had recognized himself among the portraits George had drawn.

The other ray of comfort was of quite another kind. One day the telephone rang, and it was Nebraska Crane howling his friendship over the wire:

"Hi, there, Monkus! That you? How you makin' out, boy?"

"Oh, all right, I guess," George answered, in a tone of resignation which he could not conceal even in the pleasure that he felt at hearing the hearty ring of the familiar voice.

"You sound sorta down in the mouth," said Nebraska, full of immediate concern. "What's the matter? Ain't nothin' wrong with you, is there?"

"Oh, no. No. It's nothing. Forget it." Then, shaking off the mood that had been with him for days, he began to respond with something of the warmth he felt for his old friend. "God, I'm glad to hear from you, Bras! I can't tell you how glad I am! How *are* you, Bras?"

"Oh, cain't complain," he shouted lustily. "I think maybe they're gonna give me a contrack for one more year. Looks like it, anyways. If they do, we'll be all set."

"That's swell, Bras! That's wonderful! . . . And how is Myrtle?"

"Fine! Fine! . . . Say—" he howled—"she's here now! She's the one put me up to callin' you. I never woulda thought of it. You know *me*! . . . We been readin' all about you—about that book you wrote. Myrtle's been tellin' me about it. She's cut out all the pieces from the papers. . . . That sure went over big, didn't it?"

"It's doing pretty well, I suppose," said George without enthusiasm. "It seems to be selling all right, if that's what you mean."

"Well, now, I knowed it!" said Nebraska. "Me an' Myrtle bought a copy. . . . I ain't read it yet," he added apologetically.

263

"You don't have to."

"I'm *goin'* to, I'm *goin'* to," he howled vigorously. "Just as soon as I git time."

"You're a damned liar!" George said good-naturedly. "You know you never will!"

"Why, I *will!*" Nebraska solemnly declared. "I'm just waitin' till I git a chance to settle down. . . . Boy, you shore do write 'em long, don't you?"

"Yes, it *is* pretty long."

"Longest darn book I ever seen!" Nebraska yelled enthusiastically. "Makes me tard just to tote it aroun'!"

"Well, it made me tired to write it."

"Dogged if I don't believe you! I don't see how you ever thought up all them words. . . . But I'm gonna read it! . . . Some of the boys on the Club know about it already. Jeffertz was talkin' to me about it the other day."

"Who?"

"Jeffertz—Matt Jeffertz, the ketcher."

"Has *he* read it?"

"Naw, he ain't read it yet, but his wife has. She's a big book-reader an' she knows all about you. They knowed I knowed you, an' that's how come he tells me——"

"Tells you what?" George broke in with a feeling of sudden panic.

"Why, that you got *me* in there!" he yelled. "Is that right?"

George reddened and began to stammer:

"Well, Bras, you see——"

"Well, that's what Matt's wife said!" Nebraska shouted at the top of his lungs, without waiting for an answer. "Said I'm in there so's anyone would know me! . . . What'd you say about me, Monk? You sure it's *me?*"

"Well—you see, now, Bras—it was like this——"

"What's eatin' on you, boy? It *is* me, ain't it? . . . Well, what d'you know?" he yelled with evident amazement and delight. "Ole Bras right there in the book!" His voice grew low and more excited as, evidently turning to Myrtle, he said: "It's *me*, all right!" Then, to George again: "Say, Monk—" solemnly—"you shore do make me feel mighty proud! That's what I called you up to tell you."

Chapter Twenty-Three

The Lion Hunters

In New York his book got a somewhat better reception than it enjoyed back home. The author was unknown. Nobody had any advance reason to care about what he had written one way or another. Though this was not exactly an asset, at least it gave the book a chance to be considered on its merits.

Surprisingly enough, it got pretty good reviews in most of the leading newspapers and magazines. That is, they were the kind of reviews that his publisher called "good." They said nice things about the book and made people want to buy it. George himself could have wished that some of the reviewing gentry, even some of those who hailed him as "a discovery" and studded their sentences with superlatives, had been a little more discriminating in what they said of him. Occasionally he could have asked for a little more insight into what he had been driving at. But after reading the letters from his former friends and neighbors he was in no mood to quarrel with anybody who felt disposed to speak him a soft and gentle word, and on the whole he had every reason to be well pleased with his press.

He read the notices avidly, feverishly, and sooner or later he must have seen them all, for his publisher showed him the clippings as they came in from every section of the country. He would take great bunches of them home to devour. When his eager eye ran upon a word of praise it was like magic to him, and he would stride about his room in a delirium of joy. When he read a savage, harsh, unfavorable review, he felt crushed: even though it came from some little rural paper in the South, his fingers would tremble, his face turn pale, and he would wad it up in his hand and curse it bitterly.

Whenever a notice of his work appeared in one of the best magazines or weekly journals, he could hardly bring himself to read it; neither could he go away from it and leave it unread. He would approach it as a man creeps stealthily to pick a snake up by the tail, his heart leaping at the sight of his name. He would scan the last line first, then with a rush of blood to his face he would plunge into it at once, devouring the whole of it as

265

quickly as he could. And if he saw that it was going to be "good," a feeling of such powerful joy and exultancy would well up in his throat that he would want to shout his triumph from the windows. If he saw that the verdict was going to be "thumbs down," he would read on with agonized fascination, and his despair would be so great that he would feel he was done for, that he had been exposed to the world as a fool and a failure, and that he would never be able to write another line.

After the more important reviews appeared, his mail gradually took on a different complexion. Not that the flood of damning letters from home had ceased, but now, along with them, began to come messages of another kind, from utter strangers who had read his novel and liked it. The book was doing pretty well, it seemed. It even appeared on some of the best-seller lists, and then things really began to happen. Soon his box was stuffed with fan mail, and the telephone jingled merrily all day long with invitations from wealthy and cultivated people who wanted him for lunch, for tea, for dinner, for theatre parties, for week-ends in the country—for anything at all if he would only come.

Was this Fame at last? It looked so, and in the first flush of his eager belief he almost forgot about Libya Hill and rushed headlong into the welcoming arms of people he had never seen before. He accepted invitations right and left, and they kept him pretty busy. And each time he went out it seemed to him that he was on the very point of capturing all the gold and magic he had ever dreamed of finding, and that now he was really going to take a place of honor among the great ones of the city, in a life more fortunate and good than any he had ever known. He went to each encounter with each new friend as though some wonderful and intoxicating happiness were impending for him.

But he never found it. For, in spite of all the years he had lived in New York, he was still a country boy, and he did not know about the lion hunters. They are a peculiar race of people who inhabit the upper jungles of Cosmopolis and subsist entirely on some rarefied and ambrosial ectoplasm that seems to emanate from the arts. They love art dearly—in fact, they dote on it—and they love the artists even more. So they spend their whole lives running after them, and their favorite sport is trapping literary lions. The more intrepid hunters go after nothing but the full-grown lions, who make the most splendid trophies for exhibition purposes, but others—especially the lady hunters—would rather bag a cub. A cub, once tamed and housebroken, makes a nice pet—much nicer than a lap dog—because there's just no limit to the beguiling tricks a gentle hand can teach him.

For a few weeks George was quite the fair-haired boy among these wealthy and cultivated people.

One of his new-found friends told him about an aesthetic and high-minded millionaire who was panting with eagerness to meet him. From others came further confirmation of the fact.

"The man is mad about your work," people would say to him. "He's crazy to meet you. And you ought to go to see him, because a man like that might be of great help to you."

They told George that this man had asked all kinds of questions about him, and had learned that he was very poor and had to work for a small salary as an instructor in the School for Utility Cultures. When the millionaire heard this, his great heart began to bleed for the young author immediately. It was intolerable, he said, that such a state of affairs should exist. America was the only country in the world where it would be permitted. Anywhere in Europe—yes, even in poor little Austria!—the artist would be subsidized, the ugly threat of poverty that hung over him would be removed, his best energies would be released to do his finest work—and, by God, he was going to see that this was done for George!

George had never expected anything like this to happen, and he could not see why such a thing should be done for any man. Nevertheless, when he thought of this great-hearted millionaire, he burned with eagerness to meet him and began to love him like a brother.

So a meeting was arranged, and George went to see him, and the man was very fine to him. The millionaire had George to his house for dinner several times and showed him off to all of his rich friends. And one lovely woman to whom the millionaire introduced the poor young author took him home with her that very night and granted him the highest favor in her keeping.

Then the millionaire had to go abroad on brief but urgent business, George went to the boat to see him off, and his friend shook him affectionately by the shoulder, called him by his first name, and told him that if there was anything he wanted, just to let him know by cable and he would see that it was done. He said he would be back within a month at most, and would be so busy that he wouldn't have time to write, but he would get in touch with George again as soon as he returned. With this he wrung George by the hand and sailed away.

A month, six weeks, two months went by, and George heard nothing from the man. It was well into the new year before he saw him again, and then by accident.

A young lady had invited George to have lunch with her at an expensive speakeasy. As soon as they entered the place George saw his millionaire friend sitting alone at one of the tables. Immediately George uttered a cry of joy and started across the room to meet him with his hand outstretched, and in such precipitate haste that he fell sprawling across an intervening table and two chairs. When he picked himself up from the floor, the man had drawn back with an expression of surprise and perplexity on his face, but he unbent sufficiently to take the young man's proffered hand and to say coolly, in an amused and tolerant voice:

"Ah—it's our writer friend again! How are you?"

The young man's crestfallen confusion and embarrassment were so evident that the rich man's heart was quite touched. His distant manner thawed out instantly, and now nothing would do but that George should bring the young lady over to the millionaire's table so that they could all have lunch together.

During the course of the meal the man became very friendly and attentive. It seemed he just couldn't do enough for George. He kept helping him to various dishes and filling his glass with more wine. And whenever George turned to him he would find the man looking at him with an expression of such obvious sympathy and commiseration that finally he felt compelled to ask him what the trouble was.

"Ah," he said, shaking his head with a doleful sigh, "I was mighty sorry when I read about it."

"Read about what?"

"Why," he said, "the prize."

"What prize?"

"But didn't you read about it in the paper? Didn't you see what happened?"

"I don't know what you are talking about," said George, puzzled. "What did happen?"

"Why," he said, "you didn't get it."

"Didn't get what?"

"The prize!" he cried—"the prize!"—mentioning a literary prize that was awarded every year. "I thought you would be sure to get it, but—" he paused a moment, then went on sorrowfully—"they gave it to another man. . . . You got mentioned . . . you were runner-up . . . but—" he shook his head gloomily—"you didn't get it."

So much for his good friend, the millionaire. George never saw him again after that. And yet, let no one say that he was ever bitter.

Then there was Dorothy.

Dorothy belonged to that fabulous and romantic upper crust of New York "Society" which sleeps by day and begins to come awake at sunset and never seems to have any existence at all outside of the better-known hot spots of the town. She had been expensively educated for a life of fashion, she had won a reputation in her set for being quite an intellectual because she had been known to read a book, and so, of course, when George Webber's novel was listed as a best seller she bought it and left it lying around in prominent places in her apartment. Then she wrote the author a scented note, asking him to come and have a cocktail with her. He did, and at her urging he went back to her again and again.

Dorothy was no longer as young as she had been, but she was well built, had kept her figure and her face, and was not a bad-looking wench. She had never married, and apparently felt she did not need to, for it was freely whispered about that she seldom slept alone. One heard that she had bestowed her favors not only upon all the gentlemen of her own set, but also upon such casual gallants as the milkmen on her family's estate, stray taxi drivers, writers of da-da, professional bicycle riders, wasteland poets, and plug-ugly bruisers with flat feet and celluloid collars. So George had expected their friendship to come quickly to its full flower, and he was quite surprised and disappointed when nothing happened.

His evenings with Dorothy turned out to be quiet and serious *tête-à-têtes* devoted to highly intellectual conversation. Dorothy remained as chaste as a nun, and George began to wonder whether she had not been grossly maligned by evil tongues. He found her intellectual and aesthetic interests rather on the dull side, and was several times on the point of giving her up in sheer boredom. But always she would pursue him, sending him notes and letters written in a microscopic hand on paper edged with red, and he would go back again, partly out of curiosity and a desire to find out what it was the woman was after.

He found out. Dorothy asked him to dine with her one night at a fashionable restaurant, and on this occasion she brought along her current sleeping companion, a young Cuban with patent-leather hair. George sat at the table between them. And while the Cuban gave his undivided attention to the food before him, Dorothy began to talk to George, and he learned to his chagrin that she had picked him out of all the world to be the victim of her only sacred passion.

269

"I love you, Jawge," she leaned over and whispered loudly in her rather whiskified voice. "I love you—but mah love for you is pewer!" She looked at him with a sorrowful expression. *"You,* Jawge—I love you for your *maind,"* she rumbled on, "for your *spirit!* But Miguel! Miguel!—" here her eyes roved over the Cuban as he sat tucking the food away with both hands— "Miguel—I love him for his *bawd-y!* He has no maind, but he has a fa-ine bawd-y," she whispered lustfully, "a fa-ine, beautiful bawd-y—so slim—so boyish—so *La-tin!"*

She was silent for a moment, and when she went on it was in a tone of foreboding:

"I wantcha to come with us to-night, Jawge!" she said abruptly. "I don't know what is going to happen," she said ominously, "and I wantcha *nee-ah* me."

"But what *is* going to happen, Dorothy?"

"I don't know," she muttered. "I just don't know. Anything might happen! . . . Why, last naight I thought that he was *gone!* We had a fight and he walked out on me! These La-tins are so *proud,* so *sen-sitive!* He caught me looking at another man, and he got up and left me flat! . . . If he left me I don't know what I'd do, Jawge," she panted. "I think I'd *die!* I think I'd *kill* myself!"

Her eye rested broodingly upon her lover, who at this moment was bending forward with bared teeth toward the tines of his uplifted fork on which a large and toothsome morsel of broiled chicken was impaled. Feeling their eyes upon him, he looked up with his fork poised in mid-air, smiled with satisfaction, then seized the bit of chicken in his jaws, took a drink to wash it down, and wiped his moist lips with a napkin. After that he elegantly lifted one hand to shield his mouth, inserted a fingernail between his teeth, detached a fragment of his victuals, and daintily ejected it upon the floor, while his lady's fond eye doted on him. Then he picked up the fork again and resumed his delightful gastronomic labors.

"I shouldn't worry about it, Dorothy," George said to her. "I don't think he's going to leave you for some time."

"I should *die!* I really think that it would *kill* me! . . . Jawge, you've *got* to come with us to-naight! I just wantcha to be *nee-ah* me! I feel so safe—so *secure*—when you're around! You're so *sawlid,* Jawge—so *comfawtin'!"* she said. "I wantcha to be theah to *tawk* to me—to hold mah hand and *comfawt* me—if anything should happen," she said, at the same time putting her hand on his and squeezing it.

But George did not go with her that night, nor any night thereafter. This was the last he saw of Dorothy. But surely none can say that he was ever bitter.

Again, there was the rich and beautiful young widow whose husband had died just a short time before, and who mentioned this sad fact in the moving and poignantly understanding letter she wrote to George about his book. Naturally, he accepted her kind invitation to drop in for tea. And almost at once the lovely creature offered to make the supreme sacrifice, first beginning with an intimate conversation about poetry, then looking distressed and saying it was very hot in here and did he mind if she took off her dress, then taking it off, and everything else as well, until she stood there as God made her, then getting into bed and casting the mop of her flaming red hair about on the pillow, rolling her eyes in frenzied grief, and crying out in stricken tones: "O Algernon! Algernon! Algernon!"—which was the name of her departed husband.

"O Algernon!" she cried, rolling about in grief and shaking her great mop of flaming hair—"Algie, darling, I am doing it for you! Algie, come back to me! Algie, I love you so! My pain is more than I can bear! Algernon!— No, no, poor boy!" she cried, seizing George by the arm as he started to crawl out of bed, because, to tell the truth, he did not know whether she had gone mad or was playing some wicked joke on him. "Don't go!" she whispered tenderly, clinging to his arm. "You just don't understand! I want to be so good to you—but everything I do or think or feel is Algernon, Algernon, Algernon!"

She explained that her *heart* was buried in her husband's grave, that she was really "a dead woman" (she had already told him she was a great reader of psychologies), and that the act of love was just an act of devotion to dear old Algie, an effort to be with him again and to be "a part of all this beauty."

It was very fine and high and rare, and surely no one will think that George would sneer at a beautiful emotion, although it was too fine for him to understand. Therefore he went away, and never saw this lovely and sorrowful widow any more. He knew he was not fine enough. And yet, not for a moment should you think that he was ever bitter.

Finally, there was another girl who came into George Webber's life during this period of his brief glory, and her he understood. She was a beautiful and brave woman, country-bred, and she had a good job, and a little apartment from which you could see the East River, the bridges, and all the busy traffic of the tugs and barges. She was not too rare and high for him, although she liked to take a part in serious conversations, to know worth-while people with liberal minds, and to keep up her interest in new schools and modern methods for the children. George became quite fond of her, and would stay all night and go away at daybreak when the streets were empty, and the great buildings went soaring up haggardly, incredibly, as if he were the first man to discover them, in the pale, pure, silent light of dawn.

He loved her well; and one night, after a long silence, she put her arms around him, drew him down beside her, and kissed him, whispering:

"Will you do something for me if I ask you to?"

"Darling, anything!" he said. "Anything you ask me, if I can!"

She held him pressed against her for a moment in the dark and living silence.

"I want you to use your influence to get me into the Cosmopolis Club," she whispered passionately——

And then dawn came, and the stars fell.

This was the last he saw of the great world of art, of fashion, and of letters.

And if it seems to anyone a shameful thing that I have written thus of shameful things and shameful people, then I am sorry for it. My only object is to set down here the truthful record of George Webber's life, and he, I feel quite sure, would be the last person in the world to wish me to suppress any chapter of it. So I do not think that I have written shamefully.

The only shame George Webber felt was that at one time in his life, for however short a period, he broke bread and sat at the same table with any man when the living warmth of friendship was not there; or that he ever traded upon the toil of his brain and the blood of his heart to get the body of a scented whore that might have been better got in a brothel for some greasy coins. This was the only shame he felt. And this shame was so great in him that he wondered if all his life thereafter would be long enough to wash out of his brain and blood the last pollution of its loathsome taint.

And yet, he would not have it thought that he was bitter.

Chapter Twenty-Four

Man-Creating and Man-Alive

It must be abundantly clear by now that George Webber was never bitter. What cause had he for bitterness? When he fled from the lion hunters he could always go back to the loneliness of his dismal two-room flat in Twelfth Street, and that is what he did. Also, he still had the letters from his friends in Libya Hill. They had not forgotten him. For four months and more after the publication of his book they continued to write him, and all of them took pains to let him know exactly what place he held in their affections.

Throughout this time George heard regularly from Randy Shepperton. Randy was the only one that George had left to talk to, so George, in answering Randy, unburdened himself of everything he thought and felt. Everything, that is, except upon a single topic—the rancor of his fellow-townsmen against the author who had exposed them naked to the world. Neither of the friends had ever mentioned it. Randy had set the pattern for evasion in his first letter, feeling that it was better to ignore the ugly gossip altogether and to let it die down and be forgotten. As for George, he had been too overwhelmed by it, too sunk and engulfed in it, to be able to speak of it at first. So they had chiefly confined themselves to the book itself, exchanging their thoughts and afterthoughts about it, with comments on what the various critics had said and left unsaid.

But by early March of the new year the flow of damning mail was past its flood and was thinning to a trickle, and one day Randy received from George the letter that he feared would have to come:

"I have spent most of my time this past week," George wrote, "reading and rereading all the letters that my erstwhile friends and neighbors have written me since the book came out. And now that the balloting is almost over and most of the vote is in, the result is startling and a little confusing. I have been variously compared to Judas Iscariot, Benedict Arnold, and Caesar's Brutus. I have been likened to the bird that fouls its own nest, to a viper that an innocent populace had long

273

nurtured in its bosom, to a carrion crow preying upon the blood and bones of his relatives and friends, and to an unnatural ghoul to whom nothing is sacred, not even the tombs of the honored dead. I have been called a vulture, a skunk, a hog deliberately and lustfully wallowing in the mire, a defiler of pure womanhood, a rattlesnake, a jackass, an alley-cat, and a baboon. Although my imagination has been strained trying to conceive of a creature who combined in himself all of these interesting traits—it would be worth any novelist's time to meet such a chap!—there have been moments when I have felt that maybe my accusers are right. . . ."

Behind this semblance of facetiousness, Randy could see that he was sincerely disturbed, and, knowing the capacity of George's soul for self-torture, he could pretty well imagine how deep and sore the extent of his full suffering might be. He revealed it almost immediately:

"Great God! What is it I have done? Sometimes I am overwhelmed by a sense of horrible and irrevocable guilt! Never before have I realized as I have this past week how terrible and great may be the distance between the Artist and the Man.

"As the artist, I can survey my work with a clear conscience. I have the regrets and dissatisfactions that every writer ought to have: the book should have been better, it failed to measure up to what I wanted for it. I am not ashamed of it. I feel that I wrote it as I did because of an inner necessity, that I *had* to do it, and that by doing it I was loyal to the only thing in me which is worth anything.

"So speaks Man-Creating. Then, instantly, it all changes, and from Man-Creating I become simply Man-Alive—a member of society, a friend and neighbor, a son and brother of the human race. And when I look at what I have done from this point of view, suddenly I feel lower than a dog. I see all the pain and anguish I have caused to people that I know, and I wonder how I could have done it, and how there could possibly be any justification for it—yes, even if what I wrote had been as great as *Lear*, as eloquent as *Hamlet*.

"Believe me—incredible as it may sound—when I tell you that during these weeks I have even derived a kind of grotesque and horrible pleasure from reading those letters which simply abused, cursed, or threatened me. There is, I found, a bitter relief in having someone curse me with every foul name he can think of or invent, or tell me he will put a bullet through my brain if I ever set foot in the streets of Libya Hill again. At any rate, I feel that the poor devil got some satisfaction out of writing it.

"But the letters that drive the blade into my heart and twist it around are those which neither curse nor threaten—the letters written by stunned and stricken people who never did me any
274

wrong, whose whole feeling toward me was one of kindly good will and belief, who did not know me *as I am*, and who write me now straight out of the suffering heart of man, with their spirits quivering, stripped, whipped by naked shame, to ask me over and over again in their bewilderment that terrible and insistent question: 'Why did you do it? Why? Why? Why?'

"And as I read their letters I no longer know why. I can't answer them. As Man-Creating, I thought I knew, and thought, too, that the answer was all-sufficient. I wrote about them with blunt directness, trying to put in every relevant detail and circumstance, and I did it because I thought it would be cowardly *not* to write that way, false to withhold or modify. I thought that the Thing Itself was its own and valid reason for being.

"But now that it is done, I am no longer sure of anything. I am troubled by the most maddening doubts and impossible regrets. I have moments when I feel that I would give my life if I could *un-write* my book, *un-print* its pages. For what has it accomplished, apparently, except to ruin my relatives, my friends, and everyone in town whose life was ever linked with mine? And what is there for me to salvage out of all this wreckage?

" 'The integrity of the artist,' you may say.

"Ah, yes—if I could only soothe my conscience with that solacement! For what integrity is there that is not tainted with human frailty? If only I could tell myself that every word and phrase and incident in the book had been created at the top of my bent and with the impartial judgment of unrancorous detachment! But I know it is not true. So many words come back to me, so many whip-lash phrases, that must have been written in a spirit that had nothing to do with art or my integrity. We are such stuff as dust is made of, and where we fail—we fail! Is there, then, no such thing as a pure spirit in creation?

"In all the whole wretched experience there is also a grim and horrible humor. It is insanely comical to find in almost all these letters that I am being cursed for doing things I did not do and for saying things I did not say. It is even more ludicrous to hear myself grudgingly praised for having the one thing that I have not got. Few of these letters—even those which threaten hanging, and those which deny me the remotest scrap of talent (except a genius for obscenity)—fail to commend me for what their writers call 'my memory.' Some of them accuse me of sneaking around as a little boy of eight with my pockets stuffed with notebooks, my ears fairly sprouting from my head and my eyes popping out, in my effort to spy upon and snatch up every word and act and phrase among my virtuous and unsuspecting fellow-townsmen.

" 'It's the dirtiest book I ever read,' one citizen cogently
275

remarks, 'but I'll have to give you credit for one thing—you've got a wonderful memory.'

"And that is just exactly what I have *not* got. I have to see a thing a *thousand times* before I see it *once*. This thing they call my memory, this thing they think they can themselves remember, is nothing that they ever saw. It is rather something that *I* saw after looking at the thing a thousand times, and this is what they *think* they can remember."

Randy paused in his reading of the letter, for he suddenly realized that what George said was literally true. In the weeks since the book was published, he himself had seen it proved over and over again.

He knew that there was scarcely a detail in George's book that was precisely true to fact, that there was hardly a page in which everything had not been transmuted and transformed by the combining powers of George's imagination; yet readers got from it such an instant sense of reality that many of them were willing to swear that the thing described had been not only "drawn from life," but was the actual and recorded fact itself. And that was precisely what had made the outcry and denunciation so furious.

But not only that. It was funny enough to hear people talking and arguing with each other out of a savage conviction that scenes and incidents in the book were literally true because they may have had some basis in remembered fact. It was even more grotesque to hear them testify, as some of them now did, that they had been witnesses to events which he knew to be utter fabrications of the author's imagination.

"Why," they cried, when final proof of anything was wanted, "he's got it all in! He's written it all down, just the way it happened! Nothing's changed a bit! Look at the Square!"

They always came back to the Square, for the Square had occupied a prominent place in *Home to Our Mountains*. George had pictured it with such intensity of vision that almost every brick and window-pane and cobblestone became imprinted on the reader's mind. But what was this Square? Was it the town Square of Libya Hill? Everybody said it was. Hadn't the local newspaper set it down in black and white that "our native chronicler has described the Square with a photographic eye"? Then people had read the book for themselves and had agreed.

So it was useless to argue with them—useless to point out to them how Webber's Square differed from their own, useless to mention a hundred items of variation. They had been pitiful in their anger when they first discovered that art had imitated life; now they were ludicrous in their ignorance that life was also imitating art.

With a smile and a shake of the head, Randy turned back to the letter:

"In God's name, what *have* I done?" George concluded. "Have I really acted according to some inner truth and real necessity, or did my unhappy mother conceive and give birth to a perverse monster who has defiled the dead and betrayed his family, kinsmen, neighbors, and the human race? What should I have done? What ought I to do now? If there is any help or answer in you, for Christ's sake let me have it. I feel like a dead leaf in a hurricane. I don't know where to turn. You alone can help me. Stay with me—write me—tell me what you think.

Yours ever,

George."

George's suffering had been so palpable in every sentence of his letter that Randy had winced in reading it. He had felt the naked anguish of his friend's raw wound almost as if it had been his own. But he knew that neither he nor any other man could give the help or answer that George sought. He would have to find it somehow in himself. That was the only way he had ever been able to learn anything.

So when Randy drafted his reply he deliberately made his letter as casual as he could. He did not want to let it seem that he attached too much importance to the town's reaction. He said that he did not know what he would do if he were George, since he was not a writer, but that he had always supposed a writer had to write about the life he knew. To cheer George up, he added that the people of Libya Hill reminded him of children who had not yet been told the facts of life. They still believed, apparently, in the stork. Only people who knew nothing about the world's literature could be surprised or shocked to learn where every good book came from.

And then, in a kind of mild parenthesis, he said that Tim Wagner, the town's most celebrated souse, noted for his wit in his rare intervals of sobriety, had been a warm supporter of the book from the beginning, but had made one reservation: "Why, hell! If George wants to write about a horse thief, that's all right. Only the next time I hope he don't give his street address. And there ain't no use in throwing in his telephone number, too."

Randy knew this would amuse George, and it did. In fact, George told him later that it was the most sound and valuable critical advice that he had ever had.

Randy ended his letter by assuring George that even if he *was* a writer, he still considered him a member of the human race. And he added, in what he hoped would be a comforting postscript, that there were other angry mutterings abroad. He

277

had heard a rumor, whispered by one of the town's leading business men with a great air of hush-hush and please-don't-breathe-a-word-of-this-to-anyone, that Mr. Jarvis Riggs, the president of Libya Hill's largest bank and past hero of infallibilities, was tottering on the brink of ruin.

"So you see," Randy concluded, "if that godly gentleman is capable of imperfection, there may still be hope of pardon even in creatures as vile as you."

Chapter Twenty-Five

The Catastrophe

A day or two after receiving Randy's reply, George was reading the *New York Times* one morning when his eye was caught by a small news item on an inside page. It occupied only a scant two inches or so at the bottom of a column, but the Libya Hill date line leaped out at him:

BANK FAILS IN SOUTH

Libya Hill, O. C., Mar. 12—The Citizens Trust Company of this city failed to open its doors for business this morning, and throughout the day, as news of its closing spread, conditions of near-panic mounted steadily here and in all the surrounding region. The bank was one of the largest in western Old Catawba and for years had been generally regarded as a model of conservative management and financial strength. The cause of its failure is not yet known. It is feared that the losses to the people of this community may be extensive.

The alarm occasioned by the closing of the bank was heightened later in the day by the discovery of the sudden and rather mysterious death of Mayor Baxter Kennedy. His body was found with a bullet through his head, and all the available evidence seems to point to suicide. Mayor Kennedy was a man of exceptionally genial and cheerful disposition, and is said to have had no enemies.

Whether there is any connection between the two events which have so profoundly disturbed the accustomed calm of this mountain district is not known, although their close coincidence has given rise to much excited conjecture.

"So," thought George, laying down the paper with a stunned and thoughtful air, "it has come at last! . . . What was it that Judge Rumford Bland had said to them?"

The whole scene in the Pullman washroom came back to him. He saw again the stark and speechless terror in the faces of Libya Hill's leaders and rulers as the frail but terrible old blind man suddenly confronted them and held them with his sightless eyes and openly accused them of ruining the town. As George remembered this and sat there thinking about the news he had just read, he felt quite sure there must be some direct relation between the failure of the bank and the Mayor's suicide.

There was, indeed. Things had been building up to this double climax for a long time.

Jarvis Riggs, the banker, had come from a poor but thoroughly respectable family in the town. When he was fifteen his father died and he had to quit school and go to work to support his mother. He held a succession of small jobs until, at eighteen, he was offered a modest but steady position in the Merchants National Bank.

He was a bright young fellow and a "hustler," and step by step he worked his way up until he became a teller. Mark Joyner kept a deposit at the Merchants National and used to come home and talk about Jarvis Riggs. In those days he had none of the brittle manner and pompous assurance that were to characterize him later, after he had risen to greatness. His hair, which was afterwards to turn a dead and lifeless sandy color, had glints of gold in it then, his cheeks were full and rosy, he had a bright and smiling face, and it was always briskly and cheerfully—"Good morning, Mr. Joyner!" or "Good morning, Mr. Shepperton!"—when a customer came in. He was friendly, helpful, courteous, eager to please, and withal businesslike and knowing. He also dressed neatly and was known to be supporting his mother. All these things made people like him and respect him. They wanted to see him succeed. For Jarvis Riggs was a living vindication of an American legend—that of the poor boy who profits from the hardships of his early life and "makes good." People would nod knowingly to one another and say of him:

"That young man has his feet on the ground."

"Yes," they would say, "he's *going* somewhere."

So when, along about 1912, the word began to go around that

a small group of conservative business men were talking of starting a new bank, and that Jarvis Riggs was going to be its cashier, the feeling was most favorable. The backers explained that they were not going to compete with the established banks. It was simply their feeling that a growing town like Libya Hill, with its steady increase in population and in its business interests, could use another bank. And the new bank, one gathered, was to be conducted according to the most eminently approved principles of sound finance. But it was to be a progressive bank, too, a forward-looking bank, mindful of the future, the great, golden, magnificent future that Libya Hill was sure to have—that it was even heresy to doubt. In this way it was also to be a young man's bank. And this was where Jarvis Riggs came in.

It is not too much to say that the greatest asset the new enterprise had from the beginning was Jarvis Riggs. He had played his cards well. He had offended no one, he had made no enemies, he had always remained modest, friendly, and yet impersonal, as if not wishing to intrude himself too much on the attention of men who stood for substance and authority in the town's life. The general opinion was that he knew what he was doing. He had learned about life in the highly-thought-of "university of hard knocks," he had learned business and banking in "the hard school of experience," so everybody felt that if Jarvis Riggs was going to be cashier of the new bank, then the new bank was pretty sure to be all right.

Jarvis himself went around town and sold stock in the bank. He had no difficulty at all. He made it quite plain that he did not think anyone was going to make a fortune. He simply sold the stock as a safe and sound investment, and that was how everybody felt about it. The bank was modestly capitalized at $25,000, and there were 250 shares at $100 each. The sponsors, including Jarvis, took 100 shares between them, and the remaining 150 shares were divided among "a selected group of leading business men." As Jarvis said, the bank was really "a community project whose first and only purpose is to serve the community," so no one was allowed to acquire too large an interest.

This was the way the Citizens Trust Company got started. And in no time at all, it seemed, Jarvis Riggs was advanced from cashier to vice-president, and then to president. The poor boy had come into his own.

In its early years the bank prospered modestly and conservatively. Its growth was steady but not spectacular. After the United States entered the war, it got its share of the nation's prosperity. But after the war, in 1921, there was a temporary lull, a period of "adjustment." Then the 1920's began in earnest. The only way to explain what happened then is to say that there was "a feeling in the air." Everybody seemed to sense a prospect of quick and easy money. There was thrilling and rapid expansion in all directions, and it seemed that there were possibilities of wealth, luxury, and economic power hitherto undreamed of just lying around waiting for anyone who was bold enough to seize them.

Jarvis Riggs was no more insensible to these beckoning opportunities than the next man. The time had come, he decided, to step out and show the world what he could do. The Citizens Trust began to advertize itself as "the fastest-growing bank in the state." But it did not advertize what it was growing on.

That was the time when the political and business clique which dominated the destinies of the town, and which had put amiable Baxter Kennedy in the Mayor's office as its "front," began to focus its activities around the bank. The town was burgeoning rapidly and pushing out into the wilderness, people were confident of a golden future, no one gave a second thought to the reckless increase in public borrowing. Bond issues involving staggering sums were being constantly "floated" until the credit structure of the town was built up into a teetering inverted pyramid and the citizens of Libya Hill no longer owned the streets they walked on. The proceeds of these enormous borrowings were deposited with the bank. The bank, for its part, then returned these deposits to the politicians, or to their business friends, supporters, allies, and adherents—in the form of tremendous loans, made upon the most flimsy and tenuous security, for purposes of private and personal speculation. In this way "The Ring," as it was called, which had begun as an inner circle of a few ambitious men, became in time a vast and complex web that wove through the entire social structure of the town and involved the lives of thousands of people. And all of it now centered in the bank.

But the weaving of this complicated web of frenzied finance and speculation and special favors to "The Ring" could not go on forever, though there were many who thought it could. There had to come a time when the internal strains and stresses became too great to sustain the load, a time when there would be ominous preliminary tremors to give warning of the crash that was to come. Just when this time arrived is pretty hard to say. One can observe a soldier moving forward in a battle and see him spin and tumble, and know the moment he is hit. But one cannot observe so exactly the moment when a man has been shot down by life.

So it was with the bank and with Jarvis Riggs. All that one can be sure of is that their moment came. And it came long before the mighty roar of tumbling stocks in Wall Street echoed throughout the nation. That event, which had its repercussions

281

in Libya Hill as elsewhere, was not the *prime cause* of anything. What happened in Wall Street was only the initial explosion which in the course of the next few years was to set off a train of lesser explosions all over the land—explosions which at last revealed beyond all further doubting and denial the hidden pockets of lethal gases which a false, vicious, and putrescent scheme of things had released beneath the surface of American life.

Long before the explosion came that was to blow *him* sky-high, and the whole town with him, Jarvis Riggs had felt the tremors in the thing he had created, and he knew he was a doomed and ruined man. Before long others knew it, too, and knew that they were ruined with him. But they would not let themselves believe it. They did not dare. Instead, they sought to exorcise the thing they feared by pretending it wasn't there. Their speculations only grew madder, fiercer.

And then, somehow, the cheerful, easy-going Mayor found out what some of those around him must have known for months. That was in the spring of 1928, two years before the failure of the bank. At that time he went to Jarvis Riggs and told him what he knew, and then demanded to withdraw the city's funds. The banker looked the frightened Mayor in the eye and laughed at him.

"What are you afraid of, Baxter?" he said. "Are you showing the white feather now that the pinch is on? You say you are going to withdraw the deposits of the city? All right—withdraw them. But I warn you, if you do the bank is ruined. It will have to close its doors tomorrow. And if it closes its doors, where is your town? Your precious town is also ruined."

The Mayor looked at the banker with a white face and stricken eyes. Jarvis Riggs leaned forward and his tones became more persuasive:

"Pull out your money if you like, and wreck your town. But why not play along with us, Baxter? We're going to see this thing through." He was smiling now, and wearing his most winning manner. "We're in a temporary depression—yes. But six months from now we'll be out of the woods. I know we will. We're coming back stronger than ever. You can't sell Libya Hill short," he said, using a phrase that was in great vogue just then. "We've not begun to see the progress we're going to make. But the salvation and future of this town rests in your hands. So make up your mind about it. What are you going to do?"

The Mayor made up his mind. Unhappy man.

Things drifted along. Time passed. The sands were running low.

By the fall of 1929 there began to be a vague rumor going about that all was not well at the Citizens Trust. George Webber had heard it himself when he went home in September. But it was a nebulous thing, and as often as not the person who whispered it fearfully would catch himself and say:

"Oh, pshaw! There's nothing in it. There couldn't be! You know how people talk."

But the rumor persisted through the winter, and by early March it had become a disturbing and sinister contagion. No one could say where it came from. It seemed to be distilled like a poison out of the mind and heart and spirit of the whole town.

On the surface there was nothing to account for it. The Citizens Trust maintained its usual appearance of solid substance, businesslike efficiency, and Greek-templed sanctity. Its broad plate-glass windows opening out upon the Square let in a flood of light, and the whole atmosphere was one of utter clarity. The very breadth of those windows seemed to proclaim to the world the complete openness and integrity of the bank's purpose. They seemed to say:

"Here is the bank, and here are all the people in the bank, and all the people in the bank are openly at work. Look, citizens, and see for yourselves. You see there is nothing hidden here. The bank is Libya, and Libya is the bank."

It was all so open that one did not have to go inside to know what was going on. One could stand on the sidewalk outside and look in and see everything. To the right were the tellers' cages, and to the left there was a railed-off space in which the officers sat at their sumptuous mahogany flat-topped desks. At the largest of these desks, just inside the low enclosure, sat Jarvis Riggs himself. There he sat, talking importantly and pompously, as though laying down the law, to one of his customers. There he sat, briskly reading through the pile of papers on his desk. There he sat, pausing in his work now and then to look up at the ceiling in deep thought, or to lean back in his swivel chair and gently rock in meditation.

It was all just as it had always been.

Then it happened.

March 12, 1930 was a day that will be long remembered in the annals of Libya Hill. The double tragedy set the stage as nothing else could have done for the macabre weeks to follow.

If all the fire bells in town had suddenly begun to ring out their alarm at nine o'clock that morning, the news could not have spread more rapidly that the Citizens Trust Company was closed. Word of it leapt from mouth to mouth. And almost instantly, from every direction, white-faced men and women came running toward the Square. There were housewives with their aprons on, their hands still dripping dishwater; workmen and mechanics with their warm tools in their hands; hatless business men and clerks; young mothers carrying babies in their arms. Everyone in town, it seemed, had dropped whatever he was doing and rushed out in the streets the moment the news had reached him.

The Square itself was soon a seething mass of frenzied people. Frantically, over and over, they asked each other the same questions: Was it really true? How had it happened? How bad was it?

In front of the bank itself the crowd was quieter, more stunned. To this spot, sooner or later, they all came, drawn by a common desperate hope that they would yet be able to see with their own eyes that it was not so. Like a sluggish current within that seething mass the queue moved slowly past, and as the people saw those locked and darkened doors they knew that all hope was gone. Some just stared with stricken faces, some of the women moaned and wailed, from the eyes of strong men silent tears coursed down, and from the mouths of others came the rumble of angry mutterings.

For their ruin had caught up with them. Many of the people in that throng had lost their life savings. But it was not only the bank's depositors who were ruined. Everyone now knew that their boom was over. They knew that the closing of the bank had frozen all their speculations just as they were, beyond the possibility of extricating themselves. Yesterday they could count their paper riches by ten thousands and by millions; today they owned nothing, their wealth had vanished, and they were left saddled with debts that they could never pay.

And they did not yet know that their city government was bankrupt, too—that six million dollars of public money had been lost behind those closed and silent doors.

It was a little before noon on that ill-omened day that Mayor

Kennedy was found dead. And, just to put the final touch of gruesome irony upon the whole event, a blind man found him.

Judge Rumford Bland testified at the inquest that he left his front office, upstairs in the ramshackle building that he owned there on the Square, and went out in the hall, heading in the direction of the toilet, where he proposed to perform an essential function of nature. It was dark out there, he said with his ghostly smile, and the floors creaked, but this didn't matter to him—he knew the way. He said he couldn't have lost his way even if he wanted to. At the end of the hall he could hear a punctual drip of water, dropping with its slow, incessant monotone; and besides, there was the pervasive smell of the tin urinal—all he had to do was to follow his nose.

He arrived in darkness and pushed open the door, and suddenly his foot touched something. He leaned over, his white, thin fingers groped down, and all at once they were plunged—wet, warm, sticky, reeking—into the foundering mass of what just five minutes before had been the face and brains of a living man.

—No, he hadn't heard the shot—there was all that infernal commotion out in the Square.

—No, he had no idea how *he* had got there—walked it, he supposed—the City Hall was only twenty yards away.

—No, he couldn't say why His Honor should have picked that spot to blow his brains out—there was no accounting for tastes—but if a man wanted to do it, that was probably as good a place as any.

So it was that weak, easy-going, procrastinating, good-natured Baxter Kennedy, Mayor of Libya Hill, was found—all that was left of him—in darkness, by an evil old blind man.

In the days and weeks that followed the closing of the bank, Libya Hill presented a tragic spectacle the like of which had probably never before been seen in America. But it was a spectacle that was to be repeated over and over again, with local variations, in many another town and city within the next few years.

The ruin of Libya Hill was much more than the ruin of the bank and the breakdown of the economic and financial order. True, when the bank failed, all that vast and complicated scheme of things which had been built upon it, the ramifications of which extended into every element of the community's life, toppled and crashed. But the closing of the bank was only like the action of a rip cord which, once jerked, brought the whole
285

thing down, and in doing so laid bare the deeper and more corrosive ruin within. And this deeper ruin—the essence of the catastrophe—was the ruin of the human conscience.

Here was a town of fifty thousand people who had so abdicated every principle of personal and communal rectitude, to say nothing of common sense and decency, that when the blow fell they had no inner resources with which to meet it. The town almost literally blew its brains out. Forty people shot themselves within ten days, and others did so later. And, as so often happens, many of those who destroyed themselves were among the least guilty of the lot. The rest—and this was the most shocking part of it—suddenly realizing their devastating guilt to such a degree that they could not face the results of it, now turned like a pack of howling dogs to rend each other. Cries of vengeance rose up from all their throats, and they howled for the blood of Jarvis Riggs. But these cries proceeded not so much from a conviction of wounded justice and deceived innocence as from their opposites. It was the sublime, ironic, and irrevocable justice of what had happened to them, and their knowledge that they alone had been responsible for it, that maddened them. From this arose their sense of outrage and their cries of vengeance.

What happened in Libya Hill and elsewhere has been described in the learned tomes of the overnight economists as a breakdown of "the system, the capitalist system." Yes, it was that. But it was also much more than that. In Libya Hill it was the total disintegration of what, in so many different ways, the lives of all these people had come to be. It went much deeper than the mere obliteration of bank accounts, the extinction of paper profits, and the loss of property. It was the ruin of men who found out, as soon as these symbols of their outward success had been destroyed, that they had nothing left—no inner equivalent from which they might now draw new strength. It was the ruin of men who, discovering not only that their values were false but that they had never had any substance whatsoever, now saw at last the emptiness and hollowness of their lives. Therefore they killed themselves; and those who did not die by their own hands died by the knowledge that they were already dead.

How can one account for such a complete drying up of all the spiritual sources in the life of a people? When one observes a youth of eighteen on a city street and sees the calloused scar that has become his life, and remembers the same youth as he was ten years before when he was a child of eight, one knows what has happened though the cause is hidden. One knows that there came a time when life stopped growing for that youth and the scar began; and one feels that if he could only find the reason and the cure, he would know what revolutions are.

In Libya Hill there must have been a time when life stopped growing and the scar began. But the learned economists of "the system" do not bother about this. For them, it belongs to the realm of the metaphysical—they are impatient of it, they will not trouble with it, they want to confine the truth within their little picket fence of facts. But they cannot. It is not enough to talk about the subtle complications of the credit structure, the intrigues of politics and business, the floating of bond issues, the dangers of inflation, speculation, and unsound prices, or the rise and decline of banks. When all these facts are added up, they still don't give the answer. For there is something more to say.

So with Libya Hill:

One does not know at just what moment it began, but one suspects that it began at some time long past in the lone, still watches of the night, when all the people lay waiting in their beds in darkness. Waiting for what? They did not know. They only hoped that it would happen—some thrilling and impossible fulfillment, some glorious enrichment and release of their pent lives, some ultimate escape from their own tedium.

But it did not come.

Meanwhile, the stiff boughs creaked in the cold bleakness of the corner lights, and the whole town waited, imprisoned in its tedium.

And sometimes, in furtive hallways, doors opened and closed, there was a padding of swift, naked feet, the stealthy rattling of brass casters, and behind old battered shades, upon the edge of Niggertown, the dull and fetid quickenings of lust.

Sometimes, in grimy stews of night's asylumage, an oath, a blow, a fight.

Sometimes, through the still air, a shot, the letting of nocturnal blood.

And always, through broken winds, the sounds of shifting engines in the station yards, far off, along the river's edge—and suddenly the thunder of great wheels, the tolling of the bell, the loneliness of the whistle cry wailed back, receding toward the North, and toward the hope, the promise, and the memory of the world unfound.

Meanwhile, the boughs creaked bleakly in stiff light, ten thousand men were waiting in the darkness, far off a dog howled, and the Court House bell struck three.

No answer? Impossible? . . . Then let those—if such there be—who have not waited in the darkness, find answers of their own.

But if speech could frame what spirit utters, if tongue could tell what the lone heart knows, there would be answers somewhat other than those which are shaped by the lean pickets of rusty facts. There would be answers of men waiting, who have not spoken yet.

287

Below the starred immensity of mountain night old Rumford Bland, he that is called "The Judge," strokes his sunken jaws reflectively as he stands at the darkened window of his front office and looks out with sightless eyes upon the ruined town. It is cool and sweet tonight, the myriad promises of life are lyric in the air. Gem-strewn in viewless linkage on the hills the lights make a bracelet for the town. The blind man knows that they are there, although he cannot see them. He strokes his sunken jaws reflectively and smiles his ghostly smile.

It is so cool and sweet tonight, and spring has come. There never was a year like this, they say, for dogwood in the hills. There are so many thrilling, secret things upon the air tonight—a burst of laughter, and young voices, faint, half-broken, and the music of a dance—how could one know that when the blind man smiles and strokes his sunken jaws reflectively, he is looking out upon a ruined town?

The new Court House and City Hall are very splendid in the dark tonight. But he has never seen them—they were built since he went blind. Their fronts are bathed, so people say, in steady, secret light just like the nation's dome at Washington. The blind man strokes his sunken jaws reflectively. Well, they *should* be splendid—they cost enough.

Beneath the starred immensity of mountain night there is something stirring in the air, a rustling of young leaves. And around the grass roots there is something stirring in the earth tonight. And below the grass roots and the sod, below the dew-wet pollen of young flowers, there is something alive and stirring. The blind man strokes his sunken jaws reflectively. Aye, there below, where the eternal worm keeps vigil, there is something stirring in the earth. Down, down below, where the worm incessant through the ruined house makes stir.

What lies there stir-less in the earth tonight, down where the worm keeps vigil?

The blind man smiles his ghostly smile. In his eternal vigil the worm stirs, but many men are rotting in their graves tonight, and sixty-four have bullet fractures in their skulls. Ten thousand more are lying in their beds tonight, living as shells live. They, too, are dead, though yet unburied. They have been dead so long they can't remember how it was to live. And many weary nights must pass before they can join the buried dead, down where the worm keeps vigil.

Meanwhile, the everlasting worm keeps vigil, and the blind man strokes his sunken jaws, and slowly now he shifts his sightless gaze and turns his back upon the ruined town.

Chapter Twenty-Six

The Wounded Faun

Ten days after the failure of the bank in Libya Hill, Randy Shepperton arrived in New York. He had made up his mind suddenly, without letting George know, and the motives that brought him were mixed. For one thing, he wanted to talk to George and see if he couldn't help to get him straightened out. His letters had been so desperate that Randy was beginning to be worried about him. Then, too, Randy felt he just had to get away from Libya Hill for a few days and out of that atmosphere of doom and ruin and death. And he was free now, there was nothing to keep him from coming, so he came.

He arrived early in the morning, a little after eight o'clock, and took a taxi from the station to the address on Twelfth Street and rang the bell. After a long interval and another ringing of the bell, the door lock clicked and he entered the dim-lit hall. The stairs were dark and the whole house seemed sunk in sleep. His footfalls rang out upon the silence. The air had a close, dead smell compounded of many elements, among which he could distinguish the dusty emanations of old wood and worn plankings and the ghostly reminders of many meals long since eaten. The light was out on the second-floor landing and the gloom was Stygian, so he groped along the wall until he found the door and rapped loudly with his knuckles.

In a moment the door was almost jerked off its hinges, and George, his hair disheveled, his eyes red with sleep, an old bathrobe flung hastily over his pajamas, stood framed in the opening, blinking out into the darkness. Randy was a little taken back by the change in his appearance in the six months since he had last seen him. His face, which had always had a youthful and even childish quality, had grown older and sterner. The lines had deepened. And now his heavy lip stuck out at his caller with a menacing challenge, and his whole pug-nosed countenance had a bulldog look of grim truculence.

When Randy recovered from his first surprise he cried out heartily:

"Now wait a minute! Wait a minute! Don't shoot! I'm not *that* fellow at all!"

289

At the unexpected sound of the familiar voice George looked startled, then his face broke into a broad smile of incredulity and delight. "Well, I'll be damned!" he cried, and with that he seized hold of Randy, wrung him vigorously by the hand, almost dragged him into the room, and then held him off at arm's length while he grinned his pleasure and amazement.

"That's better," said Randy in a tone of mock relief. "I was afraid it might be permanent."

They now clapped each other on the back and exchanged those boisterous and half-insulting epithets with which two men who have been old friends like to greet each other when they meet. Then, almost at once, George asked Randy eagerly about the bank. Randy told him. George listened intently to the shocking details of the catastrophe. It was even worse than he had supposed, and he kept firing questions at Randy. At last Randy said:

"Well, that's just about the whole story. I've told you all I know. But come, we can talk about that later. What I want to know is—how the hell are *you*? You're not cracking up, too, are you? Your last letters made me a little uneasy about you."

In their joy at seeing one another again and their eagerness to talk, they had both remained standing by the door. But now, as Randy put his casual finger on George's sore spot, George winced and began to pace back and forth in an agitated way without answering.

Randy saw that he looked tired. His eyes were bloodshot, as if he had not slept well, and his unshaved face made him look haggard. The old bathrobe he was wearing had all the buttons missing, and the corded rope that belonged to it was also gone and George had lashed a frayed necktie around his middle to hold the thing together. This remarkable garment added to his general appearance of weariness and exhaustion. His features as he strode about the room had the contracted intensity of nervous strain, and as he looked up quickly Randy saw the worry and apprehension in his eyes.

Suddenly he paused and faced Randy squarely, and with a grim set to his jaws said:

"All right, let me have it! What are they saying now?"

"Who? What is who saying?"

"The people back home. That's what you meant, isn't it? From what they've written me and said to my face, I can imagine what they're saying behind my back. Let's have it and get it over with. What are they saying now?"

"Why," said Randy, "I don't know that they're saying anything. Oh, they said plenty at first—just the kind of thing they wrote you. But since the bank failed I don't think I've heard your name mentioned. They've got too much real trouble to worry about now."

290

George looked incredulous, and then relieved. For a moment he studied the floor and said nothing. But as his sense of relief spread its soothing balm upon his agitated spirit he looked up and smiled broadly at his friend, and then, realizing for the first time that Randy was standing there with his back against the door, he suddenly remembered his duties as a host and burst out impulsively and warmly:

"God, Randy, I'm glad to see you! I can't get over it! Sit down! Sit down! Can't you find a chair somewhere? For Christ's sake, where *are* all the chairs in this dump?"

With that he went over to a chair that was piled high with manuscript and books, brushed these things off unceremoniously onto the floor, and shoved the chair across the room toward his friend.

He apologized now for the coldness of the place, explaining unnecessarily that the door bell had got him out of bed, and telling Randy to keep his overcoat on and that it would be warmer in a little while. Then he vanished through a doorway into a noisome cubbyhole, turned on a faucet, and came back with a coffee pot full of water. This he proceeded to pour into the spout of the radiator that stood below a window. When this was done, he got down on his hands and knees, peered about underneath, struck a match, turned some sort of valve, and applied the flame. There was an immediate blast, and pretty soon the water began to rattle and gurgle in the pipes.

"It's gas," he said, as he clambered to his feet. "That's the worst thing about this place—it gives me headaches when I have to spend long hours working here."

While this operation had been going on, Randy took a look around. The room, which was really two large rooms thrown together when the sliding doors that joined them were pushed into the wall, as now, seemed as big as a barn. The windows at the front gave onto the street, and those at the rear looked out over some bleak little squares of backyard fences to another row of buildings. The first impression Randy got was one of staleness: the whole apartment had that unmistakable look and feeling of a place where someone has lived and where something has been finished so utterly that there is no going back to it. It was not merely the disorder everywhere—the books strewn around, the immense piles of manuscript, the haphazard scattering of stray socks, shirts and collars, old shoes, and unpressed trousers inside out. It was not even the dirty cup and saucer filled with old cigarette butts, all of them stained with rancid coffee, which was set down in the vast and untidy litter of the table. It was just that life had gone out of all these things—they were finished—all as cold and tired and stale as the old dirty cup and the exhausted butts.

George was living in the midst of this dreary waste with a

kind of exasperated and unhappy transiency. Randy saw that he had caught him on the wing, in that limbo of waiting between work which is one of the most tormenting periods a writer can know. He was through with one thing, and yet not really ready to settle down in earnest to another. He was in a state of furious but exhausted ferment. But it was not merely that he was going through a period of gestation before going on with his next book. Randy realized that the reception of his first, the savagery of the attack against him in Libya Hill, the knowledge that he had done something more than write a book—that he had also torn up violently by the roots all those ties of friendship and sentiment that bind a man to home—all of this, Randy felt, had so bewildered and overwhelmed him that now he was caught up in the maelstrom of the conflict which he had himself produced. He was not ready to do another piece of work because his energies were still being absorbed and used up by the repercussions of the first.

Moreover, as Randy looked around the room and his eye took in the various objects that contributed to its incredible chaos, he saw, in a dusty corner, a small green smock or apron, wrinkled as though it had been thrown aside with a gesture of weary finality, and beside it, half-folded inward, a single small and rather muddy overshoe. The layer of dust upon them showed that they had lain there for months. These were the only poignant ghosts, and Randy knew that something which had been there in that room had gone out of it forever—that George was done with it.

Randy saw how it was with George, and felt that almost any decisive act would be good for him. So now he said:

"For God's sake, George, why don't you pick up and clear out of all this? You're through with it—it's finished—it'll only take you a day or two to wind the whole thing up. So pull yourself together and get out. Move away somewhere—anywhere—just to enjoy the luxury of waking up in the morning and finding none of this around you."

"I know," said George, going over to a sagging couch and tossing back the pile of foul-looking bedclothes that covered it and flinging himself down wearily. "I've thought of it," he said.

Randy did not press the point. He knew it would be no use. George would have to work around to it in his own way and in his own good time.

George shaved and dressed, and they went out for breakfast. Then they returned and talked all morning, and were finally interrupted by the ringing of the telephone.

George answered it. Randy could tell by the sounds which came from the transmitter that the caller was female, garrulous, and unmistakably Southern. George did nothing for a while but blurt out polite banalities:

"Well, now, that's fine. . . . I certainly do appreciate it. . . . That's mighty nice of you. . . . Well now, I'm certainly glad you called. I hope you will remember me to all of them." Then he was silent, listening intently, and Randy gathered from the contraction of his face that the conversation had now reached another stage. In a moment he said slowly, in a somewhat puzzled tone: "Oh, he is? . . . He did? . . . Well—" somewhat indefinitely—"that's mighty nice of him. . . . Yes, I'll remember. . . . Thank you very much. . . . Good-bye."

He hung up the receiver and grinned wearily.

"That," he said, "was one of the I-just-called-you-up-to-tell-you-that-I've-read-it-all-every-word-of-it-and-I-think-it's-perfectly-grand people—another lady from the South." As he went on his voice unconsciously dropped into burlesque as he tried to imitate the unction of a certain type of Southern female whose words drip molasses mixed with venom:

" 'Why, I'll declayah, we're *all* just so proud of yew-w! I'm just simply thrilled to *daith*! It's the most wondaful thing I *evah* read! Why it *is*! Why, I nevah *dreamed* that *anyone* could have such a wondaful command of lang-widge!' "

"But don't you like it just a little?" asked Randy. "Even if it's laid on with a trowel, you must get some satisfaction from it."

"God!" George said wearily, and came back and fell upon the couch. "If you only knew! That's only one out of a thousand! That telephone there"—he jerked a thumb toward it—"has played a tune for months now! I know them all—I've got 'em classified! I can tell by the tone of the voice the moment they speak whether it's going to be type B or group X."

"So the author is already growing jaded? He's already bored with his first taste of fame?"

"*Fame?*"—disgustedly. "That's not fame—that's just plain damn ragpicking!"

"Then you don't think the woman was sincere?"

"Yes—" his face and tone were bitter now—"she had all the sincerity of a carrion crow. She'll go back and tell them that she talked to me, and by the time she's finished with me she'll have a story that every old hag in town can lick her chops and cackle over for the next six months."

It sounded so unreasonable and unjust that Randy spoke up quickly:

"Don't you think you're being unfair?"

George's head was down dejectedly and he did not even look up; with his hands plunged in his trouser pockets he just snorted something unintelligible but scornful beneath his breath.

293

It annoyed and disappointed Randy to see him acting so much like a spoiled brat, so he said:

"Look here! It's about time you grew up and learned some sense. It seems to me you're being pretty arrogant. Do you think you can afford to be? I doubt if you or any man can go through life successfully playing the spoiled genius."

Again he muttered something in a sullen tone.

"Maybe that woman *was* a fool," Randy went on. "Well, a lot of people are. And maybe she hasn't got sense enough to understand what you wrote in the way you think it should be understood. But what of it? She gave the best she had. It seems to me that instead of sneering at her now, you could be grateful."

George raised his head: "You heard the conversation, then?"

"No, only what you told me."

"All right, then—you didn't get the whole story. I wouldn't mind if she'd just called up to gush about the book, but, look here!—" he leaned toward Randy very earnestly and tapped him on the knee. "I don't want you to get the idea that I'm just a conceited fool. I've lived through and found out about something these last few months that most people never have the chance to know. I give you my solemn word for it, that woman didn't call up because she liked my book and wanted to tell me so. She called up," he cried bitterly, "to pry around, and to find out what she could about me, and to pick my bones."

"Oh, look here now—" Randy began impatiently.

"Yes, she did, too! I know what I'm talking about!" he said earnestly. "Here's what you didn't hear—here's what she was working around to all the time—it came out at the end. I don't know who she is, I never heard of her before—but she's a friend of Ted Reeve's wife. And apparently he thinks I put him in the book, and has been making threats that he's going to kill me if I ever go back home."

This was true; Randy had heard it in Libya Hill.

"That's what it was about," George sneered bitterly—"that woman's call. That's what most of the calls are about. They want to talk to the Beast of the Apocalypse, feel him out, and tell him: 'Ted's all right! Now don't you believe all those things you hear! He was upset at first—but he sees the whole thing now, the way you meant it—and everything's all right.' That's what she said to me, so maybe I'm not the fool you think I am!"

He was so earnest and excited that for a moment Randy did not answer him. Besides, making allowances for the distortion of his feelings, he could see some justice in what George said.

"Have you had many calls like that?" Randy asked.

"Oh—" wearily—"almost every day. I think everyone who has been up here from home since the book was published has telephoned me. They go about it in different ways. There are those who call me up as if I were some kind of ghoul: 'How are you?'—in a small, quiet tone such as you might use to a condemned man just before they lead him to the death chamber at Sing Sing—'Are you all right?' And then you get alarmed, you begin to stammer and to stumble around: 'Why, yes! Yes, I'm fine! Fine, thanks!'—meanwhile, beginning to feel yourself all over just to see if you're all there. And then they say in that same still voice: 'Well, I just wanted to know. . . . I just called up to find out. . . . I hope you're all right.' "

After looking at Randy for a moment in a tormented and bewildered way, he burst out in an exasperated laugh:

"It's been enough to give a hippopotamus the creeps! To listen to them talk, you'd think I was Jack the Ripper! Even those who call up to laugh and joke about it take the attitude that the only reason I wrote the book was to see how much dirt and filth I could dig up on people I didn't like. Yes!" he cried bitterly. "My greatest supporters at home seem to be the disappointed little soda jerkers who never made a go of it and the frustrated hangers-on who never got into the Country Club. 'You sure did give it to that son-of-a-bitch, Jim So-and-so!' they call me up to tell me. 'You sure did burn him up! I had to laugh when I read what you said about him—boy!' Or: 'Why didn't you say something about that bastard, Charlie What's-his-name? I'd have given anything to see you take him for a ride!' . . . Jesus God!" He struck his fist upon his knee with furious exasperation. "That's all it means to them: nothing but nasty gossip, slander, malice, envy, a chance of getting back at someone—you'd think that none of them had ever read a book before. Tell me," he said earnestly, bending toward Randy, "isn't there anyone there—anyone besides yourself—who gives a damn about the book itself? Isn't there anyone who has read it as a book, who sees what it was about, who understands what I was trying to do?"

His eyes were full of torment now. It was out at last—the thing Randy had dreaded and wanted to avoid. He said:

"I should think you'd know more about that by this time than anyone. After all, you've had more opportunity than anyone else to find out."

Well, that was out, too. It was the answer that he had to have, that he had feared to get. He stared at Randy for a minute or two with his tormented eyes, then he laughed bitterly and began to rave:

"Well, then, to hell with it! To hell with all of it!" He began to curse violently. "The small two-timing bunch of crooked sons-of-bitches! They can go straight to hell! They've done their best to ruin me!"

It was ignoble and unworthy and untrue. Randy saw that he was lashing himself into a fit of violent recrimination in which all that was worst and weakest in him was coming out—distortion, prejudice, and self-pity. These were the things he would have to conquer somehow or be lost. Randy stopped him curtly:

"Now, no more of that! For God's sake, George, pull yourself together! If a lot of damn fools read your book and didn't understand it, that's not Libya Hill, that's the whole world. People there are no different from people anywhere. They thought you wrote about them—and the truth is, you did. So they got mad at you. You hurt their feelings, and you touched their pride. And, to be blunt about it, you opened up a lot of old wounds. There were places where you rubbed salt in. In saying this, I'm not like those others you complain about: you know damn well I understand what you did and why you had to do it. But just the same, there were some things that you did not have to do—and you'd have had a better book if you hadn't done them. So don't whine about it now. And don't think you're a martyr."

But he had got himself primed into a mood of martyrdom. As Randy looked at him sitting there, one hand gripping his knee, his face sullen, his head brooding down between his hulking shoulders, he could see how this mood had grown upon him. To begin with, he had been naïve not to realize how people would feel about some of the things he had written. Then, when the first accusing letters came, he had been overwhelmed and filled with shame and humility and guilt over the pain he had caused. But as time went on and the accusations became more vicious and envenomed, he had wanted to strike back and defend himself. When he saw there was no way to do that—when people answered his explanatory letters only with new threats and insults—he had grown bitter. And finally, after taking it all so hard and torturing himself through the whole gamut of emotions, he had sunk into this morass of self-pity.

George began to talk about "the artist," spouting all the intellectual and aesthetic small change of the period. The artist, it seemed, was a kind of fabulous, rare, and special creature who lived on "beauty" and "truth" and had thoughts so subtle that the average man could comprehend them no more than a mongrel could understand the moon he bayed at. The artist, therefore, could achieve his "art" only through a constant state of flight into some magic wood, some province of enchantment.

The phrases were so spurious that Randy felt like shaking him. And what annoyed him most was the knowledge that George was really so much better than this. He must know how cheap and false what he was saying really was. At last Randy said to him quietly:

"George, of all the people I have ever known, you are the least qualified to play the wounded faun."

But he was so immersed in his fantasy that he paid no attention. He just said, "Huh?"—and then was off again. Anybody who was "a real artist," he said, was doomed to be an outcast from society. His inevitable fate was to be "driven out by the tribe."

It was all so wrong that Randy lost patience with him:

"For Christ's sake, George, what's the matter with you? You're talking like a fool!" he said. "You haven't been driven out of anywhere! You've only got yourself in a little hot water at home! Here you've been ranting your head off about 'beauty' and 'truth'! God! Why in hell, then, don't you stop lying to yourself? Can't you see? The truth is that for the first time in your life you've managed to get a foothold in the thing you want to do. Your book got some good notices and has had a fair sale. You're in the right spot now to go on. So where have you been driven? No doubt all those threatening letters have made you feel like an exile from home, but hell, man!—you've been an exile for years. And of your own accord, too! You know you've had no intention of ever going back there to live. But just as soon as they started yelling for your scalp, you fooled yourself into believing you'd been driven out by force! And, as for this idea of yours that a man achieves 'beauty' by escaping somewhere from the life he knows, isn't the truth just the opposite? Haven't you written me the same thing yourself a dozen times?"

"How do you mean?" he said sullenly.

"I mean, taking your own book as an example, isn't it true that every good thing in it came, not because you withdrew from life, but because you got into it—because you managed to understand and use the life you knew?"

He was silent now. His face, which had been screwed up into a morose scowl, gradually began to relax and soften, and at last he looked up with a little crooked smile.

"I don't know what comes over me sometimes," he said. He shook his head and looked ashamed of himself and laughed. "You're right, of course," he went on seriously. "What you say is true. And that's the way it has to be, too. A man must use what he knows—he can't use what he doesn't know. . . . And that's why some of the critics make me mad," he added bluntly.

"How's that?" asked Randy, glad to hear him talking sense at last.

"Oh, you know," he said, "you've seen the reviews. Some of them said the book was 'too autobiographical.'"

This was surprising. And Randy, with the outraged howls of Libya Hill still ringing in his ears, and with George's outlandish rantings in answer to those howls still echoing in the room, could hardly believe he had heard him aright. He could only say in frank astonishment:

"Well, it *was* autobiographical—you can't deny it."

"But not 'too autobiographical,'" George went on earnestly. "If the critics had just crossed those words out and written in their place 'not autobiographical enough,' they'd have hit it squarely. That's where I failed. That's where the real fault was." There was no question that he meant it, for his face was twisted suddenly with a grimace, the scar of his defeat and shame. "My young hero was a stick, a fool, a prig, a snob, as Dædalus was—as in my own presentment of the book I was. There was the weakness. Oh, I know—there were lots of autobiographical spots in the book, and where it was true I'm not ashamed of it, but the hitching post I tied the horses to wasn't good enough. It wasn't true autobiography. I've learned that now, and learned why. The failure comes from the false personal. There's the guilt. That's where the young genius business gets in—the young artist business, what you called a while ago the wounded faun business. It gets in and it twists the vision. The vision may be shrewd, subtle, piercing, within a thousand special frames accurate and Joycean—but within the larger one, false, mannered, and untrue. And the large one is the one that matters."

He meant it now, and he was down to solid rock. Randy saw the measure of his suffering. And yet, now as before, he seemed to be going to extremes and taking it too hard. In some such measure all men fail, and Randy said:

"But was anything ever as good as it could be? Who succeeded anyway?"

"Oh, plenty did!" he said impatiently. "Tolstoy when he wrote *War and Peace*. Shakespeare when he wrote *King Lear*. Mark Twain in the first part of *Life on the Mississippi*. Of course they're not as good as they might have been—nothing ever is. Only, they missed in the right way: they might have put the shot a little further—but they were not hamstrung by their vanity, shackled by their damned self-consciousness. That's what makes for failure. That's where I failed."

"Then what's the remedy?"

"To use myself to the top of my bent. To use everything I have. To milk the udder dry, squeeze out the last drop, until there is nothing left. And if I use myself as a character, to withhold nothing, to try to try to see and paint myself as I am— the bad along with the good, the shoddy alongside of the true— just as I must try to see and draw every other character. No more false personal, no more false pride, no more pettiness and injured feelings. In short, to kill the wounded faun."

Randy nodded: "Yes. And what now? What comes next?"

"I don't know," he answered frankly. His eyes showed his perplexity. "That's the thing that's got me stumped. It's not that I don't know what to write about.—God!" he laughed suddenly. "You hear about these fellows who write one book and then can't do another because they haven't got anything else to write about!"

"You're not worried about that?"

"Lord, no! My trouble's all the other way around! I've got too much material. It keeps backing up on me—" he gestured around him at the tottering piles of manuscript that were everywhere about the room—"until sometimes I wonder what in the name of God I'm going to do with it all—how I'm going to find a frame for it, a pattern, a channel, a way to make it flow!" He brought his fist down sharply on his knee and there was a note of desperation in his voice. "Sometimes it actually occurs to me that a man may be able to write no more because he gets drowned in his own secretions!"

"So you're not afraid of ever running dry?"

He laughed loudly. "At times I almost hope I will," he said. "There'd be a kind of comfort in the thought that some day—maybe after I'm forty—I would dry up and become like a camel, living on my hump. Of course, I don't really mean that either. It's not good to dry up—it's a form of death. . . . No, that's not what bothers me. The thing I've got to find out is the way!" He was silent a moment, staring at Randy, then he struck his fist upon his knee again and cried: "The *way*! The *way*! Do you understand?"

"Yes," said Randy, "I think I do. But how?"

George's face was full of perplexity. He was silent, trying to phrase his problem.

"I'm looking for a way," he said at last. "I think it may be something like what people vaguely mean when they speak of fiction. A kind of legend, perhaps. Something—a story—composed of all the knowledge I have, of all the living I've seen. Not the facts, you understand—not just the record of my life—but something truer than the facts—something distilled out of my experience and transmitted into a form of universal application. That's what the best fiction is, isn't it?"

Randy smiled and nodded encouragement. George was all right. He needn't have worried about him. He would work his way out of the morass. So Randy said cheerfully:

"Have you started the new book yet?"

He began to talk rapidly, and again Randy saw worried tension in his eyes.

"Yes," he said, "I've written a whole lot. These ledgers here—" he indicated a great stack of battered ledgers on the table—"and all this manuscript—" he swept his arms in a wide gesture around the room—"they are full of new writing. I must have written half a million words or more."

Randy then made the blunder which laymen so often innocently make when they talk to writers.

"What's it about?" he said.

He was rewarded with an evil scowl. George did not answer. He began to pace up and down, thinking to himself with smoldering intensity. At last he stopped by the table, turned and faced Randy, and, with the redemptive honesty that was the best thing in him, bluntly said:

"No, I haven't started my new book yet! . . . Thousands of words—" he whacked the battered ledgers with a flattened palm—"hundreds of ideas, dozens of scenes, of scraps, of fragments—but no book! . . . And—" the worried lines about his eyes now deepened—"time goes by! It has been almost five months since the other book was published, and now—" he threw his arms out toward the huge stale chaos of that room with a gesture of exasperated fury—"here I am! Time gets away from me before I know that it has gone! Time!" he cried, and smote his fist into his palm and stared before him with a blazing and abstracted eye as though he saw a ghost—"Time!"

His enemy was Time. Or perhaps it was his friend. One never knows for sure.

Randy stayed in New York several days, and the two friends talked from morning till night and from night till morning. Everything that came into their heads they talked about. George would stride back and forth across the floor in his restless way, talking or listening to Randy, and suddenly would pause beside the table, scowl, look around him as though he were seeing the room for the first time, bring down his hand with a loud *whack* on a pile of manuscript, and boom out:

"Do you know what the reason is for all these words I've written? Well, I'll tell you. It's because I'm so damned lazy!"

"It doesn't look like the room of a lazy man to me," said Randy, laughing.

"It is though," George answered. "That's why it looks this way. You know—" his face grew thoughtful as he spoke—"I've got an idea that a lot of work in this world gets done by lazy people. That's the reason they work—because they're so lazy."

"I don't follow you," said Randy, "but go on—spill it—get it off your chest."

"Well," he said, quite seriously, "it's this way: you work because you're afraid not to. You work because you have to drive yourself to such a fury to begin. That part's just plain hell! It's so hard to get started that once you do you're afraid of slipping back. You'd rather do anything than go through all that agony again—so you keep going—you keep going faster all the time—you keep going till you couldn't stop even if you wanted

300

to. You forget to eat, to shave, to put on a clean shirt when you have one. You almost forget to sleep, and when you do try to you can't—because the avalanche has started, and it keeps going night and day. And people say: 'Why don't you stop sometime? Why don't you forget about it now and then? Why don't you take a few days off?' And you don't do it because you can't—you can't stop yourself—and even if you could you'd be afraid to because there'd be all that hell to go through getting started up again. Then people say you're a glutton for work, but it isn't so. It's laziness—just plain, damned, simple laziness, that's all."

Randy laughed again. He had to—it was so much like George—no one else could have come out with a thing like that. And what made it so funny was that he knew George saw the humor of it, too, and yet was desperately in earnest. He could imagine the weeks and months of solemn cogitation that had brought George to this paradoxical conclusion, and now, like a whale after a long plunge, he was coming up to spout and breathe.

"Well, I see your point," Randy said. "Maybe you're right. But at least it's a unique way of being lazy."

"No," George answered, "I think it's probably a very natural one. Now take all those fellows that you read about," he went on excitedly—"Napoleon—and—and Balzac—and Thomas Edison—" he burst out triumphantly—"these fellows who never sleep more than an hour or two at a time, and can keep going night and day—why, that's not because they love to work! It's because they're really lazy—and afraid not to work because they *know* they're lazy! Why, hell yes!" he went on enthusiastically. "I know that's the way it's been with all those fellows! Old Edison now," he said scornfully, "going around pretending to people that he works all the time because he *likes* it!"

"You don't believe that?"

"Hell, no!"—scornfully. "I'll bet you anything you like that if you could really find out what's going on in old Edison's mind, you'd find that he wished he could stay in bed every day until two o'clock in the afternoon! And then get up and scratch himself! And then lie around in the sun for a while! And hang around with the boys down at the village store, talking about politics, and who's going to win the World Series next fall!"

"Then what keeps him from it, if that's what he wants to do?"

"Why," he cried impatiently, *"laziness!* That's all. He's afraid to do it because he knows he's so damned lazy! And he's ashamed of being lazy, and afraid he'll get found out! That's why!"

"Ah, but that's another thing! Why is he ashamed of it?"

301

"Because," he said earnestly, "every time he wants to lie in bed until two o'clock in the afternoon, he hears the voice of his old man——"

"His old man?"

"Sure. His father." He nodded vigorously.

"But Edison's father has been dead for years, hasn't he?"

"Sure—but that doesn't matter. He hears him just the same. Every time he rolls over to get an extra hour or two, I'll bet you he hears old Pa Edison hollering at him from the foot of the stairs, telling him to get up, and that he's not worth powder enough to blow him sky high, and that when he was *his* age, he'd been up four hours already and done a whole day's work—poor, miserable orphan that he was!"

"Really, I didn't know that. Was Edison's father an orphan?"

"Sure—they all are when they holler at you from the foot of the stairs. And school was always at least six miles away, and they were always barefooted, and it was always snowing. God!" he laughed suddenly. "No one's old man ever went to school except under polar conditions. They all did. And that's why you get up, that's why you drive yourself, because you're afraid not to—afraid of 'that damned Joyner blood in you.' . . . So I'm afraid that's the way it's going to be with me until the end of my days. Every time I see the *Ile de France* or the *Aquitania* or the *Berengaria* backing into the river and swinging into line on Saturday, and see the funnels with their racing slant, and the white breasts of the great liners, and something catches at my throat, and suddenly I hear mermaids singing—I'll also hear the voice of the old man yelling at me from as far back as I can remember, and telling me I'm not worth the powder to blow me up. And every time I dream of tropic isles, of plucking breadfruit from the trees, or of lying stretched out beneath a palm tree in Samoa, fanned by an attractive lady of those regions clad in her latest string of beads—I'll hear the voice of the old man. Every time I dream of lying sprawled out with Peter Breughel in Cockaigne, with roast pigs trotting by upon the hoof, and with the funnel of a beer bung in my mouth—I'll hear the voice of the old man. Thus conscience doth make cowards of us all. I'm lazy—but every time I surrender to my baser self, the old man hollers from the stairs."

George was full of his own problems and talked about them constantly. Randy was an understanding listener. But suddenly one day, toward the end of Randy's visit, the thought struck George as strange that his friend should be taking so much time off from his job. He asked Randy about it. How had he managed it?

"I haven't got a job," Randy answered quietly with his little embarrassed laugh. "They threw me out."

"You mean to say that that bastard Merrit—" George began, hot with instant anger.

"Oh, don't blame him," Randy broke in. "He couldn't help it. The higher-ups were on his tail and he had to do it. He said I wasn't getting the business, and it's true—I wasn't. But what the Company doesn't know is that nobody can get the business any more. It isn't there, and hasn't been for the last year or so. You saw how it was when you were home. Every penny anybody could get hold of went into real estate speculation. That was the only business they had left down there. And now, of course, that's gone, too, since the bank failed."

"And do you mean to say," George commented, speaking the words slowly and with emphasis—"do you mean to say that Merrit seized that moment to throw you out on your ear? Why, the dirty——"

"Yes," said Randy. "I got the sack just a week after the bank closed. I don't know whether Merrit figured that was the best time to get rid of me or whether it just happened so. But what's the difference? It's been coming for a long time. I've seen it coming for a year or more. It was just a question of when. And believe me," he said with quiet emphasis, "I've been through hell. I lived from day to day in fear and dread of it, knowing it was coming and knowing there wasn't anything I could do to head it off. But the funny thing is, now it's happened I feel relieved." He smiled his old clear smile. "It's the truth," he said. "I never would have had the guts to quit—I was making pretty good money, you know—but now that I'm out, I'm glad. I'd forgotten how it felt to be a free man. Now I can hold my head up and look anybody in the eye and tell the Great Man, Paul S. Appleton himself, to go to the devil. It's a good feeling. I like it."

"But what are you going to do, Randy?" asked George with evident concern.

"I don't know," said Randy cheerfully. "I haven't any plans. All the years I was with the Company I lived pretty well, but I also managed to save a little something. And, luckily, I didn't put it in the Citizens Trust, or in real estate either, so I've still got it. And I own the old family house. Margaret and I can get along all right for a while. Of course, jobs that pay as well as the one I had don't turn up around every corner, but this is a big country and there's always a place for a good man. Did you ever hear of a good man who couldn't find work?" he said.

"Well, you can't be too sure of that," said George, shaking his head dubiously. "Maybe I'm wrong," he went on, pausing and frowning thoughtfully, "but I don't think the Stock Market crash and the bank failure in Libya Hill were isolated events.

I'm coming to feel," he said, "that we may be up against something new—something that's going to cut deeper than anything America has experienced before. The papers are beginning to take it seriously. They're calling it a depression. Everybody seems to be scared."

"Oh, pshaw!" said Randy with a laugh. "You *are* feeling low. That's because you live in New York. Here the Stock Market is everything. When it's high, times are good; when it's low, they're bad. But New York is not America."

"I know," said George. "But I'm not thinking about the Stock Market. I'm thinking about America. . . . Sometimes it seems to me," he continued slowly, like a man who gropes his way in darkness over an unfamiliar road, "that America went off the track somewhere—back around the time of the Civil War, or pretty soon afterwards. Instead of going ahead and developing along the line in which the country started out, it got shunted off in another direction—and now we look around and see we've gone places we didn't mean to go. Suddenly we realize that America has turned into something ugly—and vicious—and corroded at the heart of its power with easy wealth and graft and special privilege. . . . And the worst of it is the intellectual dishonesty which all this corruption has bred. People are *afraid* to think straight—*afraid* to face themselves—*afraid* to look at things and see them as they are. We've become like a nation of advertising men, all hiding behind catch phrases like 'prosperity' and 'rugged individualism' and 'the American way.' And the real things like freedom, and equal opportunity, and the integrity and worth of the individual—things that have belonged to the American dream since the beginning—they have become just words, too. The substance has gone out of them—they're not real any more. . . . Take your own case. You say you feel free at last because you've lost your job. I don't doubt it—but it's a funny kind of freedom. And just how free *are* you?"

"Well, free enough to suit me," said Randy heartily. "And, funny or not, I'm freer than I've ever been before. Free enough to take my time and look around a bit before I make a new connection. I don't want to get in with another outfit like the old one. I'll land on my feet," he said serenely.

"But how are you going to do it?" asked George. "There can't be anything for you in Libya Hill, with the bottom dropped out of everything down there."

"Hell, I'm not wedded to the place!" said Randy. "I'll go anywhere. Remember, I've been a salesman all my life—I'm used to traveling around. And I have friends in the game—in other lines—who'll help me. That's one good thing about being a salesman: if you can sell one thing, you can sell anything, and

304

it's easy to switch products. I know my way around," he concluded with strong confidence. "Don't you worry about me."

They said very little more about it. And when Randy left, his parting words at the station were:

"Well, so long fellow! *You're* going to be all right. But don't forget to kill that wounded faun! As for me, I don't know just what the next move is, but I'm on my way!"

With that he got aboard his train, and was gone.

But George wasn't too sure about Randy. And the more he thought about him, the less sure he became. Randy had certainly not been licked by what had happened to him, and that was good; but there was something about his attitude—his cheerful optimism in the face of disaster—that seemed spurious. He had the clearest head of anybody George knew, but it was almost as if he had shut off one compartment of his brain and wasn't using it. It was all very puzzling.

"There are tides in the affairs of men," George thought musingly—"definite periods of ebb and flow. . . . And when they come, they come, and can't be held back by wishing."

That was it, perhaps. It seemed to George that Randy was caught in the ebb and didn't know it. And that was what made it so queer and puzzling—that *he*, of all people, shouldn't know it.

Also, he had spoken about not wanting to get mixed up with another outfit like the old one. Did he think the fearful pressures he had been subject to were peculiar to the company he had been working for, and that their counterparts existed nowhere else? Did he suppose he could escape those conditions just by changing jobs? Did he believe it was possible by such a shift to enjoy all the glorious advantages he had ever dreamed of as a bright, ambitious youth—high income and good living far beyond what most men are accustomed to—and to do it without paying the cost in other ways?

"What will you have? quoth God; pay for it, and take it," said Emerson, in that wonderful essay on "Compensation" that every American ought to be required by law to read. . . . Well, that was true. One always paid for it. . . .

Good Lord! Didn't Randy know you can't go home again?

The next few years were terrible ones for all America, and especially terrible for Randy Shepperton.

He didn't get another job. He tried everything, but nothing

worked. There just weren't any jobs. Men were being let off by the thousands everywhere, and nowhere were new ones being taken on.

After eighteen months his savings were gone, and he was desperate. He had to sell the old family house, and what he got for it was a mere pittance. He and Margaret rented a small apartment, and for another year or so, by careful management, they lived on what the house had brought them. Then that, too, was gone. Randy was on his uppers now. He fell ill, and it was an illness of the spirit more than of the flesh. At last, when there was nothing else to do, he and Margaret moved away from Libya Hill and went to live with the older sister who was married, and stayed there with her husband's family—dependents on the bounty of these kindly strangers.

And at the end of all of this, Randy—he of the clear eyes and the quick intelligence—he who was nobody's fool—he who thought he loved the truth and had always been able to see straight to the heart of most things—Randy went on relief.

And by that time George thought he understood it. Behind Randy's tragedy George thought he could see a personal devil in the form of a very bright and plausible young man, oozing confidence and crying, "Faith!" when there was no faith, and dressed like a traveling salesman. Yes, salesmanship had done its job too well. Salesmanship—that commercial brand of special pleading—that devoted servant of self-interest—that sworn enemy of truth. George remembered how Randy had been able to look at *his* alien problem and see it in the abstract, whole and clear, because there was no self-interest to cast its shadow on his vision. He could save others—himself he could not save, because he could no longer see the truth about himself.

And it seemed to George that Randy's tragedy was the essential tragedy of America. America—the magnificent, unrivaled, unequaled, unbeatable, unshrinkable, supercolossal, 99-and-44-one-hundredths-percent-pure, schoolgirl-complexion, covers-the-earth, I'd-walk-a-mile-for-it, four-out-of-five-have-it, his-master's-voice, ask-the-man-who-owns-one, blueplate-special home of advertising, salesmanship, and special pleading in all its many catchy and beguiling forms.

Had not the real rulers of America—the business men—been wrong about the depression from the start? Had they not pooh-poohed it and tried to wipe it out with words, refusing to see it for what it was? Had they not kept saying that prosperity was just around the corner—long after "prosperity," so called, had vanished, and the very corner it was supposed to be around had flattened out and bent into a precipitate downward curve of hunger, want, and desperation?

Well, Randy had been right about the wounded faun. For

George knew now that his own self-pity was just his precious egotism coming between him and the truth he strove for as a writer. What Randy didn't know was that business also had its wounded fauns. And they, it seemed, were a species that you could not kill so lightly. For business was the most precious form of egotism—self-interest at its dollar value. Kill that with truth, and what would be left?

A better way of life, perhaps, but it would not be built on business as we know it.

BOOK IV

The Quest of the Fair Medusa

George took Randy's advice and moved. He did not know where to go. All he wanted was to get away as far as possible from Park Avenue, from the aesthetic jungles of the lion hunters, from the half-life of wealth and fashion that had grown like a parasite upon the sound body of America. He went to live in Brooklyn.

He had made a little money from his book, so now he paid his debts and quit the job he held as a teacher at the School for Utility Cultures. From this time on, he earned his precarious living solely by what he wrote.

For four years he lived in Brooklyn, and four years in Brooklyn are a geologic age—a single stratum of grey time. They were years of poverty, of desperation, of loneliness unutterable. All about him were the poor, the outcast, the neglected and forsaken people of America, and he was one of them. But life is strong, and year after year it went on around him in all its manifold complexity, rich with its unnoticed and unrecorded little happenings. He saw it all, he took it all in hungrily as part of his experience, he recorded much of it, and in the end he squeezed it dry as he tried to extract its hidden meanings.

And what was he like inside while these grey years were slipping by? What was he up to, what was he doing, what did he want?

That's rather hard to tell, because he wanted so many things, but the thing he wanted most was Fame. Those were the years of his concentrated quest of that fair Medusa. He had had his little taste of glory, and it was bitter in his mouth. He thought the reason was that he had not been good enough—and he had not been good enough. Therefore he thought that what he had was not Fame at all, but only a moment's notoriety. He had been a seven-day wonder—that was all.

Well, he had learned some things since he wrote his first book. He would try again.

So he lived and wrote, and wrote and lived, and lived there by himself in Brooklyn. And when he had worked for hours at a stretch, forgetting food and sleep and everything, he would rise from his desk at last and stagger forth into the nighttime streets, reeling like a drunkard with his weariness. He would eat his supper at a restaurant, and then, because his mind was feverish and he knew he could not sleep, he would walk to Brooklyn Bridge and cross it to Manhattan, and ferret out the secret heart of darkness in all the city's ways, and then at dawn come back across the Bridge once more, and so to bed in Brooklyn.

And in these nightly wanderings the old refusals dropped away, the old avowals stood. For then, somehow, it seemed to him that he who had been dead was risen, he who had been lost was found again, and he who in his brief day of glory had sold the talent, the passion, and the belief of youth into the keeping of the fleshless dead, until his heart was corrupted and all hope gone, would win his life back bloodily, in solitude and darkness. And he felt then that things would be for him once more as they had been, and he saw again, as he had once seen, the image of the shining city. Far-flung, and blazing into tiers of jeweled light, it burned forever in his vision as he walked the Bridge, and strong tides were bound around it, and the great ships called. So he walked the Bridge, always he walked the Bridge.

And by his side was that stern friend, the only one to whom he spoke what in his secret heart he most desired. To Loneliness he whispered, "Fame!"—and Loneliness replied, "Aye, brother, wait and see."

Chapter Twenty-Seven

The Locusts Have No King

The tragic light of evening falls upon the huge and rusty jungle of South Brooklyn. It falls without glare or warmth upon the faces of all the men with dead eyes and flesh of tallow-grey as they lean upon their window sills at the sad, hushed end of day.

If at such a time you walk down this narrow street, between the mean and shabby houses, past the eyes of all the men who lean there quietly at their open windows in their shirt-sleeves, and turn in at the alley here and follow the two-foot strip of broken concrete pavement that skirts the alley on one side, and go to the very last shabby house down at the end, and climb up the flight of worn steps to the front entrance, and knock loudly at the door with your bare knuckles (the bell is out of order), and then wait patiently until someone comes, and ask whether Mr. George Webber lives here, you will be informed that he most certainly does, and that if you will just come in and go down this stairway to the basement and knock at the door there on your right, you will probably find him in. So you go down the stairway to the damp and gloomy basement hall, thread your way between the dusty old boxes, derelict furniture, and other lumber stored there in the passage, rap on the door that has been indicated to you, and Mr. Webber himself will open it and usher you right into his room, his home, his castle.

The place may seem to you more like a dungeon than a room that a man would voluntarily elect to live in. It is long and narrow, running parallel to the hall from front to rear, and the only natural light that enters it comes through two small windows rather high up in the wall, facing each other at the opposite ends, and these are heavily guarded with iron bars, placed there by some past owner of the house to keep the South Brooklyn thugs from breaking in.

The room is furnished adequately but not so luxuriously as to deprive it of a certain functional and Spartan simplicity. In the back half there is an iron bed with sagging springs, a broken-down dresser with a cracked mirror above it, two kitchen

311

chairs, and a steamer trunk and some old suitcases that have seen much use. At the front end, under the yellow glow of an electric light suspended from the ceiling by a cord, there is a large desk, very much scarred and battered, with the handles missing on most of the drawers, and in front of it there is a straight-backed chair made out of some old, dark wood. In the center, ranged against the walls, where they serve to draw the two ends of the room together into aesthetic unity, stand an ancient gate-legged table, so much of its dark green paint flaked off that the dainty pink complexion of its forgotten youth shows through all over, a tier of book-shelves, unpainted, and two large crates or packing cases, their thick top boards pried off to reveal great stacks of ledgers and of white and yellow manuscript within. On top of the desk, on the table, on the book-shelves, and all over the floor are scattered, like fallen leaves in autumn woods, immense masses of loose paper with writing on every sheet, and everywhere are books, piled up on their sides or leaning crazily against each other.

This dark cellar is George Webber's abode and working quarters. Here, in winter, the walls, which sink four feet below the level of the ground, sweat continuously with clammy drops of water. Here, in summer, it is he who does the sweating.

His neighbors, he will tell you, are for the most part Armenians, Italians, Spaniards, Irishmen, and Jews—in short, Americans. They live in all the shacks, tenements, and slums in all the raw, rusty streets and alleys of South Brooklyn.

And what is that you smell?

Oh, that! Well, you see, he shares impartially with his neighbors a piece of public property in the vicinity; it belongs to all of them in common, and it gives to South Brooklyn its own distinctive atmosphere. It is the old Gowanus Canal, and that aroma you speak of is nothing but the huge symphonic stink of it, cunningly compacted of unnumbered separate putrefactions. It is interesting sometimes to try to count them. There is in it not only the noisome stenches of a stagnant sewer, but also the smells of melted glue, burned rubber, and smoldering rags, the odors of a boneyard horse, long dead, the incense of putrefying offal, the fragrance of deceased, decaying cats, old tomatoes, rotten cabbage, and prehistoric eggs.

And how does he stand it?

Well, one gets used to it. One can get used to anything, just as all these other people do. They never think of the smell, they never speak of it, they'd probably miss it if they moved away.

To this place, then, George Webber has come, and here "holed in" with a kind of dogged stubbornness touched with desperation. And you will not be far wrong if you surmise that he has come here deliberately, driven by a resolution to seek out the most forlorn and isolated hiding spot that he could find.

Mr. Marple, a gentleman who has a room on the second floor, comes stumbling down the darkened basement stairway with a bottle in his hand and knocks upon George Webber's door.

"Come in!"

Mr. Marple comes in, introduces himself, does the right thing with the bottle, sits down, and begins to make talk.

"Well, now, Mr. Webber, how d'yah like that drink I mixed for yah?"

"Oh, I like it, I like it."

"Well, now, if yah don't, I want yah t'come right out an' say so."

"Oh, I would, I would."

"I mean I'd like to know. I'd appreciate yah tellin' me. What I mean is, I made that stuff myself from a private formuler I got—I wouldn't buy no stuff from a bootlegger—I wouldn't take no chance wit' the bastards. I buy the alcohol that goes into that drink from a place I know, an' I always know what I'm gettin'—d'yah know what I mean?"

"Yes, I certainly do."

"But I'd like to know what yah think of it, I'd appreciate yah tellin' me."

"Oh, it's fine, it couldn't be better."

"I'm glad yah like it, an' you're sure I didn't disturb yah?"

"Oh, no, not at all."

"Because I was on my way in when I sees your light there in the winder, so I says to myself, now that guy may think I've got an orful nerve buttin' in like this but I'm gonna stop an' get acquainted an' ast him if he'd like a little drink."

"I'm glad you did."

"But if I disturbed yah I wantcha t'say so."

"Oh, no, not at all."

"Because here's the way it is wit' me. I'm interested in youman nature—I'm a great student of psychology—I can read faces the minute I look at a guy—it's somethin' that I always had—I guess that's why I'm in the insurance game. So when I sees a guy that interests me I wanta get acquainted wit' him an' get his reactions to things. So when I sees your light I says to myself, he may tell me to get the hell outa there but there ain't no harm in tryin'."

"I'm glad you did."

"Now Mr. Webber, I think I'm a pretty good judge of character——"

"Oh, I'm sure you are."

313

"—an' I been lookin' at yah an' sorta sizin' yah up while yah been sittin' there. Yah didn't know I was sizin' yah up but that's what I been doin' all the time yah been sittin' there because I'm a great student of youman nature, Mr. Webber, an' I gotta size up all grades an' classes every day in my business—*you* know— I'm in the insurance game. An' I wanna ast yah a question. Now if it's too personal I wantcha t'come right out an' say so, but if yah don't mind answerin' I'm gonna ast it to yah."

"Not at all. What is it?"

"Well, Mr. Webber, I already reached my own conclusions, but I'm gonna ast it to yah just t'see if it don't bear me out. Now what I'm gonna ast yah—an' yah don't have to answer if yah don't want to—is—What's your line?—What business are yah in? Now yah don't need to tell me if it's too personal."

"Not at all. I'm a writer."

"A *what*?"

"A writer. I wrote a book once. I'm trying to write another one now."

"Well now, it may surprise yah but that's just what I figgered out myself. I says to myself, now there's a guy, I says, that's in some kind of intelleckshul work where he's got t'use his head. He's a writer or a newspaperman or in the advertisin' business. Y'see I've always been a great judge of youman nature—that's *my* line."

"Yes, I see."

"An' now I wanna tell yah somethin' else, Mr. Webber. You're doin' the thing yah was cut out for, you're doin' the thing yah was born to do, it's what yah been preparin' to do all your life sinct yah was a kid—am I right or wrong?"

"Oh, I guess you're right."

"An' that's the reason you're gonna be a big success at it. Stick to writin', Mr. Webber. I'm a great judge of youman nature an' I know what I'm talkin' about. Just stick to the thing yah always wanted to be an' yah'll get there. Now some guys never find theirselves. Some guys never know what they wanna be. That's the trouble wit' some guys. Now wit' me it's different. I didn't find myself till I was a grown man. You'd have t'laugh, Mr. Webber, if I told yah what it was I wanted t'be when I was a kid."

"What was it, Mr. Marple?"

"Say, Mr. Webber—y'know it's funny—yah won't believe me—but up to the time I was about twenty years old, a grown man, I was crazy to be a railroad engineer. No kiddin'. I was nuts about it. An' I'd a-been just crazy enough to've gone ahead an' got a job on the railroad if the old man hadn't yanked me by the collar an' told me t'snap out of it. Yah know I'm a Down-Easter by birth—don't talk like it any more—I been here too long—but that's where I grew up. My old man was a plumber in
314

Augusta, Maine. So when I tells him I'm gonna be a locomotive engineer he boots me one in the seat of the pants an' tells me I ain't no such thing. 'I've sent yah to school,' he says, 'you've had ten times the schoolin' that I had, an' now yah tell me that you're gonna be a railroad hogger. Well, you're not,' the old man says, 'you're gonna be one member of the fambly that's comin' home at night wit' clean hands an' a white collar. Now you get the hell outa here an' hunt yah up a job in some decent high-class business where yah'll have a chanct t'advance an' associate wit' your social ekals.' Jesus! It was a lucky thing for me he took that stand or I'd never a-got where I am today. But I was good an' sore about it at the time. An' say, Mr. Webber— you're gonna laugh when I tell yah this one—I ain't actually over the darn thing yet. No kiddin'. When I see one of these big engines bargin' down the track I still get that funny crawly feelin' I usta have when I was a kid an' looked at 'em. The guys at the office had t'laugh about it when I told 'em, an' now when I come in they call me Casey Jones.—Well, what d'yah say yah have another little snifter before I go?"

"Thanks, I'd like to, but maybe I'd better not. I've still got a little work I ought to do before I turn in."

"Well now, Mr. Webber, I know just how it is. An' that's the way I had yah sized up from the first. That guy's a writer, I says, or in some sort of intelleckshul occupation where he's got to use his head—was I right or wrong?"

"Oh, you were right."

"Well, I'm glad to've metcha, Mr. Webber. Don't make yourself a stranger around here. Yah know, a guy gets sorta lonely sometimes. My wife died four years ago so I been livin' upstairs here ever sinct—sorta figgered that a single guy didn't need no more room than I got here. Come up to see me. I'm interested in youman nature an' I like to talk to people an' get their different reactions. So any time yah feel like chewin' the rag a bit, drop in."

"Oh, I will, I will."

"Good night, Mr. Webber."

"Good night, Mr. Marple."

Good night. Good night. Good night.

Across the basement hall, in another room similar to George Webber's, lived an old man by the name of Wakefield. He had a son somewhere in New York who paid his rent, but Mr. Wakefield rarely saw his son. He was a brisk and birdy little man with a chirping, cheerful voice; and, although he was almost ninety, he always seemed to be in good health and was

315

still immensely active. His son had provided him with a room to live in, he had a little money of his own—a few dollars a month from a pension—enough to supply his meager wants; but he lived a life of utter loneliness, seeing his son only on the occasion of a holiday or a rare visit, and the rest of the time living all by himself in his basement room.

Yet he had as brave and proud a spirit as any man on earth. He longed desperately for companionship, but he would have died rather than admit he was lonely. So independent was he, and so sensitive, that, while he was always courteous and cheerful, his tone when he responded to a greeting was a little cold and distant, lest anyone should think he was too forward and eager. But, once satisfied of one's friendliness, no one could respond more warmly or more cordially than old man Wakefield.

George grew fond of him and liked to talk with him, and the old man would invite him eagerly into his part of the basement and proudly display his room, which he kept with a soldierlike neatness. He was a veteran of the Union Army in the Civil War, and his room was filled with books, records, papers, and old clippings bearing on the war and on the part his regiment had played in it. Although he was alert and eager toward the life around him, and much too brave and hopeful a spirit to live mournfully in the past, the Civil War had been the great and central event in old man Wakefield's life. Like many of the men of his generation, both North and South, it had never occurred to him that the war was not the central event in everyone's life. Because it was so with him, he believed that people everywhere still lived and thought and talked about the war all the time.

He was a leading figure in the activities of his Grand Army Post, and was always bustling about with plans and projects for the coming year. It seemed to him that the Grand Army organization, whose thinning ranks of old and feeble men he still saw with the proud eyes of forty or fifty years before, was the most powerful society in the nation, and that its word of warning or stern reproof was enough to make all the kings of the earth quake and tremble in their boots. He was bitterly scornful and would bristle up immediately at mention of the American Legion: he fancied slights and cunning trickery on the part of this body all the time, and he would ruffle up like a rooster when he spoke of the Legionnaires, and say in an angry, chirping tone:

"It's jealousy! Nothing in the world but sheer tar-nation *jealousy*—that's what it is!"

"But why, Mr. Wakefield? Why should they be jealous of you?"

"Because we reely did some soldierin'—that's why!" he chirped angrily. "Because they know we fit the Rebels—yes!

316

and *fit* 'em good—and *licked* 'em, too!" he crackled triumphantly—"in a war that *was* a war! . . . Pshaw!" he said scornfully, in a lowered voice, looking out the window with a bitter smile and with eyes that had suddenly grown misty. "What do these fellows know about a war?—Some *bob-tail—raggedy—two-by-two*—little *jackleg* feller—of a *Legionnary!*" He spat the words out with malignant satisfaction, breaking at the end into a vindictive cackle. "Standin' to their necks all day in some old trench and never gettin' within ten miles of the enemy!" he sneered. "If they ever saw a troop of cavalry, I don't know what they'd make of it! I reckon they'd think it was the circus come to town!" he cackled. "A war! A *war!* Hell-fire, that warn't no war!" he cried derisively. "If they wanted to see a war, they should've been with us at the Bloody Angle! But, pshaw!" he said. "They'd a-run like rabbits if they'd been there! The only way you could a-kept 'em would've been to tie 'em to a tree!"

"Don't you think they could have beaten the Rebels, Mr. Wakefield?"

"Beat 'em?" he shrilled. "*Beat* 'em! Why, boy, what are you talkin' about? . . . Hell! If Stonewall Jackson ever started for that gang, he'd run 'em ragged! Yes, sir! They'd light out so fast they'd straighten out all the bends of the road as they went by!" cried old man Wakefield, cackling. "Pshaw!" he said quietly and scornfully again. "They couldn't do it! It ain't in 'em! . . . But I'll tell you this much!" he cried suddenly in an excited voice. "We're not goin' to put up with it much longer! The boys have had just about as much of it as they can stand! If they try to do us like they done last year—pshaw!" he broke off again, and looked out the window shaking his head—"Why it's all as plain as the nose on your face! It's jealousy—just plain, confounded *jealousy*—that's all in the world it is!"

"What is, Mr. Wakefield?"

"Why, the way they done us last year!" he cried. "Puttin' us way back there at the tail-end of the *pee*-rade, when by all the rights—as everybody knows—we should've come first! But we'll fix 'em!" he cried warningly. "We've got a way to fix 'em!" he said with a triumphant shake of the head. "I know the thing we're goin' to do *this* year," he cried, "if they try another trick like that on us!"

"What are you going to do, Mr. Wakefield?"

"Why," he cackled, "we won't *pee*-rade! We simply won't *pee*-rade! We'll tell 'em they can hold their derned *pee*-rade without us!" he chirped exultantly. "And I reckon that'll fix 'em! Oh, yes! That'll bring 'em round, or I miss *my* guess!" he crowed.

"It ought to, Mr. Wakefield."

"Why, boy," he said solemnly, "if we ever did a thing like that, there would be a wave of protest—a *wave* of protest—" he

317

cried with a sweeping gesture of the arm, as his voice rose strongly—"from here to Californy! . . . The people wouldn't *stand* for it!" he cried. "They'd make *those* fellers back down in a hurry!"

And as George left him, the old man would come with him to the door, shake his hand warmly, and, with an eager and lonely look in his old eyes, say:

"Come again, boy! I'm always glad to see you! . . . I got stuff in here—photygraphs, an' books, an' such as that about the war—that you ain't seen yet. No, nor no one else!" he cackled. "For no one else has got 'em! . . . Just let me know when you're comin' an' I'll be here."

Slowly the years crept by and George lived alone in Brooklyn. They were hard years, desperate years, lonely years, years of interminable writing and experimentation, years of exploration and discovery, years of grey timelessness, weariness, exhaustion, and self-doubt. He had reached the wilderness period of his life and was hacking his way through the jungles of experience. He had stripped himself down to the brutal facts of self and work. These were all he had.

He saw himself more clearly now than he had ever done before, and, in spite of living thus alone, he no longer thought of himself as a rare and special person who was doomed to isolation, but as a man who worked and who, like other men, was a part of life. He was concerned passionately with reality. He wanted to see things whole, to find out everything he could, and then create out of what he knew the fruit of his own vision.

One criticism that had been made of his first book still rankled in his mind. An unsuccessful scribbler turned critic had simply dismissed the whole book as a "barbaric yawp," accusing Webber of getting at things with his emotions rather than with his brains, and of being hostile toward the processes of the intellect and "the intellectual point of view." These charges, if they had any truth in them, seemed to George to be the kind of lifeless half-truth that was worse than no truth at all. The trouble with the so-called "intellectuals" was that they were not intellectual enough, and their point of view more often than not had no point, but was disparate, arbitrary, sporadic, and confused.

To be an "intellectual" was, it seemed, a vastly different thing from being intelligent. A dog's nose would usually lead him toward what he wished to find, or away from what he wished to avoid: this was intelligent. That is, the dog had the sense of reality in his nose. But the "intellectual" usually had no nose,

318

and was lacking in the sense of reality. The most striking difference between Webber's mind and the mind of the average "intellectual" was that Webber absorbed experience like a sponge, and made use of everything that he absorbed. He really learned constantly from experience. But the "intellectuals" of his acquaintance seemed to learn nothing. They had no capacity for rumination and digestion. They could not reflect.

He thought over a few of them that he had known:

There was Haythorpe, who when George first knew him was an aesthete of the late baroque in painting, writing, all the arts, author of one-act costume plays—"Gesmonder! Thy hands pale chalices of hot desire!" Later he became an aesthete of the primitives—the Greek, Italian, and the German; then aesthete of the nigger cults—the wood sculptures, coon songs, hymnals, dances, and the rest; still later, aesthete of the comics—of cartoons, Chaplin, and the Brothers Marx; then of Expressionism; then of the Mass; then of Russia and the Revolution; at length, aesthete of homo-sexuality; and finally, death's aesthete—suicide in a graveyard in Connecticut.

There was Collingswood, who, fresh out of Harvard, was not so much the aesthete of the arts as of the mind. First, a Bolshevik from Beacon Hill, practitioner of promiscuous, communal love as the necessary answer to "bourgeois morality"; then back to Cambridge for post-graduate study at the feet of Irving Babbitt—Collingswood is now a Humanist, the bitter enemy of Rousseau, Romanticism, and of Russia (which is, he now thinks, Rousseau in modern form); the playwright, next—New Jersey, Beacon Hill, or Central Park seen in the classic unities of the Greek drama; at length, disgusted realist—"all that's good in modern art or letters is to be found in advertisements"; then a job as a scenario writer and two years in Hollywood—all now is the moving picture, with easy money, easy love affairs, and drunkenness; and finally, back to Russia, but with his first love lacking—no sex triflings now, my comrades—we who serve the Cause and wait upon the day lead lives of Spartan abstinence—what was the free life, free love, enlightened pleasure of the proletariat ten years ago is now despised as the contemptible debauchery of "bourgeois decadence."

There was Spurgeon from the teaching days at the School for Utility Cultures—good Spurgeon—Chester Spurgeon of the Ph.D.—Spurgeon of "the great tradition"—thin-lipped Spurgeon, ex-student of Professor Stuart Sherman, and bearer-onward of the Master's Torch. Noble-hearted Spurgeon, who wrote honeyed flatteries of Thornton Wilder and his *Bridge*— "The tradition of the Bridge is Love, just as the tradition of America and of Democracy is Love. Hence—" Spurgeon hences—Love grows Wilder as the years Bridge on across

America. Oh, where now, good Spurgeon, "intellectual" Spurgeon—Spurgeon whose thin lips and narrowed eyes were always so glacial prim on Definitions? Where now, brave intellect, by passion uninflamed? Spurgeon of the flashing mind, by emotion unimpulsed, is now a devoted leader of the intellectual Communists (See Spurgeon's article entitled, "Mr. Wilder's Piffle," in the *New Masses*).—So, Comrade Spurgeon, hail! Hail, Comrade Spurgeon—and most heartily, my bright-eyed Intellectual, farewell!

Whatever George Webber was, he knew he was not an "intellectual." He was just an American who was looking hard at the life around him, and sorting carefully through all the life he had ever seen and known, and trying to extract some essential truth out of this welter of his whole experience. But, as he said to his friend and editor, Fox Edwards:

"What *is* truth? No wonder jesting Pilate turned away. The truth, it has a thousand faces—show only one of them, and the *whole* truth flies away! But how to show the whole? That's the question. . . .

"Discovery in itself is not enough. It's not enough to find out what things are. You've also got to find out where they come from, where each brick fits in the wall."

He always came back to the wall.

"I think it's like this," he said. "You see a wall, you look at it so much and so hard that one day you see clear through it. Then, of course, it's not just one wall any longer. It's every wall that ever was."

He was still spiritually fighting out the battle of his first book, and all the problems it had raised. He was still searching for a way. At times he felt that his first book had taught him nothing—not even confidence. His feelings of hollow desperation and self-doubt seemed to grow worse instead of better, for he had now torn himself free from almost every personal tie which had ever bound him, and which formerly had sustained him in some degree with encouragement and faith. He was left, therefore, to rely almost completely on his own resources.

There was also the insistent, gnawing consciousness of work itself, the necessity of turning toward the future and the completion of a new book. He was feeling, now as never before, the inexorable pressure of time. In writing his first book, he had been unknown and obscure, and there had been a certain fortifying strength in that, for no one had expected anything of him. But now the spotlight of publication had been turned upon him, and he felt it beating down with merciless intensity. He was pinned beneath the light—he could not crawl out of it. Though he had not won fame, still he was known now. He had

320

been examined, probed, and talked about. He felt that the world was looking at him with a critic eye.

It had been easy in his dreams to envision a long and fluent sequence of big books, but now he was finding it a different matter to accomplish them. His first book had been more an act of utterance than an act of labor. It was an impassioned expletive of youth—something that had been pent up in him, something felt and seen and imagined and put down at white-hot heat. The writing of it had been a process of spiritual and emotional evacuation. But that was behind him now, and he knew he should never try to repeat it. Henceforth his writing would have to come from unending labor and preparation.

In his effort to explore his experience, to extract the whole, essential truth of it, and to find a way to write about it, he sought to recapture every particle of the life he knew down to its minutest details. He spent weeks and months trying to put down on paper the exactitudes of countless fragments—what he called, "the dry, caked colors of America"—how the entrance to a subway looked, the design and webbing of the elevated structure, the look and feel of an iron rail, the particular shade of rusty green with which so many things are painted in America. Then he tried to pin down the foggy color of the brick of which so much of London is constructed, the look of an English doorway, of a French window, of the roofs and chimney pots of Paris, of a whole street in Munich—and each of these foreign things he then examined in contrast to its American equivalent.

It was a process of discovery in its most naked, literal, and primitive terms. He was just beginning really to see thousands of things for the first time, to see the relations between them, to see here and there whole series and systems of relations. He was like a scientist in some new field of chemistry who for the first time realizes that he has stumbled upon a vast new world, and who will then pick out identities, establish affiliations, define here and there the outlines of sub-systems in crystalline union, without yet being aware what the structure of the whole is like, or what the final end will be.

The same processes now began to inform his direct observation of the life around him. Thus, on his nocturnal ramblings about New York, he would observe the homeless men who prowled in the vicinity of restaurants, lifting the lids of garbage cans and searching around inside for morsels of rotten food. He saw them everywhere, and noticed how their numbers increased during the hard and desperate days of 1932. He knew what kind of men they were, for he talked to many of them; he knew what they had been, where they had come from, and even what kind of scraps they could expect to dig out of the garbage cans. He found out the various places all over the city where such men slept at night. A favorite rendezvous was a corridor of the subway station at Thirty-third Street and Park Avenue in Manhattan. There one night he counted thirty-four huddled together on the cold concrete, wrapped up in sheathings of old newspaper.

It was his custom almost every night, at one o'clock or later, to walk across the Brooklyn Bridge, and night after night, with a horrible fascination, he used to go to the public latrine or "comfort station" which was directly in front of the New York City Hall. One descended to this place down a steep flight of stairs from the street, and on bitter nights he would find the place crowded with homeless men who had sought refuge there. Some were those shambling hulks that one sees everywhere, in Paris as well as New York, in good times as well as bad—old men, all rags and bags and long white hair and bushy beards stained dirty yellow, wearing tattered overcoats in the cavernous pockets of which they carefully stored away all the little rubbish they lived on and spent their days collecting in the streets—crusts of bread, old bones with rancid shreds of meat still clinging to them, and dozens of cigarette butts. Some were the "stumble bums" from the Bowery, criminal, fumed with drink or drugs, or half insane with "smoke." But most of them were just flotsam of the general ruin of the time—honest, decent, middle-aged men with faces seamed by toil and want, and young men, many of them mere boys in their teens, with thick, unkempt hair. These were the wanderers from town to town, the riders of freight trains, the thumbers of rides on highways, the uprooted, unwanted male population of America. They drifted across the land and gathered in the big cities when winter came, hungry, defeated, empty, hopeless, restless, driven by they knew not what, always on the move, looking everywhere for work, for the bare crumbs to support their miserable lives, and finding neither work nor crumbs. Here in New York, to this obscene meeting place, these derelicts came, drawn into a common stew of rest and warmth and a little surcease from their desperation.

George had never before witnessed anything to equal the indignity and sheer animal horror of the scene. There was even a kind of devil's comedy in the sight of all these filthy men squatting upon those open, doorless stools. Arguments and savage disputes and fights would sometimes break out among them over the possession of these stools, which all of them wanted more for rest than for necessity. The sight was revolting, disgusting, enough to render a man forever speechless with very pity.

He would talk to the men and find out all he could about

them, and when he could stand it no more he would come out of this hole of filth and suffering, and there, twenty feet above it, he would see the giant hackles of Manhattan shining coldly in the cruel brightness of the winter night. The Woolworth Building was not fifty yards away, and a little farther down were the silvery spires and needles of Wall Street, great fortresses of stone and steel that housed enormous banks. The blind injustice of this contrast seemed the most brutal part of the whole experience, for there, all around him in the cold moonlight, only a few blocks away from this abyss of human wretchedness and misery, blazed the pinnacles of power where a large portion of the entire world's wealth was locked in mighty vaults.

They were now closing up the restaurant. The tired waitresses were racking the chairs upon the tables, completing the last formalities of their hard day's work in preparation for departure. At the cash register the proprietor was totting up the figures of the day's take, and one of the male waiters hovered watchfully near the table, in a manner politely indicating that while he was not in a hurry he would be glad if his last customer would pay his bill and leave.

George called for his check and gave the man some money. He took it and in a moment returned with the change. He pocketed his tip and said, "Thank you, sir." Then as George said good night and started to get up and leave, the waiter hesitated and hung around uncertainly as if there was something he wanted to say but scarcely knew whether he ought to say it or not.

George looked at him inquiringly, and then, in a rather embarrassed tone, the waiter said:

"Mr. Webber . . . there's . . . something I'd like to talk over with you sometime. . . . I—I'd like to get your advice about something—that is, if you have time," he added hastily and almost apologetically.

George regarded the waiter with another inquiring look, in which the man evidently read encouragement, for now he went on quickly, in a manner of almost beseeching entreaty:

"It's—it's about a story."

The familiar phrase awakened countless weary echoes in Webber's memory. It also resolved that hard and honest patience with which any man who ever sweated to write a living line and to earn his bread by the hard, uncertain labor of his pen will listen, as an act of duty and understanding, to any other man who says he has a tale to tell. His mind and will wearily

323

composed themselves, his face set in a strained smile of mechanical anticipation, and the poor waiter, thus encouraged, went on eagerly:

"It's—it's a story a guy told me several years ago. I've been thinking about it ever since. The guy was a foreigner," said the waiter impressively, as if this fact was enough to guarantee the rare color and fascinating interest of what he was about to reveal. "He was an Armenian," said the waiter very earnestly. "Sure! He came from over there!" He nodded his head emphatically. "And this story that he told me was an *Armenian* story," said the waiter with solemn emphasis, and then paused to let this impressive fact sink in. "It was a story that he knew about—he told it to me—and I'm the only other guy that knows about it," said the waiter, and paused again, looking at his patron with a very bright and feverish eye.

George continued to smile with wan encouragement, and in a moment the waiter, after an obvious struggle with his soul, a conflict between his desire to keep his secret and to tell it, too, went on:

"Gee! You're a writer, Mr. Webber, and you know about these things. I'm just a dumb guy working in a restaurant—but if I could put it into words—if I could get a guy like you who knows how it's done to tell the story for me—why—why" he struggled with himself, then burst out enthusiastically— "there'd be a fortune in it for the both of us!"

George felt his heart sink still lower. It was turning out just as he knew it would. But he still continued to smile pallidly. He cleared his throat in an undecided fashion, but then said nothing. And the waiter, taking silence for consent, now pressed on impetuously:

"Honest, Mr. Webber—if I could get somebody like you to help me with this story—to write it down for me the way it ought to be—I'd—I'd—" for a moment the waiter struggled with his lower nature, then magnanimity got the better of him and he cried out with the decided air of a man who is willing to make a generous bargain and stick to it—"I'd go fifty-fifty with him! I'd—I'd be willing to give him half! . . . And there's a fortune in it!" he cried. "I go to the movies and I read *True Story Magazine*—and I never seen a story like it! It's got 'em all beat! I've thought about it for years, ever since the guy told it to me—and I know I've got a gold mine here if I could only write it down! . . . It's—it's——"

Now, indeed, the waiter's struggle with his sense of caution became painful to watch. He was evidently burning with a passionate desire to reveal his secret, but he was also obviously tormented by doubts and misgivings lest he should recklessly give away to a comparative stranger a treasure which the other might appropriate to his own use. His manner was very much

324

that of a man who has sailed strange seas and seen, in some unknown coral island, the fabulous buried cache of forgotten pirates' plundering, and who is now being torn between two desperate needs—his need of partnership, of outward help, and his imperative need of secrecy and caution. The fierce interplay of these two powers discrete was waged there on the open battlefield of the waiter's countenance. And in the end he took the obvious way out. Like an explorer who will take from his pocket an uncut gem of tremendous size and value and cunningly hint that in a certain place he knows of there are many more like it, the waiter decided to tell a little part of his story without revealing all.

"I—I can't tell you the whole thing tonight," he said apologetically. "Some other night, maybe, when you've got more time. But just to give you an idea of what's in it—" he looked around stealthily to make sure he was in no danger of being overheard, then bent over and lowered his voice to an impressive whisper—"just to give you an idea, now—there's one scene in the story where a woman puts an advertisement in the paper that she will give a ten-dollar gold piece and as much liquor as he can drink to any man who comes around to see her the next day!" After imparting this sensational bit of information, the waiter regarded his patron with glittering eyes. "Now!" said the waiter, straightening up with a gesture of finality. "You never heard of anything like *that*, did you? You ain't never seen *that* in a story!"

George, after a baffled pause, admitted feebly that he had not. Then, when the waiter continued to regard him feverishly, with a look that made it plain that he was supposed to say something more, he inquired doubtfully whether this interesting event had really happened in Armenia.

"Sure!" cried the waiter, nodding vigorously. "That's what I'm telling you! The whole thing happens in Armenia!" He paused again, torn fiercely between his caution and his desire to go on, his feverish eyes almost burning holes through his questioner. "It's—it's—" he struggled for a moment more, then surrendered abjectly—"well, I'll tell you," he said quietly, leaning forward, with his hands resting on the table in an attitude of confidential intimacy. "The idea of the story runs like this. You got this rich dame to begin with, see?"

He paused and looked at George inquiringly. George did not know what was expected of him, so he nodded to show that his mind had grasped this important fact, and said hesitantly:

"In Armenia?"

"Sure! Sure!" The waiter nodded. "This dame comes from over there—she's got a big pile of dough—I guess she's the richest dame in Armenia. And then she falls for this guy, see?" he went on. "He's nuts about her, and he comes to see her every night. The way the guy told it to me, she lives up at the top of this big house—so every night the guy comes and climbs up there to see her—oh, a hell of a long ways up—" the waiter said—"thirty floors or more!"

"In Armenia?" George asked feebly.

"Sure!" cried the waiter, a little irritably. "That's where it all takes place! That's what I'm telling you!"

He paused and looked searchingly at George, who finally asked, with just the proper note of hesitant thoughtfulness, why the lover had had to climb up so far.

"Why," said the waiter impatiently, "because the dame's old man wouldn't let him in! That was the only way the guy could get to her! The old man shut her up way up there at the top of the house because he didn't want the dame to get married! . . . But then," he went on triumphantly, "the old man dies, see? He dies and leaves all his dough to this dame—and then she ups and marries this guy!"

Dramatically, with triumph written in his face, the waiter paused to let this startling news soak into the consciousness of his listener. Then he continued:

"They lived together for a while—the dame's in love with him—and for a year or two they're sitting pretty. But then the guy begins to drink—he's a booze hound, see?—only she don't know it—she's been able to hold him down for a year or two after they get married. . . . Then he begins to step out again. . . . The first thing you know he's staying out all night and running around with a lot of hot blondes, see? . . . Well, then, you see what's coming now, don't you?" said the waiter quickly and eagerly.

George had no notion, but he nodded his head wisely.

"Well, that's what happens," said the waiter. "The first thing you know the guy ups and leaves the dame and takes with him a lot of her dough and joolry. . . . He just disappears—just like the earth had opened and swallowed him up!" the waiter declared, evidently pleased with his poetic simile. "He leaves her cold, and the poor dame's almost out of her head. She does everything—she hires detectives—she offers rewards—she puts ads in the paper begging him to come back. . . . But it's no use—she can't find him—the guy's lost. . . . Well, then," the waiter continued, "three years go by while the poor dame sits and eats her heart out about this guy. . . . And then—" here he paused impressively, and it was evident that he was now approaching the crisis—"then she has an idea!" He paused again, briefly, to allow this extraordinary accomplishment on the part of his heroine to be given due consideration, and in a moment, very simply and quietly, he concluded: "She opens up a night club."

The waiter fell silent now, and stood at ease with his hands clasped quietly before him, with the modest air of a man who has given his all and is reasonably assured it is enough. It now became compellingly apparent that his listener was supposed to make some appropriate comment, and that the narrator could not continue with his tale until this word had been given. So George mustered his failing strength, moistened his dry lips with the end of his tongue, and finally said in a halting voice:

"In—in Armenia?"

The waiter now took the question, and the manner of its utterance, as signs of his listener's paralyzed surprise. He nodded his head victoriously and cried:

"Sure! You see, the dame's idea is this—she knows the guy's a booze hound and that sooner or later he'll come to a place where there's lots of bar-flies and fast women. That kind always hang together—sure they do! . . . So she opens up this joint—she sinks a lot of dough in it—it's the swellest joint they got over there. And then she puts this ad in the paper."

George was not sure that he had heard aright, but the waiter was looking at him with an expression of such exuberant elation that he took a chance and said:

"What ad?"

"Why," said the waiter, "this come-on ad that I was telling you about. You see, that's the big idea—that's the plan the dame dopes out to get him back. So she puts this ad in the paper saying that any man who comes to her joint the next day will be given a ten-dollar gold piece and all the liquor he can drink. She figures that will bring him. She knows the guy is probably down and out by this time and when he reads this ad he'll show up. . . . And that's just what happens. When she comes down next morning she finds a line twelve blocks long outside, and sure enough, here's this guy the first one in the line. Well, she pulls him out of the line and tells the cashier to give all the rest of 'em their booze and their ten bucks, but she tells this guy he ain't gonna get nothing. 'What's the reason I ain't?' he says—you see, the dame is wearing a heavy veil so he don't recognize her. Well, she tells him she thinks there's something phoney about him—gives him the old line, you know—tells him to come upstairs with her so she can talk to him and find out if he's O.K. . . . Do you get it?"

George nodded vaguely. "And then what?" he said.

"Why," the waiter cried, "she gets him up there—and then—" he leaned forward again with fingers resting on the table, and his voice sank to an awed whisper—"*she—takes—off—her—veil!*"

There was a reverential silence as the waiter, still leaning forward with his fingers arched upon the table, regarded his listener with bright eyes and a strange little smile. Then he straightened up slowly, stood erect, still smiling quietly, and a

327

long, low sigh like the coming on of evening came from his lips, and he was still. The silence drew itself out until it became painful, and at length George squirmed wretchedly in his chair and asked:

"And then—then what?"

The waiter was plainly taken aback. He stared in frank astonishment, stunned speechless by the realization that anybody could be so stupid.

"Why—" he finally managed to say with an expression of utter disillusion—"that's *all*! Don't you see. That's all there is! The dame takes off her veil—he recognizes her—and there you are! . . . She's found him! . . . She's got him back! . . . They're together again! . . . *That's* the story!" He was hurt, impatient, almost angry as he went on: "Why, anybody ought to be able to see——"

"Good night, Joe."

The last waitress was just going out and had spoken to the waiter as she passed the table. She was a blonde, slender girl, neatly dressed. Her voice was quiet and full of the casual familiarity of her daily work and association; it was a pleasant voice, and it was a little tired. Her face, as she paused a moment, was etched in light and shadow, and there were little pools of violet beneath her clear grey eyes. Her face had the masklike fragility and loveliness, the almost hair-drawn fineness, that one often sees in young people who have lived in the great city and who have never had wholly enough of anything except work and their own hard youth. One felt instantly sorry for the girl, because one knew that her face would not long be what it was now.

The waiter, interrupted in the flood of his impassioned argument, had been a little startled by the casual intrusion of the girl's low voice, and turned toward her. When he saw who it was, his manner changed at once, and his own seamed face softened a little with instinctive and unconscious friendliness.

"Oh, hello, Billie. Good night, kid."

She went out, and the sound of her brisk little heels clacked away on the hard pavement. For a moment more the waiter continued to look after her, and then, turning back to his sole remaining customer with a queer, indefinable little smile hovering in the hard lines about his mouth, he said very quietly and casually, in the tone men use to speak of things done and known and irrecoverable:

"Did you see that kid? . . . She came in here about two years ago and got a job. I don't know where she came from, but it was some little hick town somewhere. She'd been a chorus girl—a hoofer in some cheap road show—until her legs gave out. . . . You find a lot of 'em in this game—the business is full of 'em. . . . Well, she worked here for about a year, and then she began

328

going with a cheap gigolo who used to come in here. You know the kind—you can smell 'em a mile off—they stink. I could've told her! But, hell, what's the use? They won't listen to you—you only get yourself in dutch all around—they got to find out for themselves—you can't teach 'em. So I left it alone—that's the only way. . . . Well, six or eight months ago, some of the girls found out she was pregnant. The boss let her out. He's not a bad guy—but, hell, what can you expect? You can't keep 'em around a place like this when they're in that condition, can you? . . She had the kid three months ago, and then she got her job back. I understand she's put the kid in a home somewhere. I've never seen it, but they say it's a swell kid, and Billie's crazy about it—goes out there to see it every Sunday. . . . She's a swell kid, too."

The waiter was silent for a moment, and there was a far-off look of tragic but tranquil contemplation in his eyes. Then, quietly, wearily, he said:

"Hell, if I could tell you what goes on here every day—the things you see and hear—the people you meet and all that happens. Jesus, I get sick and tired of it. Sometimes I'm so fed up with the whole thing that I don't care if I never see the joint again. Sometimes I get to thinking how swell it would be not to have to spend your whole life waiting on a lot of mugs—just standing around and waiting on 'em and watching 'em come in and out . . . and feeling sorry for some little kid who's fallen for some dope you wouldn't wipe your feet on . . . and wondering just how long it'll be before she gets the works. . . . Jesus, I'm fed up with it!"

Again he was silent. His eyes looked off into the distance, and his face was set in that expression of mildly cynical regret and acceptance that one often notices in people who have seen much of life, and experienced its hard and seamy side, and who know that there is very little they can do or say. At last he sighed deeply, shook himself, threw off the mood, and resumed his normal manner.

"Gee, Mr. Webber," he said with a return of his former eagerness, "it must be great to be able to write books and stories—to have the gift of gab—all that flow of language—to go anywhere you like—to work when you want to! Now, take that story I was telling you about," he said earnestly. "I never had no education—but if I could only get some guy like you to help me—to write it down the way it ought to be—honest, Mr. Webber, it's a great chance for somebody—there's a fortune in it—I'd go fifty-fifty!" His voice was pleading now. "A guy I knew one time, he told it to me—and me and him are the only two that knows it. This guy was an Armenian, like I said, and the whole thing happened over there. . . . There'd be a gold mine in it if I only knew how to do it."

It was long after midnight, and the round disk of the moon was sinking westward over the cold, deserted streets of slumbering Manhattan.

The party was in full swing now.

The gold and marble ballroom of the great hotel had been converted into a sylvan fairyland. In the center a fountain of classic nymphs and fauns sent up its lighted sprays of water, and here and there about the floor were rustic arbors with climbing roses trailing over them, heavy with scented blossoms. Flowering hot-house trees in tubs were banked around the walls, the shining marble pillars were wreathed about with vines and garlands, and overhead gay lanterns had been strung to illuminate the scene with their gentle glow. The whole effect was that of an open clearing in a forest glade upon Midsummer Night where Queen Titania had come to hold her court and revels.

It was a rare, exotic spectacle, a proper setting for the wealthy, carefree youth for whom it had been planned. The air was heavy with the fragrance of rich perfumes, and vibrant with the throbbing, pulsing rhythms of sensuous music. Upon the polished floor a hundred lovely girls in brilliant evening gowns danced languidly in the close embrace of pink-cheeked boys from Yale and Harvard, their lithe young figures accentuated smartly by the black and white of faultless tailoring.

This was the coming-out party of a fabulously rich young lady, and the like of it had not been seen since the days before the market crashed. The papers had been full of it for weeks. It was said that her father had lost millions in the debacle, but it was apparent that he still had a few paltry dollars left. So now he was doing the right thing, the expected thing, the necessary and inescapable thing, for his beautiful young daughter, who would one day inherit all that these ruinous times had left him of his hard-earned savings. Tonight she was being "presented to Society" (whose members had known her since her birth), and all "Society" was there.

And from this night on, the girl's smiling face would turn up with monotonous regularity in all the rotogravure sections of the Sunday papers, and daily the nation would be kept posted on all the momentous trivia of her life—what she ate, what she wore, where she went, who went with her, what night clubs had been honored by her presence, what fortunate young gentleman had been seen accompanying her to what race track, and what benefits she had sponsored and poured tea for. For one whole year, from now until another beautiful and rich young lady from next season's crop of beautiful and rich young ladies was chosen by the newspaper photographers to succeed her as America's leading débutante, this gay and care-free creature would be for Americans very much what a royal princess is for Englishmen, and for very much the same reason—because she was her father's daughter, and because her father was one of the rulers of America. Millions would read about her every move and envy her, and thousands would copy her as far as their means would let them. They would buy cheap imitations of her costly dresses, hats, and underclothes, would smoke the same cigarettes, use the same lipsticks, eat the same soups, sleep on the same mattresses that she had allowed herself to be pictured wearing, smoking, using, eating, and sleeping on in the handsome colored advertisements on the back covers of magazines—and they would do it, knowing full well that the rich young lady had set these fashions for a price—was she not her father's daughter?—all, of course, for the sake of sweet charity and commerce.

Outside the great hotel, on the Avenue in front of it and on all the side streets in the near vicinity, sleek black limousines were parked. In some of them the chauffeurs slouched dozing behind their wheels. Others had turned on their inside lights and sat there reading the pages of the tabloids. But most of them had left their cars and were knotted together in little groups, smoking, talking, idling the time away until their services should be needed again.

On the pavement near the entrance of the hotel, beside the huge marquee which offered shelter from the wind, the largest group of them, neat in their liveried uniforms, had gathered in debate. They were discussing politics and theories of international economy, and the chief disputants were a plump Frenchman with a waxed mustache, whose sentiments were decidedly revolutionary, and an American, a little man with corky legs, a tough, seamed face, the beady eyes of a bird, and the quick, impatient movements of the city. As George Webber came abreast of them, brought thither by the simple chance of his nightly wanderings, the argument had reached its furious climax, and he stopped a while to listen.

The scene, the situation, and the contrast between the two principal debaters made the whole affair seem utterly grotesque. The plump Frenchman, his cheeks glowing with the cold and his own excitement, was dancing about in a frenzy, talking and gesticulating volubly. He would lean forward with thumb and forefinger uplifted and closed daintily in a descriptive circle—a gesture that eloquently expressed the man's conviction that the case he had been presenting for immediate and bloody world
331

revolution was complete, logical, unshakable, and beyond appeal. When any of the others interposed an objection, he would only grow more violent and inflamed.

At last his little English began to break down under the strain imposed upon it. The air about him fairly rang with objurations, expletives, impassioned cries of *"Mais oui! . . . Absolument! . . . C'est la vérité!"*—and with laughs of maddened exasperation, as if the knowledge that anyone could be so obtuse as not to see it as he saw it was more than he could endure.

"Mais non! Mais non!" he would shout. *"Vous avez tort! . . . Mais c'est stupide!"* he would cry, throwing his plump arms up in a gesture of defeat, and turning away as if he could stand it no longer and was departing—only to return immediately and begin all over again.

Meanwhile, the chief target of this deluge, the little American with the corky legs and the birdy eyes, let him go on. He just leaned up against the building, took an occasional puff at his cigarette, and gave the Frenchman a steady look of cynical impassivity. At last he broke in to say:

"O.K. . . . O.K., Frenchy. . . . When you get through spoutin', maybe *I'll* have somethin' to say."

"Seulement un mot!" replied the Frenchman, out of breath. "One vord!" he cried impressively, drawing himself up to his full five feet three and holding one finger in the air as if he were about to deliver Holy Writ—"I 'ave to say one vord more!"

"O.K.! O.K.!" said the corky little American with cynical weariness. "Only don't take more than an hour and a half to say it!"

Just then another chauffeur, obviously a German, with bright blue eyes and a nut-cracker face, rejoined the group with an air of elated discovery.

"Noos! I got noos for you!" he said. "I haf been mit a drifer who hass in Rooshia liffed, and he says that conditions there far *worser* are——"

"Non! Non!" the Frenchman shouted, red in the face with anger and protest. *"Pas vrai! . . . Ce n'est pas possible!"*

"Oh, for Christ's sake," the American said, tossing his cigarette away with a gesture of impatience and disgust. "Why don't you guys wake up? This ain't Russia! You're in America! The trouble with you guys," he went on, "is that you've been over there all your life where you ain't been used to nothin'—and just as soon as you get over here where you can live like a human bein' you want to tear it all down."

At this, others broke in, and the heated and confused dialogue became more furious than ever. But the talk just went round and round in circles.

George walked away into the night.

The lives of men who have to live in our great cities are often tragically lonely. In many more ways than one, these dwellers in the hive are modern counterparts of Tantalus. They are starving to death in the midst of abundance. The crystal stream flows near their lips but always falls away when they try to drink of it. The vine, rich-weighted with its golden fruit, bends down, comes near, but springs back when they reach to touch it.

Melville, at the beginning of his great fable, *Moby Dick,* tells how the city people of his time would, on every occasion that was afforded them, go down to the dock, to the very edges of the wharf, and stand there looking out to sea. In the great city of today, however, there is no sea to look out to, or if there is, it is so far away, so inaccessible, walled in behind such infinite ramifications of stone and steel, that the effort to get to it is disheartening. So now, when the city man looks out, he looks out on nothing but crowded vacancy.

Does this explain, perhaps, the desolate emptiness of city youth—those straggling bands of boys of sixteen or eighteen that one can always see at night or on a holiday, going along a street, filling the air with raucous jargon and senseless cries, each trying to outdo the others with joyless catcalls and mirthless quips and jokes which are so feeble, so stupidly inane, that one hears them with strong mixed feelings of pity and of shame? Where here, among these lads, is all the merriment, high spirits, and spontaneous gayety of youth? These creatures, millions of them, seem to have been born but half made up, without innocence, born old and stale and dull and empty.

Who can wonder at it? For what a world it is that most of them were born into! They were suckled on darkness, and weaned on violence and noise. They had to try to draw out moisture from the cobblestones, their true parent was a city street, and in that barren universe no urgent sails swelled out and leaned against the wind, they rarely knew the feel of earth beneath their feet and no birds sang, their youthful eyes grew hard, unseeing, from being stopped forever by a wall of masonry.

In other times, when painters tried to paint a scene of awful desolation, they chose the desert or a heath of barren rocks, and there would try to picture man in his great loneliness—the prophet in the desert, Elijah being fed by ravens on the rocks. But for a modern painter, the most desolate scene would be a street in almost any one of our great cities on a Sunday afternoon.

Suppose a rather drab and shabby street in Brooklyn, not

quite tenement perhaps, and lacking therefore even the gaunt savagery of poverty, but a street of cheap brick buildings, warehouses, and garages, with a cigar store or a fruit stand or a barber shop on the corner. Suppose a Sunday afternoon in March—bleak, empty, slaty grey. And suppose a group of men, Americans of the working class, dressed in their "good" Sunday clothes—the cheap machine-made suits, the new cheap shoes, the cheap felt hats stamped out of universal grey. Just suppose this, and nothing more. The men hang around the corner before the cigar store or the closed barber shop, and now and then, through the bleak and empty street, a motor car goes flashing past, and in the distance they hear the cold rumble of an elevated train. For hours they hang around the corner, waiting—waiting—waiting——

For what?

Nothing. Nothing at all. And that is what gives the scene its special quality of tragic loneliness, awful emptiness, and utter desolation. Every modern city man is familiar with it.

And yet—and yet——

It is also true—and this is a curious paradox about America—that these same men who stand upon the corner and wait around on Sunday afternoons for nothing are filled at the same time with an almost quenchless hope, an almost boundless optimism, an almost indestructible belief that something is bound to turn up, something is sure to happen. This is a peculiar quality of the American soul, and it contributes largely to the strange enigma of our life, which is so incredibly mixed of harshness and of tenderness, of innocence and of crime, of loneliness and of good fellowship, of desolation and of exultant hope, of terror and of courage, of nameless fear and of soaring conviction, of brutal, empty, naked, bleak, corrosive ugliness, and of beauty so lovely and so overwhelming that the tongue is stopped by it, and the language for it has not yet been uttered.

How explain this nameless hope that seems to lack all reasonable foundation? I cannot. But if you were to go up to this fairly intelligent-looking truck driver who stands and waits there with his crowd, and if you put to him your question, and if he understood what you were talking about (he wouldn't), and if he were articulate enough to frame in words the feelings that are in him (he isn't)—he might answer you with something such as this:

"Now is duh mont' of March, duh mont' 'of March—now it is Sunday afternoon in Brooklyn in duh mont' of March, an' we stand upon cold corners of duh day. It's funny dat dere are so many corners in duh mont' of March, here in Brooklyn where no corners are. Jesus! On Sunday in duh mont' of March we sleep late in duh mornin', den we get up an' read duh papers—duh funnies an' duh sportin' news. We eat some chow.

334

An' den we dress up in duh afternoon, we leave our wives, we leave duh funnies littered on duh floor, an' go outside in Brooklyn in duh mont' of March an' stand around upon ten t'ousand corners of duh day. We need a corner in duh mont' of March, a wall to stand to, a shelter an' a door. Dere must be *some* place inside in duh mont' of March, but we never found it. So we stand around on corners where duh sky is cold an' ragged still wit' winter, in our good clothes we stand around wit' a lot of udder guys we know, before duh barber shop, just lookin' for a door."

Ah, yes, for in summer:

It is so cool and sweet tonight, a million feet are walking here across the jungle web of Brooklyn in the dark, and it's so hard now to remember that it ever was the month of March in Brooklyn and that we couldn't find a door. There are so many million doors tonight. There's a door for everyone tonight, all's open to the air, all's interfused tonight: remote the thunder of the elevated trains on Fulton Street, the rattling of the cars along Atlantic Avenue, the glare of Coney Island seven miles away, the mob, the racket, and the barkers shouting, the cars swift-shuttling through the quiet streets, the people swarming in the web, lit here and there with livid blurs of light, the voices of the neighbors leaning at their windows, harsh, soft, all interfused. All's illusive in the liquid air tonight, all mixed in with the radios that blare from open windows. And there is something over all tonight, something fused, remote, and trembling, made of all of this, and yet not of it, upon the huge and weaving ocean of the night in Brooklyn—something that we had almost quite forgotten in the month of March. What's this?—a sash raised gently?—a window?—a near voice on the air?—something swift and passing, almost captured, there below?—there in the gulf of night the mournful and yet thrilling voices of the tugs?—the liner's blare? Here—there—some otherwhere—was it a whisper?—a woman's call?—a sound of people talking behind the screens and doors in Flatbush? It trembles in the air throughout the giant web tonight, as fleeting as a step—near—as soft and sudden as a woman's laugh. The liquid air is living with the very whisper of the thing that we are looking for tonight throughout America—the very thing that seemed so bleak, so vast, so cold, so hopeless, and so lost as we waited in our good clothes on ten thousand corners of the day in Brooklyn in the month of March.

If George Webber had never gone beyond the limits of the neighborhood in which he lived, the whole chronicle of the earth would have been there for him just the same. South Brooklyn was a universe.

The people in the houses all around him, whose lives in the cold, raw days of winter always seemed hermetic, sterile, and remote, as shut out from him as though they were something sealed up in a tin, became in spring and summer so real to him it seemed that he had known them from his birth. For, as the days and nights grew warmer, everybody kept their windows open, and all the dwellers in these houses conducted their most intimate affairs in loud and raucous voices which carried to the street and made the casual passer-by a confidant of every family secret.

God knows he saw squalor and filth and misery and despair enough, violence and cruelty and hate enough, to crust his lips forever with the hard and acrid taste of desolation. He found a sinister and demented Italian grocer whose thin mouth writhed in a servile smile as he cringed before his customers, and the next moment was twisted in a savage snarl as he dug his clawlike fingers into the arm of his wretched little son. And on Saturdays the Irishmen would come home drunk, and then would beat their wives and cut one another's throats, and the whole course and progress of their murderous rages would be published nakedly from their open windows with laugh, shout, scream, and curse.

But he found beauty in South Brooklyn, too. There was a tree that leaned over into the narrow alley where he lived, and George could stand at his basement window and look up at it and watch it day by day as it came into its moment's glory of young and magic green. And then toward sunset, if he was tired, he could lie down to rest a while upon his iron bed and listen to the dying birdsong in the tree. Thus, each spring, in that one tree, he found all April and the earth. He also found devotion, love, and wisdom in a shabby little Jewish tailor and his wife, whose dirty children were always tumbling in and out of the dingy suffocation of his shop.

In the infinite variety of such common, accidental, oft-unheeded things one can see the web of life as it is spun. Whether we wake at morning in the city, or lie at night in darkness in the country towns, or walk the streets of furious noon in all the dusty, homely, and enduring lights of present time, the universe around us is the same. Evil lives forever—so does good. Man alone has knowledge of these two, and he is such a little thing.

For what is man?

First, a child, soft-boned, unable to support itself on its rubbery legs, befouled with its excrement, that howls and laughs by turns, cries for the moon but hushes when it gets its mother's teat; a sleeper, eater, guzzler, howler, laugher, idiot, and a chewer of its toe; a little tender thing all blubbered with its spit, a reacher into fires, a beloved fool.

After that, a boy, hoarse and loud before his companions, but afraid of the dark; will beat the weaker and avoid the stronger; worships strength and savagery, loves tales of war and murder, and violence done to others; joins gangs and hates to be alone; makes heroes out of soldiers, sailors, prize fighters, football players, cowboys, gunmen, and detectives; would rather die than not out-try and out-dare his companions, wants to beat them and always to win, shows his muscle and demands that it be felt, boasts of his victories and will never own defeat.

Then the youth: goes after girls, is foul behind their backs among the drugstore boys, hints at a hundred seductions, but gets pimples on his face; begins to think about his clothes, becomes a fop, greases his hair, smokes cigarettes with a dissipated air, reads novels, and writes poetry on the sly. He sees the world now as a pair of legs and breasts; he knows hate, love, and jealousy; he is cowardly and foolish, he cannot endure to be alone; he lives in a crowd, thinks with the crowd, is afraid to be marked off from his fellows by an eccentricity. He joins clubs and is afraid of ridicule; he is bored and unhappy and wretched most of the time. There is a great cavity in him, he is dull.

Then the man: he is busy, he is full of plans and reasons, he has work. He gets children, buys and sells small packets of everlasting earth, intrigues against his rivals, is exultant when he cheats them. He wastes his little three score years and ten in spendthrift and inglorious living; from his cradle to his grave he scarcely sees the sun or moon or stars; he is unconscious of the immortal sea and earth; he talks of the future and he wastes it as it comes. If he is lucky, he saves money. At the end his fat purse buys him flunkeys to carry him where his shanks no longer can; he consumes rich food and golden wine that his wretched stomach has no hunger for; his weary and lifeless eyes look out upon the scenery of strange lands for which in youth his heart was panting. Then the slow death, prolonged by costly doctors, and finally the graduate undertakers, the perfumed carrion, the suave ushers with palms outspread to leftwards, the fast motor hearses, and the earth again.

This is man: a writer of books, a putter-down of words, a painter of pictures, a maker of ten thousand philosophies. He grows passionate over ideas, he hurls scorn and mockery at another's work, he finds the one way, the true way, for himself, and calls all others false—yet in the billion books upon the shelves there is not one that can tell him how to draw a single fleeting breath in peace and comfort. He makes histories of the universe, he directs the destiny of nations, but he does not know his own history, and he cannot direct his own destiny with dignity or wisdom for ten consecutive minutes.

This is man: for the most part a foul, wretched, abominable creature, a packet of decay, a bundle of degenerating tissues, a creature that gets old and hairless and has a foul breath, a hater of his kind, a cheater, a scorner, a mocker, a reviler, a thing that kills and murders in a mob or in the dark, loud and full of brag surrounded by his fellows, but without the courage of a rat alone. He will cringe for a coin, and show his snarling fangs behind the giver's back; he will cheat for two sous, and kill for forty dollars, and weep copiously in court to keep another scoundrel out of jail.

This is man, who will steal his friend's woman, feel the leg of his host's wife below the table cloth, dump fortunes on his whores, bow down to worship before charlatans, and let his poets die. This is man, who swears he will live only for beauty, for art, for the spirit, but will live only for fashion, and will change his faith and his convictions as soon as fashion changes. This is man, the great warrior with flaccid gut, the great romantic with the barren loins, the eternal knave devouring the eternal fool, the most glorious of all the animals, who uses his brain for the most part to make himself a stench in the nostrils of the Bull, the Fox, the Dog, the Tiger, and the Goat.

Yes, this is man, and it is impossible to say the worst of him, for the record of his obscene existence, his baseness, lust, cruelty, and treachery, is illimitable. His life is also full of toil, tumult, and suffering. His days are mainly composed of a million idiot repetitions—in goings and comings along hot streets, in sweatings and freezings, in the senseless accumulation of fruitless tasks, in decaying and being patched, in grinding out his life so that he may buy bad food, in eating bad food so that he may grind his life out in distressful defecations. He is the dweller in that ruined tenement who, from one moment's breathing to another, can hardly forget the bitter weight of his uneasy flesh, the thousand diseases and distresses of his body, the growing incubus of his corruption. This is man, who, if he can remember ten golden moments of joy and happiness out of all his years, ten moments unmarked by care, unseamed by aches or itches, has power to lift himself with his expiring breath and say: "I have lived upon this earth and known glory!"

This is man, and one wonders why he wants to live at all. A third of his life is lost and deadened under sleep; another third is given to a sterile labor; a sixth is spent in all his goings and his comings, in the moil and shuffle of the streets, in thrusting, shoving, pawing. How much of him is left, then, for a vision of the tragic stars? How much of him is left to look upon the everlasting earth? How much of him is left for glory and the making of great songs? A few snatched moments only from the barren glut and suck of living.

338

Here, then, is man, this moth of time, this dupe of brevity and numbered hours, this travesty of waste and sterile breath. Yet if the gods could come here to a desolate, deserted earth where only the ruin of man's cities remained, where only a few marks and carvings of his hand were legible upon his broken tablets, where only a wheel lay rusting in the desert sand, a cry would burst out of their hearts and they would say: "He lived, and he was here!"

Behold his works:

He needed speech to ask for bread—and he had Christ! He needed songs to sing in battle—and he had Homer! He needed words to curse his enemies—and he had Dante, he had Voltaire, he had Swift! He needed cloth to cover up his hairless, puny flesh against the seasons—and he wove the robes of Solomon, he made the garments of great kings, he made the samite for the young knights! He needed walls and a roof to shelter him—and he made Blois! He needed a temple to propitiate his God—and he made Chartres and Fountains Abbey! He was born to creep upon the earth—and he made great wheels, he sent great engines thundering down the rails, he launched great wings into the air, he put great ships upon the angry sea!

Plagues wasted him, and cruel wars destroyed his strongest sons, but fire, flood, and famine could not quench him. No, nor the inexorable grave—his sons leaped shouting from his dying loins. The shaggy bison with his thews of thunder died upon the plains; the fabled mammoths of the unrecorded ages are vast scaffoldings of dry, insensate loam; the panthers have learned caution and move carefully among tall grasses to the water hole; and man lives on amid the senseless nihilism of the universe.

For there is one belief, one faith, that is man's glory, his triumph, his immortality—and that is his belief in life. Man loves life, and, loving life, hates death, and because of this he is great, he is glorious, he is beautiful, and his beauty is everlasting. He lives below the senseless stars and writes his meanings in them. He lives in fear, in toil, in agony, and in unending tumult, but if the blood foamed bubbling from his wounded lungs at every breath he drew, he would still love life more dearly than an end of breathing. Dying, his eyes burn beautifully, and the old hunger shines more fiercely in them—he has endured all the hard and purposeless suffering, and still he wants to live.

Thus it is impossible to scorn this creature. For out of his strong belief in life, this puny man made love. At his best, he *is* love. Without him there can be no love, no hunger, no desire.

So this is man—the worst and best of him—this frail and petty thing who lives his day and dies like all the other animals, and is forgotten. And yet, he is immortal, too, for both the good and evil that he does live after him. Why, then, should any living man ally himself with death, and, in his greed and blindness, batten on his brother's blood?

Chapter Twenty-Eight

The Fox

During all these desperate years in Brooklyn, when George lived and worked alone, he had only one real friend, and this was his editor, Foxhall Edwards. They spent many hours together, wonderful hours of endless talk, so free and full that it combed the universe and bound the two of them together in bonds of closest friendship. It was a friendship founded on many common tastes and interests, on mutual liking and admiration of each for what the other was, and on an attitude of respect which allowed unhampered expression of opinion even on those rare subjects which aroused differences of views and of belief. It was, therefore, the kind of friendship that can exist only between two men. It had in it no element of that possessiveness which always threatens a woman's relations with a man, no element of that physical and emotional involvement which, while it serves nature's end of bringing a man and woman together, also tends to thwart their own dearest wish to remain so by throwing over their companionship a constricting cloak of duty and obligation, of right and vested interest.

The older man was not merely friend but father to the younger. Webber, the hot-blooded Southerner, with his large capacity for sentiment and affection, had lost his own father many years before and now had found a substitute in Edwards. And Edwards, the reserved New Englander, with his deep sense of family and inheritance, had always wanted a son but had had five daughters, and as time went on he made of George a kind of foster son. Thus each, without quite knowing that he did it, performed an act of spiritual adoption.

So it was to Foxhall Edwards that George now turned whenever his loneliness became unbearable. When his inner turmoil, confusion, and self-doubts overwhelmed him, as they often did, and his life went dead and stale and empty till it sometimes seemed that all the barren desolation of the Brooklyn streets had soaked into his very blood and marrow——then he would seek out Edwards. And he never went to him in vain. Edwards, busy though he always was, would drop whatever he was doing and would take George out to lunch or dinner, and in his quiet, casual, oblique, and understanding way would talk to him and draw him out until he found out what it was that troubled him. And always in the end, because of Edwards' faith in him, George would be healed and find himself miraculously restored to self-belief.

What manner of man was this great editor and father-confessor and true friend—he of the quiet, shy, sensitive, and courageous heart who often seemed to those who did not know him well an eccentric, cold, indifferent fellow—he who, grandly christened Foxhall, preferred to be the simple, unassuming Fox?

The Fox asleep was a breathing portrait of guileless innocence. He slept on his right side, legs doubled up a little, hands folded together underneath the ear, his hat beside him on the pillow. Seen so, the sleeping figure of the Fox was touching—for all his five and forty years, it was so plainly boylike. By no long stretch of fancy the old hat beside him on the pillow might have been a childish toy brought to bed with him the night before—and this, in fact, it was!

It was as if, in sleep, no other part of Fox was left except the boy. Sleep seemed to have resumed into itself this kernel of his life, to have excluded all transitions, to have brought the man back to his acorn, keeping thus inviolate that which the man, indeed, had never lost, but which had passed through change and time and all the accretions of experience—and now had been restored, unwoven back into the single oneness of itself.

And yet it was a guileful Fox, withal. Oh, guileful Fox, how innocent in guilefulness and in innocence how full of guile! How straight in cunning, and how cunning-straight, in all directions how strange-devious, in all strange-deviousness how direct! Too straight for crookedness, and for envy too serene, too fair for blind intolerance, too just and seeing and too strong for hate, too honest for base dealing, too high for low suspiciousness, too innocent for all the scheming tricks of swarming villainy—yet never had been taken in a horse trade yet!

So, then, life's boy is he, life's trustful child; life's guileful-guileless Fox is he, but not life's angel, not life's fool. Will get at all things like a fox—not full-tilt at the fences, not head-on, but

341

through coverts peering, running at fringes of the wood, or by the wall; will swing round on the pack and get behind the hounds, cross them up and be away and gone when they are looking for him where he's not—he will not mean to fox them, but he will.

Gets round the edges of all things the way a fox does. Never takes the main route or the worn handle. Sees the worn handle, what it is, says, "Oh," but knows it's not right handle though most used: gets right handle right away and uses it. No one knows how it is done, neither knows the Fox, but does it instantly. It seems so easy when Fox does it, easy as a shoe, because he has had it from his birth. It is a genius.

Our Fox is never hard or fancy, always plain. He makes all plays look easy, never brilliant; it seems that anyone can do it when Fox does it. He covers more ground than any other player in the game, yet does not seem to do so. His style is never mannered, seems no style at all; the thrilled populace never holds its breath in hard suspense when he takes aim, because no one ever saw the Fox take aim, and yet he never misses. Others spend their lives in learning to take aim: they wear just the proper uniform for taking aim, they advance in good order, they signal to the breathless world for silence—"We are taking aim!" they say, and then with faultless style and form, with flawless execution, they bring up their pieces, take aim—and *miss*! The great Fox never seems to take aim, and never misses. Why? He was just born that way—fortunate, a child of genius, innocent and simple—and a Fox!

"And ah!—a cunning Fox!" the Aimers and the Missers say. "A damned subtle, devilish, and most cunning Fox!" they cry, and grind their teeth. "Be not deceived by his appearance—'tis a cunning Fox! Put not your faith in Foxes, put not your faith in this one, he will look so shy, and seem so guileless and so bewildered—but he will never miss!"

"But how—" the Aimers and the Missers plead with one another in exasperation—"how does he do it? What has the fellow got? He's nothing much to look at—nothing much to talk to. He makes no appearance! He never goes out in the world—you never see him at receptions, parties, splendid entertainments—he makes no effort to meet people—no, or to talk to them! He hardly talks at all! . . . What has he got? Where does it come from? Is it chance or luck? There is some mystery
——"

"Well, now," says one, "I'll tell you what my theory is——" Their heads come close, they whisper craftily together until

"No!" another cries. "It is not that. I tell you what he does, it's——"

And again they whisper close, argue and deny, get more

confused than ever, and finally are reduced to furious impotence:

"Bah!" cries one. "How does the fellow do it, anyway? How does he get away with it? He seems to have no sense, no knowledge, no experience. He doesn't get around the way we do, lay snares and traps. He doesn't seem to know what's going on, or what the whole thing's all about—and yet——"

"He's just a *snob!*" another snarls. "When you try to be a good fellow, he high-hats you! You try to kid him, he just looks at you! He never offers to shake hands with you, he never slaps you on the back the way real fellows do! You go out of your way to be nice to him—to show him you're a real guy and that you think he is, too—and what does he do? He just looks at you with that funny little grin and turns away—and wears that damned hat in the office all day long—I think he *sleeps* with it! He never asks you to sit down—and gets up while you're talking to him—leaves you cold—begins to wander up and down outside, staring at everyone he sees—his own associates—as if he were some half-wit idiot boy—and wanders back into his office twenty minutes later—stares at you as if he never saw your face before—and jams that damned hat further down around his ears, and turns away—takes hold of his lapels—looks out the window with that crazy grin—then looks at you again, looks you up and down, stares at your face until you wonder if you've changed suddenly into a baboon—and turns back to the window without a word—then stares at you again—finally *pretends* to recognize you, and says: 'Oh, it's you!' . . . I tell you he's a *snob,* and that's his way of letting you know you don't *belong!* Oh, I know about him—I know what he is! He's an old New Englander—older than God, by God! Too good for anyone but God, by God!—and even God's a little doubtful! An aristocrat—a rich man's son—a Groton-Harvard boy—too fine for the likes of us, by God!—too good for the 'low bounders' who make up this profession! He thinks we're a bunch of business men and Babbitts—and that's the reason that he looks at us the way he does—that's the reason that he grins his grin, and turns away, and catches at his coat lapels, and doesn't answer when you speak to him——"

"Oh, no," another quickly interrupts. "You're wrong there! The reason that he grins that grin and turns away is that he's trying hard to hear—the reason that he doesn't answer when you speak to him is that he's deaf——"

"Ah, deaf!" says still another in derision. "Deaf, hell! Deaf as a Fox, *he* is! That deafness is a stall—a trick—a gag! He hears you when he wants to hear you! If it's anything he wants to hear, *he'll* hear you though you're forty yards away and talking in a whisper! He's a Fox. I tell you!"

"Yes, a Fox, a Fox!" they chorus in agreement. "That much is certain—the man's a Fox!"

So the Aimers and the Missers whisper, argue, and deduce. They lay siege to intimates and friends of Fox, ply them with flattery and strong drink, trying thus to pluck out the heart of Fox's mystery. They find out nothing, because there's nothing to find out, nothing anyone can tell them. They are reduced at length to exasperated bafflement and finish where they started. They advance to their positions, take aim—and miss!

And so, in all their ways, they lay cunning snares throughout the coverts of the city. They lay siege to life. They think out tactics, crafty stratagems. They devise deep plans to bag the game. They complete masterly flanking operations in the night-time (while the great Fox sleeps), get in behind the enemy when he isn't looking, are sure that victory is within their grasp, take aim magnificently—and fire—and shoot one another painfully in the seats of their expensive pants!

Meanwhile, the Fox is sleeping soundly through the night, as sweetly as a child.

Night passes, dawn comes, eight o'clock arrives. How to describe him now as he awakes?

A man of five and forty years, not really seeming younger, yet always seeming something of the boy. Rather, the boy is there within that frame of face, behind the eyes, within the tenement of flesh and bone—not imprisoned, just held there in a frame—a frame a little worn by the years, webbed with small wrinkles round the eyes—invincibly the same as it has always been. The hair, once fair and blond, no longer fair and blond now, feathered at the temples with a touch of grey, elsewhere darkened by time and weather to a kind of steel-grey—blondness really almost dark now, yet, somehow, still suggesting fair and blond. The head well set and small, boy's head still, the hair sticking thick and close to it, growing to a V in the center of the forehead, then back straight and shapely, full of natural grace. Eyes pale blue, full of a strange misty light, a kind of far weather of the sea in them, eyes of a New England sailor long months outbound for China on a clipper ship, with something drowned, sea-sunken in them.

The general frame and structure of the face is somewhat lean and long and narrow—face of the ancestors, a bred face, face of people who have looked the same for generations. A stern, lonely face, with the enduring fortitude of granite, face of the New England seacoast, really his grandfather's face, New England statesman's face, whose bust sits there on the mantel, looking at the bed. Yet something else has happened on Fox's face to transfigure it from the primeval nakedness of granite: in its essential framework, granite still, but a kind of radiance and warmth of life has enriched and mellowed it. A light is burning in the Fox, shining outward through the face, through every gesture, grace, and movement of the body, something swift, mercurial, mutable, and tender, something buried and withheld, but passionate—something out of his mother's face, perhaps, or out of his father's, or his father's mother's—something that subdues the granite with warmth —something from poetry, intuition, genius, imagination, living, inner radiance, and beauty. This face, then, with the shapely head, the pale, far-misted vision of the eyes, held in round bony cages like a bird's, the strong, straight nose, curved at the end, a little scornful and patrician, sensitive, sniffing, swift-nostriled as a hound's—the whole face with its passionate and proud serenity might almost be the face of a great poet, or the visage of some strange and mighty bird.

But now the sleeping figure stirs, opens its eyes and listens, rouses, starts up like a flash.

"What?" says Fox.

The Fox awake now.

"FOXHALL MORTON EDWARDS."

The great name chanted slowly through his brain—someone had surely spoken it—it filled his ears with sound—it rang down solemnly through the aisles of consciousness—it was no dream—the very walls were singing with its grave and proud sonorities as he awoke.

"What?" cried Fox again.

He looked about him. There was no one there. He shook his head as people do when they shake water from their ears. He inclined his good right ear and listened for the sound again. He tugged and rubbed his good right ear—yes, it was unmistakable—the good right ear was ringing with the sound.

Fox looked bewildered, puzzled, searched around the room again with sea-pale eyes, saw nothing, saw his hat beside him on the pillow, said, "Oh," in a slightly puzzled tone, picked up the hat and jammed it on his head, half covering the ears, swung out of bed and thrust his feet into his slippers, got up, pajamaed and behatted, walked over to the door, opened it, looked out, and said:

"What? Is anybody there?— Oh!"

For there was nothing—just the hall, the quiet, narrow hall of morning, the closed door of his wife's room, and the stairs.

He closed the door, turned back into his room, still looking puzzled, intently listening, his good right ear half-turned and searching for the sounds.

Where had they come from then? The name—he thought he

heard it still, faintly now, mixed in with many other strange, confusing noises. But where? From what direction did they come? Or had he heard them? A long, droning sound, like an electric fan—perhaps a motor in the street? A low, retreating thunder—an elevated train, perhaps? A fly buzzing? Or a mosquito with its whining bore? No, it could not be: it was morning, springtime, and the month of May.

Light winds of morning fanned the curtains of his pleasant room. An old four-poster bed, a homely, gay old patch-quilt coverlet, an old chest of drawers, a little table by his bed, piled high with manuscripts, a glass of water and his eyeglasses, and a little ticking clock. Was that what he had heard? He held it to his ear and listened. On the mantel, facing him, the bust of his grandfather, Senator William Foxhall Morton, far-seeing, sightless, stern, lean, shrewd with decision; a chair or two, and on the wall an engraving of Michelangelo's great Lorenzo Medici. Fox looked at it and smiled.

"A *man*," said he in a low voice. "The way a man *should* look!" The figure of the young Caesar was mighty-limbed, enthroned; helmeted for war; the fine hand half-supporting the chin of the grand head, broodingly aware of great events and destiny; thought knit to action, poetry to fact, caution to boldness, reflection to decision—the Thinker, Warrior, Statesman, Ruler all conjoined in one. "And what a man *should* be," thought Fox.

A little puzzled still, Fox goes to his window and looks out, pajamaed and behatted still, the fingers of one hand back upon his hips, a movement lithe and natural as a boy's. The head goes back, swift nostrils sniff, dilate with scorn. Light winds of morning fan him, gauzy curtains are blown back.

And outside, morning, and below him, morning, sky-shining morning all above, below, around, across from him, cool-slanting morning, gold-cool morning, and the street. Bleak fronts of rusty brown across from him, the flat fronts of Turtle Bay.

Fox looks at morning and the street with sea-pale eyes, as if he never yet had seen them, then in a low and husky voice, a little hoarse, agreeable, half-touched with whisper, he says with slow recognition, quiet wonder, and—somehow, somewhy—resignation:

"Oh. . . . I see."

Turns now and goes into his bathroom opposite, surveys himself in the mirror with the same puzzled, grave, and sea-pale wonder, looks at his features, notes the round cages that enclose his eyes, sees Boy-Fox staring gravely out at him, bethinks him suddenly of Boy-Fox's ear, which stuck out at right angles forty years ago, getting Boy-Fox gibes at Groton—so jams hat further down about the ear, so stick-out ear that's stick-out ear no longer won't stick out!

So standing, he surveys himself for several moments, and finding out at length that this indeed is he, says, as before, with the same slightly puzzled, slow, and patiently resigned acceptance:

"Oh. I see."

Turns on the shower faucet now—the water spurts and hisses in jets of smoking steam. Fox starts to step beneath the shower, suddenly observes pajamas on his person, mutters slowly—"Oh-h!"—and takes them off. Unpajamaed now, and as God made him, save for hat, starts to get in under shower with hat on—and remembers hat, remembers it in high confusion, is forced against his will to acknowledge the unwisdom of the procedure—so snaps his fingers angrily, and, in a low, disgusted tone of acquiescence, says:

"Oh, well, then! *All* right!"

So removes his hat, which is now jammed on so tightly that he has to take both hands and fairly wrench and tug his way out of it, hangs the battered hulk reluctantly within easy reaching distance on a hook upon the door, surveys it for a moment with an undecided air, as if still not willing to relinquish it—and then, still with a puzzled air, steps in beneath those hissing jets of water hot enough to boil an egg!

Puzzled no longer, my mad masters, ye may take it, Fox comes out on the double-quick, and loudly utters, "Damn!"—and fumes and dances, snaps his fingers, loudly utters "Damn!" again—but gets his water tempered to his hide this time, and so, without more peradventure, takes his shower.

Shower done, hair brushed at once straight back *around* his well-shaped head, on goes the hat at once. So brushes teeth, shaves with a safety razor, walks out naked but behatted into his room, starts to go downstairs, remembers clothing—"Oh!"—looks round, bepuzzled, sees clothing spread out neatly on a chair by womenfolks the night before—fresh socks, fresh underwear, a clean shirt, a suit, a pair of shoes. Fox never knows where they come from, wouldn't know where to look, is always slightly astonished when he finds them. Says "Oh!" again, goes back and puts clothes on, and finds to his amazement that they fit.

They fit him beautifully. Everything fits the Fox. He never knows what he has on, but he could wear a tow-sack, or a shroud, a sail, a length of canvas—they would fit the moment that he put them on, and be as well the elegance of faultless style. His clothes just seem to grow on him: whatever he wears takes on at once the grace, the dignity, and the unconscious ease of his own person. Never exercises much, but never has to; loves

347

to take a walk, is bored by games and plays none; has same figure that he had at twenty-one—five feet ten, one hundred and fifty pounds, no belly and no fat, the figure of a boy.

Dressed now, except for necktie, picks up necktie, suddenly observes it, a very gay one with blue polka dots, and drops it with dilating nostrils, muttering a single word that seems to utter volumes:

"Women!"

Then searches vaguely on a tie rack in his closet, finds a modest grey cravat, and puts it on. So, attired now, picks up a manuscript, his pince-nez glasses, opens the door, and walks out in the narrow hall.

His wife's door closed and full of sleep, the air touched subtly with a faint perfume. The Fox sniffs sharply, with a swift upward movement of his head, and, looking with scorn, mixed with compassion, pity, tenderness, and resignation, inclines his head in one slow downward movement of decision, and says:

"Women!"

So, down the narrow, winding staircase now, his head thrown sharply back, one hand upon his lapel, the other holding manuscript, and reaches second floor. Another narrow hall. Front, back and to the side, three more closed doors of sleep and morning, and five daughters——

"Women!"

Surveys the door of Martha, the oldest, twenty, a——

Woman!

And next the door of Eleanor, aged eighteen, and Amelia, just sixteen, but——

Women!

And finally, with a gentle scorn, touched faintly with a smile, the door of the two youngest, Ruth, fourteen, little Ann, just seven, yet——

Women!

So, sniffing sharply the woman-laden air, descends now to the first floor, enters living room, and scornfully surveys the work of——

Women!

The carpets are rolled up, the morning sunlight slants on the bare boards. The chairs, the sofas, and upholstery have been ripped open, the stuffing taken out. The place smells of fresh paint. The walls, brown yesterday, are robin's-egg blue this morning. Buckets of paint are scattered round the floor. Even the books that lined the walls have been taken from the tall, indented shelves. The interior decorators are at their desperate work again, and all because of——

Women!

Fox sniffs the fresh paint with sharp disgust, crosses the

room, mounts winding steps, which also have been painted robin's-egg blue, and goes out on the terrace. Gay chairs and swings and tables, gay-striped awnings, and in an ashtray several cigarette butts with telltale prints upon them——

Women!

The garden backs of Turtle Bay are lyrical with tender green, with birdsong and the hidden plash of water—the living secret of elves' magic embedded in the heart of the gigantic city—and beyond, like some sheer, terrific curtain of upward-curving smoke, the frontal cliff of the sky-waving towers.

Fox sniffs sharply the clean green fragrance of the morning, sea-pale eyes are filled with wonder, strangeness, recognition. Something passionate and far transforms his face—and something rubs against his leg, moans softly. Fox looks down into the melancholy, pleading eyes of the French poodle. He observes the ridiculous barbering of the creature—the fuzzy muff of kinky wool around the shoulders, neck, and head, the skinned nakedness of ribs and loins, wool-fuzzy tail again, tall, skinny legs—a *half*-dressed female creature with no wool at all just where the wool is needed most—no dog at all, but just a frenchified parody of dog—an absurd travesty of all the silly fashions, mannerisms, coquettishness, and irresponsibility of a

——

Woman!

Fox turns in disgust, leaves terrace, descends steps to the living room again, traverses barren boards, threads way around the disemboweled furnishings, and descends the stairs to the basement floor.

"What's *this*?"

In entrance hall below, a lavish crimson carpet where yesterday there was a blue one, cream-white paint all over walls today, which yesterday were green, the wall all chiseled into, a great sheet of mirror ready to be installed where yesterday no mirror was.

Fox traverses narrow hallway, past the kitchen, through the cloakroom—this, too, redolent of fresh paint—and into little cubbyhole that had no use before.

"Good God, what's *this*?"

Transfigured now to Fox's "cozy den" (Fox wants no "cozy den"—will have none!), walls are painted, bookshelves built, a reading lamp and easy chairs in place, the Fox's favorite books (Fox groans!) transplanted from their shelves upstairs and brought down here where Fox can never find them.

Fox bumps his head against the low doorway in going out, traverses narrow hall again, at last gets into dining room. Seats himself at head of the long table (six women make a table long!), looks at the glass of orange juice upon his plate, does nothing to it, makes no motion toward it, just sits there waiting in a state of patient and resigned dejection, as who should say: "It's no one but the Old Grey Mule."

Portia enters—a plump mulatto, nearing fifty, tinged so imperceptibly with yellow that she is almost white. She enters, stops, stares at Fox sitting motionless there, and titters coyly. Fox turns slowly, catches his coat lapels, and looks at her in blank astonishment. She drops her eyelids shyly, tittering, and spreads plump fingers over her fat mouth. Fox surveys her steadily, as if trying to peer through her fingers at her face, then with a kind of no-hope expression in his eyes, he says slowly, in a sepulchral tone:

"Fruit salad."

And Portia, anxiously:

"What fo' you don't drink yo' orange juice, Mistah Edwahds? Doesn't you like it?"

"Fruit salad," repeats Fox tonelessly.

"What fo' you always eats dat ole fruit salad, Mistah Edwahds? What fo' you wants dat ole canned stuff when we fixes you de nice fresh orange juice?"

"Fruit salad," echoes Fox dolefully, utter resignation in his tone.

Portia departs protesting, but presently fruit salad is produced and put before him. Fox eats it, then looks round and up at Portia, and, still with no-hope resignation in his voice, says low and hoarsely:

"Is that—all?"

"Why, no suh, Mistah Edwahds," Portia replies. "You can have anything you likes if you jest lets us know. We nevah knows jest what you's goin' to awdah. All las' month you awdahed fish fo' brek-fus'—is dat what you wants?"

"Breast of guinea hen," says Fox tonelessly.

"Why, Mistah Edwahds!" Portia squeals. "Breas' of guinea hen fo' brek-fus'?"

"Yes," says Fox, patient and enduring.

"But, Mistah Edwahds!" Portia protests. "You know you doesn't want breas' of guinea hen fo' brek-fus'!"

"Yes," says Fox in his hopeless tone, "I do." And he regards her steadily with sea-misted eyes, with proud and scornful features, eloquent with patient and enduring bitterness as if to say: "Man is born of woman and is made to mourn."

"But Mistah Edwahds," Portia pleads with him, "fokes don't eat breas' of guinea hen fo' brek-fus'! Dey eats ham an' aiggs, an' toast an' bacon—things like dat."

Fox continues to regard her fixedly.

"Breast of guinea hen," he says wearily, implacably as before.

"B-b-b-but, Mistah Edwahds," Portia stammers, thoroughly

demoralized by this time, "we ain't *got* no breas' of guinea hen."

"We had some night before last," says Fox.

"Yes, suh, yes, suh!" Portia almost tearfully agrees. "But dat's all gone! We et up all dere was! . . . Besides, you been eatin' breas' of guinea hen ev'ry night fo' dinnah de las' two weeks, an' Miz Edwahds—she say you had enough—she say de chillun gettin' tired of it—she tol' us to get somep'n else! . . . If you tol' us dat you wanted guinea hen fo' *brek*-fus', we'd a-had it. But you nevah tol' us, Mistah Edwahds." Portia is on the verge of open tears by now. "You nevah tells us what you wants—an' dat's why we nevah knows. One time you wanted cream chicken fo' yo' brek-fus' ev'ry mawnin' fo' a month. . . . Den you changed aroun' to codfish balls, an' had dat fo' a long, long time. . . . An' now it's guinea hen," she almost sobs—"an' we ain't *got* none, Mistah Edwahds. You nevah tol' us what you wanted. We got ham an' aiggs—we got bacon—we got——"

"Oh, well," says Fox wearily, "bring what you have, then— anything you like."

He turns away full of patient scorn, enduring and unhoping bitterness—and "aiggs" are brought him. Fox eats them with relish; toast, too, three brown slices, buttered; and drinks two cups of strong hot coffee.

Just at half-past eight something entered the dining room as swift and soundless as a ray of light. It was a child of fourteen years, a creature of surpassing loveliness, the fourth daughter of the Fox, named Ruth. It was the Fox in miniature: a little creature, graceful as a bird, framed finely as some small and perfect animal. The small, lean head was shaped and set exactly as the head of Fox, the dark blonde hair grew cleanly to it, the child's face was of an ivory transparency, the features and the sensitivity of expression were identical with those of Fox, transformed to femininity, and the lines of the whole face were cut and molded with the exquisite delicacy of a cameo.

The shyness of this little girl was agonizing; it was akin to ter- ror. She entered the room breathlessly, noiselessly, stricken, with her head lowered, her arms held to her side, her eyes fixed on the floor. The ordeal of passing by her father, and of speaking to him, was obviously a desperate one; she glided past as if she almost hoped to escape notice. Without raising her eyes, she said, "Good morning, daddy," in a timid little voice, and was about to duck into her chair, when Fox looked up, startled, got up quickly, put his arms around her, and kissed her. In answer to his kiss, she pecked her cheek toward him like a bird, still keeping her eyes desperately on the floor.

The face of Fox was illuminated by a radiant tenderness as, in a low, deaf, slightly hoarse tone, he said:

"Good morning, darling."

Still without looking at him, stricken, desperate, she tried to get away from him, yet, even in the act, her affection for the Fox was eloquent. Her heart was beating like a triphammer, her eyes went back and forth like a frightened fledgling's, she wanted to vanish through the walls, dart out of doors, turn into a shadow—anything, *anything,* if only she could utterly escape notice, having no one look at her, pay any attention to her, above all, *speak* to her. So she fluttered there in his embrace like a dove caught in a snare, tried to get away from him, was in a state of agony so acute and sensitive that it was painful to watch her or to do anything that would in any way increase the embarrassment and desperate shyness of this stricken little girl.

Fox's embrace tightened around her as she tried to escape, and he grew full of solicitude and anxiety as he looked at her.

"Darling!" he whispered, in a low and troubled tone. He shook her gently. *"What,* darling?" he demanded. *"Now* what?" he finally demanded, with a touch of the old scorn.

"But *nothing,* daddy!" she protested, her timid little voice rising in a note of desperate protest. *"Nothing,* daddy!" She squirmed a little to get free. Reluctantly Fox let her go. The child ducked right down into her chair, still with her eyes averted, and concluded with a little gasping laugh of protest: "You're so *funny,* daddy!"

Fox resumed his seat and still continued to regard her sternly, gravely, with alarmed solicitude, and a little scorn. She shot a frightened look at him and ducked her head down toward her plate.

"Is anything *wrong?*" said Fox, in a low voice.

"But *naturally—not!*"—a protesting and exasperated little gasp of laughter. "Why should anything be *wrong?* Honestly, you're so *strange,* daddy!"

"Well, then," said Fox, with patient resignation.

"But *nothing!* I keep *telling* you, there's *nothing!* That's what I've told you from the *feerst!*"

All of the children of the Fox say "feerst" for "first," "beerst" for "burst," "theerst" for "thirst." Why, no one knows. It seems to be a tribal accent, not only among all of Fox's children, but among all of their young cousins on the Fox's side. It is almost as if they were creatures of some isolated family, immured for generations on some lonely island, cut off from the world, and speaking some lost accent that their ancestors spoke three hundred years ago. Moreover, their tone is characterized by a kind of *drawl*—not the languorous drawl of the deep South, but a protesting drawl, a wearied-out,

352

exasperated drawl, as if they have almost given up hope of making Fox—or *someone*—understand what ought to be obvious without any explanation whatsoever. Thus:

"But *nothing,* daddy! I've told you that from the *f-e-e-r-s-t!*"

"Well, then, what *is* it, darling?" Fox demanded. "Why do you *look* like that?"—with an emphatic downward movement of the head.

"But look like *what?*" the child protested. "Oh, *daddy,* honestly—" she gasped, with a little strained laugh, and looked away—"I don't know what you're talking about."

Portia brought smoking oatmeal and put it down before her, and the girl, saying timidly, "Good morning, Portia," ducked her head and began to eat hastily.

Fox continued to look at the child sternly, gravely, with a troubled expression in his eyes. Looking up suddenly, she put down her spoon, and cried:

"But, *daddy—wha-a-t?*"

"Are those scoundrels going to be here again today?" said Fox.

"Oh, daddy, *what* scoundrels? . . . Honestly!" She twisted in her chair, gasped a little, tried to laugh, picked up her spoon, started to go on eating, then put her spoon down again.

"Those scoundrels," said the Fox, "that—you *women*—" he inclined his head with scornful emphasis—"have brought in to destroy my home."

"But *who* are you *talking* about?" she protested, looking around like a hunted animal for a means of escape. "I don't know who you *mean.*"

"I mean," said Fox, "those interior decorating *fellows*—" here his voice was filled with the dismissal of an unutterable contempt—"that you and your *mother* have imported to wreck the house."

"But *I* had nothing to do with it!" the girl protested. "Oh, daddy, you're *so*—" she broke off, squirmed, and turned away with a little laugh.

"So—*what?*" said Fox, low, hoarse, and scornful.

"Oh, I don't know—so—so *stra-a-nge!* You say such funny *thi-i-ngs!*"

"Have you *women,*" Fox went on, "decided when you're going to let me have a little peace in my own house?"

"Let you have a little *pe-a-ce?* . . . What have *I* done? If you don't want the decorators, why don't you speak to *mo-o-ther?*"

"*Because*—" Fox inclined his head with a slow, ironic emphasis upon the word—"because—I—don't—count! I'm only the—Old—Grey—Mule—among six women—and, of course, *anything* is good enough for me!"

"But what have *we* done? *We* haven't done anything to you!

353

Why do you act so *p-e-e-r*-secuted? . . . Oh, daddy, honestly!"
She squirmed desperately, tried to laugh, turned away, and
ducked her head down toward her plate again.

Sitting back in his chair, one hand clasped upon the arm, his
whole being withdrawn, remote, in an attitude eloquent of deep,
unhoping patience, Fox continued to regard the child gravely
for a moment. Then he thrust his hand into his pocket, pulled
his watch out and looked at it, glanced at the child again, and
shook his head in a movement packed with stern reproach and
silent accusation.

She looked up, quick and startled, laid her spoon down, and
gasped:

"*Now* what? What are you shaking your *he-a-ad* for? What
is it *now*?"

"Is your mother up?"

"But *naturally*, I don't *kno-o-w*!"

"Are your sisters up?"

"But, *da-a-dy*, how can I tell?"

"Did you get to bed early?"

"Ye-e-e-s," in a drawl of protest.

"What time did your sisters get to bed?"

"But, of course, I have no way of *kno-o-wing*! Why don't you
ask *the-e-m*?"

Fox looked at the watch again, then at the child, and shook
his head once more.

"Women!" he said quietly, and put the watch back into his
pocket.

The child by now has finished with her oatmeal—all she
wants of it. Now she slides out of her chair and, with face
averted, tries to glide past Fox, out of the room. Fox gets up
quickly, puts his arms around her, says in a low, quick, worried
tone:

"Oh, *darling*, where are you going?"

"But to *sch-o-o-ol*, of course!"

"*Darling*, stay and *eat* your breakfast!"

"But I've *e-e-a-ten*!"

"Oh, you *haven't*!" whispers Fox impatiently.

"But I've eaten all I *wa-a-a-nt*!"

"You haven't eaten *anything*!" he whispers scornfully.

"But I don't *want* any more," she protests, looks desperately
about, and struggles to free herself. "Oh, let me *go-o-o*, daddy!
I'll be *late*!"

"Then *be* late!" whispers the great watch-watcher and head-
shaker scornfully. "*Stay* and *eat* your *breakfast*!"—punctuating
these decisive words with slow nods of emphasis.

"But I *ca-a-n't*! I've got to read a *pa-a-per*."

"A—what?"

"A *t-e-e-r-m* paper—for Miss Allen's class—it comes at nine o'clock."

"Oh," says Fox slowly, "I see." In a low, almost inaudible tone, "On—*Whitman?*"

"Ye-e-e-s."

"Oh. . . . Did you read the book I gave you—the one with his war diary and notes?"

"Ye-e-e-s."

"Astonishing!" whispers Fox. "Isn't it *astonishing?* You can see just how he *did* it, can't you? He—he *got right up* on everything," Fox whispers, "just as if he were the thing itself—as if it were happening to *him!*"

"Ye-e-e-s." She looks desperately around, then with averted eyes blurts out: "You were right about the other thing, too."

"What other thing?"

"About night—how there's so much night and darkness in him—his—his feeling for night."

"Oh," Fox whispers slowly, his sea-pale eyes misted with reflection. "Did you tell about that, too?"

"Ye-e-s. It's *tr-u-e.* After you told me, I read him again, and it's *tr-u-e.*"

Shy, desperate, timid, stricken as she is, she nevertheless knows it's true when it's true.

"That's *fine!*" Fox whispers, and shakes his head sharply with immense satisfaction. "I'll bet it's *good!*"

The girl's ivory features flush crimson. Like Fox, she loves praise, yet cannot stand to have it spoken. She squirms, is terrified, is hoping against hope——

"I don't *kno-o-ow*," she gasps. "Miss Allen didn't like the last paper I wrote—what I said about Mark Twain."

"Then," Fox whispers, low and scornfully, "let Miss Allen *not* like it. That was a *fine* paper," he whispers. "What—what you said about the *River* was just right."

"I *kno-o-ow!* And that was the part she didn't like. She didn't seem to know what I was talking about—said it was immature and not sound, and gave me a 'C'."

"Oh," says Fox absently, thinking all the time with an immense satisfaction of the spirit: "What a girl this *is!* She has a *fine* mind. She—she *understands* things!"

"You see, darling," Fox whispers gently, coming back to Miss Allen, "it's not their fault. These people do the best they can—but—but they just can't seem to *understand*," he whispers. "You see, Miss Allen is an—an academic kind of person—I guess, kind of an old maid, *really*," he whispers, with an emphatic movement of the head—"and that kind of person, darling, just wouldn't be able to understand what Whitman and Mark Twain and Keats are like. . . . It's—it's a shame," Fox

355

mutters, and shakes his head, his eyes troubled with regret
—"it's a shame we've got to hear about these people first in—
in schools—from—from people like Miss Allen. You see,
darling," Fox says gently, his face cocked sideways, his good
ear pointing toward the girl, his language simple as a shoe, his
face keen, shrewd, thoughtful, and absorbed, and radiant as a
blade of light, as it always is when interest and reflection hold
the wise serpent of his brain—"you see, darling, schools are all
right, really—but the *Thing* they do is different from the *Thing*
that Keats and Whitman and Mark Twain do. . . . People like
that really have no place in schools. A—a *school*," Fox
whispers, "is an *academic* kind of place, you see—and the
people that you find in schools are academic people—and these
other kind of people—the *poets*," whispers Fox, "are not
academic people—they're—they're really *against* what the
academic people do—they are people who—who *discover*
things for themselves," Fox whispers, "who burst through and
make another world—and the academic people cannot
understand them—so that's why what the academic people say
about them is—is *not much good*," Fox whispers. For a
moment he is silent, then shakes his head and mutters in a low
tone of profound regret: "It's a *pity*! Too *bad* you've got to hear
about it first in schools—but—but just do the best you can with
it—get what you can from it—and—and when *those people*"
—whisper mixed with understanding, pity, and contempt
—"have gone as far as they can go, just forget about the *rest*
they tell you."

"I kno-o-w! But, really, daddy, when Miss Allen starts
drawing charts and diagrams upon the blackboard, showing
how they *did* it—it's—it's *aw-w-ful*! I can't *be-e-ar* it—it just
makes everything so—*te-er-rible*! . . . Oh, daddy, let me go!"
She squirms to free herself again, her tender features tortured
with self-consciousness. "*Please,* daddy! I've *got* to! I'll be *late*!"

"How are you going?"

"But *naturally*, the way I always go."

"By taxi?"

"But of *course* not, I take the *stre-e-e-t* car."

"Oh. . . . What street car?"

"The Lexington A-a-a-venue."

"Alone?" says Fox in a low, grave, troubled tone.

"But, of *course*, daddy!"

He looks at her sternly with a sorrow-troubled face, and
shakes his head.

"But what's wrong with taking the *str-e-e-t* car? Oh, daddy,
you're *so-o*"—she squirms, looks off indefinitely, her face
touched by a smile of agonized embarrassment. "*Please*, daddy!
Let me *go-o-o*! I tell you I'll be *late*!"

She pushes a little to release herself, he kisses her, and lets her go reluctantly.

"Good-bye, darling"—low, hoarse, tender, troubled with grave solicitude. "You *will* take care, won't you?"

"But, of *course!*" A little agonized laugh. "There's nothing to take *care*." Then, suddenly, in a timid little voice, "Good-bye, daddy"—and she is gone, swiftly, silently, like fading light.

Fox, hands upon his hips, with a look half-trouble and half-tenderness, follows her with sea-pale eyes until she has gone. Then he turns back to the table, sits down again, and picks up the paper.

News.

Chapter Twenty-Nine

"The Hollow Men"

Fox picks up the paper and settles back to read it with keen relish. The paper is the *Times*. (He read the *Tribune* late last night: waited up for it, would not miss it, has never missed it, could not sleep if he had not read it.) Morning now, Fox reads the *Times*.

How does he read the *Times*?

He reads it the way Americans have always read the paper. He also reads it as few Americans have ever read the paper— with nostrils sensitive, dilating with proud scorn, sniffing for the news behind the news.

He loves it—even loves the *Times*—loves Love unlovable— and don't we all? Ink-fresh papers, millions of them—ink-fresh with morning, orange juice, waffles, eggs and bacon, and cups of strong hot coffee. How fine it is, here in America, at ink-fresh, coffee-fragrant morning, to read the paper!

How often have we read the paper in America! How often have we seen it *blocked* against our doors! Little route-boys fold and block it, so to throw it—and so we find it and unfold it, crackling and ink-laden, at our doors. Sometimes we find it tossed there lightly with flat *plop*; sometimes we find it thrown with solid, whizzing *whack* against the clapboards (clapboards here, most often, in America); sometimes, as now in Turtle Bay, servants find just freshly folded sheets laid neatly down in doorways, and take them to the table for their masters. No matter how it got there, we always find it.

How we do love the paper in America! How we do love the paper, all!

Why do we love the paper in America? Why do we love the paper, all?

Mad masters, I will tell ye why.

Because the paper is "the news" here in America, and we love the *smell* of news. We love the smell of news that's "fit to print." We also love the smell of news *not* fit to print. We love, besides, the smell of *facts* that news is made of. Therefore we love the paper because the news is so fit-printable—so unprintable—and so fact-printable.

Is the news, then, like America? No, it's not—and Fox, unlike the rest of you, mad masters, turns the pages knowing it is just the news and not America that he reads there in his *Times*.

The news is *not* America, nor is America the *news*—the news is *in* America. It is a kind of light at morning, and at evening, and at midnight in America. It is a kind of growth and record and excrescence of our life. It is not good enough—it does not tell our story—yet it is the news!

Fox reads (proud nose sharp-sniffing with a scornful relish):

An unidentified man fell or jumped yesterday at noon from the twelfth story of the Admiral Francis Drake Hotel, corner of Hay and Apple Streets, in Brooklyn. The man, who was about thirty-five years old, registered at the hotel about a week ago, according to the police, as C. Green. Police are of the opinion that this was an assumed name. Pending identification, the body is being held at the King's County Morgue.

This, then, is news. Is it also the whole story, Admiral Drake? No! Yet we do not supply the whole story—we who have known all the lights and weathers of America—as Fox supplies it now:

Well, then, it's news, and it happened in your own hotel, brave Admiral Drake. It didn't happen in the Penn-Pitt at Pittsburgh, nor the Phil-Penn at Philadelphia, nor the York-Albany at Albany, nor the Hudson-Troy at Troy, nor the Libya-Ritz at Libya Hill, nor the Clay-Calhoun at Columbia, nor the Richmond-Lee at Richmond, nor the George

Washington at Easton, Pennsylvania, Canton, Ohio, Terre Haute, Indiana, Danville, Virginia, Houston, Texas, and ninety-seven other places; nor at the Abraham Lincoln at Springfield, Massachusetts, Hartford, Connecticut, Wilmington, Delaware, Cairo, Illinois, Kansas City, Missouri, Los Angeles, California, and one hundred and thirty-six other towns; nor at the Andrew Jackson, the Roosevelt (Theodore or Franklin—take your choice), the Jefferson Davis, the Daniel Webster, the Stonewall Jackson, the U. S. Grant, the Commodore Vanderbilt, the Waldorf-Astor, the Adams House, the Parker House, the Palmer House, the Taft, the McKinley, the Emerson (Waldo or Bromo), the Harding, the Coolidge, the Hoover, the Albert G. Fall, the Harry Daugherty, the Rockefeller, the Harriman, the Carnegie or the Frick, the Christopher Columbus or the Leif Ericsson, the Ponce-de-Leon or the Magellan, in the remaining eight hundred and forty-three cities of America—but at the Francis Drake, brave Admiral—your own hotel—so, of course, you'll want to know what happened.

"An unidentified man"—well, then, this man was an American. "About thirty-five years old" with "an assumed name"—well, then, call him C. Green as he called himself ironically in the hotel register. C. Green, the unidentified American, "fell or jumped," then, "yesterday at noon . . . in Brooklyn"—worth nine lines of print in today's *Times*—one of seven thousand who died yesterday upon this continent—one of three hundred and fifty who died yesterday in this very city (see dense, close columns of obituaries, page 15: begin with "Aaronson," so through the alphabet to "Zorn"). C. Green came here "a week ago"——

And came from where? From the deep South, or the Mississippi Valley, or the Middle West? From Minneapolis, Bridgeport, Boston, or a little town in Old Catawba? From Scranton, Toledo, St. Louis, or the desert whiteness of Los Angeles? From the pine barrens of the Atlantic coastal plain, or from the Pacific shore?

And so—was *what*, brave Admiral Drake? Had seen, felt, heard, smelled, tasted—*what*? Had known—*what*?

Had known all our brutal violence of weather: the burned swelter of July across the nation, the smell of the slow, rank river, the mud, the bottom lands, the weed growth, and the hot, coarse, humid fragrance of the corn. The kind that says, "Jesus, but it's hot!"—pulls off his coat, and mops his face, and goes in shirt-sleeves in St. Louis, goes to August's for a Swiss on rye with mustard, and a mug of beer. The kind that says, "Damn! It's hot!" in South Carolina, slouches in shirt sleeves and straw hat down South Main Street, drops into Evans Drug Store for a dope, says to the soda jerker, "Is it hot enough fer you today,

Jim?" The kind that reads in the paper of the heat, the deaths, and the prostrations, reads it with a certain satisfaction, hangs on grimly day by day and loses sleep at night, can't sleep for heat, is tired in the morning, says, "Jesus! It can't last forever!" as heat lengthens into August, and the nation gasps for breath, and the green that was young in May now mottles, fades and bleaches, withers, goes heat-brown. Will boast of coolness in the mountains, Admiral Drake. "Always cool at night! May get a little warm around the middle of the day, but you'll sleep with blankets every night."

Then summer fades and passes, and October comes. Will smell smoke then, and feel an unsuspected sharpness, a thrill of nervous, swift elation, a sense of sadness and departure. C. Green doesn't know the reason, Admiral Drake, but lights slant and shorten in the afternoon, there is a misty pollen of old gold in light at noon, a murky redness in the lights of dusk, a frosty stillness, and the barking of the dogs; the maples flame upon the hills, the gums are burning, bronze the oak leaves, and the aspens yellow; then come the rains, the sodden dead-brown of the fallen leaves, the smoke-stark branches—and November comes.

Waiting for winter in the little towns, and winter comes. It is really the same in big towns and the cities, too, with the bleak enclosure of the winter multiplied. In the commerce of the day, engaged and furious, then darkness, and the bleak monotony of "Where shall we go? What shall we do?" The winter grips us, closes round each house—the stark, harsh light encysts us— and C. Green walks the streets. Sometimes hard lights burn on him, Admiral Drake, bleak faces stream beneath the lights, amusement signs are winking. On Broadway, the constant blaze of sterile lights; in little towns, no less, the clustered raisins of hard light on Main Street. On Broadway, swarming millions up to midnight; in little towns, hard lights and frozen silence—no one, nothing, after ten o'clock. But in the hearts of C. Greens everywhere, bleak boredom, undefined despair, and "Christ! Where shall I go now? When will winter end?"

So longs for spring, and wishes it were Saturday, brave Admiral Drake.

Saturday night arrives with the thing that we are waiting for. Oh, it will come tonight; the thing that we have been expecting all our lives will come tonight, on Saturday! On Saturday night across America we are waiting for it, and ninety million Greens go mothwise to the lights to find it. Surely it will come tonight! So Green goes out to find it, and he finds—hard lights again, saloons along Third Avenue, or the Greek's place in a little town—and then hard whiskey, gin, and drunkenness, and brawls and fights and vomit.

Sunday morning, aching head.

Sunday afternoon, and in the cities the chop-suey signs wink on and flash their sterile promises of unborn joy.

Sunday night, and the hard stars, and the bleak enclosures of our wintry weather—the buildings of old rusty brick, in cold enclosed, the fronts of old stark brown, the unpainted houses, the deserted factories, wharves, piers, warehouses, and office buildings, the tormented shabbiness of Sixth Avenues; and in the smaller towns, bleak Main Streets, desolate with shabby store fronts and be-raisined clusters of lamp standards, and in the residential streets of wooden houses (dark by ten o'clock), the moaning of stark branches, the stiff lights, limb-be-patterned, shaking at street corners. The light shines there with wintry bleakness on the clapboard front and porch of a shabby house where the policeman lives—blank and desolate upon the stuffy, boxlike little parlor where the policeman's daughter amorously receives—and *almost*—not *quite*—gives. Hot, fevered, fearful, and insatiate, it is all too close to the cold street light—too creaking, panting, flimsy-close to others in the flimsy house—too close to the policeman's solid and slow-creaking tread—yet somehow valiant, somehow strong, somehow triumphant over the stale varnish of the little parlor, the nearness of the street, the light, the creaking boughs, and papa's tread—somehow triumphant with hot panting, with rose lips and tender tongue, white underleg and tight-locked thighs—by these intimacies of fear and fragrant hot desire will beat the ashen monotone of time and even the bleak and grey duration of the winter out.

Does this surprise you, Admiral Drake?

"But Christ!"—Green leaves the house, his life is bitter with desire, the stiff light creaks. "When will it end?" thinks Green. "When will spring come?"

It comes at last unhoped for, after hoping, comes when least expected, and when given up. In March there is a day that's almost spring, and C. Green, strong with will to have it so, says, "Well, it's here"—and it is gone like smoke. You can't look spring too closely in the eye in March. Raw days return, and blown light, and gusty moanings of the wind. Then April comes, and small, soaking rain. The air is wet and raw and chilled, but with a smell of spring now, a smell of earth, of grass exploding in small patches, here and there a blade, a bud, a leaf. And spring comes, marvelous, for a day or two—"It's here!" Green thinks. "It's here at last!"—and he is wrong again. It goes, chill days and greyness and small, soaking rains return. Green loses hope. "There is no spring!" he says. "You never get spring any more; you jump from winter into summer—we'll have summer now and the hot weather before you know it."

Then spring comes—explodes out of the earth in a green radiance—comes up overnight! It's April twenty-eighth—the

361

tree there in the city backyard is smoke-yellow, feathered with the striplings of young leaf! It's April twenty-ninth—the leaf, the yellow, and the smoke have thickened overnight. April thirtieth—you can watch it grow and thicken with your eye! Then May the first—the tree's in leaf now, almost full and dense, young, feather-fresh! The whole spring has exploded from the earth!

All's explosive with us really, Admiral Drake—spring, the brutal summer, frost, October, February in Dakota with fifty-one below, spring floods, two hundred drowning along Ohio bottoms, in Missouri, in New England, all through Pennsylvania, Maryland, and Tennessee. Spring shot at us overnight, and everything with us is vast, explosive, floodlike. A few hundred dead in floods, a hundred in a wave of heat, twelve thousand in a year by murder, thirty thousand with the motor car—it all means nothing here. Floods like this would drown out France; death like this would plunge England in black mourning; but in America a few thousand C. Greens more or less, drowned, murdered, killed by motor cars, or dead by jumping out of windows on their heads—well, it just means nothing to us—the next flood, or next week's crop of death and killings, wash it out. We do things on a large scale, Admiral Drake.

The tar-smell in the streets now, children shouting, and the smell of earth; the sky shell-blue and faultless, a sapphire sparkle everywhere; and in the air the brave stick-candy whippings of a flag. C. Green thinks of the baseball games, the raw-hide arm of Lefty Grove, the resilient crack of ashwood on the horsehide ball, the waiting pockets of the well-oiled mitts, the warm smell of the bleachers, the shouted gibes of shirt-sleeved men, the sprawl and monotone of inning after inning. (Baseball's a dull game, really; that's the reason that it is so good. We do not love the game so much as we love the sprawl and drowse and shirt-sleeved apathy of it.) On Saturday afternoon, C. Green goes out to the ball park and sits there in the crowd, awaiting the sudden sharpness and the yell of crisis. Then the game ends and the crowd flows out across the green turf of the playing field. Sunday, Green spends the day out in the country in his flivver, with a girl.

Then summer comes again, heat-blazing summer, humid, murked with mist, sky-glazed with brutal weariness—and C. Green mops his face and sweats and says, "Jesus! Will it ever end?"

This, then, is C. Green, "thirty-five years old"—"unidentified" —and an American. In what way an American? In what way different from the men *you* knew, old Drake?

When the ships bore home again and Cape St. Vincent blazed in Spaniard's eye—or when old Drake was returning with his men, beating coastwise from strange seas abreast, past the Scilly

Isles toward the slant of evening fields, chalk cliffs, the harbor's arms, the town's sweet cluster and the spire—where was Green?

When, in red-oak thickets at the break of day, coon-skinned, the huntsmen of the wilderness lay for bear, heard arrows rattling in the laurel leaves, the bullets' whining *plunk*, and waited with cocked musket by the tree—where was Green?

Or when, with strong faces turning toward the setting sun, hawk-eyed and Indian-visaged men bore gunstocks on the western trails and sternly heard the fierce war-whoops around the Painted Buttes—where, then, was Green?

Was never there with Drake's men in the evening when the sails stood in from the Americas! Was never there beneath the Spaniard's swarthy eye at Vincent's Cape! Was never there in the red-oak thicket in the morning! Was never there to hear the war-cries round the Painted Buttes!

No, no. He was no voyager of unknown seas, no pioneer of western trails. He was life's little man, life's nameless cipher, life's manswarm atom, life's American—and now he lies disjected and exploded on a street in Brooklyn!

He was a dweller in mean streets, was Green, a man-mote in the jungle of the city, a resident of grimy steel and stone, a mole who burrowed in rusty brick, a stunned spectator of enormous salmon-colored towers, hued palely with the morning. He was a renter of shabby wooden houses in a little town, an owner of a raw new bungalow on the outskirts of the town. He was a waker in bleak streets at morning, an alarm-clock watcher, saying, "Jesus, I'll be late!"—a fellow who took short cuts through the corner lot, behind the advertising signs; a fellow used to concrete horrors of hot day and blazing noon; a man accustomed to the tormented hodgepodge of our architectures, used to broken pavements, ash cans, shabby store fronts, dull green paint, the elevated structure, grinding traffic, noise, and streets be-tortured with a thousand bleak and dismal signs. He was accustomed to the gas tanks going out of town, he was an atom of machinery in an endless flow, going, stopping, going to the winking of the lights; he tore down concrete roads on Sundays, past the hot-dog stands and filling stations; he would return at darkness; hunger lured him to the winking splendor of chop-suey signs; and midnight found him in The Coffee Pot, to prowl above a mug of coffee, tear a coffee-cake in fragments, and wear away the slow grey ash of time and boredom with other men in grey hats and with skins of tallow-grey, at Joe the Greek's.

C. Green could read (which Drake could not), but not too accurately; could write, too (which the Spaniard couldn't), but not too well. C. Green had trouble over certain words, spelled them out above the coffee mug at midnight, with a furrowed brow, slow-shaping lips, and "Jesus!" when news stunned him—for he read the news. Preferred the news with pictures, too, girls with voluptuous legs crossed sensually, dresses above the knees, and plump dolls' faces full of vacant lechery. Green liked news "hot"—not as Fox knows it, not subtly sniffing with strange-scornful nostrils for the news *behind* the news—but straight from the shoulder—socko!—biff!—straight off the griddle, with lots of mustard, shapely legs, roadside wrecks and mutilated bodies, gangsters' molls and gunmen's hide-outs, tallow faces of the night that bluntly stare at flashlight lenses—this and talk of "heart-balm," "love-thief," "sex-hijacker"—all of this liked Green.

Yes, Green liked the news—and now, a bit of news himself (nine lines of print in *Times*), has been disjected and exploded on a Brooklyn pavement!

Well, such was our friend, C. Green, who read, but not too well; and wrote, but not too easily; who smelled, but not too strongly; felt, but not too deeply; saw, but not too clearly—yet had smelled the tar in May, smelled the slow, rank yellow of the rivers, and the clean, coarse corn; had seen the slants of evening on the hill-flanks in the Smokies, and the bronze swell of the earth, the broad, deep red of Pennsylvania barns, proud-portioned and as dominant across the fields as bulls; had felt the frost and silence in October; had heard the whistles of the train wail back in darkness, and the horns of New Year's Eve, and —"Jesus! There's another year gone by! What now?"

No Drake was he, no Spaniard, no coon-skin cap, no strong face burning west. Yet, in some remote and protoplasmic portion, he was a little of each of these. A little Scotch, perhaps, was Green, a little Irish, English, Spanish even, and some German—a little of each part, all compacted and exploded into nameless atom of America!

No. Green—poor little Green—was not a man like Drake. He was just a cinder out of life—for the most part, a thinker of base thoughts, a creature of unsharpened, coarse perceptions. He was meager in the hips, he did not have much juice or salt in him. Drake gnawed the beef from juicy bones in taverns, drank tankards of brown ale, swore salty curses through his whiskers, wiped his mouth with the back of his hard hand, threw the beef bone to his dog, and pounded with his tankard for more ale. Green ate in cafeterias, prowled at midnight over coffee and a doughnut or a sugar-coated bun, went to the chop-suey joint on Saturday nights and swallowed chow mein, noodle soup, and rice. Green's mouth was mean and thin and common, it ran to looseness and a snarl; his skin was grey and harsh and dry; his eyes were dull and full of fear. Drake was self-contained: the world his oyster, seas his pastures, mighty distances his wings. His eyes were sea-pale (like the eyes of Fox); his ship was England. Green had no ship, he had a motor car, and tore down concrete roads on Sunday, and halted with the lights against him with the million other cinders hurtling through hot space. Green walked on level concrete sidewalks and on pavements grey, through hot and grimy streets past rusty tenements. Drake set his sails against the west, he strode the buoyant, sea-washed decks, he took the Spaniard and his gold, and at the end he stood in to the sweet enfoldments of the spire, the clustered town, the emerald fields that slope to Plymouth harbor—then Green came!

We who never saw brave Drake can have no difficulty conjuring up an image of the kind of man he was. With equal ease we can imagine the bearded Spaniard, and almost hear his swarthy oaths. But neither Drake nor Spaniard could ever have imagined Green. Who could have foreseen him, this cipher of America, exploded now upon a street in Brooklyn?

Behold him, Admiral Drake! Observe the scene now! Listen to the people! Here is something strange as the Armadas, the gold-laden cargoes of the bearded Spaniards, the vision of unfound Americas!

What do you see here, Admiral Drake?

⚓

Well, first, a building—your own hotel—such a building as the folk of Plymouth never saw. A great block of masonry, pale-hued, grimy-white, fourteen stories tall, stamped in an unvarying pattern with many windows. Sheeted glass below, the store front piled with medicines and toilet articles, perfumes, cosmetics, health contrivances. Within, a soda fountain, Admiral Drake. The men in white with monkey caps, soda jerkers sullen with perpetual overdriven irritation. Beneath the counter, pools of sloppy water, filth, and unwashed dishes. Across the counter, Jewesses with fat rouged lips consuming ice cream sodas and pimento sandwiches.

Outside upon the concrete sidewalk lies the form of our exploded friend, C. Green. A crowd has gathered round—taxi drivers, passers-by, hangers-on about the subway station, people working in the neighborhood, and the police. No one has dared to touch exploded Green as yet—they stand there in a rapt and fascinated circle, looking at him.

Not much to look at either, Admiral Drake; not even those who trod your gory decks would call the sight a pretty one. Our friend has landed on his head—"taken a nose dive," as we say—and smashed his brains out at the iron base of the second lamp post from the corner. (It is the same lamp post as heretofore described, to be found throughout America—a "standard," standardized, supporting five hard grapes of frosted glass.)

So here Green lies, on the concrete sidewalk all disjected. No head is left, the head is gone now, head's exploded; only brains are left. The brains are pink, and almost bloodless, Admiral Drake. (There's not much blood here—we shall tell you why.) But brains exploded are somewhat like pale sausage meat, fresh-ground. Brains are stuck hard to the lamp post, too; there is a certain driven emphasis about them, as if they had been shot hydraulically out of a force-hose against the post.

The head, as we have said, is gone completely; a few fragments of the skull are scattered round—but of the face, the features, forehead—nothing! They have all been blown *out,* as by some inner explosion. Nothing is left but the back of the skull, which curiously remains, completely hollowed out and vacant, and curved over, like the rounded handle of a walking stick.

The body, five feet eight or nine of it, of middling weight, is lying—we were going to say "face downward"; had we not better say "stomach downward"?—on the sidewalk. It is well-dressed, too, in cheap, neatly pressed, machine-made clothes: tan shoes and socks with a clocked pattern, suit of a light texture, brownish red in hue, a neat canary-colored shirt with attached collar—obviously C. Green had a nice feeling for proprieties! As for the body itself, save for a certain indefinable and curiously "disjected" quality, one could scarcely tell that every bone in it is broken. The hands are still spread out, half-folded and half-clenched, with a still-warm and startling eloquence of recent life. (It happened just four minutes ago!)

Well, where's the blood, then, Drake? You're used to blood; you'd like to know. Well, you've heard of casting bread upon the waters, Drake, and having it return—but never yet, I'll vow, of casting blood upon the streets—and having it run away—and then come back to you! But here it comes now, down the street—down Apple Street, round the corner into Hay, across the street now toward C. Green, the lamp post, and the crowd!—a young Italian youth, blunt-featured, low-browed, and bewildered, his black eyes blank with horror, tongue mumbling thickly, arm held firmly by a policeman, suit and shirt all drenched with blood, and face be-spattered with it! A stir of sudden interest in the crowd, sharp nudges, low-toned voices whispering:

"Here he is! Th' guy that 'got it'! . . . Sure, that's him—you know him, that Italian kid that works inside in the newsstand—he was standin' *deh* beside the post! Sure, *that's* the guy!—talkin' to anotheh guy—he got it all! *That's* the reason you didn't see more blood—*this* guy got it!—Sure! The guy just missed him by six inches!—Sure! I'm tellin' you I *saw* it, ain't I? I looked up an' saw him in the air! He'd a hit this guy, but when he saw that he was goin' to hit the lamp post, he put out his

366

hands an' tried to keep away! *That's* the reason that he didn't hit this guy! . . . But this guy heard him when he hit, an' turned around—and zowie!—he got all of it right in his face!"

And another, whispering and nudging, nodding toward the horror-blank, thick-mumbling Italian boy: "Jesus! Look at th' guy, will yah! . . . He don't know what he's doing! . . . He don't know yet what happened to him! . . . Sure! He got it *all.* I tell yuh! He was standin' deh beside the post, wit a package undehneath one ahm—an' when it happened—when he got it— he just stahted runnin' . . . He don't know yet what's happened! . . . That's what I'm tellin' yuh—th' guy just stahted runnin' when he got it."

And one policeman (to another): ". . . Sure, I yelled to Pat to stop him. He caught up with him at Borough Hall. . . . He just kept on runnin'—he don't know yet what happened to him."

And the Italian youth, thick-mumbling: ". . . Jeez! W'at happened? . . . Jeez! . . . I was standin' talkin' to a guy—I heard it hit. . . . Jeez! . . . W'at happened, anyway? . . . I got it all oveh me! . . . Jeez! . . . I just stahted runnin' . . . Jeez! I'm sick!"

Voices: "Here, take 'im into the drug store! . . . Wash 'im off! . . . That guy needs a shot of liquor! . . . Sure! Take him into the drug stoeh *deh*! . . . *They'll* fix him up!"

The plump, young, rather effeminate, but very intelligent young Jew who runs the newsstand in the corridor, talking to everyone around him, excitedly and indignantly: ". . . Did I *see* it? Listen! I saw *everything*! I was coming across the street, looked up, and saw him in the air! . . . *See* it? . . . *Listen!* If someone had taken a big ripe watermelon and dropped it on the street from the twelfth floor you'd have some idea what it was like! . . . *See* it! *I'll* tell the world I saw it! I don't want to see anything like *that* again!" Then excitedly, with a kind of hysterical indignation: "Shows no consideration for other people, that's all *I've* got to say! If a man is going to do a thing like that, why does he pick a place like *this*—one of the busiest corners in Brooklyn? . . . How did *he* know he wouldn't hit someone? Why, if that boy had been standing six inches nearer to the post, he'd have killed him, as sure as you live! . . . And here he does it right in front of all these people who have to look at it! It shows he had no consideration for other people! A man who'd do a thing like that. . . ."

(Alas, poor Jew! As if C. Green, now past considering, had considered nice "considerations.")

A taxi driver, impatiently: "That's what I'm tellin' yuh! . . . I watched him for five minutes before he jumped. He crawled out on the window sill an' stood there for *five* minutes, makin' up his mind! . . . Sure, I saw him! Lots of people saw him!" Impatiently, irritably: "Why didn't we *do* somethin' to stop him? F'r Chri' sake, what was there to do? A guy who'd do a thing like that is nuts to start with! You don't think he'd listen to anything *we* had to say, do you? . . . Sure, we *did* yell at him! . . . Jesus! . . . We was almost *afraid* to yell at him—we made motions to him to get back—tried to hold his attention while the cops sneaked round the corner into the hotel. . . . Sure, the cops got there just a second after he jumped—I don't know if he jumped when he heard 'em comin', or what happened, but Christ!—he stood there gettin' ready for five minutes while we watched!"

And a stocky little Czech-Bohemian, who works in the delicatessen-fruit store on the corner, one block down: "Did I *hear* it! Say, you could have heard it for six blocks! Sure! *Everybody* heard it! The minute that I heard it, I knew what had happened, too! I come runnin'!"

People press and shuffle in the crowd. A man comes round the corner, presses forward to get a better look, runs into a little fat, bald-headed man in front of him who is staring at the Thing with a pale, sweating, suffering, fascinated face, by accident knocks off the little fat man's straw hat. The new straw hat hits the pavement dryly, the little fat, bald-headed man scrambles for it, clutches it, and turns around on the man who has knocked it off, both of them stammering frantic apologies:

"Oh, excuse me! . . . 'Scuse me! . . . 'Scuse me! . . . Sorry!"

"Quite all right. . . . All right! . . . All right."

Observe now, Admiral, with what hypnotic concentration the people are examining the grimy-white façade of your hotel. Watch their faces and expressions. Their eyes go traveling upward slowly—up—up—up. The building seems to widen curiously, to be distorted, to flare out wedgelike till it threatens to annihilate the sky, overwhelm the will, and crush the spirit. (These optics, too, American, Admiral Drake.) The eyes continue on past story after story up the wall until they finally arrive and come to rest with focal concentration on that single open window twelve floors up. It is no jot different from all the other windows, but now the vision of the crowd is fastened on it with a fatal and united interest. And after staring at it fixedly, the eyes come traveling slowly down again—down—down—down—the faces strained a little, mouths all slightly puckered as if something set the teeth on edge—and slowly, with fascinated measurement—down—down—down—until the eyes reach sidewalk, lamp post, and—the Thing again.

The pavement finally halts all, stops all, answers all. It is the American pavement, Admiral Drake, our universal city sidewalk, a wide, hard stripe of grey-white cement, blocked accurately with dividing lines. It is the hardest, coldest, cruellest, most impersonal pavement in the world: all of the indifference, the atomic desolation, the exploded nothingness of one hundred million nameless "Greens" is in it.

In Europe, Drake, we find worn stone, all hollowed out and rubbed to rounded edges. For centuries the unknown lives of men now buried touched and wore this stone, and when we see it something stirs within our hearts, and something strange and dark and passionate moves our souls, and—"They were here!" we say.

Not so, the streets, the sidewalks, the paved places of America. Has *man* been here? No. Only unnumbered nameless Greens have swarmed and passed here, and none has left a mark.

Did ever the eye go seaward here with searching for the crowded sail, with longing for the strange and unknown coasts of Spain? Did ever beauty here come home to the heart and eyes? Did ever, in the thrusting crowd, eye look to eye, and face to face, and heart to heart, and know the moment of their meeting—stop and pause, and be oblivious in this place, and make one spot of worn pavement sacred stone? You won't believe it, Admiral Drake, but it is so—these things *have* happened on the pavements of America. But, as you see yourself, they have not left their mark.

You, old Drake, when last your fellow townsmen saw you at the sailing of the ships, walked with the crowd along the quay, past the spire and cluster of the town, down to the cool lap of the water; and from your deck, as you put out, you watched the long, white, fading arm of your own coast. And in the town that you had left were streets still haunted by your voice. There was your worn tread upon the pavement, there the tavern table dented where you banged your tankard down. And in the evening, when the ships were gone, men waited for your return.

But no return is here among us in America. Here are no streets still haunted by departed men. Here is no street at all, as you knew streets. Here are just our cement Mobways, unannealed by time! No place in Mobway bids you pause, old Drake. No spot in Mobway bids you hold your mind a moment in reflection, saying: "He was here!" No square of concrete slab says: "Stay, for I was built by men." Mobway never knew the hand of man, as your streets did. Mobway was laid down by great machines, for one sole purpose—to unimpede and hurry up the passing of the feet.

Where did Mobway come from? What produced it?

It came from the same place where all our mob ways come from—from Standard Concentrated Production Units of America, No. 1. This is where all our streets, sidewalks, and lamp posts (like the one on which Green's brains are spattered) come from, where all our white-grimy bricks (like those of which your hotel is constructed) come from, where the red façades of our standard-unit tobacco stores (like the one across the street) come from, where our motor cars come from, where

369

our drug stores and our drug store windows and displays come from, where our soda fountains (complete, with soda jerkers attached) come from, where our cosmetics, toilet articles, and the fat, rouged lips of our Jewesses come from, where our soda water, slops and syrups, steamed spaghetti, ice cream, and pimento sandwiches come from, where our clothes, our hats (neat, standard stamps of grey), our faces (also stamps of grey, not always neat), our language, conversation, sentiments, feelings, and opinions come from. All these things are made for us by Standard Concentrated Production Units of America, No. 1.

So here we are, then, Admiral Drake. You see the street, the sidewalk, the front of your hotel, the constant stream of motor cars, the drug store and the soda fountain, the tobacco store, the traffic lights, the cops in uniform, the people streaming in and out of the subway, the rusty, pale-hued jungle of the buildings, old and new, high and low. There is no better place to see it, Drake. For this is Brooklyn—which means ten thousand streets and blocks like this one. Brooklyn, Admiral Drake, is the Standard Concentrated Chaos No 1 of the Whole Universe. That is to say, it has no size, no shape, no heart, no joy, no hope, no aspiration, no center, no eyes, no soul, no purpose, no direction, and no anything—just Standard Concentrated Units everywhere—exploding in all directions for an unknown number of square miles like a completely triumphant Standard Concentrated Blot upon the Face of the Earth. And here, right in the middle—no, that is wrong, for Standard Concentrated Blots don't have a middle—but, if not in the middle, at least right slap-bang out in the open, upon a minute portion of this magnificent Standard Concentrated Blot, where all the Standard Concentrated Blotters can stare at him, and with the brains completely out of him——

—Lies Green!

And this is bad—most bad—oh, *very* bad—and should not be allowed! For, as our young Jewish friend has just indignantly proclaimed, it "shows no consideration for other people"—which means, for other Standard Concentrated Blotters. Green has no right to go falling in this fashion in a public place. He has no right to take unto himself any portion of this Standard Concentrated Blot, however small. He has no business *being* where he is at all. A Standard Concentrated Blotter is not supposed to *be* places, but to *go* places.

You see, dear Admiral, this is not a street to amble in, to ride along, to drift through. It is a channel—in the words of the Standard Concentrated Blotter-Press, an "artery." This means that it is not a place where one drives, but a place where one is driven—not really a street at all, but a kind of tube for a projectile, a kind of groove for millions and millions of projectiles, all driven past incessantly, all beetling onward, bearing briefly white slugged blurs of driven flesh.

As for the sidewalk, this Standard Concentrated Mobway is not a place to walk on, really. (Standard Concentrated Blotters have forgotten how to walk.) It is a place to swarm on, to weave on, to thrust and dodge on, to scurry past on, to crowd by on. It is not a place to stand on, either. One of the earliest precepts in a Concentrated Blotter's life is: "Move on there! Where th' hell d'you think you are, anyway—in a cow pasture?" And, most certainly, it is not a place to lie on, to sprawl out on.

But look at Green! Just *look* at him! No wonder the Jewish youth is angry with him!

Green has willfully and deliberately violated every Standard Concentrated Principle of Blotterdom. He has not only gone and dashed his brains out, but he has done it in a public place— upon a piece of Standard Concentrated Mobway. He has messed up the sidewalk, messed up another Standard Concentrated Blotter, stopped traffic, taken people from their business, upset the nerves of his fellow Blotters—and now *lies* there, all *sprawled* out, in a place where he has no right to *be*. And, to make his crime unpardonable, C. Green has——

—Come to Life!

Consider *that*, old Drake! We can understand some measure of *your* strangeness, because we heard you swearing in the tavern and saw your sails stand to the west. Can you now do the same for *us*? Consider strangeness, Drake—and look at Green! For you have heard it said by your own countryman, and in your living generation: "The times have been that, when the brains were out, the man would die." But now, old Drake, what hath Time wrought? There is surely here some strangeness in us that you could never have foretold. For the brains are "out" now—and the man has——

—Come to Life!

What's that, Admiral? You do not understand it? Small wonder, though it's really very simple:

For just ten minutes since, C. Green was a Concentrated Blotter like the rest of us. Ten minutes since, he, too, might hurry in and out of the subway, thrust and scurry on the pavement, go hurtling past with whited blur in one of our beetles of machinery, a nameless atom, cipher, cinder, swarming with the rest of us, just another "guy" like a hundred million other "guys." But now, observe him! No longer is he just "another guy"—already he has become a "special guy"—he has become "*The* Guy." C. Green at last has turned into a—*Man!*

Four hundred years ago, brave Admiral Drake, if we had seen you lying on your deck, your bronze gone pale and cold, imbrued in your own blood, and hewn to the middle by the Spaniards' steel, we could have understood that, for there was

371

blood in you. But Green—this Concentrated Blotter of ten minutes since—made in our own image, shaped in our own dust, compacted of the same grey stuff of which our own lives are compacted, and filled, we thought, with the same Standard Concentration of embalming fluid that fills *our* veins—oh, Drake, we did not know the fellow had such *blood* in him! We could not have thought it was so red, so rich, and so abundant!

Poor, shabby, and corrupted cipher! Poor, nameless, and exploded atom! Poor little guy! He fills us Concentrated Blotters of the Universe with fear, with shame, with awe, with pity, and with terror—for we see ourselves in him. If he was a man with blood in him, then so are we! If he, in the midst of his always-driven life, could at last be driven to this final and defiant gesture of refusal to remain a Concentrated Blotter, then we, too, might be driven to a point of equal desperation! And there are other methods of defiance, other ways of ultimate refusal, other means of exercising one's last-remaining right of manhood—and some of them are no less terrifying to contemplate than this! So our fascinated eyes go up and up, past floor after floor of Standard Concentrated brick, and fasten on the open window where he stood—and suddenly we crane our necks along the ridges of our collars, look away with constricted faces, and taste the acrid bitterness of steel upon our lips!

It is too hard, and not to be endured—to know that little Green, speaking our own tongue and stuffed with our own stuffing, had yet concealed in him some secret, dark, and frightful thing more terrible than anything that we have ever known—that he bore within him some black and hideous horror, some depth of madness or of courage, and could stand *there*—upon the sheer and nauseating verge of that grey window ledge for five full minutes—and know the thing he was about to do—and tell himself he *must* now!—that he *had* to!—that the compulsion of every horror-fascinated eye down in the gulf below had *now* made escape impossible—and then, horror-sick past all regeneration, see, too, before he jumped, his fall, the downward-hurtling plunge, and his own exploded body—feel the bones crack and fly apart, and the brutal obliteration of the instant when his brains would shoot out against the lamp post—and even while his soul drew back from that sheer verge of imagined terror, shame, and unutterable self-loathing, crying, "I cannot do it!"—then jumped!

And *we*, brave Drake? We try to see it, but we cannot see. We try to fathom it, but we cannot plunge. We try to comprehend the hell of hells, the hundred lives of horror, madness, anguish, and despair that were exhausted *in five minutes* by that shabby creature crouched there on the window ledge. But we cannot understand, or look at it any longer. It is too hard, too hard, and not to be endured. We turn away with nausea, hollowness, blind fear, and unbelief within us.

One man stares, cranes his neck, wets his lips, and whispers: "Jesus! To do a thing like that takes *guts*!"

Another, harshly: "Nah! It don't take guts! A guy who'd do a thing like that is crazy! He don't know what he's doin' to begin with!"

And others, doubtfully, half-whispering, with eyes focused on the ledge: "But Jesus!"

A taxi driver, turning away and moving toward his cab, with an attempt at casual indifference that does not ring entirely true: "Oh, well! Just another guy, I guess!"

Then one man, turning to his companion with a little puckered smile: "Well, what about it, Al? You still feel like eating?"

And his companion, quietly: "Eating, hell! I feel like two or three stiff shots of rye! Come on, let's go around to Steve's!"

They go. The Concentrated Blotters of the World cannot abide it. They must somehow blot it out.

So a policeman comes around the corner now with an old tarpaulin, with which he covers the No-Head. The crowd remains. Then the green wagon from the morgue. The Thing, tarpaulin and all, is pushed into it. It drives away. A policeman with thick-soled boots scuffs and pushes skull-pieces and brain-fragments into the gutter. Someone comes with sawdust, strews it. Someone from the drug store with formaldehyde. Later, someone with a hose and water. From the subway come an adolescent boy and girl with the hard, tough faces of the city; they walk past it, deliberately and arrogantly step among it, look at the lamp post, then at each other, and laugh!

All's over now, all's gone, the crowd's departed. Something else remains. It cannot be forgotten. There's a sick, humid smell upon the air, what was light and clear and crystal has gone out of day, and something thick and glutinous—half taste, half smell, and all impalpable—remains upon your tongue.

There would have been a time and place for such a thing, brave Admiral Drake, if he, our fellow Green, had only fallen as a hollow man and landed dryly, or if he had opened to disperse a grey embalming fluid in the gutter. It would have been all right if he had just been blown away like an old paper, or if he had been swept aside like remnants of familiar litter, and then subsumed into the Standard Concentrated stuff from which he came. But C. Green would not have it so. He exploded to drench our common substance of viscous grey with the bright indecency of blood, to resume himself from number, to become before our eyes a Man, and to identify a single spot of all our general Nothingness with the unique passion, the awful terror, and the dignity of Death.

So, Admiral Drake—"an unidentified man fell or jumped yesterday at noon" from a window of your own hotel. That was the news. Now you've had the story.

We are "the hollow men, the hollow men"? Brave Admiral, do not be too sure.

Chapter Thirty

The Anodyne

Fox read it instantly, the proud nose sniffing upward sharply: —"man fell or jumped . . . Admiral Francis Drake Hotel . . . Brooklyn." The sea-pale eyes took it in at once, and went on to more important things.

Fox was cold, then? Hard? Selfish? Lacking in understanding? Unsympathetic? Unimaginative? By no means.

Could not have known Green, then? Was too much the patrician to know Green? Was too high, too rare, too subtle, too fine-fibered to know Green? None of these.

Fox knew everything, or almost everything. (If there's a lack here, we will smell it out.) Fox had been born with everything, and had learned much, yet his learning had not made him mad, or ever blunted the keen blade of knowing. He saw all things as they were: had never (in his mind and heart) called man a "white man" yet, because Fox saw man was not "white man"— man was pink man tinged with sallow, man was sallow tinged with grey, man was pink-brown, red-bronze, or white-red-sallow, but not white.

So Fox (in mind and heart) would call it as it was. This was the boy's straight eye. Yet his clarities were obscured for other men. His straightness was thought cunning by crude-cunning rogues, his warmth seemed ice to all the hearty-false, and to the false-sincere Fox was a twister. Not one of these things was true of him.

Fox knew Green all right—knew him better than we, the Concentrated Blotters of Green's ilk. For, being of the ilk, we

374

grow confused, struggle with Green (so with ourselves), argue, debate, deny, are tarred with the same brush, and so lose judgment.

Not so, Fox. Not of Green's ilk, yet was he still of the whole family of earth. Fox knew at once that Green had blood in him. Fox placed him instantly: saw sky above him, Admiral Drake Hotel behind him, lamp post, pavement, people, Brooklyn corner, cops, rouged Jewesses, the motor cars, the subway entrance, and exploded brains—and, had he been there, would have said in a low, somewhat puzzled, and abstracted tone:

"Oh. . . . I see."

Would have seen, too, my mad masters; never doubt it. Would have seen clearly and seen whole, without our agony, without confusion, without struggling with the surface of each brick, each square inch of concrete pavement, each scale of rust upon the fire escapes, the raw-green paint of the lamp post, the sterile red-front brightness of the cigar store, the shapes of windows, ledges, cornices, and doorways, the way the shops were set into old houses along the street, all the heartsick ugliness exploded into the nothingness of Brooklyn. Fox would have seen it instantly, without having to struggle to see all, know all, hold all clearly, singly, permanently, in the burning crystal of the brain.

And if Fox had lived in Brooklyn, he would have got much else as well—got it clear and straight—while we were trying to make our maddened ears spread out like funnels to absorb it—every whispered word in Flatbush, every rhythmic-creaking spring in the back bedrooms of whore's Sand Street (by old yellow shades concealed), every barker's cry in Coney, all the jargons of each tenement from Red Hook to Brownsville. Yes, while we wrestled with our five senses there in Jungletown, our tormented brain caught in the brutal chaos of "Gewirr! Gewirr!"—Fox would have got it all, without madness, agony, or the fevered eye, and would have murmured:

"Oh. . . . I see."

Wherever he was, Fox was one to get the little things—the little, most important things that tell you everything. He never picked a little thing because it was a little thing, to show he was a devilish cunning, subtle, rare, and most aesthetic fellow: he picked a little thing because it was the *right* thing—and he never missed.

Fox was a great fox, and a genius. He was no little Pixy of the Aesthetes. He did not write nine-page reviews on "How Chaplin Uses Hands in Latest Picture"—how it really was not slap-stick, but the tragedy of Lear in modern clothes; or on how Enters enters; or on how Crane's poetry can only be defined, reviewed, and generally exposited in terms of mathematical formulae—ahem! ahem, now!—as:

$$\frac{\sqrt{an + pxt}}{237} = \frac{n - F_3(B^{18} + 11)}{2}$$

(Bring on the Revolution, Comrades; it is Time!)

Fox did not go around making discoveries nine years after Boob McNutt had made them. He didn't find out that Groucho was funny seven years too late, and then inform the public *why* he was. He did not write: "The opening *Volte* of the Ballet is the historic method amplified in history, the production of historic fullness without the literary cliché of the historic spate." He had no part in any of the fine horse-manure with which we have allowed ourselves to be bored, maddened, whiff-sniffed, hound-and-hornered, nationed, new-republicked, dialed, spectatored, mercuried, storied, anviled, new-massed, new-yorkered, vogued, vanity-faired, timed, broomed, transitioned, and generally shat upon by the elegant, refined, and snobified Concentrated Blotters of the Arts. He had nothing to do with any of the doltish gibberings, obscene quackeries, phoney passions, and six-months-long religions of fools, joiners, and fashion-apes a trifle brighter and quicker on the uptake than the fools, joiners, and fashion-apes they prey upon. He was none of your little franky-panky, seldesey-weldesey, cowley-wowley, tatsey-watesy, hicksy-picksy, wilsony-pilsony, jolasy-wolasy, steiny-weiny, goldy-woldly, sneer-puss fellows. Neither, in more-conventional guise, was he one of your groupy-croupy, cliquey-triquey, meachy-teachy, devoto-bloato wire-pullers and back-scratchers of the world.

No, Fox was none of these. He looked at the whole thing, whatever it was, and got it straight, said slowly, "Oh. . . . I see," then like a fox would begin to pick up things around the edges. An eye here, a nose there, a cleft of lip, a length of chin elsewhere—and suddenly, within the frame of a waiter's face, he would see the grave, thought-lonely visage of Erasmus. Fox would turn away reflectively and drink his drink, glance casually from time to time as the man approached him, catch his coat lapels and turn, stare fixedly at the waiter's face again, turn back to the table, turn again and stare, bend over, staring right up into the waiter's face:

The waiter, troubled now, and smiling doubtfully: "Sir? . . . Is there anything wrong, sir?"

Fox, slowly, almost in a whisper: "Did you ever hear of— Erasmus?"

And the waiter, still smiling, but more doubtfully than ever: "No sir."

And Fox, turning away and whispering hoarsely with astounded conviction: "Simply *astonishing!*"

376

Or, again, it will be a hat-check girl at the place where he has lunch—a little tough-voiced, pert, hard-boiled girl. Fox will suddenly stop one day and look at her keenly with his sea-pale eyes, and will give her a dollar as he goes out.

"But Fox," friends will protest, "in God's name, why did you give that girl a dollar?"

"But *isn't* she the *nicest* person?" Fox will say, in a low and earnest whisper.

And they will stare at him in blank amazement. *That* girl! That little tough, gold-digging, hard-boiled—oh, well, what's the use? They give it up! Rather than shatter the illusions and wound the innocence of this trusting child, they'll hold their tongues and leave him to his dream.

And she, the little hard-boiled hat-check girl, in a hoarse, confiding tone to the other hat-check girl, excitedly: "Say! Do you know that guy that comes in here every day for lunch—the queer one that always orders guinea hen—an' that didn't usta wanna let us have his hat at all?"

The other, nodding: "Sure, *I* know! He usta try to wear it w'ile he's eatin'! You awmost had to throw 'im down an' take it from 'im befoeh he'd letcha have it."

She, rapidly, nodding: "Yeah! That's him!" Then, lowering her voice to an excited whisper: "Well, y'know, he's been givin' me a dollah tip every day for the last mont'!"

The other, staring, stunned: "G'wan!"

She: "Honest t' Gawd!"

The other: "Has he made any passes atcha yet?—any wisecracks?—any funny tawk?"

She, with a puzzled look in her eye: "That's the funny paht of it—I can't make 'im out! He tawks funny awright—but—he don't mean what I thought he did. The first time he said somethin' I thought he was goin' t' be fresh. He comes up t' get his hat one day, an' stands lookin' at me with that funny look until I got the willies. So I says, 'So what?' 'Married?' he says—just like that. Just stands lookin' at me an' says, 'Married?' "

The other: "Gee! That *was* fresh!" Eagerly: "Well, go on— w'atcha say to 'im? W'atcha tell 'im?"

She: "Well, I says to myse'f, 'Oh, ho! I knew *this* was comin'! This dollah-a-day stuff can't keep up forever! Well,' I thinks, 'you can't hang onto a good thing all yoeh life!'—so I decides to let 'im have it befoeh he has the chanct to staht gettin' funny. So I lies to 'im: 'Sure!' I says, an' looks 'im right in the eye—'I'm *good* an' married! Ain't *you?*' I thought that ought to hold 'im."

The other: "An' w'at did he say t' *that?*"

She: "He just stood lookin' at me with that funny look. Then he shook his head at me—as if I'd *done* somep'n—as if it was *my* fault—as if he was *disgusted* wit' me. 'Yes,' he says, an' gets his hat, an' leaves his dollah, an' walks out. Tie *that* one down! Well, I gets to thinkin' it oveh, an' I figure that next day he's goin' t' spring it—staht givin' me the old oil about how his wife don't undehstand 'im, or how he's not livin' wit' her an' how lonesome he is—an' how about it?—can't we get togetheh some night for dinneh?"

And number two, rapt: "So w'at happens?"

And she: "When he comes to get his hat next day he just stands there lookin' at me for a long time in that funny way of his that used to get me noivous—as if I'd *done* somep'n—so I says again, 'So what?' An' he says in that funny voice—it's so low sometimes you can't hahdly hear it—he says, 'Any children?'—just like *that*! Gee, it was funny! It wasn't what I expected 'im t' say at all! I didn't know what t' say, so fine'ly I says, 'No.' So, wit' that, he just stands there lookin' at me, an' he shakes his head at me like he was disgusted wit' me for not havin' any. So then I gets sore, I forget I'm not married—the way he shakes his head at me as if it was *my* fault for not havin' any children gets me good an' sore—an' I says to 'im: 'So *what*? What if I *haven't*? Have *you*?' "

Number two, now fascinated: "So w'at happens? W'at does he tell yah?"

She: "He stands lookin' at me, an' says, 'Five!'—just like that. An' then he shakes his head again—'All *women*,' he says, as if he was disgusted wit' me—'Like *yourself*,' he says. An' then he takes his hat, an' leaves his dollah, an' walks out!"

Number two, in an aggrieved tone: "*Say-y!* who does he think he is, anyway? How does he get that way? That guy's pretty fresh, *I'd* say!"

She: "Well, I get to thinkin' about it an' I get sore. The *noive* of 'im, tawkin' about women like that! So the next day when he comes to get his hat I says: 'Listen,' I says, 'what's eatin' on you, anyway? What are yah—a woman-hatah or somep'n? Whatcha got against women, anyway? What'd they eveh do to *you*?' 'Nothing,' he says, 'nothing—except *act like women*!' Gee! The way he said that! An' stood there shakin' his head at me in that disgusted way like I'd done somep'n! He takes his hat then, leaves his dollah, an' goes out. . . . So afteh that I decide t' kid 'im along a little, seein' he's not tryin' t' get funny wit' me. So every day afteh that I make some wisecrack about women, tryin' to get a rise out of 'im, but I neveh do! Say! You *can't* get a rise outa that guy! I've tried an' I know! He don't even *know* when you're tryin' t' get a rise out of 'im! . . . So then he stahts t' ast me questions about my husband—an' gee!—was *I* embarrassed? He ast me all kinds of questions about 'im—what did he do, an' how old was he, an' where did he come from, an' was his mother livin', an' what did *he* think about women? Gee! It usta keep me busy from one day to anotheh wonderin' what he was goin' to ast me next, an' what t'say to 'im. . . . Then he stahted astin' me about my mother, an' my sisters an' brothers, an' what did *they* do, an' how old were they—an' I could tell 'im those because I knew the answers."

Number two: "An' you told 'im?"

She: "Sure. W'y not?"

Number two: "Gee, Mary, y' shouldn't do *that*! You don't know th' guy! How do you know *who* he is?"

She, abstracted, in a softer tone: "Oh, I don't know. *That* guy's all right!" With a little shrug: "*You* know! You can always tell."

Number two: "Yeah, but all the same, y' neveh can tell! You don't know anything about th' guy! I kid 'em along, but I neveh tell 'em anything."

She: "Oh, sure. *I* know. I do the same. Only, it's diff'rent wit' this guy. Gee, it's funny! I musta told 'em awmost everything—all about mama, an' Pat, an' Tim, an' Helen—I guess he knows the history of the whole damn fam'ly now! I neveh tawked so much to a stranger befoeh in my whole life. But it's funny, he neveh seems to say anything himse'f. He just stands there an' looks at you, an' turns his head to one side as if he's listenin'—an' you spill the beans. When he's gone you realize you've done *all* the tawkin'. 'Listen,' I says to 'im the otheh day, 'you know everything else now, I've told you the truth about everything else, so I'll come clean on this, too—that wasn't true about me bein' married.' Gee! He was about to drive me nuts astin' a new question every day about my husband! 'I lied to you about that,' I says. 'I neveh was married. I haven't got a husband.' "

Number two, hungrily: "So w'at does he say to that?"

She: "Just looks at me an' says, 'So—*what*?' " Laughing: "Gee, it was funny to hear 'im say *that*! I guess I taught it to 'im. He says it all the time now. But it's funny the way he says it—like he don't know exactly what it means. 'So—*what*?' he says. So I says, 'What d'you mean, so what? I'm tellin' you that I'm not married, like I said I was.' 'I knew that all the time,' he says. '*How* did you know?' I says. 'How could you *tell*?' 'Because,' he says, an' shakes his head at me in that disgusted way—'because you're a *woman*!' "

Number two: "Can you imagine *that*? The *noive* of 'im! I hope you told 'im somep'n!"

She: "Oh, sure! I always come right back at 'im! But *still*, you neveh can be sure he means it! I think he's kiddin' half the time. He may be kiddin' when he shakes his head at you in that disgusted way. Anyway, that guy's all right! I don't know, but somehow you can tell." A pause, then with a sigh: "But gee! If only he'd go an' get himse'f a——"

Number two: "*Hat!*"

She: "Can yah *beat* it?"
Number two: "Ain't it a *scream*?"
They regard each other silently, shaking their heads.

Fox gets at all things around the edges in this way—sees the whole thing, whole, clear, instant, unperplexed, then all the little things as well. Will see a man in the crowd, notice the way his ear sticks out, his length of chin, his short upper lip, the way his face is formed, something about the cheek bones—a man well dressed and well behaved, conventional in appearance, no one but the Fox would look a second time at him—and suddenly the Fox will find himself looking into the naked eyes of a wild animal. Fox will see the cruel and savage tiger prowling in that man, let loose in the great jungle of the city, sheathed in harmless and deceptive grey—a wild beast, bloody, rending, fierce, and murderous—and stalking free and unsuspected on the sheep of life! And Fox will turn away appalled and fascinated, look at the people all around him with astonishment—"Can't *they* see? Don't they *know*?"—then will return again and walk past the tiger with hands clutching coat lapels, will bend, crane his head, and stare fixedly into tiger's eye until tiger's eye, discovered and unguarded now, blazes back at Fox—and all the people, puzzled and perturbed, are staring at Fox, too. Like children, they don't know what to make of it: "*What* does that guy see?" And Fox, astounded: "*Can't* they see?"

Sees all life foxwise, really: has acute animal perceptions—does not let concrete, brick, stone, skyscrapers, motor cars, or clothes obscure the thing itself. Finds the tiger looking out at life, and then sees all the people who are lions, bulls, mastiffs, terriers, bulldogs, greyhounds, wolves, owls, eagles, hawks, rabbits, reptiles, monkeys, apes, and—foxes. Fox knows the world is full of them. He sees them every day. He might have found one in C. Green, too—cat, rabbit, terrier, or snipe—could he have seen him.

He reads the news in this way, sniffing sharply, with keen relish, at the crisp, ink-pungent pages. He also reads the paper with a kind of eager hopelessness. Fox has no hope, really; he is beyond despair. (If there's a lack, we'll smell it out. Is this not one? Is this not a lack-American? Can Fox be wholly of us if he has no hope?) Fox really has no hope that men will change, that life will ever get much better. He knows the forms will change: perhaps new changes will bring better forms. The shifting forms of change absorb him—this is why he loves the news. Fox would give his life to keep or increase virtue—to save the savable, to grow the growable, to cure the curable, to keep the good. But for the thing unsavable, for life ungrowable, for the ill incurable, he has no care. Things lost in nature hold no interest for him.

Thus will grow grey at the temples, haggard-eyed, and thin if one of his children has an ailment. One daughter has been in a motor wreck, escapes unhurt apparently, days later has a slight convulsion. It comes a second time, returns weeks later, goes away, and comes again—not much, not long, just a little thing, but Fox grows grey with worry. He takes the girl from college, gets doctors, specialists, the best people in the world, tries everything, can find nothing wrong, yet the attacks continue; at length comes through it, finds out the trouble, pulls the girl out, and sees her married. His eyes are clear again. Yet if the girl had had a cureless ailment, Fox would not have worried much.

He goes home, sleeps soundly, seems indifferent, shows no worry, the night the daughter has a child. Next morning, when informed he is a grandfather, looks blank, puzzled, finally says, "Oh"—then, turning away with a disdainful sniffing of the nose, says scornfully:

"Another *woman*, I suppose?"

Informed it is a man-child, says, "Oh," dubiously, then whispers contemptuously:

"I had supposed such a phenomenon was impossible in *this* family."

And for some weeks thereafter persists in referring to his grandson as "She," to the indignation, resentment, excited protest of the——

Women!

(A cunning Fox—knows slyly how to tease.)

So, then, unhoping hopefulness, and resigned acceptance; patient fatality, and unflagging effort and unflinching will. Has no hope, really, for the end, the whole amount of things; has hope incessant for the individual things themselves. Knows we lose out all along the line, but won't give in. Knows how and when we win, too, and never gives up trying for a victory. Considers it disgraceful to stop trying—will try everything— will lay subtle, ramified, and deep-delved plans to save people from avertible defeat: a man of talent drowning in his own despair, some strong and vital force exploding without purpose, some precious, misused thing gone wickedly to ruin. These things *can* be helped, they *must* be helped and saved, to see them lost, to see them thrown away, is not to be endured—Fox will move mountains to prevent them. But gone? Lost? Destroyed? Irretrievably thrown away? The grave face will be touched with sadness, the sea-pale eyes filled with regret, the low voice hoarse and indignant:

"It was a shame! A *shame*! Everything would have come out
381

all right . . . he had it in his grasp . . . and he just let it go! He *just gave in!*"

Yes, for failure such as this, a deep, indignant sadness, a profound regret. But for other things foreordained and inevitable, not savable by any means, then a little sadness —"Too bad"—but in the end a tranquil fatality of calm acceptance: the thing had to be, it couldn't be helped.

Is therefore like Ecclesiastes: has the tragic sense of life, knows that the day of birth is man's misfortune—but, knowing this, will then "lay hold." Has never, like the Fool, folded his hands together and consumed his flesh, but, seeing work to be done, has taken hold with all his might and done it. Knows that the end of all is vanity, but says: "Don't whine, and don't repine, but *get work done.*"

Is, therefore, not afraid to die; does not court death, but knows death is a friend. Does not hate life, is rather passionately involved with life, yet does not hug it like a lover— it would not be torn bitterly from reluctant fingers. There is no desperate hug of mortality in Fox—rather, the sense of mystery and strangeness in the hearts of men, the thrilling interest of the human adventure, the unending fascination of the whole, tangled, grieved, vexed, and unfathomed pattern. As he reads the *Times* now, he sniffs sharply, shakes his head, smiles, scans the crowded columns of the earth, and whispers to himself:

"What a world! And what a life! Will we ever get to the bottom of it all? . . . And what a *time* we live in! I don't dare go to sleep at night without the paper. I cannot wait until the next one has come out—things change so fast, the whole world's in such a state of flux, the course of history may change from one edition to another. The whole thing's so fascinating, I wish I could live a hundred years to see what's going to happen! If it weren't for that—and for the children——"

A slow perplexity deepens in his eyes. What will become of them? Five tender lambs to be turned loose out of the fold into the howling tumults of this dangerous and changeful earth. Five fledglings to be sent forth, bewildered and defenseless, to meet the storms of fury, peril, adversity, and savage violence that beat across the whole vexed surface of the earth—unsheltered, ignorant, unprepared, and——

"Women." Scorn, touched now deeply with compassion; trouble, with a tender care.

Is there a way out, then? Yes, if only he can live to see each of them married to—to—to a *good* husband (the sense of trouble deepens in the sea-pale eyes—the world in printed columns there before him seethes with torment—no easy business). . . . But to find *good* husbands, foxes all of them—to see his fleecelings safely folded, shielded from the storms—

382

each—each with fleecelings of her own—yes!—that's the thing!
Fox clears his throat and rattles the pages with decision. That's
the thing for——

—Women!

—To be folded, sheltered, guarded, kept from all the danger,
violence, and savagery, the grimed pollution of this earth's
coarse thumb, each to ply her needle, learn to keep her house,
do a woman's work, be wifely, and—and—"lead the sort of life
a woman ought to lead," Fox whispers to himself—"the kind of
life she was intended for."

Which is to say, produce more fleecelings for the fold, Fox?
Who will, in turn, find "good" husbands, and a fold, learn
sewing, housewifery, and "lead the sort of life a woman ought
to lead," produce still other fleecelings, and so on, *ad infinitum,*
to world's end forever, or until——

—The day-of wrath, the huge storm howling through the
earth again—again the Terror and Jemappes!—again November and Moscow!—the whole flood broke through, the
mighty river re-arisen, the dark tide flowing in the hearts of
men, and a great wind howling through the earth, good Fox,
that tears off rooftops like a sheet of paper, bends the strongest
oak trees to the ground, knocks down the walls, and levels the
warmest, strongest, and most solid folds that ever sheltered
fleecelings in security—leaving fleecelings where?

O Fox, is there no answer?

Leaving fleecelings there to knit a pattern of fine needlework
on the hurricane? Leaving fleecelings there to ply housewifery
on the flood? Leaving fleecelings to temper the bleak storms of
misery to the perfumed tenderness of fleeceling hides? To find
"good" husbands in the maelstrom's whirl? To produce more
fleecelings in order to be secure, protected, in doing a woman's
work, in leading "the kind of life she was intended for"——

Oh, where, Fox, where?

—To draw compassion from the cobblestones? Security
from iron skies? Solicitude from the subduer's bloody hand?
Arthurian gallantries from the brutal surge of the on-marching
mass?

Still no answer, subtle Fox?

What, then? Will not hoarse voices fogged with blood and
triumph soften to humility when they behold the fleeceling
loveliness? And while the blind mob fills the desolated streets,
will not a single cloak be thrown down for dainty fleeceling feet
to tread upon? Will the shattered masonries of all those (as we
thought) impregnable securities, with which the Foxes of the
world have sheltered fleecelings, no longer give the warmth and
safety which once were so assured and certain? And must those
fountains so unfailing in the flow of milk and honey, on which

fleecelings feed, be withered at their source? Must they be fountains, rather, dyed with blood—blood of the lamb, then? Fleeceling blood?

O Fox, we cannot think of it!

Fox reads on, intent, with the keen hunger of a fascinated interest, the shade of a deep trouble in his eye. The sober, close-set columns of the *Times* give up their tortured facts, revealing a world in chaos, man bewildered, life in chains. These substantial pages, so redolent of morning and sobriety—of breakfast in America, the pungency of ham and eggs, the homes of prosperous people—yield a bitter harvest of madness, hatred, dissolution, misery, cruelty, oppression, injustice, despair, and the bankruptcy of human faith. What have we here, mad masters?—for surely if ye be masters of such hell-on-earth as sober *Times* portrays, then ye be mad!

Well, here's a little item:

It is announced, my masters, that on Saturday next, in the Land of the Enchanted Forest, land of legends and the magic of the elves, land of the Venusberg and the haunting beauties of the Gothic towns, land of the truth-lover and the truth-seeker, land of the plain, good, common, vulgar, and all-daring Sense of Man, land where the great monk nailed his blunt defiance to the doors at Wittenberg, and broke the combined powers, splendors, pomps, and menaces of churchly Europe with the sledgehammer genius of his coarse and brutal speech—land from that time onward of man's common noble dignity, and of the strong truth of sense and courage, shaking its thick fist into the face of folly—yes! land of Martin Luther, land of Goethe, land of Faust, land of Mozart and Beethoven—land where immortal music was created, glorious poetry written, and philosophy cultivated—land of magic, mystery, matchless loveliness, and unending treasure-hordes of noble art—land where the Man of Weimar, for the last time in the modern world, dared to make the whole domain of art, culture, and learning the province of his gigantic genius—land, too, of noble, consecrated youth, where young men sang and wrote, loved truth, went through apprenticeships devoted to the aspiration of a high and passionate ideal—well, mad masters, it is announced that this same enchanted land will consecrate the devotion of another band of youth *this* Saturday—when the young men of the nation will burn books before the Town Halls, in all the public squares of Germany!

Well, then, Fox?

And elsewhere on this old tormented globe, goes it much better? Fire, famine, flood, and pestilence—these trials we have always had. And hatred—most firelike, faminelike, floodlike, and most pestilential of all evils—yes, we have always had *that,* too. And yet, Great God! When has our old unhappy earth been stricken with such universal visitation? When has she ached in every joint as she aches now? When has she had such a universal itch, been so spavined, gouty, poxy, so broken out in sores all over?

The Chinese hate the Japanese, the Japanese the Russians, the Russians also hate the Japanese, and the hordes of India the English. The Germans hate the French, the French hate the Germans, and then look wildly around to find other nations to help them hate the Germans, but find they hate almost everyone as much as they hate Germans; they can't find enough to hate outside of France, and so divide themselves into thirty-seven different cliques and hate each other bitterly from Calais to Menton—the Leftists hate Rightists, the Centrists hate Leftists, the Royalists hate Socialists, the Socialists hate Communists, the Communists hate Capitalists, and all unite in hatred of one another. In Russia, the Stalinites hate Trotskyites, the Trotskyites hate Stalinites, and both hate Republicans and Democrats. Everywhere the Communists (so they say) hate their cousin Fascists, and the Fascists hate the Jews.

In this year of Our Gentle Lord 1934, "expert" observers say, Japan is preparing to go to war again with China within two years, Russia will join in with China, Japan will ally herself with Germany, Germany will make a deal with Italy, and then make war on France and England, America will try to stick her head into the sand, and so keep out of it, but will find it cannot be done and will be drawn in. And in the end, after everybody has fought everybody else up and down the globe, the whole Capitalistic world will join up finally against Russia in an effort to crush Communism—which eventually must win—will lose—is bound to triumph—will be wiped out—will supplant Capitalism, which is on its last legs—which is only suffering a temporary relapse—which grows more dropsical, greedy, avaricious, bloated, and monopolistic all the time—which is mending its ways and growing better all the time—which must be preserved at all costs if the "American System" is to endure—which must be destroyed at all costs if America is to endure—which is just beginning—which is ending—which is gone already—which will never go——

And so it goes—around, around, around the tortured circumference of this aching globe—around, around, and back again, and up and down, with stitch and counterstitch until this whole earth and all the people in it are caught up in one gigantic web of hatred, greed, tyranny, injustice, war, theft, murder, lying, treachery, hunger, suffering, and devilish error!

385

And we, old Fox? How goes it in our own fair land—our great America?

Fox winces quickly, cranes his neck into his collar, and mutters hoarsely a passionate regret:

"Too *bad*! Too *bad*! We should have *had* it! We were just beginning—we should have had it fifty years ago, as Rome had it, and as England had it! But all this turmoil came too soon—we didn't have it long enough! Too *bad*! Too *bad*!"

Yes, Fox, it *is* too bad. Too bad, indeed, that in our pride, our self-respect, and our taut horror the Medusa-visage of the whole tormented earth may be an anodyne for us, lest we have to look too closely at the honor of our own America.

Chapter Thirty-One

The Promise of America

For four years George Webber lived and wrote in Brooklyn, and during all this time his life was about as solitary as any that a modern man can know. Loneliness, far from being a rare and curious circumstance, is and always has been the central and inevitable experience of every man. Not only has this been true of the greatest poets, as evidenced by the huge unhappiness of their published grief, but now it seemed to George to apply with equal force to all the nameless ciphers who swarmed about him in the streets. As he saw them in their strident encounters with each other, and overheard their never-varying exchanges of abuse, contempt, distrust, and hatred, it became increasingly clear to him that one of the contributing causes of their complaint was loneliness.

To live alone as George was living, a man should have the confidence of God, the tranquil faith of a monastic saint, the stern impregnability of Gibraltar. Lacking these, he finds that there are times when anything, everything, all and nothing, the most trivial incidents, the most casual words, can in an instant strip him of his armor, palsy his hand, constrict his heart with frozen horror, and fill his bowels with the grey substance of shuddering impotence and desolation. Sometimes it would be a sly remark dropped by some all-knowing literary soothsayer in the columns of one of the more leftish reviews, such as:

"Whatever has become of our autobiographical and volcanic friend, George Webber? Remember him? Remember the splash he made with that so-called 'novel' of his a few years back? Some of our esteemed colleagues thought they detected signs of promise there. We ourselves should have welcomed another book from him, just to prove that the first was not an accident. But *tempus fugit*, and where is Webber? Calling Mr. Webber! No answer? Well, a pity, perhaps; but then, who can count the number of one-book authors? They shoot their bolt, and after that they go into the silence and no more is heard from them. Some of us who were more than a little doubtful about that book of Webber's, but whose voices were drowned out by the Oh's and Ah's of those who rushed headlong to proclaim a new star rising in the literary firmament, could now come forward, if we weren't too kindly disposed toward our more emotional brethren of the critical fraternity, and modestly say, 'We told you so!'"

Sometimes it would be nothing but a shadow passing on the sun, sometimes nothing but the gelid light of March falling on the limitless, naked, sprawling ugliness and squalid decencies of Brooklyn streets. Whatever it was, at such a time all joy and singing would go instantly out of day, Webber's heart would drop out of him like a leaden plummet, hope, confidence, and conviction would seem lost forever to him, and all the high and shining truth that he had ever found and lived and known would now turn false to mock him. Then he would feel like one who walked among the dead, and it would be as if the only things that were not false on earth were the creatures of the death-in-life who moved forever in the changeless lights and weathers of red, waning, weary March and Sunday afternoon.

These hideous doubts, despairs, and dark confusions of the soul would come and go, and George knew them as every lonely man must know them. For he was united to no image save that image which he himself created. He was bolstered by no knowledge save that which he gathered for himself out of his own life. He saw life with no other vision save the vision of his own eyes and brain and senses. He was sustained and cheered and aided by no party, was given comfort by no creed, and had no faith in him except his own.

That faith, though it was made up of many articles, was at bottom a faith in himself, a faith that if he could only succeed in capturing a fragment of the truth about the life he knew, and make it known and felt by others, it would be a more glorious accomplishment than anything else he could imagine. And through it all, animating this faith and sustaining it with a promise of rewards to come, was a belief—be it now confessed—that if he could only do this, the world would thank him for it, and would crown him with the laurel of its fame.

The desire for fame is rooted in the hearts of men. It is one of the most powerful of all human desires, and perhaps for that very reason, and because it is so deep and secret, it is the desire that men are most unwilling to admit, particularly those who feel most sharply its keen and piercing spur.

The politician, for example, would never have us think that it is love of office, the desire for the notorious elevation of public place, that drives him on. No, the thing that governs him is his pure devotion to the common weal, his selfless and high-minded statesmanship, his love of his fellow man, and his burning idealism to turn out the rascal who usurps the office and betrays the public trust which he himself, as he assures us, would so gloriously and devotedly maintain.

So, too, the soldier. It is never love of glory that inspires him to his profession. It is never love of battle, love of war, love of all the resounding titles and the proud emoluments of the heroic conqueror. Oh, no. It is devotion to duty that makes him a soldier. There is no personal motive in it. He is inspired simply by the selfless ardor of his patriotic abnegation. He regrets that he has but one life to give for his country.

So it goes through every walk of life. The lawyer assures us that he is the defender of the weak, the guardian of the oppressed, the champion of the rights of defrauded widows and beleagured orphans, the upholder of justice, the unrelenting enemy, at no matter what cost to himself, of all forms of chicanery, fraud, theft, violence, and crime. Even the businessman will not admit to selfish motive in his money-getting. On the contrary, he is the developer of the nation's resources. He is the benevolent employer of thousands of working men who would be lost and on the dole without the organizing genius of his great intelligence. He is the defender of the American ideal of rugged individualism, the shining exemplar to youth of what a poor country boy may achieve in this nation through a devotion to the national virtues of thrift, industry, obedience to duty, and business integrity. He is, he assures us, the backbone of the country, the man who makes the wheels go round, the leading citizen, Public Friend No. 1.

All these people lie, of course. They know they lie, and everyone who hears them also knows they lie. The lie, however, has become a part of the convention of American life. People listen to it patiently, and if they smile at it, the smile is weary, touched with resignation and the indifferent dismissals of fatigue.

Curiously enough, the lie has also invaded the world of

creation—the one place where it has no right at all to exist. There was a time when the poet, the painter, the musician, the artist of whatever sort, was not ashamed to confess that the desire for fame was one of the driving forces of his life and labor. But what a transformation from that time to this! Nowadays one will travel far and come back fruitless if he hopes to find an artist who will admit that he is devoted to anything except the service of some ideal—political, social, economic, religious, or aesthetic—which is outside himself, and to which his own humble fame-forsaking person is reverently and selflessly consigned.

Striplings of twenty assure us that the desire for fame is naïvely childish, the fruit of an outworn cult of "romantic individualism." From all the falseness and self-deception of this cult these young gentlemen tell us they are free—without troubling to explain, however, by what process of miraculous purgation they achieved their freedom. It took Goethe, the strongest soul of modern times, some three and eighty years to free his mighty spirit of this last infirmity. Milton, old and blind, forsaken, and past fifty, is said to have won free of it by the end of Cromwell's revolution, in whose employment he destroyed his sight. And yet, can we be sure that even he was ever wholly clear, for what is the tremendous edifice of *Paradise Lost* except a man's final and triumphant suit against eternity?

Poor, blind Milton!

> Fame is the spur that the clear spirit doth raise
> (That last infirmity of Noble mind)
> To scorn delights, and live laborious dayes;
> But the fair Guerdon when we hope to find,
> And think to burst out into sudden blaze,
> Comes the blind Fury with th'abhorred shears,
> And slits the thin-spun life. But not the praise,
> Phoebus repli'd, and touch'd my trembling ears;
> Fame is no plant that grows on mortal soil,
> Nor in the glistering foil
> Set off to th'world, nor in broad rumour lies,
> But lives and spreds aloft by those pure eyes,
> And perfet witnes of all judging Jove;
> As he pronounces lastly on each deed,
> Of so much fame in Heav'n expect thy meed.

Deluded man! Poor vassal of corrupted time! How fair a thing for us to know that we are not such men as he and Goethe were! We live in more stirring times, and our very striplings are secure in their collective selflessness. We have freed ourselves of all degrading vanities, choked off the ravening desire for individual immortality, and now having risen out of the ashes of our father's earth into the untainted ethers of collective consecration, we are clear at last of all that vexed, corrupted earth—clear of the sweat and blood and sorrow, clear of the grief and joy, clear of the hope and fear and human agony of which our father's flesh and that of every other man alive before us was ever wrought.

And yet, having achieved this glorious emancipation; having laid all petty dreams aside; having learned to think of life, not in terms of ourselves, but in terms of the whole mass; having learned to think of life, not as it is today, but as it is to be five hundred years from now, when all the revolutions have been made, and all the blood has been shed, and all the hundreds of millions of vain and selfish little lives, each concerned with its own individual and romantic breath, have been ruthlessly wiped out in order to usher in the collective glory that will be—having become marvelously and, as it were, overnight such paragons of collective selflessness and such scorners of the vanity of personal fame, is it not strange that though we have new phrases, yet their meaning is still the same? Is it not strange that, feeling only an amused and pitying contempt for those who are still naïve enough to long for glory, we should yet lacerate our souls, poison our minds and hearts, and crucify our spirits with bitter and rancorous hatred against those who are fortunate enough to achieve fame?

Or do we err? Are we mistaken in assuming that these words we read so often are really words of hatred, malice, envy, ridicule, and jeering mockery? Are we mistaken in assuming that the whole vocabulary of abuse which is exhausted every week in the journals of our red and pink-complexioned comrades—the sneers against a man's talent, the bitter denials that his work has any substance, sincerity, truth, or reality whatever—is really what it seems to be? No doubt we *are* mistaken. It would be more charitable to believe that these pure spirits of the present day are what they say they are—collective, selfless, consecrated—and that the words they use do not mean what they seem to mean, and do not betray the romantic and deluded passions that seem to animate them, but are really words used coldly, without passion, for the purposes of collective propaganda—in operations completely surgical, whereby the language of the present day, with all its overtones of superstition, prejudice, and false knowledge, is employed clinically, scientifically, simply to further the Idea of the Future State!

No more, no more! Of what avail to crush these vermin beneath our heavy boot? The locusts have no king, and lice will multiply forever. The poet must be born, and live, and sweat, and suffer, and change, and grow, yet somehow maintain the changeless selfhood of his soul's integrity among all the crawling fashions of this world of lice. The poet lives, and dies, and is immortal; but the eternal trifler of all complexions never dies. The eternal trifler comes and goes, sucks blood of living men, is filled and emptied with the surfeit of each changing fashion. He gorges and disgorges, and is never fed. There is no nurture in him, and he draws no nurture from the food he feeds on. There is no heart, no soul, no blood, no living faith in him: the eternal trifler simply swallows and remains.

And we? Made of our father's earth, blood of his blood, bone of his bone, flesh of his flesh—born like our father here to live and strive, here to win through or be defeated—here, like all the other men who went before us, not too nice or dainty for the uses of this earth—here to live, to suffer, and to die— O brothers, like our fathers in their time, we are burning, burning, burning in the night.

Go, seeker, if you will, throughout the land and you will find us burning in the night.

There where the hackles of the Rocky Mountains blaze in the blank and naked radiance of the moon, go make your resting stool upon the highest peak. Can you not see us now? The continental wall juts sheer and flat, its huge black shadow on the plain, and the plain sweeps out against the East, two thousand miles away. The great snake that you see there is the Mississippi River.

Behold the gem-strung towns and cities of the good, green East, flung like star-dust through the field of night. That spreading constellation to the north is called Chicago, and that giant wink that blazes in the moon is the pendant lake that it is built upon. Beyond, close-set and dense as a clenched fist, are all the jeweled cities of the eastern seaboard. There's Boston, ringed with the bracelet of its shining little towns, and all the lights that sparkle on the rocky indentations of New England. Here, southward and a little to the west, and yet still coasted to the sea, is our intensest ray, the splintered firmament of the towered island of Manhattan. Round about her, sown thick as grain, is the glitter of a hundred towns and cities. The long chain of lights there is the necklace of Long Island and the Jersey shore. Southward and inland, by a foot or two, behold the duller glare of Philadelphia. Southward further still, the twin constellations—Baltimore and Washington. Westward, but still within the borders of the good, green East, that night-time glow and smolder of hell-fire is Pittsburgh. Here, St. Louis, hot and humid in the cornfield belly of the land, and bedded on the mid-length coil and fringes of the snake. There at the snake's mouth, southward six hundred miles or so, you see the jeweled crescent of old New Orleans. Here, west and south again, you see the gemmy glitter of the cities on the Texas border.

Turn now, seeker, on your resting stool atop the Rocky Mountains, and look another thousand miles or so across moon-blazing fiend-worlds of the Painted Desert and beyond Sierras' ridge. That magic congeries of lights there to the west, ringed like a studded belt around the magic setting of its lovely harbor, is the fabled town of San Francisco. Below it, Los Angeles and all the cities of the California shore. A thousand miles to north and west, the sparkling towns of Oregon and Washington.

Observe the whole of it, survey it as you might survey a field. Make it your garden, seeker, or your backyard patch. Be at ease in it. It's your oyster—yours to open if you will. Don't be frightened, it's not so big now, when your footstool is the Rocky Mountains. Reach out and dip a hatful of cold water from Lake Michigan. Drink it—we've tried it—you'll not find it bad. Take your shoes off and work your toes down in the river oozes of the Mississippi bottom—it's very refreshing on a hot night in the summertime. Help yourself to a bunch of Concord grapes up there in northern New York State—they're getting good now. Or raid that watermelon patch down there in Georgia. Or, if you like, you can try the Rockyfords here at your elbow, in Colorado. Just make yourself at home, refresh yourself, get the feel of things, adjust your sights, and get the scale. It's your pasture now, and it's not so big—only three thousand miles from east to west, only two thousand miles from north to south—but all between, where ten thousand points of light prick out the cities, towns, and villages, there, seeker, you will find us burning in the night.

Here, as you pass through the brutal sprawl, the twenty miles of rails and rickets, of the South Chicago slums—here, in an unpainted shack, is a Negro boy, and, seeker, he is burning in the night. Behind him is a memory of the cotton fields, the flat and mournful pineland barrens of the lost and buried South, and at the fringes of the pine another nigger shack, with mammy and eleven little niggers. Farther still behind, the slave-driver's whip, the slave ship, and, far off, the jungle dirge of Africa. And before him, what? A roped-in ring, a blaze of lights, across from him a white champion; the bell, the opening, and all around the vast sea-roaring of the crowd. Then the lightning feint and stroke, the black panther's paw—the hot, rotating presses, and the rivers of sheeted print! O seeker, where is the slave ship now?

Or there, in the clay-baked piedmont of the South, that lean and tan-faced boy who sprawls there in the creaking chair

392

among admiring cronies before the open doorways of the fire department, and tells them how he pitched the team to shut-out victory today. What visions burn, what dreams possess him, seeker of the night? The packed stands of the stadium, the bleachers sweltering with their unshaded hordes, the faultless velvet of the diamond, unlike the clay-baked outfields down in Georgia. The mounting roar of eighty thousand voices and Gehrig coming up to bat, the boy himself upon the pitching mound, the lean face steady as a hound's; then the nod, the signal, and the wind-up, the rawhide arm that snaps and crackles like a whip, the small white bullet of the blazing ball, its loud report in the oiled pocket of the catcher's mitt, the umpire's thumb jerked upward, the clean strike.

Or there again, in the East-Side Ghetto of Manhattan, two blocks away from the East River, a block away from the gas-house district and its thuggery, there in the swarming tenement, shut in his sweltering cell, breathing the sun-baked air through opened window at the fire escape, celled there away into a little semblance of privacy and solitude from all the brawling and vociferous life and argument of his family and the seething hive around him, the Jew boy sits and pores upon his book. In shirt-sleeves, bent above his table to meet the hard glare of a naked bulb, he sits with gaunt, starved face converging to his huge beaked nose, the weak eyes squinting painfully through his thick-lens glasses, his greasy hair roached back in oily scrolls above the slanting cage of his painful and constricted brow. And for what? For what this agony of concentration? For what this hell of effort? For what this intense withdrawal from the poverty and squalor of dirty brick and rusty fire escapes, from the raucous cries and violence and never-ending noise? For what? Because, brother, he is burning in the night. He sees the class, the lecture room, the shining apparatus of gigantic laboratories, the open field of scholarship and pure research, certain knowledge, and the world distinction of an Einstein name.

So, then, to every man his chance—to every man, regardless of his birth, his shining, golden opportunity—to every man the right to live, to work, to be himself, and to become whatever thing his manhood and his vision can combine to make him— this, seeker, is the promise of America.

BOOK V

Exile and Discovery

After four long years in Brooklyn, George Webber came out of the wilderness, looked around him, and concluded he had had enough of it. During this period he had learned much, both about himself and about America, but now he was seized again with wanderlust. His life had always seemed to shift between the poles of anchored loneliness and foot-loose voyagings— between wandering forever, and then the earth again—and now the old and restless urgings of "Where shall we go? And what shall we do?" again became insistent, would not down, and demanded of him a new answer.

Ever since his first book had been published he had been looking for a way to form and shape his next. Now he thought that he had found it. It was not the way, perhaps, but it was a way. The hundreds and thousands of separate and disjointed notes that he had written down had fallen at last into a pattern in his mind. He needed only to weave them all together, and fill in the blanks, and he would have a book. He felt that he could do this final job of organization and revision better if he made a clean break in the monotony of his life. New scenes, new faces, and new atmospheres might clear his head and sharpen his perspective.

It would be a good thing, too, to get away from America for a while. Too much was happening here—it was too exciting and disturbing. The whole thing was in such a state of flux, in such a prophetic condition of becoming, that the sheer exhilaration of watching it made it hard to concentrate upon the immediate job he had to do. Perhaps in the older civilization of Europe, where life was fixed and certain, molded by the heritage of centuries, there would be fewer distractions to keep him from his work. He decided to go abroad, to England, and there drop anchor, there find even keel in placid waters—there complete his book.

So in the late summer of 1934 he sailed from New York, went straight to London, took a flat, and settled down to hard, intensive labor. All through the fall and winter of that year he lived in London in his self-imposed exile. It was a memorable time for him, a time during which, as he was later to realize, he discovered an entire new world. All the events, the experiences, and the people that he met became engraved indelibly upon his life.

And the event which exercised the most profound influence upon him in that alien air was his meeting with the great American author, Mr. Lloyd McHarg. Everything seemed to lead up to that. And what made his meeting with Mr. McHarg so important to him was that now, for the first time, he met a living embodiment of his own dearest and most secret dream. For when Mr. Lloyd McHarg swept like a cyclone through his life, George knew that he was having his first encounter in the flesh with that fair Medusa, Fame herself. Never before had he beheld the lady, or witnessed the effects of her sweet blandishments. Now he saw the whole thing for himself.

Chapter Thirty-Two

The Universe of Daisy Purvis

On arriving in London, George had the good fortune to sublet a flat in Ebury Street. The young military gentleman who condescended to let him have the place possessed one of those resounding double-jointed names that one comes across so often among the members of the upper or would-be-upper branches of English society. George was never able to get all the mouth-filling syllables of that grand name quite straight, but suffice it to say that his landlord was a Major Somebody Somebody Somebody Bixley-Dunton.

He was a good-looking man, tall, young, ruddy, with the lean and well-conditioned figure of a cavalryman. He was an engaging kind of fellow, too—so engaging that when he made the arrangements which permitted George to take over the premises, he managed to insinuate into his bill for rent a thumping sum that covered all the electricity and gas he had used in the preceding two quarters. And electricity and gas, as George was to discover, came high in London. You read and worked by one, sometimes not only through the night, but also through the pea-soup opacity of a so-called day. And you bathed and shaved and cooked and feebly warmed yourself by the other. George never did figure out just exactly how the engaging Major Bixley-Dunton did it, but he managed it so adroitly that George was halfway back to America some six months later before it dawned on his unsuspecting mind that he had occupied his modest dwelling only two quarters but had paid four whacking assessments for a whole year's gas and electricity.

George thought he was getting a bargain at the time, and perhaps he was. He paid Major Bixley-Dunton in quarterly installments—in advance, of course—at the rate of two pounds ten shillings a week, and for this sum he had the advantage of being the sole occupant, at night at least, of a very small but distinctly authentic London house. It was really a rather tiny house, and certainly a very inconspicuous one, in a section noted for the fashionable spaciousness and magnificence of its dwellings. The building was three stories tall, and George had the top floor. Below him a doctor had his offices, and the ground floor was occupied by a small tailor shop. These other tenants both lived elsewhere and were present only during the day, so at night George had the whole house to himself.

He had a good deal of respect for the little tailor shop. The venerable and celebrated Irish writer, Mr. James Burke, had his pants pressed there, and George had the honor of being present in the shop one night when the great man called for them. It was a considerable moment in Webber's life. He felt that he was assisting at an impressive and distinguished ceremony. It was the first time he had ever been in such intimate contact with such exalted literary greatness, and most fair-minded people will agree that there are few things in the world more intimate than a pair of pants. Also, even at the moment that Mr. Burke entered the shop and demanded his trousers, George was requesting the return of his own. This homely coincidence gave him a feeling of perfectly delightful understanding and identity of purpose with a gentleman whose talents had for so many years been an object of his veneration. It gave him an easy and casual sense of belonging to the inner circle, and he could imagine someone saying to him:

"Oh, by the way, have you seen anything of James Burke lately?"

"Oh yes," he could nonchalantly reply, "I ran into him the other day in the place where we both go to have our pants pressed."

And night after night as he worked in his sitting room on the third floor, at that hour the solitary lord and master of that little house, toiling on the composition of a work which he hoped, but did not dare believe, might rival in celebrity some of James Burke's own, he would get at times the most curious and moving sense of companionship, as if a beneficent and approving spirit were there beneath that roof with him; and through the watches of the night it would speak to him with the eloquence of silence, saying:

"Toil on, son, and do not lose heart or hope. Let nothing you dismay. You are not utterly forsaken. I, too, am here—here in the darkness waiting, here attentive, here approving of your labor and your dream.

Ever sincerely yours,
James Burke's Pants"

One of the most memorable experiences of George Webber's six months in London was his relationship with Daisy Purvis.

Mrs. Purvis was a charwoman who lived at Hammersmith and for years had worked for "unmarried gentlemen" in the fashionable districts known as Mayfair and Belgravia. George had inherited her, so to speak, from Major Bixley-Dunton, and when he went away he gave her back to him, to be passed on to the next young bachelor gentleman—a man, George hoped, who would be worthy of her loyalty, devotion, idolatry, and humble slavery. He had never had a servant in his life before. He had known Negro servants during his boyhood in the South; since then he had had people come in once or twice a week to clean up the various places where he had lived; but never before had he owned a servant body and soul, to the degree that her interests became his interests and her life his life; never before had he had anyone whose whole concern was the preservation of his comfort and welfare.

In appearance, Mrs. Purvis might have been the prototype of a whole class. She was not one of those comic figures so often pictured in the drawings of Belcher and Phil May, those pudgy old women who wear shawls and little Queen Victoria bonnets perched upon their heads, whose most appropriate locale seems to be the pub, and whom one actually does see in London pubs, sodden with beer and viciousness. Mrs. Purvis was a self-respecting female of the working class. She was somewhere in her forties, a woman inclined to plumpness, of middling height, fair-haired, blue-eyed, and pink-complexioned, with a pleasant, modest face, and a naturally friendly nature, but inclined to be somewhat on her dignity with strangers. At first, although she was at all times courteous, her manner toward her new employer was a little distant. She would come in in the morning and they would formally discuss the business of the day—what they were going to have for lunch, the supplies they were going to "git in," the amount of money it would be necessary to "lay out."

"What would you like for lunch today, sir?" Mrs. Purvis would say. "'Ave you decided?"

"No, Mrs. Purvis. What would you suggest? Let's see. We had the chump chop yesterday, didn't we, and the sprouts?"

"Yes, sir," Mrs. Purvis would reply, "and the day before—Monday, you may recall—we 'ad rump steak with potato chips."

"Yes, and it was good, too. Well, then, suppose we have rump steak again?"

"Very good, sir," Mrs. Purvis would say, with perfect courtesy, but with a rising intonation of the voice which somehow suggested, delicately and yet unmistakably, that he could do as he pleased, but that she rather thought his choice was not the best.

Feeling this, George would immediately have doubts. He would say:

"Oh, wait a minute. We've been having steak quite often, haven't we?"

"You 'ave 'ad it quite a bit, sir," she would say quietly, not with reproof, but with just a trace of confirmation. "Still, of course—" She would not finish, but would pause and wait.

"Well, rump steak is good. All that we've had was first-rate. Still, maybe we could have something else today, for a change. What do you think?"

"Should think so, sir, if you feel that way," she said quietly. "After all, one does like a bit of variety now and then, *doesn't* one?"

"Of course. Well, then, what shall it be? What would you suggest, Mrs. Purvis?"

"Well, sir, if I may say so, a bit of gammon and peas is rather nice sometimes," with just a trace of shyness and diffidence, mixed with an engaging tinge of warmth as she relented into the informality of mild enthusiasm. "I 'ad a look in at the butcher's as I came by this mornin', and the gammon was nice, sir. It *was* a prime bit, sir," she said now with genuine warmth. "Prime."

After this, of course, he could not tell her that he had not the faintest notion what gammon was. He could only look delighted and respond:

"Then, by all means, let's have gammon and peas. I think it's just the thing today."

"Very good, sir." She had drawn herself up again; the formal intonation of the words had put her back within the fortress of aloofness, and had put him back upon his heels.

It was a curious and disquieting experience, one that he was often to have with English people. Just when he thought that finally the bars were down and the last barriers of reserve broken through, just when they had begun to talk with mutual warmth and enthusiasm, these English would be back behind the barricade, leaving him to feel that it was all to do over again.

"Now for your breakfast tomorrow mornin'," Mrs. Purvis would continue. " 'Ave you decided what you'd like?"

"No, Mrs. Purvis. Have we anything on hand? How are our supplies holding out?"

"They *are* a bit low, sir," she admitted. "We 'ave eggs. There is still butter left, and 'arf a loaf of bread. We're gettin' low on tea, sir. But you could 'ave eggs, sir, if you like."

Something in the faint formality of the tone informed him that even though he might like to have eggs, Mrs. Purvis would not approve, so he said quickly:

"Oh, no, Mrs. Purvis. Get the tea, of course, but no more eggs. I think we've had too many eggs, don't you?"

"You *'ave*, sir, you know," she said gently—"for the last

three mornin's, at any rate. Still——" Again she paused, as if to say that if he was determined to go on having eggs, he should have them.

"Oh, no. We mustn't have eggs again. If we keep on at this rate, we'll get to the point where we can't look an egg in the face again, won't we?"

She laughed suddenly, a jolly and full-throated laugh. "We will, sir, won't we?" said Mrs. Purvis, and laughed again. "Excuse me for larfin', sir, but the way you put it, I 'ad to larf. It was quite amusin', really."

"Well, then, Mrs. Purvis, maybe you've got some ideas. It's not going to be eggs, that's one thing sure."

"Well, sir, 'ave you tried kippers yet? Kippers are quite nice, sir," she went on, with another momentary mellowing into warmth. "If you're lookin' for a change, you could do worse than kippers. Really you could, sir."

"Well, then, we'll have kippers. They're the very thing."

"Very good, sir." She hesitated a moment and then said: "About your supper, sir—I was thinkin'——"

"Yes, Mrs. Purvis?"

"It just occurred to me, sir, that, seein' as I'm not here at night to cook you a 'ot meal, we might lay in somethin' you could prepare for yourself. I was thinkin' the other day, sir, workin' as you do, you must get 'ungry in the middle of the night, so it wouldn't be a bad idea, would it, sir, if you could have somethin' on 'and?"

"I think it would be a wonderful idea, Mrs. Purvis. What do you have in mind?"

"Well, sir," she paused briefly again, reflecting quietly, "we might git in a bit of tongue, you know. A bit of cold tongue is very tasty. I should think you'd find it most welcome in the middle of the night. Or a bit of 'am. Then, sir, you would 'ave your bread and butter and your mustard pickle, and I could even git in a jar of chutney, if you like, and you know 'ow to make tea yourself, don't you, sir?"

"Of course. It's a good idea. By all means, get in tongue or ham and chutney. Is that all, now?"

"Well, sir," she reflected a moment longer, went to the buffet sideboard, opened it, and looked in. "I was just wonderin' 'ow you are for beer, sir. . . . Ah-h," she exclaimed, nodding with satisfaction, "it *is* gittin' a bit low, sir. You 'ave only two bottles left. Shall we lay in a 'arf-dozen bottles?"

"Yes. No—wait a minute. Better make it a dozen, then you won't have to be running out to order it again so soon."

"Very good, sir." Again the formal rising intonation, this time, he thought, with approval. "And what do you prefer, the Worthington or Bass?"

"Oh, I don't know. Which is better?"

"They're both first-rate, sir. Some people prefer one kind and some another. The Worthington, perhaps, is a trifle lighter, but you won't go wrong, sir, whichever one you order."

"All right, then, I'll tell you what you do—suppose you order half a dozen of each."

"Very good, sir." She turned to go.

"Thank you, Mrs. Purvis."

" 'Kew," she said, most formally and distantly now, and went out quietly, closing the door gently but very firmly after her.

As the weeks went by, her excessive formality toward George began to thaw out and drop away. She became more and more free in communicating to him whatever was on her mind. Not that she ever forgot her "place." Quite the contrary. But, while always maintaining the instinctive manner of an English servant toward her master, she also became increasingly assiduous in her slavish attentions, until at last one would almost have thought that her duty toward him was her very life.

Her devotion, however, was not quite as whole and absolute as it appeared to be. For three or four hours of the day she had another master, who shared with George her service and her expense. This was the extraordinary little man who kept doctor's offices on the floor below. In truth, therefore, Mrs. Purvis had a divided loyalty, and yet, in a curious way, she also managed to convey to each of her employers a sense that her whole-souled obligation belonged to him, and to him alone.

The little doctor was a Russian of the old régime, who had been a physician at the court of the Czar, and had accumulated a large fortune, which of course had been confiscated when he fled the country during the revolution. Penniless, he had come to England, and had made another fortune by a practice about which Mrs. Purvis, with a kind of haughty aloofness mixed with loyalty, had invented a soothing little fiction, but concerning which the doctor himself became in time quite candid. From one o'clock in the afternoon until four or thereabouts, the door bell tinkled almost constantly, and Mrs. Purvis was kept busy padding up and down the narrow stairs, admitting or ushering out an incessant stream of patients.

George had not been long in the place before he made a surprising discovery concerning this thriving practice. He and the little doctor had the same telephone, by a plug-in arrangement which permitted each to use the instrument in his own quarters while sharing the same number and the same bill. Sometimes the telephone would ring at night, after the doctor had departed for his home in Surrey, and George observed that the callers were always women. They would demand the doctor in voices that varied from accents of desperate entreaty to tones that fairly crooned with voluptuous and sensual complaint. Where *was* the doctor? When George informed them that he was at his home, some twenty miles away, they would moan that it couldn't be true, that it wasn't possible, that fate could assuredly not play them so cruel a joke. When told that it was indeed so, they would then sometimes suggest that perhaps George himself could render them some assistance on his own account. To these requests he was forced to reply, often with reluctance, that he was not a physician, and that they would have to seek help in some other quarter.

These calls sharpened his curiosity, and he began to keep his eye peeled during the doctor's office hours in the afternoon. He would go to the window and look out each time the door bell rang, and in a little while he became convinced of what he had already begun to suspect, that the doctor's practice was devoted exclusively to women. Their ages ranged from young womanhood to elderly haghood, they were of all kinds and conditions, but the one thing that was true of these patients was that they all wore skirts. No man ever rang that door bell.

George would sometimes tease Mrs. Purvis about this unending procession of female visitors, and would openly speculate on the nature of the doctor's practice. She had a capacity for self-deception which one often encounters among people of her class, although the phenomenon is by no means confined to it. No doubt she guessed some of the things that went on below stairs, but her loyalty to anyone she served was so unquestioning that when George pressed her for information her manner would instantly become vague, and she would confess that, although she was not familiar with the technical details of the doctor's practice, it was, she believed, devoted to "the treatment of nervous diseases."

"Yes, but what kind of nervous diseases?" George would ask. "Don't the gentlemen ever get nervous, too?"

"Ah-h," said Mrs. Purvis, nodding her head with an air of knowing profundity that was very characteristic of her. "Ah-h, *there* you 'ave it!"

"Have what, Mrs. Purvis?"

" 'Ave the hanswer," she said. "It's this Moddun Tempo. That's what Doctor says," she went on loftily, in that tone of unimpeachable authority with which she always referred to him and quoted his opinions. "It's the pace of Moddun Life—cocktail parties, stayin' up to all hours, and all of that. In America, I believe, conditions are even worse," said Mrs. Purvis. "Not, of course, that they *really* are," she added quickly, as if fearing that her remark might inadvertently have wounded the patriotic sensibilities of her employer. "I mean, after all, not 'avin' been there myself, I wouldn't know, would I?"

Her picture of America, derived largely from the pages of the tabloid newspapers, of which she was a devoted reader, was so delightfully fantastic that George could never find it in his heart to disillusion her. So he dutifully agreed that she was right, and even managed, with a few skillful suggestions, to confirm her belief that almost all American women spent their time going from one cocktail party to another—in fact, practically never got to bed.

"Ah, then," said Mrs. Purvis, nodding her head wisely with an air of satisfaction, "then *you* know what this Moddun Tempo means!" And, after a just perceptible pause: "Shockin' I calls it!"

She called a great many things shocking. In fact, no choleric Tory in London's most exclusive club could have been more vehemently and indignantly concerned with the state of the nation than was Daisy Purvis. To listen to her talk one might have thought she was the heir to enormous estates that had been chief treasures of her country's history since the days of the Norman conquerors, but which were now being sold out of her hands, cut up piece-meal, ravaged and destroyed because she could no longer pay the ruinous taxes which the government had imposed. She would discuss these matters long and earnestly, with dire forebodings, windy sighs, and grave shakings of the head.

George would sometimes work the whole night through and finally get to bed at six or seven o'clock in the dismal fog of a London morning. Mrs. Purvis would arrive at seven-thirty. If he was not already asleep he would hear her creep softly up the stairs and go into the kitchen. A little later she would rap at his door and come in with an enormous cup, smoking with a beverage in whose soporific qualities she had the utmost faith.

"'Ere's a nice 'ot cup of Ovaltine," said Mrs. Purvis, "to git you off to sleep."

He was probably nearly "off to sleep" already, but this made no difference. If he was not "off to sleep," she had the Ovaltine to "git him off." And if he *was* "off to sleep," she woke him up and gave him the Ovaltine to "git him off" again.

The real truth of the matter was that she wanted to talk with him, to exchange gossip, and especially to go over the delectable proceedings of the day's news. She would bring him fresh copies of *The Times* and *The Daily Mail,* and she would have, of course, her own tabloid paper. Then, while he propped himself up in bed and drank his Ovaltine, Mrs. Purvis would stand in the doorway, rattle her tabloid with a premonitory gesture, and thus begin:

"Shockin', I calls it!"

"What's shocking this morning, Mrs. Purvis?"

"Why, 'ere now, listen to this, if you please!" she would say indignantly, and read as follows: " 'It was announced yesterday, through the offices of the Messrs. Merigrew & Raspe, solicitors to 'Is Grace, the Duke of Basingstoke, that 'Is Grace 'as announced for sale 'is estate at Chipping Cudlington in Gloucestershire. The estate, comprisin' sixteen thousand acres, of which eight thousand are in 'untin' preserve, and includin' Basingstoke Hall, one of the finest examples of early Tudor architecture in the kingdom, 'as been in the possession of 'Is Grace's family since the fifteenth century. Representatives of the Messrs. Merigrew & Raspe stated, 'owever, that because of the enormous increase in the estate and income taxes since the war, 'Is Grace feels that it is no longer possible for 'im to maintain the estate, and 'e is accordingly puttin' it up for sale. This means, of course, that the number of 'Is Grace's private estates 'as now been reduced to three, Fothergill 'All in Devonshire, Wintringham in Yawkshire, and the Castle of Loch McTash, 'is 'untin' preserve in Scotland. 'Is Grace, it is said, 'as stated recently to friends that if somethin' is not done to check the present ruinous trend toward 'igher taxation, there wil not be a single great estate in England remainin' in the 'ands of its original owners within a 'undred years. . . .'

"Ah-h," said Mrs. Purvis, nodding with an air of knowing confirmation as she finished reading this dolorous item. "There you 'ave it! Just as 'Is Grace says, we're losin' all our great estates. And what's the reason? Why the owners can no longer afford to pay the taxes. Ruinous 'e calls 'em, and 'e's right. If it keeps up, you mark my words, the nobility'll 'ave no place left to live. A lot of 'em are migratin' already," she said darkly.

"Migrating where, Mrs. Purvis?"

"Why," she said, "to France, to Italy, places on the Continent. There is Lord Cricklewood, livin' somewhere in the south of France. And why? Because the taxes got too 'igh for 'im. Let all 'is places go 'ere. Ah-h, lovely places they were, too," she said, with appetizing tenderness. "And the Earl of Pentateuch, Lady Cynthia Wormwood, and 'Er Ladyship, the Dowager Countess of Throttlemarsh—where are they all? They've all left, that's where they are. Packed up and got out. Let their estates go. They've gone abroad to live. And why? Because the taxes are too 'igh. Shockin', I calls it!"

By this time Mrs. Purvis's pleasant face would be pink with indignation. It was one of the most astonishing demonstrations of concern George had ever seen. Again and again he would try to get to the bottom of it. He would bang down his cup of Ovaltine and burst out:

"Yes, but good Lord, Mrs. Purvis, why should *you* worry so much about it. Those people aren't going to starve. Here you get ten shillings a week from me and eight shillings more from the doctor. He says he's retiring and going abroad to live at the end of this year. I'll be going back to America pretty soon after that. You don't even know where you'll be or what you'll be doing this time next year. Yet you come in here day after day and read me this stuff about the Duke of Basingstoke or the Earl of Pentateuch having to give up one of his half dozen estates, as if you were afraid the whole lot of them would have to go on the dole. You're the one who will have to go on the dole if you get out of work. Those people are not going to suffer, not really, not the way you'll have to."

"Ah-h yes," she answered quietly, in a tone that was soft and gentle, as if she were speaking of the welfare of a group of helpless children, "but then, we're used to it, *aren't* we? And *they,* poor things, they're not."

It was appalling. He couldn't fathom it. He just felt as if he'd come up smack against an impregnable wall. You could call it what you liked—servile snobbishness, blind ignorance, imbecilic stupidity—but there it was. You couldn't shatter it, you couldn't even shake it. It was the most formidable example of devotion and loyalty he had ever known.

These conversations would go on morning after morning until there was scarcely an impoverished young viscount whose grandeurs and miseries had not undergone the reverent investigation of Mrs. Purvis's anguished and encyclopaedic care. But always at the end—after the whole huge hierarchy of saints, angels, captains of the host, guardians of the inner gate, and chief lieutenants of the right hand had been tenderly inspected down to the minutest multicolored feather that blazed in their heraldic wings—silence would fall. It was as if some great and unseen presence had entered the room. Then Mrs. Purvis would rattle her crisp paper, clear her throat, and with holy quietness pronounce the sainted name of " 'E."

Sometimes this moment would come as a sequel to her fascinated discussion of America and the Moddun Tempo, as, after enlarging for the hundredth time upon the shocking and unfortunate lot of the female population in the United States, she would add:

"I must say, though," tactfully, after a brief pause, "that the

American ladies *are* very smart, aren't they, sir? They're all so well turned out. You can always tell one when you see one. And then they're *very* clever, aren't they, sir? I mean, quite a number of 'em 'ave been received at court, 'aven't they, sir? And some of 'em 'ave married into the nobility, too. And of course—" her voice would fall to just the subtlest shade of unction, and George would know what was coming—"of course, sir, 'E . . ."

Ah, there it was! Immortal " 'E," who lived and moved and loved and had his being there at the center of Daisy Purvis's heaven! Immortal " 'E," the idol of all the Purvises everywhere, who, for *their* uses, *their* devotions, had no other name and needed none but " 'E."

"Of course, sir," Mrs. Purvis said, " '*E* likes 'em, doesn't 'E? I'm told 'E's very fond of 'em. The American ladies *must* be very clever, sir, because 'E finds 'em so amusin'. There was a picture of 'Im in the news just recently with a party of 'Is friends, and a new American lady was among 'em. At least I'd never seen *'er* face before. And very smart she was, too—a Mrs. Somebody-or-other—I can't recall the name."

Again, something in the day's news would bring the reverent tone to her voice and the glow of tenderness to her face, as:

"Well, I see by the paper 'ere that 'E's got back from the Continent. I wonder what 'E's up to now." And suddenly she laughed, a jolly and involuntary laugh that flushed her pink cheeks almost crimson and brought a mist to her blue eyes. "Ah! I tell you what," she said, " 'E *is* a deep one. You never know what 'E's been up to. You pick the paper up one day and read where 'E's visitin' some friends in Yawkshire. The next day, before you know it, 'E turns up in Vienna. This time they say 'E's been in Scandinavia—it wouldn't surprise me if 'E's been over there visitin' one of them young princesses. Of course—" her tone was now tinged with the somewhat pompous loftiness with which she divulged her profounder revelations to the incondite Mr. Webber—"of course there's been talk about *that* for some time past. Not that 'E would care! Not *'Im*! 'E's too independent, *'E* is! 'Is mother found that out long ago. She tried to manage 'Im the way she does the others. Not *'Im*! That chap's got a will of 'Is own. 'E'll do what 'E wants to do, and no one will stop 'Im—that's 'ow independent 'E is."

She was silent a moment, reflecting with misty eyes upon the object of her idolatry. Then suddenly her pleasant face again suffused with ruddy color, and a short, rich, almost explosive laugh burst from her as she cried:

"The dev-*ill*! You know, they do say 'E was comin' 'ome one night not long ago, and"—her voice lowered confidingly —"they do say 'E'd 'ad a bit too much, and"—her voice sank still lower, and in a tone in which a shade of hesitancy was mixed with laughter, she went on—"well, sir,

407

they do say 'E was 'avin' 'Is troubles in gittin' 'ome. They say that really 'E was 'avin' to support 'Imself, sir, by the fence around St. James's Palace. But they do say, sir, that—ooh! ha-ha-ha!"—she laughed suddenly and throatily. "You must excuse me, sir, but I 'ave to larf when I think of it!" And then, slowly, emphatically, with an ectsasy of adoration, Mrs. Purvis whispered: "They say, sir, that the bobby on duty just outside the palace saw 'Im, and came up to 'Im and said, 'Can I 'elp you, sir?' But not *'Im*! 'E wouldn't be 'elped! 'E's too proud, *'E* is! That's the way 'E's always been. I'll tell you what—'E *is* a dev-*ill*!" And, still smiling, her strong hands held before her in a worn clasp, she leaned against the door and lapsed into the silence of misty contemplation.

"But, Mrs. Purvis," George remarked presently, "do you think he'll ever get married? I mean, do you really, now? After all, he's no chicken any longer, is he? And he must have had lots of chances, and if he was going to do anything about it——"

"Ah!" said Mrs. Purvis, in that tone of somewhat lofty recognition that she always used at such a time. "*Ah*! What I always say to *that* is, 'E *will*! 'E'll make up 'Is mind to it when 'E 'as to, but not before! 'E won't be driven into it, not 'Im! But 'E'll do it when 'E knows it is the proper time."

"Yes, Mrs. Purvis, but what *is* the proper time?"

"Well," she said, "after all, there *is* 'Is father, isn't there? And 'Is father is not as young as 'e used to be, *is* 'e?" She was silent for a moment, diplomatically allowing the tactful inference to sink in by itself. "Well, sir," she concluded very quietly, "I mean to say, sir, a time *will* come, sir, won't it?"

"Yes, Mrs. Purvis," George persisted, "but *will* it?" I mean, can you be sure? You know, you hear all sorts of things—even a stranger like myself hears them. For one thing, you hear he doesn't want it very much, and then, of course, there *is* his brother, isn't there?"

"Oh, *'im*," said Mrs. Purvis, "*'im!*" For a brief interval she remained silent, but had she filled an entire dictionary with the vocabulary of bitter and unyielding hostility, she could not have said more than she managed to convey in the two letters of that mutilated little pronoun "*'im.*"

"Yes," George persisted somewhat cruelly, "but after all, he *wants* it, doesn't he?"

"'E does," said Mrs. Purvis grimly.

"And he *is* married, isn't he?"

"'E is," said Mrs. Purvis, if anything a trifle more grimly than before.

"And *he* has children, hasn't he?"

"'E *as*, yes," said Mrs. Purvis, somewhat more gently. In fact, for a moment her face glowed with its look of former tenderness, but it grew grim again very quickly as she went on:

"But 'im! Not 'im!" She was deeply stirred by this imagined threat to the ascendancy of her idol. Her lips worked tremulously, then she shook her head with a quick movement of inflexible denial and said, "Not 'im." She was silent for a moment more, as if a struggle were going on between her desire to speak and the cool barrier of her natural reserve. Then she burst out: "I tell you, sir, I never liked the look of 'im! Not that one—no!" She shook her head again in a half-convulsive movement; then, in a tone of dark confidingness, she almost whispered: "There's somethin' *sly* about 'is face that I don't like! 'E's a sly one, 'e is, but 'e don't fool *me*!" Her face was now deeply flushed, and she nodded her head with the air of a person who had uttered her grim and final judgment and would not budge from it. "That's my opinion, if you ask me, sir! That's the way I've always felt about 'im. And 'er. *'Er! She* wouldn't like it, *would* she? Not 'arf she wouldn't!" She laughed suddenly, the bitter and falsetto laugh of an angry woman. "Not *'er*! Why, it's plain as day, it's written all over 'er! But a lot of good it'll do 'em," she said grimly, "*We* know what's what!" She shook her head again with grim decision. "The *people* know. They can't be fooled. So let 'em git along with it!"

"You don't think, then, that they———"

"Them!" said Mrs. Purvis strongly. *"Them!* Not in a million years, sir! Never! Never! . . . 'E"—her voice fairly soared to a cry of powerful conviction— " 'E's the one! 'E's *always* been the one! And when the time comes, sir, *'E—'E* will be King!"

In the complete and unquestioning loyalty of her character, Mrs. Purvis was like a large and gentle dog. Indeed, her whole relation to life was curiously animal-like. She had an intense concern for every member of brute creation, and when she saw dogs or horses in the streets she always seemed to notice first the animal and then the human being that it belonged to. She had come to know and recognize all the people in Ebury Street through the dogs they owned. When George questioned her one day about a distinguished-looking old gentleman with a keen hawk's face whom he had passed several times on the street, Mrs. Purvis answered immediately, with an air of satisfaction:

"Ah-h, yes. 'E's the one that 'as the rascal in 27. Ah-h, and 'e *is* a rascal, too," she cried, shaking her head and laughing with affectionate remembrance. "Big, shaggy fellow 'e is, you know, comin' along, swingin' 'is big shoulders, and lookin' as if butter wouldn't melt in 'is mouth. 'E is a *rascal*."

George was a little bewildered by this time and asked her if she meant the gentleman or the dog.

"Oh, the dog," cried Mrs. Purvis. "The dog! A big Scotch shepherd 'e is. Belongs to the gentleman you were speakin' of. Gentleman's some sort of scholar or writer or professor, I believe. Used to be up at Cambridge. Retired now. Lives in 27."

Or again, looking out of the window one day into the pea-soup drizzle of the street, George saw an astonishingly beautiful girl pass by upon the other side. He called Mrs. Purvis quickly, pointed out the girl, and excitedly demanded:

"Who is she? Do you know her? Does she live here on the street?"

"I can't say, sir," Mrs. Purvis answered, looking puzzled. "It seems I must 'ave seen 'er before, but I can't be sure. But I will just keep my eyes open and I'll let you know if I find out where she lives."

A few days later Mrs. Purvis came in from her morning's shopping tour, beaming with satisfaction and full of news. "Ah-h," she said, "I 'ave news for you. I found out about the girl."

"What girl?" he said, looking up startled from his work.

"The girl you asked about the other day," said Mrs. Purvis. "The one you pointed out to me."

"Oh yes," he said, getting up. "And what about her? Does she live here in the street?"

"Of course," said Mrs. Purvis. "I've seen 'er a 'undred times. I should 'ave known 'er in a second the other day, only she didn't 'ave *'im* with 'er."

"Him? Who?"

"Why, the rascal down at 46. That's who she is."

"That's who who is, Mrs. Purvis?"

"Why, the great Dane, of course. You must 'ave seen *'im.* 'E's big as a Shetland pony," she laughed. " 'E's always with 'er. The only time I ever saw 'er without 'im was the other day, and that's why," she cried triumphantly, "I didn't know 'er. But today, they were out takin' a walk together and I saw 'em comin'. Then I knew who she was. They're the ones in 46. And the rascal—" here she laughed affectionately—"ah-h, what a rascal 'e is! Oh, a fine fellow, you know. So big and strong 'e is. I sometimes wonder where they keep 'im, 'ow they found a 'ouse big enough to put 'im in."

Hardly a morning passed that she didn't return from her little tour of the neighborhood flushed with excitement over some new "rascal," some "fine fellow," some dog or horse she had observed and watched. She would go crimson with anger over any act of cruelty or indifference to an animal. She would come in boiling with rage because she had passed a horse that had been tightly bridled:

". . . And I gave 'im a piece of my mind, too," she would cry, referring to the driver. "I told 'im that a man as mistreated a hanimal in that way wasn't fit to 'ave one. If there'd been a constable about, I'd 'ave 'ad 'im took in custody, that's what I'd 'ave done. I told 'im so, too. Shockin', I calls it. The way some people can b'ave to some poor, 'elpless beast that 'as no tongue to tell what it goes through. Let 'em 'ave a bridle in *their* mouth a bit! Let 'em go around for a while with *their* faces shut up in a muzzle! Ah-h," she would say grimly, as if the idea afforded her a savage pleasure, "that'd teach 'em! They'd know then, all right!"

There was something disturbing and unwholesome about the extravagance of this feeling for animals. George observed Mrs. Purvis closely in her relations with people and found out that she was by no means so agitated at the spectacle of human suffering. Her attitude toward the poor, of whom she was one, was remarkable for its philosophic acceptance. Her feeling seemed to be that the poor are always with us, that they are quite used to their poverty, and that this makes it unnecessary for anybody to bother about it, least of all the miserable victims themselves. It had certainly never entered her head that anything should be done about it. The sufferings of the poor seemed to her as natural and as inevitable as the London fog, and to her way of thinking it was just as much a waste of honest emotion to get worked up about the one as about the other.

Thus, on the same morning that she would come in blazing with indignation over the mistreatment of a dog or a horse, George would sometimes hear her speak sharply, curtly, and without a trace of feeling to the dirty, half-starved, and half-naked devil of a boy who always delivered the beer from the liquor shop. This wretched child was like some creature out of Dickens—a living specimen of that poverty which, at its worst, has always seemed to be lower and more degraded in England than anywhere else. The thing that gives it its special horror is that in England people of this type appear to be stogged in their misery, sucked down in a swamp of inherited wretchedness which is never going to be any better, and from which they know they can never escape.

So it was with this God-forsaken boy. He was one of the Little People—that race of dwarfs and gnomes which was suddenly and terribly revealed to George that winter in London. George discovered that there are really two different orders of humanity in England, and they are so far apart that they hardly seem to belong to the same species. They are the Big People and the Little People.

The Big People are fresh-skinned, ruddy, healthy, and alert; they show by their appearance that they have always had

411

enough to eat. At their physical best, they look like great bulls of humanity. On the streets of London one sees these proud and solid figures of men and women, magnificently dressed and cared for, and one observes that their faces wear the completely vacant and imperturbable expressions of highly bred cattle. These are the British Lords of Creation. And among the people who protect and serve them, and who are really a part of their own order, one also sees some magnificent specimens— strapping Guardsmen, for example, six feet five inches tall and as straight as lances, with the same assured look in their faces, which says plainly that though they may not be the Lords of Creation themselves, at any rate they are the agents and instruments of the Lords.

But if one stays in England long enough, all of a sudden one day he is going to discover the Little People. They are a race of gnomes who look as if they have burrowed in tunnels and lived for so many centuries in underground mines that they have all become pale and small and wizened. Something in their faces and in the gnarled formations of their bodies not only shows the buried lives they live, but also indicates that their fathers and mothers and grandparents for generations before them were similarly starved for food and sunlight and were bred like gnomes in the dark and deep-delved earth.

One hardly notices them at first. But then, one day, the Little People swarm up to the surface of the earth, and for the first time one sees them. That is the way the revelation came to George Webber, and it was an astounding discovery. It was like a kind of terrible magic to realize suddenly that he had been living in this English world and seeing only one part of it, thinking it was the whole. It was not that the Little People were few in number. Once he saw them, they seemed to be almost the whole population. They outnumbered the Big People ten to one. And after he saw them, he knew that England could never look the same to him again, and that nothing he might read or hear about the country thereafter would make sense to him if it did not take the Little People into account.

The wretched boy from the liquor shop was one of them. Everything about him proclaimed eloquently that he had been born dwarfed and stunted into a world of hopeless poverty, and that he had never had enough to eat, or enough clothes to warm him, or enough shelter to keep the cold fogs from seeping through into the very marrow of his bones. It was not that he was actually deformed, but merely that his body seemed to be shriveled and shrunk and squeezed of its juices like that of an old man. He may have been fifteen or sixteen years old, though there were times when he seemed younger. Always, however, his appearance was that of an undergrown man, and one had

412

the horrible feeling that his starved body had long since given up the unequal struggle and would never grow any more.

He wore a greasy, threadbare little jacket, tightly buttoned, from the sleeves of which his raw wrists and large, grimy, work-reddened hands protruded with almost indecent nakedness. His trousers, tight as a couple of sausage skins, were equally greasy and threadbare, and were inches too short for him. His old and broken shoes were several sizes too big, and from the battered look of them they must have helped to round the edges of every cobblestone in stony-hearted London. This costume was completed by a shapeless old hulk of a cap, so large and baggy that it slopped over on one side of his head and buried the ear.

What his features were like it was almost impossible to know, because he was so dirty. His flesh, what one could see of it through the unwashed grime, had a lifeless, opaque pallor. The whole face was curiously blurred and blunted, as if it had been molded hastily and roughly out of tallow. The nose was wide and flat, and turned up at the end to produce great, flaring nostrils. The mouth was thick and dull, and looked as if it had been pressed into the face with a blunt instrument. The eyes were dark and dead.

This grotesque little creature even spoke a different language. It was cockney, of course, but not sharp, decisive cockney; it was a kind of thick, catarrhal jargon, so blurred in the muttering that it was almost indecipherable. George could hardly understand him at all. Mrs. Purvis could make better sense of it, but even she confessed that there were times when she did not know what he was talking about. George would hear her beginning to rail at him the instant he came staggering into the house beneath the weight of a heavy case of beer:

"'Ere, now, mind where you're goin', won't you? And try not to make so much noise with those bottles! Why can't you wipe those muddy boots before you come in the 'ouse? Don't come clumpin' up the stairs like an 'orse! . . . Oh," she would cry in despair, turning to George, "'e *is* the clumsiest chap I ever saw! . . . And why can't you wash your face once in a while?" she would say, striking again at the urchin with her sharp tongue. "A great, growin' chap like you ought to be ashamed goin' about where people can see you with a face like that!"

"Yus," he muttered sullenly, "goin' abaht wiv a fyce lahk that. If you 'ad to go abaht the wye I do, you'd wash your fyce, wouldn't yer?"

Then, still muttering resentfully to himself, he would clump down the stairs and go away, and from the front window George would watch him as he trudged back up the street toward the wine and liquor shop in which he worked.

This store was small, but since the neighborhood was

413

fashionable the place had that atmosphere of mellow luxury and quiet elegance—something about it a little worn, but all the better for being a little worn—that one finds in small, expensive shops of this sort in England. It was as if the place were mildly tinctured with fog, touched a little with the weather, and with the indefinable but faintly exciting smell of soft coal smoke. And over everything, permeating the very woods of the counter, shelves, and floor, hung the fragrance of old wines and the purest distillations of fine liquors.

You opened the door, and a little bell tinkled gently. You took a half-step down into the shop, and immediately its atmosphere made you feel at peace. You felt opulent and secure. You felt all the powerful but obscure seductions of luxury (which, if you have money, you can feel in England better than anywhere else). You felt rich and able to do anything. You felt that the world was good, and overflowing with delectable delicacies, and that all of them were yours for the asking.

The proprietor of this luxurious little nest of commerce seemed just exactly the man for such an office. He was middle-aged, of medium height, spare of build, with pale brown eyes and brown mustaches—wispy, rather long, and somewhat lank. He wore a wing collar, a black necktie, and a scarfpin. He usually appeared in shirt-sleeves, but he dispelled any suggestion of improper informality by wearing arm protectors of black silk. This gave him just the proper touch of unctuous yet restrained servility. He was middle class—not middle class as America knows it, not even middle class as the English usually know it—but a very special kind of middle class, *serving* middle class, as befitted a purveyor of fine comforts to fine gentlemen. He was there to serve the gentry, to live upon the gentry, to exist by, through, and for the gentry, and always to bend a little at the waist when gentry came.

As you entered the shop, he would come forward behind his counter, say "Good evening, sir" with just the proper note of modified servility, make some remark about the weather, and then, arching his thin, bony, sandily-freckled hands upon the counter, he would bend forward slightly—wing collar, black necktie, black silk arm protectors, mustache, pale brown eyes, pale, false smile, and all the rest of him—and with servile attentiveness, not quite fawning, would wait to do your bidding.

"What is good today? Have you a claret, a sound yet modestly-priced vintage you can recommend?"

"A claret, sir?" in silken tones. "We have a good one, sir, and not expensive either. A number of our patrons have tried it. They all pronounce it excellent. You'll not go wrong, sir, if you try this one."

"And how about a Scotch whiskey?"

"A Haig, sir?" Again the silken tones. "You'll not go wrong on Haig, sir. But perhaps you'd like to try another brand, something a trifle rare, a little more expensive, perhaps a little more mature. Some of our patrons have tried this one, sir. It costs a shilling more, but if you like the smoky flavor you'll find it worth the difference."

Oh, the fond, brisk slave! The fond, neat slave! The fond slave bending at the waist, with bony fingers arched upon his counter! The fond slave with his sparse hair neatly parted in the middle, and the narrow forehead arched with even cor-rugations of pale wrinkles as the face lifted upward with its thin, false smile! Oh, this fond, brisk pander to fine gentlemen—and that wretched boy! For suddenly, in the midst of all this show of eager servitude, this painted counterfeit of warmth, the man would turn like a snarling cur upon that miserable child, who stood there sniffling through his catarrhal nose, shuffling his numbed feet for circulation, and chafing his reddened, chapped, work-coarsened hands before the cheerful, crackling fire of coals:

"Here, now, what are you hanging around the shop for? Have you delivered that order to Number 12 yet? Be on your way, then, and don't keep the gentleman waiting any longer!"

And then immediately the grotesque return to silken courtesy, to the pale, false smile again, to the fawning unctions of his "Yes, sir. A dozen bottles, sir. Within thirty minutes, sir. The Number 42—oh, quite so, sir. Good night."

And good night, good night, good night to you, my fond, brisk slave, you backone of a nation's power. Good night to you, staunch symbol of a Briton's rugged independence. Good night to you, and to your wife, your children, and your mongrel tyranny over their lives. Good night to you, my little autocrat of the dinner table. Good night to you, my lord and master of the Sunday leg of mutton. Good night to you, my gentlemen's pander in Ebury Street.

And good night to you, as well, my wretched little boy, my little dwarf, my gnome, my grimy citizen from the world of the Little People.

The fog drifts thick and fast tonight into the street. It sifts and settles like a cloak, until one sees the street no longer. And where the shop light shines upon the fog, there burns a misty glow, a blurred and golden bloom of radiance, of comfort, and of warmth. Feet pass the shop, men come ghostwise from the fog's thick mantle, are for a moment born, are men again, are heard upon the pavement, then, wraithlike, vanish into fog, are ghosts again, are lost, are gone. The proud, the mighty, and the titled of the earth, the lovely and protected, too, go home—home to their strong and sheltered walls behind the golden nimbus of other lights, fog-flowered. Four hundred yards away

415

the tall sentries stamp and turn and march again. All's glory here. All's strong as mortared walls. All's loveliness and joy within this best of worlds.

And you, you wretched child, so rudely and unfitly wrenched into this world of glory, wherever you must go tonight, in whatever doorway you must sleep, upon whatever pallet of foul-smelling straw, within whatever tumbled warren of old brick, there in the smoke, the fog-cold welter, and the swarming web of old, unending London—sleep well as can be, and hug the ghosts of warmth about you as you remember the forbidden world and its imagined glory. So, my little gnome, good night. May God have mercy on us all.

Chapter Thirty-Three

Enter Mr. Lloyd McHarg

*During the late Autumn and early Winter of that year oc-*cured an event which added to Webber's chronicle the adventure of an extraordinary experience. He had received no news from America for several weeks when, suddenly in November, he began to get excited letters from his friends informing him of a recent incident that bore directly on his own career.

The American novelist, Mr. Lloyd McHarg, had just published a new book which had been instantly and universally acclaimed as a monument of national significance, as well as the crowning achievement in McHarg's brilliant literary career. George had read in the English press brief accounts of the book's tremendous success, but now he began to receive enlargements on the news from his friends at home. Mr. Mc-Harg, it seemed, had given an interview to reporters, and to the astonishment of everyone had begun to talk, not about his own book, but about Webber's. Cuttings of the interview were sent to George. He read them with astonishment, and with the deepest and most earnest gratitude.

George had never met Mr. Lloyd McHarg. He had never had occasion to communicate with him in any way. He knew him only through his books. He was, of course, one of the chief figures in American letters, and now, at the zenith of his career, when he had won the greatest ovation one could win, he had seized the occasion, which most men would have employed for purposes of self-congratulation, to praise enthusiastically the work of an obscure young writer who was a total stranger to him and who had written only one book.

It seemed to George then, as it seemed to him ever afterwards, one of the most generous acts he had ever known, and when he had somewhat recovered from the astonishment and joy which this unexpected news had produced in him, he sat down and wrote to Mr. McHarg and told him how he felt. In a short time he had an answer from him—a brief note, written from New York. Mr. McHarg said that he had spoken as he had because he felt that way about Webber's book, and that he was happy to have had the opportunity of giving public acknowledgment to his feeling. He said that he was about to be awarded an honorary degree by one of America's leading universities—an event which, he confessed with pardonable pride, pleased him all the more because the award was to be made out of season, in special recognition of his last book, and because the ceremony attending it was not to be part of the usual performance of trained seals at commencement time. He said that he was sailing for Europe immediately afterwards and would spend some time on the Continent, that he would be in England a little later, and that he hoped to see Webber then. George wrote back and told him he was looking forward to their meeting, gave him his address, and there for a time the matter rested.

Mrs. Purvis was a party to George's elation, which was so exultant that he could not have kept the reason a secret from her if he had tried. She was almost as excited about his impending meeting with Mr. McHarg as he was. Together they would scan the papers for news of Mr. McHarg. One morning she brought the "nice 'ot cup" of Ovaltine, rattled the pages of her tabloid paper, and said:

"I see where 'e is on 'is way. 'E's sailed already from New York."

A few days later George smacked the crisp sheets of *The Times* and cried: "He's there! He's landed! He's in Europe! It won't be long now!"

Then came the never-to-be-forgotten morning when she brought the usual papers, and with them the day's mail, and in the mail a letter from Fox Edwards, enclosing a long clipping from *The New York Times*. This was a full account of the ceremonies at which Mr. McHarg had been awarded his honorary degree. Before a distinguished gathering at the great university Mr. McHarg had made a speech, and the clipping contained an extended quotation of what he had had to say.

417

George had not foreseen it. He had not imagined it could happen. His name shot up at him from the serried columns of close print and exploded in his eyes like shrapnel. A hard knot gathered in his throat and choked him. His heart leaped, skipped, hammered at his ribs. McHarg had put Webber in his speech, had spoken of him there at half a column's length. He had hailed the younger man as a future spokesman of his country's spirit, an evidence of a fruition that had come, of a continent that had been discovered. He called Webber a man of genius, and held his name before the mighty of the earth as a pledge of what America was, and a token of where it would go.

And suddenly George remembered who he was, and saw the journey he had come. He remembered Locust Street in Old Catawba twenty years before, and Nebraska, Randy, and the Potterhams, Aunt Maw and Uncle Mark, his father and the little boy that he had been, with the hills closing in around him, and at night the whistles wailing northward toward the world. And now his name, whose name was nameless, had become a shining thing, and a boy who once had waited tongueless in the South had, through his language, opened golden gateways to the Earth.

Mrs. Purvis felt it almost as much as he did. He pointed speechless to the clipping. He tapped the shining passages with trembling hand. He thrust the clipping at her. She read it, flushed crimson in the face, turned suddenly, and went away.

After that they waited daily for McHarg's coming. Week lengthened into week. They searched the papers every morning for news of him. He seemed to be making a tour of Europe, and everywhere he went he was entertained and fêted and interviewed and photographed in the company of other famous men. Now he was in Copenhagen. Now he was staying in Berlin a week or two. Later he had gone to Baden-Baden for a cure.

"Oh Lord!" George groaned dismally. "How long does that take?"

Again he was in Amsterdam; and then silence. Christmas came.

"I should 'ave thought," said Mrs. Purvis, "'e'd be 'ere by now."

New Year's came, and still there was no word from Lloyd McHarg.

One morning about the middle of January, after George had worked all night, and now, in bed, was carrying on his usual chat with Mrs. Purvis, he had just spoken of McHarg's long-deferred arrival rather hopelessly—when the phone rang. Mrs. Purvis went into the sitting room and answered it. George could hear her saying formally:

"Yes. Who shall I say? Who's callin', please?" A waiting silence. Then, rather quickly, "Just a moment, sir." She entered

George's room, her face flushed, and said, "Mr. Lloyd Mc'Arg is on the wire."

To say that George got out of bed would be to give a hopelessly inadequate description of a movement which hurled him into the air, bedclothes and all, as if he had been shot out of a cannon. He landed squarely in his bedroom slippers, and in two strides, still shedding bedclothes as he went, he was through the door, into the sitting room, and had the receiver in his hand.

"Hello, hello, hello!" he stammered. "Who—what—is that?"

McHarg was even quicker. His voice, rapid, feverish, somewhat nasal and high-pitched, unmistakably American, stabbed nervously across the wire and said:

"Hello, hello. Is that you, George?" He called him by his first name immediately. "How are you, son? How are you, boy? How are they treating you?"

"Fine, Mr. McHarg!" George yelled. "It *is* Mr. McHarg, isn't it? Say, Mr. McHarg——"

"Now take it easy! Take it easy!" he cried feverishly. "Don't shout so loud!" he yelled. "I'm not in New York, you know!"

"I know you're not," George screamed. "That's what I was just about to say!"—laughing idiotically. "Say, Mr. McHarg, when can we——"

"Now wait a minute, wait a minute! Let me do the talking. Don't get so excited. Now listen, George!" His voice had the staccato rapidity of a telegraph ticker. Even though one had never seen him, one would have got instantly an accurate impression of his feverishly nervous vitality, wire-taut tension, and incessant activity. "Now listen!" he barked. "I want to see you and talk to you. We'll have lunch together and talk things over."

"Fine! F-fine!" George stuttered. "I'll be delighted! Any time you say. I know you're busy. I can meet you tomorrow, next day, Friday—next week if that suits you better."

"Next week, hell!" he rasped. "How much time do you think I've got to wait around for lunch? You're coming here for lunch today. Come on! Get busy! Get a move on you!" he cried irritably. "How long will it take you to get here, anyway?"

George asked him where he was staying, and he gave an address on one of the streets near St. James's and Piccadilly. It was only a ten-minute ride in a taxi, but since it was not yet ten o'clock in the morning George suggested that he arrive there around noon.

"What? Two hours? For Christ's sake!" McHarg cried in a high-pitched, irritated voice. "Where the hell do you live anyway? In the north of Scotland?"

George told him no, that he was only ten minutes away, but that he thought he might want to wait two or three hours before he had his lunch.

"Wait two or three hours?" he shouted. "Say, what the hell is this, anyway? How long do you expect me to wait for lunch? You don't keep people waiting two or three hours every time you have lunch with them, do you, George?" he said, in a milder but distinctly aggrieved tone of voice. "Christ, man! A guy'd starve to death if he had to wait on you!"

George was getting more and more bewildered, and wondered if it was the custom of famous writers to have lunch at ten o'clock in the morning, but he stammered hastily:

"No, no, certainly not, Mr. McHarg. I can come any time you say. It will only take me twenty minutes or half an hour."

"I thought you said you were only ten minutes away?"

"I know, but I've got to dress and shave first."

"Dress! Shave!" McHarg yelled. "For Christ's sake, you mean to tell me you're not out of bed yet? What do you do? Sleep till noon every day? How in the name of God do you ever get any work done?"

By this time George felt so crushed that he did not dare tell McHarg that he was not only not out of bed, but that he'd hardly been to bed yet; somehow it seemed impossible to confess that he had worked all night. He did not know what new explosion of derision or annoyance this might produce, so he compromised and mumbled some lame excuse about having worked late the night before.

"Well, come on, then!" he cried impatiently, before the words were out of George's mouth. "Snap out of it! Hop into a taxi and come on up here as soon as you can. Don't stop to shave," he said curtly. "I've been with a Dutchman for the last three days and I'm hungry as hell!"

With these cryptic words he banged the receiver up in George's ear, leaving him to wonder, in a state of stunned bewilderment, just why being with a Dutchman for three days should make anyone hungry as hell.

Mrs. Purvis already had a clean shirt and his best suit of clothes laid out for him by the time he returned to his room. While he put them on she got out the brush and the shoe polish, took his best pair of shoes just beyond the open door into the sitting room, and went right down on her knees and got to work on them. And while she labored on them she called in to him, a trifle wistfully:

"I do 'ope 'e gives you a good lunch. We was 'avin' gammon and peas again today. Ah-h, a prime bit, too. I 'ad just put 'em on when 'e called."

"Well, I hate to miss them, Mrs. Purvis," George called back, as he struggled into his trousers. "But you go on and eat them, and don't worry about me. I'll get a good lunch."

" 'E'll take you to the Ritz, no doubt," she called again a trifle loftily.

"Oh," George answered easily as he pulled on his shirt, "I don't think he likes those places. People of that sort," he shouted with great assurance, as if he were on intimate terms with "people of that sort"—"they don't go in for swank as a rule. He's probably bored stiff with it, particularly after all he's been through these past few weeks. He'd probably much rather go to some simple place."

"Um. Shouldn't wonder," said Mrs. Purvis reflectively. "Meetin' all them artists and members of the nobility. Probably fed up with it, I should think," she said. "I know I should be," which meant that she would have given only her right eye for the opportunity. "You might take 'im to Simpson's, you know," she said in the offhand manner that usually accompanied her most important contributions.

"There's an idea," George cried. "Or to Stone's Chop House in Panton Street."

"Ah yes," she said. "That's just off the 'Ay Market, isn't it?"

"Yes, runs between the Hay Market and Leicester Square," George said, tying his tie. "An old place, you know, two hundred years or more, not quite so fancy as Simpson's, but he might like it better on that account. They don't let women in," he added with a certain air of satisfaction, as if this in itself would probably recommend the place to his distinguished host.

"Yes, and their ale, they say, is grand," said Mrs. Purvis.

"It's the color of mahogany," George said, throwing on his coat, "and it goes down like velvet. I've tried it, Mrs. Purvis. They bring it to you in a silver tankard. And after two of them you'd send flowers to your own mother-in-law."

She laughed suddenly and heartily and came bustling in with the shoes, her pleasant face suffused with pink color.

"Excuse me, sir," she said, setting the shoes down. "But you do 'ave a way of puttin' things. I 'ave to larf sometimes. . . . Still, in Simpson's—you won't go wrong in Simpson's, you know," said Mrs. Purvis, who had never seen any of these places in her whole life. "If 'e likes mutton—ah-h, I tell you what," she said with satisfaction, "you do get a prime bit of mutton there."

He put on his shoes and noted that only ten minutes had passed since Mr. McHarg hung up. He was now dressed and ready, so he started out the door and down the stairs, flinging on his overcoat as he descended. Despite the early hour, his appetite had been whetted by his conversation, and he felt that he would be able to do full justice to his lunch. He had reached the street and was hailing a taxi when Mrs. Purvis came running after him, waving a clean handkerchief, which she put neatly in the breast pocket of his coat. He thanked her and signaled again to the taxi.

It was one of those old, black, hearselike contraptions with a baggage rack on top which, to an American, used to the gaudy, purring thunderbolts of the New York streets, seem like Victorian relics, and which are often, indeed, driven by elderly Jehus with walrus mustaches who were driving hansom cabs at the time of Queen Victoria's jubilee. This ancient vehicle now rolled sedately toward him, on the wrong side of the street as usual—which is to say, on the right side for the English.

George opened the door, gave the walrus the address, and told him to make haste, that the occasion was pressing. He said, "Very good, sir," with courteous formality, wheeled the old crate around, and rolled sedately up the street again at exactly the same pace, which was about twelve miles an hour. They passed the grounds of Buckingham Palace, wheeled into the Mall, turned up past St. James's Palace into Pall Mall, thence into St. James's Street, and in a moment more drew up before McHarg's address.

It was a bachelors' chambers, one of those quiet and sedate-looking places that one finds in England, and that are so wonderfully comfortable if one has the money. Inside, the appointments suggested a small and very exclusive club. George spoke to a man in the tiny office. He answered:

"Mr. McHarg? Of course, sir. He is expecting you. . . . John," to a young man in uniform and brass buttons, "take the gentleman up."

They entered the lift. John closed the door carefully, gave a vigorous tug to the rope, and sedately they crept up, coming to a more or less accurate halt, after a few more manipulations of the rope, at one of the upper floors. John opened the door, stepped out with an "If you please, sir," and led off down the hall to a door which stood partially open and from which there came a confused hum of voices. John rapped gently, entered in response to the summons, and said quietly:

"Mr. Webber calling, sir."

There were three men in the room, but so astonishing was the sight of McHarg that at first George did not notice the other two. McHarg was standing in the middle of the floor with a glass in one hand and a bottle of Scotch whiskey in the other, preparing to pour himself a drink. When he saw George he looked up quickly, put the bottle down, and advanced with his hand extended in greeting. There was something almost terrifying in his appearance. George recognized him instantly. He had seen McHarg's pictures many times, but he now realized how beautifully unrevealing are the uses of photography. He was fantastically ugly, and to this ugliness was added a devastation of which George had never seen the equal.

The first and most violent impression was his astonishing redness. Everything about him was red—hair, large protuberant ears, eyebrows, eyelids, even his bony, freckled, knuckly hands. (As George noticed the hands he understood why everyone who knew him called him "Knuckles.") Moreover, it was a most alarming redness. His face was so red that it seemed to throw off heat, and if at that moment smoke had begun to issue from his nostrils and he had burst out in flames all over, George would hardly have been surprised.

His face did not have that fleshy and high-colored floridity that is often seen in men who have drunk too long and too earnestly. It was not like that at all. McHarg was thin to the point of emaciation. He was very tall, six feet two or three, and his excessive thinness and angularity made him seem even taller. George thought he looked ill and wasted. His face, which was naturally a wry, puckish sort of face—as one got to know it better, a pugnacious but very attractive kind of face, full of truculence, but also with an impish humor and a homely, Yankee, freckled kind of modesty that were wonderfully engaging—this face now looked as puckered up as if it were permanently about to swallow a half-green persimmon, and it also seemed to be all dried out and blistered by the fiery flames that burned in it. And out of this face peered two of the most remarkable-looking eyes in all the world. Their color must originally have been light blue, but now they were so bleached and faded that they looked as if they had been poached.

He came toward George quickly, with his bony, knuckled hand extended in greeting, his lips twitching nervously over his large teeth, his face turned wryly upward and to one side in an expression that was at once truculent, nervously apprehensive, and yet movingly eloquent of something fiercely and permanently wounded, something dreadfully lacerated, something so tender and unarmed in the soul and spirit of the man that life had got in on him at a thousand points and slashed him to ribbons. He took George's hand and shook it vigorously, at the same time bristling up to him with his wry and puckered face like a small boy to another before the fight begins, as if to say: "Go on, now, go on. Knock that chip off my shoulder. I dare and double-dare you." This was precisely his manner now, except that he said:

"Why you—why you monkeyfied—why you monkeyfied bastard, you! Just look at him!" he cried suddenly in a high-pitched voice, half turning to his companions. "Why you—who the hell ever told you you could write, anyway?" Then cordially: "George, how are you? Come on in, come on over here!"

And, still holding Webber's hand in his bony grip, and taking his arm with his other hand, he led him across the room toward his other guests. Then, suddenly releasing him, and striking a pompous oratorical attitude, he began to declaim in the florid accents of an after-dinner speaker:

"Ladies and gentlemen, it is my peculiar privilege, and I may even say my distinguished honor, to present to the members of the Hog Head Hollow Ladies Leeterary, Arteestic, and Mutual Culshural Society our esteemed guest of honor—a man who writes books that are so God-damned long that few people can even pick 'em up. A man whose leeterary style is distinguished by such a command of beautiful English as she is wrote that he has rarely been known to use less than twenty-one adjectives where four would do."

He changed abruptly, dropped his oratorical attitude, and laughed a sudden, nervous, dry, falsetto laugh, at the same time mauling Webber in the ribs with a bony finger. "How do you like that, George?" he said with immediate friendly warmth. "Does that get 'em? Is that the way they do it? Not bad, eh?" He was obviously pleased with his effort.

"George," he now continued in a natural tone of voice, "I want you to meet two friends of mine. Mr. Bendien, of Amsterdam," he said, presenting Webber to a heavy-set, red-faced, elderly Dutchman, who sat by the table within easy reaching distance of a tall brown crock of Holland gin, of which, to judge from his complexion, he had already consumed a considerable quantity.

"Ladies and gentlemen," cried McHarg, striking another attitude, "allow me to introduce that stupendous, that death-defying, that thrill-packed wonder of the ages, that hair-raising and spine-tingling act which has thrilled most of the crowned heads of Europe and all of the deadheads of Amsterdam. Now appearing absolutely for the first time under the big tent. Ladies and gentlemen, I now take pleasure in introducing Mynheer Cornelius Bendien, the Dutch maestro, who will perform for you his celebrated act of balancing an eel on the end of his nose while he swallows in rapid succession, without pausing for breath, three—count 'em—three brown jugs of the finest imported Holland gin. Mr. Bendien, Mr. Webber. . . . How was that, boy, how was that?" said McHarg, laughing his shrill falsetto, and turning and prodding Webber again with an eager finger.

Then, somewhat more curtly, he said: "You may have met Mr. Donald Stoat before. He tells me that he knows you."

The other man looked out from underneath his heavy

eyebrows and inclined his head pompously. "I believe," he said, "I have had the honor of Mr. Webber's acquaintance."

George remembered him, although he had seen him only once or twice, and that some years before. Mr. Stoat was not the kind of man one easily forgets.

It was plain to see that McHarg was on edge, terribly nervous, and also irritated by Stoat's presence. He turned away abruptly, muttering: "Too—too—too much—too much." And then, wheeling about suddenly: "All right, George. Have a drink. What's it going to be?"

"My own experience," said Mr. Stoat with unctuous pomposity, "is that the best drink in the morning—" he leered significantly with his bushy eyebrows—"a gentleman's drink, if I may say so—is a glawss of dry sherry." He had a "glawss" of this beverage in his hand at the moment, and, lifting it with an air of delicate connoisseurship, at the same time working his eyebrows appraisingly, he sniffed it—an action which seemed to irritate McHarg no end. "Allow me," continued Mr. Stoat, with rotund deliberation, "to recommend it to your consideration."

McHarg began to pace rapidly up and down. "Too much— too much," he muttered. "All right, George," he said irritably, "what'll you have to drink—Scotch?"

Mynheer Bendien put in his oar at this point. Holding up his glass and leaning forward with a hand on one fat knee, he said with guttural solemnity: "You should trink chin. Vy don't you try a trink of Holland chin?"

This advice also seemed to annoy Mr. McHarg. He glared at Bendien with his flaming face, then, throwing up his bony hands with a quick, spasmodic movement, he cried, "Oh, for God's sake!" He turned and began to pace up and down again, muttering: "Too much—too much—too—too—too much." Then abruptly, in a voice shrill with irritation: "Let him drink what he wants, for Christ's sake! Go ahead, Georgie," he said roughly. "Drink what you like. Pour yourself some Scotch." And suddenly turning to Webber, his whole face lighting up with an impish smile, his lips flickering nervously above his teeth: "Isn't it wonderful, Georgie? Isn't it marvelous? K-k-k-k-k—" prodding Webber in the ribs with bony forefinger, and laughing a high, dry, feverish laugh—"Can you beat it?"

"I confess," said Mr. Donald Stoat at this point, with rotund unction, "that I have not read our young friend's opus, which, I believe—" unction here deepening visibly into rotund sarcasm—"which, I believe, has been hailed by certain of our cognoscenti as a masterpiece. After all, there are so many masterpieces nowadays, aren't there? Scarcely a week goes by but what I pick up my copy of *The Times*—I refer, of course, to *The Times* of London, as distinguished from its younger and

425

somewhat more immature colleague, *The New York Times*—to find that another of our young men has enriched English literature with another masterpiece of im—per—ish—able prose."

All this was uttered in ponderous periods with leerings and twitchings of those misplaced mustaches that served the gentleman for eyebrows. McHarg was obviously becoming more and more annoyed, and kept pacing up and down, muttering to himself. Mr. Stoat, however, was too obtuse by nature, and too entranced by the rolling cadences of his own rhetoric, to observe the warning signals. After leering significantly with his eyebrows again, he went on:

"I can only hope, however, that our young friend here is a not too enthusiastic devotee of the masters of what I shall call The School of Bad Taste."

"What are you talking about?" said McHarge, pausing suddenly, half turning, and glaring fiercely. "I suppose you mean Hugh Walpole, and John Galsworthy, and other dangerous radicals of that sort, eh?"

"No, sir," said Mr. Stoat deliberately. "I was not thinking of them. I was referring to that concocter of incoherent nonsense, that purveyor of filth, that master of obscenity, who wrote that book so few people can read, and no one can understand, but which some of our young men are hailing enthusiastically as the greatest masterpiece of the century."

"What book are you talking about anyway?" McHarg said irritably.

"Its name, I believe," said Mr. Stoat pompously, "is *Ulysses.* Its author, I have heard, is an Irishman."

"Oh," cried McHarg with an air of enlightenment, and with an impish gleam in his eye that was quite lost on Mr. Stoat. "You're speaking of George Moore, aren't you?"

"That's it! That's it!" cried Mr. Stoat quickly, nodding his head with satisfaction. He was getting excited now. His eyebrows twitched more rapidly than ever. "That's the fellow! And the book—" he sputtered—"pah!" He spat out the word as though it had been brought up by an emetic, and screwed his eyebrows around across his domy forehead in an expression of nausea. "I tried to read a few pages of it once," he whispered sonorously and dramatically, "but I let it fall. I let it fall. As though I had touched a tainted thing, I let it fall. And then," he said hoarsely, "I washed my hands, with a very—strong—soap."

"My dear sir," cried McHarg suddenly, with an air of sincere conviction, at the same time being unable to keep his eye from gleaming more impishly than ever, "you are absolutely right. I absolutely agree with you."

Mr. Stoat, who had been very much on his dignity up to now,

thawed visibly under the seducing cajolery of this unexpected confirmation of his literary judgment.

"You are positively and unanswerably correct," said Knuckles, now standing in the middle of the room with his long legs spread wide apart, his bony hands hanging to the lapels of his coat. "You have hit the nail right smack—dead—square on the top of its head." As he uttered these words, he jerked his wry face from side to side to give them added emphasis. "There has never been a dirtier—filthier—more putrid—and more corrupt writer than George Moore. And as for that book of his, *Ulysses,*" McHarg shouted, "that is unquestionably the vilest——"

"—the rottenest—" shouted Mr. Stoat——

"—the most obscene—" shrilled McHarg——

"—the most vicious—" panted Mr. Stoat——

"—unadulterated——"

"—piece of tripe—" choked Mr. Stoat with rapturous agreement——

"—that has ever polluted the pages, defiled the name, and besmirched the record——"

"—of English literature!" gasped Mr. Stoat happily, and paused, panting for breath. "Yes," he went on when he had recovered his power of speech, "and that other thing—that play of his—that rotten, vile, vicious, so-called tragedy in five acts—what was the name of that thing, anyway?"

"Oh," cried McHarg with an air of sudden recognition—"you mean *The Importance of Being Earnest,* don't you?"

"No, no," said Mr. Stoat impatiently. "Not that one. This one came later on."

"Oh yes." McHarg exclaimed, as if it had suddenly come to him. "You're speaking of *Mrs. Warren's Profession,* aren't you?"

"That's it, that's it!" cried Mr. Stoat. "I took my wife to see it—I took my *wife*—my *own* wife——"

"His *own* wife!" McHarg repeated, as if astounded. "Well I'll be God-damned," he said. "What do you know about that!"

"And would you believe it, sir?" Mr. Stoat's voice again sank to a whisper of loathing and revulsion, and his eyebrows worked ominously about his face. "I was so ashamed—I was *so ashamed*—that I could not look at her. We got up and left, sir, before the end of the first act—before anyone could see us. I went away with head bowed, as one who had been forced to take part in some nasty thing."

"Well what do you know about that?" said McHarg sympathetically. "Wasn't that just too damned bad? *I call it perfectly damned awful!*" he shouted suddenly, and turned away, his jaw muscles working convulsively as he muttered again, "Too much—too much." He halted abruptly in front of Webber with his puckered face aflame and his lips twitching nervously, and began to prod him in the ribs, laughing his high, falsetto laugh. "He's a publisher," he squeaked. "He publishes books. K-k-k-k-k—Can you beat it, Georgie?" he squeaked almost inaudibly. Then, jerking a bony thumb in the direction of the astonished Stoat, he shrieked: "In the name of Christ Almighty—a *publisher*!" and resumed his infuriated pacing of the room.

Chapter Thirty-Four

The Two Visitors

Ever since George entered the room he had been wondering about the presence of McHarg's two strangely assorted visitors. Anyone could see at a glance that Bendien and Stoat were not clever men, not men of the spirit, and that neither possessed any qualities of intellect or of perception that could interest a person like Lloyd McHarg. What, then, were they doing here in this simulation of boon companionship so early in the morning?

Mynheer Bendien was obviously just a business man, a kind of Dutch Babbitt. He was, indeed, a hard-bargaining, shrewd importer who plied a constant traffic between England and Holland, and was intimately familiar with the markets and business practices of both countries. His occupation had left its mark upon him, that same mark which is revealed in a coarsening of perception and a blunting of sensitivity among people of his kind the world over.

As George observed the signs that betrayed what Bendien was beyond any mistaking, he felt confirmed in an opinion that had been growing on him of late. He had begun to see that the true races of mankind are not at all what we are told in youth that they are. They are not defined either by national frontiers or by the characteristics assigned to them by the subtle investigations of anthropologists. More and more George was coming to believe that the real divisions of humanity cut across these barriers and arise out of differences in the very souls of men.

George had first had his attention called to this phenomenon by an observation of H. L. Mencken. In his extraordinary work on the American language, Mencken gave an example of the

American sporting writers' jargon—"Babe Smacks Forty-second with Bases Loaded"—and pointed out that such a headline would be as completely meaningless to an Oxford don as the dialect of some newly discovered tribe of Eskimos. True enough; but what shocked George to attention when he read it was that Mencken drew the wrong inference from his fact. The headline would be meaningless to the Oxford don, not because it was written in the American language, but because the Oxford don had no knowledge of baseball. The same headline might be just as meaningless to a Harvard professor, and for the same reason.

It seemed to George that the Oxford don and the Harvard professor had far more kinship with each other—a far greater understanding of each other's ways of thinking, feeling, and living—than either would have with millions of people of his own nationality. This observation led George to realize that academic life has created its own race of men who are set apart from the rest of humanity by the affinity of their souls. This academic race, it seemed to him, had innumerable peculiar characteristics of its own, among them the fact that, like the sporting gentry, they had invented their own private languages for communication with one another. The internationalism of science was another characteristic: there is no such thing as English chemistry or American physics or (Stalin to the contrary notwithstanding) Russian biology, but only chemistry, physics, and biology. So, too, it follows that one tells a good deal more about a man when one says he is a chemist than when one says he is an Englishman.

In the same way, Babe Ruth would probably feel more closely akin to the English professional cricketer, Jack Hobbs, than to a professor of Greek at Princeton. This would be true also among prize fighters. George thought of that whole world that is so complete within itself—the fighters, the trainers, the managers, the promoters, the touts, the pimps, the gamblers, the grafters, the hangers-on, the newspaper "experts" in New York, London, Paris, Berlin, Rome, and Buenos Aires. These men were not really Americans, Englishmen, Frenchmen, Germans, Italians, and Argentines. They were simply citizens of the world of prize fighting, more at home with one another than with other men of their respective nations.

Throughout all the years of his life, George Webber had been soaking up experience like a sponge. This process never ceased with him, but within the last few years he had noticed a change in it. Formerly, in his insatiable hunger to know everything—to see all the faces in a crowd at once, to remember every face that passed him on a city street, to hear all the voices in a room and through the vast, perplexing blur to distinguish what each was saying—he had often felt that he was drowning in some vast sea

429

of his own sensations and impressions. But now he was no longer so overwhelmed by Amount and Number. He was growing up, and out of the very accumulation of experience he was gaining an essential perspective and detachment. Each new sensation and impression was no longer a single, unrelated thing: it took its place in a pattern and sifted down to form certain observable cycles of experience. Thus his incessantly active mind was free to a much greater degree than ever before to remember, digest, meditate, and compare, and to seek relations between all the phenomena of living. The result was an astonishing series of discoveries as his mind noted associations and resemblances, and made recognitions not only of surface similarities but of identities of concept and of essence.

In this way he had become aware of the world of waiters, who, more than any other class of men, seemed to him to have created a special universe of their own which had almost obliterated nationality and race in the ordinary sense of those words. For some reason George had always been especially interested in waiters. Possibly it was because his own beginnings had been small-town middle class, and because he had been accustomed from birth to the friendship of working people, and because the experience of being served at table by a man in uniform had been one of such sensational novelty that its freshness had never worn off. Whatever the reason, he had known hundreds of waiters in many different countries, had talked to them for hours at a time, had observed them intimately, and had gathered tremendous stores of knowledge about their lives—and out of all this had discovered that there are not really different nationalities of waiters but rather a separate race of waiters, whole and complete within itself. This seemed to be true even among the French, the most sharply defined, the most provincial, and the most unadaptive nationality George had ever known. It surprised him to observe that even in France the waiters seemed to belong to the race of waiters rather than to the race of Frenchmen.

This universe of waiterdom has produced a type whose character is as precisely distinguished as that of the Mongolian. It has a spiritual identity that unites it as no mere feelings of patriotism could ever do. And this spiritual identity—a unity of thought, of purpose, and of conduct—has produced unmistakable physical characteristics. After George became aware of this, he got so that he could recognize a waiter no matter where he saw him, whether in the New York subway or on a Paris bus or in the streets of London. He tested his observation many times by accosting men he suspected of being waiters and engaging them in conversation, and nine times out of ten he found that his guess had been right. Something in the feet and legs gave them away, something in the way they moved and walked and stood. It was not merely that these men had spent most of their lives standing on their feet and hurrying from kitchen to table in the execution of their orders. Other classes of men, such as policemen, also lived upon their feet, and yet no one could mistake a policeman in mufti for a waiter. (The police of all countries, George discovered, formed another separate race.)

The gait of an old waiter can best be described as gingery. It is a kind of gouty shuffle, painful, rheumatic, and yet expertly nimble, too, as if the man has learned by every process of experience to save his feet. It is the nimbleness that comes from years of "Yes, sir. Right away, sir," or of "*Oui, monsieur, Je viens. Toute de suite.*" It is the gait of service, of despatch, of incessant haste to be about one's orders, and somehow the whole soul and mind and character of the waiter is in it.

If one wishes an instant insight into the emotional and spiritual differences between the race of waiters and the race of policemen, all one needs to do is to observe the gaits of each. Compare a waiter as he approaches a table at the peremptory command of an impatient customer, and a policeman, whether in New York, London, Paris, or Berlin, as he approaches the scene of a disorder or accident. A man is lying stretched out on the pavement, let us say: he has had a heart attack, or has been struck by a motor car, or has been assaulted and beaten by thugs. People are standing around in a circle. Watch the policeman as he comes up. Does he hurry? Does he rush to the scene? Does he come forward with the quick, shuffling, eager, and solicitous movement of the waiter? He does not. He advances deliberately, ponderously, with a heavy and flat-footed tread, taking the scene in slowly as he approaches, with an appraising and unrelenting look. He is coming not to take orders but to give them. He is coming to assume command of the situation, to investigate, to disperse the crowd, to do the talking, and not to be talked back to. His whole bearing expresses a certain primitive brutality of vested authority, as well as all the other related mental and spiritual qualities that proceed from the exercise of licensed power. And in all these things which issue from his own peculiar vision of life and of the world, he is almost the exact reverse of the waiter.

Since this is true, can anyone doubt that waiters and policemen belong to separate races? Does it not follow that a French waiter is more closely akin to a German waiter than to a French gendarme?

Mynheer Bendien had attracted George's interest from the first. It was not merely that he was Dutch. That fact was unmistakable. He had a Halsian floridity, a Halsian heartiness and gusto, a Halsian heaviness—a kind of Dutch grossness that is quite different from German grossness in that it is mixed with a certain delicacy, or rather smallness. This delicacy or smallness is most often evident in the expression and shape of the mouth. So, now, with Mynheer Bendien. His lip was full and pouting, but also a little prim and smug. It was the characteristic Dutch lip—the lip of a small and cautious people, with a very good notion about which side their bread is buttered on. In any town throughout Holland one can see them behind the shuttered windows of their beautiful and delicate houses—see them quietly and privily enjoying the very best of everything and smacking those full, pouting, sensual little lips together.

Holland is a wonderful little country, and the Dutch are a wonderful little people. Just the same, it *is* a little country, they *are* a little people, and George did not like little countries or little people. For in the look of those little, fat, wet, pouting mouths there is also something cautious and self-satisfied, something that kept nicely out of war in 1914 while its neighbors were bleeding to death, something that feathered its nest and fattened its purse at the expense of dying men, something that maintained itself beautifully clean, beautifully prim, and beautifully content to live very quietly and simply in those charming, beautiful houses, without any show or fuss whatever upon the best of everything.

In all these respects Mynheer Bendien was indubitably Dutch. But he was also something else as well, and this was what made George observe him with fascinated interest. For, alongside his Dutchness, he also wore that type look which George had come to recognize as belonging to the race of small business men. It was a look which he had discovered to be common to all members of this race whether they lived in Holland, England, Germany, France, the United States, Sweden, or Japan. There was a hardness and grasping quality in it that showed in the prognathous jaw. There was something a little sly and tricky about the eyes, something a little amoral in the sleekness of the flesh, something about the slightly dry concavity of the face and its vacuous expression in repose which indicated a grasping self-interest and a limited intellectual life. It was the kind of face that is often thought of as American. But it was not American. It belonged to no nationality. It belonged simply and solely to the race of small business men everywhere.

He was obviously the kind of man who would have found an instant and congenial place for himself among his fellow business men in Chicago, Detroit, Cleveland, St. Louis, or Kalamazoo. He would have felt completely at home at one of the weekly luncheons of the Rotary Club. He would have chewed his cigar with the best of them, wagged his head approvingly as the president spoke of some member as having "both feet on the ground," entered gleefully into all the horseplay, the heavy-handed kind of humor known as "kidding," and joined in the roars of laughter that greeted such master strokes of wit as collecting all the straw hats in the cloak room, bringing them in, throwing them on the floor, and gleefully stamping them to pieces. He would also have nodded his red face in bland agreement as the speaker aired again all the quackery about "service," "the aims of Rotary," and its "plans for world peace."

George could easily imagine Mynheer Bendien pounding across the continental breadth of the United States in one of the crack trains, striking up a conversation with other men of substance in the smoking room of the Pullman car, pulling fat cigars from his pocket and offering them to his new-found companions, chewing on his own approvingly and nodding with ponderous affirmation as someone said: "I was talking to a man in Cleveland the other day, one of the biggest glue and mucilage producers in the country, a fellow who has learned his business from the ground up and *knows* what he's talking about——" Yes, Mynheer Bendien would have recognized his brother, his kinsman, his twin spirit wherever he found him, and would instantly have established a connection and a footing of proper familiarity with him, as McHarg and Webber could never have done, even though the stranger might be an American like themselves.

George knew McHarg's antipathy for this kind of man. It was an antipathy which he had savagely expressed in swingeing and satiric fiction—an antipathy which, George had felt, had a quality of almost affectionate concern in its hatred, but which was hatred nonetheless. Why, then, had McHarg invited this man to his room? Why had he sought out his companionship?

The reason became plain enough as he thought about it. Although McHarg and Webber could never belong to Bendien's world, there was something of Bendien in both of them—more in McHarg, perhaps, than in himself. Though they belonged to separate worlds, there was still another world to which each of them could find a common entry. This was the world of natural humanity, the world of the earthly, eating, drinking, companionable, and company-loving man. Every artist feels the need of this world desperately. His nature is often torn between opposing poles of loneliness and gregariousness. Isolation he must have to do his work. But fellowship is also a necessity without which he is lost, since the lack of it removes him from all the naturalness of life which he demands more than any other man alive, and which he must share in if he is to grow and prosper in his art. But his need for companionship often betrays him through its very urgency. His hunger and thirst for life often lay him open to the stupidity of fools and the trickery and dishonesty of Philistines and rascals.

George could see what had happened to McHarg. He himself had gone through the same experience many times. McHarg, it is true, was a great man, a man famous throughout the world, a man who had now attained the highest pinnacle of success to which a writer could aspire. But on just this account his disillusionment and disappointment must have been so much the greater and the more crushing.

And what disillusionment, what disappointment, was this? It was a disappointment that all men know—the artist most of all. The disappointment of reaching for the flower and having it fade the moment your fingers touch it. It was the disappointment that comes from the artist's invincible and unlearning youth, from the spirit of indomitable hope and unwavering adventure, the spirit that is defeated and cast down ten thousand times but that is lost beyond redemption never, the spirit that, so far from learning wisdom from despair, acceptance from defeat, cynicism from disillusionment, seems to grow stronger at every rebuff, more passionate in its convictions the older it grows, more assured of its ultimate triumphant fulfillment the more successive and conclusive its defeats.

McHarg had accepted his success and his triumph with the exultant elation of a boy. He had received the award of his honorary degree, symbolizing the consummation of his glory, with blazing images of impossible desire. And then, almost before he knew it, it was over. The thing was his, it had been given to him, he had it, he had stood before the great ones of the earth, he had been acclaimed and lauded, *all* had happened— and yet, nothing had happened.

Then, of course, he took the inevitable next step. With a mind surcharged with fire, with a heart thirsting for some impossible fulfillment, he took his award, and copies of all the speeches programs, and tributes, sailed for Europe, and began to go from place to place, looking for something that he had no name for, something that existed somewhere, perhaps—but where he did not know. He went to Copenhagen—wine, women, aquavit, and members of the press; then women, wine, members of the press, and aquavit again. He went to Berlin—members of the press, wine, women, whiskey, women, wine, and members of the press. So then to Vienna—women, wine, whiskey, members of the press. Finally to Baden-Baden for a "cure"—cure, call it, if you will, for wine, women, and members of the press—cure, really, for life-hunger, for life-thirst, for life-triumph, for life-defeat, life-disillusionment, life-loneliness, and life-boredom —cure for devotion to men and for disgust of them, cure for love of life and for weariness of it—last of all, cure for the cureless, cure for the worm, for the flame, for the feeding mouth, for the thing that eats and rests not ever till we die. Is there not some medicine for the irremediable? Give us a cure, for God's sake, for what ails us! Take it! Keep it! Give it back again! Oh, let us have it! Take it from us, damn you, but for God's sake bring it back! And so good night.

Therefore this wounded lion, this raging cat of life, forever prowling past a million portals of desire and destiny, had flung himself against the walls of Europe, seeking, hunting, thirsting, starving, and lashing himself into a state of frenzied bafflement, and at last had met—a red-faced Dutchman from the town of Amsterdam, and had knocked about with the red-faced Dutchman for three days on end, and now hates red-faced Dutchman's guts and would to God that he could pitch him out of the window, bag and baggage, and wonders how in God's name the whole thing began, and how he can ever win free from it and be alone again—and so now is here, pacing the carpet of his hotel room in London.

The presence of Mr. Donald Stoat was more puzzling. Mynheer Bendien at least had a certain earthy congeniality to recommend him to McHarg's interest. Mr. Stoat had nothing. Everything about the man was calculated to rub McHarg the wrong way. He was pompous and pretentious, his judgments, such as they were, were governed by a kind of moral bigotry that was infuriating, and, to cap it all, he was a complete and total fool.

He had inherited from his father a publishing business with a good name and a record of respected accomplishment. Under his leadership it had degenerated into a business largely devoted to the fabrication of religious tracts and textbooks for the elementary grades. Its fiction list was pitiful. Mr. Stoat's literary and critical standards were derived from a pious devotion to the welfare of the *jeune fille*. "Is it a book," he would whisper hoarsely to any aspiring new author, at the same time rolling his eyebrows about—"is it a book that you would be willing for your young daughter to read?" Mr. Stoat had no young daughter, but in his publishing enterprises he always acted on the hypothesis that he did have, and that no book should be printed which he would be unwilling to place in her hands. The result, as may be imagined, was fudge and taffy, slop and goo.

George had met Mr. Stoat quite casually some years before and had later been invited to his house. He was married to a large, full-bosomed female with a grim jaw who wore a perpetually frozen grin around the edges of her mouth and eyeglasses which were attached to a cord of black silk. This formidable lady was devoted to art and had not let her marriage to Mr. Stoat interfere with that devotion. Indeed she had not let marriage interfere even with her name, but had clung to her resounding maidenly title of Cornelia Fosdick Sprague. She and Mr. Stoat maintained a salon, to which a great many people who shared Cornelia Fosdick Sprague's devotion to art repaired at regular intervals, and it was to one of these meetings of the elect that George had been invited. He still remembered it vividly. Mr. Stoat had telephoned him a few days after their first casual meeting and had pressed the invitation upon him.

"You must come, my boy," Mr. Stoat had wheezed over the wire. "You can't afford to miss this, you know. Henrietta Saltonstall Spriggins is going to be there. You must meet her. And Penelope Buchanan Pipgrass is going to give a reading from her poems. And Hortense Delancey McCracken is going to read her latest play. You simply must come, by all means."

So urged, George accepted and went, and it was quite an occasion. Mr. Stoat met him at the door and with a pontifical flourish of the eyebrows led him into the presence of Cornelia Fosdick Sprague. After he had made his obeisances Mr. Stoat piloted the young man about the room and with repeated flourishes of the eyebrows introduced him to the other guests. There was an astonishing number of formidable-looking females, and, like the imposing Cornelia, most of them had three names. As Mr. Stoat made the introductions he fairly smacked his lips over the triple-barreled sonority of their titles.

George noticed with amazement that all of these women bore a marked resemblance to Cornelia Fosdick Sprague. Not that they really looked like her in feature. Some were tall, some were short, some were angular, some were fat, but all of them had a certain overwhelming quality in their bearing. This quality became a crushing air of absolute assurance and authority when they spoke of art. And they spoke of art a great deal. Indeed, it was the purpose of these meetings to speak of art. Almost all of these ladies were not only interested in art, but were "artists" themselves. That is to say, they were writers. They wrote one-act plays for the Little Theatre, or they wrote novels, or essays and criticism, or poems and books for children.

Henrietta Saltonstall Spriggins read one of her wee stories for tiny tots about a little girl waiting for Prince Charming. Penelope Buchanan Pipgrass read some of her poems, one about a quaint organ grinder, and another about a whimsical old rag man. Hortense Delancey McCracken read her play, a sylvan fantasy laid in Central Park, with two lovers sitting on a bench in the springtime and Pan prancing around in the background, playing mad music on his pipes and leering slyly out at the lovers from behind trees. In all of these productions there was not a line that could bring the blush of outraged modesty to the cheek of the most innocent young girl. Indeed, the whole thing was just too damned delightful for words.

After the readings they all sat around and drank pale tea and discussed what they had read in fluty voices. George remembered vaguely that there were two or three other men present, but they were pallid figures who faded into the mist, hovering in the background like wan ghosts, submissive and obscure attendants, husbands even, to the possessors of those sonorous and triple-barreled names.

George never went back again to Cornelia Fosdick Sprague's salon, and had seen nothing more of Mr. Donald Stoat. Yet here he was, the last person in the world he would have expected to find in Lloyd McHarg's apartment. If Mr. Stoat had ever read any of McHarg's books—a most improbable circumstance— his moral conscience must have been outraged by the mockery with which, in almost every one of them, McHarg had assaulted the cherished ideals and sacred beliefs that Mr. Stoat held dear. Yet here he was sipping his dry sherry in McHarg's room with all the aplomb of one who was accustomed to such familiar intimacy.

What was he doing here? What on earth did it mean?

George did not have to wait long for an answer. The telephone rang. McHarg snapped his fingers sharply and sprang for the instrument with an exclamation of overwrought relief.

"Hello, hello!" He waited a moment, his inflamed and puckered face twisted wryly to one side. "Hello, hello, hello!" he said feverishly and rattled the receiver hook. "Yes, yes. Who? Where?" A brief pause. "Oh, it's New York," he cried, and then impatiently: "All right, then! Put them through!"

George had never before seen the transatlantic telephone in operation, and he watched with feelings of wonder and disbelief. A vision of the illimitable seas passed through his mind. He remembered the storms that he had been in and the way great ships were tossed about; he thought of the enormous curve of the earth's surface and of the difference in time; and yet in a moment McHarg, his voice calm now, began to speak quietly as if he were talking to someone in the next room:

"Oh, hello Wilson," he said. "Yes, I can hear you perfectly. Of course. . . . Yes, yes, it's true. Of course it is!" he cried, with a return to his former manner of feverish annoyance. "No, I've broken with him completely. . . . No, I don't know where I'm going. I haven't signed up with anyone yet. . . . All right, all right," impatiently. "Wait a minute," he said curtly. "Let me do the talking. I won't do anything until I see you. . . . No that's *not* a promise to go with you," he said angrily. "It's just a promise that I won't go anywhere else till I see you." A moment's pause while McHarg listened intently. "You're sailing when? . . . Oh, tonight! The *Berengaria*. Good. I'll see you here then next week. . . . All right. Good-bye, Wilson," he snapped, and hung up.

Turning away from the phone, he was silent a moment, looking a little rueful in his wry, puckered way. Then, with a shrug of his shoulders and a little sigh, he said:

"Well, cat's out of the bag, I guess. The news has got around. They all know I've left Bradford-Howell. I suppose they'll all be on my tail now. That was Wilson Fothergill," he said, mentioning the name of one of America's largest publishers. "He's sailing tonight." Suddenly his face was twisted with demonic glee. He laughed a high, dry cackle. "Christ, Georgie!" he squeaked, prodding Webber in the ribs. "Isn't it wonderful? Isn't it marvelous? Can you beat it?"

Mr. Donald Stoat cleared his throat with premonitory emphasis and arched his eyebrows significantly. "I hope," he said, "that before you come to any terms with Fothergill, you will talk to me and listen to what I have to say." There was a weighty pause, then he concluded pontifically: "Stoat—the House of Stoat—would like to have you on its list."

"What's that? What's that?" said McHarg feverishly. "Stoat!" he cried suddenly. "Stoat?" He winced nervously in a kind of convulsion of jangled nerves, then paused, trembling and undecided, as if he did not know whether to spring upon Mr. Stoat or to spring out the window. Snapping his bony fingers sharply, he turned to Webber and shrieked again in a shrill, falsetto cackle: "Did you hear it, Georgie? Isn't it wonderful? K-k-k-k-k— Stoat!" he squeaked, prodding Webber in the ribs again. "The House of Stoat! Can you beat it? Isn't it marvelous? Isn't it— All right, all right," he said, breaking off abruptly and turning upon the astounded Mr. Stoat. "All right, Mr. Stoat, we'll talk about it. But some other time. Come in to see me next week," he said feverishly.

With that he grasped Mr. Stoat by the hand, shook it in farewell, and with his other arm practically lifted that surprised gentleman from his chair and escorted him across the room. "Good-bye, good-bye! Come in next week. . . . Good-bye Bendien!" he now said to the Dutchman, seizing him by the hand, lifting him from the chair, and repeating the process. He herded the two before him with his bony arms outstretched as if he were shooing chickens, and finally got them out of the door, talking rapidly all the time, saying: "Good-bye, good-bye. Thanks for coming in. Come back to see me again. Georgie and I have to go to lunch now."

At last he closed the door on them, turned, and came back in the room. He was obviously unstrung.

Chapter Thirty-Five

A Guest in Spite of Himself

*When Bendien and Stoat were so suddenly and uncere-*moniously ushered from the room, George rose from his chair in some excitement, not knowing what to do with himself. McHarg now looked at him wearily.

"Sit down, sit down!" McHarg gasped, and fell into a chair. He crossed his bony legs with a curiously pathetic and broken attitude. "Christ!" he said, letting out a long sigh, "I'm tired. I feel as if I've been run through a sausage grinder. That damned Dutchman! I went out with him in Amsterdam, and we've been going it ever since. God, I can't remember having eaten since I left Cologne. That was four days ago."

He looked it, too. George was sure that he had spoken the literal truth and that he had not paused to eat for days. He was a wreck of jangled nerves and utterly exhausted weariness. As he sat there with his bony shanks crossed like two pieces of limp string, his gaunt figure had the appearance of being broken in two at the waist. He looked as if he would never be able to get out of that chair again without assistance. Just at that moment, however, the telephone rang sharply, and McHarg leaped up as if he had received an electric shock.

"Jesus Christ!" he shrilled. "What's that?" He darted for the phone, snatched it up savagely, and snapped, "Hello, who's there?" Then feverishly but very cordially: "Oh, hello; hello, Rick—you bastard, you! Where the hell have you been, anyway? I've been trying to reach you all morning. . . . No! No! I just got here last night. . . . Of course I'm going to see you. That's one of the reasons I'm here. . . . No, no, you don't need to come for me. I've got my own car here. We'll drive down. I'm bringing someone with me. . . . *Who?*" he cackled suddenly in his shrill falsetto. "You'll see, you'll see. Wait till we get there.

. . . For dinner? Sure, I'll make it. How long does it take? . . . Two hours and a half? Seven o'clock. We'll be there with time to spare. Wait a minute. Wait a minute. What's the address? Wait till I get it down."

He seated himself abruptly at the writing desk, fumbled for a moment with pen and paper, and then passed them impatiently toward George, saying, "Write it down, George, as I give it to you." The address was in Surrey, a farm on a country road several miles away from a small town. The directions for finding it were quite complicated, involving detours and crossroads, but George finally got it all down correctly. Then McHarg, feverishly assuring his host that *they* would be there for dinner, with time to spare, hung up.

"Well, now," he said impatiently, springing to his feet with another exhibition of that astounding vitality which seemed to burn in him all the time, "come on, Georgie! Let's snap out of it! We'll have to get going!"

"*W-w-w-we?*" George stammered. "Y-y-y-you mean me, Mr. McHarg?"

"Sure, sure!" McHarg said impatiently. "Rick's expecting us to dinner. We can't keep him waiting. Come on! Come on! Let's get started! We're getting out of London! We're going places!"

"P-p-p-places?" George stammered again, dumbfounded. "But w-w-w-where are we going, Mr. McHarg?"

"West of England," he barked out instantly. "We'll go down to Rick's and spend the night. But tomorrow—tomorrow," he muttered, pacing up and down and speaking with ominous decision, "we'll be on our way. West of England," he muttered again, pacing and hanging to his coat lapels with bony fingers. "Cathedral towns," he said. "Bath, Bristol, Wells, Exeter, Salisbury, Devonshire, coast of Cornwall," he cried feverishly, getting his geography and his cathedrals hopelessly confused, but covering, nevertheless, a large portion of the kingdom in a single staccato sentence. "Keep out of cities," he went on. "Stay away from swank hotels—joints like this one. Hate them. Hate all of them. Want the country—the English countryside," he said with relish.

George's heart sank. He had not bargained for anything like this. He had come to England to finish his new book. The work had been going well. He had established the beat and cadence of daily hours at his writing, and the prospect of breaking the rhythm of it just when he was going at full swing was something that he dreaded. Moreover, God only knew where such a jaunt as McHarg spoke of would end. McHarg, meanwhile, was still talking, pacing nervously back and forth and letting his enthusiasm mount as his mind built up the idyllic picture of what he had suddenly taken it into his head to do.

"Yes, the English countryside—that's the thing," he said with

440

relish. "We'll put up at night by the side of the road and cook our own meals, or stay at some old inn—some real English country inn," he said with deliberate emphasis. "Tankards of musty ale," he muttered. "A well-done chop by the fireside. A bottle of old port, eh Georgie?" he cried, his scorched face lighting up with great glee. "Did it all before one time. Toured the whole country several years ago with my wife. Used a trailer. Went from place to place. Slept in our trailer at night and did our own cooking. Wonderful! Marvelous!" he barked. "The real way to see the country. The only way."

George said nothing. At the moment he was unable to say anything. For weeks he had looked forward to his meeting with McHarg. He had leaped to do his bidding when McHarg had summoned him to get out of bed instantly and come to lunch. But he had never dreamed of being abducted as a traveling and talking companion on an expedition that might last for days and even weeks, and end up almost anywhere. He had no desire or intention of going with McHarg if he could avoid it. And yet— his mind groped frantically for a way out—what was he to do? He did not want to offend him. He had too great an admiration and respect for McHarg to do anything that might, wittingly or unwittingly, hurt him or wound his feelings. And how could he reject the invitation of a man who, with the most generous and unselfish enthusiasm, had used the power and elevation of his high place to try to lift him out of the lower channel in which his own life ran?

In spite of the brevity of their acquaintance, George had already seen clearly and unmistakably what a good and noble human being McHarg really was. He knew how much integrity and courage and honesty was contained in that tormented tenement of fury and lacerated hurts. Regardless of all that was jangled, snarled, and twisted in his life, regardless of all that had become bitter, harsh, and acrid, McHarg was obviously one of the truly good, the truly high, the truly great people of the world. Anyone with an atom of feeling and intelligence, George thought, must have seen this at once. And as he continued to watch and study McHarg, and took in again the shock of his appearance—the inflamed face, the poached blue eyes, the emaciated figure and nervously shaking hands—an image flashed into his mind which seemed to represent the essential quality of the man, and this, curiously, was the image of Abraham Lincoln. Save for McHarg's tallness and gauntness, there was no physical similarity to Lincoln. The resemblance came, George thought, from a certain homely identity, from a kind of astonishing ugliness which was so marked that it was hard to see how it escaped the grotesque, and yet it was not grotesque. It was an ugliness which somehow, no matter what extravagances of gesture, tone, and manner McHarg indulged in, never lost its quality of enormous, latent dignity. This strange and troubling resemblance became strikingly evident in repose.

For now, his decision having been arrived at with explosive violence, McHarg sat quietly in a chair, his bony legs crossed lankly, and with the fingers of one freckled and large-knuckled hand fumbled in the breast pocket of his coat for his checkbook and his wallet. He got them out at last, his hands still shaking as with palsy, but even that did not disturb the suggestion of quiet dignity and strength. He put wallet and checkbook on his knees, fumbled in a pocket of his vest, took out an old, worn spectacle case, snapped it open, and deliberately extracted a pair of spectacles. They were the most extraordinary spectacles George had ever seen. They looked as if they might have belonged to Washington, or to Franklin, or to Lincoln himself. The rims, the nose clasp, and the handles were of plain old silver. McHarg opened them carefully, and then, using both hands, slowly adjusted them and settled the handles over his large and freckled ears. This done, he bent his head, took up the wallet, opened it, and very carefully began to count the contents. The transforming effect of this simple act was astonishing. The irritable, rasping, overwrought man of a few minutes before was gone completely. This lank and ugly figure in the chair, with its silver-rimmed spectacles, its wry and puckered face lowered in calculation, its big bony hands deliberately fingering each note inside the wallet, was an image of Yankee shrewdness, homely strength, plain dignity, and assured power. His very tone had changed. Still counting his money, without lifting his head, he spoke to George, saying quietly:

"Ring that bell over there, George. We'll have to get some more money. I'll send John out to the bank."

George rang, and shortly the young man with buttons rapped at the door and entered. McHarg glanced up and, opening his checkbook and, taking out his fountain pen, said quietly:

"I need some money, John. Will you take this check around to the bank and cash it?"

"Very good, sir," said John. "And 'Enry is 'ere, sir, with the car. 'E wants to know if 'e should wait."

"Yes," said McHarg, still writing out the check. "Tell him I'll need him. Tell him we'll be ready in twenty minutes." He tore out the check and handed it to the man. "And by the way," he said, "when you come back will you pack some things—shirts, underwear, socks, and so on—in a small bag? We're going out of town."

"Very good, sir," John said quietly, and went out.

McHarg was silent and thoughtful for a moment. Then he capped his fountain pen, restored it to his pocket, put away his wallet and checkbook, took off his old spectacles with the same grave and patient movement, folded them and laid them in the case, snapped it to and put it in the pocket of his vest, and then, with a much quieter and more genial friendliness than he had yet displayed, brought one hand down smartly on the arm of his chair and said:

"Well, George, what are you doing now? Working on another book?"

Webber told him that he was.

"Going to be good?" he demanded.

Webber said he hoped so.

"A nice, big, fat one like the first? Lots of meat on it, is there? Lots of people?"

Webber told him that there would be.

"That's the stuff," he said. "Go to it and give 'em people," he said quietly. "You've got the feeling for 'em. You know how to make 'em live. Go on and put 'em in. You'll hear a lot of bunk," he went on. "You've probably heard it already. There'll be a lot of bright young men who will tell you how to write, and tell you that what you do is wrong. They'll tell you that you have no style, no sense of form. They'll tell you that you don't write like Virginia Woolf, or like Proust, or like Gertrude Stein, or like someone else that you ought to write like. Take it all in, as much of it as you can. Believe all of it that you're able to believe. Try to get all the help from it you can, but if you know it's not true, don't pay too much attention to it."

"Will you be able to know whether it's true or not?"

"Oh, yes," he said quietly. "You always know if it's true. Christ, man, you're a writer, you're not a bright young man. If you were a bright young man you wouldn't know whether it was true or not. You'd only say you did. But a writer always knows. The bright young men don't think he does. That's the reason they're bright young men. They think a writer is too dumb or too pig-headed to listen to what they say, but the real truth of the matter is that the writer knows much more about it than they can ever know. Once in a while they say something that hits the nail on the head. But that's only one time in a thousand. When they do, it hurts, but it's worth listening to. It's probably something that you knew about yourself, that you knew you'd have to look at finally, but that you've been trying to dodge and that you hoped no one else would discover. When they punch one of those raw nerves, listen to them, even though it hurts like hell. But usually you'll find that you've known everything they say a long time before they say it, and that what they think is important doesn't amount to a damn."

443

"Then what's a man to do?" Webber said. "It looks pretty much as if he's got to be his own doctor, doesn't it? It looks as if he's got to find the answer for himself."

"I never found any other way," said McHarg. "I don't think you will, either. So get going. Keep busy. For Christ's sake, don't freeze up. Don't stall around. I've known a lot of young fellows who froze up after their first book, and it wasn't because they had only that one book in them, either. That's what the bright young men thought. That's what they always think, but it just ain't true. Good God, man, you've got a hundred books in you! You can keep on turning them out as long as you live. There's no danger of your drying up. The only danger is of freezing up."

"How do you mean? Why should a man freeze up?"

"Usually," said McHarg, "because he loses his nerve. He listens to the bright young men. His first book gets him pretty good reviews. He takes them seriously. He begins to worry about every little bit of criticism that's sandwiched in with the praise. He begins to wonder if he can do it again. His next book is really going to be as good as his first, maybe better. He has been a natural slugger to begin with, with a one-ton punch. Now he begins to shadow-box. He listens to everything they tell him. How to jab and how to hook. How to counter with his right. How to keep out of the way. How to weave and how to bob. How to take care of his feet. He learns to skip the rope, but forgets to use that paralyzing punch that he was born with, and the first thing you know some palooka comes along and knocks him for a row of ash cans. For God's sake, don't let it happen to you. Learn all you can. Improve all you can. Take all the instruction you can absorb. But remember that no amount of instruction can ever take the place of the wallop in the old right hand. If you lose that, you may learn all the proper ways that other men have used to do the job, but you'll have forgotten your own way. As a writer, you'll be through. So for God's sake, get going and keep going. Don't let them slow you down. Make your mistakes, take your chances, look silly, but keep on going. Don't freeze up."

"You think that can happen? Do you think a man can freeze up if he really has talent?"

"Yes," McHarg said quietly, "that can happen. I've seen it happen. You'll find out, as you go on, that most of the things they say, most of the dangers that they warn you of, do not exist. They'll talk to you, for instance, about prostituting your talent. They'll warn you not to write for money. Not to sell your soul to Hollywood. Not to do a dozen other things that have nothing whatever to do with you or with your life. You won't prostitute yourself. A man's talent doesn't get prostituted just because someone waves a fat check in his face. If your talent is prostituted, it is because you are a prostitute by nature. The number of writers in this world who weep into their Scotch and tell you of the great books they would have written if they hadn't sold out to Hollywood or to the *Saturday Evening Post* is astonishingly large. But the number of great writers who have sold out is not large. In fact, I don't believe there are any at all. If Thomas Hardy had been given a contract to write stories for the *Saturday Evening Post*, do you think he would have written like Zane Grey or like Thomas Hardy? I can tell you the answer to that one. He would have written like Thomas Hardy. He couldn't have written like anyone else but Thomas Hardy. He would have kept on writing like Thomas Hardy whether he wrote for the *Saturday Evening Post* or *Captain Billy's Whizbang*. You can't prostitute a great writer, because a great writer will inevitably be himself. He couldn't sell himself out if he wanted to. And a good many of them, I suppose, *have* wanted to, or thought they did. But he can freeze up. He can listen too much to the bright young men. He can learn to shadow-box, to feint and jab and weave, and he can lose his punch. So whatever you do, don't freeze up."

There was a rap at the door, and in response to McHarg's summons John came in, carrying in his hand a bundle of crisp, brand-new Bank of England notes.

"I think you will find these right, sir," he said, as he handed the money to McHarg. "I counted them. One 'undred pounds, sir."

McHarg took the notes, folded them into a wad, and thrust it carelessly into his pocket. "All right, John," he said. "And now will you pack a few things?"

He got up, looked about him absently, and then, with a sudden resumption of his former feverish manner, he barked out:

"Well, George, get on your coat! We've got to be on our way!"

"B-b-but—" George began to temporize—"don't you think we'd better get some lunch before we start out, Mr. McHarg? If you haven't eaten for so long, you'll need food. Let's go somewhere now and get something to eat."

George spoke with all the persuasiveness he could put into his voice. By this time he was beginning to feel very hungry, and thought longingly of the "prime bit" of gammon and peas that Mrs. Purvis had prepared for him. Also he hoped that if he could only get McHarg to have lunch before starting, he could use the occasion diplomatically to dissuade him from his intention of departing forthwith, and taking him along willy-nilly, on a tour that was apparently designed to embrace a good portion of the British Isles. But McHarg, as if he foresaw Webber's design, and also feared, perhaps, the effect of further delay upon his almost exhausted energies, snapped curtly, with inflexible decision:

"We'll eat somewhere on the road. We're getting out of town at once."

George saw that it was useless to argue, so he said nothing more. He decided to go along, wherever McHarg was going, and to spend the night, if need be, at his friend's house in the country, trusting in the hope that the restorative powers of a good meal and a night's sleep would help to alter McHarg's purpose. Therefore he put on his coat and hat, descended with McHarg in the lift, waited while he left some instructions at the desk, and then went out with him to the automobile that was standing at the curb.

McHarg had chartered a Rolls-Royce. When George saw this magnificent car he felt like roaring with laughter, for if this was the vehicle in which he proposed to explore the English countryside, cooking out of a frying pan and sleeping beside the road at night, then the tour would certainly be the most sumptuous and the most grotesque vagabondage England had ever seen. John had already come down and had stowed away a small suitcase on the floor beside the back seat. The driver, a little man dressed appropriately in livery, touched the visor of his cap respectfully, and he and George helped McHarg into the car. He had suddenly gone weak, and almost fell as he got in. Once in, he asked George to give the driver the address in Surrey, and, having said this, he collapsed: his face sank forward on his chest, and he had again that curious broken-in-two look about the waist. He had one hand thrust through the loop of a strap beside the door, and if it had not been for this support he would have slumped to the floor. George got in and sat down beside him, still wondering desperately what to do, how in the name of God he was going to get out of it.

It was well after one o'clock when they started off. They rolled smoothly into St. James's Street, turned at the bottom into Pall Mall, went around St. James's Palace and into the Mall, and headed toward Buckingham Palace and Webber's own part of town. Coming out of the Mall and wheeling across the great place before the palace, McHarg roused himself with a jerk, peered through the drizzle and the reek—it was a dreary day—at the magnificent sentries stamping up and down in front of the palace, stamping solemnly, facing at the turns, and stamping back again, and was just about to slump back when George caught him up sharply.

At that moment Ebury Street was very near, and it seemed very dear to him. George thought with desire and longing of his

446

bed, of Mrs. Purvis, and of his untouched gammon and peas. That morning's confident departure already seemed to be something that had happened long ago. He smiled bitterly as he remembered his conversation with Mrs. Purvis and their speculations about whether Mr. McHarg would take him to lunch at the Ritz, or at Stone's in Panton Street, or at Simpson's in the Strand. Gone now were all these Lucullan fantasies. At that point he would joyfully have compromised on a pub and a piece of cheese and a pint of bitter beer.

As the car wheeled smoothly past the palace, he felt his last hope slipping away. Desperately he jogged his companion by the elbow before it should be too late and told him he lived just around the corner in Ebury Street, and could he please stop off a moment there to get a toothbrush and a safety razor, that it would take only a minute. McHarg meditated this request gravely and finally mumbled that he could, but to "make it snappy." Accordingly, George gave the driver the address, and they drove down around the palace, turned into Ebury Street, and slowed down as they approached his modest little house. McHarg was beginning to look desperately ill. He hung on grimly to his strap, but when the car stopped he swayed in his seat and would have gone down if George had not caught him.

"Mr. McHarg," George said, "you ought to have something to eat before we go on farther. Won't you come upstairs with me and let the woman give you something? She has fixed me a good lunch. It's all ready. We could eat and be out again in twenty minutes."

"No food," he muttered and glared at George suspiciously. "What are you trying to do—run out on me?"

"No, of course not."

"Well, get your toothbrush then, and hurry up. We're going to get out of town."

"All right. Only I think you're making a mistake not to eat first. It's there waiting for you if you'll take it."

George made it as persuasive as he could. He stood at the open door, with one foot upon the running board. McHarg made no answer; he lay back against the seat with his eyes closed. But a moment later he tugged on the strap, pulled himself partly erect, and, with just a shade of obstinate concession, said:

"You got a cup of tea up there?"

"Of course. She'll have it for you in two minutes."

He pondered this information for a moment, then half unwillingly said: "Well, I don't know. I might take a cup of tea. Maybe it would brace me up."

"Come on," George said quickly, and took him by the arm.

The driver and George helped him out of the car. George told the man to wait for them, that they would be back within thirty minutes, which McHarg quickly amended to fifteen. Then George opened the street door with his key and, slowly, carefully, helping the exhausted man, began to propel the tall and angular form up the narrow stairs. They finally got there. George opened the door, led him through into his sitting room, and seated McHarg in his most comfortable chair, where he immediately let his head slump forward on his breast again. George lit the little open gas radiator which provided the room with the only heat it had, called Mrs. Purvis, who had heard them and was already coming from the kitchen, whispered quickly to her the circumstance of his being there and the identity of his distinguished visitor, and dispatched her at once to make the tea.

When she left the sitting room McHarg roused himself a little and said: "Georgie, I feel all shot to hell. God, I could sleep a month."

"I've just sent Mrs. Purvis for the tea," George answered. "She'll have it ready in a minute. That'll make you feel better."

But almost instantly, as if the effort to speak had used up his last energies, McHarg sank back in the chair and collapsed completely. By the time Mrs. Purvis entered with her tray and teapot, he no longer needed tea. He was buried in comatose oblivion—past tea or travel now, past everything.

She saw instantly what had happened. She put the tray down quietly and whispered to George: " 'E's not goin' anywhere just yet. 'E will be needin' sleep."

"Yes," George said. "That's what he does need, badly."

"It's a shame to leave 'im in that chair. If we could only get 'im up, sir," she whispered, "and into your room, 'e could lie down in your bed. It'd be more comfortable for 'im."

George nodded, stooped beside the chair, got one of McHarg's long, dangling arms around his neck and his own arm around McHarg's waist, and, heaving, said encouragingly: "Come on, Mr. McHarg. You'll feel better if you lie down and stretch out." He made a manful effort and got out of the chair, and took the few steps necessary to enter the bedroom and reach the bed, where he again collapsed, this time face downward. George rolled him over on his back, straightened him out, undid his collar, and took off his shoes. Then Mrs. Purvis covered him from the raw chill and cold, which seemed to soak right into the little bedroom from the whole clammy reek of fog and drizzle outside. They piled a number of blankets and comforters upon him, brought in a small electric heat reflector and turned it on in such a way that its warmth would reach him, then they pulled the curtains together at the window, darkened the room, closed the doors, and left him.

Mrs. Purvis was splendid.

"Mr. McHarg is very tired," George said to her. "A little sleep will do him good."

"Ah, yes," she said, and nodded wisely and sympathetically. "You can see it's the strain 'e's been under. Meetin' all them people. And then 'avin' to travel so much. It's easy to see," she went on loftily, "that 'e's still sufferin' from the fatigue of the journey. But you," she said quickly—"should think you'd feel tired yourself, what with the excitement and 'avin' no lunch and all. Do come," she said persuasively, "and 'ave a bite to eat. The gammon is nice, sir. I could 'ave it for you in a minute."

Her proposal had George's enthusiastic endorsement. She hastened to the kitchen, and soon came in again and told him lunch was ready. He went at once to the little dining room and ate a hearty meal—gammon, peas, boiled potatoes, a crusty apple tart with a piece of cheese, and a bottle of Bass ale.

After that he returned to the sitting room and decided to stretch out on the sofa. It was a small sofa and much too short for him, but he had had no sleep for more than twenty-four hours and it looked inviting. He lay down with his legs dangling over the end, and almost instantly fell asleep.

Later he was faintly conscious that Mrs. Purvis had come softly in, had put his feet upon a chair, and had spread a blanket over him. He was also dimly aware that she had drawn the curtains, darkened the room, and gone softly out.

Later still, as she prepared to leave for the day, George heard her open the door and listen for a moment; then, very quietly, she tiptoed across the floor and opened the bedroom door and peered in. Evidently satisfied that all was well, she tiptoed out again, closing the doors gently as she went. He heard her creep softly down the stairs, and presently the street door closed. He fell asleep again and slept soundly for some time.

When George woke again it had grown completely dark outside, and McHarg was up and stirring about in the bedroom, evidently looking for the light. George got up and switched the light on in the sitting room, and McHarg came in.

Again there was an astonishing transformation in him. His short sleep seemed to have restored his vitality, and restored it to a degree and in a direction George had not wanted. He had hoped that a few hours of sleep would calm McHarg and make him see the wisdom of getting a really sound rest before proceeding farther on his travels. Instead, the man had wakened like a raging lion, and was now pacing back and forth like a caged beast, fuming at their delay and demanding with every breath that George get ready to depart instantly.

"Are you coming?" he said. "Or are you trying to back out of it? What are you going to do, anyway?"

George had waked up in a semi-daze, and he now became conscious that the door bell was ringing, and had been ringing for some time. It was probably this sound which had aroused them both. Telling McHarg that he'd be back in a moment, George ran down the stairs and opened the door. It was, of course, McHarg's chauffeur. In the excitement and fatigue of the afternoon's event he had completely forgotten him, and the poor fellow had been waiting all this time there in his glittering chariot drawn up before Webber's modest door. It was not yet quite five o'clock in the afternoon, but dark comes early in the dismal wintry days of London's ceaseless fog and drizzle, and it was black as midnight outside. The street lights were on, and the shop fronts were shining out into the fog with a blurred and misty radiance. The street itself was still and deserted, but high up over the roof tops the wind was beginning to swoop in fitful gusts, howling faintly in a way that promised a wild night.

The little chauffeur stood patiently before George when he opened the door, holding his visored cap respectfully in his hands, but he had an air of restrained anxiety about him which he could not conceal. "I beg your pardon, sir," he said, "but I wonder if you know whether Mr. Mc'Arg 'as changed 'is plans?"

"Plans? Plans?" George stammered, still not quite awake, and he shook his head like a dog coming out of the water in an effort to compose himself and bring order to his own bewilderment. "What plans?"

"About going to Surrey, sir," the little man said gently, yet giving George a quick and rather startled look. Already the painful suspicion, which later in the evening was to become a deep-rooted conviction, that he was alone and under the criminal direction of two dangerous maniacs, had begun to shape itself in the chauffeur's consciousness, but as yet he betrayed his apprehension only by an attitude of solicitous and somewhat tense concern. "You know, sir," he continued quietly, in a tone of apologetic reminder, "that's where we started for hearlier in the hafternoon."

"Oh, yes, yes. Yes, I remember," George said, running his fingers through his hair and speaking rather distractedly. "Yes, we did, didn't we?"

"Yes, sir," he said gently. "And you see," he went on, almost like a benevolent elder speaking to a child—"you see, sir, one is not supposed to park 'ere in the street for so long a time as we've been 'ere. The bobby," he coughed apologetically behind his hand, " 'as just spoken to me, sir, and 'as told me that I've been 'ere too long and will 'ave to move. So I thought it best to tell you, sir, and to find out if you know what Mr. Mc'Arg intends to do."

"I—I think he intends to go on with it," George said. "That is, to go on to Surrey as we started out to do. But—you say the bobby has ordered you to move?"

"Yes, sir," the chauffeur said patiently, and held his visored cap and looked up at George and waited.

"Well, then—" George thought desperately for a moment, and then burst out: "Look here, I'll tell you what you do. Drive around the block—drive around the block——"

"Yes, sir," the chauffeur said, and waited.

"And come back here in five minutes. I'll be able to tell you then what we're going to do."

"Very good, sir." He inclined his head in a brief nod of agreement, put on his cap, and got into his car.

George closed the door and went back up the stairs. When he entered the sitting room, McHarg had on his overcoat and hat and was pacing restlessly up and down.

"It was your driver," George said. "I forgot about him, but he's been waiting there all afternoon. He wants to know what we're going to do."

"What we're going to do?" McHarg shrilled. "We're going to get a move on! Christ Almighty, man, we're four hours late already! Come on, come on, George!" he rasped. "Let's get going!"

George saw that he meant it and that it was useless to try to change his purpose. He took his brief case, crammed toothbrush, tooth paste, razor, shaving cream and brush, and a pair of pajamas into it, put on his hat and coat, switched off the lights, and led the way into the hall, saying: "All right. I'm ready if you are. Let's go."

When they got out into the foggy drizzle of the street, the car was just wheeling to a halt at the curb. The chauffeur jumped out and opened the door for them. McHarg and Webber got in. The chauffeur climbed back into his seat, and they drove swiftly away, down the wet street, with a smooth, cupped hissing of the tires. They reached Chelsea, skirted the Embankment, crossed Battersea Bridge, and began to roll southwestward through the vast, interminable ganglia of outer London.

It was a journey that Webber remembered later with nightmare vividness. McHarg had begun to collapse again before they crossed the Thames at Battersea. And no wonder! For weeks, in the letdown and emptiness that had come upon him as a sequel to his great success, he had lashed about in a frenzy of seeking for he knew not what, going from place to place, meeting new people, hurling himself into fresh adventures. From this impossible quest he had allowed himself no pause or rest. And at the end of it he had found exactly nothing. Or, to be more exact, he had found Mynheer Bendien in Amsterdam. It was easy to see just what had happened to McHarg after that. For if, at the end of the trail, there was nothing but a red-faced Dutchman, then, by God, he'd at least find out what kind of stuff a red-faced Dutchman was made of. Then for several days more, in his final fury of exasperation, he had put the Dutchman to the test, driving him even harder than he had driven himself, not even stopping to eat, until at last the Dutchman, sustained by gin and his own phlegmatic constitution, had used up what remained of McHarg's seemingly inexhaustible energies. So now he was all in. The flare of new vitality with which he had awakened from his nap had quickly burnt itself out: he lay back in the seat of the car, drained and emptied of the fury which had possessed him, too exhausted even to speak, his eyes closed, his head rolling gently with the motion of the car, his long legs thrust out limply before him. George sat beside him, helpless, not knowing what to do or where he was going or how and when it would end, his gaze fixed upon the head of the little driver, who was hunched up behind the wheel, intent upon the road, steering the car skillfully through the traffic and the fog-bound night.

The enormous ganglia of unending London rolled past them—street after street wet with a dull gleam of rain-fogged lamps, mile after mile of brick houses, which seemed steeped in the fog and soot and grime of uncounted days of dismal weather, district after district in the interminable web, a giant congeries of uncounted villages, all grown together now into this formless, monstrous sprawl. They would pass briefly through the high streets of these far-flung warrens. For a moment there would be the golden nimbus of the fog-blurred lights, the cheerful radiance of butcher shops, with the red brawn of beef, the plucked plumpness and gangling necks of hung fowls, and the butchers in their long white aprons; then the wine and liquor stores, and the beer-fogged blur and warmth and murmur of the pubs, with the dull gleam of the rain-wet pavement stretching out in front; then pea-soup darkness again, and again the endless rows of fog-drear houses.

At last they began to come to open country. There was the darkness of the land, the smell of the wet fields, the strung spare lights of night across the countryside. They began to feel the force of the wind as it swooped down at them across the fields and shivered against the sides of the car. It was blowing the fog away and the sky was lifting. And now, against the damp, low, thick, and dismal ceiling of the clouds, there was an immense corrupted radiance, as if all the swelter, smoke, and fury of London's unending life had been caught up and resumed there.

With every revolution of the wheels the glow receded farther behind them.

And now, with the lonely countryside all around him, George became conscious of the mysterious architecture of night. As he felt the abiding strength and everlastingness of the earth, he began to feel also a sense of exultation and release. It was a feeling he had had many times before, a feeling that every man who lives in a vast modern city must feel when, after months within the hive of the city's life—months of sweat and noise and violence, months of grimy brick and stone, months of the incessant thrust and intershift and weaving of the endless crowd, months of tainted air and tainted life, of treachery, fear, malice, slander, blackmail, envy, hatred, conflict, fury, and deceit, months of frenzy and the tension of wire-taut nerves and the changeless change—he leaves the city and is free at last, out beyond the remotest filament of that tainted and tormented web. He that has known only a jungle of mortared brick and stone where no birds sing, where no blade grows, has now found earth again. And yet, unfathomable enigma that it is, he has found earth and, finding it, has lost the world. He has found the washed cleanliness of vision and of soul that comes from earth. He feels himself washed free of all the stains of ancient living, its evil and its lust, its filth and cruelty, its perverse and ineradicable pollution. But curiously, somehow, the wonder and the mystery of it all remains, its beauty and its magic, its richness and its joy, and as he looks back upon that baleful glow that lights the smoky blanket of the sky, a feeling of loss and loneliness possesses him, as if in gaining earth again he has relinquished life.

The car sped onward and still onward, until finally the last outpost of London was left behind and the glow in the sky was gone. They were driving now through dark country and night toward their journey's end. McHarg had not uttered a word. He still sat with legs sprawled out and head thrown back, swaying with the motion of the car but held in position by one limp arm which was hooked in the strap beside him. George was getting more and more alarmed at the thought of bringing him in this exhausted state to the house of an old friend whom he had not seen for years. At last he stopped the car and told the driver to wait while he pleaded with his master.

He switched on the overhead light and shook him, and to his surprise McHarg opened his eyes right away and by his responses showed that his mind was completely clear and alert. George told him that, worn out as he must be, he could not possibly enjoy a visit with his friend. He begged him to change his mind, to return to London for the night, to let him telephone his friend from the nearest town to say that he had been delayed and would see him in a day or two, but by all means to defer his visit until he felt better able to make it. After McHarg's former display of obstinate determination, George had little hope of success, but to his amazement McHarg now proved most reasonable. He agreed to everything George said, confessed that he himself thought it would be better not to see his friend that night, and said he was prepared to embrace any alternative George might propose, except—on this he was most blunt and flat—he would not go back to London. All day his desire to get out of London had had the force and urgency of an obsession, so George pressed no further on that point. He agreed that they should not turn back, but asked McHarg if he had any preference about where they should go. McHarg said he didn't care, but after meditating with chin sunk forward on breast for several moments, he said suddenly that he would like the sea.

This remark did not seem at all astonishing to George at the time. It became astonishing only as he thought of it later. He accepted the proposal of going to the sea as naturally as a New Yorker might accept a suggestion of riding on a Fifth Avenue bus to see Grant's tomb. If McHarg had said he wanted to go to Liverpool or to Manchester or to Edinburgh, it would have been the same—George would have felt no astonishment whatever. Once out of London, both of these Americans, in their unconscious minds, were as little impressed by the dimensions of England as they would have been by a half-acre lot. When McHarg said he'd like the sea, George thought to himself: "Very well. We'll just drive over to the other side of the island and take a look at it."

So George thought the idea an excellent one and fell in with it enthusiastically, remarking that the salt air, the sound of the waves, and a good night's sleep would do them both a world of good, and would make them fit and ready for further adventures in the morning. McHarg, too, began to show wholehearted warmth for the plan. George asked him if he had any special place in mind. He said no, that it didn't matter, that any place was good as long as it was on the sea. In rapid order they named over seacoast towns which they had either heard of or at one time or another had visited—Dover, Folkstone, Bournemouth, Eastbourne, Blackpool, Torquay, Plymouth.

"Plymouth! Plymouth!" cried McHarg with enthusiastic decision. "That's the very place! I've been in there in ships dozens of times, but never stopped off. True, it's in the harbor, but that doesn't matter. It always looked like a nice little town. Let's go there for the night."

"Oh, sir," spoke up the chauffeur, who till now had sat quietly at his wheel, listening to two maniacs dismember the geography of the British Isles. "Oh, sir," he repeated, with an intonation of quite evident alarm, "you can't do that, you know.

Not tonight, sir. It's quite himpossible to make Plymouth tonight."

"What's the reason it is?" McHarg demanded truculently.

"Because, sir," said the drive, "it's a good two 'undred and fifty miles, sir. In this weather, what with rain and never knowing when the fog may close in again, it would take quite all of eight hours, sir, to do it. We should not arrive there, sir, until the small hours of the morning."

"Well, then, all right," McHarg cried impatiently. "We'll go somewhere else. How about Blackpool? Blackpool, eh, Georgie?" he said, turning to Webber feverishly, his lips lifting in a grimace of puckered nervousness. "Let's try Blackpool. Never been there. Like to see the place."

"But, sir—" the driver was now obviously appalled— "Blackpool—Blackpool, sir, is in the north of England. Why, sir," he whispered, "Blackpool is even farther away than Plymouth is. It must be all of three 'undred miles, sir," he whispered, and the awe in his tone could not have been greater if they had just proposed an overnight drive from Philadelphia to the Pacific coast. "We couldn't reach Blackpool, sir, before tomorrow morning."

"Oh, well, then," said McHarg in disgust. "Have it your own way. You name a place, George," he demanded.

Webber thought earnestly for a long minute, then, fortified with memories of scenes from Thackeray and Dickens, he said hopefully: "Brighton. How about Brighton?"

Instantly he knew that he had hit it. The driver's voice vibrated with a tone of unspeakable relief. He turned around in his seat and whispered with almost fawning eagerness:

"Yes, sir! Yes, sir! Brighton! We can do that very nicely, sir."

"How long will it take?" McHarg demanded.

"I should think, sir," said the driver, "I could do it from 'ere in about two and a 'arf hours. A bit late for dinner, sir, but still, it *is* within reach."

"Good. All right," McHarg said, nodding his head with decision and settling back in his seat. "Go ahead." He waved one bony hand in a gesture of dismissal. "We're going to Brighton."

They started off again, and at the next crossroad changed their course to hunt for the Brighton road.

From that time on, their journey became a nightmare of halts and turnings and changes of direction. The little driver was sure they were headed toward Brighton, but somehow he could not find the road. They twisted this way and that, driving for miles

455

through towns and villages, then out into the open country again, and getting nowhere. At last they came to an intricate and deserted crossroad where the driver stopped the car to look at the signs. But there was none to Brighton, and he finally admitted that he was lost. At these words, McHarg roused and pulled himself wearily forward in his seat, peered out into the dark night, then asked George what he thought they ought to do. The two of them knew even less about where they were than the driver, but they had to go somewhere. When George hazarded a guess that Brighton ought to be off to the left somewhere, McHarg commanded the man to take the first left fork and see where he came out, then sank back in his seat and closed his eyes again. At each intersection after that McHarg or Webber would tell the driver what to do, and the little Londoner would obey them dutifully, but it was evident that he harbored increasing misgivings at the thought of being lost in the wilds of Surrey and subject to the unpredictable whim of two strange Americans. For some inexplicable reason it never occurred to either of them to stop and ask their way, so they only succeeded in getting more lost than ever. They shuttled back and forth, first in one direction, then in another, and after a while George had the feeling that they must have covered a good part of the whole complex system of roads in the region south of London.

The driver himself was being rapidly reduced to a nervous wreck. The little man was now plainly terrified. He agreed with frenzied eagerness to everything that was said to him, but his voice trembled when he spoke. From his manner, he obviously felt that he had fallen into the clutches of two madmen, that he was now at their mercy in the lonely countryside, and that something dreadful was likely to happen at any moment. George could see him bent over the wheel, his whole figure contracted with the tenseness of his terror. If either of the crazy Americans on the back seat had chosen to let out a blood-curdling war whoop, the wretched man would not have been surprised, but he would certainly have died instantly.

Under these special circumstances the very geography of the night seemed sinister and was conducive to an increase of his terror. As the hours passed, the night grew wilder. It became a stormy and demented kind of night, such as one sometimes finds in England in the winter. A man alone, if he had adventure in his soul, might have found it a thrilling and wildly beautiful night. But to this quiet little man, who was probably thinking bitterly of a glass of beer and the snug haven of his favorite pub, the demoniac visage of the night must have been appalling. It was one of those nights when the beleaguered moon drives like a spectral ship through the scudding storm rack of the sky, and the wind howls and shrieks like a demented fiend. They could hear it roaring all around them through the storm-tossed

456

branches of the barren trees. Then it would swoop down on them with an exultant scream, and moan and whistle round the car, and sweep away again while gusts of beating rain drove across their vision. Then they would hear it howling far away—remote, demented, in the upper air, rocking the branches of the trees. And the spectral moon kept driving in and out, now casting a wild, wan radiance over the stormy landscape, now darting in behind a billowing mass of angry-looking clouds and leaving them to darkness and the fiendish howling of the wind. It was a fitting night for the commission of a crime, and the driver, it was plain to see, now feared the worst.

Somewhere along the road, after they had spent hours driving back and forth and getting nowhere, McHarg's amazing reserves of energy and vitality ran completely out. He was sitting sprawled out as before, with head thrown back, when suddenly he groped blindly with a hand toward George and said:

"I'm done in, George! Stop the car! I can't go on."

George stopped the car at once. There by the roadside in the darkness, in stormy wind and scudding rain, they halted. In the wan and fitful light of the spectral moon McHarg's appearance was ghastly. His face now looked livid and deathlike. George was greatly alarmed and suggested that he get out of the car and see if the cold air wouldn't make him feel better.

McHarg answered very quietly, with the utter finality of despair. "No," he said. "I just feel as if I'd like to die. Leave me alone." He slumped back into his corner, closed his eyes, and seemed to resign himself entirely into George's keeping. He did not speak again during the remainder of that horrible journey.

In the half-darkness, illuminated only by the instrument panel of the car and the eerie light of the moon, George and the driver looked at each other in mute and desperate interrogation. Presently the driver moistened his dry lips and whispered:

"What are we to do now, sir? Where shall we go?"

George thought for a moment, then answered: "We'll have to go back to his friend's house, I think. Mr. McHarg may be very ill. Turn around quickly, and let's get there as soon as possible."

"Yes, sir! Yes, sir!" the driver whispered. He backed the car around and started off again.

From that point on, the journey was just pure nightmare. The directions they had received were complicated and would have been hard enough to follow if they had kept to the road they had first intended to take. But now they were lost and off their course, and had somehow to find their way back to it. Through what seemed to George nothing less than a miracle, this was finally accomplished. Then their instructions required them to look carefully for several obscure crossroads, make the proper turns at each, and at the end of all this find the lonely country lane up which McHarg's friend lived. In attempting it, they lost their way again and had to go back to a village, where the driver got his bearings and the true directions. It was after ten-thirty before they finally found the lane leading up to the house which was their destination.

And now the prospect was more sinister and weird than any they had seen. George could not believe that they were still in England's Surrey. He had always thought of Surrey as a pleasant and gentle place, a kind of mild and benevolent suburb of London. The name had called to his mind a vision of sweet, green fields, thick-sown with towns and villages. It was, he had thought, a place of peace and tranquil spires, as well as a kind of wonderful *urbs in rure,* a lovely countryside of which all parts were within an hour's run of London, a place where one could enjoy bucolic pleasures without losing any of the convenient advantages of the city, and a place where one was never out of hailing distance of his neighbor. But the region they had now come to was not at all like this. It was densely wooded, and as wild and desolate on that stormy night as any spot he had ever seen. As the car ground slowly up the tortuous road, it seemed to George that they were climbing the fiendish slope of Nightmare Hill, and he rather expected that when the moon broke from the clouds again they would find themselves in a cleared and barren circle in the forest, surrounded by the whole witches' carnival of Walpurgis Night. The wind howled through the rocking trees with insane laughter, the broken clouds scudded across the heavens like ghosts in flight, and the car lurched, bumped, groaned, and lumbered its way up a road which must have been there when the Romans came to Rye, and which, from the feel of it, had not been repaired or used since. There was not a house or a light in sight.

George began to feel that they were lost again, and that surely no one would choose to live in this inaccessible wilderness. He was ready to give up and was about to command the driver to turn back when, as they rounded a bend, he saw, away to the right, a hundred yards or so off the road and at some elevation above it, a house—and from its windows issued the beaconing assurance of light and warmth.

Chapter Thirty-Six

The House in the Country

The chauffeur brought the car to a jolting halt.

"This must be it, sir," he whispered. "It's the only 'ouse there is." His tone indicated heightened tension rather than relief.

George agreed that it was probably the place they were looking for.

All the way up the hill McHarg had given no signs of life. George was seriously alarmed about him, and his anxiety had been increased the last few miles by the inanimate flappings and jerkings of the long, limp arms and bony hands of the exhausted figure every time the car hit a new bump in the road or lurched down into another rut. George spoke to him, but there was no answer. He did not want to leave him, so he suggested to the chauffeur that he'd better get out and go up to the house and find out if Mr. McHarg's friend really lived there; if so, George told him to ask the man to come down to the car.

This request was more than the chauffeur could bear in his already terrified state. If before he had been frightened to be *with* them, he seemed now even more frightened at the thought of being *without* them. What he was afraid of George did not know, but he spoke as if he thought the other members of their bloody gang were in that house, just waiting for him.

"Oh, sir," he whispered, "I couldn't go up there, sir. Not to that 'ouse," he shuddered. "Really, sir, I couldn't. I'd much rather you'd go, sir."

Accordingly, George got out, took a deep breath to brace himself, and started reluctantly up the path. He felt trapped in a grotesque and agonizing predicament. He had no idea whom he was going to meet. He did not even know the name of McHarg's friend. McHarg had spoken of him only as Rick, which George took to be an abbreviation or a nickname. And he could not be certain that the man lived here. All he knew was that after a day filled with incredible happenings, and a nightmarish ride in a Rolls-Royce with a terrified driver, he was now advancing up a path with rain and wind beating in his face toward a house he had never seen before to tell someone whose name he did not know that one of the most distinguished of American novelists was lying exhausted at his door, and would he please come out and see if he knew him.

So he went on up the path and knocked at the door of what appeared to be a rambling old farmhouse that had been renovated. In a moment the door opened and a man stood before him, and George knew at once that he must be, not a servant, but the master of the place. He was a well-set and well-kept Englishman of middle age. He wore a velvet jacket, in the pockets of which he kept his hands thrust while he stared out with distrust at his nocturnal visitor. He had on a wing collar and a faultless bow tie in a polka-dot pattern. This touch of formal spruceness made George feel painfully awkward and embarrassed, for he knew what a disreputable figure he himself must cut. He had not shaved for two days, and his face was covered with a coarse smudge of stubbly beard. Save for the afternoon's brief nap, he had not slept for thirty-six hours, and his eyes were red and bloodshot. His shoes were muddy, and his old hat, which was jammed down on his head, was dripping with the rain. And he was tired out, not only by physical fatigue, but by nervous strain and worry as well. It was plain that the Englishman thought him a suspicious character, for he stiffened and stood staring at him without a word.

"You're—I—" George began—"that is to say, if you're the one I'm looking for——"

"Eh?" the man said in a startled voice. "What!"

"It's Mr. McHarg," George tried again. "If you know him ——"

"Eh?" he repeated, and then almost at once, "Oh!" The rising intonation of the man's tone and the faint howl of surprise and understanding that he put into the word made it sound like a startled, sharply uttered "Ow!" He was silent a moment, searching George's face. "Ow!" he said again, and then quietly, "Where is he?"

"He—he's out here in his car," George said eagerly, feeling an overwhelming sense of relief.

"Ow!" the Englishman cried again, and then, impatiently: "Well, then, why doesn't he come in? We've been waiting for him."

"I think if you'd go down and speak to him—" George began, and paused.

"Ow!" the gentleman cried, looking at George with a solemn air. "Is he—that is to say—? . . . Ow!" he cried, as if a great light had suddenly burst upon him. "Hm-m!" he muttered meditatively. "Well, then," he said in a somewhat firmer voice, stepping out into the path and closing the door carefully behind him, "suppose we just go down and have a look at him. Shall we?"

The last squall of rain had passed as quickly as it had blown up, and the moon was sailing clear again as they started down the path together. Halfway along, the Englishman stopped, looked apprehensive, and shouted to make himself heard above the wind:

"I say—is he—I mean to say," he coughed, "is he—*sick?*"

George knew by the emphasis on that final word, as well as from previous experience with the English, that when he said "sick" he meant only one thing. George shook his head.

"He looks very ill," he said, "but he is not *sick.*"

"Because," the gentleman went on with howling apprehensiveness, "if he's sick—ow, dear me!" he exclaimed. "I'm very fond of Knuck, you know—I've known him for years—but if he's going to get *sick!*" He shuddered slightly. "If you don't mind, I'd rather not. I don't want to know about it!" he shouted rapidly. "I—I don't want to hear about it! I—I don't want to be around when it's going on! I—I—I wash my hands of the whole business!" he blurted out.

George reassured him that Mr. McHarg had not been sick but was merely desperately ill, so they went on down the path until they got to the car. The Englishman, after a moment's hesitation, stepped up and opened the door, thrust his head inside, and, peering down at McHarg's crumpled figure, called out:

"Knuck! I say, Knuck!"

McHarg was silent, save for his hoarse breathing, which was almost a snore.

"Knuck, old chap!" the Englishman cried again. "I say, Knuck!" he cried more loudly. "Are you there, old boy?"

McHarg very obviously *was* there, but he gave no answer.

"I say, Knuck! Speak up, won't you, man? It's Rick!"

McHarg only seemed to snore more hoarsely at this announcement, but after a moment he shifted one long jackknifed leg a few inches and, without opening his eyes, grunted, " 'Lo, Rick." Then he began to snore again.

"I say, Knuck!" the Englishman cried with sharper insistence. "Won't you get up, man? We're waiting for you at the house!"

There was no response except the continued heavy breathing. The Englishman made further efforts but nothing happened, and at length he withdrew his head out of the car and, turning to George, said:

"I think we'd better help him inside. Knuck has worn himself out again, I fancy."

"Yes," said George anxiously. "He looks desperately ill, as if he were on the point of complete physical and nervous collapse. We'd better call a doctor, hadn't we?"

"Ow, no," said the Englishman cheerfully. "I've known
461

Knuck a long time and seen this happen before when he got all keyed up. He drives himself mercilessly, you know—won't rest—won't stop to eat—doesn't know how to take care of himself. It would kill anybody else, the way he lives. But not Knuck. It's nothing to worry about, really. He'll be all right. You'll see."

With this comforting assurance they helped McHarg out of the car and stood him on his feet. His emaciated form looked pitifully weak and frail, but the cold air seemed to brace him up. He took several deep breaths and looked about him.

"That's fine," said the Englishman encouragingly. "Feel better now, old chap?"

"Feel Godawful," said McHarg. "All in. Want to go to bed."

"Of course," said the Englishman. "But you ought to eat first. We've kept dinner waiting. It's all ready."

"No food," said McHarg brusquely. "Sleep. Eat tomorrow."

"All right, old man," the Englishman said amiably. "Whatever you say. But your friend here must be starved. We'll fix you both up. Do come along," he said, and took McHarg by the arm.

The three of them started to move up the path together.

"But, sir," spoke a plaintive voice at George's shoulder, for he was on the side nearest the car. Full of their own concerns, they had completely forgotten the little driver. "But, sir," he now leaned out of the window and whispered, "what shall I do with the car, sir? Will—" he moistened his lips nervously—"will you be needing it again tonight, sir?"

The Englishman took immediate charge of the situation.

"No," he said crisply, "we shan't be needing it. Just drive it up behind the house, won't you, and leave it there."

"Yes, sir, yes, sir," the driver gasped. What he was still afraid of not even he could have said. "Drive it up be'ind the 'ouse, sir," he repeated mechanically. "Very good, sir. And—and—" again he moistened his dry lips.

"And, ow yes!" the Englishman cried, suddenly recollecting. "Go into the kitchen when you're through. My butler will give you something to eat."

Then, turning cheerfully and taking McHarg by the arm again, he led the way up the path, leaving the stricken driver behind to mutter, "Yes, sir, yes, sir," to the demented wind and scudding moon.

After the blind wilderness of storm and trouble, the house, as they entered it, seemed very warm and bright with lights. It was a lovely house, low-ceilinged, paneled with old wood. Its

462

mistress, a charming and beautiful woman much younger than her husband, came forward to greet them. McHarg spoke a few words to his hostess and then immediately repeated his desire for sleep. The woman seemed to take in the situation at once and led the way upstairs to the guest room, which had already been prepared for them. It was a comfortable room with deep-set windows. A fire had been kindled in the grate. There were two beds, the covers of which had been folded neatly down, the white linen showing invitingly.

The women left them, and her husband and George did what they could to help McHarg get to bed. He was dead on his feet. They took off his shoes, collar, and tie, then propped him up while they got his coat and vest off. They laid him on the bed, straightened him out, and covered him. By the time all this was done and they were ready to leave the room, McHarg was lost to the world in deep and peaceful slumber.

The two men went downstairs again, and now for the first time remembered that in the confusion of their meeting they had not thought to introduce themselves. George told his name, and was pleased and flattered to learn that his host knew it and had even read his book. His host had the curious name of Rickenbach Reade. He informed George later in the evening that he was half German. He had lived in England all his life, however, and in manner, speech, and appearance he was pure British.

Reade and Webber had been a little stiff with each other from the start. The circumstances of Webber's arrival had not been exactly conducive to easy companionship or the intimacy of quick understanding. After introductions were completed with a touch of formal constraint, Reade asked Webber if he did not want to wash up a bit, and ushered him into a small washroom. When George emerged, freshened up as much as soap and water and comb and brush could accomplish, his host was waiting for him and, still with a trace of formality, led him into the dining room, where the lady had preceded them. They all sat down at the table.

It was a lovely room, low-ceilinged, warm, paneled with old wood. The lady was lovely, too. And the dinner, although it had been standing for hours, was nevertheless magnificent. While they were waiting for the soup to come on, Reade gave George a glass of fine dry Sherry, then another, and still another. The soup came in at last, served by a fellow with a big nose and a sharp, shrewd, cockney sort of face, correctly dressed for the occasion in clean but somewhat faded livery. It was a wonderful soup, thick tomato, the color of dark mahogany. George could not conceal his hunger. He ate greedily, and, with the evidence of that enthusiastic appetite before them, all the stiffness that was left began to melt away.

The butler brought in an enormous roast of beef, then boiled potatoes and Brussels sprouts. Reade carved a huge slab of meat for George, and the lady garnished his plate generously with the vegetables. They ate, too, but it was evident that they had already had their dinner. They took only small portions and left their plates unfinished, but they went through the motions just to keep George company. The beef vanished from his own plate in no time at all.

"I say!" cried Reade, seizing the carving knife again. "Do let me give you some more. You must be starved."

"I should think you'd be famished," said his wife in a musical voice.

So George ate again.

The butler brought in wine—old, full-toned Burgundy in a cobwebbed bottle. They polished that off. Then for dessert there was a deep and crusty apple pudding and a large slice of cheese. George ate up everything in sight. When he had finished he heaved a great sigh of satisfied appeasement and looked up. At that instant their three pairs of eyes suddenly met, and with one accord they leaned back in their chairs and roared with laughter.

It was the mutual and spontaneous kind of laughter that one almost never hears. It was a booming, bellowing, solid, and ungovernable "haw-haw-haw" that exploded out of them in a rib-splitting paroxysm and bounded and reverberated all around the walls until the very glasses on the sideboard started jingling. Once begun, it swelled and rose and mounted till it left them exhausted and aching, reduced to wheezing gasps of almost inaudible mirth, and then, when it seemed that they didn't have another gasp left in them and that their weary ribs could stand no more, it would begin again, roaring and rolling and reverberating around the room with renewed force. Twice while this was going on the butler came to the swinging door, opened it a little, and craftily thrust his startled face around. Each time the sight of him set them off again. At length, when they were subsiding into the last faint wheezes of their fit, the butler thrust his face around the door again and said:

"Please, sir. The driver's 'ere."

This wretched little man now reappeared, standing nervously in the doorway, fingering his cap, and moistening his dry lips apprehensively.

"Please, sir," he finally managed to whisper. "The car. Will you be wanting it to stay be'ind the 'ouse all night, sir, or shall I take it to the nearest village?"

"How far is the nearest village?" George wheezed faintly.

"It's about six miles, sir, I understand," he whispered, with a look of desperation and terror in his eyes.

The expression on his face was too much for them. A

464

strangled scream burst from Webber's throat. Mrs. Reade bent forward, thrusting her wadded napkin over her mouth. As for Rickenbach Reade, he just lay back in his chair with lolling head and roared like one possessed.

The driver stood there, rooted to the spot. It was clear that he thought his time had come. These maniacs had him at their mercy now, but he was too paralyzed to flee. And they could do nothing to allay his nameless fear. They could not speak to him, they could not explain, they could not even look at him. Every time they tried to say something and glanced in his direction and caught sight of the little man's blanched and absurdly tortured face, they would strangle with new whoops and yells and shrieks of helpless laughter.

But at last it was over. The mood was spent. They felt drained and foolish and sober and ashamed of themselves because of the needless fright they had given the little driver. So, calmly and gently, they told him to leave the car where it was and forget about it. Reade asked his butler to take care of the driver and put him up for the night in his own quarters.

"Yes, sir, yes, sir," mumbled the little driver automatically.

"Very good, sir," said the butler briskly, and led the man away.

They now arose from the table and went into the living room. In a few minutes the butler brought in a tray with coffee. They sat around a cheerful fire and drank it, and had brandy afterwards. It was wonderfully warm and comforting to sit there and listen to the fury of the storm outside, and under the spell of it they felt drawn together, as if they had all known each other a long time. They laughed and talked and told stories without a trace of self-consciousness. Reade, seeing that George was still worried about McHarg, tried in various ways to allay his fears.

"My dear fellow," he said, "I've known Knuck for years. He drives himself to exhaustion and I've seen him do it a dozen times, but it always comes out all right in the end. It's astonishing how he does it. I'm sure I couldn't. No one else could, but he can. The man's vitality is amazing. Just when you think he's done himself in, he surprises you by bounding up and beginning all over again, as fresh as a daisy."

George had already seen enough to know that this was true. Reade told of incidents which verified it further. Some years before, McHarg had come to England to work on a new book. Even then his way of life had been enough to arouse the gravest apprehensions among those who knew him. Few people believed that he could long survive it, and his writing friends did not understand how he could get any work done.

"We were together one night," Reade continued, "at a party that he gave in a private room at the Savoy. He had been going

465

it for days, driving himself the way he does, and by ten o'clock that night he was all in. He just seemed to cave in, and went to sleep at the table. We laid him out on a couch and went on with the party. Later on, two of us, with the assistance of a couple of porters, got him out of the place into a taxi and took him home. He had a flat in Cavendish Square. The next day," Reade went on, "we had arranged to have lunch together. I had no idea—not the faintest—that the man would be able to make it. In fact, I very much doubted whether he would be out of his bed for two or three days. Just the same, I stopped in a little before one o'clock to see how he was."

Reade was silent a moment, looking into the fire. Then, with a sharp expiration of his breath, he said:

"Well! He was sitting there at his desk, in front of his typewriter, wearing an old dressing gown over his baggy old tweeds, and he was typing away like mad. There was a great sheaf of manuscript beside him. He told me he'd been at it since six o'clock and had done over twenty pages. As I came in, he just looked up and said: 'Hello, Rick. I'll be with you in a minute. Sit down, won't you?' . . . Well!"—again the sharp expiration of his breath—"I *had* to sit down! I simply fell into a chair and stared at him. It was the most astonishing thing I had ever seen."

"And was able to go to lunch with you?"

"Was he able!" cried Reade. "Why, he fairly bounded from his chair, flung on his coat and hat, pulled me out of my seat, and said: 'Come on! I'm hungry as a bear.' And what was most astounding," Reade continued, "was that he remembered everything that had happened the night before. He remembered everything that had been said, too—even the things that were said during the time when I should have sworn he was unconscious. It is an astonishing creature! Astonishing!" cried the Englishman.

In the warming glow of the fire and their new-found intimacy they had several more brandies, smoked endless cigarettes, and talked on and on for hours, forgetting the passage of time. It was the kind of talk which, freed of all constricting traces of self-consciousness, lets down the last barriers of natural reserve and lays bare the souls of men. George's host was in high spirits and told the most engaging stories about himself, his wife, and the good life they were making here in the isolated freedom of their rural retreat. He made it seem not only charming and attractive, full of wholesome country pleasures, but altogether desirable and enviable. It was an idyllic picture that he

466

painted—such a picture of rugged independence, with its simple joys and solid comforts, as has at one time or another haunted the imagination of almost every man in the turmoil, confusion, and uncertainties of the complex world we live in. But as George listened to his host and felt the nostalgic attractiveness of the images that were unfolded before him, he also felt a disquieting sense of something else behind it all which never quite got into the picture, but which lent colorings of doubt and falsity to every part of it.

For Rickenbach Reade, George began to see after a while, was one of those men who are unequal to the conditions of modern life, and who have accordingly retreated from the tough realities which they could not face. The phenomenon was not a new one to George. He had met and observed a number of people like this. And it was now evident to him that they formed another group or family or race, another of those little worlds which have no boundary lines of country or of place. One found a surprising number of them in America, particularly in the more sequestered purlieus of Boston, Cambridge, and Harvard University. One found them also in New York's Greenwich Village, and when even that makeshift Little Bohemia became too harsh for them, they retired into a kind of desiccated country life.

For all such people the country became the last refuge. They bought little farms in Connecticut or Vermont, and renovated the fine old houses with just a shade too much of whimsey or of restrained good taste. Their quaintness was a little too quaint, their simplicity a little too subtle, and on the old farms that they bought no utilitarian seeds were sown and no grain grew. They went in for flowers, and in time they learned to talk very knowingly about the rarer varieties. They loved the simple life, of course. They loved the good feel of "the earth." They were just a shade too conscious of "the earth," and George had heard them say, the women as well as the men, how much they loved to work in it.

And work in it they did. In spring they worked on their new rock garden, with the assistance of only one other man—some native of the region who hired himself out for wages, and whose homely virtues and more crotchety characteristics they quietly observed and told amusing stories about to their friends. Their wives worked in the earth, too, attired in plain yet not unattractive frocks, and they even learned to clip the hedges, wearing canvas gloves to protect their hands. These dainty and lovely creatures became healthily embrowned: their comely forearms took on a golden glow, their faces became warm with soaked-up sunlight, and sometimes they even had a soft, faint down of gold just barely visible above the cheekbone. They were good to see.

In winter there were also things to do. The snows came down, and the road out to the main highway became impassable to cars for three weeks at a time. Not even the trucks of the A. & P. could get through. So for three whole weeks on end they had to plod their way out on foot, a good three-quarters of a mile, to lay in provisions. The days were full of other work as well. People in cities might think that country life was dull in winter, but that was because they simply did not know. The squire became a carpenter. He was working on his play, of course, but in between times he made furniture. It was good to be able to do something with one's hands. He had a workshop fitted up in the old barn. There he had his studio, too, where he could carry on his intellectual labors undisturbed. The children were forbidden to go there. And every morning, after taking the children to school, the father could return to his barn-studio and have the whole morning free to get on with the play.

It was a fine life for the children, by the way. In summer they played and swam and fished and got wholesome lessons in practical democracy by mingling with the hired man's children. In winter they went to an excellent private school two miles away. It was run by two very intelligent people, an expert in planned economy and his wife, an expert in child psychology, who between them were carrying on the most remarkable experiments in education.

Life in the country was really full of absorbing interests which city folk knew nothing about. For one thing, there was local politics, in which they had now become passionately involved. They attended all the town meetings, became hotly partisan over the question of a new floor for the bridge across the creek, took sides against old Abner Jones, the head selectman, and in general backed up the younger, more progressive element. Over week-ends, they had the most enchanting tales to tell their city friends about these town meetings. They were full of stories, too, about all the natives, and could make the most sophisticated visitor howl with laughter when, after coffee and brandy in the evening, the squire and his wife would go through their two-part recital of Seth Freeman's involved squabble and lawsuit with Rob Perkins over a stone fence. One really got to know his neighbors in the country. It was a whole world in itself. Life here was simple, yet it was so good.

In this old farmhouse they ate by candlelight at night. The pine paneling of the dining room had been there more than two hundred years. They had not changed it. In fact, the whole front part of the house was just the same as it had always been. All they had added was the new wing for the children. Of course, they had had to do a great deal when they bought the place. It had fallen into shocking disrepair. The floors and sills were rotten and had had to be replaced. They had also built a concrete basement and installed an oil furnace. This had been costly, but it was worth the price. The people who had sold them the house were natives of the region who had gone to seed. The farm had been in that one family for five generations. It was incredible, though, to see what they had done to the house. The sitting room had been covered with an oilcloth carpet. And in the dining room, right beside the beautiful old revolutionary china chest, which they had persuaded the people to sell with the house, had been an atrocious phonograph with one of those old-fashioned horns. Could one imagine that?

Of course they had had to furnish the house anew from cellar to garret. Their city stuff just wouldn't do at all. It had taken time and hard work, but by going quietly about the countryside and looking into farmers' houses, they had managed to pick up very cheaply the most exquisite pieces, most of them dating back to revolutionary times, and now the whole place was in harmony at last. They even drank their beer from pewter mugs. Grace had discovered these, covered with cobwebs, in the cellar of an old man's house. He was eighty-seven, he said, and the mugs had belonged to his father before him. He'd never had no use for 'em himself, and if she wanted 'em he calc'lated that twenty cents apiece would be all right. Wasn't it delicious! And everyone agreed it was.

The seasons changed and melted into one another, and they observed the seasons. They would not like to live in places where no seasons were. The adventure of the seasons was always thrilling. There was the day in late summer when someone saw the first duck flying south, and they knew by this token that the autumn of the year had come. Then there was the first snowflake that melted as it fell to usher in the winter. But the most exciting of all was the day in early spring when someone discovered that the first snowdrop had opened or that the first starling had come. They kept a diary of the seasons, and they wrote splendid letters to their city friends:

"I think you would like it now. The whole place is simply frantic with spring. I heard a thrush for the first time today. Overnight, almost, our old apple trees have burst into full bloom. If you wait another week, it will be too late. So do come, won't you? You'll love our orchard and our twisted, funny, dear old apple trees. They've been here, most of them, I suspect, for eighty years. It's not like modern orchards, with their little regiments of trees. We don't get many apples. They are small and sharp and tart, and twisted like the trees themselves, and there are never too many of them, but always just enough. Somehow we love them all the better for it. It's *so* New England."

So year followed year in healthy and happy order. The first
469

year the rock garden got laid down and the little bulbs and alpine plants set out. Hollyhocks were sown all over the place, against the house and beside the fences. By the next year they were blooming in gay profusion. It was marvelous how short a time it took. That second year he built the studio in the barn, doing most of the work with his own hands, with only the simple assistance of the hired man. The third year—the children were growing up now; they grow fast in the country— he got the swimming pool begun. The fourth year it was finished. Meanwhile he was busy on his play, but it went slowly because there was so much else that had to be done.

The fifth year—well, one did miss the city sometimes. They would never think of going back there to live. This place was wonderful, except for three months in the winter. So this year they were moving in and taking an apartment for the three bad months. Grace, of course, loved music and missed the opera, while he liked the theatre, and it *would* be good to have again the companionship of certain people whom they knew. That was the greatest handicap of country life—the natives made fine neighbors, but one sometimes missed the intellectual stimulus of city life. And so this year he had decided to take the old girl in. They'd see the shows and hear the music and renew their acquaintance with old friends and find out what was going on. They might even run down to Bermuda for three weeks in February. Or to Haiti. That was a place, he'd heard, that modern life had hardly touched. They had windmills and went in for voodoo worship. It was all savage and most primitively colorful. It would get them out of the rut to go off somewhere on a trip. Of course they'd be back in the country by the first of April.

Such was the fugitive pattern in one of its most common manifestations. But it also took other forms. The American expatriates who had taken up residence in Europe were essentially the same kind of people, though theirs was a more desolate and more embittered type of escapism. George Webber had known them in Paris, in Switzerland, and here in England, and it seemed to him that they represented one of the extremest breeds among the race of futilitarians. These were the Americans who had gone beyond even the pretense of being nature-lovers and earth-discoverers and returners to the simple life of native virtue in rural Yankeedom. These were the ones to whom nothing was left except an encyclopaedic sneer—a sneer at everything American. It was a sneer which was derived from what they had read, from what others had said, or from some easy rationalization of self-defense. It was a sneer that did not have in it the sincerity of passion or the honesty of true indignation, and it became feebler year after year. For these people had nothing left but drink and sneering, the dreary round of café life with its endless repetition of racked saucers—nothing left but a blurred vision of the world, a sentimental fantasy of "Paris," or of "England," or of "Europe," which was as unreal as if all their knowledge had been drawn from the pages of a fairy tale, and as if they had never set foot upon these shores which they professed to understand so well and to cherish so devotedly.

And always with this race of men it seemed to George that the fundamental inner structure of illusion and defeat was the same, whether they followed the more innocuous formula of flight to the farm, with its trumped-up interest in rock gardening, carpentry, hollyhock culture, and the rest of it, or whether they took the more embittered route of retreat to Europe and the racked saucers. And it made no difference whether they were Americans, Englishmen, Germans, or Hottentots. All of them betrayed themselves by the same weaknesses. They fled a world they were not strong enough to meet. If they had talent, it was a talent that was not great enough to win for them the fulfillment and success which they pretended to scorn, but for which each of them would have sold the pitifully small remnant of his meager soul. If they wanted to create, they did not want it hard enough to make and shape and finish something in spite of hell and heartbreak. If they wanted to work, they did not want it genuinely enough to work and keep on working till their eyeballs ached and their brains were dizzy, to work until their loins were dry, their vitals hollow, to work until the whole world reeled before them in a grey blur of weariness and depleted energy, to work until their tongues clove to their mouths and their pulses hammered like dry mallets at their temples, to work until no work was left in them, until there was no rest and no repose, until they could not sleep, until they could do nothing and could work no more—and then work again. They were the pallid half-men of the arts, more lacking in their lack, possessing half, than if their lack had been complete. And so, half full of purpose, they eventually fled the task they were not equal to—and they pottered, tinkered, gardened, carpentered, and drank.

Such a man, in his own way, was this Englishman, Rickenbach Reade. He was, as he confided to George later in the evening, a writer—as he himself put it, with a touch of bitter whimsey, "a writer of sorts." He had had a dozen books published. He took them from their shelves with a curious eagerness that was half apology and showed them to George. They were critical biographies of literary men and politicians, and were examples of the "debunking school" of historical writing. George later read one or two of them, and they turned out to be more or less what he had expected. They were the kind of books that debunked everything except themselves. They were the lifeless products of a padded Stracheyism: their author, lacking Strachey's wit and shirking the labors of his scholarship, succeeded at best in a feeble mimicry of his dead vitality, his moribund fatigue, his essential foppishness. So these books, dealing with a dozen different lives and periods, were really all alike, all the same—the manifestations of defeat, the jabs of an illusioned disillusion, the skeptical evocations of a fantastic and unliving disbelief.

Their author, being the kind of man he was, could not write otherwise than as he had written. Having no belief or bottom in himself, he found no belief or bottom in the lives he wrote about. Everything was bunk, every great man who ever lived had been built up into the image of greatness by a legend of concocted bunk; truth, therefore, lay in the debunking process, since all else was bunk, and even truth itself was bunk. He was one of those men who, by the nature of their characters and their own defeat, could believe only the worst of others. If he had written about Caesar, he could never have convinced himself that Caesar looked—as Caesar looked; he would assuredly have found evidence to show that Caesar was a miserable dwarf, the butt of ridicule among his own troops. If he had written about Napoleon, he would have seen him only as a fat and pudgy little man who got his forelock in the soup and had grease spots on the lapels of his marshal's uniform. If he had written about George Washington, he would have devoted his chief attention to Washington's false teeth, and would have become so deeply involved with them that he would have forgotten all about George Washington. If he had written about Abraham Lincoln, he would have seen him as a deified Uriah Heep, the grotesque product of backwoods legendry, a country lawyer come to town, his very fame a thing of chance, the result of a fortuitous victory and a timely martyrdom. He could never have believed that Lincoln really said the things that Lincoln said, or that he really wrote what he is known to have written. Why? Because the things said and written were too much like Lincoln. They were too good to be true. Therefore they were myths. They had not been said at all. Or, if they had been said, then somebody else had said them. Stanton had said them, or Seward had said them, or a newspaper reporter had said them—anybody could have said them except Lincoln.

Such was the tone and temper of Reade's books, and such was the quality of disbelief that had produced them. In consequence, they fooled no one except the author. They did not even have the energy of an amusing or persuasive slander. They were stillborn the moment they issued from the press. No one read them or paid any attention to them.

And how did he rationalize to himself his defeat and failure? In the easy, obvious, and inevitable way. He had been rash enough, he told George with a smile of faint, ironic bitterness, to expose some of the cherished figures of public worship and, with his cold, relentless probing for the truth, to shatter the false legends that surrounded them. Naturally, his reward had been anathema and abuse, the hatred of the critics and the obstinate hostility of the public. It had been a thankless business from beginning to end, so he was done with it. He had turned his back on the prejudice, bigotry, stupidity, and hypocrisy of the whole fickle and idolatrous world, and had come here to the country to find solitude and seclusion. One gathered that he would write no more.

And this life certainly had its compensations. The old house which Reade had bought and renovated, making it a trifle too faultlessly agricultural, with a workbench for mending harness in the kitchen, was nevertheless a charming place. His young wife was gracious and lovely, and obviously cared a great deal for him. And Reade himself, apart from the literary pretensions which had embittered his life, was not a bad sort of man. When one understood and accepted the nature of his illusions and defeat, one saw that he was a likable and good-hearted fellow.

It was growing late, but they had not noticed and were surprised when the clock in the hall chimed two. The three of them talked quietly for a few minutes after that, had a final glass of brandy, then said good night. George went upstairs, and shortly afterwards he heard Mr. and Mrs. Reade come softly up and go to their room.

McHarg lay motionless, just as they had left him. He had not stirred a muscle, but seemed to be sunk in the untroubled sleep of childhood. George spread another blanket over him. Then he undressed, turned out the lights, and crawled into his own bed.

He was exhausted, but so excited by all the strange events of the day that he was beyond the desire for sleep. He lay there thinking over what had happened and listening to the wind. It would rush at the house and shiver the windows, then swoop around the corners and the eaves, howling like a banshee. Somewhere a shutter flapped and banged insanely. Now and then, in the momentary lulls between the rushes of the wind, a dog barked mournfully in the faint distance. He heard the clock in the downstairs hall chime three.

It was some time after that when he finally dropped off. The storm was still howling like a madman round the house, but he was no longer aware of it.

473

Chapter Thirty-Seven

The Morning After

George lay in merciful and dreamless sleep, as leaden as if he had been knocked senseless by a heavy club. How long he had slept he did not know, but it hardly seemed five minutes when he was awakened suddenly by someone shaking him by the shoulder. He opened his eyes and started up. It was McHarg. He stood there in his underwear, prancing around on his storklike legs like an impatient sprinter straining at the mark.

"Get up, George, get up!" he cried shrilly. "For Christ's sake, man, are you going to sleep all day?"

George stared at him dumbfounded. "What—what time is it?" he managed finally to say.

"It's after eight o'clock," McHarg cried. "I've been up an hour. Shaved and had a bath, and now," he smacked his bony hands together with an air of relish and sniffed zestfully at the breakfast-laden air, "boy, I could eat a horse! Don't you smell it?" he cried gleefully. "Oatmeal, eggs and bacon, grilled tomatoes, toast and marmalade, coffee. Ah!" he sighed with reverent enthusiasm. "There's nothing like an English breakfast. Get up, George, get up!" he cried again with shrill insistence. "My God, man, I let you sleep a whole hour longer than I did because you looked as if you needed it! So get your clothes on! We don't want to keep breakfast waiting!"

George groaned, dragged his legs wearily from the covers, and stood groggily erect. He felt as if he wanted nothing so much as to sleep for two days on end. But under the feverish urging of this red fury, he had nothing left to do except to awake and dress. Like a man in a trance, he pulled on his clothes with slow, fumbling motions, and all the while McHarg fumed up and down, demanding every two seconds that he get a move on and not be all day about it.

When they got downstairs the Reades were already at the table. McHarg bounced in as if he had a rubber core, greeted both of them cheerfully, took a seat, and instantly fell to. He put away an enormous breakfast, talking all the time and crackling with electricity. His energy was astounding. It was really incredible. It seemed impossible that the exhausted wreck of a few hours before could now be miraculously transformed into this dynamo of vitality. He was in uproarious spirits, and full of stories and adventures. He told wonderful yarns about the ceremonies at which his degree had been presented and about all the people there. Then he told about Berlin, and about people he had met in Germany and in Holland. He told of his meeting with Mynheer Bendien, and gave a side-splitting account of their madhouse escapades. He was full of plans and purposes. He asked about everyone he knew in England. His mind seemed to have a thousand brilliant facets. He took hold of everything, and whatever he touched began to crackle with the energy and alertness of his own dynamic power. He was a delightful companion. George realized that he was now seeing McHarg at his best, and his best was wonderfully and magnificently good.

After breakfast they all took a walk together. It was a rare, wild morning. The temperature had dropped several degrees during the night and the fitful rain had turned to snow, which was now coming down steadily, swirling and gusting through the air upon the howling wind and piling up in soft, fleecy drifts. Overhead, the branches of the bare trees thrashed about and moaned. The countryside was impossibly wild and beautiful. They walked long and far, filled with the excitement of the storm, and with a strange, wild joy and sorrow, knowing that the magic could not last.

When they came back to the house, they sat beside the fire and talked together. McHarg's gleeful exuberance of the morning had subsided, but in its place had come a quiet power—the kind of Lincolnesque dignity of repose and strength which George had observed in him the day before. He took out his old silver-rimmed spectacles and put them on his homely, wry, and curiously engaging face. He read some letters which he had in his pocket and had not opened, and after that he talked to his old friend. What they talked about was not important in itself. What *was* important, and what George would always remember, was the way McHarg looked, and the way he sat and talked, with his bony knuckles arched and clasped before him in an attitude of unconscious power, and the dignity, wisdom, and deep knowledge of his speech. Here was a man with greatness in him, a man who was now showing the basic sources of his latent strength. His speech was full of quiet affection for his old friend. One felt something unshakable and abiding in him—a loyalty that would not change, that would

475

remain always the same, even though he might not see his friend again for twenty years.

They had a good lunch together. Wine was served, but McHarg partook sparingly of it. After lunch, to Webber's great relief, McHarg told him quietly that they were returning to London in the afternoon. He said nothing about the projected tour of England which he had depicted in such glowing colors the day before. Whether that had been just a passing whim, or whether he had given up the idea because he sensed George's lack of enthusiasm for it, George did not know. McHarg did not refer to it at all. He merely announced their return to London as a fact and let it go at that.

But now, as if the thought of going back to the city was more than he could bear, he immediately underwent another of his astonishing transformations. Almost at once his manner again became feverish and impatient. By three o'clock, when they left, he had worked himself into a state of inflamed distemper. He seemed on edge, like one who wanted to get some disagreeable business over and done with.

They drove cautiously down the whitened, trackless lane, over which no car had passed that day, leaving behind them the low-eaved comfort of that fine old house, now warmly fleeced in its blanket of snow, and George felt again the almost unbearable sadness that always came to him when he said good-bye to people whom he knew he would never see again. The lovely woman stood in the doorway and watched them go, with Reade beside her, his hands thrust deep in the pockets of his velvet jacket. As the car took the turn McHarg and George looked back. Reade and his wife waved, and they waved back, and something tightened in George's throat. Then they were out of sight. McHarg and George were alone again.

They reached the highroad and turned north and sped onward toward London. Both men were silent, each absorbed in his own thoughts. McHarg sat back in his corner, quiet, abstracted, sunk deep into his inner world. Darkness came, and they said nothing.

And now the lights were up, and there against the sky George saw again the vast corrupted radiance of the night—the smoke, the fury, and the welter of London's unending life. And after a little while the car was threading its way through the jungle warren of that monstrous sprawl, and at last it turned into Ebury Street and stopped. George got out and thanked McHarg; they shook hands, exchanged a few words, and then said good-bye. The little driver shut the door, touched his cap respectfully, and climbed back into his seat. The big car purred and drove off smoothly into the darkness.

George stood at the curb and looked after it until it

disappeared. And he knew that he and McHarg might meet and speak and pass again, but never as they had in this, their first meeting; for something had begun which now was finished, and henceforth they would have to take their separate courses, he to his own ending, McHarg to his—and which to the better one no man knew.

BOOK VI

"I Have a Thing to Tell You"

(,,Nun Will Ich Ihnen 'Was Sagen")

By spring, when George returned to New York, it seemed to him that he had his new book almost finished. He took a small apartment near Stuyvesant Square and buckled down to a steady daily grind to wind it up. He thought two months more would surely see him through, but he always fooled himself about time, and it was not till six months later that he had a manuscript that satisfied him. That is to say, he had a manuscript that he was willing to turn over to his publisher, for he was never really satisfied with anything he wrote. There was always that seemingly unbridgeable gulf between the thing imagined and the thing accomplished, and he wondered if any writer had ever been able to look calmly at something he had done and honestly say:

"This conveys precisely the ideas and feelings I wanted it to convey—no more, no less. The thing is just right, and cannot be improved."

In that sense he was not at all satisfied with his new book. He knew its faults, knew all the places where it fell short of his intentions. But he also knew that he had put into it everything he had at that stage of his development, and for this reason he was not ashamed of it. He delivered the bulky manuscript to Fox Edwards, and as its weight passed from his hands to Fox's he felt as if a load that he had been carrying for years had been lifted from his mind and conscience. He was done with it, and he wished to God he could forget it and never have to see a line of it again.

That, however, was too much to hope for. Fox read it, told him in his shy, straight way that it was good, and then made a few suggestions—for cutting it here, for adding something there, for rearranging some of the material. George argued hotly with Fox, then took the manuscript home and went to work on it again and did the things Fox wanted—not because Fox wanted them, but because he saw that Fox was right. Two more months went into that. Then there were proofs to read and correct, and by the time this was done another six weeks had gone. The better part of a year had passed since his return from England, but now the job was really finished and he was free at last.

Publication was scheduled for the spring of 1936, and as the time approached he became increasingly apprehensive. When his first book had come out, wild horses could not have dragged him from New York; he had wanted to be on hand so he could be sure not to miss anything. He had waited around, and read all the reviews, and almost camped out in Fox's office, and had expected from day to day some impossible fulfillment that never came. Instead, there had been the letters from Libya Hill and his sickening adventures with the lion hunters. So now he was gun-shy of publication dates, and he made up his mind to go away this time—as far away as possible. Although he did not believe there would be an exact repetition of those earlier experiences, just the same he was prepared for the worst, and when it happened he was determined not to be there.

Suddenly he thought of Germany, and thought of it with intense longing. Of all the countries he had ever seen, that was the one, after America, which he liked the best, and in which he felt most at home, and with whose people he had the most natural, instant, and instinctive sympathy and understanding. It was also the country above all others whose mystery and magic haunted him. He had been there several times, and each time its spell over him had been the same. And now, after the years of labor and exhaustion, the very thought of Germany meant peace to his soul, and release, and happiness, and the old magic again.

So in March, two weeks before the publication of his book, with Fox at the pier to see him off and reassure him that everything was going to be all right, he sailed again for Europe.

Chapter Thirty-Eight

The Dark Messiah

George had not been in Germany since 1928 and the early months of 1929, when he had had to spend weeks of slow convalescence in a Munich hospital after a fight in a beer hall. Before that foolish episode, he had stayed for a while in a little town in the Black Forest, and he remembered that there had been great excitement because an election was being held. The state of politics was chaotic, with a bewildering number of parties, and the Communists polled a surprisingly large vote. People were disturbed and anxious, and there seemed to be a sense of impending calamity in the air.

This time, things were different. Germany had changed.

Ever since 1933, when the change occurred, George had read, first with amazement, shock, and doubt, then with despair and a leaden sinking of the heart, all the newspaper accounts of what was going on in Germany. He found it hard to believe some of the reports. Of course, there were irresponsible extremists in Germany as elsewhere, and in times of crisis no doubt they got out of hand, but he thought he knew Germany and the German people, and on the whole he was inclined to feel that the true state of affairs had been exaggerated and that things simply could not be as they were pictured.

And now, on the train from Paris, where he had stopped off for five weeks, he met some Germans who gave him reassurance. They said there was no longer any confusion or chaos in politics and government, and no longer any fear among the people, because everyone was so happy. This was what George wanted desperately to believe, and he was prepared to be happy, too. For no man ever went to a foreign land under more propitious conditions than those which attended his arrival in Germany early in May, 1936.

It is said that Byron awoke one morning at the age of twenty-four to find himself famous. George Webber had to wait eleven years longer. He was thirty-five when he reached Berlin, but it was magic just the same. Perhaps he was not really very famous, but that didn't matter, because for the first and last

481

time in his life he felt as if he were. Just before he left Paris a letter had reached him from Fox Edwards, telling him that his new book was having a great success in America. Then, too, his first book had been translated and published in Germany the year before. The German critics had said tremendous things about it, it had had a very good sale, and his name was known. When he got to Berlin the people were waiting for him.

The month of May is wonderful everywhere. It was particularly wonderful in Berlin that year. Along the streets, in the Tiergarten, in all the great gardens, and along the Spree Canal the horse chestnut trees were in full bloom. The crowds sauntered underneath the trees on the Kurfürstendamm, the terraces of the cafés were jammed with people, and always, through the golden sparkle of the days, there was a sound of music in the air. George saw the chains of endlessly lovely lakes around Berlin, and for the first time he knew the wonderful golden bronze upon the tall poles of the kiefern trees. Before, he had visited only the south of Germany, the Rhinelands and Bavaria; now the north seemed even more enchanting.

He planned to stay all summer, and one summer seemed too short a time to encompass all the beauty, magic, and almost intolerable joy which his life had suddenly become, and which he felt would never fade or tarnish if only he could remain in Germany forever. For, to cap it all, his second book was translated and brought out within a short time of his arrival, and its reception exceeded anything he had ever dared to hope for. Perhaps his being there at the time may have had something to do with it. The German critics outdid each other in singing his praises. If one called him "the great American epic writer," the next seemed to feel he had to improve on that, and called him "the American Homer." So now everywhere he went there were people who knew his work. His name flashed and shone. He was a famous man.

Fame shed a portion of her loveliness on everything about him. Life took on an added radiance. The look, feel, taste, smell, and sound of everything had gained a tremendous and exciting enhancement, and all because Fame was at his side. He saw the world with a sharper relish of perception than he had ever known before. All the confusion, fatigue, dark doubt, and bitter hopelessness that had afflicted him in times past had gone, and no shadow of any kind remained. It seemed to him that he had won a final and utterly triumphant victory over all the million forms of life. His spirit was no longer tormented, exhausted, and weighted down with the ceaseless effort of his former struggles with Amount and Number. He was wonderfully aware of everything, alive in every pore.

Fame even gave a tongue to silence, a language to unuttered speech. Fame was with him almost all the time, but even when he was alone without her, in places where he was not known and his name meant nothing, the aura which Fame had shed still clung to him and he was able to meet each new situation with a sense of power and confidence, of warmth, friendliness, and good fellowship. He had become the lord of life. There had been a time in his youth when he felt that people were always laughing at him, and he had been ill at ease with strangers and had gone to every new encounter with a chip on his shoulder. But now he was life's strong and light-hearted master, and everyone he met and talked to—waiters, taxi drivers, porters in hotels, elevator boys, casual acquaintances in trams and trains and on the street—felt at once the flood of happy and affectionate power within him, and responded to him eagerly, instinctively, with instant natural liking, as men respond to the clean and shining light of the young sun.

And when Fame was with him, all this magic was increased. He could see the wonder, interest, respect, and friendly envy in the eyes of men, and the frank adoration in the eyes of women. The women seemed to worship at the shrine of Fame. George began to get letters and telephone calls from them, with invitations to functions of every sort. The girls were after him. But he had been through all of that before and he was wary now, for he knew that the lion hunters were the same the whole world over. Knowing them now for what they were, he found no disillusion in his encounters with them. Indeed, it added greatly to his pleasure and sense of power to turn the tactics of designing females on themselves: he would indulge in little gallantries to lead them on, and then, just at the point where they thought they had him, he would wriggle innocently off the hook and leave them wondering.

And then he met Else. Else von Kohler was not a lion hunter. George met her at one of the parties which his German publisher, Karl Lewald, gave for him. Lewald liked to give parties; he just couldn't do enough for George, and was always trumping up an excuse for another party. Else did not know Lewald, and took an instinctive dislike to the man as soon as she saw him, but just the same she had come to his party, brought there uninvited by another man whom George had met. At first sight, George fell instantly in love with her, and she with him.

Else was a young widow of thirty who looked and was a perfect type of the Norse Valkyrie. She had a mass of lustrous yellow hair braided about her head, and her cheeks were two ruddy apples. She was extremely tall for a woman, with the long, rangy legs of a runner, and her shoulders were as broad and wide as a man's. Yet she had a stunning figure, and there was no suggestion of an ugly masculinity about her. She was as completely and as passionately feminine as a woman could be. Her somewhat stern and lonely face was relieved by its spiritual depth and feeling, and when it was lighted by a smile it had a sudden, poignant radiance, a quality of illumination which in its intensity and purity was different from any other smile George had ever seen.

At the moment of their first meeting, George and Else had been drawn to each other. From then on, without the need of any period of transition, their lives flowed in a single channel. They spent many wonderful days together. Many, too, were the nights which they filled with the mysterious enchantments of a strong and mutually shared passion. The girl became for George the ultimate reality underlying everything he thought and felt and was during that glorious and intoxicating period of his life.

And now all the blind and furious Brooklyn years, all the years of work, all the memories of men who prowled in garbage cans, all the years of wandering and exile, seemed very far away. In some strange fashion, the image of his own success and this joyous release after so much toil and desperation became connected in George's mind with Else, with the kiefern trees, with the great crowds thronging the Kurfürstendamm, with all the golden singing in the air—and somehow with a feeling that for everyone grim weather was behind and that happy days were here again.

It was the season of the great Olympic games, and almost every day George and Else went to the stadium in Berlin. George observed that the organizing genius of the German people, which has been used so often to such noble purpose, was now more thrillingly displayed than he had ever seen it before. The sheer pageantry of the occasion was overwhelming, so much so that he began to feel oppressed by it. There seemed to be something ominous in it. One sensed a stupendous concentration of effort, a tremendous drawing together and ordering in the vast collective power of the whole land. And the thing that made it seem ominous was that it so evidently went beyond what the games themselves demanded. The games were overshadowed, and were no longer merely sporting competitions to which other nations had sent their chosen teams. They became, day after day, an orderly and overwhelming demonstration in which the whole of Germany had been schooled and disciplined. It was as if the games had been chosen as a symbol of the new collective might, a means of showing to the world in concrete terms what this new power had come to be.

With no past experience in such affairs, the Germans had

constructed a mighty stadium which was the most beautiful and most perfect in its design that had ever been built. And all the accessories of this monstrous plant—the swimming pools, the enormous halls, the lesser stadia—had been laid out and designed with this same cohesion of beauty and of use. The organization was superb. Not only were the events themselves, down to the minutest detail of each competition, staged and run off like clockwork, but the crowds—such crowds as no other great city has ever had to cope with, and the like of which would certainly have snarled and maddened the traffic of New York beyond hope of untangling—were handled with a quietness, order, and speed that was astounding.

The daily spectacle was breath-taking in its beauty and magnificence. The stadium was a tournament of color that caught the throat; the massed splendor of the banners made the gaudy decorations of America's great parades, presidential inaugurations, and World's Fairs seem like shoddy carnivals in comparison. And for the duration of the Olympics, Berlin itself was transformed into a kind of annex to the stadium. From one end of the city to the other, from the Lustgarten to the Brandenburger Tor, along the whole broad sweet of Unter den Linden, through the vast avenues of the faëry Tiergarten, and out through the western part of Berlin to the very portals of the stadium, the whole town was a thrilling pageantry of royal banners—not merely endless miles of looped-up bunting, but banners fifty feet in height, such as might have graced the battle tent of some great emperor.

And all through the day, from morning on, Berlin became a mighty Ear, attuned, attentive, focused on the stadium. Everywhere the air was filled with a single voice. The green trees along the Kurfürstendamm began to talk: from loud-speakers concealed in their branches an announcer in the stadium spoke to the whole city—and for George Webber it was a strange experience to hear the familiar terms of track and field translated into the tongue that Goethe used. He would be informed now that the *Vorlauf* was about to be run—and then the *Zwischenlauf*—and at length the *Endlauf*—and the winner: "Owens—Oo Ess Ah!"

Meanwhile, through those tremendous banner-laden ways, the crowds thronged ceaselessly all day long. The wide promenade of Unter den Linden was solid with patient, tramping German feet. Fathers, mothers, children, young folks, old—the whole material of the nation was there, from every corner of the land. From morn to night they trudged, wide-eyed, full of wonder, past the marvel of those banner-laden ways. And among them one saw the bright stabs of color of Olympic jackets and the glint of foreign faces: the dark features of Frenchmen and Italians, the ivory grimace of the Japanese, the straw hair and blue eyes of the Swedes, and the big Americans, natty in straw hats, white flannels, and blue coats crested with the Olympic seal.

And there were great displays of marching men, sometimes ungunned but rhythmic as regiments of brown shirts went swinging through the streets. By noon each day all the main approaches to the games, the embannered streets and avenues of the route which the Leader would take to the stadium, miles away, were walled in by the troops. They stood at ease, young men, laughing and talking with each other—the Leader's bodyguards, the Schutz Staffel units, the Storm Troopers, all the ranks and divisions in their different uniforms—and they stretched in two unbroken lines from the Wilhelm-strasse up to the arches of the Brandenburger Tor. Then, suddenly, the sharp command, and instantly there would be the solid smack of ten thousand leather boots as they came together with the sound of war.

It seemed as if everything had been planned for this moment, shaped to this triumphant purpose. But the people—they had not been planned. Day after day, behind the unbroken wall of soldiers, they stood and waited in a dense and patient throng. These were the masses of the nation, the poor ones of the earth, the humble ones of life, the workers and the wives, the mothers and the children—and day after day they came and stood and waited. They were there because they did not have money enough to buy the little cardboard squares that would have given them places within the magic ring. From noon till night they waited for just two brief and golden moments of the day: the moment when the Leader went out to the stadium, and the moment when he returned.

At last he came—and something like a wind across a field of grass was shaken through that crowd, and from afar the tide rolled up with him, and in it was the voice, the hope, the prayer of the land. The Leader came by slowly in a shining car, a little dark man with a comic-opera mustache, erect and standing, moveless and unsmiling, with his hand upraised, palm outward, not in Nazi-wise salute, but straight up, in a gesture of blessing such as the Buddha or Messiahs use.

From the beginning of their relationship, and straight through to the end, Else refused to discuss with George anything even remotely connected with the Nazi regime. That was a closed subject between them. But others were not so discreet. The first weeks passed, and George began to hear some ugly things. From time to time, at parties, dinners, and the like, when George would speak of his enthusiasm for Germany and the German people, various friends that he had made would, if they had had enough to drink, take him aside afterwards and, after looking around cautiously, lean toward him with an air of great secrecy and whisper:

"But have you heard . . . ? And have you heard . . . ?"

He did not see any of the ugly things they whispered about. He did not see anyone beaten. He did not see anyone imprisoned, or put to death. He did not see any men in concentration camps. He did not see openly anywhere the physical manifestations of a brutal and compulsive force.

True, there were men in brown uniforms everywhere, and men in black uniforms, and men in uniforms of olive green, and everywhere in the streets there was the solid smack of booted feet, the blare of brass, the tootling of fifes, and the poignant sight of young faces shaded under iron helmets, with folded arms and ramrod backs, precisely seated in great army lorries. But all of this had become so mixed in with his joy over his own success, his feeling for Else, and the genial temper of the people making holiday, as he had seen and known it so many pleasant times before, that even if it did not now seem good, it did not seem sinister or bad.

Then something happened. It didn't happen suddenly. It just happened as a cloud gathers, as fog settles, as rain begins to fall.

A man George had met was planning to give a party for him and asked him if he wanted to ask any of his friends. George mentioned one. His host was silent for a moment; he looked embarrassed; then he said that the person George had named had formerly been the editorial head of a publication that had been suppressed, and that one of the people who had been instrumental in its suppression had been invited to the party, so would George mind——?

George named another, an old friend named Franz Heilig whom he had first met in Munich years before, and who now lived in Berlin, and of whom he was very fond. Again the anxious pause, the embarrassment, the halting objections. This person was—was—well, George's host said he knew about this peson and knew he did not go to parties—he would not come if he were invited—so would George mind——?

George next spoke the name of Else von Kohler, and the response to this suggestion was of the same kind. How long had he known this woman? Where, and under what circumstances, had he met her? George tried to reassure his host on all these scores. He told the man he need have no fear of any sort about Else. His host was instant, swift, in his apologies: oh, by no means—he was sure the lady was eminently all right—only, nowadays—with a mixed gathering—he had tried to pick a group of people whom George had met and who all knew one

487

another—he had thought it would be much more pleasant that way—strangers at a party were often shy, constrained, and formal—Frau von Kohler would not know anybody there—so would George mind——?

Not long after this baffling experience a friend came to see him. "In a few days," his friend said, "you will receive a phone call from a certain person. He will try to meet you, to talk to you. Have nothing to do with this man."

George laughed. His friend was a sober-minded German, rather on the dull and heavy side, and his face was so absurdly serious as he spoke that George thought he was trying to play some lumbering joke upon him. He wanted to know who this mysterious personage might be who was so anxious to make his acquaintance.

To George's amazement and incredulity, his friend named a high official in the government.

But why, George asked, should this man want to meet him? And why, if he did, should he be afraid of him?

At first his friend would not answer. Finally he muttered circumspectly:

"Listen to me. Stay away from this man. I tell you for your own good." He paused, not knowing how to say it; then: "You have heard of Captain Roehm? You know about him? You know what happened to him?" George nodded. "Well," his friend went on in a troubled voice, "there were others who were not shot in the purge. This man I speak of is one of the bad ones. We have a name for him—it is 'The Prince of Darkness.'"

George did not know what to make of all this. He tried to puzzle it out but could not, so at last he dismissed it from his mind. But within a few days the official whom his friend had named did telephone, and did ask to meet him. George offered some excuse and avoided seeing the man, but the episode was most peculiar and unsettling.

Both of these baffling experiences contained elements of comedy and melodrama, but those were the superficial aspects. George began to realize now the tragedy that lay behind such things. There was nothing political in any of it. The roots of it were much more sinister and deep and evil than politics or even racial prejudice could ever be. For the first time in his life he had come upon something full of horror that he had never known before—something that made all the swift violence and passion of America, the gangster compacts, the sudden killings, the harshness and corruption that infested portions of American business and public life, seem innocent beside it. What George began to see was a picture of a great people who had been psychically wounded and were now desperately ill with some dread malady of the soul. Here was an entire nation, he now realized, that was infested with the contagion of an ever-

488

present fear. It was a kind of creeping paralysis which twisted and blighted all human relations. The pressures of a constant and infamous compulsion had silenced this whole people into a sweltering and malignant secrecy until they had become spiritually septic with the distillations of their own self-poisons, for which now there was no medicine or release.

As he began to see and understand the true state of affairs, George wondered if anyone could be so base as to exult at this great tragedy, or to feel hatred for the once-mighty people who were the victims of it. Culturally, from the eighteenth century on, the German was the first citizen of Europe. In Goethe there was made sublimely articulate a world spirit which knew no boundary lines of nationality, politics, race, or religion, which rejoiced in the inheritance of all mankind, and which wanted no domination or conquest of that inheritance save that of participating in it and contributing to it. This German spirit in art, literature, music, science, and philosophy continued in an unbroken line right down to 1933, and it seemed to George that there was not a man or woman alive in the world who was not, in one way or another, the richer for it.

When he first visited Germany, in 1925, the evidence of that spirit was manifest everywhere in the most simple and unmistakable ways. For example, one could not pass the crowded window of a bookshop in any town without instantly observing in it a reflection of the intellectual and cultural enthusiasm of the German people. The contents of the shop revealed a breadth of vision and of interest that would have made the contents of a French bookshop, with its lingual and geographic constrictions, seem paltry and provincial. The best writers of every country were as well known in Germany as in their own land. Among the Americans, Theodore Dreiser, Sinclair Lewis, Upton Sinclair, and Jack London had particularly large followings; their books were sold and read everywhere. And the work of America's younger writers was eagerly sought out and published.

Even in 1936 this noble enthusiasm, although it had been submerged and mutilated by the regime of Adolph Hitler, was still apparent in the most touching way. George had heard it said that good books could no longer be published and read in Germany. This, he found, was not true, as some of the other things he had heard about Germany were not true. And about Hitler's Germany he felt that one must be very true. And the reason one needed to be very true was that the thing in it which every decent person must be against was false. You could not turn the other cheek to wrong, but also, it seemed to him, you could not be wrong about wrong. You had to be right about it. You could not meet lies and trickery with lies and trickery, although there were some people who argued that you should.

So it was not true that good books could no longer be published and read in Germany. And because it was not true, the tragedy of the great German spirit was more movingly evident, in the devious and distorted ways in which it now manifested itself, than it would have been if it were true. Good books were still published if their substance did not, either openly or by implication, criticize the Hitler regime or contravert its dogmas. And it would simply be stupid to assert that any book must criticize Hitler and contravert his doctrines in order to be good.

For these reasons, the eagerness, curiosity, and enthusiasm of the Germans for such good books as they were still allowed to read had been greatly intensified. They wanted desperately to find out what was going on in the world, and the only way they had left was to read whatever books they could get that had been written outside of Germany. This seemed to be one basic explanation of their continued interest in American writing, and that they *were* interested was a fact as overwhelming as it was pathetic. Under these conditions, the last remnants of the German spirit managed to survive only as drowning men survive—by clutching desperately at any spar that floated free from the wreckage of their ship.

So the weeks, the months, the summer passed, and everywhere about him George saw the evidences of this dissolution, this shipwreck of a great spirit. The poisonous emanations of suppression, persecution, and fear permeated the air like miasmic and pestilential vapors, tainting, sickening, and blighting the lives of everyone he met. It was a plague of the spirit—invisible, but as unmistakable as death. Little by little it sank in on him through all the golden singing of that summer, until at last he felt it, breathed it, lived it, and knew it for the thing it was.

Chapter Thirty-Nine

"One Big Fool"

The time had come for George to go. He knew he had to leave, but he had kept putting it off. Twice he had booked his passage back to America and made all his preparations for departure, and twice, as the day approached, he had canceled the arrangements.

He hated the thought of quitting Germany, for he felt, somehow, that he would never again be able to return to this ancient land he loved so much. And Else—where, and under what alien skies, could he hope to see her again? Her roots were here, his were elsewhere. This would be a last farewell.

So, after delaying and delaying, once more he booked his passage and made his plans to leave Berlin on a day toward the middle of September. The postponement of the dreaded moment had only made it more painful. He would be foolish to draw it out any further. This time he would really go.

And at last came the fateful dawn.

The phone beside his bed rang quietly. He stirred, then roused sharply from that fitful and uneasy sleep which a man experiences when he has gone to bed late, knowing that he has to get up early. It was the porter. His low, quiet voice had in it the quality of immediate authority.

"It is seven o'clock," he said.

"All right." George answered. "Thank you, I'm awake."

Then he got up, still fighting dismally with a stale fatigue which begged for sleep, as well as with a gnawing tension of anxiety which called for action. One look about the room reassured him. His old leather trunk lay open on the baggage rest. It had been packed the night before with beautiful efficiency by the maid. Now there was very little more to do except to shave and dress, stow toilet things away, pack the brief case with a few books and letters and the pages of manuscript that always accumulated wherever he was, and drive to the station. Twenty minutes' steady work would find him ready. The train was not due until half-past eight, and the station was not three minutes distant in a taxicab. He thrust his feet into his slippers, walked over to the windows, tugged the cord, and pulled up the heavy wooden blinds.

It was a grey morning. Below him, save for an occasional motor car, the quiet thrum of a bicycle, or someone walking briskly to his work with a lean, spare clack of early morning, the Kurfürstendamm was bare and silent. In the center of the street, above the tram tracks, the fine trees had already lost their summer freshness—that deep and dark intensity of German green which is the greenest green on earth and which has a kind of forest darkness, a legendary sense of coolness and of magic. The leaves looked faded now, and dusty. They were already touched here and there by the yellowing tinge of autumn. A tram, cream-yellow, spotless, shining like a perfect toy, slid past with a hissing sound upon the rails and at the contacts of the trolley. Except for this, the tram car made no noise. Like everything the Germans built, the tram and its roadbed were perfect in their function. The rattling and metallic clatter of an American street car were totally absent. Even the little cobblestones that paved the space between the tracks were as clean and spotless as if each of them had just been gone over thoroughly with a whisk broom, and the strips of grass that bordered the tracks were as green and velvety as Oxford sward.

On both sides of the street, the great restaurants, cafés, and terraces of the Kurfürstendamm had the silent loneliness that such places always have at that hour of the morning. Chairs were racked upon the tables. Everything was clean and bare and empty. Three blocks away, at the head of the street, the clock on the Gedächtnis-kirche belatedly struck seven times. He could see the great, bleak masses of the church, and in the trees a few birds sang.

Someone knocked upon the door. He turned and crossed and opened it. The waiter stood there with his breakfast tray. He was a boy of fifteen, a blond-haired, solemn child with a fresh pink face. He wore a boiled shirt, and a waiter's uniform which was spotless-clean, but which had obviously been cut off and shortened down a little from the dimensions of some more mature former inhabitant. He marched in solemnly, bearing his tray before him straight toward the table in the center of the room, stolidly uttering in a guttural and toneless voice his three phrases of English which were:

"Goot morning, sir," as George opened the door—

"If you bleeze, sir," as he set the tray down upon the table, and then—

"Dank you ferry much, sir," as he marched out and turned to close the door behind him.

The formula had always been the same. All summer it had not varied by a jot, and now as he marched out for the last time George had a feeling of affection and regret. He called to the boy to wait a moment, got his trousers, took some money, and gave it to him. His pink face reddened suddenly with happiness. George shook hands with him, and the boy said gutturally:

"Dank you ferry much, sir." And then, very quietly and earnestly, *"Gute reise, mein Herr."* He clicked his heels together and bowed formally, and then closed the door.

George stood there for a moment with that nameless feeling of affection and regret, knowing that he would never see the boy again. Then he went back to the table and poured out a cup of the hot, rich chocolate, broke a crusty roll, buttered it, spread it with strawberry jam, and ate it. This was all the breakfast he wanted. The pot was still half full of chocolate, the dish was still piled with little scrolls of creamy butter, there was enough of the delicious jam, enough of the crusty rolls and flaky croissants, to make half a dozen breakfasts, but he was not hungry.

He went over to the wash basin and switched on the light. The large and heavy porcelain bowl was indented in the wall. The wall and the floor beneath were substantial and as perfect as a small but costly bathroom. He brushed his teeth and shaved, packed all the toilet things together in a little leather case, pulled the zipper, and put it away in the old trunk. Then he dressed. By seven-twenty he was ready.

Franz Heilig came in as George was ringing for the porter. He was an astonishing fellow, an old friend of the Munich days, and George was devoted to him.

When they had first met, Heilig had been a librarian in Munich. Now he had a post in one of the large libraries of Berlin. In this capacity he was a public functionary, with the prospect of slow but steady advancement through the years. His income was small and his scale of living modest, but such things did not bother Heilig. He was a scholar, with the widest range of knowledge and interests that George had ever known in anyone. He read and spoke a dozen languages. He was German to the very core of his learned soul, but his English, which he spoke less well than any other language he had studied, was not the usual German rendering of Shakespeare's tongue. There were plenty of Germanic elements in it, but in addition Heilig had also borrowed accents and inflections from some of his other linguistic conquests, and the result was a most peculiar and amusing kind of bastard speech.

As he entered the room and saw George he began to laugh, closing his eyes, contorting his small features, and snuffling through his sourly puckered lips as if he had just eaten a half-ripe persimmon. Then his face went sober and he said anxiously:

"You are ready, zen? You are truly going?"

George nodded. "Yes," he said. "Everything's all ready. How do you feel, Franz?"

He laughed suddenly, took off his spectacles, and began to polish them. Without his glasses, his small puckered face had a tired and worn look, and his weak eyes were bloodshot and weary from the night before.

"O Gott!" he cried, with a kind of gleeful desperation. "I feel perfectly *dret-ful*! I haf not efen been to bett! After I left you I could not sleep. I valked and valked, almost up to Grunewald.

493

. . . May I tell you somesing?" he said earnestly, and peered at George with the serious intensity with which he always uttered these oracular words. "I feel like hell—I really do."

"Then you haven't been to bed at all? You've had no sleep?"

"Oh, yes," he said wearily. "I haf slept an hour. I came back home. My girl vas asleep—I did not vant to get into ze bett wiz her—I did not vant to vake her up. So I laid down upon ze couch. I did not efen take off my clothes. I vas afraid zat I vould come too late to see you at ze station. And zat," he said, peering at George most earnestly again, "vould be too dret-ful!"

"Why don't you go back home and sleep today after the train goes?" George said. "I don't think you'll be able to do much work, feeling as you do. Wouldn't it be better if you took the day off and caught up on your sleep?"

"Vell, zen," said Heilig abruptly, yet rather indifferently, "I vill tell you somesing." He peered at George earnestly and intently again, and said: "It does not matter. It really does not matter. I vill take somesing—some coffee or somesing," he said indifferently. "It vill not be too bad. But Gott!"—again the desperately gleeful laugh—"how I shall sleep tonight! After zat I shall try to get to know my girl again."

"I hope so, Franz. She's a nice girl. I'm afraid she hasn't seen much of you the last month or so."

"Vell, zen," said Heilig, as before, "I vill tell you somesing. It does not matter. It really does not matter. She is a good girl— she knows about zese sings—you like her, yes?"—and he peered at George eagerly, earnestly, again. "You sink she is nice?"

"Yes, I think she's very nice."

"Vell, zen," said Heilig, "I vill tell you somesing. She *is* very nice. I am glad if you like her. She is very good for me. Ve get along togezzer very vell. I hope zat zey vill let me keep her," he said quietly.

"They? Who do you mean by 'they,' Franz?"

"Oh," he said, wearily, and his small face puckered in an expression of disgust, "zese people—zese stupid people—zat you know about."

"But good Lord, Franz! Surely they have not yet forbidden *that*, have they? A man is still allowed to have a girl, isn't he? Why you can step right into the Kurfürstendamm and get a dozen girls before you've walked a block."

"Oh," said Heilig, "you mean ze little whores. Yes, you may still go to ze little whores. Zat's quite anozzer matter. You may go to ze little whores and perhaps zey give you somesing—a little poison. But zat is quite all right. You see, my dear shap," here his face puckered in a look of impish malice, and he began to speak in the tone of exaggerated and mincing refinement that characterized some of his more vicious utterances, "I vill now

494

tell you somesing. Under ze *Dritte Reich* ve are all so happy, everysing is so fine and healsy, zat it is perfectly Gott-tam dretful," he sneered. "Ve may go to ze little whores in ze Kurfürstendamm. Zey vill take you to zeir rooms, or zey vill come wiz you. Yes," he said earnestly, nodding, "zey vill come wiz you to vhere you live—to your room. But you cannot haf a girl. If you haf a girl you must marry her, and—may I tell you?" he said frankly—"I cannot marry. I do not make enough money. It vould be *quite* impossible!" he said decisively. "And may I tell you zis?" he continued, pacing nervously up and down and taking rapid puffs at his cigarette. "If you haf a girl, zen you must haf two rooms. And zat also is quite impossible! I haf not efen money enough to afford two rooms."

"You mean, if you are living with a girl you are compelled by law to have two rooms?"

"It is ze law, yes," said Heilig quietly, nodding with the air of finality with which a German states established custom. "You must. If you are liffing wiz a girl, she must haf a room. Zen you can say," he went on seriously, "zat you are not liffing wiz each ozzer. She may haf a room right next to you, but zen you can say zat she is not your girl. You may sleep togezzer every night, all you Gott-tam please. But zen, you see, you vill be good. You vill not do some sings against ze Party. . . . Gott!" he cried, and, lifting his impish, bitterly puckered face, he laughed again. "It is all quite dret-ful."

"But if they find, Franz, that you're living with her in a single room?"

"Vell, zen," he said quietly, "I may tell you zat she vill haf to go." And then, wearily, dismissingly, in a tone of bitter indifference: "It does not matter. I do not care. I pay no attention to zese stupid people. I haf my vork, I haf my girl. And zat is all zat matters. Ven I am finished wiz my vork, I go home to my little room. My girl is zere, and zis little dog," he said, and his face lighted up gleefully again. "Zis little dog—may I tell you somesing?—zis little dog—Pooki—ze little Scottie zat you know—I haf become quite fond of him. He is really quite nice," said Heilig earnestly. "Ven he first came to us I hated him. My girl saw him and she fall in love wiz zis little animal," said Heilig. "She said zat she must haf him—zat I must be buying him for her. Vell, zen," said Heilig, quickly flipping the ash from his cigarette and moving up and down the room, "I said to her zat I vill not haf zis Gott-tam little beast about my place." He fairly shouted these words to show the emphasis of his intention. "Vell, zen, ze girl cry. She talk alvays about zis little dog. She say zat she must haf him, zat she is going to die. Gott!" he cried gleefully again, and laughed. "It vas perfectly dret-ful. Zere vas no more peace for me. I vould go home at night and instantly she vould begin to cry and say she vill be dying if I do

495

not buy zis little dog. So finally I say: 'All right, haf it your own vay. I vill buy zis little animal!' " he said viciously—" 'Only for Gott's sake, shut your crying!' So, zen," said Heilig impishly, "I vent to buy zis little dog, and I looked at him." Here his voice became very droll, and with a tremendous sense of comic exaggeration his eyes narrowed, his small face puckered to a grimace, and his discolored teeth gritted together as he snarled softly and gleefully: "I looked at zis little dog and I said—'All right, you—you-u-u buh-loody little animal—you-u-u aww-ful —dret-ful—little bee-e-est—I vill take you home wiz me—but you—you-u-u damned little beast, you—' " here he gleefully and viciously shook his fist at an imaginary dog—" 'if you do some sings I do not like—if you vill be making some buh-loody awful messes in my place, I vill give you somesing to eat zat you will not enchoy.' . . . But zen," said Heilig, "after ve had him, I became quite fond of him. He is quite nice, really. Sometime ven I come home at night and everysing has gone badly and zere haf been so many of zese dret-ful people, he vill come and look at me. He vill talk to me. He vill say he knows zat I am so unhappy. And zat life is very hard. But zat he is my friend. Yes, he is really very nice. I like him very much."

During this conversation the porter had come in and was now waiting for his orders. He asked George if everything was in the leather trunk. George got down on hands and knees and took a final look under the bed. The porter opened doors and drawers. Heilig himself peered inside the big wardrobe and, finding it empty, turned to George with his characteristic expression of surprise and said:

"Vell, zen, I may tell you zat I sink you have it all."

Satisfied on this score, the porter closed the heavy trunk, locked it, and tightened the straps, while Heilig helped George stuff manuscripts, letters, and a few books into the old brief case. Then George fastened the brief case and gave it to the porter. He dragged the baggage out into the hall and said he would wait for them below.

George looked at his watch and found that it still lacked three-quarters of an hour until train time. He asked Heilig if they should go on immediately to the station or wait at the hotel.

"Ve can vait here," he said. "I sink it vould be better. If you vait here anozzer half an hour, zere vould still be time."

He offered George a cigarette and struck a match for him. Then they sat down, George at the table, Heilig upon the couch against the wall. And for a minute or two they smoked in silence.

"Vell, zen," said Heilig quietly, "zis time is to be good-bye. . . . Zis time you will really go?"

"Yes, Franz. I've got to go this time. I've missed two boats already. I can't miss another one."

They smoked in silence for a moment more, and then suddenly, earnestly and anxiously, Heilig said:

"Vell, zen, may I tell you somesing? I am sorry."

"And I, too, Franz."

Again they smoked in troubled and uneasy silence.

"You vill come back, of gourse," said Heilig presently. And then, decisively: "You must, of gourse. Ve like you here." Another pause, then very simply and quietly, "You know, ve do so luff you."

George was too moved to say anything, and Heilig, peering at him quickly and anxiously, continued:

"And you like it here? You like us? Yes!" he cried emphatically, in answer to his own question. "Of gourse you do!"

"Of course, Franz."

"Zen you must come back," he said quietly. "It vould be quite dret-ful if you did not." He looked at George searchingly again, but George said nothing. In a moment Heilig said, "And I—I shall hope zat ve shall meet again."

"I hope so, too, Franz," said George. And then, trying to throw off the sadness that had fallen on them, he went on as cheerfully as he could, voicing his desire more than his belief: "Of course we shall. I shall come back some day, and we shall sit together talking just the same as we are now."

Heilig did not answer immediately. His small face became contorted with the look of bitter and malicious humor which George had seen upon it so often. He took off his glasses quickly, polished them, wiped his tired, weak eyes, and put his glasses on again.

"You sink so?" he said, and smiled his wry and bitter smile.

"I'm sure of it," George said positively, and for the moment he almost believed it. "You and I and all the friends we know— we'll sit together drinking, we'll stay up all night and dance around the trees and go to Aenna Maentz at three o'clock in the morning for chicken soup. All of it will be the same."

"Vell, zen, I hope zat you are right. But I am not so sure," said Heilig quietly. "I may not be here."

"You!" George laughed derisively. "Why what are you talking about? You know you wouldn't be happy anywhere else. You have your work, it's what you always wanted to do, and at last you're in the place where you always wanted to be. Your future is mapped out clearly before you—it's just a matter of hanging on until your superiors die off or retire. You'll always be here!"

"I am not so sure," he said. He puffed at his cigarette, and then continued rather hesitantly. "You see—zere are zese fools—zese stupid people!" He ground his cigarette out viciously in the ash tray, and, his face twisted in a wry smile of defiant, lacerated pride, he cried angrily: "Myself—I do not care. I do not vorry for myself. Right now I haf my little life—my little chob—my little girl—my little room. Zese people—zese fools!" he cried—"I do not notice zem. I do not see zem. It does not bozzer me," he cried. And now, indeed, his face had become a grotesque mask. "I shall always get along," he said. "If zey run me out—vell, zen, I may tell you zat I do not care! Zere are ozzer places!" he cried bitterly. "I can go to England, to Sveden. If zey take my chob, my girl," he cried scornfully and waved his hand impatiently, "may I tell you zat it does not matter. I shall get along. And if zese fools—zese stupid people—if zey take my life—I do not sink zat is so terrible. You sink so? Yes?"

"Yes, I do think so, Franz. I should not like to die."

"Vell, zen," said Heilig quietly, "wiz you it is a different matter. You are American. Wiz us, it is not ze same. I haf seen men shot, in Munich, in Vienna—I do not sink it is too bad." He turned and looked searchingly at George again. "No, it is not too bad," he said.

"Oh hell, you're talking like an idiot," George said. "No one's going to shoot you. No one's going to take your job or girl away. Why, man, your job is safe. It has nothing to do with politics. And they'd never find another scholar like you. Why, they couldn't do without you."

He shrugged his shoulders indifferently and cynically. "I do not know," he said. "Myself—I think ve can do wizout everybody if ve must. And perhaps ve must."

"Must? What do you mean by that, Franz?"

Heilig did not answer for a moment. Then he said abruptly:

"Now I sink zat I vill tell you somesing. In ze last year here, zese fools haf become quite dret-ful. All ze Chews haf been taken from zier vork, zey haf nozzing to do any more. Zese people come around—some stupid people in zeir uniform—" he said contemptuously—"and zey say zat everyone must be an Aryan man—zis vonderful plue-eyed person eight feet tall who has been Aryan in his family since 1820. If zere is a little Chew back zere—zen it is a pity," Heilig jeered. "Zis man can no more vork—he is no more in ze Cherman spirit. It is all quite stupid." He smoked in silence for a minute or two, then continued: "Zis last year zese big fools haf been coming round to me. Zey demand to know who I am, vhere I am from—whezzer or not I haf been born or not. Zey say zat I must prove to zem zat I am an Aryan man. Ozzervise I can no longer vork in ze library."

"But my God, Franz!" George cried, and stared at him in

498

stupefaction. "You don't mean to tell me that—why, you're not a Jew," he said, "*are* you?"

"Oh Gott no!" Heilig cried, with a sudden shout of gleeful desperation. "My dear shap, I am so Gott-tam Cherman zat it is perfectly dret-ful."

"Well, then," George demanded, puzzled, "what's the trouble? Why should they bother you? Why worry about it if you're a German?"

Heilig was silent a little while, and the look of wry, wounded humor in his small, puckered face had deepened perceptibly before he spoke again.

"My dear Chorge," he said at last, "now I may tell you somesing. I am completely Cherman, it is true. Only, my poor dear mozzer—I do so luff her, of course—but Gott!" He laughed through his closed mouth, and there was bitter merriment in his face. "Gott! She is such a fool! Zis poor lady," he said, a trifle contemptuously, "luffed my fazzer very much—so much, in fact, zat she did not go to ze trouble to marry him. So zese people come and ask me all zese questions, and say, 'Vhere is your fazzer!' And of gourse I cannot tell zem. Because, alas, my dear old shap, I am zis bastard. Gott!" he cried again, and with eyes narrowed into slits he laughed bitterly out of the corner of his mouth. "It is all so dret-ful—so stupid—and so horribly funny!"

"But Franz! Surely you must know who your father is—you must have heard his name."

"My Gott, yes!" he cried. "Zat is vhat makes it all so funny."

"You mean you know him, then? He is living?"

"But of gourse," said Heilig. "He is living in Berlin."

"Do you ever see him?"

"But of gourse," he said again. "I see him every veek. Ve are *quite* good friends."

"But—then I don't see what the trouble is—unless they can take your job from you because you're a bastard. It's embarrassing, of course, and all that, both for your father and yourself—but can't you tell them? Can't you explain it to them? Won't your father help you out?"

"I am sure he vould," said Heilig, "if I told zis sing to him. Only, I cannot tell him. You see," he went on quietly, "my fazzer and I are quite good friends. Ve never speak about zis sing togezzer—ze vay he knew my mozzer. And now, I vould not ask him—I vould not tell him of zis trouble—I vould not vant him to help me—because it might seem zat I vas taking an adwantage. It might spoil everysing."

"But your father—is he known here? Would these people know his name if you mentioned it?"

"Oh Gott yes!" Heilig cried out gleefully, and snuffled with bitter merriment. "Zat is vhat makes it all so horrible—and so dret-fully amusing. Zey vould know his name at vonce. Perhaps zey vill say zat I am zis little Chew and t'row me out because I am no Aryan man—and my fazzer—" Heilig choked and, snuffling, bent half over in his bitter merriment—"my fazzer is zis loyal Cherman man—zis big Nazi—zis most important person in ze Party!"

For a moment George looked at his friend—whose name, ironically, signified "the holy one"—and could not speak. This strange and moving illumination of his history explained so much about him—the growing bitterness and disdain toward almost everyone and everything, the sense of weary disgust and resignation, the cold venom of his humor, and that smile which kept his face almost perpetually puckered up. As he sat there, fragile, small, and graceful, smiling his wry smile, the whole legend of his life became plain. He had been life's tender child, so sensitive, so affectionate, so amazingly intelligent. He had been the fleeceling lamb thrust out into the cold to bear the blast and to endure want and loneliness. He had been wounded cruelly. He had been warped and twisted. He had come to this, and yet he had maintained a kind of bitter integrity.

"I'm so sorry, Franz," George said. "So damned sorry. I never knew of this."

"Vell, zen," said Heilig indifferently, "I may tell you zat it does not matter. It really does not matter." He smiled his tortured smile, snuffling a little through his lips, flicked the ash from his cigarette, and shifted his position. "I shall do somesing about it. I haf engaged one of zese little men—zese dret-ful little people—vhat do you call zem?—lawyers!—O Gott, but zey are dret-ful!" he shouted gleefully. "I haf bought one of zem to make some lies for me. Zis little man wiz his papers—he vill feel around until he discover fazzers, mozzers, sisters, brozzers—everysing I need. If he cannot, if zey vill not believe—vell, zen," said Heilig, "I must lose my chob. But it does not matter. I shall do somesing. I shall go somevhere else. I shall get along somehow. I haf done so before, and it vas not too terrible. . . . But zese fools—zese dret-ful people!" he said with deep disgust. "Some day, my dear Chorge, you must write a bitter book. You must tell all zese people just how horrible zey are. Myself—I haf no talent. I cannot write a book. I can do nozzing but admire vhat ozzers do and know if it is good. But you must tell zese dret-ful people vhat zey are. . . . I haf a little fantasy," he went on with a look of impish glee. "Ven I feel bad—ven I see all zese dret-ful people valking up and down in ze Kurfürstendamm and sitting at ze tables and putting food into zeir faces—zen I imagine zat I haf a little ma-chine gun. So I take zis little ma-chine gun and go up and down, and ven I see one of zese dret-ful people I go—ping-ping-ping-ping-ping!" As he uttered these words in a rapid, childish key, he took aim with his hand and hooked his finger rapidly. "O Gott!" he cried ecstatically. "I should so enchoy it if I could go around wiz zis little ma-chine gun and use it on all zese stupid fools! But I cannot. My machine gun is only in imagination. Wiz you it is different. You haf a ma-chine gun zat you can truly use. And you must use it," he said earnestly. "Some day you must write zis bitter book, and you must tell zese fools vhere zey belong. Only," he added quickly, and turned anxiously toward George, "you must not do it yet. Or if you do, you must not say some sings in zis book zat vill make zese people angry wiz you here."

"What kind of things do you mean, Franz?"

"Zese sings about—" he lowered his voice and glanced quickly toward the door—"about politics—about ze Party. Sings zat vould bring zem down on you. It would be quite dret-ful if you did."

"Why would it?"

"Because," he said, "you have a great name here. I don't mean wiz zese fools, zese stupid people, but wiz ze people left who still read books. I may tell you," he said earnestly, "zat you have ze best name here now of any foreign writer. If you should spoil it now—if you should write some sings now zat zey vould not like—it vould be a pity. Ze *Reichsschriftskammer* vould forbid your books—vould tell us zat ve could no longer read you—and ve could not get your books. And zat vould be a pity. Ve do so like you here—I mean ze people who understand. Zey know so vell about you. Zey understand ze vay you feel about sings. And I may tell you zat ze translations are quite marvelous. Ze man who does zem is a poet, and he luffs you— he gets you in, ze vay you feel—your images—ze rhythmus of your writing. And ze people find it very vonderful. Zey cannot believe zat zey are reading a translation. Zey say zat it must haf been written in Cherman in ze beginning. And—O Gott!" he shouted gleefully again—"zey call you everysing—ze American Homer, ze American epic writer. Zey like and understand you so much. Your writing is so full of juice, so round and full of blood. Ze feeling is like feeling zat ve haf. Wiz many people you haf ze greatest name of any writer in ze world today."

"That's a good deal more than I've got at home, Franz."

"I know. But zen, I notice, in America zey luff everyvun a year—and zen zey spit upon him. Here, wiz many people you haf zis great name," he said earnestly, "and it vould be too dret-ful—it vould be such a pity—if you spoil it now. You vill not?" he said, and again looked anxiously and earnestly at George.

George looked off in space and did not answer right away; then he said:

"A man must write what he must write. A man must do what he must do."

"Zen you mean zat if you felt zat you had to say some sings—about politics—about zese stupid fools—about——"

"What about life?" George said. "What about people?"

"You vould say it?"

"Yes, I would."

"Efen if it did you harm? Efen if it spoiled you here? Efen if ve could no longer read vhat you write?" With his small face peering earnestly at George, he waited anxiously for his reply.

"Yes, Franz, even if that happened."

Heilig was silent a moment, and then, with apparent hesitancy, he said:

"Efen if you write somesing—and zey say to you zat you cannot come back?"

George, too, was silent now. There was much to think of. But at last he said:

"Yes, even if they told me that."

Heilig straightened sharply, with a swift intake of anger and impatience. "Zen I vill tell you somesing," he said harshly. "You are one big fool." He rose, flung his cigarette away, and began to pace nervously up and down the room. "Vhy should you go and spoil yourself?" he cried. "Vhy should you go and write sings now zat vill make it so zat you cannot come back. You do so luff it here!" he cried; then turned sharply, anxiously, and said, "You do, of gourse?"

"Yes, I do—better than almost any other place on earth."

"And ve alzo!" cried Heilig, pacing up and down. "Ve do so luff you, too. You are no stranger to us, Chorge. I see ze people look at you ven you go by upon ze street and zey all smile at you. Zere is somesing about you zat zey like. Ze little girls in ze shirt shop ven ve vent to buy ze shirt for you—zey all said, 'Who is he?' Zey all vanted to know about you. Zey kept ze shop open two hours late, till nine o'clock zat night, so zat ze shirt vould be ready for you. Efen ven you speak zis poor little Cherman zat you speak, all ze people like it. Ze vaiters in ze restaurants come and do sings for you before everybody else, and not because zey vant a tip from you. You are at home here. Everybody understands you. You have zis famous name—to us you are zis great writer. And for a little politics," he said bitterly, "because zere are zese stupid fools, you vould now go and spoil it all."

George made no answer. So Heilig, still walking feverishly up and down, went on:

"Vhy should you do it? You are no politician. You are no propaganda Party man. You are not one of zese Gott-tam little New York *Salon-Kommunisten*." He spat the word out viciously, his pale eyes narrowed into slits. "May I now tell you somesing?" He paused abruptly, looking at George. "I hate zese bloody little people—zese damned aest'etes—zese little

502

propaganda literary men." Puckering his face into an expression of mincing disdain, advancing with two fingers pressed together in the air before him, and squinting at them with delicately lidded eyes, he coughed in an affected way—"U-huh, u-huh!"—and then, in a tone of mincing parody, he quoted from an article he had read: " 'If I may say so, ze transparence of ze *Darstellung* in Vebber's vork. . . .' U-huh, u-huh!" he coughed again. "Zis bloody little fool who wrote zat piece about you in *Die Dame*—zis damned little aest'ete wiz zese phrases about 'ze transparence of ze *Darstellung*'—may I tell you somesing?" he shouted violently. "I spit upon zese bloody people! Zey are everyvhere ze same. You find zem in London, Paris, Vienna. Zey are bad enough in Europe—but in America!" he shouted, his face lighting up with impish glee—"O Gott! If I may tell you so, zey are perfectly dret-ful! Vhere do you get zem from? Efen ze European aest'ete says, 'My Gott! zese bloody men, zese people, zese damned aest'etes from ze Oo Ess Ah—zey are too dret-ful!' "

"Are you talking now of Communists? You began on them, you know!"

"Vell now," he said, curtly and coldly, with the arrogant dismissal that was becoming more and more characteristic of him, "it does not matter. It does not matter vhat zey call zemselves. Zey are all ze same. Zey are zese little expressionismus, surréalismus, *Kommunismus* people—but really zey can call zemselves anysing, everysing, for zey are nozzing. And may I tell you zat I hate zem. I am so tired of all zese belated little people," he said, and turned away with an expression of weariness and disgust. "It does not matter. It simply does not matter vhat zey say. For zey know nozzing."

"You think then, Franz, that all of Communism is like that—that all Communists are just a crowd of parlor fakes?"

"Oh, *die Kommunisten*," said Heilig wearily. "No, I do not sink zat zey are all fakes. And *Kommunismus*—" he shrugged his shoulders—"vell, zen, I sink zat it is very good. I sink zat some day ze vorld may live like zat. Only, I do not sink zat you and I vill see it. It is too great a dream. And zese sings are not for you. You are not one of zese little propaganda Party people—you are a writer. It is your duty to look around you and to write about ze vorld and people as you see zem. It is not your duty to write propaganda speeches and call zem books. You could not do zat. It is quite impossible."

"But suppose I write about the world and people as I see them, and come in conflict with the Party—what then?"

"Zen," he said roughly, "you vill be one big fool. You can write everysing you need to write wizout zese Party people coming down on you. You do not need to mention zem. And if you do mention zem, and do not say nice sings, zen ve can no

503

longer read you, and you cannot come back. And for vhat vould you do it? If you vere some little propaganda person in New York, you could say zese sings and zen it vould not matter. Because zey can say anysing zey like—but zey know nozzing of us, and it costs zem nozzing. But you—you have so much to lose."

Heilig paced back and forth in feverish silence, puffing on his cigarette, then all at once he turned and demanded truculently:

"You sink it is so bad here now?—ze vay sings are wiz ze Party and zese stupid people? You sink it vould be better if zere vas anozzer party, like in America? Zen," he said, not waiting for an answer, "I sink you are mistaken. It *is* bad here, of gourse, but I sink it vill be soon no better wiz you. Zese bloody fools—you find zem everyvhere. Zey are ze same wiz you, only in a different vay." Suddenly he looked at George earnestly and searchingly. "You sink zat you are free in America—no?" He shook his head and went on: "I do not sink so. Ze only free ones are zese dret-ful people. Here, zey are free to tell you vhat you must read, vhat you must believe, and I sink zat is also true in America. You must sink and feel ze vay zey do—you must say ze sings zey vant you to say—or zey kill you. Ze only difference is zat here zey haf ze power to do it. In America zey do not haf it yet, but just vait—zey vill get it. Ve Chermans haf shown zem ze vay. And zen, you vould be more free here zan in New York, for here you haf a better name, I sink, zan in America. Here zey admire you. Here you are American, and you could efen write and say sings zat no Cherman could do, so long as you say nozzing zat is against ze Party. Do you sink zat you could do zat in New York?"

He paced the floor in silence for a long moment, pausing to look searchingly at George. At length he answered his own question:

"No, you could not. Zese people here—zey say zat zey are Nazis. I sink zat zey are more honest. In New York, zey call zemselves by some fine name. Zey are ze *Salon-Kommunisten*. Zey are ze Daughters of ze Revolution. Zey are ze American Legion. Zey are ze business men, ze Chamber of Commerce. Zey are one sing and anozzer, but zey are all ze same, and I sink zat zey are Nazis, too. You vill find everyvhere zese bloody people. Zey are not for you. You are not a propaganda man."

Again there was a silence. Heilig continued to pace the floor, waiting for George to say something; when he did not, Heilig went on again. And in his next words he revealed a depth of cynicism and indifference which was greater than George had ever before suspected, and of which he would not have thought Heilig's sensitive soul was capable.

"If you write somesing now against ze Nazis," said Heilig, "you vill please ze Chews, but you cannot come back to

504

Chermany again, and zat for all of us vould be quite dret-ful. And may I tell you somesing?" he cried harshly and abruptly, and glared at George. "I do not like zese Gott-tam Chews any more zan I like zese ozzer people. Zey are just as bad. Ven all is going vell wiz zem, zey say, 'Ve spit upon you and your bloody country because ve are so vunderful.' And ven sings are going bad wiz zem, zey become zese little Chewish men zat veep and wring zeir hands and say, 'Ve are only zese poor, downtrodden Chews, and look vhat zey are doing to us.' And may I tell you," he cried harshly, "zat I do not care. I do not sink it matters very much. I sink zat it is stupid vhat zese bloody fools are doing to zese Chews—but I do not care. It does not matter. I haf seen zese Chews ven zey were high and full of power, and really zey vere dret-ful. Zey were only for zemselves. Zey spit upon ze rest of us. So it does not matter," he repeated harshly. "Zey are as bad as all ze ozzers, zese great, fat Chews. If I had my little ma-chine gun, I vould shoot zem, too. Ze only sing I care about any more is vhat zese dret-ful fools vill do to Chermany—to ze people." Anxiously, he looked at George and said, "You do so like ze people, Chorge?"

"Enormously," said George, almost in a whisper, and he was filled with such an overwhelming sadness—for Germany, for the people, and for his friend—that he could say no more. Heilig caught the full implications of George's whispered tone. He glanced at him sharply. Then he sighed deeply, and his bitterness dropped away.

"Yes," he said quietly, "you must, of gourse." Then he added gently: "Zey are really a good lot. Zey are big fools, of gourse, but zey are not too bad."

He was silent a moment. He ground out his cigarette in the ash tray, sighed again, and then said, a little sadly:

"Vell, zen, you must do vhat you must do. But you are one big fool." He looked at his watch and put his hand upon George's arm. "Come on, old shap. Now it is time to go."

George got up, and for a moment they stood looking at each other, then they clasped each other by the hand.

"Good-bye, Franz," George said.

"Good-bye, dear Chorge," said Heilig quietly. "Ve shall miss you very much."

"And I you," George answered.

Then they went out.

Chapter Forty

Last Farewell

When they got downstairs the bill was made up and ready, and George paid it. There was no need to count it up, because there never had been a cheat or error in their reckoning. George distributed extra largess to the head porter—a grey, chunky, sternly able Prussian—and to the head waiter. He gave a mark to the smiling boy beside the lift, who clicked his heels together and saluted. He took one final look at the faded, ugly, curiously pleasant furnishings of the little foyer, and said good-bye again, and went swiftly down the steps into the street.

The porter was already there. He had the baggage on the curb. A taxi was just drawing up, and he stowed the baggage in. George tipped him and shook hands. He also tipped the enormous doorman, a smiling, simple, friendly fellow who had always patted him upon the back as he went in and out. Then he got into the taxi, sat down by Heilig, and gave the driver the address—Bahnhof Am Zoo.

The taxi wheeled about and started up along the other side of the Kurfürstendamm, turned and crossed into the Joachimtalen-strasse, and, three minutes later, drew in before the station. They still had some minutes to wait before the train, which was coming from the Friedrich-strasse, would be there. They gave the baggage to a porter, who said he would meet them on the platform. Then Heilig thrust a coin into the machine and bought a platform ticket. They passed by the ticket inspectors and went up the stairs.

A considerable crowd of travelers was already waiting on the platform. A train was just pulling in out of the west, from the direction of Hanover and Bremen. A number of people got off. On other tracks the glittering trains of the Stadtbahn were moving in and out; their beautiful, shining cars—deep maroon, red, and golden yellow—going from east to west, from west to east, and to all the quarters of the city's compass, were heavily loaded with morning workers. George looked down the tracks toward the east, in the direction from which his train must come, and saw the semaphores, the lean design of tracks, the tops of houses, and the massed greens of the Zoologic Garden. The Stadtbahn trains kept sliding in and out, swiftly, almost noiselessly, discharging streams of hurrying people, taking in others. It was all so familiar, so pleasant, and so full of morning. It seemed that he had known it forever, and he felt as he always did when he left a city—a sense of sorrow and regret, of poignant unfulfillment, a sense that here were people he could have known, friends he could have had, all lost now, fading, slipping from his grasp, as the inexorable moment of the departing hour drew near.

Far down the platform the doors of the baggage elevator clanged, and the porters pulled trucks loaded with great piles of baggage out upon the platform. And presently George saw his porter advancing with a truck, and among the bags and trunks upon it he could see his own. The porter nodded to him, indicating at about what point he ought to stand.

At this same moment he turned and saw Else coming down the platform toward him. She walked slowly, at her long and rhythmic stride. People followed her with their eyes as she passed by. She was wearing a rough tweed jacket of a light, coarse texture and a skirt of the same material. Everything about her had a kind of incomparable style. She could have worn anything with the same air. Her tall figure was stunning, a strange and moving combination of delicacy and power. Under her arm she was carrying a book, and as she came up she gave it to George. He took her hands, which for so large a woman were amazingly lovely and sensitive, long, white, and slender as a child's, and George noticed that they were cold, and that the fingers trembled.

"Else, you have met Herr Heilig, haven't you? Franz, you remember Frau von Kohler?"

Else turned and surveyed Heilig coldly and sternly. Heilig answered her look with a stare that was equally unrelenting and hostile. There was a formidable quality in the mutual suspicion they displayed as their eyes met. George had observed the same phenomenon many times before in the encounters of Germans who were either total strangers or who did not know each other well. At once their defenses would be up, as if each distrusted the other on sight and demanded full credentials and assurances before relenting into any betrayal of friendliness and confidence. George was used to this sort of thing by now. It was what was to be expected. Just the same, it never failed to be alarming to him when it happened. He could not accustom himself to it and accept it as an inevitable part of life, as so many of these Germans seemed to have done, because he had never seen anything like it at home, or anywhere else in the world before.

Moreover, between these two, the usual manifestations of

507

suspicion were heightened by an added quality of deep, instinctive dislike. As they stood regarding each other, something flashed between them that was as cold and hard as steel, as swift and naked as a rapier thrust. These feelings of distrust and antagonism were communicated in a single moment's silence; then Else inclined her head slightly and sternly and said in her excellent English, which had hardly a trace of accent and revealed its foreignness only by an occasional phrase and the undue precision of her enunciation:

"I believe we have met, at Grauschmidt's party for George."

"I belief so," Heilig said. And then, after surveying her a moment longer with a look of truculent hostility, he said coldly: "And Grauschmidt's drawing in ze *Tageblatt*—you did not like it—no?"

"Of George!" she spoke derisively, incredulously. Her stern face was suddenly illuminated with a radiant smile. She laughed scornfully and said: "This drawing by your friend, Grauschmidt—you mean the one that made George look like a wonderful and charming sugar-tenor?"

"You did not like it, zen?" said Heilig coldly.

"But *ja*!" she cried. "As a drawing of a *Zuckertenor*—as a drawing of Herr Grauschmidt, the way he is himself, the way he sees and feels—it is quite perfect! But George! It looks no more like George than you do!"

"Zen I may tell you somesing," said Heilig coldly and venomously. "I sink zat you are very stupid. Ze drawing vas egg-zellent—everybody sought so. Grauschmidt himself said zat it vas vun of ze very best zat he has effer done. He likes it very much."

"But *naturlich*!" Else said ironically, and laughed scornfully again. "Herr Grauschmidt likes so many things. First of all, he likes himself. He likes everything he does. And he likes music of Puccini," she went on rapidly. "He sings *Ave Maria*. He likes sob-songs of Hilbach. He likes dark rooms with a red light and silken pillows. He is romantic and likes to talk about his feelings. He thinks: 'We artists!'"

Heilig was furious. "If I may tell you somesing—" he began.

But Else now could not be checked. She took a short and angry step away, then turned again, with two spots of passionate color in her cheeks:

"Your friend, Herr Grauschmidt," she continued, "likes to talk of art. He says, 'This orchestra is wonderful!'—he never hears the music. He goes to see Shakespeare, saying, 'Mayer is a wonderful actor.' He——"

"If I may tell you somesing—" Heilig choked.

"He likes little girls with high heels," she panted. "He is in the Ess Ah. When he shaves, he wears a hair-dress cap. Of course his nails are polished. He has a lot of photographs—of himself
508

and other great people!" And, panting but triumphant, she turned and walked away a few paces to compose herself.

"Zese bloody people!" Heilig grated. "O Gott, but zey are dret-ful!" Turning to George, he said venomously: "If I may tell you somesing—zis person—zis voman—zis von Kohler zat you like so much—she *iss* a fool!"

"Wait a minute, Franz. I don't think she is. You know what I think of her."

"Vell, zen," said Heilig, "you are wrong. You are mistaken. If I may say so, you are again also one big fool. Vell, zen, it does not matter," he cried harshly. "I vill go and buy some cigarettes, and you can try to talk to zis damn stupid voman." And, still choking with rage, he turned abruptly and walked away down the platform.

George went up to Else. She was still excited, still breathing rapidly. He took her hands and they were trembling. She said: "This bitter little man—this man whose name it means 'the holy one'—he is so full of bitterness—he hates me. He is so jealous for you. He wants to keep you for himself. He has told you lies. He has tried to say things against me. I hear them!" she went on excitedly. "People come to me with them! I do not listen to them!" she cried angrily. "O George, George!" she said suddenly, and took him by the arms. "Do not listen to this bitter little man. Last night," she whispered, "I had a strange dream. It was a so strange, a so good and wonderful dream that I had for you. You must not listen to this bitter man!" she cried earnestly, and shook him by the arms. "You are religious man. You are artist. And the artist *is* religious man."

Just then Lewald appeared on the platform and came toward them. His pink face looked fresh and hearty as always. His constant exuberance had in it a suggestion of alcoholic stimulation. Even at this hour of the morning he seemed to be bubbling over with a winy exhilaration. As he barged along, swinging his great shoulders and his bulging belly, people all along the platform caught the contagion of his gleeful spirits and smiled at him, and yet their smiles were also tinged with respect. In spite of his great pink face and his enormous belly, there was nothing ridiculous in Lewald's appearance. One's first impression was that of a strikingly handsome man. One did not think of him as being fat; rather, one thought of him as being big. And as he rolled along, he dominated the scene with a sense of easy and yet massive authority. One would scarcely have taken him for a business man, and a very shrewd and crafty one to boot. Everything about him suggested a natural and instinctive Bohemianism. Looking at him, one felt that here, probably, was an old army man, not of the Prussian military type, but rather a fellow who had done his service and who had thoroughly enjoyed the army life—the boisterous camaraderie of men, the eating and drinking bouts, the adventures with the girls—as, indeed, he had.

A tremendous appetite for life was plainly legible all over him. People recognized it the moment they saw him, and that is why they smiled. He seemed so full of wine, so full of spacious, hearty unconventionality. His whole manner proclaimed him to be the kind of man who has burst through all the confines of daily, routine living with the force of a natural element. He was one of those men who, immediately somehow, shine out luminously in all the grey of life, one of those men who carry about their persons a glamorous aura of warmth, of color, and of temperament. In any crowd he stood out in dominant and exciting isolation, drawing all eyes to himself with a vivid concentration of interest, so that one would remember him later even though one had seen him only for an instant, just as one would remember the one room in an otherwise empty house that had furniture and a fire in it.

So now, as he approached, even when he was still some yards away, he began to shake his finger at George waggishly, at the same time moving his great head from side to side. As he came up, he sang out in a throaty, vinous voice the opening phrases of an obscene song which he had taught to George, and which the two of them had often sung together during those formidable evenings at his house:

"Lecke du, lecke du, lecke du die Katze am Arsch . . ."

Else flushed, but Lewald checked himself quickly at the penultimate moment and, wagging his finger at George again, cried:

"Ach du!" And then, in an absurdly sly and gleeful croon, his small eyes twinkling roguishly: "Naught-ee boy-ee! Naught-ee boy-ee!"—wagging a finger all the time. "My old Chorge!" he cried suddenly and heartily. "Where haf you been—you naught-ee boy-ee? I look for you last night and I cannot see you anyvheres!"

Before George could answer, Heilig returned, smoking a cigarette. George remembered that the two men had met before, but now they gave no sign of recognition. Indeed, Lewald's hearty manner dropped away at sight of the little Heilig, and his face froze into an expression of glacial reserve and suspicion. George was so put out by this that he forgot his own manners, and instead of presenting Else to Lewald, he stammered out an introduction of Heilig. Lewald then acknowledged the other's presence with a stiff and formal little bow. Heilig merely inclined his head slightly and returned Lewald's look coldly. George was feeling very uncomfortable and embarrassed when Lewald took the situation in hand again. Turning his back on Heilig, he now resumed his former manner of hearty exuberance and, seizing George's arm in one meaty fist and pounding affectionately upon it with the other, he cried out loudly:

"Chorge! Vhere haf you been, you naught-ee boy-ee? Vhy do you not come in to see me dese last days? I vas eggsbecting you."

"Why—I—I—" George began, "I really meant to, Karl. But I knew you would be here to see me off, and I just didn't get around to dropping in at your office. I've had a great deal to do, you know."

"And I al*zo*!" cried Lewald, his voice rising in droll emphasis on the last word. "I al*zo*!" he repeated. "But me—I alvays haf time for mein friends," he said accusingly, still beating away on George's arm to show that his pretended hurt had not really gone very deep.

"Karl," George now said, "you remember Frau von Kohler, don't you?"

"*Aber natürlich!*" he cried with the boisterous gallantry that always marked his manner with women. "Honorable lady," he said in German, "how are you? I shall not be likely to forget the pleasure you gave me by coming to one of my parties. But I have not seen you since that evening, and I have seen less and less of old Chorge since then." Relapsing into English at this point, he turned to George again and shook his finger at him, saying: "You naught-ee boy-ee, you!"

This playful gallantry had no effect on Else. Her face did not relax any of its sternness. She just looked at Lewald with her level gaze and made no effort to conceal the scorn she felt for him. Lewald, however, appeared not to notice, for once more he turned to her and addressed her in his exuberant German:

"Honorable lady, I can understand the reason why the Chorge has deserted me. He has found more exciting adventures than anything the poor old Lewald had to offer him." Here he turned back to George again and, with his small eyes twinkling mischievously, he wagged his finger beneath George's nose and crooned slyly, absurdly: "Naught-ee boy-ee! Naught-ee boy-ee!"—as if to say: "Aha, you rascal, you! I've caught you now!"

This whole monologue had been delivered almost without a pause in Lewald's characteristic manner—a manner that had been famous throughout Europe for thirty years. His waggishness with George was almost childishly naïve and playful, while his speech to Else was bluff, high-spirited, hearty, and good-humored. Through it all he gave the impression of a man who was engagingly open and sincere, and one who was full of jolly good will toward mankind. It was the manner George had seen him use many times—when he was meeting some new author, when he was welcoming someone to his office, when he was talking over the telephone, or inviting friends to a party.

But now again, George was able to observe the profound difference between the manner and the man. That bluff and hearty openness was just a mask which Lewald used against the world with all the deceptive grace and subtlety of a great matador preparing to give the finishing stroke to a charging bull. Behind that mask was concealed the true image of the man's soul, which was sly, dexterous, crafty, and cunning. George noticed again how really small and shrewd were the features. The big blond head and the broad shoulders and the great, pink, vinous jowls gave an effect of massive size and grandeur, but that general effect was not borne out by the smaller details. The mouth was amazingly tiny and carnal; it was full of an almost obscene humor, and it had a kind of mousing slyness, as if its fat little chops were fairly watering for lewd titbits. The nose was also small and pointed, and there was a sniffing shrewdness about it. The eyes were little, blue, and twinkled with crafty merriment. One felt that they saw everything—that they were not only secretly and agreeably aware of the whole human comedy, but were also slyly amused at the bluff and ingenuous part that their owner was playing.

"But come, now!" Lewald cried suddenly, throwing back his shoulders and seeming to collect himself to earnestness with a jerk. "I bring somet'ing to you from mein hosband. . . . *Was?*" He looked around at all three of them with an expression of innocent, questioning bewilderment as George grinned.

It was a familiar error of his broken English. He always called his wife his "hosband," and frequently told George that some day he, too, would get a "good hosband." But he used the word with an expression of such droll innocence, his little blue eyes twinkling in his pink face with a look of cherubic guilelessness, that George was sure he knew better and was making the error deliberately for its comic effect. Now, as George laughed, Lewald turned to Else, then to Heilig, with a puzzled air, and in a lowered voice said rapidly:

"Was, denn? Was meint Chorge? Wie sagt man das? Ist das nicht richtig englisch?"

Else looked pointedly away as though she had not heard him and wished to have nothing more to do with him. Heilig's only answer was to continue looking at him coldly and suspiciously. Lewald, however, was not in the least put out by the unappreciativeness of his audience. He turned back to George with a comical shrug, as if the whole thing were quite beyond him, and then slipped into George's pocket a small flask of German brandy, saying that it was the gift his "hosband" had sent. Next he took out a thin and beautifully bound little

512

volume which one of his authors had written and illustrated. He held it in his hand and fingered through it lovingly.

It was a comic memoir of Lewald's life, from the cradle to maturity, done in that vein of grotesque brutality which hardly escapes the macabre, but which nevertheless does have a power of savage caricature and terrible humor such as no other race can equal. One of the illustrations showed the infant Lewald as the infant Hercules strangling two formidable-looking snakes, which bore the heads of his foremost publishing rivals. Another showed the adolescent Lewald as Gargantua, drowning out his native town of Kolberg in Pomerania. Still another pictured Lewald as the young publisher, seated at a table in Aenna Maentz café and biting large chunks out of a drinking glass and eating them—an operation which he had actually performed on various occasions in the past, in order, he said, "to make propaganda for meinself and mein business."

Lewald had inscribed and autographed this curious little book for George, and underneath the inscription had written the familiar and obscene lines of the song: *"Lecke du, lecke du, lecke du die Katze am Arsch."* Now he closed the book and thrust it into George's pocket.

And even as he did so there was a flurry of excitement in the crowd. A light flashed, the porters moved along the platform. George looked up the tracks. The train was coming. It bore down swiftly, sweeping in around the edges of the Zoologic Garden. The huge snout of the locomotive, its fenders touched with trimmings of bright red, advanced bluntly, steamed hotly past, and came to a stop. The dull line of the coaches was broken vividly in the middle with the glittering red of the Mitropa dining car.

Everybody swung into action. George's porter, heaving up his heavy baggage, clambered quickly up the steps and found a compartment for him. There was a blur of voices all around, an excited tumult of farewell.

Lewald caught George by the hand, and with his other arm around George's shoulder half pounded and half hugged him, saying, "My old Chorge, *auf wiedersehn!*"

Heilig shook hands hard and fast, his small and bitter face contorted as if he were weeping, while he said in a curiously vibrant, deep, and tragic voice, "Good-bye, good-bye, dear saying, "My old Chorge, *auf wiedersehen!*"

The two men turned away, and Else put her arms around him. He felt her shoulders shake. She was weeping, and he heard her say: "Be good man. Be great one that I know. Be religious man." And as her embrace tightened, she half gasped, half whispered, "Promise." He nodded. Then they came together: her thighs widened, closed about his leg, her voluptuous figure yielded, grew into him, their mouths clung

513

fiercely, and for the last time they were united in the embrace of love.

Then he climbed into the train. The guard slammed the door. Even as he made his way down the narrow corridor toward his compartment, the train started. These forms, these faces, and these lives all began to slide away.

Heilig kept walking forward, waving his hat, his face still contorted with the grimace of his sorrow. Behind him, Else walked along beside the train, her face stern and lonely, her arm lifted in farewell. Lewald whipped off his hat and waved it, his fair hair in disarray above his flushed and vinous face. The last thing George heard was his exuberant voice raised in a shout of farewell. "Old Chorge, *auf wiedersehen!*" And then he cupped his hands around his mouth and yelled, *"Lecke du—!"* George saw his shoulders heave with laughter.

Then the train swept out around the curve. And they were lost.

Chapter Forty-One

Five Passengers for Paris

The train gathered speed, the streets and buildings in the western part of the city slipped past—those solid, ugly streets, those massive, ugly buildings in the Victorian German style, which yet, with all the pleasant green of trees, the window boxes bright with red geraniums, the air of order, of substance, and of comfort, had always seemed as familiar and as pleasant to George as the quiet streets and houses of a little town. Already they were sweeping through Charlottenburg. They passed the station without halting, and on the platforms George saw, with the old and poignant feeling of regret and loss, the people waiting for the Stadtbahn trains. Upon its elevated track the great train swept on smoothly toward the west, gathering momentum steadily. They passed the Funkturma. Almost before he knew it they were rushing through the outskirts of the city toward the open country. They passed an aviation field. He saw the hangars and a flock of shining planes. And as he looked, a great silver-bodied plane moved out, sped along the runway, lifted its tail, broke slowly from the earth, and vanished.

And now the city was left behind. Those familiar faces, forms, and voices of just six minutes past now seemed as remote as dreams, imprisoned there as in another world—a world of massive brick and stone and pavements, a world hived of four million lives, of hope and fear and hatred, of anguish and despair, of love, of cruelty and devotion, that was called Berlin.

And now the land was stroking past, the level land of Brandenburg, the lonely flatland of the north which he had always heard was so ugly, and which he had found so strange, so haunting, and so beautiful. The dark solitude of the forest was around them now, the loneliness of the kiefern trees, tall, slender, towering, and as straight as sailing masts, bearing upon their tops the slender burden of their needled and eternal green. Their naked poles shone with that lovely gold-bronze color which is like the material substance of a magic light. And all between was magic, too. The forest dusk beneath the kiefern trees was gold-brown also, the earth gold-brown and barren, and the trees themselves stood alone and separate, a polelike forest filled with haunting light.

Now and then the light would open and the woods be gone, and they would sweep through the level cultivated earth, tilled thriftily to the very edges of the track. He could see the clusters of farm buildings, the red-tiled roofs, the cross-quarterings of barns and houses. Then they would find the haunting magic of the woods again.

George opened the door of his compartment and went in and took a seat beside the door. On the other side, in the corner by the window, a young man sat and read a book. He was an elegant young man and dressed most fashionably. He wore a sporting kind of coat with a small and fancy check, a wonderful vest of some expensive doelike grey material, cream-grey trousers pleated at the waist, also of a rich, expensive weave, and grey suede gloves. He did not look American or English. There was a foppish, almost sugared elegance about his costume that one felt, somehow, was Continental. Therefore it struck George with a sense of shock to see that he was reading an American book, a popular work in history which had the title, *The Saga of Democracy*, and bore the imprint of a well-known firm. But while he pondered on this puzzling combination of the familiar and the strange there were steps outside along the corridor, voices, the door was opened, and a woman and a man came in.

They were Germans. The woman was small and no longer young, but she was plump, warm, seductive-looking, with hair so light it was the color of bleached straw, and eyes as blue as sapphires. She spoke rapidly and excitedly to the man who accompanied her, then turned to George and asked if the other places were unoccupied. He replied that he thought so, and looked questioningly at the dapper young man in the corner. This young man now spoke up in somewhat broken German, saying that he believed the other seats were free, and adding that he had got on the train at the Friedrich-strasse station and had seen no one else in the compartment. The woman immediately and vigorously nodded her head in satisfaction and spoke with rapid authority to her companion, who went out and presently returned with their baggage—two valises, which he arranged upon the rack above their heads.

They were a strangely assorted pair. The woman, although most attractive, was obviously much the older of the two. She appeared to be in her late thirties or early forties. There were traces of fine wrinkles at the corners of her eyes, and her face gave an impression of physical maturity and warmth, together with the wisdom that comes from experience, but it was also apparent that some of the freshness and resilience of youth had gone out of it. Her figure had an almost shameless sexual attraction, the kind of naked allure that one often sees in people of the theatre—in a chorus girl or in the strip-tease woman of a burlesque show. Her whole personality bore a vague suggestion of the theatrical stamp. In everything about her there was that element of heightened vividness which seems to set off and define people who follow the stage.

Beside her assurance, her air of practice and authority, her sharply vivid stamp, the man who accompanied her was made to seem even younger than he was. He was probably twenty-six or thereabouts, but he looked a mere stripling. He was a tall, blond, fresh-complexioned, and rather handsome young German who conveyed an indefinable impression of countrified and slightly bewildered innocence. He appeared nervous, uneasy, and inexperienced in the art of travel. He kept his head down or averted most of the time, and did not speak unless the woman spoke to him. Then he would flush crimson with embarrassment, the two flags of color in his fresh, pink face deepening to beetlike red.

George wondered who they were, why they were going to Paris, and what the relation between them could be. He felt, without exactly knowing why, that there was no family connection between them. The young man could not be the woman's brother, and it was also evident that they were not man and wife. It was hard not to fall back upon an ancient parable and see in them the village hayseed in the toils of the city siren—to assume that she had duped him into taking her to Paris, and that the fool and his money would soon be parted. Yet there was certainly nothing repulsive about the woman to substantiate this conjecture. She was decidedly a most attractive and engaging creature. Even her astonishing quality of sexual

516

magnetism, which was displayed with a naked and almost uncomfortable openness, so that one felt it the moment she entered the compartment, had nothing vicious in it. She seemed, indeed, to be completely unconscious of it, and simply expressed herself sensually and naturally with the innocent warmth of a child.

While George was busy with these speculations the door of the compartment opened again and a stuffy-looking little man with a long nose looked in, peered about truculently, and rather suspiciously, George thought, and then demanded to know if there was a free seat in the compartment. They all told him that they thought so. Upon receiving this information, he, too, without another word, disappeared down the corridor, to reappear again with a large valise. George helped him stow it away upon the rack. It was so heavy that the little man could probably not have managed it by himself, yet he accepted this service sourly and without a word of thanks, hung up his overcoat, fidgeted and worried around, took a newspaper from his pocket, sat down opposite George and opened it, banged the compartment door shut rather viciously, and, after peering around mistrustfully at the other people, rattled his paper and began to read.

While he read his paper George had a chance to observe this sour-looking customer from time to time. Not that there was anything sinister about the man—decidedly there was not. He was just a drab, stuffy, irascible little fellow of the type that one sees a thousand times a day upon the streets, muttering at taxicabs or snapping at imprudent drivers—the type that one is always afraid he is going to encounter on a trip but hopes fervently he won't. He looked like the kind of fellow who would always be slamming the door of the compartment to, always going over and banging down the window without asking anyone else about it, always fidgeting and fuming about and trying by every crusty, crotchety, cranky, and ill-tempered method in his equipment to make himself as unpleasant, and his traveling companions as uncomfortable, as possible.

Yes, he was certainly a well-known type, but aside from this he was wholly unremarkable. If one had passed him in the streets of the city, one would never have taken a second look at him or remembered him afterwards. It was only when he intruded himself into the intimacy of a long journey and began immediately to buzz and worry around like a troublesome hornet that he became memorable.

It was not long, in fact, before the elegant young gentleman in the corner by the window almost ran afoul of him. The young fellow took out an expensive-looking cigarette case, extracted a cigarette, and then, smiling engagingly, asked the lady if she objected to his smoking. She immediately answered, with great warmth and friendliness, that she minded not at all. George received this information with considerable relief, and took a package of cigarettes from his pocket and was on the point of joining his unknown young companion in the luxury of a smoke when old Fuss-and-Fidget rattled his paper viciously, glared sourly at the elegant young man and then at George, and, pointing to a sign upon the wall of the compartment, croaked dismally:

"*Nicht Raucher.*"

Well, all of them had known that at the beginning, but they had not supposed that Fuss-and-Fidget would make an issue of it. The young fellow and George glanced at each other with a slightly startled look, grinned a little, caught the lady's eye, which was twinkling with the comedy of the occasion, and were obediently about to put their cigarettes away unsmoked when old Fuss-and-Fidget rattled his paper, looked sourly around at them a second time, and then said bleakly that as far as he was concerned it was all right—he didn't personally mind their smoking—he just wanted to point out that they were in a non-smoking compartment. The implication plainly was that from this time on the crime was on their own heads, that he had done what he could as a good citizen to warn them, but that if they proceeded with their guilty plot against the laws of the land, it was no further concern of his. Being thus reassured, they produced their cigarettes again and lighted up.

Now while George smoked, and while old Fuss-and-Fidget read his paper, George had further opportunity to observe this unpleasant companion of the voyage. And his observations, intensified as they were by subsequent events, became fixed as an imperishable image in his mind. The image which occurred to him as he sat there watching the man was that of a sour-tempered Mr. Punch. If you can imagine Mr. Punch without his genial spirits, without his quick wit, without his shrewd but kind intelligence, if you can imagine a crotchety and cranky Mr. Punch going about angrily banging doors and windows shut, glaring around at his fellow-travelers, and sticking his long nose into everybody's business, then you will get some picture of this fellow. Not that he was hunchbacked and dwarfed like Mr. Punch. He was certainly small, he was certainly a drab, unlovely little figure of a man, but he was not dwarfed. But his face had the ruddy glow that one associates with Mr. Punch, and its contour, like that of Mr. Punch, was almost cherubic, except that the cherub had gone sour. The nose also was somewhat Punchian. It was not grotesquely hooked and beaked, but it was a long nose, and its fleshy tip drooped over as if it were fairly sniffing with suspicion, fairly stretching with

518

eagerness to pry around and stick itself into things that did not concern it.

George fell asleep presently, leaning against the side of the door. It was a fitful and uneasy coma of half-sleep, the product of excitement and fatigue—never comfortable, never whole—a dozing sleep from which he would start up from time to time to look about him, then doze again. Time after time he came sharply awake to find old Fuss-and-Fidget's eyes fixed on him in a look of such suspicion and ill-temper that it barely escaped malevolence. He woke up once to find the man's gaze fastened on him in a stare that was so protracted, so unfriendly, that he felt anger boiling up in him. It was on the tip of his tongue to speak hotly to the fellow, but he, as if sensing George's intent, ducked his head quickly and busied himself again with his newspaper.

The man was so fidgety and nervous that it was impossible to sleep longer than a few minutes at a time. He was always crossing and uncrossing his legs, always rattling his newspaper, always fooling with the handle of the door, doing something to it, jerking and pulling it, half opening the door and banging it to again, as if he were afraid it was not securely closed. He was always jumping up, opening the door, and going out into the corridor, where he would pace up and down for several minutes, turn and look out of the windows at the speeding landscape, then fidget back and forth in the corridor again, sour-faced and distempered-looking, holding his hands behind him and twiddling his fingers nervously and impatiently as he walked.

All this while, the train was advancing across the country at terrific speed. Forest and field, village and farm, tilled land and pasture stroked past with the deliberate but devouring movement of high velocity. The train slackened a little as it crossed the Elbe, but there was no halt. Two hours after its departure from Berlin it was sweeping in beneath the arched, enormous roof of the Hanover station. There was to be a stop here of ten minutes. As the train slowed down, George awoke from his doze. But fatigue still held him, and he did not get up.

Old Fuss-and-Fidget arose, however, and, followed by the woman and her companion, went out on the platform for a little fresh air and exercise.

George and the dapper young man in the corner were now left alone together. The latter had put down his book and was looking out of the window, but after a minute or two he turned

519

to George and said in English, marked by a slight accent:

"Where are we now?"

George told him they were at Hanover.

"I'm tired of traveling," the young man said with a sigh. "I shall be glad when I get home."

"And where is home for you?" George asked.

"New York," he said, and, seeing a look of slight surprise on George's face, he added quickly: "Of course I am not American by birth, as you can see from the way I talk. But I am a naturalized American, and my home is in New York."

George told him that he lived there, too. Then the young man asked if George had been long in Germany.

"All summer," George replied. "I arrived in May."

"And you have been here ever since—in Germany?"

"Yes," said George, "except for ten days in the Tyrol."

"When you came in this morning I thought at first that you were German. I believe I saw you on the platform with some German people."

"Yes, they were friends of mine."

"But then when you spoke I saw you could not be a German from your accent. When I saw you reading the Paris *Herald* I concluded that you were English or American."

"I am American, of course."

"Yes, I can see that now. I," he said, "am Polish by birth. I went to America when I was fifteen years old, but my family still lives in Poland."

"And you have been to see them, naturally?"

"Yes. I have made a practice of coming over every year or so to visit them. I have two brothers living in the country." It was evident that he came from landed people. "I am returning from there now," he said. He was silent for a moment, and then said with some emphasis: "But not again! Not for a long time will I visit them. I have told them that it is enough—if they want to see me now, they must come to New York. I am sick of Europe," he went on. "Every time I come I am fed up. I am tired of all this foolish business, these politics, this hate, these armies, and this talk of war—the whole damned stuffy atmosphere here!" he cried indignantly and impatiently, and, thrusting his hand into his breast pocket, he pulled out a paper—"Will you look at this?"

"What is it?" George said.

"A paper—a permit—the damn thing stamped and signed which allows me to take twenty-three marks out of Germany. Twenty-three marks!" he repeated scornfully—"as if I want their God-damn money!"

"I know," George said. "You've got to get a paper every time you turn around. You have to declare your money when you come in, you have to declare it when you go out. If you send home for money, you have to get a paper for that, too. I made a little trip to Austria as I told you. It took three days to get the papers that would allow me to take my own money out. Look here!" he cried, and reached in his pocket and pulled out a fistful of papers. "I got all of these in one summer."

The ice was broken now. Upon a mutual grievance they began to warm up to each other. It quickly became evident to George that his new acquaintance, with the patriotic fervor of his race, was passionately American. He had married an American girl, he said. New York, he asserted, was the most magnificent city on earth, the only place he cared to live, the place he never wished to leave again, the place to which he was aching to return.

And America?

"Oh," he said, "it will be good after all this to be back there where all is peace and freedom—where all is friendship—where all is love."

George felt some reservations to this blanket endorsement of his native land, but he did not utter them. The man's fervor was so genuine that it would have been unkind to try to qualify it. And besides, George, too, was homesick now, and the man's words, generous and whole-hearted as they were, warmed him with their pleasant glow. He also felt, beneath the extravagance of the comparison, a certain truth. During the past summer, in this country which he had known so well, whose haunting beauty and magnificence had stirred him more deeply than had any other he had ever known, and for whose people he had always had the most affectionate understanding, he had sensed for the first time the poisonous constrictions of incurable hatreds and insoluble politics, the whole dense weave of intrigue and ambition in which the tormented geography of Europe was again enmeshed, the volcanic imminence of catastrophe with which the very air was laden, and which threatened to erupt at any moment.

And George, like the other man, was weary and sick at heart, exhausted by these pressures, worn out with these tensions of the nerves and spirit, depleted by the cancer of these cureless hates which had not only poisoned the life of nations but had eaten in one way or another into the private lives of all his friends, of almost everyone that he had known here. So, like his new-found fellow countryman, he too felt, beneath the extravagance and intemperance of the man's language, a certain justice in the comparison. He was aware, as indeed the other must have been, of the huge sum of all America's lacks. He knew that all, alas, was not friendship, was not freedom, was not love beyond the Atlantic. But he felt, as his new friend must

521

also have felt, that the essence of America's hope had not been wholly ruined, its promise of fulfillment not shattered utterly. And like the other man, he felt that it would be very good to be back home again, out of the poisonous constrictions of this atmosphere—back home where, whatever America might lack, there was still air to breathe in, and winds to clear the air.

His new friend now said that he was engaged in business in New York. He was a member of a brokerage concern in Wall Street. This seemed to call for some similar identification on George's part, and he gave the most apt and truthful statement he could make, which was that he worked for a publishing house. The other then remarked that he knew the family of a New York publisher, that they were, in fact, good friends of his. George asked him who these people were, and he answered:

"The Edwards family."

Instantly, a thrill of recognition pierced George. A light flashed on, and suddenly he knew the man. He said:

"I know the Edwardses. They are among the best friends I have, and Mr. Edwards is my publisher. And you—" George said—"your name is Johnnie, isn't it? I have forgotten your last name, but I have heard it."

He nodded quickly, smiling. "Yes, Johnnie Adamowski," he said. "And you?—what is your name?"

George told him.

"Of course," he said. "I know of you."

So instantly they were shaking hands delightedly, with that kind of stunned but exuberant surprise which reduces people to the banal conclusion that "It's a small world after all." George's remark was simply: "I'll be damned!" Adamowski's, more urbane, was: "It is quite astonishing to meet you in this way. It is very strange—and yet in life it always happens."

And now, indeed, they began to establish contact at many points. They found that they knew in common scores of people. They discussed them enthusiastically, almost joyfully. Adamowski had been away from home just one short month, and George but five, but now, like an explorer returning from the isolation of a polar voyage that had lasted several years, George eagerly demanded news of his friends, news from America, news from home.

———

By the time the other people returned to the compartment and the train began to move again, George and Adamowski were deep in conversation. Their three companions looked somewhat startled to hear this rapid fire of talk and to see this evidence of acquaintance between two people who had apparently been strangers just ten minutes before. The little blonde woman smiled at them and took her seat; the young man also. Old Fuss-and-Fidget glanced quickly, sharply, from one to the other of them and listened attentively to all they said, as if he thought that by straining his ears to catch every strange syllable he might be able somehow to fathom the mystery of this sudden friendship.

The cross fire of their talk went back and forth, from George's corner of the compartment to Adamowski's. George felt a sense of embarrassment at the sudden intrusion of this intimacy in a foreign language among fellow travelers with whom he had heretofore maintained a restrained formality. But Johnnie Adamowski was evidently a creature of great social ease and geniality. He was troubled not at all. From time to time he smiled in a friendly fashion at the three Germans as if they, too, were parties to the conversation and could understand every word of it.

Under this engaging influence, everyone began to thaw out visibly. The little blonde woman began to talk in an animated way to her young man. After a while Fuss-and-Fidget chimed in with those two, so that the whole compartment was humming with the rapid interplay of English and German.

Adamowski now asked George if he would not like some refreshment.

"Of course I myself am not hungry," Adamowski said indifferently. "In Poland I have had to eat too much. They eat all the time, these Polish people. I had decided that I would eat no more until I got to Paris. I am sick of food. But would you like some Polish fruits?" he said, indicating a large paper-covered package at his side. "I believe they have prepared some things for me," he said casually—"some fruits from my brother's estate, some chickens and some partridges. I do not care for them myself. I have no appetite. But wouldn't you like something?"

George told him no, that he was not hungry either. Thereupon Adamowski suggested that they might seek out the *Speisewagen* and get a drink.

"I still have these marks," he said indifferently. "I spent a few for breakfast, but there are seventeen or eighteen left. I shall not want them any longer. I should not have used them. But now that I have met you, I think it would be nice if I could spend them. Shall we go and see what we can find?"

To this George agreed. They arose, excused themselves to their companions, and were about to go out when old Fuss-and-Fidget surprised them by speaking up in broken English and asking Adamowski if he would mind changing seats.

523

He said with a nervous, forced smile that was meant to be ingratiating that Adamowski and the other gentleman, nodding at George, could talk more easily if they were opposite each other, and that for himself, he would be glad of the chance to look out the window. Adamowski answered indifferently, and with just a trace of the unconscious contempt with which a Polish nobleman might speak to someone in whom he felt no interest:

"Yes, take my seat, of course. It does not matter to me where I sit."

They went out and walked forward through several coaches of the hurtling train, carefully squeezing past those passengers who, in Europe, seem to spend as much time standing in the narrow corridors and staring out of the windows as in their own seats, and who flatten themselves against the wall or obligingly step back into the doors of compartments as one passes. Finally they reached the *Speisewagen*, skirted the hot breath of the kitchen, and seated themselves at a table in the beautiful, bright, clean coach of the Mitropa service.

Adamowski ordered brandy lavishly. He seemed to have a Polish gentleman's liberal capacity for drink. He tossed his glass off at a single gulp, remarking rather plaintively:

"It is very small. But it is good and does no harm. We shall have more."

Pleasantly warmed by brandy, and talking together with the ease and confidence of people who had known each other for many years—for, indeed, the circumstances of their meeting and the discovery of their many common friends did give them just that feeling of old intimacy—they now began to discuss the three strangers in their compartment.

"The little woman—she is rather nice," said Adamowski, in a tone which somehow conveyed the impression that he was no novice in such appraisals. "I think she is not very young, and yet, quite charming, isn't she? A personality."

"And the young man with her?" George inquired. "What do you make of him? You don't think he is her husband?"

"No, of course not," replied Adamowski instantly. "It is most curious," he went on a puzzled tone. "He is much younger, obviously, and not the same—he is much simpler than the lady."

"Yes. It's almost as if he were a young fellow from the country, and she——"

"Is like someone in the theatre," Adamowski nodded. "An actress. Or perhaps some music-hall performer."

"Yes, exactly. She is very nice, and yet I think she knows a great deal more than he does."

"I should like to know about them," Adamowski went on

524

speculatively, in the manner of a man who has a genuine interest in the world about him. "These people that one meets on trains and ships—they fascinate me. You see some strange things. And these two—they interest me. I should like so much to know who they are."

"And the other man?" George said. "The little one? The nervous, fidgety fellow who keeps staring at us—who do you suppose he is?"

"Oh, that one," said Adamowski indifferently, impatiently. "I do not know. I do not care. He is some stuffy little man—it doesn't matter. . . . But shall we go back now?" he said. "Let's talk to them and see if we can find out who they are. We shall never see them again after this. I like to talk to people in trains."

George agreed. So his Polish friend called the waiter, asked for the bill, and paid it—and still had ten or twelve marks left of his waning twenty-three. Then they got up and went back through the speeding train to their compartment.

Chapter Forty-Two

The Family of Earth

The woman smiled at them as they came in, and all three of their fellow passengers looked at them in a way that showed wakened curiosity and increased interest. It was evident that George and Adamowski had themselves been subjects of speculation during their absence.

Adamowski now spoke to the others. His German was not very good but it was coherent, and his deficiencies did not bother him at all. He was so self-assured, so confirmed in his self-possession, that he could plunge boldly into conversation in a foreign language with no sense whatever of personal handicap. Thus encouraged, the three Germans now gave free expression to their curiosity, to the speculations which the meeting of George and Adamowski and their apparent recognition of each other had aroused.

The woman asked Adamowski where he came from—"*Was für ein Landsmann sind sie?*"

He replied that he was an American.

"Ach, so?" She looked surprised, then added quickly: "But not by birth? You were not born in America?"

"No," said Adamowski. "I am Polish by birth. But I live in America now. And my friend here—" they all turned to stare curiously at George—"is an American by birth."

They nodded in satisfaction. And the woman, smiling with good-humored and eager interest, said:

"And your friend—he is an artist, isn't he?"

"Yes," said Adamowski.

"A painter?" The woman's tone was almost gleeful as she pursued further confirmation of her own predictions.

"He is not a painter. He is *ein Dichter*."

The word means "poet," and George quickly amended it to *"ein Schriftsteller"*—a writer.

All three of them thereupon looked at one another with nods of satisfaction, saying, ah, they thought so, it was evident. Old Fuss-and-Fidget even spoke up now, making the sage observation that it was apparent "from the head." The others nodded again, and the woman then turned once more to Adamowski, saying:

"But you—you are not an artist, are you? You do something else?"

He replied that he was a business man—*"ein Geschäfts-mann"*—that he lived in New York, and that his business was in Wall Street. The name apparently had imposing connotations for them, for they all nodded in an impressed manner and said "Ah!" again.

George and Adamowski went on then and told them of the manner of their meeting, how they had never seen each other before that morning, but how each of them had known of the other through many mutual friends. This news delighted everyone. It was a complete confirmation of what they had themselves inferred. The little blonde lady nodded triumphantly and burst out in excited conversation with her companion and with Fuss-and-Fidget, saying:

"What did I tell you? I said the same thing, didn't I? It's a small world after all, isn't it?"

Now they were all really wonderfully at ease with one another, all talking eagerly, excitedly, naturally, like old friends who had just met after a long separation. The little lady began to tell them all about herself. She and her husband, she said, were proprietors of a business near the Alexander-platz. No—smiling—the young man was not her husband. He, too, was a young artist, and was employed by her. In what sort of business? She laughed—one would never guess. She and her husband manufactured manikins for show-window displays. No, it was not a shop, exactly—there was a trace of modest pride here—it was more like a little factory. They made their own figures. Their business, she implied, was quite a large one. She said that they employed over fifty workers, and formerly had had almost a hundred. That was why she had to go to Paris as often as she could, for Paris set the fashion in manikins just as it did in clothes.

Of course, they did not *buy* the Paris models. *Mein Gott!*— that was impossible with the money situation what it was. Nowadays it was hard enough for a German business person even to get out of his own country, much less buy anything abroad. Nevertheless, hard as it was, she had to get to Paris somehow once or twice a year, just in order to keep up with "what was going on." She always took an artist with her, and this young man was making his first trip in this capacity. He was a sculptor by profession, but he earned money for his art by doing commercial work in her business. He would make designs and draw models of the latest show-window manikins in Paris, and would duplicate them when he returned; then the factory would turn them out by the hundreds.

Adamowski remarked that he did not see how it was possible, under present circumstances, for a German citizen to travel anywhere. It had become difficult enough for a foreigner to get in and out of Germany. The money complications were so confusing and so wearisome.

George added to this an account of the complications that had attended his own brief journey to the Austrian Tyrol. Ruefully he displayed the pocketful of papers, permits, visas, and official stamps which he had accumulated during the summer.

Upon this common grievance they were all vociferously agreed. The lady affirmed that it was stupid, exhausting, and, for a German with business outside the country, almost impossible. She added quickly, loyally, that of course it was also necessary. But then she went on to relate that her three- or four-day trips to Paris could only be managed through some complicated trade arrangement and business connection in France, and as she tried to explain the necessary details of the plan she became so involved in the bewildering complexities of checks and balances that she finally ended by waving her hand charmingly in a gesture of exhausted dismissal, saying:

"*Ach, Gott!* It is all too complicated, too confusing! I cannot tell you how it is—I do not understand it myself!"

Old Fuss-and-Fidget put in here with confirmations of his own. He was, he said, an attorney in Berlin—"*ein Rechtsanwalt*"—and had formerly had extensive professional connections in France and in other portions of the Continent. He had visited America as well, and had been there as recently

527

as 1930, when he had attended an international congress of lawyers in New York. He even spoke a little English, which he unveiled with evident pride. And he was going now, he said, to another international congress of lawyers which was to open in Paris the next day, and which would last a week. But even so brief a trip as this now had its serious difficulties. As for his former professional activities in other countries, they were now, alas, impossible.

He asked George if any of his books had been translated and published in Germany, and George told him they had. The others were all eagerly and warmly curious, wanting to know the titles and George's name. Accordingly, he wrote out for them the German titles of the books, the name of the German publisher, and his own name. They all looked interested and pleased. The little lady put the paper away in her pocketbok and announced enthusiastically that she would buy the books on her return to Germany. Fuss-and-Fidget, after carefully copying the paper, folded the memorandum and tucked it in his wallet, saying that he, too, would buy the books as soon as he came home again.

The lady's young companion, who had shyly and diffidently, but with growing confidence, joined in the conversation from time to time, now took from an envelope in his pocket several postcard photographs of sculptures he had made. They were pictures of muscular athletes, runners, wrestlers, miners stripped to the waist, and the voluptuous figures of young nude girls. These photographs were passed around, inspected by each of them, and praised and admired for various qualities.

Adamowski now picked up his bulky paper package, explained that it was filled with good things from his brother's estate in Poland, opened it, and invited everyone to partake. There were some splendid pears and peaches, some fine bunches of grapes, a plump broiled chicken, some fat squabs and partridges, and various other delicacies. The three Germans protested that they could not deprive him of his lunch. But Adamowski insisted vigorously, with the warmth of generous hospitality that was obviously characteristic of his nature. On the spur of the moment he reversed an earlier decision and informed them that he and George were going to the dining car for luncheon anyway, and that if they did not eat the food in the package it would go to waste. On this condition they all helped themselves to fruit, which they pronounced delicious, and the lady promised that she would later investigate the chicken.

At length, with friendly greetings all around, George and his Polish friend departed a second time and went forward to the *Speisewagen.*

They had a long and sumptuous meal. It began with brandy, proceeded over a fine bottle of Bernkasteler, and wound up over coffee and more brandy. They were both determined to spend the remainder of their German money—Adamowski his ten or twelve marks, George his five or six—and this gave them a comfortable feeling in which astute economy was thriftily combined with good living.

During the meal they discussed their companions again. They were delighted with them and immensely interested in the information they had gathered from them. The woman, they both agreed, was altogether charming. And the young man, although diffident and shy, was very nice. They even had a word of praise for old Fuss-and-Fidget now. After his crusty shell had been cracked, the old codger was not bad. He really was quite friendly underneath.

"And it goes to show," said Adamowski quietly, "how good people really are, how easy it is to get along with one another in this world, how people really like each other—if only——"

"—if only——" George said, and nodded.

"—if only it weren't for these God-damned politicians," Adamowski concluded.

At the end they called for their bill. Adamowski dumped his marks upon the table and counted them.

"You'll have to help me out," he said. "How many have you got?"

George dumped his out. Together, they had enough to pay the bill and to give the waiter something extra. And there was also enough left over for another double jolt of brandy and a good cigar.

So, grinning with satisfaction, in which their waiter joined amiably as he read their purpose, they paid the bill, ordered the brandy and cigars, and, full of food, drink, and the pleasant knowledge of a job well done, they puffed contentedly on their cigars and observed the landscape.

They were now running through the great industrial region of western Germany. The pleasant landscape was gone, and everything in sight had been darkened by the grime and smoke of enormous works. The earth was dotted with the steely skeletons of great smelting and refining plants, and disfigured with mountainous dumps and heaps of slag. It was brutal, smoky, dense with life and labor and the grim warrens of industrial towns. But these places, too, had a certain fascination—the thrill of power in the raw.

The two friends talked about the scene and about their trip. Adamowski said they had done well to spend their German money. Outside of the Reich its exchange value would be lower, and they were already almost at the border; since their own coach went directly through to Paris, they would have no additional need of German currency for porters' fees.

George confided to him, somewhat apprehensively, that he had some thirty dollars in American currency for which he had no German permit. Almost all of his last week in Berlin had been consumed, he said, in the red tape of departure—pounding wearily from one steamship office to another in an effort to secure passage home, cabling to Fox Edwards for more money, then getting permits for the money. At the last moment he had discovered that he still had thirty dollars left for which he had no official permit. When he had gone in desperation to an acquaintance who was an official in a travel agency, and had asked him what to do, this man had told him wearily to put the money in his pocket and say nothing; that if he tried now to get a permit for it and waited for the authorities to act on it, he would miss the boat; so to take the chance, which was, at most, he thought, a very slight one, and go ahead.

Adamowski nodded in agreement, but suggested that George take the uncertified money, thrust it in the pocket of his vest, where he would not seem to hide it, and then, if he were discovered and questioned, he could say that he had put the money there and had forgotten to declare it. This he decided to do, and made the transfer then and there.

This conversation brought them back to the thorny problem of the money regulations and the difficulties of their fellow travelers who were Germans. They agreed that the situation was hard on their new-found friends, and that the law which permitted foreigners and citizens alike to take only ten marks from the country, unless otherwise allowed, was, for people in the business circumstances of the little blonde woman and old Fuss-and-Fidget, very unfair indeed.

Then Adamowski had a brilliant inspiration, the fruit of his generous and spontaneous impulses.

"But why——" he said—"why can't we help them?"

"How do you mean? In what way can we help them?"

"Why," he said, "I have here a permit that allows me to take twenty-three marks out of the country. You have no permit, but everyone is allowed——"

"—to take ten marks," George said. "So you mean, then," he concluded, "that each of us has spent his German money——"

"—but can still take as much as is allowed out of the country. Yes," he said. "So we could at least suggest it to them."

"You mean that they should give us some of their marks to keep in our possession until we get across the frontier?"

Adamowski nodded. "Yes. I could take twenty-three. You could take ten. It is not much, of course, but it might help."

No sooner said than seized upon. They were almost jubilantly elated at this opportunity to do some slight service for these people to whom they had taken such a liking. But even as they sat there smiling confirmation at each other, a man in uniform came through the car, paused at their table—which was the only one now occupied, all the other diners having departed—and authoritatively informed them that the Pass-Control had come aboard the train, and that they must return at once to their compartment to await examination.

They got up immediately and hastened back through the swaying coaches. George led the way, and Adamowski whispered at his shoulder that they must now make haste and propose their offer to their companions quickly, or it would be too late.

As soon as they entered the compartment they told their three German friends that the officials were already on the train and that the inspection would begin shortly. This announcement caused a flurry of excitement. They all began to get ready. The woman busied herself with her purse. She took out her passport, and then, with a worried look, began to count her money.

Adamowski, after watching her quietly for a moment, took out his certificate and held it open in his hand, remarking that he was officially allowed twenty-three marks, that he had had that sum at the beginning, but that now he had spent it. George took this as his cue and said that he, too, had spent all of his German money, and that, although he had no permit, he was allowed ten marks. The woman looked quickly, eagerly, from one to the other and read the friendship of their purpose.

"Then you mean——" she began. "But it would be wonderful, of course, if you would!"

"Have you as much as twenty-three marks above what you are allowed?" asked Adamowski.

"Yes," she nodded quickly, with a worried look. "I have more than that. But if you would take the twenty-three and keep them till we are past the frontier——"

He stretched out his hand. "Give them to me," he said.

She gave them to him instantly, and the money was in his pocket in the wink of an eye.

531

Fuss-and-Fidget now counted out ten marks nervously, and without a word passed them across to George. George thrust the money in his pocket, and they all sat back, a little flushed, excited but triumphant, trying to look composed.

A few minutes later an official opened the door of the compartment, saluted, and asked for their passports. He inspected Adamowski's first, found everything in order, took his certificate, saw his twenty-three marks, stamped the passport, and returned it to him.

Then he turned to George, who gave him his passport and the various papers certifying his possession of American currency. The official thumbed through the pages of the passport, which were now almost completely covered with the stamps and entries which had been made every time George cashed a check for register-marks. On one page the man paused and frowned, scrutinizing carefully a stamp showing reëntrance into Germany from Kufstein, on the Austrian border; then he consulted again the papers George had handed him. He shook his head. Where, he asked, was the certificate from Kufstein?

George's heart jumped and pounded hard. He had forgotten the Kufstein certificate! There had been so many papers and documents of one kind and another since then that he no longer thought the Kufstein certificate was needed. He began to paw and thumb through the mass of papers that remained in his pocket. The officer waited patiently, but with an air of perturbation in his manner. Everyone else looked at George apprehensively, except Adamowski, who said quietly:

"Just take your time. It ought to be there somewhere."

At last George found it! And as he did, his own sharp intake of relief found echo among his companions. As for the official, he, too, seemed glad. He smiled quite kindly, took the paper and inspected it, and returned the passport.

Meanwhile, during the anxious minutes that George had taken to paw through his papers, the official had already inspected the passports of the woman, her companion, and Fuss-and-Fidget. Everything was apparently in order with them, save that the lady had confessed to the possession of forty-two marks, and the official had regretfully informed her that he would have to take from her everything in excess of ten. The money would be held at the frontier and restored to her, of course, when she returned. She smiled ruefully, shrugged her shoulders, and gave the man thirty-two marks. All other matters were now evidently in order, for the man saluted and withdrew.

So it was over, then! They all drew deep breaths of relief, and commiserated the charming lady upon her loss. But they were all quietly jubilant, too, to know that her loss had been no greater, and that Adamowski had been able in some degree to lessen it.

George asked Fuss-and-Fidget if he wanted his money returned now or later. He replied that he thought it would be better to wait until they had crossed the frontier into Belgium. At the same time he made a casual remark, to which none of them paid any serious attention just then, to the effect that for some reason, which they did not follow, his ticket was good only to the frontier, and that he would utilize the fifteen minutes' wait at Aachen, which was the frontier town, to buy a ticket for the remainder of the trip to Paris.

They were now approaching Aachen. The train was beginning to slacken speed. They were going once more through a lovely countryside, smiling with green fields and gentle hills, unobtrusively, mildly, somehow unmistakably European. The seared and blasted district of the mines and factories was behind them. They were entering the outskirts of a pleasant town.

This was Aachen. Within a few minutes more, the train was slowing to a halt before the station. They had reached the frontier. Here there would be a change of engines. All of them got out—Fuss-and-Fidget evidently to get a ticket, the others to stretch their legs and get a breath of air.

Chapter Forty-Three

The Capture

*Adamowski and George stepped out on the platform to-gether and walked forward to inspect the locomotive. The German engine, which had here reached the end of its journey and would soon be supplanted by its Belgian successor, was a magnificent machine of tremendous power and weight, almost as big as one of the great American engines. It was beautifully streamlined for high velocity, and its tender was a wonderful affair, different from any other that George had ever seen. It seemed to be a honeycomb of pipes. One looked in through some slanting bars and saw a fountainlike display composed of thousands of tiny little jets of steaming water. Every line of this intricate and marvelous apparatus bore evidence of the organizing skill and engineering genius that had created it.

Knowing how important are the hairline moments of transition, how vivid, swift, and fugitive are the poignant first impressions when a traveler changes from one country to another, from one people to another, from one standard of conduct and activity to another, George waited with intense interest for the approach of the Belgian locomotive in order to see what it might indicate of the differences between the powerful, solid, and indomitable race they were leaving and the little people whose country they were now about to enter.

While Adamowski and George were engaged in observations and speculations on this subject, their own coach and another, which was also destined for Paris, were detached from the German train and shifted to a string of coaches on the opposite side of the platform. They were about to hasten back when a guard informed them that they still had ample time, and that the train was not scheduled to depart for another five minutes. So they waited a little longer, and Adamowski remarked that it was a pitiful evidence of the state Europe was in that a crack train between the two greatest cities on the Continent should be carrying only two through coaches, and these not even filled.

But the Belgian locomotive still did not come, and now, glancing up at the station clock, they saw that the moment for departure had arrived. Fearful of being left behind if they waited any longer, they started back along the platform. They found the little blonde-haired lady and, flanking her on each side, they hastened toward their coach and their own compartment.

As they approached, it was evident that something had happened. There were no signs of departure. The conductor and the station guard stood together on the platform. No warning signal had been given. When they came alongside of their car, people were clustered in the corridor, and something in the way they stood indicated a subdued tension, a sense of crisis, that made George's pulse beat quicker.

George had observed this same phenomenon several times before in the course of his life and he knew the signs. A man has leaped or fallen, for example, from a high building to the pavement of a city street; or a man has been shot or struck by a motor car, and now lies dying quietly before the eyes of other men—and always the manifestation of the crowd is just the same. Even before you see the faces of the people, something about their backs, their posture, the position of their heads and shoulders tells you what has happened. You do not know, of course, the precise circumstances, but you sense immediately the final stage of tragedy. You know that someone has just died

534

or is dying. And in the terrible eloquence of backs and shoulders, the feeding silence of the watching men, you also sense another tragedy which is even deeper. This is the tragedy of man's cruelty and his lust for pain—the tragic weakness which corrupts him, which he loathes, but which he cannot cure. As a child, George had seen it on the faces of men standing before the window of a shabby little undertaker's place, looking at the bloody, riddled carcass of a Negro which the mob had caught and killed. Again, as a boy of fourteen, he had seen it on the faces of men and women at a dance, as they watched a fight in which one man beat another man to death.

And now, here it was again. As George and his two companions hastened along beside the train and saw the people gathered in the corridor in that same feeding posture, waiting, watching, in that same deadly fascinated silence, he was sure that once again he was about to witness death.

That was the first thought that came to him—and it came also, instantaneously, without a word of communication between them, to Adamowski and the little blonde woman—the thought that someone had died. But as they started to get on the train, what suddenly stunned them and stopped them short, appalled, was the realization that the tragedy, whatever it was, had happened in their own compartment. The shades were tightly drawn, the door closed and locked, the whole place sealed impenetrably. They stared in silence, rooted to the platform. Then they saw the woman's young companion standing at the window in the corridor. He motioned to them quickly, stealthily, a gesture warning them to remain where they were. And as he did so it flashed over all three of them that the victim of this tragic visitation must be the nervous little man who had been the companion of their voyage since morning. The stillness of the scene and the shuttered blankness of that closed compartment were horrible. They all felt sure that this little man who had begun by being so disagreeable, but who had gradually come out of his shell and become their friend, and to whom they had all been taking only fifteen minutes before, had died, and that authority and the law were now enclosed there with his body in the official ceremony that society demands.

Even as they stared appalled and horror-stricken at that fatally curtained compartment, the lock clicked sharply, the door was opened and closed quickly, and an official came out. He was a burly fellow in a visored cap and a jacket of olive green—a man of forty-five or more with high, blunt cheekbones, a florid face, and tawny mustaches combed out sprouting in the Kaiser Wilhelm way. His head was shaven, and there were thick creases at the base of his skull and across his fleshy neck. He came out, climbed down clumsily to the platform, signaled and called excitedly to another officer, and climbed back into the train again.

He belonged to a familiar and well-known type, one which George had seen and smiled at often, but one which now became, under these ominous and unknown circumstances, sinisterly unpleasant. The man's very weight and clumsiness, the awkward way he got down from the train and climbed up again, the thickness of his waist, the width and coarseness of his lumbering buttocks, the way his sprouting mustaches quivered with passion and authority, the sound of his guttural voice as he shouted to his fellow officer, his puffing, panting air of official indignation—all these symptoms which ran true to type now became somehow loathsome and repellent. All of a sudden, without knowing why, George felt himself trembling with a murderous and incomprehensible anger. He wanted to smash that fat neck with the creases in it. He wanted to pound that inflamed and blunted face into a jelly. He wanted to kick square and hard, bury his foot dead center in the obscene fleshiness of those lumbering buttocks. Like all Americans, he had never liked the police and the kind of personal authority that is sanctified in them. But his present feeling, with its murderous rage, was a good deal more than that. For he knew that he was helpless, that all of them were, and he felt impotent, shackled, unable to stir against the walls of an unreasonable but unshakable authority.

The official with the sprouting mustaches, accompanied by the colleague he had summoned, opened the curtained door of the compartment again, and now George saw that two other officers were inside. And the nervous little man who had been their companion—no, he was not dead!—he sat all huddled up, facing them. His face was white and pasty. It looked greasy, as if it were covered with a salve of cold, fat sweat. Under his long nose his mouth was trembling in a horrible attempt at a smile. And in the very posture of the two men as they bent over him and questioned him there was something revolting and unclean.

But the official with the thick, creased neck had now filled the door and blotted out the picture. He went in quickly, followed by his colleague. The door closed behind them, and again there was nothing but the drawn curtains and that ill-omened secrecy.

All the people who had gathered around had gotten this momentary glimpse and had simply looked on with stupefied surprise. Now those who stood in the corridor of the train began to whisper to one another. The little blonde woman went over and carried on a whispered conversation with the young man and several other people who were standing at the open window. After conferring with them with subdued but growing

536

excitement for a minute or two, she came back, took George and Adamowski by the arm, and whispered:

"Come over here. There is something I want to tell you."

She led them across the platform, out of hearing. Then, as both of the men said in lowered voices, "What is it?"—she looked around cautiously and whispered:

"That man—the one in our compartment—he was trying to get out of the country—and they've caught him!"

"But why? What for? What has he done?" they asked, bewildered.

Again she glanced back cautiously and, drawing them together till their three heads were almost touching, she said in a secretive whisper that was full of awe and fright:

"They say he is a Jew! And they found money on him! They searched him—they searched his baggage—he was taking money out!"

"How much?" asked Adamowski.

"I don't know," she whispered. "A great deal, I think. A hundred thousand marks, some say. Anyhow, they found it!"

"But how?" George began. "I thought everything was finished. I thought they were done with all of us when they went through the train."

"Yes," she said. "But don't you remember something about the ticket? He said something about not having a ticket the whole way. I suppose he thought it would be safer—wouldn't arouse suspicion in Berlin if he bought a ticket only to Aachen. So he got off the train here to buy his ticket for Paris—and that's when they caught him!" she whispered. "They must have had their eye on him! They must have suspected him! That's why they didn't question him when they came through the train!" George remembered now that "they" had not. "But they were watching for him, and they caught him here!" she went on. "They asked him where he was going, and he said to Paris. They asked him how much money he was taking out. He said ten marks. Then they asked him how long he was going to remain in Paris, and for what purpose, and he said he was going to be there a week, attending this congress of lawyers that he spoke about. They asked him, then, how he proposed to stay in Paris a week if all he had was ten marks. And I think," she whispered, "that that's where he got frightened! He began to lose his head! He said he had twenty marks besides, which he had put into another pocket and forgotten. And then, of course, they had him! They searched him! They searched his baggage! And they found more—" she whispered in an awed tone—"much, much more!"

They all stared at one another, too stunned to say a word.

Then the woman laughed in a low, frightened sort of way, a little, uncertain "O-hoh-hoh-hoh-hoh," ending on a note of incredulity.

"This man—" she whispered again—"this little Jew——"

"I didn't know he was a Jew," George said. "I should not have thought so."

"But he is!" she whispered, and looked stealthily around again to see if they were being overheard or watched. "And he was doing what so many of the others have done—he was trying to get out with his money!" Again she laughed, the uncertain little "Hoh-hoh-hoh" that mounted to incredulous amazement. Yet George saw that her eyes were troubled, too.

All of a sudden George felt sick, empty, nauseated. Turning half away, he thrust his hands into his pockets—and drew them out as though his fingers had been burned. The man's money—he still had it! Deliberately, now, he put his hand into his pocket again and felt the five two-mark pieces. The coins seemed greasy, as if they were covered with sweat. George took them out and closed them in his fist and started across the platform toward the train. The woman seized him by the arm.

"Where are you going?" she gasped. "What are you going to do?"

"I'm going to give the man his money. I won't see him again. I can't keep it."

Her face went white. "Are you mad?" she whispered. "Don't you know that that will do no good? You'll only get yourself arrested! And, as for him—he's in trouble enough already. You'll only make it so much worse for him. And besides," she faltered, "God knows what he has done, what he has said already. If he has lost his head completely—if he has told that we have transferred money to one another—we'll all be in for it!"

They had not thought of this. And as they realized the possible consequences of their good intentions, they just stood there, all three, and stared helplessly at one another. They just stood there, feeling dazed and weak and hollow. They just stood there and prayed.

And now the officers were coming out of the compartment. The curtained door opened again, and the fellow with the sprouting mustaches emerged, carrying the little man's valise. He clambered down clumsily onto the platform and set the valise on the floor between his feet. He looked around. It seemed to George and the others that he glared at them. They just stood still and hardly dared to breathe. They thought they were in for it, and expected now to see all of their own baggage come out.

But in a moment the other three officials came through the door of the compartment with the little man between them.

538

They stepped down to the platform and marched him along, white as a sheet, grease standing out in beads all over his face, protesting volubly in a voice that had a kind of anguished lilt in it. He came right by the others as they stood there. The man's money sweated in George's hand, and he did not know what to do. He made a movement with his arm and started to speak to him. At the same time he was hoping desperately that the man would not speak. George tried to look away from him, but could not. The little man came toward them, protesting with every breath that the whole thing could be explained, that it was an absurd mistake. For just the flick of an instant as he passed the others he stopped talking, glanced at them, white-faced, still smiling his horrible little forced smile of terror; for just a moment his eyes rested on them, and then, without a sign of recognition, without betraying them, without giving any indication that he knew them, he went on by.

George heard the woman at his side sigh faintly and felt her body slump against him. They all felt weak, drained of their last energies. Then they walked slowly across the platform and got into the train.

The evil tension had been snapped now. People were talking feverishly, still in low tones but with obvious released excitement. The little blonde woman leaned from the window of the corridor and spoke to the fellow with the sprouting mustaches, who was still standing there.

"You—you're not going to let him go?" she asked hesitantly, almost in a whisper. "Are—are you going to keep him here?"

He looked at her stolidly. Then a slow, intolerable smile broke across his brutal features. He nodded his head deliberately, with the finality of a gluttonous and full-fed satisfaction:

"*Ja,*" he said. "*Er bleibt.*" And, shaking his head ever so slightly from side to side, "*Geht nicht!*" he said.

They had him. Far down the platform the passengers heard the shrill, sudden fife of the Belgian engine whistle. The guard cried warning. All up and down the train the doors were slammed. Slowly the train began to move. At a creeping pace it rolled right past the little man. They had him, all right. The officers surrounded him. He stood among them, still protesting, talking with his hands now. And the men in uniform said nothing. They had no need to speak. They had him. They just stood and watched him, each with a faint suggestion of that intolerable slow smile upon his face. They raised their eyes and looked at the passengers as the train rolled past, and the line of travelers standing in the corridors looked back at them and caught the obscene and insolent communication in their glance and in that intolerable slow smile.

And the little man—he, too, paused once from his feverish effort to explain. As the car in which he had been riding slid by, he lifted his pasty face and terror-stricken eyes, and for a moment his lips were stilled of their anxious pleading. He looked once, directly and steadfastly, at his former companions, and they at him. And in that gaze there was all the unmeasured weight of man's mortal anguish. George and the others felt somehow naked and ashamed, and somehow guilty. They all felt that they were saying farewell, not to a man, but to humanity; not to some pathetic stranger, some chance acquaintance of the voyage, but to mankind; not to some nameless cipher out of life, but to the fading image of a brother's face.

The train swept out and gathered speed—and so they lost him.

Chapter Forty-Four

The Way of No Return

"Well," said Adamowski, *turning to George, "I think this is a* sad end to our journey."

George nodded but said nothing. Then they all went back into their compartment and took their former seats.

But it seemed strange and empty now. The ghost of absence sat there ruinously. The little man had left his coat and hat; in his anguish he had forgotten them. Adamowski rose and took them, and would have given them to the conductor, but the woman said:

"You'd better look into the pockets first. There may be something in them. Perhaps—" quickly, eagerly, as the idea took her—"perhaps he has left money there," she whispered.

Adamowski searched the pockets. There was nothing of any value in them. He shook his head. The woman began to search the cushions of the seats, thrusting her hands down around the sides.

"It might just be, you know," she said, "that he hid money
540

here." She laughed excitedly, almost gleefully. "Perhaps we'll all be rich!"

The young Pole shook his head. "I think they would have found it if he had." He paused, peered out of the window, and thrust his hand into his pocket. "I suppose we're in Belgium now," he said. "Here's your money." And he returned to her the twenty-three marks she had given him.

She took the money and put it in her purse. George still had the little man's ten marks in his hand and was looking at them. The woman glanced up, saw his face, then said quickly, warmly:

"But you're upset about this thing! You look so troubled."

George put the money away. Then he said:

"I feel exactly as if I had blood-money in my pocket."

"No," she said. She leaned over, smiling, and put her hand reassuringly upon his arm. "Not blood-money—Jew-money!" she whispered. "Don't worry about it. He had plenty more!"

George's eyes met Adamowski's. Both were grave.

"This is a sad ending to our trip," Adamowski said again, in a low voice, almost to himself.

The woman tried to talk them out of their depression, to talk herself into forgetfulness. She made an effort to laugh and joke.

"These Jews!" she cried. "Such things would never happen if it were not for them! They make all the trouble. Germany has had to protect herself. The Jews were taking all the money from the country. Thousands of them escaped, taking millions of marks with them. And now, when it's too late, we wake up to it! It's too bad that foreigners must see these things—that they've got to go through these painful experiences—it makes a bad impression. They don't understand the reason. But it's the Jews!" she whispered.

The others said nothing, and the woman went on talking, eagerly, excitedly, earnestly, persuasively. But it was as if she were trying to convince herself, as if every instinct of race and loyalty were now being used in an effort to excuse or justify something that had filled her with sorrow and deep shame. For even as she talked and laughed, her clear blue eyes were sad and full of trouble. And at length she gave it up and stopped. There was a heavy silence. Then, gravely, quietly, the woman said:

"He must have wanted very badly to escape."

They remembered, then, all that he had said and done throughout the journey. They recalled how nervous he had been, how he had kept opening and shutting the door, how he had kept getting up to pace along the corridor. They spoke of the suspicion and distrust with which he had peered round at them when he first came in, and of the eagerness with which he had asked Adamowski to change places with him when the Pole had got up to go into the dining car with George. They recalled his explanations about the ticket, about having to buy passage from the frontier to Paris. All of these things, every act and word and gesture of the little man, which they had dismissed at the time as trivial or as evidence simply of an irascible temper, now became invested with a new and terrible meaning.

"But the ten marks!" the woman cried at length, turning to George. "Since he had all this other money, why, in God's name, did he give ten marks to you? It was so stupid!" she exclaimed in an exasperated tone. "There was no reason for it!"

Certainly they could find no reason, unless he had done it to divert suspicion from their minds about his true intent. This was Adamowski's theory, and it seemed to satisfy the woman. But George thought it more likely that the little man was in such a desperate state of nervous frenzy and apprehension that he had lost the power to reason clearly and had acted blindly, wildly, on the impulse of the moment. But they did not know. And now they would never find out the answer.

George was still worried about getting the man's ten marks returned to him. The woman said that she had given the man her name and her address in Paris, and that if he were later allowed to complete his journey he could find her there. George then gave her his own address in Paris and asked her to inform the man where he was if she should hear from him. She promised, but they all knew that she would never hear from him again.

Late afternoon had come. The country had closed in around them. The train was winding through a pleasant, romantic landscape of hills and woods. In the slant of evening and the waning light there was a sense of deep, impenetrable forest and of cool, darkling waters.

They had long since passed the frontier, but the woman, who had been looking musingly and a little anxiously out of the window, hailed the conductor as he passed along the corridor and asked him if they were really in Belgium now. He assured her that they were. Adamowski gave him the little man's hat and coat, and explained the reason. The conductor nodded, took them, and departed.

The woman had her hand upon her breast, and now when the conductor had gone she sighed slowly with relief. Then, quietly and simply, she said:

"Do not misunderstand me. I am a German and I love my
542

country. But—I feel as if a weight has lifted from me *here*." She put her hand upon her breast again. "You cannot understand, perhaps, just how it feels to us, but—" and for a moment she was silent, as if painfully meditating what she wished to say. Then, quickly, quietly: "We are so happy to be—*out!*"

Out? Yes, that was it. Suddenly George knew just how she felt. He, too, was "out" who was a stranger to her land, and yet who never had been a stranger in it. He, too, was "out" of that great country whose image had been engraved upon his spirit in childhood and youth, before he had ever seen it. He, too, was "out" of that land which had been so much more to him than land, so much more than place. It had been a geography of heart's desire, an unfathomed domain of unknown inheritance. The haunting beauty of that magic land had been his soul's dark wonder. He had known the language of its spirit before he ever came to it, had understood the language of its tongue the moment he had heard it spoken. He had framed the accents of its speech most brokenly from that first hour, yet never with a moment's trouble, strangeness, or lack of comprehension. He had been at home in it, and it in him. It seemed that he had been born with this knowledge.

He had known wonder in this land, truth and magic in it, sorrow, loneliness, and pain in it. He had known love in it, and for the first time in his life he had tasted there the bright, delusive sacraments of fame. Therefore it was no foreign land to him. It was the other part of his heart's home, a haunted part of dark desire, a magic domain of fulfillment. It was the dark, lost Helen that had been forever burning in his blood—the dark, lost Helen he had found.

And now it was the dark, found Helen he had lost. And he knew now, as he had never known before, the priceless measure of his loss. He knew also the priceless measure of his gain. For this was the way that henceforth would be forever closed to him—the way of no return. He was "out." And, being "out," he began to see another way, the way that lay before him. He saw now that you can't go home again—not ever. There was no road back. Ended now for him, with the sharp and clean finality of the closing of a door, was the time when his dark roots, like those of a pot-bound plant, could be left to feed upon their own substance and nourish their own little self-absorbed designs. Henceforth they must spread outward—away from the hidden, secret, and unfathomed past that holds man's spirit prisoner—outward, outward toward the rich and life-giving soil of a new freedom in the wide world of all humanity. And there came to him a vision of man's true home, beyond the ominous and cloud-engulfed horizon of the here and now, in the green and hopeful and still-virgin meadows of the future.

"Therefore," he thought, "old master, wizard Faust, old father of the ancient and swarm-haunted mind of man, old earth, old German land with all the measure of your truth, your glory, beauty, magic, and your ruin; and dark Helen burning in our blood, great queen and mistress, sorceress—dark land, dark land, old ancient earth I love—farewell!"

BOOK VII

A Wind Is Rising, and the Rivers Flow

The experiences of that final summer in Germany had a profound effect upon George Webber. He had come face to face with something old and genuinely evil in the spirit of man which he had never known before, and it shook his inner world to its foundations. Not that it produced a sudden revolution in his way of thinking. For years his conception of the world and of his own place in it had been gradually changing, and the German adventure merely brought this process to its climax. It threw into sharp relief many other related phenomena which George had observed in the whole temper of the times, and it made plain to him, once and for all, the dangers that lurk in those latent atavistic urges which man has inherited from his dark past.

Hitlerism, he saw, was a recrudescence of an old barbarism. Its racial nonsense and cruelty, its naked worship of brute force, its suppression of truth and resort to lies and myths, its ruthless contempt for the individual, its anti-intellectual and anti-moral dogma that to one man alone belongs the right of judgment and decision, and that for all others virtue lies in blind, unquestioning obedience—each of these fundamental elements of Hitlerism was a throwback to that fierce and ancient tribalism which had sent waves of hairy Teutons swooping down out of the north to destroy the vast edifice of Roman civilization. That primitive spirit of greed and lust and force had always been the true enemy of mankind.

But this spirit was not confined to Germany. It belonged to no one race. It was a terrible part of the universal heritage of man. One saw traces of it everywhere. It took on many disguises, many labels. Hitler, Mussolini, Stalin—each had his own name for it. And America had it, too, in various forms. For wherever ruthless men conspired together for their own ends, wherever the rule of dog-eat-dog was dominant, there it bred. And wherever one found it, one also found that its roots sank down into something primitive in man's ugly past. And these roots would somehow have to be eradicated, George felt, if man was to win his ultimate freedom and not be plunged back into savagery and perish utterly from the earth.

When George realized all this he began to look for atavistic yearnings in himself. He found plenty of them. Any man can find them if he is honest enough to look for them. The whole year that followed his return from Germany, George occupied himself with this effort of self-appraisal. And at the end of it he knew, and with the knowledge came the definite sense of new direction toward which he had long been groping, that the dark ancestral cave, the womb from which mankind emerged into the light, forever pulls one back—but that you can't go home again.

The phrase had many implications for him. You can't go back home to your family, back home to your childhood, back home to romantic love, back home to a young man's dreams of glory and of fame, back home to exile, to escape to Europe and some foreign land, back home to lyricism, to singing just for singing's sake, back home to aestheticism, to one's youthful idea of "the artist" and the all-sufficiency of "art" and "beauty" and "love," back home to the ivory tower, back home to places in the country, to the cottage in Bermuda, away from all the strife and conflict of the world, back home to the father you have lost and have been looking for, back home to someone who can help you, save you, ease the burden for you, back home to the old forms and systems of things which once seemed everlasting but which are changing all the time—back home to the escapes of Time and Memory.

In a way, the phrase summed up everything he had ever learned. And what he now knew led inexorably to a decision which was the hardest he had ever had to make. Throughout the year he wrestled with it, talked about it with his friend and editor, Foxhall Edwards, and fought against doing what he realized he would have to do. For the time had come to leave Fox Edwards. They had reached a parting of the ways. Not that Fox was one of the new barbarians. God, no! But Fox— well, Fox—Fox understood. And George knew that whatever happened, Fox would always remain his friend.

So in the end, after all their years together, they parted. And when it was over, George sat down and wrote to Fox. He wanted to leave the record clear. And this is what he wrote:

Chapter Forty-Five

Young Icarus

I have of late, dear Fox [George wrote,] *been thinking of* you very much, and of your strange but most familiar face. I never knew a man like you before, and if I had not known you, I never could have imagined you. And yet, to me you are inevitable, so that, having known you, I cannot imagine what life would have been for me without you. You were a polestar in my destiny. You were the magic thread in the great web which, being woven now, is finished and complete: the circle of our lives rounds out, full swing, and each of us in his own way now has rounded it: there is no further circle we can make. This, too—the end as the beginning—was inevitable: therefore, dear friend and parent of my youth, farewell.

Nine years have passed since first I waited in your vestibule. And I was not repulsed. No: I was taken in, was welcomed, was picked up and sustained just when my spirit reached its lowest ebb, was given life and hope, the restoration of my self-respect, the vindication of my self-belief, the renewal of my faith by the assurance of your own belief; and I was carried on, through all the struggle, doubt, confusion, desperation, effort of the years that were to follow, by your help and by the noble inspiration of your continued faith.

But now it ends—the road we were to go together. We two alone know how completely it has ended. But before I go, because few men can ever know, from first to last, a circle of such whole, superb finality, I leave this picture of it.

You may think it a little premature of me to start summing up my life at the age of thirty-seven. That is not my purpose here. But, although thirty-seven is not an advanced age at which one can speak of having learned many things, neither is it too early to have learned a few. By that time a man has lived long enough to be able to look back over the road he has come and see certain events and periods in a proportion and a perspective which he could not have had before. And because certain of the periods of my life represent to me, as I now look back on them, stages of marked change and development, not only in the spirit which animates the work I do, but also in my views on men and living, and my own relation to the world, I am going to tell you about them. Believe me, it is not egotism that prompts me to do this. As you will see, my whole experience swings round, as though through a predestined orbit, to you, to this moment, to this parting. So bear with me—and then, farewell.

To begin at the beginning (all is clear from start to finish):

Twenty years ago, when I was seventeen years old and a sophomore at Pine Rock College, I was very fond, along with many of my fellows, of talking about my "philosophy of life." That was one of our favorite subjects of conversation, and we were most earnest about it. I'm not sure now what my "philosophy" was at the time, but I am sure I had one. Everybody had. We were deep in philosophy at Pine Rock. We juggled such formidable terms as "concepts," "categorical imperatives," and "moments of negation" in a way that would have made Spinoza blush.

And if I do say so, I was no slouch at it myself. At the age of seventeen I had an A-1 rating as a philosopher. "Concepts" held no terrors for my young life, and "moments of negation" were my meat. I could split a hair with the best of them. And now that I have turned to boasting, I may as well tell you that I made a One in Logic, and it was said to be the only One that had been given in that course for many a year. So when it comes to speaking of philosophy, I am, you see, a fellow who is privileged to speak.

I don't know how it goes with students of this generation, but to those of us who were in college twenty years ago philosophy was serious business. We were always talking about "God." In our interminable discussions we were forever trying to get at the inner essence of "truth," "goodness," and "beauty." We were full of notions about all these things. And I do not laugh at them today. We were young, we were impassioned, and we were sincere.

One of the most memorable events of my college career occurred one day at noon when I was walking up a campus path and encountered, coming toward me, one of my classmates whose name was D. T. Jones. D. T.—sometimes known more familiarly as Delirium Tremens—was also a philosopher. And the moment I saw him approaching I knew that D. T. was in the throes. He came from a family of Primitive Baptists, and he was red-haired, gaunt, and angular, and now as he came toward me

548

everything about him—hair, eyebrows, eyelids, eyes, freckles, even his large and bony hands—shone forth in the sunlight with an excessive and almost terrifying redness.

He was coming up from a noble wood in which we held initiations and took our Sunday strolls. It was also the sacred grove to which we resorted, alone, when we were struggling with the problems of philosophy. It was where we went when we were going through what was known as "the wilderness experience," and it was the plane from which, when "the wilderness experience" was done, we triumphantly emerged.

D. T. was emerging now. He had been there, he told me later, all night long. His "wilderness experience" had been a good one. He came bounding toward me like a kangaroo, leaping into the air at intervals, and the only words he said were:

"I've had a Concept!"

Then, leaving me stunned and leaning for support against an ancient tree, he passed on down the path. high-bounding every step or two, to carry the great news to the whole brotherhood.

And still I do not laugh at it. We took philosophy seriously in those days, and each of us had his own. And, together, we had our own "Philosopher." He was a venerable and noble-hearted man—one of those great figures which almost every college had some years ago, and which I hope they still have. For half a century he had been a dominant figure in the life of the entire state. In his teaching he was a Hegelian. The process of his scholastic reasoning was intricate: it came up out of ancient Greece and followed through the whole series of "developments" down to Hegel. After Hegel—well, he did not supply the answer. But it didn't matter, for *after* Hegel we had *him* —he was our own Old Man.

Our Philosopher's "philosophy," as I look back upon it, does not seem important now. It seems to have been, at best, a tortuous and patched-up scheme of other men's ideas. But what *was* important was the man himself. He was a great teacher, and what he did for us, and for others before us for fifty years, was not to give us his "philosophy"—but to communicate to us his own alertness, his originality, his power to think. He was a vital force because he supplied to many of us, for the first time in our lives, the inspiration of a questioning intelligence. He taught us not to be afraid to think. to question; he taught us to examine critically the most sacrosanct of our native prejudices and superstitions. So of course, throughout the state, the bigots hated him; but his own students worshiped him to idolatry. And the seed he planted grew—long after Hegel, "concepts," "moments of negation," and all the rest of it had vanished into the limbo of forgotten things.

It was at about this time that I began to write. I was editor of
549

the college newspaper, and I wrote stories and poems for our literary magazine, *The Burr,* of which I was also a member of the editorial staff. The war was going on then. I was too young to be in service, but my first literary attempts may be traced to the patriotic inspiration of the war. I remember one poem (my first, I believe) which was aimed directly at the luckless head of Kaiser Bill. It was called, defiantly, "The Gauntlet," and was written in the style and meter of "The Present Crisis," by James Russell Lowell. I remember, too, that it took a high note from the very beginning. The poet, it is said, is the prophet and the bard—the awkward tongue of all his folk. I was all of that. In the name of embattled democracy I let the Kaiser have the works. And I remember two lines in particular that seemed to me to ring out with the very voice of outraged Freedom:

"Thou hast given us the challenge—
Pay, thou dog, the cost, and go!"

I remember these lines because they were the occasion of an editorial argument. The more conservative members of the magazine's staff felt that the epithet, "thou dog," was too strong—not that the Kaiser didn't deserve it, but that it jarred rudely upon the high moral elevation of the poem and upon the literary quality of *The Burr*. Over my vigorous protest, and without regard for the meter of the line, the two words were deleted.

Another poem that I wrote that year was a cheerful one about a peasant in a Flanders field who ploughed up a skull, and then went on quietly about his work while the great guns blasted away and "the grinning skull its grisly secret kept." I also remember a short story—my first—which was called "A Winchester of Virginia," and was about the recreant son of an old family who recovered his courage and vindicated his tarnished honor in the charge over the top that took his life. These, so far as I can recall them, were my first creative efforts; it will be seen what an important part the last war played in them.

I mention all this merely to fix the point from which I started. This was the beginning of the road.

In recent years there have been several attempts to explain what has happened to me since that time in terms of something that happened to me in college. I believe, Fox, that I never told you about that episode. Not that I was ashamed of my part in it or was afraid to talk about it. It just never came up; in a way, I had forgotten it. But now, at this moment of our parting, I think I had better speak of it, because it is vitally important to me to make one thing clear: that I am not the victim or the embittered martyr of anything that ever happened in the past. Oh, yes, there was a time, as you well know, when I was full of bitterness. There was a time when I felt that life had betrayed me. But that preciousness is gone now, and with it has gone my bitterness. This is the simple truth.

But to get back to this episode I spoke of:

As you know, Fox, when my first book was published, feeling ran high against me at home. Then it was that an effort was made to explain what was called the "bitterness" of the book in terms of my disfranchisement when I was at college. Now, the Pine Rock case is famous in Old Catawba, but the names of its chief actors had been almost forgotten when the book appeared. Then, because I was one of them, people began to talk about the case again, and the whole horrible tragedy was exhumed.

It was recalled how five of us (and God have mercy on the souls of those who kept silent at the time) had taken our classmate Bell out to the playing field one night, blindfolded him, and compelled him to dance upon a barrel. It was recalled how he stumbled and toppled from the barrel, fell on a broken bottle neck, severed his jugular, and bled to death within five minutes. It was recalled, then, how the five of us—myself and Randy Shepperton, John Brackett, Stowell Anderson, and Dick Carr—were expelled, brought up for trial, released in the custody of our parents or nearest relatives, and deprived of the rights of citizenship by legislative act.

All this was true. But the construction which people put upon it when the book appeared was false. None of us, I think, was "ruined" and "embittered"—and our later records prove that we were not. There is no doubt that the tragic consequences of our act (and of the five who suffered disfranchisement, at least three—I will not say which three—were present only in the group of onlookers) left its dark and terrible imprint on our young lives. But, as Randy whispered to me on that dreadful night, as we stood there white-faced and helpless in the moonlight, watching that poor boy as he bled to death:

"We're not guilty of anything—except of being plain damned fools!"

That was the way we felt that night—all of us—as we knelt, sick with horror, around the figure of that dying boy. And I know that was the way Bell felt, too, for he saw the terror and remorse in our white faces and, dying though he was, he tried to smile and speak to us. The words would not come, but all of us knew that if he could have spoken he would have said that he was sorry for us—that he knew there was no evil in us—no evil but our own stupidity.

We had killed the boy—our thoughtless folly killed him—but with his dying breath that would have been his only judgment on us. And we broke the heart of Plato Grant, our Old Man, our own Philosopher; but all *he* said to us that night as he turned toward us from poor Bell was, quietly:

"My God, boys, what have you done?"

And that was all. Even Bell's father said no more to us. And after the first storm had passed, the cry of outrage and indignation that went up throughout the state—that was our punishment: the knowledge of the *Done* inexorable, the merciless insistence in our souls of that fatal and irrevocable "Why?"

Swiftly, people came to see and feel this, too. The first outburst of wrath that resulted in our disfranchisement was quickly over. Even our citizenship was quietly restored to us within three years. (As for myself, I was only eighteen when it happened, and cannot even be said to have missed a legal vote because of it.) Each of us was allowed to return to college the next year after our expulsion, and finish the full course. The sentiment of people everywhere not only softened: the verdict quickly became: "They didn't mean to do it. They were just damned fools." Later, by the time of our reënfranchisement, public sentiment actually became liberal in its tone of pardon. "They've been punished enough," people said by then. "They were just kids—and they didn't mean to do it. Besides—" this became an argument in our favor—"it cost a life, but it killed hazing in the state."

As to the later record of the five—Randy Shepperton is dead now; but John Brackett, Stowell Anderson, and Dick Carr have all enjoyed a more than average measure of success in their communities. When I last saw Stowell Anderson—he is an attorney, and the political leader of his district—he told me quietly that, far from having been damaged in his career by the experience, he thought he had been helped.

"People," he said, "are willing to forget a past mistake if they see you're regular. They're not only willing to forgive—on the whole, I think they're even glad to give a helping hand."

"If they see you're regular!" Without commenting on the meanings of that, I think it sums up the matter in a nutshell. There has not only been no question since about the "regularity" of the other three—Brackett, Anderson, and Carr—but I think any natural tendencies they may have had toward regularity were intensified by their participation in the Pine Rock case. I believe, too, that the denunciations of my "irregularity," following the publication of my first book, might

552

have been even more virulent and vicious than they were had it not been for the respectable fellowship of Brackett, Anderson, and Carr.

Well, Fox, I have taken the trouble to tell you about this unrecorded incident in my life because I thought you might hear of it sometime and might possibly put a strained construction on it. There were those in Libya Hill who thought it offered a reasonable and complete explanation of what had happened to me when I wrote the book. So, too, you might come to believe that it twisted and embittered me and somehow had something to do with what has happened now. With nine-tenths of your mind and heart you understand perfectly why I have to leave you, but with that remaining tenth you are still puzzled, and I can see that you will go on wondering about it. You have, from time to time, tried to reason with me about what you called, half seriously, my "radicalism." I don't believe there is any radicalism in me—or, if there is, it is certainly not what the word implies when you use it.

So, believe me, the Pine Rock case has nothing to do with it. It explains nothing. Rather, the natural assumption, for me as for the others who were involved in it, would be that the experience should have established me in a more staunch and regular conformity than I should otherwise have known.

You have a friend, Fox, named Hunt Conroy. You introduced me to him. He is only a few years my senior, but he is very fixed in his assertion of what he calls "The Lost Generation"—a generation of which, as you know, he has been quite vociferously a member, and in which he has tried enthusiastically to include me. Hunt and I used to argue about it.

"You belong to it, too," he used to say grimly. "You came along at the same time. You can't get away from it. You're a part of it whether you want to be or not."

To which my vulgar response was:

"Don't you-hoo me!"

If Hunt *wants* to belong to The Lost Generation—and it really is astonishing with what fond eagerness some people hug the ghost of desolation to their breast—that's *his* affair. But he can't have me. If I have been elected, it was against my knowledge and my will—and I resign. I do not feel that I belong to a Lost Generation, and I have never felt so. Indeed, I doubt very much the existence of a Lost Generation, except insofar as every generation, groping, must be lost. Recently, however, it has occurred to me that if there is such a thing as a Lost Generation in this country, it is probably made up of those men of advanced middle age who still speak the language that was spoken before 1929, and who know no other. These men indubitably *are* lost. But I am not one of them.

Although I don't believe, then, that I was ever part of any Lost Generation anywhere, the fact remains that, as an individual, I was lost. Perhaps that is one reason, Fox, why for so long I needed you so desperately. For I was lost, and was looking for someone older and wiser to show me the way, and I found you, and you took the place of my father who had died. In our nine years together you did help me find the way, though you could hardly have been aware just how you did it, and the road now leads off in a direction contrary to your intent. For the fact is that now I no longer feel lost, and I want to tell you why.

When I returned to Pine Rock and finished my course and graduated—I was only twenty then—I don't suppose it would have been possible to find a more confused and baffled person than I was. I had been sent to college to "prepare myself for life," as the phrase went in those days, and it almost seemed that the total effect of my college training was to produce in me a state of utter unpreparedness. I had come from one of the most conservative parts of America, and from one of the most conservative elements in those parts. All of my antecedents, until a generation before, had been country people whose living had been in one way or another drawn out of the earth.

My father, John Webber, had been all of his life a working man. He had done hard labor with his hands since the time he was twelve years old. As I have often told you, he was a man of great natural ability and intelligence. But, like many other men who have been deprived of the advantages of formal education, he was ambitious for his son: he wanted more than anything else in the world to see me go to college. He died just before I was prepared to enter, but it was on the money he left me that I went. It is only natural that people like my father should endow formal education with a degree of practicality which it does not and should not possess. College seemed to him a kind of magic door which not only opened to a man all the reserves of learning, but also admitted him to free passage along any highroad to material success which he might choose to follow after he had passed through the pleasant academic groves. It was only natural, too, that such a man as my father should believe that this success could be most easily arrived at along one of the more familiar and more generally approved roads.

The road he had chosen for me before his death was a branch of engineering. He stubbornly opposed the Joyner choice, which was the law. The old man had small use for the law as a profession, and very little respect for the lawyer as a man; his usual description of lawyers was "a gang of shysters." When I went to see him as he lay dying, his last advice to me was:

"Learn to *do* something, learn to *make* something—that's what college should be for."

His bitterest regret was that the poverty of his early years had prevented him from learning any skill beyond that of a carpenter and a mason. He was a good carpenter, a good mason—in his last days he liked to call himself a builder, which indeed he was—but I think he felt in himself, like a kind of dumb and inarticulate suffering, the unachieved ability to *design* and *shape*. Certainly he would have been profoundly disappointed if he could have known what strange forms his own desires for "doing" and for "making" were to achieve in me. I cannot say what extremity—law or writing—would have filled him with the most disgust.

But by the time I left college it was already apparent that whatever talents I might have, they were neither for engineering nor the law. I had not the technical ability for the one, and, in view of what I was to discover for myself in later years, I think I was too honest for the other. But what to do? My academic career, with the crowning disgrace of complicity in the Pine Rock case and temporary expulsion from college, had not been distinguished by any very glittering records in scholarship except that One in Logic. I had failed both my father and the Joyner side of the house in any ambitions they had had for me. My father was dead, and the Joyners were now done with me.

For all these reasons, it was difficult to admit, even to myself, the stirrings of an urge so fantastic and impractical as the desire to write. It would only have confirmed the worst suspicions that my people had of me—suspicions, I fear, which had begun to eat into my own opinion of myself. Consequently, the first admission I made to myself was evasive. I told myself that I wanted to go into journalism. Now, looking back at it, I can see the reason for this decision clearly enough. I doubt very much that I had, at the age of twenty, the burning enthusiasm for newspaper work which I thought I had, but I managed to convince myself of it because newspaper work would provide me with the only means I knew whereby I could, in some fashion, write, and also earn a living, and thus prove to the world and to myself that I was not wasting my time.

To have confessed openly to my family that I wanted to be a

writer would have been impossible. To be a writer was, in modern phrase, "nice work if you could get it." In the Joyner consciousness, as well as in my own, "a writer" was a very remote kind of person. He was a romantic figure like Lord Byron, or Longfellow, or—or—Irvin S. Cobb—who in some magical way was gifted with the power to put words together into poems or stories or novels which got printed in books or in the pages of magazines like the *Saturday Evening Post*. He was therefore, quite obviously, a very strange, mysterious, sort of creature who lived a very strange, mysterious, and glittering sort of life, and who came from some strange and mysterious and glittering world very far away from the life and world *we* knew. For a boy who had grown up in the town of Libya Hill to assert openly that he wanted to be a writer would have seemed to everyone at that time to border on lunacy. It would have harked back to the days of Uncle Rance Joyner, who wasted his youth learning to play the violin, and who in later life borrowed fifty dollars from Uncle Mark to take a course in phrenology. I had always been told that there was a strong resemblance between myself and Uncle Rance, and now I knew that if I confessed my secret desires, everyone would have thought the likeness more pronounced than ever.

It was a painful situation, and one which is now amusing to look back on. But it was also very human—and very American. Even today I don't think the Joyners have altogether recovered from their own astonishment at the fact that I have actually become "a writer." This attitude, which was also my own at the age of twenty, was to shape the course of my life for years.

So, fresh from college, I took what remained of the small inheritance my father had left me, and, with an exultant sense that I had packed my secret into my suitcase along with my extra pants, I started out, boy and baggage, on the road to fame and glory. That is to say, I came to New York to look for a job on a newspaper.

I did look for the job, but not too hard, and I didn't find it. Meanwhile I had enough money to live on and I began to write. Later, when the money ran out, I condescended to become an instructor in one of the great educational factories of the city. This was another compromise, but it had one virtue—it enabled me to live and go on writing.

During that first year in New York I shared an apartment with a group of boys, transplanted Southerners like myself, whom I had known in college. Through one of them I made the acquaintance of some artistic young fellows who were living in what I swiftly learned to call "The Village." Here, for the first time, I was thrown into the company of sophisticated young men of my own age—at least they seemed very sophisticated to me. For instead of being like me, an uncouth yokel from the backwoods, all rough edges, who felt within himself the timid but unspoken flutterings of a desire to write, these young gentlemen had come down from Harvard, they had the easy manner of men of the world, and they casually but quite openly told me that they *were* writers. And so they were. They wrote, and were published, in some of the little experimental magazines which were springing up on all sides during that period. How I envied them!

They were not only able to assert openly that they were writers, but they also asserted openly that a great many other people that I had thought were writers—most dismally were not. When I made hesitant efforts to take part in the brilliant conversation that flashed around me, I began to discover that I would have to be prepared for some very rude shocks. It was decidedly disconcerting, for example, to ask one of these most superior young men, so carelessly correct in their rough tweeds and pink cheeks: "Have you ever read Galsworthy's *Strife?*"—and to have him raise his eyebrows slowly, exhale a slow column of cigarette smoke, slowly shake his head, and then say in an accent of resigned regret: "I can't read him. I simply can't read him. Sorry—" with a rising inflection as if to say that it was too bad, but that it couldn't be helped.

They were sorry about a great many things and people. The theatre was one of their most passionate concerns, but it seemed that there was hardly a dramatist writing in those days who escaped their censure. Shaw was amusing, but he was not a dramatist—he had never really learned how to write a play. O'Neill's reputation was grossly exaggerated: his dialogue was clumsy, and his characters stock types. Barrie was insufferable on account of his sentimentality. As for Pinero and others of that ilk, their productions were already so dated that they were laughable.

In a way, this super-criticality was a very good thing for me. It taught me to be more questioning about some of the most venerated names and reputations whose authority had been handed down to me by my preceptors and accepted by me with too little thought. But the trouble with it was that I soon became involved, along with the others, in a niggling and overrefined aestheticism which was not only pallid and precious, but too detached from life to provide the substance and the inspiration for high creative work.

It is interesting to look back now and see just what it was we believed fifteen years ago—those of us who were the bright young people of the time and wanted to produce something of value in the arts. We talked a great deal about "art" and "beauty"—a great deal about "the artist." A great deal too much, in fact. For the artist as we conceived him was a kind of aesthetic monster. Certainly he was not a living man. And if the artist is not first and foremost a living man—and by this I mean a man of life, a man who belongs to life, who is connected with it so intimately that he draws his strength from it—then what manner of man is he?

The artist we talked about was not such a man at all. Indeed, if he had any existence outside of our imaginations he must have been one of the most extraordinary and inhuman freaks that nature ever created. Instead of loving life and believing in life, our "artist" hated life and fled from it. That, in fact, was the basic theme of most of the stories, plays, and novels we wrote. We were forever portraying the sensitive man of talent, the young genius, crucified by life, misunderstood and scorned of men, pilloried and driven out by the narrow bigotry and mean provincialism of the town or village, betrayed and humiliated by the cheapness of his wife, and finally crushed, silenced, torn to pieces by the organized power of the mob. So conceived, the artist that we talked about so much, instead of being in union with life, was in perpetual conflict with it. Instead of belonging to the world he lived in, he was constantly in a state of flight from it. The world itself was like a beast of prey, and the artist, like some wounded faun, was forever trying to escape from it.

It seems to me now, as I look back on it, that the total deposit of all this was bad. It gave to young people who were deficient in the vital materials and experiences of life, and in the living contacts which the artist ought to have with life, the language and formulas of an unwholesome preciosity. It armed them with a philosophy, an aesthetic, of escapism. It tended to create in those of us who were later to become artists not only a special but a privileged character: each of us tended to think of himself as a person who was exempt from the human laws that govern other men, who was not subject to the same desires, the same feelings, the same passions—who was, in short, a kind of beautiful disease in nature, like a pearl in an oyster.

The effect of all this upon such a person as myself may easily be deduced. Now, for the first time, I was provided with a protective armor, a glittering and sophisticated defense to shield my own self-doubts, my inner misgivings, my lack of confidence in my power and ability to accomplish what I wanted to do. The result was to make me arrogantly truculent where my own desires and purposes were concerned. I began to talk the jargon just as the others did, to prate about "the artist," and to refer scornfully and contemptuously to the bourgeoisie, the Babbitts, and the Philistines—by which all of us meant anyone who did not belong to the very small and precious province we had fashioned for ourselves.

Looking back, in an effort to see myself as I was in those days, I am afraid I was not a very friendly or agreeable young man. I was carrying a chip on my shoulder, and daring the whole world to knock it off. And the reason I so often took a high tone with people who, it seemed to me, doubted my ability to do the thing I wanted to do, was that, inwardly, I was by no means sure that I could do it myself. It was a form of whistling to keep one's courage up.

That was the kind of man I was when you first knew me, Fox. Ah, yes, I spoke about the work I wished to do in phrases of devotion and humility, but there was not much of either in me. Inside, I was full of the disdainful scorn of the small and precious snob. I felt superior to other people and thought I belonged to a rare breed. I had not yet learned that one cannot really be superior without humility and tolerance and human understanding. I did not yet know that in order to belong to a rare and higher breed one must first develop the true power and talent of selfless immolation.

Chapter Forty-Six

Even Two Angels Not Enough

Since childhood [George wrote to Fox] *I had wanted what all* men want in youth: to be famous, to be loved. These two desires went back through all the steps, degrees, and shadings of my education; they represented what we younglings of the time had been taught to believe in and to want.

Love and Fame. Well, I have had them both.

You told me once, Fox, that I did not want them, that I only thought I did. You were right. I wanted them desperately before I had them, but once they were mine I found that they were not enough. And I think, if we speak truth, the same thing holds for every man who ever lived and had the spark of growth in him.

It has never been dangerous to admit that Fame is not enough—one of the world's greatest poets called it "that last infirmity of Noble mind"—but it is dangerous, for reasons which everybody understands, to admit the infirmity of Love. Perhaps Love's image may suffice some men. Perhaps, as in a drop of shining water, Love may hold in microcosm the reflection of the sun and the stars and the heavens and the whole universe of man. Mighty poets dead and gone have said that this was true, and people have professed it ever since. As for that, I can only say that I do not think a frog pond or a Walden Pond contains the image of the ocean, even though there be water in both of them.

"Love is enough, though the world be a-waning," wrote William Morris. We have his word for it, and can believe it or not as we like. Perhaps it was true for him, yet I doubt it. It may have been true at the moment he wrote it, but not in the end, not when all was said and done.

As for myself, I did not find it so.

For, even while I was most securely caught up and enclosed within the inner circle of Love's bondage, I began to discover a larger world outside. It did not dawn upon me in a sudden and explosive sense, the way the world of Chapman's *Homer* burst upon John Keats:

> "Then felt I like some watcher of the skies
> When a new planet swims into his ken."

It did not come like that at all. It came in on me little by little, almost without my knowing it.

Up to that time I had been merely the sensitive young fellow in conflict with his town, his family, the life around him—then the sensitive young fellow in love, and so concerned with his little Universe of Love that he thought it the whole universe. But gradually I began to observe things in life which shocked me out of this complete absorption with the independent entities of self. I caught glimpses of the great, the rich, the fortunate ones of all the earth living supinely upon the very best of everything and taking the very best for granted as their right. I saw them enjoying a special privilege which had been theirs so long that it had become a vested interest: they seemed to think it was a law ordained by nature that they should be forever life's favorite sons. At the same time I began to be conscious of the submerged and forgotten Helots down below, who with their toil and sweat and blood and suffering unutterable supported and nourished the mighty princelings at the top.

Then came the cataclysm of 1929 and the terrible days that followed. The picture became clearer now—clear enough for all with eyes to see. Through those years I was living in the jungle depths of Brooklyn, and I saw as I had never seen before the true and terrifying visage of the disinherited of life. There came to me a vision of man's inhumanity to man, and as time went on it began to blot out the more personal and self-centered vision of the world which a young man always has. Then it was, I think, that I began to learn humility. My intense and passionate concern for the interests and designs of my own little life were coming to seem petty, trifling, and unworthy, and I was coming more and more to feel an intense and passionate concern for the interests and designs of my fellow men and of all humanity.

Of course I have vastly oversimplified the process in my telling of it. While it was at work in me I was but dimly aware of it. It is only now, as I look back upon those years, that I can see in true perspective the meaning of what was happening to me then. For human nature is, alas, a muddy pool, too full of sediment, too murky with the deposits of time, too churned up by uncharted currents in the depths and on the surface, to reflect a sharp, precise, and wholly faithful image. For that, one has to wait until the waters settle down. It follows, then, that one can never hope, however much he wishes that he could, to shed the old integuments of the soul as easily and completely as a snake sloughs off its outworn skin.

For, even at the time when this new vision of the outer world was filtering in and making its strange forms manifest to me, I was also more involved than I had ever been before with my inner struggle. Those were the years of the greatest doubt and desperation I had ever known. I was wrestling with the problems of my second book, and I could take in what my eyes beheld only in brief glimpses, flashes, snatches, fragments. As I was later to discover, the vision etched itself upon some sensitive film within, but it was not until that later time, when the second book was finished and out of the way, that I saw it whole and knew what the total experience had done to me.

And all the while, of course, I was still enamored of that fair Medusa, Fame. My desire for her was a relic of the past. All the guises of Fame's loveliness—phantasmal, ghostwise, like something flitting in a wood—I had dreamed of since my early youth, until her image and the image of the loved one had a thousand times been merged together. I had always wanted to be loved and to be famous. Now I had known Love, but Fame was still elusive. So in the writing of my second book I courted her.

Then, for the first time, I saw her. I met Mr. Lloyd McHarg. That curious experience should have taught me something. And in a way I suppose it did. For in Lloyd McHarg I met a truly great and honest man who had aspired to Fame and won her, and I saw that it had been an empty victory. He had her more completely than I could ever hope to have her, yet it was apparent that, for him, Fame was not enough. He needed something more, and he had not found it.

I say I should have learned from that. And yet, how could I? Does one ever really learn from others till one is ready for the lesson? One may read the truth in another's life and see it plain and still not make the application to oneself. Does not one's glorious sense of "I"—this wonderful, unique "I" that never was before since time began and never will be again hereafter—does not this "I" of tender favor come before the eye of judgment and always plead exception. I thought: "Yes, I see how it is with Lloyd McHarg, but with me it will be different—because I am *I*." That is how it has always been with me. I could never learn anything except the hard way. I must experience it for myself before I knew.

So with Fame. In the end I had to have her. She was another woman—of all Love's rivals, as I was to find by a strange paradox, the only one by women and by Love beloved. And I had her, as she may be had—only to discover that Fame, like Love, was not enough.

By then life's weather had soaked in, although I was not fully conscious yet what seepings had begun, or where, in what directions, the channel of my life was flowing. All I knew was that I was exhausted from my labor, respiring from the race, conscious only, as is a spent runner, that the race was over, the tape breasted, and that in such measure I had won. This was the only thought within me at the time: the knowledge that I had met the ordeal a second time and at last had conquered—conquered my desperation and self-doubt, the fear that I might never come again to a whole and final accomplishment.

Then the circle went full swing, the cycle drew to its full close. For several months, emptied, hollow, worn out, my life marked time while my exhausted spirit drew its breath. But after a while the world came in again, upon the flood tide of reviving energy. The world came in, the world kept coming in, and there was something in the world, and in my heart, that I had not known was there.

I had gone back for rest, for recreation, for oblivion, to that land which, of all the foreign lands that I had visited, I loved the best. Many times during the years of desperate confinement and labor on the book I had thought of it with intense longing, as men in prison, haltered to all the dusty shackles of the hour, have longed for the haunted woods and meadows of Cockaigne. Many times I had gone back to it in my dreams—to the sunken bell, the Gothic towns, the plash of waters in the midnight fountain, the Old Place, the broken chime, and the blonde flesh of secret, lavish women. Then at last came the day when I walked at morning through the Brandenburger Tor, and into the enchanted avenues of the faëry green Tiergarten, and found blossoms of the great horsechestnut trees, and felt like Tamerlane, that it was passing fine to be a king and move in triumph through Persepolis—and be a famous man.

After those long and weary years of labor, and the need of proof to give some easement to my tormented soul, this was the easement I had dreamed of, the impossible thing so impossibly desired, now brought magically to fulfillment. And now it seemed to me, who had so often gone a stranger and unknown to the great cities of the world, that Berlin was mine. For weeks there was a round of pleasure and celebration, and the wonderful thrill of meeting in a foreign land and in a foreign tongue a hundred friends, now for the first time known and captured. There was the sapphire sparkle in the air, the enchanted brevity of northern darkness, the glorious wine in slender bottles, and morning, and green fields, and pretty women—all of these were mine now, they seemed to have been created for me, to have been waiting for me, and to exist now in all their loveliness just for my possession.

The weeks passed so—and then it happened. Little by little the world came in. At first it sifted in almost unnoticed, like dark down dropped in passing from some avenging angel's wing. Sometimes it came to me in the desperate pleading of an eye, the naked terror of a startled look, the swift concealment of a sudden fear. Sometimes it just came and went as light comes, just soaked in, just soaked in—in fleeting words and speech and actions.

After a while, however, in the midwatches of the night, behind thick walls and bolted doors and shuttered windows, it came to me full flood at last in confessions of unutterable despair. I don't know why it was that people so unburdened themselves to me, a stranger, unless it was because they knew the love I bore them and their land. They seemed to feel a desperate need to talk to someone who would understand. The thing was pent up in them, and my sympathy for all things German had burst the dam of their reserve and caution. Their tales of woe and fear unspeakable gushed forth and beat upon my ears. They told me stories of their friends and relatives who had said unguarded things in public and disappeared without a trace, stories of the Gestapo, stories of neighbors' quarrels and petty personal spite turned into political persecution, stories of concentration camps and pogroms, stories of rich Jews stripped and beaten and robbed of everything they had and then denied the right to earn a pauper's wage, stories of well-bred Jewesses despoiled and turned out of their homes and forced to kneel and scrub off anti-Nazi slogans scribbled on the sidewalks while young barbarians dressed like soldiers formed a ring and prodded them with bayonets and made the quiet places echo with the shameless laughter of their mockery. It was a picture of the Dark Ages come again—shocking beyond belief, but true as the hell that man forever creates for himself.

Thus it was that the corruption of man's living faith and the inferno of his buried anguish came to me—and I recognized at last, in all its frightful aspects, the spiritual disease which was poisoning unto death a noble and a mighty people.

But even as I saw it and knew it for what it was, there came to me, most strangely, another thing as well. For while I sat the night through in the darkened rooms of German friends, behind the bolted doors and shuttered windows—while their whispered voices spoke to me of the anguish in their hearts, and I listened, stricken in my chair to see the tears and the graven lines of mortal sorrow form on faces which only a short time before, in the presence of others, had been masked in expressions of carefree unconcern—while I heard and saw these things my heart was torn asunder, and from its opened depths came forth into my consciousness a knowledge that I had not fully known was there. For then it was, most curiously, that all the grey weather of unrecorded days in Brooklyn, which had soaked through into my soul, came flooding back upon me. Came back, too, the memory of my exploration of the jungle trails of night. I saw again the haggard faces of the homeless men, the wanderers, the disinherited of America, the aged workers who had worked and now could work no more, the callow boys who had never worked and now could find no work to do, and who, both together, had been cast loose by a society that had no need of them and left to shift in any way they could—to find their food in garbage cans, to seek for warmth and fellowship in foul latrines like the one near New York's City Hall, to sleep wrapped up in old newspapers on the concrete floors of subway corridors.

It all came back to me, all the separate fragments of the vision I had seen, together with the sinister remembrance of that upper world of night, glittering with its riches, and its soft, sophisticated pleasures, and its cold indifference to the misery and injustice on which its very life was founded. It all came back, but now it was an integrated picture.

564

So it was, in this far place and under these profoundly moving and disturbing alien circumstances, that I realized fully, for the first time, how sick America was, and saw, too, that the ailment was akin to Germany's—a dread world-sickness of the soul. One of my German friends, Franz Heilig, later told me this same thing. In Germany it was hopeless: it had already gone too far to be checked now by any measures short of death, destruction, and total ruin. But in America, it seemed to me, it was not mortal, not incurable—not yet. It was desperate, and would become more desperate still if in America, as in Germany, men became afraid to look into the face of fear itself, to probe behind it, to see what caused it, and then to speak the truth about it. America was young, America was still the New World of mankind's hope, America was not like this old and worn-out Europe which seethed and festered with a thousand deep and uncorrected ancient maladies. America was still resilient, still responsive to a cure—if only—if only—men could somehow cease to be afraid of truth. For the plain and searching light of truth, which had here, in Germany, been darkened to extinction, was the remedy, the only one, that could cleanse and heal the suffering soul of man.

After such a night of seeing whole at last, day would come again, the cool glow of morning, the bronze gold of the kiefern trees, the still green pools of lucid water, the enchanted parks and gardens—but none of it was the same as it had been before. For now I knew that there was something else in life as new as morning and as old as hell, a universal ill of man seen here in Germany at its darkest, and here articulated for the first time in a word, regimented now in a scheme of phrases and a system of abominable works. And day by day the thing soaked in, and kept soaking in, until everywhere, in every life I met and touched, I saw the ruin of its unutterable pollutions.

So now another layer had been peeled off the gauzes of the seeing eye. And what the eye had seen and understood, I knew that it could nevermore forget or again be blind to.

Chapter Forty-Seven

Ecclesiasticus

Now I have told you [*George wrote to Fox*] *some of the* things that have happened to me and the effect they had upon me. But what has all of this to do with you?—you may ask. I am coming to that now.

In the beginning I spoke about my "philosophy of life" when I was a student in college twenty years ago. I didn't tell you what it was because I don't think I really had one then. I'm not sure I have one now. But I think it is interesting and important that I should have *thought* I had one at the age of seventeen, and that people still talk about "a philosophy of life" as though it were a concrete object that you could pick up and handle and take the weight and dimensions of. Just recently I was asked to contribute to a book called *Modern-Day Philosophies*. I tried to write something for it but gave it up, because I was unwilling and unready to say that I had a "modern-day philosophy." And the reason that I was unwilling and unready was not that I felt confusion and doubt about what I think and now believe, but that I felt confusion and doubt about saying it in formalistic and final terms.

That was what was wrong with most of us at Pine Rock College twenty years ago. We had a "concept" about Truth and Beauty and Love and Reality—and that hardened our ideas about what all these words stood for. After that, we had no doubt about them—or, at any rate, could not admit that we did. This was wrong, because the essence of belief is doubt, the essence of reality is questioning. The essence of Time is Flow, not Fix. The essence of faith is the knowledge that all flows and that everything must change. The growing man is Man-Alive, and his "philosophy" must grow, must flow, with him. When it does not, we have—do we not?—the Unfixed Man, the Eternal Trifler, the Ape of Fashion—the man too fixed today, unfixed tomorrow—and his body of beliefs is nothing but a series of fixations.

I cannot attempt, therefore, to define for you your own

"philosophy"—for to define so is to delimit the "closed" and academic man, and you, thank God, are not of that ilk. And to define so would be to call upon me once again your own and curious scorn, your sudden half-amused contemptuousness. For how could anyone pin down neatly the essence of your New Englandness—so sensitively proud, so shy, so shrinking and alone, but at bottom, as I think, so unafraid?

I shall not define you, then, dear Fox. But I may state, may I not? I may say how "it seems to me"?—how Fox appears?—and what I think of it?

Well, first of all, Fox seems to me to be Ecclesiasticus. I think that this is fair, and, insofar as definition goes, I think you will agree. Do you know of any definition that could possibly go further? I do not. In thirty-seven years of thinking, feeling, dreaming, working, striving, voyaging, and devouring, I have come across no other that could fit you half so well. Perhaps something has been written, painted, sung, or spoken in the world that would define you better: if it has, I have not seen it; and if I did see it, then I should feel like one who came upon a Sistine Chapel greater than the first, which no man living yet has heard about.

So far as I can see from nine years of observing you, yours is the way of life, the way of thought, of feeling, and of acting, of the Preacher in Ecclesiastes. I know of no better way. For of all that I have ever seen or learned, that book seems to me the noblest, the wisest, and the most powerful expression of man's life upon this earth—and also earth's highest flower of poetry, eloquence, and truth. I am not given to dogmatic judgments in the matter of literary creation, but if I had to make one I could only say that Ecclesiastes is the greatest single piece of writing I have ever known, and the wisdom expressed in it the most lasting and profound.

And I should say that it expresses your own position as perfectly as anything could. I have read it over many times each year, and I do not know of a single word or stanza in it with which you would not instantly agree.

You would agree—to quote just a few precepts which come to mind from that noble book—that a good name is better than precious ointment; and I think you would also agree that the day of death is better than the day of one's birth. You would agree with the great Preacher that all things are full of labor; that man cannot utter it; that the eye is not satisfied with seeing, nor the ear filled with hearing. I know you would agree also that the thing that hath been, is that which shall be; and that that which is done, is that which shall be done: and that there is no new thing under the sun. You would agree that it is vexation of spirit to give one's heart to know wisdom, and to know madness and folly. I know you would agree—for you have so admonished me many times—that to everything there is a season, and a time to every purpose under the heaven.

"Vanity of vanities, saith the Preacher; all is vanity." You would agree with him in that; but you would also agree with him that the fool foldeth his hands together and eateth his own flesh. You would agree with all your being that "Whatsoever thy hand findeth to do, do it with thy might; for there is no work, nor device, nor knowledge, nor wisdom, in the grave, whither thou goest."

Is this abridgment and this definition just, dear Fox? Yes, for I have seen every syllable of it in you a thousand times. I have learned every accent of it from yourself. You said one time, when I had spoken of you in the dedication of a book, that what I had written would be your epitaph. You were mistaken. Your epitaph was written many centuries ago: Ecclesiastes is your epitaph. Your portrait had been drawn already in the portrait the great Preacher had given of himself. You are he, his words are yours so perfectly that if he had never lived or uttered them, all of him, all of his great and noble Sermon, could have been derived afresh from you.

If I could, therefore, define your own philosophy—and *his* —I think I should define it as the philosophy of a *hopeful* fatalism. Both of you are in the essence pessimists, but both of you are also pessimists with hope. From both of you I learned much, many true and hopeful things. I learned, first of all, that one must work, that one must do what work he can, as well and ably as he can, and that it is only the fool who repines and longs for what is vanished, for what might have been but is not. I learned from both of you the stern lesson of acceptance: to acknowledge the tragic underweft of life into which man is born, through which he must live, out of which he must die. I learned from both of you to accept that essential fact without complaint, but, having accepted it, to try to do what was before me, what I could do, with all my might.

And, curiously—for here comes in the strange, hard paradox of our twin polarity—it was just here, I think, where I was so much and so essentially in confirmation with you, that I began to disagree. I think almost that I could say to you: "I believe in everything you say, but I do not agree with you"—and so state the root of our whole trouble, the mystery of our eventual cleavage and our final severance. The little tongues will wag— have wagged, I understand, already—will propose a thousand quick and ready explanations (as they have)—but really, Fox, the root of the whole thing is here.

In one of the few letters that you ever wrote to me—a wonderful and moving one just recently—you said:

"I know that you are going now. I always knew that it would happen. I will not try to stop you, for it had to be. And the strange thing is, the hard thing is, I have never known another man with whom I was so profoundly in agreement on all essential things."

And that *is* the strange, hard thing, and wonderful and mysterious; for, in a way the little clacking tongues can never know about, it is completely true. Still, there is our strange paradox: it seems to me that in the orbit of our world you are the North Pole, I the South—so much in balance, in agreement—and yet, dear Fox, the whole world lies between.

'Tis true, our view of life was very much the same. When we looked out together, we saw man burned with the same sun, frozen by the same cold, beat upon by the hardships of the same impervious weathers, duped by the same gullibility, self-betrayed by the same folly, misled and baffled by the same stupidity. Each on the opposing hemisphere of his own pole looked out across the spinning orbit of this vexed, tormented world, and at the other, and what each saw, the picture that each got, was very much the same. We not only saw the stupidity and the folly and the gullibility and the self-deception of man, but we saw his nobility, courage, and aspiration, too. We saw the wolves that preyed upon him and laid him waste—the wild scavengers of greed, of fear, of privilege, of power, of tyranny, of oppression, of poverty and disease, of injustice, cruelty, and wrong—and in what we saw of this as well, dear Fox, we were agreed.

Why, then, the disagreement? Why, then, the struggle that ensued, the severance that has now occurred? We saw the same things, and we called them by the same names. We abhorred them with the same indignation and disgust—and yet, we disagreed, and I am making my farewell to you. Dear friend, the parent and the guardian of my spirit in its youth, the thing has happened and we know it. Why?

I know the answer, and the thing I have to tell you now is this:

Beyond the limits of my own mortality, the stern acknowledgment that man was born to live, to suffer, and to die—your own and the great Preacher's creed—I am not, cannot be, confirmed to more fatality. Briefly, you thought the ills which so beset mankind were irremediable: that just as man was born to live, to suffer, and to die, so was he born to be eternally beset and preyed upon by all the monsters of his own creation—by fear and cruelty, by tyranny and power, by poverty and wealth. You felt, with the stern fatality of resignation which is the granite essence of your nature, that these things were doomed to be, and be forever, because they had always been, and were inherent in the tainted and tormented soul of man.

Dear Fox, dear friend, I heard you and I understood you—but could not agree. You felt—I heard you and I understood—that if old monsters were destroyed, new ones would be created in their place. You felt that if old tyrannies were overthrown, new ones, as sinister and evil, would reign after them. You felt that all the glaring evils in the world around us—the monstrous and perverse unbalance between power and servitude, between want and plenty, between privilege and burdensome discrimination—were inevitable because they had always been the curse of man and were the prime conditions of his being. The gap between us widened. You stated and affirmed—I heard you, but could not agree.

To state your rule and conduct plainly, I think I never knew a kinder or a gentler man, but I also never knew a man more fatally resigned. In practice—in life and conduct—I have seen the Sermon of the Preacher work out in you like a miracle. I have seen you grow haggard and grey because you saw a talent wasted, a life misused, work undone that should be done. I have seen you move mountains to save something which, you felt, was worth the effort and could be saved. I have seen you perform prodigies of labor and patience to pull a drowning man of talent out of the swamp of failure into which his life was sinking; and at each successive slipping back, so far from acknowledging defeat with resignation and regret, you made your eyes flash fire and your will toughen to the hardness of forged steel as I saw you strike your hand upon the table and heard you whisper, with an almost savage intensity of passion: "He must not go. He is not lost. I *will* not, and he *must* not, let it happen!"

To give this noble virtue of your life the etching of magnificence it deserves, it is your due to have it stated here. For, without it, there can be no proper understanding of your worth, your true dimension. To describe the acquiescence of your stern fatality without first describing the inspired tenacity of your effort would be to give a false and insufficient picture of the strangest and the most familiar, the most devious and the most direct, the simplest and the most complex figure that this nation and this generation have produced.

To say that you looked on at all the suffering and injustice of this vexed, tormented world with the toleration of resigned fatality without telling also of your own devoted and miraculous effort to save what could be saved, would not do justice to you. No man ever better fulfilled the injunction of the Preacher to lay about him and to do the work at hand with all his might. No man ever gave himself more wholly, not only to the fulfillment of that injunction for himself but to the task of saving others who had failed to do it, and who might be saved. But no man ever accepted the irremediable with more quiet unconcern. I think you would risk your life to save that of a friend who put himself uselessly and wantonly in peril, but I know, too, that you would accept the fact of unavoidable death without regret. I have seen you grow grey-faced and hollow-eyed with worry over the condition of a beloved child who was suffering from a nervous shock or ailment that the doctors could not diagnose. You found the cause eventually and checked it; but I know that if the cause had been fatal and incurable, you would have accepted that fact with a resignation as composed as your own effort was inspired.

All of this makes the paradox of our great difference as hard and strange as the paradox of our polarity. And in this lies the root of trouble and the seed of severance. Your own philosophy has led you to accept the order of things as they are because you have no hope of changing them; and if you could change them, you feel that any other order would be just as bad. In everlasting terms—those of eternity—you and the Preacher may be right: for there is no greater wisdom that the wisdom of Ecclesiastes, no acceptance finally so true as the stern fatalism of the rock. Man was born to live, to suffer, and to die, and what befalls him is a tragic lot. There is no denying this in the final end. *But we must, dear Fox, deny it all along the way.*

Mankind was fashioned for eternity, but Man-Alive was fashioned for a day. New evils will come after him, but it is with the present evils that he is now concerned. And the essence of all faith, it seems to me, for such a man as I, the essence of religion for people of my belief, is that man's life can be, and will be, better; that man's greatest enemies, in the forms in which they now exist—the forms we see on every hand of fear, hatred, slavery, cruelty, poverty, and need—can be conquered and destroyed. But to conquer and destroy them will mean nothing less than the complete revision of the structure of society as we know it. They cannot be conquered by the sorrowful acquiescence of resigned fatality. They cannot be destroyed by the philosophy of acceptance—by the tragic hypothesis that things as they are, evil as they are, are as good and as bad as, under any form, they will ever be. The evils that we hate, you no less than I, cannot be overthrown with shrugs and sighs and shakings of the head however wise. It seems to me that they but mock at us and only become more bold when we retreat before them and take refuge in the affirmation of man's tragic average. To believe that new monsters will arise as vicious

571

as the old, to believe that the great Pandora's box of human frailty, once opened, will never show a diminution of its ugly swarm, is to help, by just that much, to make it so forever.

You and the Preacher may be right for all eternity, but we Men-Alive, dear Fox, are right for Now. And it is for Now, and for us the living, that we must speak, and speak the truth, as much of it as we can see and know. With the courage of the truth within us, we shall meet the enemy as they come to us, and they *shall* be ours. And if, once having conquered them, new enemies approach, we shall meet them from that point, from there proceed. In the affirmation of that fact, the continuance of that unceasing war, is man's religion and his living faith.

Chapter Forty-Eight

Credo

I have never before made a statement of belief [George wrote in his conclusion to Fox], although I have believed in many things and said that I believed in them. But I have never stated my belief in concrete terms because almost every element of my nature has been opposed to the hard framework, the finality, of formulation.

Just as you are the rock of life, I am the web; just as you are Time's granite, so, I think, am I Time's plant. My life, more than that of anyone I know, has taken on the form of growth. No man that I have known was ever more deeply rooted in the soil of Time and Memory, the weather of his individual universe, than was I. You followed me through the course of that whole herculean conflict. For four years, as I lived and worked and explored the jungle depths of Brooklyn—jungle depths coincident with those of my own soul—you were beside me, you followed, and you stuck.

You never had a doubt that I would finish—make an end—round out the cycle—come to the whole of it. The only doubt was mine, enhanced, tormented by my own fatigue and desperation, and by the clacking of the feeble and malicious little tongues which, knowing nothing, whispered that I would never make an end again because I could not begin. We both knew how grotesquely false this was—so false and so grotesque that it was sometimes the subject of an anguished and exasperated laugh. The truth was so far different that my own fears were just the opposite: that I might never make an end to anything again because I could never get through telling what I knew, what I felt and thought and *had* to say about it.

That was a giant web in which I was caught, the product of my huge inheritance—the torrential recollectiveness, derived out of my mother's stock, which became a living, million-fibered integument that bound me to the past, not only of my own life, but of the very earth from which I came, so that nothing in the end escaped from its inrooted and all-feeling explorativeness. The way the sunlight came and went upon a certain day, the way grass felt between bare toes, the immediacy of noon, the slamming of an iron gate, the halting skreak upon the corner of a street car, the liquid sound of shoe leather on the pavements as men came home to lunch, the smell of turnip greens, the clang of ice tongs, and the clucking of a hen—and then Time fading like a dream, Time melting to oblivion, when I was two years old. Not only this, but all lost sounds and voices, forgotten memories exhumed with a constant pulsing of the brain's great ventricle, until I lived them in my dreams, carrying the stupendous and unceasing burden of them through the unresting passages of sleep. Nothing that had ever been was lost. It all came back in an endless flow, even the blisters of the paint upon the mantelpiece in my father's house, the smell of the old leather sofa with my father's print upon it, the smell of dusty bottles and of cobwebs in the cellar, the casual stomping of a slow, gaunt hoof upon the pulpy lumber of a livery stable floor, the proud lift and flourish of a whisking tail, and the oaty droppings. I lived again through all times and weathers I had known—through the fag-ends of wintry desolation in the month of March and the cold, bleak miseries of ragged red at sunset, the magic of young green in April, the blind horror and suffocation of concrete places in mid-summer sun where no limits were, and October with the smell of fallen leaves and wood smoke in the air. The forgotten moments and un-numbered hours came back to me with all the enormous cargo of my memory, together with lost voices in the mountains long ago, the voices of the kinsmen dead and never seen, and the houses they had built and died in, and the rutted roads they trod upon, and every unrecorded moment that Aunt Maw had told me of the lost and obscure lives they led long, long ago. So did it all revive in the ceaseless pulsings of the giant ventricle, so did the plant go back, stem by stem, root by root, and filament by filament, until it was complete and whole, compacted of the very earth that had produced it, and of which it was itself the last and living part.

You stayed beside me like the rock you are until I unearthed the plant, followed it back through every fiber of its pattern to its last and tiniest enrootment in the blind, dumb earth. And now that it is finished, and the circle come full swing—we, too, are finished, and I have a thing to say:

I believe that we are lost here in America, but I believe we shall be found. And this belief, which mounts now to the catharsis of knowledge and conviction, is for me—and I think for all of us—not only our own hope, but America's everlasting, living dream. I think the life which we have fashioned in America, and which has fashioned us—the forms we made, the cells that grew, the honeycomb that was created—was self-destructive in its nature, and must be destroyed. I think these forms are dying, and must die, just as I know that America and the people in it are deathless, undiscovered, and immortal, and must live.

I think the true discovery of America is before us. I think the true fulfillment of our spirit, of our people, of our mighty and immortal land, is yet to come. I think the true discovery of our own democracy is still before us. And I think that all these things are certain as the morning, as inevitable as noon. I think I speak for most men living when I say that our America is Here, is Now, and beckons on before us, and that this glorious assurance is not only our living hope, but our dream to be accomplished.

I think the enemy is here before us, too. But I think we know the forms and faces of the enemy, and in the knowledge that we know him, and shall meet him, and eventually must conquer him is also our living hope. I think the enemy is here before us with a thousand faces, but I think we know that all his faces wear one mask. I think the enemy is single selfishness and compulsive greed. I think the enemy is blind, but has the brutal power of his blind grab. I do not think the enemy was born yesterday, or that he grew to manhood forty years ago, or that he suffered sickness and collapse in 1929, or that we began without the enemy, and that our vision faltered, that we lost the way, and suddenly were in his camp. I think the enemy is old as Time, and evil as Hell, and that he has been here with us from the beginning. I think he stole our earth from us, destroyed our
574

wealth, and ravaged and despoiled our land. I think he took our people and enslaved them, that he polluted the fountains of our life, took unto himself the rarest treasures of our own possession, took our bread and left us with a crust, and, not content, for the nature of the enemy is insatiate—tried finally to take from us the crust.

I think the enemy comes to us with the face of innocence and says to us:

"I am your friend."

I think the enemy deceives us with false words and lying phrases, saying:

"See, I am one of you—I am one of your children, your son, your brother, and your friend. Behold how sleek and fat I have become—and all because I am just one of you, and your friend. Behold how rich and powerful I am—and all because I am one of you—shaped in your way of life, of thinking, of accomplishment. What I am, I am because I am one of you, your humble brother and your friend. Behold," cries Enemy, "the man I am, the man I have become, the thing I have accomplished—and reflect. Will you destroy this thing? I assure you that it is the most precious thing you have. It is yourselves, the projection of each of you, the triumph of your individual lives, the thing that is rooted in your blood, and native to your stock, and inherent in the traditions of America. It is the thing that all of you may hope to be," says Enemy, "for—" humbly—"am I not just one of you? Am I not just your brother and your son? Am I not the living image of what each of you may hope to be, would wish to be, would desire for his own son? Would you destroy this glorious incarnation of your own heroic self? If you do, then," says Enemy, "you destroy yourselves—you kill the thing that is most gloriously American, and in so killing, kill yourselves."

He lies! And now we know he lies! He is not gloriously, or in any other way, ourselves. He is not our friend, our son, our brother. And he is not American! For, although he has a thousand familiar and convenient faces, his own true face is old as Hell.

Look about you and see what he has done.

Dear Fox, old friend, thus we have come to the end of the road that we were to go together. My tale is finished—and so farewell.

But before I go, I have just one more thing to tell you:

575

Something has spoken to me in the night, burning the tapers of the waning year; something has spoken in the night, and told me I shall die, I know not where. Saying:

"To lose the earth you know, for greater knowing; to lose the life you have, for greater life; to leave the friends you loved, for greater loving; to find a land more kind than home, more large than earth——

"—Whereon the pillars of this earth are founded, toward which the conscience of the world is tending—a wind is rising, and the rivers flow."

THE END